ALSO BY TERRI BRUCE

The Afterlife Series
Hereafter (Afterlife #1)
Thereafter (Afterlife #2)

Whereafter

Terri Bruce

♦ Mictlan Press ♦

Whereafter (Afterlife #3)
Copyright © 2016 Terri Bruce

Cover artwork by Shelby Robinson
Cover models Chelsea Howard and Justin Kalin
Cover design by Jennifer Stolzer

Digital ISBN: 978-0-9913036-5-6
Print ISBN: 978-0-9913036-4-9

Printed in the United States of America
First Edition

To Christopher,
Who always hates my endings but reads my stories
anyway.

ACKNOWLEDGEMENTS

As always, there are too many people to thank individually. A book is a team effort—from the friends and family who cheerlead and encourage the writer, to the spouse who brings a steady supply of hot beverages, food, and back rubs when things are going well (or, at least, steadily) and chocolate and hugs when they aren't, to the coworkers who tolerantly and indulgently let the author ramble about each milestone, to the bloggers who read, review, support, and promote the author and his/her works, to the amazing strangers who sign up to be on the author's street team. To all of you, thank you!

A great big thank you (as always) to cover artist Shelby Robinson for her amazing, amazing artwork and to models Chelsea Howard and Justin Kalin for bringing Irene and Jonah to life. Thank you also to cover layout artist Jennifer Stolzer for always finding the perfect symbol for the spine! That little touch is always my favorite part of the covers.

Any parts of this book that you like are probably the work of my fabulous critique partners T.W. Fendley, Beth Hayes, Jeremy Hughes, Aimee Hyndman, Sean Jenan, Anna Priemaza, and Leann Rko. Each and every one of them are not only fabulous critique partners—they always know just where a story has gone off the rails and how to get it back on track—but amazing writers in their own right. You should run right out and buy some of their books—right now. I'll wait...

Any parts of this book that are readable due to proper grammar and punctuation are the work of my fabulous editor Morgen Rich. You should go buy her books, too.

Prologue

The tiny, brass bell over the magic shop's door jingled as Jonah Johnson crossed the threshold. Without intending to, he held his breath. Perhaps the shop had changed, or maybe it wasn't the way he remembered it. Maybe, despite the sign over the door declaring it to be "Madame Majicka's Shop of Mysteries," Madame Majicka was no longer here. God, he hoped not—he'd exhausted almost all his other avenues.

One quick survey of the small store's crowded and dimly-lit interior, however, instantly alleviated his fears. He smiled as he closed the door and the overpowering scent of sandalwood incense hit him. Though it had been nearly three years since he'd last been here, the shop looked exactly as he remembered it. Typical occult paraphernalia—crystals, tarot cards, incense, crystal balls, and the like—crowded every available surface: they were crammed on the dingy, white, laminated countertop that ran around the perimeter of the room, overflowing from the various knick-knack tables, wooden bookshelves, and display cases that fought for floor space, and dangled from curtain rods and light fixtures. Interspersed with the usual and expected items were stranger things, like dried roots, small, desiccated turtles—still in their shells—and tiny vials of glittering, jewel-toned liquids.

Surely, something in here could help him.

Whispers of memory tugged at him, and a wave of melancholy hit him. When he'd last been here, he'd been with Irene, the ghost woman he'd helped to cross over to the other side.

Irene.

Just as quickly as it arose, the nostalgia was replaced by the ever-present anxiety and dread that ate at him. It had been a month since Irene had inexplicably cut off contact. *A month* — and he was no closer to finding a way to contact or locate her.

A voluptuous woman of indeterminate age — neatly dressed in a tailored suit of dark emerald green and with a hint of the Mediterranean in her dark features and hair — bustled through the bead curtain hanging in the back of the shop. Jonah's smile returned. Madame Majicka was still the same, too.

"Sale today! Twenty-five percent off," the woman sang out as the swaying beads knocked together behind her. She stopped short, recognition lighting up her face. "My dear!" she cried with delight. "How are you? So good to see you!"

"You remember me?" Jonah asked.

"Of course I remember! I never forget a face. The boy who can see dead people! It's been such a long time. How have you been?"

It had been a long time — two and a half years to be exact. He could account for every second of that time, too. A year and a half of gut-wrenching loneliness after Irene had crossed over, followed by eight months of letters once she had started writing to him from the other side, followed by one month of agonizing silence after she had inexplicably cut off contact.

"I'm good." Unbidden, images flashed through his mind: a burning lake of fire, snarling, black-bristled beasts with long claws and even longer teeth, grotesque demons with too many eyes and mouths peeling the flesh from human victims, and in every scene, a red-haired woman sobbing in pain and terror, crying out to him for help. He tried to shake the images, but it was futile: they haunted him day and night, awake or asleep.

"And your friend—the ghost woman? How is she?" Madame Majicka clucked reproachfully as she ushered Jonah toward one of the stools flanking a pub-style table in the back of the shop. "I've never seen such a difficult aura."

Despite himself, Jonah's lips twisted into a wry grin—difficult was certainly one way to describe Irene. However, despite the humor in Madame Majicka's word choice, a lump constricted his throat when he replied. "She crossed over."

"Oh? Interesting—I didn't expect that. Well, it's for the best, I'm sure."

Jonah's grin disappeared, replaced by a scowl, and the ever-present guilt roiled in his belly. Best would be if she had stayed. Best would be if she were here—where it was safe. Best would be if she were around—where he could talk to her. "Actually, that's why I'm here..." He reached into the front pocket of his jeans, pulled out the carefully folded flyer tucked there, unfolded it, and passed it to Madame Majicka across the table. On the flyer, a smiling Madame Majicka waved a hand over a crystal ball. Thick, black words proclaimed the peace of knowing your loved ones were safe and happy in the Great Beyond that could be gained from speaking to them through the services of a medium, such as herself.

"I want to arrange for a séance."

A worried pucker creased Madame Majicka's forehead as she looked at the ad. "I think we better have some tea."

He didn't want tea; he wanted Irene—a way to contact her, a way to look in on her, a way to know she wasn't being tortured over and over by demons or hell hounds or harpies or...

Madame Majicka bustled away through the bead curtain.

His heart sank. Tea from Madame Majicka meant serious business—usually a soft let down. Was she going to refuse to help him? The psychic tended to have strict views on the land of the living and the land of the dead staying separate. Frankly, he was surprised she offered séance services at all. It seemed like the kind of thing she'd frown upon. He wouldn't have come to her at all except he knew she was the real deal—she could actually see dead people. He knew she wouldn't fake contact or try to cheat him.

Grimly, he ran a hand through his hair, impatiently pushing aside the pale, straw-colored strands, mentally steeling himself for a fight. If Madame Majicka was unwilling to help him, it would be hard to change her mind.

Since there was never any hurrying Madame Majicka, especially when it came to tea, he dropped his backpack on the floor and shrugged out of his light-weight jacket. *Might as well get comfortable.*

He surveyed the shop and then wandered to the nearest shelf, looking over the various occult paraphernalia. The empty sockets of a grinning skull watched him from the one side of the room, and he glanced at it out of the corner of his eye, trying to determine if it was real. Knowing Madame Majicka, it probably was. He wasn't really sure what would require the use of a skull, and he sidled away from it, not sure he really wanted to find out.

The shop was actually two separate shops—one that served the living and one that served the dead stuck on earth as ghosts—sandwiched back to back and connected only by the opening covered by the bead-curtain Madame Majicka had disappeared through. Irene had jokingly referred to it as the "Oreo cookie of occult shops."

Jonah smiled faintly at the memory and then, just as quickly, grew somber again as the deep, dull, ever-present ache in his gut intensified.

When he'd last visited, he had been in the mystical trance that let him separate his spirit from his body— basically he'd been a ghost, which was how he'd been able to see Irene. Today, however, he was in his body, and it felt strange and uncomfortable to be standing here, thick and heavy with the encumbrance of a physical form. He suddenly realized how tired he was. God, he'd forgotten what it was like to be tired. In his ghost form, he didn't need to sleep.

He ran his hand through his hair again. Pushing the chin-length strands back from his face, he let his gaze wander around the shop, comparing this side—the side for the living—with his memories of the dead side, mentally making note of anything that might help him in his quest. Though the shelves on this side were just as cluttered and crammed as those on the dead side, these mostly seemed to be full of stuff like incense, crystals, and Ouija boards—useless junk. The turtles, roots, and various herbal remedies seemed just as irrelevant.

Madame Majicka bustled back through the bead curtain with the tea tray. "You strike me as an Earl Grey sort."

"Uh, sure?" He disliked all teas equally, so it didn't really matter what she served him. He slid onto a stool. "So, about a séance?"

Madame Majicka talked as she poured out two cups of steaming hot liquid. "Why on earth do you need a séance? You can already see the dead."

"I can see the dead here. I want to contact someone on the other side. Or, at least, locate them."

Madame Majicka set the pot down so hard the lid rattled. She looked flummoxed for a moment. Then her eyes grew sad. "Oh, my dear, I am sorry, but it doesn't work like that."

"What do you mean?"

"I mean a séance is only so the dead still here on earth can talk to the living and vice versa."

Jonah frowned. "But your flyer says you help people contact spirits in the 'Great Beyond.' "

Madame Majicka gave him a faint smile as she picked up the teapot and resumed pouring. "Well, my dear, it's all one and the same to the living. Not everyone is like you and me, you know. We can see the dead, but the rest of the living... well, they're blissfully unaware that there are spirits all around us and happy to remain unaware."

Jonah stared at her. "So, you mean that during a séance the ghost just stands here, next to you, and you just repeat whatever they say? But that's a... a... cheap trick!" He flapped his hands for a second, trying to come up with the words to express his disappointment. It wasn't exactly a trick, but it wasn't really "mystical," either. It was just parroting what someone said. It required no special skills, and, even worse, it barely involved the supernatural.

"It's hardly a trick," Madame Majicka said with some asperity. "For the living, it *is* the Great Beyond."

Jonah usually found Madame Majicka's word games and prevarications amusing, but not today. He'd spent the year and a half after Irene left missing her terribly and wondering if she was okay, then he'd spent the eight months they had corresponded across the divide separating the land of the living from the land of the dead worried that something was wrong, and then he'd spent the month since he'd last heard from her certain that something terrible had happened. All told, he'd spent two years, three months, four days, and seventeen hours worrying and wondering. Even another minute seemed untenable. He needed to find a way to contact her — and fast. If she was in trouble, there wasn't a moment to lose.

"So what happens when someone wants you to contact someone who has crossed over?" he asked.

Madame Majicka pursed her lips for a second as she added sugar to the two teacups and passed one to Jonah. "Not every séance results in a successful connection, you know," she said, and he had the impression that she was giving him the rehearsed line she used on her customers. "I'm only able to help a very small fraction of those who come to me. However, there are ways of passing messages to spirits on the other side…"

"Yeah, I know about those." He'd been communicating with Irene through letters left on her grave — right up until the moment when she'd abruptly cut off contact, curtly and incomprehensibly ordering him to stop writing to her. "I don't need to send someone a message; I need to locate them — to know exactly where in the afterlife they are."

The afterlife, it turned out, was rather vast. Jonah had learned early on that all the myths and stories of the afterlife were true—including the innumerable "lands" detailed in every culture's beliefs and mythology. Valhalla, Heaven, T'ian, the Elysian Fields, the Happy Hunting Grounds, Hades—they all existed. Irene could be in any one of a hundred planes of the afterlife.

"Oh no, my dear! I'm afraid that's not possible." She gave him another sad look as if she wanted to say something additional. Instead, she took a sip of tea, watching him over the rim of her cup.

"There's got to be some way. What about scrying or… or…" He desperately searched his memory for the few "magical" practices he'd ever heard of but came up blank. In these, he was out of his depth—afterlife mythology had turned out to be true, but the same couldn't be said for magic. He knew because he'd tried. Casting spells, summoning demons—none of it had worked to find Irene.

"Well, you could always just ask them where they are."

A burning, acrid lump rose in his throat at the bitter memory of Irene's last letter to him, of his hands shaking so badly he could barely read the cold, remorseless words and of the ringing in his ears that deafened him to everything but the sound of his thudding heart.

This will be my last letter…

His fists clenched beneath the table. "That's not an option."

Madame Majicka just looked at him with sympathetic eyes and sipped her tea.

He breathed in hard through his nose, pushing from his mind the searing image of the carefully flowing script of Irene's letter superimposed over a lake of fire. "Okay, fine. If there's no way to locate someone from this side, then is there a way to visit the other side? Like astral projection or dream walking or contacting a spirit guide or something like that?"

Madame Majicka shook her head. "Really, my dear, I am sorry."

"But there are stories, from dozens of cultures throughout history, of people visiting the land of the dead to reclaim lost souls and bring them back to the land of the living. Orpheus. Gilgamesh. Hercules, King Mu and Zaofu, Aeneas, Pwyll, Indra, Gesar, Izanagi and Izanami, Hermodr—what about them? How'd they do it?" Irene had crossed over to the afterlife via a tunnel of light—one that he, because he was living, couldn't see, even in his ghost form. So while the meditation he'd learned allowed him to see the dead stuck on earth as ghosts, it did not allow him to travel to the "Great Beyond" or any of the realms of the dead. Whatever else the meditation did, it did not actually simulate death. He was, unfortunately, still very much alive.

But somehow, in the handful of stories he had found, the living did manage to find their way to the other side. In rare instances, they even managed to bring someone back to the land of the living—and to life—with them. Unfortunately, the stories contained maddeningly few details on how it was done. All the stories started with the hero at the gates of the Underworld and being able to magically walk right in. He knew how to find the tunnel of light that would let him cross over—the problem was that he couldn't see it. Or cross it. That was the rather key detail he was missing.

Madame Majicka shook her head. "I'm afraid you're outside my area of expertise."

"Well then, what about near death experiences? Is there a way to simulate one of those?"

Madame Majicka set her tea down hard and blinked at him in horror. "Good heavens!"

He realized he'd gone too far, had revealed too much, and was venturing into territory where Madame Majicka would outright refuse to help him. He forced himself to relax. He couldn't risk alienating her by coming on too strong. She was his one solid lead at the moment. He took a deep breath and sat back. To soothe Madame Majicka, he took a sip of his tea and then had to hide his grimace of distaste. He quickly set the cup back down.

He tried to keep his thoughts focused squarely on the cup of tea and in looking placid so he didn't give away what he was thinking, his mind working furiously to come up with another line of attack, another question he could ask that Madame Majicka might be willing to answer. She never gave out information freely, but sometimes she could be coaxed into dropping hints.

The psychic gave him another pitying look, then brightened, though her smile seemed a little brittle, as if her gaiety was forced. "But come, let us talk of more pleasant things. So, how are you?"

"I'm fine," he said, desperately wishing he had Irene's knack for steamrolling over people's objections to get what she wanted. "Look, what about—"

"Really? You look a little tired. Are you sleeping well? I have the loveliest lavender powder to help with insomnia. Really, you should try it." She began to rise from the table.

She was obviously trying to change the subject, to derail him. He grabbed her arm to prevent her from getting up. "Are you sure there's nothing you can think of that might help?"

Madame Majicka's eyes became a little less warm, and her tone was steely as she replied, "Now really, I've told you everything I can."

So she couldn't—or wouldn't—help. He unwrapped his fingers from her sleeve, defeated. "Okay, fine," he said absently, already rising to his feet and reaching for his jacket as his mind jumped three steps ahead to his next move. "Look, I should get going." He grabbed his backpack from the floor. "Thanks for the tea."

"Well, I'm sorry I couldn't be more help," Madame Majicka said, her eyes, dark and inscrutable, watching him closely. "But listen, how about—"

Jonah gave her a thin smile. "It's okay. Thanks anyway." He shouldered his backpack and headed for the door. The bell tinkled as he left.

Once outside, he stood on the sidewalk, blankly watching the throng of people on the street. The shop—or, at least, this side of it—opened out onto a main street in downtown Boston, and the living bustled by on their way to work or to catch a train. Many talked on cell phones, gesturing wildly with their hands. He watched them absently, feeling numb and far removed from it all. These people got up, went to work, came home, watched television, ate dinner, did the dishes, then went to bed and did it all again the next day. It all seemed so boring, so pointless, and with every passing day, it all seemed even more pointless and dreamlike, as if everything in the ghost world was real and these people the ghosts.

He slumped against the building and slid into a sitting position, not sure what to do next. A month since Irene had cut off all contact and he was still at square one.

Initially, after Irene had first crossed more than two years ago, he'd done as he'd promised; he had given up spending time with the dead, though it had been the hardest thing he'd ever had to do. He had never forgotten about her, though, never stopped thinking about her. The moment she had entered the tunnel of light, he'd known they'd both made a terrible mistake—she in going and he in letting her go—or, at least, letting her go alone. That knowledge ate at him, day and night, always in the back of his mind, surfacing at night in his dreams. Soon, it was easier to just stay in ghost form, where he didn't have to sleep, to avoid the nightmares altogether.

Being awake wasn't always better though; whenever he saw the flash of a red dress or mahogany hair or a silver BMW, his heart would jump. She'd returned! She'd realized what a mistake it was to leave, and she'd come back. He'd get a job and an apartment, and they could live there, just the two of them. No parents to tell him what to do and no responsibilities for her. He'd keep her company, keep her from being sad that she was dead, and they'd go out exploring the ghost world every day, and everything would be okay for both of them.

Whenever the urge to try and find her became almost overwhelming, he'd write her a letter and leave it on her grave. A year and a half had gone by. Then, suddenly, one day, a letter had arrived from Irene—she needed his help. It was almost as if she had never left. She was still the one person he could talk to, who didn't treat him like a kid, and she still needed him, needed his help. In fact, in her letters, she talked as if no time at all had passed since she had crossed over. She acted as if she'd only just arrived on the other side, and strangely, there was never any mention of what had happened to her in the year and a half she'd been gone. He'd wondered—hoped, even—that maybe time worked differently on the other side.

Almost immediately upon receiving her first letter, he'd suspected something was seriously wrong. Her letters were so careful, so guarded. She was hiding something, holding something back—and she was desperately trying to get out of wherever she was. Before she left, Irene had worried that she might be going to Hell or, at least, somewhere unpleasant, and Jonah was afraid she'd been right. What else would she hide from him? When she abruptly cut off contact—after eight months of correspondence—with no explanation, no reason other than to say she didn't want him to end up like her, he knew she was in serious trouble, and there was *no* way he was just going to leave her there—wherever there was.

Irene.

His stomach clenched again. She was out there, somewhere. Alone. Unprotected.

Don't send me any more letters. I won't read them.

What could have happened to make her say such a thing?

A shiver of fear went through him. There were things—terrible things—in the land of the dead. Hell hounds and lakes of fire were just the tip of the iceberg. Irene was smart and gutsy, but she was also head-strong and impetuous—and had no people skills whatsoever. And like most people these days, she had made no preparations for afterlife journey. Hell, she hadn't even packed a coin for the ferryman and had had to write to him, asking for one. Without proper preparation, a dead person's chances of making it through the Underworld were slim to none. It didn't matter that she hadn't been alone. According to her letters, she'd been traveling with two guys—a nineteenth-century American cowboy and a twelfth-century Spanish knight.

His eyes narrowed. She'd been exceedingly tight-lipped about both men. She'd been hiding something about them. Annoyance flashed through him. What was so great about those guys, anyway? Obviously not much if they had been stuck in the same place for hundreds of years. Leave it to Irene to find the two biggest losers in the entire afterlife.

His cell phone buzzed. He reached into his pocket and pulled it out. His mother. He sent the call to voicemail. He was supposed to be dropping off a college application today; she was calling to check up on him.

The situation at home was becoming untenable; he'd need to find a new base of operations if the search for Irene continued to drag on like this. Having skipped two grades, he had been close to graduating when Irene's letters had stopped. Since he'd been sixteen and legally able, he'd simply dropped out of school. He'd hardly been going anyway and looking for Irene was much more important. His parents had flipped when they found out, threatening to throw him out of the house if he didn't go back and finish his senior year, which was not going to happen no matter how much they yelled about it. The compromise had been to get his GED, but then, predictably, they hadn't been satisfied with that. Now they wanted him to go to college. Once again, they were threatening to throw him out of the house; this time they wanted him to either get a job or enroll in community college at the very least.

His phone buzzed again. This time it was his father. He ignored that call, too.

Unfortunately, he had to live somewhere while he searched for Irene, and it turned out that without a job, he couldn't afford an apartment — not that anyone would rent one to a seventeen-year-old, anyway.

His phone vibrated — this time with a text message.
ANSWER YOUR DAMNED PHONE.

He deleted the message and turned off his phone. He leaned his head against the cool stone of the magic shop and contemplated his few remaining options.

Beside him, the bell jangled, startling him, as the door opened. Madame Majicka stuck her head out and looked at him, hardly pausing before she spoke. "You wouldn't, by any chance, be interested in a job, would you?"

One

Irene Dunphy's eyes flew open as the boat she was on came to rest against the shore with a bump. Around her, the world came muzzily into focus, as if she were just waking up from a dream. She blinked rapidly, trying to orient herself to her surroundings. The world underfoot bobbed gently, making it hard to keep her balance, while the world in front of her eyes refused to resolve itself into anything discernable. It took a moment for her to realize the problem wasn't her eyes but the sun high overhead, blinding her.

She was dead — at only thirty-six, a victim of her own folly by driving drunk after a night bar-hopping — and traveling through the afterlife. Most recently, she'd boarded a ferry — a large, flat-bottomed skiff that seemed to navigate of its own accord, to cross the proverbial River Styx — and now she was... here — wherever here was.

The land she'd just left — what could only be described as purgatory — had had a sort of indeterminateness to it, the sky and the ground all melding together in a seamless, gun-metal gray, giving no indication of day or night. Here, as there, the sky and ground ran together, but this time, all was clothed in the brittle, blinding hues of burning gold so bright it hurt the eyes. Irene found she couldn't look at anything directly or her eyes started to water.

She held up a hand to block the sunlight as she surveyed the landscape spread before her. Her traveling companion, a former twelfth-century Spanish knight named Andras, stood beside her and similarly shielded his eyes.

The landscape was flat and unending, spreading away to the horizon, its only feature some kind of tall grass.

Lots and lots and lots of gold-colored grass.

Swell.

A light breeze played about her, teasing her long, dark auburn hair and the gauzy skirt of her short dress while the river water sloshed against the sides of the boat. With the wind and sun and water, she could almost imagine she was enjoying a day at the beach—almost. Too bad she couldn't forget she was dead.

Andras, a man of few words and with a knight's taciturn personality, grunted—his usual response to most things. He made quite a picture, standing there, tall and broad-shouldered, tense and alert, his dark eyes looking to the horizon as he assessed the landscape for danger. In the bronze light, his dark features—typical of a southern Spaniard—appeared bronzed as well, and an aura of golden light framed him.

"This is not Heaven," Andras said.

Irene bit her lip. No, it most definitely did not seem to be Heaven.

Heaven was what Andras had expected when he boarded the boat with her, despite the fact she'd told him she wasn't trying to reach Heaven—she was trying to find her way back to the land of the living.

Andras was looking at her expectantly, waiting for her to disembark, so she steeled herself and stepped warily off the long, low boat into the tall grass as gracefully as she could. The thin, golden stalks tickled her legs and thighs as she hopped down and stepped away from the boat. She was still wearing the clothes she had died in—thigh-length, spaghetti-strapped candy-apple red dress—though she'd swapped her three-inch sling-back shoes for sensible, black, lace-ups with rubber soles, like the kind nurses might wear, and added an olive-green menswear suit coat—a gift from her friend Jonah — the fourteen-year-old boy who had helped her cross over.

She also still had her rattan beach bag of possessions — items she'd collected on Earth before leaving or had been sent by Jonah after she'd arrived in the land of the dead — and she clutched it tightly to her as she tentatively moved through the long, golden stalks, assessing how she felt about them.

Scratchy.

She risked a glance at Andras as he stepped down from the boat. He'd died in battle, and his body had been looted of everything of value, leaving him to travel the afterlife in his underclothes — what basically looked to Irene like long johns. He didn't even have shoes — though he never complained about being barefoot.

"What the hell is this stuff?" she asked, trailing a hand over the fuzzy tops.

Andras peered at the sweeping fields, squinting against the harsh, burning light. "Wheat," he grunted.

"Wheat?" Irene surveyed the landscape again. Andras had lived in the Dark Ages, so she assumed he would know more about it than she. The closest she'd ever come to wheat growing in a field was pictures on a cereal box. "Well, at least this plane is a lot more brightly colored than the last one."

Andras grunted.

The breeze tangled in her hair, and Irene impatiently brushed the long, silky strands from her eyes as she tried to determine what they were supposed to do next. She was attempting to return to the land of the living in the same way that someone in Ohio was heading back to Connecticut via China. The indirectness of her route was partly due to her own inability to navigate the afterlife — it turned out to be a lot harder than going from point A to point B to point C like one did in the physical world — and partly due to the fact that she was trying to return as something other than a ghost, since being a ghost had turned out to pretty much suck. She didn't know what the other options were, but the

Guide, the strange sort of afterlife mentor who popped up occasionally to give her advice, had assured her they existed—she just had to keep moving forward, traversing the planes of the afterlife.

She turned in a circle and then stopped short. Behind them, the place where the boat and river had been only a second ago was now also wheat; the boat and river were both gone. Now, in their place, a lone cow stood, eyes half closed, slowly chewing its cud.

Irene blinked, double-checking what she was seeing, but somehow wasn't surprised. Since crossing into the afterlife, she'd seen more weird than she ever thought possible: angels, little brown spirits of the hearth that attacked you if you didn't give them housework to do, a mysterious cat that came and went when it pleased, and the Guide himself— squat, bald, and dressed in a toga of bright, rainbow stripes. The landscape of the afterlife so far was just as fantastical as the creatures: an opulent hotel, an abandoned city, a desolate forest, and a desert. So why not a wheat field and a disappearing boat—it made as much sense as everything else she'd encountered.

Hesitantly, she and Andras approached the cow. The cow opened one lazy eye to study them. Irene poked it. The cow didn't respond. She looked at Andras. Andras shrugged.

"It's a cow," Irene said.

"Aye."

"Okay, I was just checking." She looked around once more, her gaze sweeping the vast, empty expanse. "Weren't there other people on the boat with us?" she asked, as indistinct memories bubbled through the lingering disorientation. As before, whenever she had made a transition between one layer of the afterlife and the next, she felt unsettled, like she was missing a chunk of time. Memories, too, perhaps. Already, the events of the past plane of existence were fading—as if they were just a dream. Maybe there had been people on the boat with them; maybe not. Maybe there hadn't even been a boat. She couldn't seem to recall for certain. One minute she'd been beside the River Acheron, saying goodbye to the people there, and the next, she'd been here. She frowned, trying to recall just what had happened in between.

Andras shrugged and, once again, grunted, his dark eyes also sweeping the landscape with a wariness that suggested he expected hidden dangers or an attack. The light breeze lifted a tail of his long, night-gownesque shirt, and Irene tried not to laugh. Instead, she raised an eyebrow at his tense stance. "It's wheat. I don't think it's going to bite."

"Have you forgotten the Nephilim?" Andras said, his deep, gravelly voice tinged with what might have been a hint of sardonic humor. Or it might be rebuke. It was so hard to tell with him. "They could be lurking anywhere."

The creatures, worshipped for centuries as angels and, before that, as gods of the afterlife, had chased them, injured them, and tried to kill them—she remembered it all quite clearly, thank you very much. "No, I haven't forgotten them, but unless they can make themselves invisible or the thickness of a stalk of wheat, there's no place for them to hide."

Irene impatiently pushed her hair back from her face again, tucking the long strands behind her ear, and swept her gaze across the landscape once more. There weren't any clear indicators of which direction they should head. There also weren't any clear indicators of what their goal was, either. Other than the Guide telling her to keep moving forward—"you have to go forward to go back," he'd said— she had no idea what she was supposed to be doing.

"Okay, well, I guess we just set out," she said, hoping Andras would feel free to jump in with a better idea.

Andras frowned doubtfully.

"I'm open to suggestions."

Andras spread his hands, palms up, in a gesture of submission.

"Yeah, well, I don't like setting off at random any better than you, but look around. It's not like there's a giant sign saying, 'Through traffic, straight ahead.' So, let's just pick a direction and see what we see. Maybe we'll find something that we can use to match this place up to one of the afterlife stories so we can figure out where we are and maybe get a clue of what we're supposed to do next."

"We could trust that God will reveal the way to us."

Now it was Irene's turn to frown. "That worked out so well for you at the river," she said, partly exasperated, partly teasing. Andras, for want of a coin to pay the ferryman, had been stuck by the River Acheron for eight hundred years.

A twinkle came into Andras's eyes though his face was completely deadpanned when he spoke. "It worked out very well. With nothing more than faith and hardly any effort on my part, I was able to traverse the river. God provided – as I knew he would."

"Oh, sure, and it only took you eight hundred years!"

One side of Andras's mouth ticked up in a faint smile. "A much-deserved and relaxing rest."

Irene laughed and threw up her hands. "Okay, Mr. Smart-Ass, fine. God provided me to get you across the river. Any chance he's going to provide you with a clue on what we're supposed to do next?"

Placidly, Andreas replied, "I follow where you lead."

He was only half joking. Andras truly did believe that God had sent Irene to lead him – and the rest of the dead – out of the underworld and into Heaven – or paradise or the Great Beyond or whatever you wanted to call it. Irene had tried to explain that she was actually trying to head in the opposite direction – away from the afterlife and back to the land of the living. Never mind that it was patently ridiculous to believe that God – a concept she didn't believe in – would choose her of all people as a messiah. But even in the face of her outright assertions she wasn't trying to get to Heaven, Andras had chosen to accompany her anyway. She found his strange – and complicated – mix of old-fashioned chivalry, misdirected protectiveness, and pig-headed stubbornness exasperating most of the time, and his blind devotion to his faith even more so; and yet, for all that, she was grateful for his company and glad that he was here.

Irene playfully narrowed her eyes. "Why is it that I'm suddenly the one unquestionably in charge whenever it's completely unclear what we're supposed to do next?"

Andras gave her one of his rare, wolfish grins.

"Oh... you...!" she sputtered, giving him a mock glare. "Fine. If God sent me to lead you out of the wilderness, then as His instrument, I'm feeling a divinely-granted urge to head... that way." She randomly pointed into the distance. She hefted the rattan beach bag of treasured possessions into a more secure position on her shoulder and then set off. Andras fell in step beside her.

They walked without speaking, the only sound the swish of the wheat as they passed. Though the sunlight was blinding, the air itself shimmering so that it hurt the eyes, there was no discernable sun-like object overhead, just a burning, bronze-hued expanse impossible to look at directly. The wheat blazed so brightly and the air glowed so warmly that Irene expected to feel as if she was in a furnace; she should be sweltering, but she wasn't.

You can't sweat, Irene reminded herself, *or feel hot and cold. You don't have a body. Even if it were a million degrees, you wouldn't feel it.*

The reminder didn't work. While intellectually she knew the dead didn't have bodies and, therefore, couldn't actually feel physical sensations or have physical needs—such as eating and sleeping—she had a hard time internalizing that fact. She still felt hot and cold, hunger and thirst, pain and fatigue, no matter how much anyone tried to convince her.

There were dark shapes up ahead, moving against the wheat, though they were too far away to see distinctly. Irene's steps slowed as she squinted, trying to see what they might be. They might be people—other ghosts—but they might be Nephilim, too. From the way he was shading his eyes and peering into the distance, Irene could tell Andras had seen them, too.

Their pace slowed to a crawl as they moved cautiously, tense and ready, the dark spots growing steadily closer as Irene and Andras slowly closed the distance. Irene reached into her bag and pulled out the tire iron, holding it defensively in front of her while she held herself in readiness to run at a moment's notice.

At last, they reached a distance at which it was clear to see that the dark shapes were people and not Nephilim. However, there was something strange about them — it was as if the people were all in the shade; they were dark and featureless from the tops of their heads to the tips of their toes.

As Irene and Andras drew closer, fear prickled along Irene's spine. These weren't people — at least, not people as she generally thought of them. These were… people-shaped shadows. Not flat and two-dimensional like regular shadows; no, instead, these were three-dimensional, fully formed and free-standing as if they were people, though inky black from head to foot with no discernable facial features, hair, or clothing.

The hair on the back of Irene's neck stood up. She slowed and then stopped, afraid to get any closer.

There were maybe a dozen of the shadow people, and they seemed to be tending the wheat — at least, that's what Irene thought they were doing. It was hard to tell — they had no tools, and yet they passed their hands to and fro as if threshing with invisible scythes.

Irene put a hand on Andras's arm, but he didn't need the warning. Without a word, he angled away from the shadows, not approaching any closer. The shadows seemed unconcerned by Andras's and Irene's presence and continued whatever it was they were doing, without paying any attention to them.

Andras and Irene were silent until they were well away from the shadows.

"What do you think those were?" Irene asked.

Andras grunted. "Demons."

"If they were demons, wouldn't they have attacked us?"

Andras grunted.

Irene frowned as she puzzled over the strange people. Maybe they should have talked to them—seen if they could have provided information.

"You are making a strange face," Andras said.

"Sorry... I was just thinking."

"About what?"

"The shadow people... and all this wheat. I'm trying to figure out which afterlife we're in—you know, from the stories. But so far, I don't remember anything about wheat fields... unless this is the Elysian Fields from the Greeks, though I'm not really sure what Elysian is. Maybe it's a kind of wheat?" She frowned. "Though, if I remember correctly, the Elysian Fields were like Heaven. This is not my idea of Heaven."

"Have you no way to ask the boy?"

By "the boy," Andras meant Jonah. Irene grimaced, immediately assailed by a stabbing pang of heartache at the reminder of her one friend—*former* friend—among the living. She pressed her lips together, hard.

Jonah, genius that he was, had figured out a way to send her letters in the afterlife, and she, using what he'd taught her about the afterlife, had figured out a way to send letters back. Those letters had been her lifeline, comforting and guiding her through the dark and gloomy world, populated by Hungry Ghosts, Nephilim, and other dangers, that she had just passed through.

Even more than giving comfort, Jonah had saved her life—once again—by sending her a coin so she could board the ferry that would let her escape across the river to the next stage of her journey. Without Jonah, she would still be stuck beside the river—for all eternity.

Andras knew that she'd left behind the altar of stones that allowed her to send letters to Jonah so that coins could continue to be sent over to help future arrivals. What he didn't know was that even if she still had the altar, she wouldn't use it. She had cut all ties between herself and

Jonah in order to ensure that Jonah stayed safely in the land of the living—where he belonged.

"I told him not to write to me anymore," she said grimly, refusing to meet Andras's inquiring gaze. She recalled with another sharp pang the letter she'd had to send to Jonah, cutting off all contact for his own good. Jonah needed to focus on being among the living, and she'd tried to express how much she wanted him to be happy and have a good life. She hadn't been able to fully explain, though, why happiness meant staying in the land of the living. If she'd told him how terrible the afterlife had turned out to be, he would have worried about her and possibly even risked trying to come after her. So instead, in the hope that it would make him hate her, she'd made it sound like she was dropping him because he was of no further use to her. The best outcome would be if he never thought of her again.

She wasn't sure which was worse: knowing she'd hurt him or knowing she should have done it sooner. Jonah's interest in the dead wasn't just a hobby, the way some kids became obsessed with dinosaurs or Jedi knights. No, his interest was deeper, much deeper, and much more dangerous.

Irene felt another stab of guilt, this one even stronger. The letter wasn't even the worst of it. She had known from nearly the first moment she'd met him that something wasn't quite right with Jonah's life—that he was achingly lonely and sad, that he didn't have many friends, and that he wasn't being quite truthful about the origin of his interest in the afterlife. She should have dug deeper, should have questioned, should have confronted—and more. She should have burned that damn book—the one containing the secret of how to cross into the spirit realm, spanked him and sent him home with a good talking to about the stupidity of suicide, and sent a letter to his parents, warning them to keep a closer eye on him. Instead, she'd done nothing, blithely ignoring that which was so very obvious.

No, that wasn't true—she'd done worse than nothing. She'd selfishly led him deeper into the afterlife, made it even more appealing by allowing him to help her. No, that wasn't right. She'd *demanded* he help her and, in doing so, gave him a reason to keep visiting the afterlife, to pull further and further away from the land of the living, to think that death was not just okay, but even cool.

The Guide had revealed the level of her culpability when he'd pulled back the veil between worlds and shown her Jonah sleeping beside her grave, day and night. He'd looked half dead — thin, pale, and so very small and alone. That image was burned into her mind — it haunted her, ate at her, terrified her. If anything happened to Jonah, if he died screwing around with the afterlife or worse, killed himself so he could cross over, it would be entirely her fault.

"Why did you tell him to stop writing? His help was invaluable."

Irene wasn't going to be able to keep the tears back for much longer, and she hated to show any kind of weakness in front of Andras. Andras was a "boot straps up" kind of guy. Tears were "women's weakness" — a sign of inferiority. Andras only accompanied her because he thought she was some sort of savior sent by God. He had only the most grudging of tolerance for her personally, and crying would almost certainly destroy what little credibility she had with him.

She attempted to change the subject. "Of course, this whole place probably isn't even real." She pointed to their feet, which were sunk into the earth as if it were mist. They were wading through the ground as if it were water, rather than walking on top of it. "We've gone so far from the physical plane that our brains can't even process what we're seeing and experiencing. I think they've just given up trying to have it make sense and are just doing the best they can to make it seem plausible. Otherwise, we'd probably go insane."

The afterlife tended to be as much metaphor as physical — most of what they saw and heard and felt was their brains' best interpretation of their actual surroundings, using familiar sights and sounds from their lives as a kind of shorthand for conveying what was actually happening. They were now, after all, non-corporeal bundles of energy—without ears and eyes and skin—so their brains did the best they could to translate.

Andras grunted. "Perhaps we are already insane. This may be the divine madness of which the poets speak."

Irene shook her head but couldn't hide a smile. "You're pretty quick with the jokes for someone who spent his life in a religious order. I thought knights in the Holy Order of Saint Whoever—"

"Sant Iago."

"—were supposed to be serious and noble and devout?"

"Cannot a knight also have wit?"

"I don't know; you tell me. What do I know about knights, especially since you won't tell me anything about them?"

Andras frowned, and Irene cut in quickly before he could give her the same old lecture about the "needless melancholy" of rehashing their lives before death. "Look, why don't we—"

But Andras was like a dog with a bone and would not be deterred from his original line of questioning. "But the boy, why would you—"

"Stop calling him that; you make it sound like he's a little kid. He's fourteen."

"Ah." Andras nodded knowingly. "My brother's bride was fourteen at the time of their marriage."

"Ewww! And how old was your brother?" She quickly held up a hand. "Wait, don't answer that; there's no good answer to that question." Irene screwed up her face in disgust and glared at him. "In my time, that's considered a crime. And I certainly hope you're not thinking that Jonah and I—because that's disgusting! Jonah is... well, he's not a kid, but he's not an adult either. Our relationship is hard to explain. He's... that voice in my head—the one that urges you to be a better version of yourself, you know? Like Jiminy Cricket."

At Andras's quizzical look, Irene was reminded of the gulf between them. Most of the time, she could forget there was eight hundred years of history separating them, but occasionally they came to a "same planet, different world" kind of impasse there was no way to bridge.

"There's this story about a wooden puppet who wants to be a real boy, and then this fairy comes and makes him into a real boy, and there's this cricket that serves as the boy's conscience because, obviously, being made out of wood, he doesn't have one..." Irene trailed off at the look on Andras's face. "I sound like a crazy person, don't I?"

Andras grinned and nodded. However, his eyes, dark and serious, probed hers. "Why then did you tell the boy to stop writing?"

"You just don't give up, do you? I thought you wanted me to let go of the past. Well, Jonah is most definitely the past. Cutting off contact with him seems like the kind of thing you'd approve of." Andras, however, continued to hold her gaze with his own, clearly not buying that explanation. She threw up her hands. "Because I had to, for his own good, okay? He's better off without me, trust me."

"Perhaps he is better off without you, but are you better off without him?"

"Yes, well, for once it's not all about what's best for me," she answered blithely. "Apparently, I'm growing as a person. You should be honored – this is a rare and special moment." Andras opened his mouth to retort, and Irene cut him off. "Look, how about we stop for a second?" Wandering clearly wasn't doing them any good. The landscape was unchanging – just wheat, wheat, wheat. It was hard to imagine they were going to find anything at all, let alone a way back to the land of the living. She was going to need to call on her "ghost senses," the internal compass that, on occasion, let her navigate the planes of the afterlife. The sensation, like a deep, low-down flame in her chest – not like her lungs or her heart or her stomach, but something more basic and elemental, something that was part of her but part of the universe, too, as if a piece of her beat in time with the heartbeat of creation—was like a third eye or psychic intuition. She wasn't always able to connect to it, but when she did, the flame would surge within her, steady and sure, and she could use it to guide her way. Sometimes, it came to her out of the blue when she was thinking about something else, but mostly, it came to her when she was desperate and filled with longing for a particular thing—safety, solace, home.

Andras's response was swift. "During training to become a knight, we had to stand for hours at a time on guard. If the master-at-arms caught us napping, he beat our arms and legs with a stick and then made us stand with our arms out straight, holding buckets of sand. We learned quickly to ignore our fatigue."

At least he wasn't talking about Jonah anymore. Irene shook her head ruefully. "Your stories are always so cheerful." She plucked at the wheat, sliding a stalk through her fingers, exploring its texture and testing its realness. It seemed real enough, and yet, there was something unreal about it, as well—a misplaced silkiness, a kind of thinness to the material of which it was made. Absently, Irene twisted the stalk around her finger, as she had done with blades of grass as a child, making herself a ring.

"You know, the Guide said that everything that ever was and ever will be is all layered together. I think that means, technically, we could time travel. We could go back to your time, and you could show me what it was like."

Andras shielded his eyes against the blazing light reflecting off the wheat and grunted, a note of humor in the sound. "I am having a hard time picturing you as a demure lady of the court."

"Yeah, well, I didn't say I wanted to spend an extended time there. Just that we could pop by and see. Besides, we'd be ghosts, so we'd be invisible. I wouldn't have to blend in."

Andras dropped his hand and stepped closer, concern etched on his face. "What is wrong?" he asked, his dark eyes probing hers.

"What do you mean?"

"You are delaying."

"This isn't delaying; it's making conversation." Okay, so maybe she was delaying a little; half the time, her attempts to use her ghost senses just fell flat, and she hated to look like an idiot in front of Andras. But she'd also been feeling him out on the idea of returning to the land of the living.

Irene sighed. Eventually, he was going to realize there was no redemption to be found in following her, that she wasn't leading him to Heaven after all, that she was, in fact, leading him to the one place he absolutely didn't want to go—back to the land of the living. He couldn't make it any clearer that he had no desire to spend even a second there—the mere suggestion that they travel back to his time so they could peek in on the living had been immediately shut down. What was he going to do when he realized she'd been sincere when she'd told him that was where she was headed? If he'd come with her thinking she'd change her mind along the way or that she'd somehow stumble upon Heaven and be so enamored of it she'd forget wanting to return to Earth, then he was very, very wrong. The longer she stayed in the land of the dead, the greater her desire to return to the land of the living—that was for sure.

So, when he finally realized that was truly where she was heading, what would happen? There would, of course, be the inevitable messy break-up. Andras would hate her for taking him farther from where he wanted to be, and he would leave. And she didn't blame him—their goals were incompatible. They had been from the very beginning. Her greater concern was what would happen to Andras after he left. As little as she knew about navigating the afterlife, he knew even less. If he struck out on his own, the likelihood of him finding his way was pretty slim, especially the farther and farther they went. They were likely to reach a point where he'd never find his way back onto the path he wanted.

She could pick a fight now, before they reached the point where Andras would be hopelessly lost. She could make him hate her so he'd stop following her, the way she had with Jonah—if there was one thing she was good at, it was getting people, especially guys, to hate her—but she wasn't sure it would help. There was no way to send Andras back to the last plane—where he might have some hope of getting back on track to where he wanted to go—since the boat had disappeared. Maybe she should take a page out of his book and pray for a miracle—maybe they'd stumble across Heaven on the way to the land of the living, and she could drop him off.

She looked down, avoiding meeting his eyes. "I was just trying to show an interest in your life and learn more about you. That's all."

Andras grunted, the sound filled with suspicion. Irene bent down to tie her shoelace, as much to avoid eye contact as anything. When she straightened up, something in the distance caught her eye, shimmering like a mirage. She squinted, not sure she was really seeing what she thought she saw.

"You know, now might be a good time for you to tell me what it was like to live in a castle," she said.

Andras shook his head, sadly, as if Irene had disappointed him. "You cling too much to the past. Forget the trappings of life. Free your mind from these longings, and so, free your soul. Only then will we be able to escape these shackles and enter Heaven to rest at the side of God."

Why did he always have to argue about everything? "For *God's* sake," she said, exasperated, "just answer the question!"

"Wherefore?"

Irene pointed to the hulking structure in the distance. "Because," she said as Andras whirled around to see what she was pointing at, "correct me if I'm wrong, but that looks like a castle."

Two

Jonah glanced up as the bell over the magic shop's door jangled. He blinked in surprise. A girl had entered the shop, about his age or maybe a little younger, tiny, with elfin features and straight, waist-length, jet-black hair streaked with vivid purple. She wore a tight, black tank top, short, flouncy skirt, purple- and black-striped tights, and black, knee-high, lace-up combat boots. Even stranger, she had come in the ghost side of the store even though she didn't have the blue-white shimmer of the dead.

"Er... can I help you?" Jonah asked, cautiously straightening up from the list of inventory he'd been updating.

"Uh, hi. Where's Auntie?"

Jonah's forehead creased in confusion. "Auntie?" He looked the girl over once more, verifying that she was indeed alive and not a ghost. For the first time, he noticed she held a large duffel bag.

At that moment, Madame Majicka swept into the room. "Char! My dear!" She flung open her arms and enveloped the girl in a hug, which the girl, dropping her duffel bag, returned just as enthusiastically. After a moment, Madame Majicka released the girl and held her at arm's length. "Let me look at you! Oh, my dear, you've grown!"

The girl, dwarfed by Madame Majicka's statuesque height, beamed. Jonah stared at the two of them.

"Jonah, this is my niece Chartreuse," Madame Majicka said, fluttering a hand in Jonah's direction. She glanced at Jonah then and, seeing his surprised expression, said, "Didn't I mention my niece was coming for a visit?"

"Uh... no."

Madame Majicka hadn't really mentioned much at all. In the six months he'd been working at the shop, he'd hardly seen Madame Majicka. She was always off to some meeting or other, some resupply trip or other, some aura-cleansing retreat or other. He was practically running the store at this point.

The girl eyed Jonah with interest. Alarmed and slightly annoyed at being scrutinized, he looked at the duffel bag again. She wasn't staying here, was she? He had his life well-ordered to a perfectly synchronized routine now, including the side business to fund his hunt for Irene that he was running out of the magic shop—which Madame Majicka didn't know about. A visiting niece meant, at the very least, that Madame Majicka was likely going to be around more, which would be rather inconvenient.

Before he could ask any of the obvious questions—what the girl was doing here, how long she would be staying, and where she was staying—Madame Majicka abruptly said, as if making a grave pronouncement, "I have to go out." She held up a hand, as if silencing a protest. "Don't worry. I will return."

With that, she swept out the door, closing it decidedly behind her.

Jonah and the girl looked at each other in surprised silence for a long moment.

Finally, Jonah cleared his throat. "Your name is Chartreuse?" he asked, not sure he'd heard Madame Majicka correctly.

"Char," the girl said quickly. "Just call me Char."

Jonah raised an eyebrow, not sure what else to say. There was another long, awkward pause. Jonah glanced at his watch. "Uh, look—I actually have to go out and do some stuff..."

The girl quickly affected a disinterested expression, but not before a look of disappointment crossed her face. "Oh. Well, that's fine—I can watch the shop by myself."

"Oh, no, I didn't mean that you... I'll just lock up—"

"No, really, it's fine."

"I can't just leave you here alone," he said, annoyed the girl couldn't see this rather obvious fact. Even if she was Madame Majicka's niece, that didn't mean she could be left alone to watch the shop. He certainly wasn't going to leave her with the cash register and all the merchandise—or with the "special" customers who might come in looking for him.

The girl shuffled the duffel bag from one hand to the other and shifted her weight from foot to foot. "I've watched the shop before."

"Madame Majicka didn't say anything about you watching—"

"She's *my* aunt, which practically makes it *my* store." The girl dropped the duffel bag with a thump and crossed her arms over her chest. She cast Jonah a suspicious glance. "More than it's yours anyway."

Before Jonah could fire back, a bell jangled, catching him by surprise. He looked at the door, but no one was there. The sound must have come from the other door, the one on the living side of the shop. Madame Majicka apparently hadn't locked the door before she left.

He and Char both headed for the bead curtain separating the two sides of the shop. The girl shot Jonah a confused, annoyed look as they both tried to squeeze through the narrow doorway at the same time. Jonah, torn between exasperation at her pushiness and ingrained good manners, stepped back and let her go first.

On the other side of the store, a heavy-set, middle-aged woman in a gauzy summer dress and sandals browsed through a rack of crystals.

"Can I help you?" Jonah asked, trying to maneuver in front of Char. The woman ignored him.

"CAN I HELP YOU?" he repeated more loudly, in case she was hard of hearing.

Char glared at him. "Duh! The living can't see the dead!" she hissed at him under her breath. Then, to the woman, she said, "Good afternoon! Can I help you?"

"What?" said Jonah. "I'm not—" He looked down at himself as he spoke. "Oh, shit, I forgot." He was in his ghost form. After he'd expressed—to a customer—his belief that the only cleansing properties of incense came from the rank smell which annoyed the spirits into leaving more than it acted upon them in any mystical way, Madame Majicka usually manned the living side of the store, leaving him free to interact with the dead side, which suited him fine.

Char's attention had already left him, focused instead on the woman, who was speaking. "Oh, yes. I'm looking for some Blue Agate."

"Hey," Jonah said to Char, and then again, louder, "Hey! I'm not dead."

Char shot him a quelling look and then moved across the room to a rack of small crystal pendants on leather cords.

Jonah was about to protest the girl's intrusive intervention but realized there wasn't much he could do at the moment. The customer couldn't see him. He stood there, arms dangling at his sides, feeling useless as Char bustled busily to the customer's aid.

"Oh, we have some of that right over here," Char said. She picked up one of the necklaces and handed it to the woman.

"We have some of that right here," Jonah mimicked under his breath.

The woman crossed to Char and reached gratefully for the pendant. "Oh, thank goodness! I've been to three stores looking for this!"

"Well, if you're looking for something for tranquility and balance, we also have Alexandrite," Char added.

The woman shook her head. "Actually, what I need is something for purification."

"What kind of purification—what's the space, and what are you trying to remove?"

"It's for my home. I want to clear it of negative influences. I'm hosting a birthday party for my six-year-old niece, and I want to make sure everything goes off without a hitch."

"Oh, well, then what you really want is Alum."

Char set down the agate necklace and picked up a small pyramid made of a vibrant magenta-colored stone. The woman gave the pyramid a dubious look, "Alum? I've never heard of it."

Jonah watched, torn between exasperation and amusement, as Char gave the woman a dazzling — and obviously fake — smile of reassurance. "Trust me — this is what you really want. It purifies and protects and is stronger than agate."

"Well... alright then," the woman said. "I'll take both the pyramid and the necklace."

"Great!"

Char rang up and bagged the purchase. As soon as the customer was out of the shop, Char turned to Jonah with a smug smile and folded her arms over her chest. He rolled his eyes and went to check that the door was locked.

"Just out of curiosity," he said, "why Alum?" Alum was little known in the modern age outside of the beauty industry; he only knew of it because it had been used in olden times to repel demons.

"It's lesser known, but it's actually better for dispelling negative influences and protecting against harm, especially since it was for a child's party. It's been used since ancient times to guard children and homes from evil influences."

"Huh." He looked the girl over again, surprised she knew this rather obscure bit of knowledge. Impressed despite himself, he flashed her a grudging half-grin. Maybe her staying here wouldn't be such a bad thing after all.

Char smiled back. "I've never met another psychic my own age, before."

"I'm not—"

"You're not really what I expected, you know?" She paused for a second, and then it was as if a floodgate

21

opened. "I mean, I don't know what I expected. It's not like I've met a lot of psychics. Only, the ones I have met are usually a little more free-spirited — or pretentious — but you're sort of... normal. Which is cool —"

"Yeah, but I'm not —"

" — Of course, I haven't really met any other psychics my own age. Well, I haven't met any outside of my own family, actually. It's not like there's tons around —"

"Hey!" Jonah said, raising his voice to talk over her. "Do I get to say something at some point?"

Char blinked at him in surprise. "What? Oh... sorry."

"Look, I'm not psychic."

"What?" Char peered at Jonah, as if trying to see him more clearly. "Look, the only people who can see the dead are ghosts or psychics. You have to be one or the other, and you said you weren't dead, so —"

"Dead, psychic, or someone who has learned a mystical meditation that lets them separate their spirit from their body."

Char's eyes widened with disbelief. Then she burst into peals of laughter. She had a deep, rolling belly-laugh. "Are you serious?"

"Why is that funny?"

Char couldn't seem to stop laughing. "Sorry," she managed to gasp out around her laughter. "It's just the way you said that." She puffed herself up in a pantomime of a big, burly man. "'Learned a mystical mediation that lets them separate their spirit blah blah blah.'" She doubled over laughing again.

Jonah waited for Char to stop. When she didn't, he glared at her. "Okay, well it's been nice talking to you. I'm going to get back to work now."

"No, wait! I'm sorry." Char wiped at her eyes though she still chuckled. "So how on earth did you learn to do that?"

"From a book."

Char gaped at him and then looked like she was about to burst out laughing again.

Jonah flushed. He shrugged as nonchalantly as he could. "I found it in my school library." Which reminded him, he needed to get to the Boston Public Library before it closed. He crossed to the door and locked it. Then he turned and headed back through the bead curtain to the dead side of the shop.

"Uh huh," Char said, following him.

"No, really," Jonah said flatly, wondering how he could change the subject without being too obvious. He crossed the room, locked the door, and turned the open sign to "closed."

"Look, I have to go—"

When he turned around, Char was standing in front of him, blocking his path. She crossed her arms and cocked one hip in challenge. "Well, okay, but if this is you out of your body, then where's your body?"

"Upstairs, in one of your aunt's spare rooms," he said, the words slipping out before he could stop them, then he mentally kicked himself; why had he told her that? Most people would run screaming upon being told there was a body lying around in a spare bedroom.

"What?" Char stared at Jonah. "Nuh-uh."

Jonah glared at her, trying to look menacing. "Okay, you know what—just forget it." He tried to move past Char, but she blocked his way.

"No, hang on..." For a second, she chewed her lip in thought. Then she lit up, mischievousness written on her face.

"Oh no...!" Jonah said, but Char was already in motion, shrieking with laughter and tearing through the shop. Jonah raced after her. "Hey! Stop!"

However, Char was too fast. She dodged around the various displays and raced up the stairs, which she took two at a time. She exploded onto the second-floor landing and tore down the narrow hall, combat boots pounding against the faded shag carpet, heading for the last room. She reached the door a half second ahead of him. She threw it open, burst into the room, and then stopped short. Jonah, unable to stop in time, banged into her.

Char hardly seemed to notice. Her eyes were wide as she stared at Jonah's body, which was stretched out on the bed. He had to admit it looked like a corpse laid out for visiting hours on top of the bed's crocheted, white coverlet, his arms folded protectively across the thick, black book — his guide to the afterlife — resting on his chest.

Char's eyes slid to Jonah and then back again to the body on the bed. "Whoa!" she said softly. She crept closer and then leaned over the body, studying his face, and then turned to look at him again. "That's really you."

"Yeah," Jonah said, shifting uncomfortably. There was a reason he didn't tell people about the afterlife book or about his ability to separate his spirit from his body — namely, because they'd think he was either crazy or weird. *Oh, you see dead people and walk around like a ghost? Here's a nice padded jacket we'd like you to try on.* Even someone like Madame Majicka who could see ghosts wasn't too keen on his spirit walking around separate from his body. She'd been none too subtle in her efforts to get him to spend less time as a ghost, sending him on errands among the living and refusing to serve him tea or food when he was in his spirit form.

"Can I touch it?" she asked.

"What do you mean touch it? Touch me where?"

Char's smile turned coy. "That depends; where do you want me to touch you?"

Jonah choked in surprise. "You know, you kind of have boundary issues."

Char laughed and bounced up from the bed, ignoring the reprimand. "I wish I had a marker. I'd give you a little mustache."

"Okay, that's it." Jonah said. He grabbed her arm and shoved her toward the door.

"Hey! I was just joking!" Char cried as Jonah thrust her into the hall and slammed the door shut after her. Silently, he cursed the fact there was no lock.

In one smooth motion, he turned toward the bed as he spoke the "password" that would rouse him from the meditation, thereby returning his spirit to his body. There was the usual sudden jolt, as if he had just been startled awake from a dream, and a moment of darkness. Then he was lying on the bed, staring up at the ceiling. He was just sitting up when Char threw open the door and re-entered the room.

She looked around and then came closer, peering at his face. "That's you in there, isn't it? You..." she gestured vaguely with her hands, trying to indicate two halves being fitted together, "...rejoined your body?"

"Yeah." Jonah stood up and dropped the book that had been on his chest onto the bed. He took a step back, putting some distance between them since she was right up close, practically nose-to-nose with him.

Char smiled. "That is so cool! You have to teach me how to do it!"

He paused. "What for? You can already see dead people."

"Yeah, but... you know... it's just cool."

Jonah raised an eyebrow. "Cool" was not the response he usually got. Char suddenly looked uncomfortable, and her eyes darted away, as if she was embarrassed. She looked around the room, clearly searching for a change in topic. He saw her notice the books, clothes, and other items scattered about the tiny room, bare except for the bed, a small bureau, and a desk. "Are you staying here?" she asked.

Jonah flushed. "Uh, yeah... Madame Majicka said I could crash here while I'm helping out. It's easier than going back and forth from home every day. If it makes you uncomfortable, I can—"

"Oh, no, it's fine," Char said quickly. "It'll be cool to have someone else around. It gets kind of lonely here sometimes." Char looked embarrassed again. This time she covered by shaking back her hair and assuming what was clearly a forced air of casual bravado. "I mean, you're not a perv or anything, right? I carry mace, just so you know."

25

Jonah snorted. "Don't worry. You're safe from me."

"Oh, you're gay?"

"What? No, I'm not gay! I just meant you're not my... listen, I actually have some work to do—"

"Work?" Char noticed the jumble of papers and books on the desk. Her eyes widened, and she came closer. "Whoa, what is all this?"

Jonah cut in front of her and hastily swept everything into an untidy pile, covering some of the more incriminating notes with books. "Nothing... just research, is all."

"Research? What kind of research?"

"For school," he said hurriedly. Char continued to eye him doubtfully. He huffed. "Look, I need to finish this—"

"I thought you said you had to go out?"

"Yeah, well it's too late now, so I'll just have to go tomorrow."

"So, do you want to go do something?"

"I just finished saying I had something I needed to do." He pointedly nodded at the door.

"Oh... right." Char's eyes swept downward, and she flushed and moved to the door. "Well, I'll see you at dinner, I guess..."

"Actually, it's been a long day, and I'm pretty tired. I'll probably just go straight to bed once I'm done."

"Oh." Char put a hand on the doorknob, hesitated as if about to say something else, and then yanked open the door. "Night, then."

Jonah shut the door after her and then collapsed against it with a sigh of relief. God, she was exhausting. Under normal circumstances, he might have been more excited by the prospect of meeting someone, especially someone his own age, who knew something about the spirit realm and could see the dead. In this case, however, the girl seemed more of a pain than anything: she had the attention span of a gnat and tried to turn everything into a joke. Plus, she was showing an annoying propensity for prying and snooping— she'd barged into his room without permission, and he'd seen the way she'd eyed the stuff on his desk.

He was going to need to get a lock for his door.

His eyes swept the room, looking for what else he should hide in case Char decided to barge back in again. His gaze fell on his cell phone, sitting on the desk; he could see an alert on the screen, notifying him of a voicemail. He'd learned early on that electronics and the afterlife didn't mix. He could cross the phone over and get a ghost cell phone, but little good that did him. He couldn't call a living phone with it—not that the living would be able to hear him as a ghost anyway—and he didn't know any ghosts he could call. Plus, once he had crossed the phone over, there didn't seem to be any way to reintegrate the spirit with the shell, so then, in the land of the living, he just ended up with a dead phone.

He crossed the room and checked his missed calls list in case there was anything urgent—like a call from one of the professors he'd reached out to for help with his afterlife research. But no, nothing like that—just calls from his parents. He tossed the phone aside, not bothering to listen to the messages.

He turned his attention to the jumble of books on the desk with a sinking heart as he thought of all the hours he'd already spent searching for Irene. He'd gone through these books so many times, and yet, he wasn't any closer to finding a way to the other side. Soon though, soon he'd have enough money to travel to the places where the heroes of old had traveled through doorways to the underworld: Lake Avernus, Pluto's Gates, Twins Caves, Luxor, the City of Ghosts, the Acheron river, the gate at Taenarus, Mount Osore, Masaya, Actun Tunichil Muknal. One of them had to be real, and that's all he needed. Just one.

Hang on, he thought. *Just hang on. I'm coming.*

There was still so much to do: maps, translations, securing supplies, prioritizing the list of prospects, figuring out transportation and logistics. There was the slight problem of getting a passport without his parents' permission since he wasn't yet eighteen, but he'd cross that bridge when he came to it. There were always fake I.D.s if need be. One of his ghost connections must know something about how to get one of those.

He straightened up with a sigh and crossed to the bed. He picked up the black book with its thick, bark-like cover. He moved to the desk and swept everything to one side, clearing a space to work. He plopped the book on the desk, opened it to a marked page, pulled a sheaf of papers from a nearby pile, and sat down to begin the tedious process of comparing the two in an attempt to translate the difficult passage.

Three

"Wow!" Irene said, her eyes roving over the dark, crenellated structure hulking in the far distance. It gleamed dully, the color of burnt blood in a fading afternoon sun. "What the hell do you think that is?"

Andras grunted. "As you said — Hell."

Irene frowned at him, but her lips quirked in amusement. "Why do you have to be so negative? It could just as easily be Heaven. God is supposed to live in a palace, right — the whole 'my father's house has many rooms' thing? A castle is just a type of palace."

Andras gave her a dry look. "Does that look like Heaven?"

Irene was on the verge of agreeing that the castle did not in any way look how she imagined Heaven when it shimmered, as if the fading sunlight had been redirected by mirrors. Light rippled across the castle's surface and the dull, dark, burnt-blood color transformed into gleaming, bright, silver-white. Crisp white pennants flapped from the corners as if whipped by wind. Irene thought she could hear them snapping crisply.

Irene looked at Andras, and he looked at her. His expression made it clear that he had seen the same transformation she had. It was as if the building was trying to trick them into coming closer.

"That… was unsettling," Irene said, feeling goose bumps rise on her arms. Even though the place looked more appealing now than it had a few seconds ago, she wanted to head toward it even less. Unfortunately, the castle was still the only feature, other than wheat and the shadows, in the entire landscape; they didn't have a lot of other options or leads. "Should we still check it out?" she asked, hoping Andras would say no.

Andras just grunted. "I follow where you lead."

Irene sighed. "Why did I know you were going to say that?" With another, deeper, sigh, this time of resignation, she shouldered her bag once more and gestured for Andras to precede her to the castle. They walked in silence, Irene trailing slightly behind, the wheat tickling and scratching as she went.

She mentally ran through a list of all the afterlife myths she knew—most of which had been pounded into her brain by Jonah in a kind of strange, torturous final exam-esque cram session. At the time, she hadn't really appreciated the constant stories and trivia. Only now was she coming to understand the value of what he'd given her—he'd been trying to prepare her for the day when she'd need to manage on her own.

It only took a minute for her to realize the only castles she'd ever heard mentioned in the stories were the homes of the rulers of the afterlife: the Egyptian goddess Ma'at, the Greek god Hades, the Sumerian goddess Ereshkigal.

Irene's stomach lurched uneasily as she called up what little she knew of these various underworld rulers. Most of the stories made them all sound pretty unpleasant and made it clear they were best avoided. Worse, if the Greeks she'd met at the river were to be believed, all the beings worshipped as rulers of the afterlife were actually Nephilim—winged monsters that resided in the land of the dead. If that was true, then the castle could be filled with Nephilim. She and Andras had barely escaped their two run-ins with the creatures on the last plane, and they were even less equipped to deal with Nephilim now than they had been then. Here, they had no weapons, no ability to launch a surprise attack, and no place to hide. Tangling with Nephilim was definitely not something she wanted to do — now or ever.

They passed more of the shadow workers, who, like the previous group, paid Irene and Andras no mind. In the distance, Irene could see more dark shapes she assumed were also shadows. They seemed to be growing more plentiful.

The sound of the wheat swishing as they walked seemed to grow in accordance with Irene's rising unease, becoming unbearably loud.

"We don't actually think Heaven is inside a castle, do we? I mean, we're going for more of a figurative meaning to 'pearly gates,' right?" she asked, her unease growing with each step.

"It does not matter what we think. Heaven is what it is, with or without our approval."

Irene rolled her eyes. "Okay, fine. I guess that was a not-so-subtle way of asking what you're expecting Heaven to be like."

Andras stopped short and heaved a theatrical sigh. "Needless —"

"Needless speculation, I know. We've covered that... quite thoroughly. I would just like to get clear in my mind what, exactly, it is that you're expecting at the end of this journey. I mean, do you really think you're going to literally meet God?" Irene raised a hand to stop Andras's protest. "Don't think of it as speculation. Think of it as an opportunity to convert an unbeliever." She gave him a perky smile.

Andras responded with a quelling frown. "We were taught that our reward for faithful and diligent service is to be invited to sit at the right hand of God. We will be the Saboath, the heavenly host, the army of the Lord."

"I thought Heaven was supposed to be relaxing, a chance to kick back as a reward for a job well done?"

"There is no greater reward than to serve."

Irene cast him a sidelong glance. "That sounds like the old, 'the reward for a job well done is more work' catch-22."

Andras didn't respond. Instead, he turned away and resumed walking.

Irene sighed and followed after; she'd disappointed him... again. Why was there never any middle ground with the guy? Every time she thought they had reached a place where they could be easy with each other he'd bristle and rebuff her. He was as prickly as a cactus.

"So, you had a brother," she said searching desperately for some other topic of conversation.

Andras grunted in response.

"Any other siblings?"

This time, Andras made a noise that sounded a lot like a growl.

"Have you seen him since you died?"

Silence.

"You told me that your family line had died out, so you must have looked them up at some point."

"And what of you?" Andras countered, stopping short and rounding on her. "Did you seek your family at the river?"

"Ouch," she said. "That's a low blow. My situation is a little different than yours. Everyone would have wanted to know why I had died so young, and unlike you, I wasn't heroically defending the holy land from invaders. I was drunk and accidentally drove my car off a bridge. Not exactly something I want my poor, sweet grandmother to know about, you know?"

She had never told Andras how she had died, and she found herself unconsciously holding her breath as she waited for his reaction. Now that the truth was out there, she expected disappointment, condemnation, even disgust.

However, Andras didn't even seem to notice what she'd said, let alone care. "My death was hardly heroic," he said flatly."I was conquered in battle, my sword and armor stolen by looters, and the land I was defending—the holy land—

was overrun by infidels. There is no limit to the depths of my dishonor."

Even though Andras tended to look on the dark side of things, this level of bitterness surprised Irene. She knew Andras regretted the way in which he'd died and had abhorred the treatment of his comrades' bodies upon death—the Moors had left the defenders unburied, allowing them to rot in the open and be picked apart by vultures. Irene hadn't bothered to tell Andras that, for some cultures, this was considered a proper burial. She knew he would hardly find that a consolation.

Irene had always thought Andras's feelings of guilt and unworthiness were his own personal feelings, though. It had never occurred to her that other people, including his family, might actually think the same thing, that he might actually have been dishonored and that his family had been ashamed of him.

She cast him a sidelong glance. "I would have thought that dying in defense of the holy land would have made you a hero. But even if that wasn't enough for them, you were dead. People overlook those kinds of things when you die. I mean they were heartbroken that you were gone and memorialized all the good things you did, right?"

Andras stared straight ahead. "My name was struck from their rolls."

Irene stopped dead in her tracks. "They disowned you?" Andras neither stopped nor answered. "Jesus! What a bunch of assholes." She hurried to catch up. No wonder Andras was so... Andras. What a family to grow up with. She tried to process this new information and the light it shed on him. The man had spent his entire life serving God—doing good, helping the poor, defending pilgrims to holy shrines. People didn't come much more saintly than that. But because he and those with him had been outnumbered in battle, his family had decided to ignore all the good he had done and just focus on the failure. Even worse, Andras somehow believed this was right and fitting—he thought he deserved to be dishonored and forgotten. She wished there was something she could say or do to convince him he was wrong, that he'd more than earned his place in Heaven. Even if his earthly life hadn't made him worthy, his eight hundred years of helping and protecting the dead had. However, she knew there was nothing she could say – her opinion held very little weight with him. Only hearing it directly from God would change his mind.

Irene shook her head. "Yeah, well, their loss," she said loud enough for Andras to hear. He gave no indication, however, that he'd heard.

Something small and gossamer floated past her face as she cast Andras a sly glance, and she absently brushed it away as she spoke. "You do have one advantage over me – you've been here for eight hundred years, so you've had the opportunity to see what future generations of your family did. You must have taken a peek. So tell me, how'd they turn out?"

Andras considered the question for a moment, his brows drawing together in thought. "It is a strange thing to look on a distant descendant and try to recognize anything of one's self in him. It is easier to look back than to look forward."

Irene bobbed her head in agreement, absently waving away another speck that floated past. She supposed Andras was right. Looking back, there was a link, a chain, connecting people. She'd heard stories from her parents and grandmother about her great grandparents and great aunts and uncles. She may never have met them, but she felt like she knew them. Anyone who had been born after Irene had died, however, would just be a face and a name. There weren't any stories or shared history connecting them.

"It is snowing," Andras said flatly, a note of disapproval in his tone.

She blinked in surprise. Tiny, white flakes were indeed swirling in the air. Irene held out a hand and caught a few. She studied them for a moment and then stuck out her tongue to taste them. Andras raised an eyebrow, and she grinned in response. "You're right – it's snow." She laughed.

Andras harrumphed. "This does not disturb you?"

"The snow?"

"Snow on a bright, cloudless day —"

"It's also a sunless day, if you want to get technical."

"Then, snow in a warm, temperate —"

"Technically, it's not really hot or cold. It's sort of... nothing."

Andras cast her a furious look.

Irene held up her hands in surrender. "Okay! Okay! Look, it's already stopped."

And indeed, it had, leaving behind no trace that any snow had fallen.

"Maybe we should take a rest break," Irene said.

Andras's scowl deepened. Irene held up her hands again. "I know, I know. We don't need to rest. It just seemed like you were getting upset, so I thought —"

"I am not upset."

"It seemed like you were."

"I assure you I am not."

"Are you sure, because —"

"I AM NOT UPSET!"

"Okay! Geesh! I was just trying to —" Something large fluttered past Irene's face. She gasped and jerked back. "What the..."

It was a butterfly.

A rather large one, at that — it was nearly the size of her hand. She watched as it flitted back and forth between her and Andras, the vibrant blue of its wings electric against the pale golden landscape.

Andras batted it away.

"Aww, don't do that," Irene said. "It's not going to hurt you."

Skepticism passed over Andras's face. "And how do you know that?"

Irene opened her mouth and then abruptly closed it. She supposed she didn't know for a fact that it wasn't dangerous, but it was, after all, just a butterfly.

A slight smirk marred Andras's otherwise placid countenance. "Exactly," he said. "I am not afraid of butterflies. It is demons disguised as butterflies that worry me."

Irene made dismissive noise with her tongue. "I don't think these are demons."

"You also thought that cat was just a cat."

Irene glared. "Yeah, well, it wasn't a demon, either. It helped us, remember?"

Another butterfly danced past her ear, and now there were two, bouncing about in the air as if dangled on a string held by unseen hands. Irene smiled. "They're kind of cute."

She reached out a finger to the nearest one, expecting it to dart away. Instead, it landed on her outstretched finger, and she gasped in surprise. Then she grinned and held the butterfly up for Andras's inspection. "Look!" This close, she could see all the lines of the patterns traced in black on its wings, the slight fuzz of its dark body, and the antenna on its head waving in the breeze. Its wings opened and closed, rhythmically, as if it were breathing through the motion.

Andras watched her with an expression she couldn't quite place, possibly bewilderment, possibly amusement. However, when he saw that she was looking at him, he growled and turned away, resuming the trek toward the castle.

The butterfly seemed content to stay just where it was, so Irene followed along with her finger held out in front of her. Two more butterflies appeared, scurrying through the air around them and then several more. In a moment, the air was full of them, fluttering back and forth between her and Andras. They flew so close their wings brushed Irene's skin, and she couldn't help but giggle at the tickling sensation. The one on her finger took off, flitted about for a moment, and then landed on her shoulder. Irene stopped, waiting to see what it would do. However, the butterfly just sat there, substantial enough that she could feel its wing brushing against her hair. Another one landed on the top of Andras's head and remained, like a jaunty hat. Irene couldn't help it — she laughed. Andras glanced at her and then looked upward as he became aware of the butterfly on his head. He waved a hand and shooed it off with a look that clearly said he wasn't amused.

A sound caught Irene's attention — so soft that it took a moment for it to bubble into her consciousness. It was low and breathy, like whispering. Irene looked around, searching for the source.

"Do you hear something?" she asked Andras, who still walked several paces ahead of her.

Andras shook his head without looking at her. "No."

She had thought it was perhaps the butterflies' wings, but the sound seemed to get louder when she turned to the right. The butterfly was still sitting there on her shoulder. Irene put her ear up close to it. The sound, still too faint to be clearly made out, grew louder. The butterfly suddenly took off, its wings tickling the side of her face as it did so.

"Seriously, you don't hear anything? Like... voices?"

Andras stiffened and then cocked his head, listening hard. After a moment, he shook his head.

Irene, eyes narrowed, reached out and caught one of the butterflies between loosely cupped hands. It fluttered for a second then went still. She held it up so she could see it properly, peering at it between her fingers. Then she brought it closer, holding it up to her ear, and this time it was clear: the sound was coming from the butterfly. Irene gasped, her hands flying apart with surprise, releasing the captured butterfly. "It's the butterflies — they're talking!"

Andras had resumed walking in the meanwhile, and at this, he stopped and turned to look at her, annoyance written in every line of his face. "Butterflies cannot speak."

"I'm telling you they're talking!"

"Then they are not butterflies."

Irene rolled her eyes at this pronouncement. "Fine, maybe not, mister-last-word-freak, but they're definitely talking."

Andras reached out and snagged one in his hands, holding it surprisingly gently. He gave it a dubious look and then moved it toward his ear, as Irene had done. Partway to his ear, he paused and glared at Irene. "If this is a jest..."

Irene laughed. "No, it's not a joke; I'm serious — though it would have been hysterical if it were."

With another warning look, Andras held the butterfly up to his ear. His face screwed up in concentration for a moment. "I hear nothing."

Irene caught another butterfly and held it up to her ear; she was sure she heard whispering, though it was too low for her to make out any words. She released the butterfly and snagged a third one. When she held this one up to her ear, she heard the same whispering sound. "They're definitely saying something."

Andras reluctantly held his butterfly up to his ear again and listened carefully. Then his face changed to one of surprise mingled with fear. He quickly released his butterfly and then crossed himself.

"Well?"

Andras set his jaw. "Evil often comes in a pretty package."

"Are you talking about me or the butterflies?"

One side of Andras's mouth lifted in a reluctant smile. "It applies equally to both."

Irene laughed. "Be serious. What do you think they are?"

"Why ask me? You understand this world better than I."

Irene shrugged in bewilderment. "I've got nothing. I have no idea what they are."

"Truly?" he replied, clearly surprised. "You know of no legend involving butterflies?"

Irene bit her lip, feeling a rush of pleasure that Andras saw her as an expert on the afterlife. Desperately not wanting to let him down, she searched through the knowledge in her brain. The only thing she could think of was something her grandmother had told he when she was a child. "Well... after my grandfather died, my grandmother said that if you whisper a message to a butterfly, it will carry the message up to Heaven for you."

"And the boy? He never spoke of them?"

Irene made a disgruntled noise. "I told you not to call him that. He has a name. And no, *Jonah* never told me any afterlife stories involving butterflies." She let her butterfly go and then dusted off her hands, her good mood evaporating. "Come on, let's keep going."

Andras cast her an incredulous look. "What, no argument? No demand to linger. No 'Come on, they are just butterflies?'"

The modern-day expression sounded strange coming from his mouth, and Irene smiled despite herself. "No, not this time. If you think the sweet, harmless-looking butterflies are actually evil demons, they probably are — so we should just keep going."

Andras cast her a suspicious look. "Are you feeling unwell? You are, perhaps, ill?"

"Ha. Ha." However, she grinned as she said it. "Come on."

This time, as they walked, Andras kept pace, walking close beside her, his eyes darting around suspiciously.

They had only gone about fifty feet when the air rippled and shimmered like oil on water for a moment, obscuring everything in view, and then the butterflies changed to schools of large, vibrantly colored fish in shades of purple and green, swimming placidly through the air around them. The fish glittered in the too-bright light, their iridescent scales reflecting like mirrors. Irene whipped around, her face nearly colliding with a fish by her ear. "What the…"

Andras crossed himself.

Irene reached out and touched one of the fish, reassuring herself they were real. Her finger connected; the fish was solid — cool and slick like a fish should be.

The fish didn't seem to notice her poking it.

Just as her finger made contact, the world rippled and shimmered again, the ground rolling beneath Irene's feet. The wheat changed to burning, arid sand, burnt umber in the blazing sun, the fish still swimming lazily through the air, as if it were water.

Andras began to mutter in Spanish. He was praying. The ground bucked beneath their feet once more, and Irene reached out and grabbed his arm, clinging to him for dear life. The world heaved again, giving out beneath them, and the air became water. Irene plummeted down into it, breaking the surface, and then she was falling, falling, falling — sinking through the depths as schools of fish placidly swam by.

Four

"What are we looking at?"

"Jesus Christ!" Jonah, crouching behind a gravestone, lurched forward and hit his head on the hard granite. He quickly steadied himself and rocked back on his heels, rubbing his head and glaring up at Char, who stood over him. He grabbed her arm and pulled her down beside him. "Get down before they see you," he hissed.

It was a quarter past midnight, and they were in the Forest Hills cemetery, one of the few active cemeteries in Boston. Five hundred yards away, the area hummed with the commotion of a construction site as a group of ghosts worked to break down a stack of ghostly coffins into their component parts. Saws buzzed, hammers pounded, and workers bustled as they separated the materials into piles.

Char craned her neck, trying to see around the headstone. "Who are we hiding from?"

"I'm not hiding," Jonah said, sinking down into a sitting position, his back against the headstone for support. "I'm waiting. And what the hell are you doing here anyway?" He'd made doubly sure to be as quiet as possible when he'd snuck out of the magic shop, in case Char was a light sleeper. The last thing he'd needed was her asking where he was going or why. Somehow, though, she'd not only seen him but apparently decided to follow him as well.

"I could ask you the same thing," she retorted. "This doesn't seem like normal behavior."

"Shhhh!" Jonah admonished, chancing another glance at the group to be sure they hadn't seen or heard them. "Look, this doesn't concern you, so why don't you go back to the shop?"

Char glared at Jonah, her expression clearly indicating she wasn't going to go away without an answer.

Jonah ground his teeth. "Okay, look, I don't know how much you know about ghost stuff—"

"Oh, I know pretty much everything," Char interjected breezily.

"Well," Jonah said pointedly, "then you know that when someone dies, it takes seven days for their spirit to separate from their body and that anything with the body crosses into the spirit realm, too—including coffins. Those guys over there are breaking down the coffins—fabric for clothes, wood for buildings, hinges for doors—and then sending them on to the other side—to the land of the dead. I'm trying to find out how, exactly, they send the stuff across."

"Why?"

"Because there has to be a portal or doorway of some kind."

Char's brow creased with confusion. "Why do you want to find a doorway to the other side?"

Jonah glanced at her out of the corner of his eye and then looked away. "I just do."

"Well, why don't you just ask those guys where the door is, then?"

Jonah's lips compressed into a thin line. "I know where the door is. I just can't get through it."

"So the plan is to…?"

"Sit here—*alone*—until they move the stuff and then go with them."

Char raised an eyebrow.

Jonah looked away, stubbornly refusing to make eye contact and hoping she'd give up and leave. No such luck. Char stood up, one hip cocked, arms folded across her chest.

Jonah ground his teeth even harder. "Okay, fine, look, those guys are kind of skittish, okay, so could you sit? And keep your voice down. I'll tell you—just sit."

Char narrowed her eyes, as if she didn't quite trust him, but complied, dropping cross-legged into the grass beside him. Jonah sighed and readjusted his position against the headstone. He regarded Char for a moment and then reached for the nearby paper bag that held the remainder of his dinner—one half of a ghostly tuna fish sandwich. He took a bite and chewed slowly, trying to figure out how best to frame his explanation. "I can't get through the door myself because I'm not actually a ghost. Those guys will let me cross through with them, if I stay out of the way while they're working." Ghosts involved in coffin reclamation tended to be no-nonsense, nose-to-the-grindstone types and highly secretive about just how the entire process worked. Coffin reclamation was, after all, a highly competitive business, especially in Boston. There weren't a lot of active cemeteries left inside the city.

Jonah had no problem staying out of sight until the group was ready to head for the doorway. He just hoped Char's presence wouldn't make them change their mind about allowing him to cross over with them. Getting them to agree hadn't been cheap.

Char regarded him for a moment, as if assessing the veracity of his words. Then she tilted her head, her expression changing to one of curiosity. "So... how do you know about all this stuff, anyway? For someone who isn't psychic, you sure do know a lot about ghosts and the afterlife."

Jonah continued to avoid Char's gaze. He let his eyes wander over the landscape of carved stone and neatly trimmed grass as he carefully picked over his words, not sure how much he should share. He didn't know Char, and he didn't know where she stood on the living and the dead mingling. If she shared her aunt's views, then she wasn't going to like anything he had to say and would likely blow his chances of trying to cross over tonight. However, she'd made it clear she wasn't going to give up and go away without an answer of some kind, so he had to say something. He settled for the vaguest possible version of the truth. "I had this friend who was a ghost. She needed help figuring out how to cross over, and I ended up learning about this stuff."

"This friend have a name?"

Jonah gripped his sandwich hard. "Irene," he said tightly; even just saying her name hurt.

This will be my last letter...

He looked down and saw the sandwich was now flattened and torn. With a sigh, he threw it into the bag and then crumpled up the bag.

"This Irene — is she pretty?"

Jonah's head jerked up. "What? Why?"

"Because you're blushing."

Jonah's face heated. "You can't see that — it's dark out!"

There were, however, street lights and a nearly full moon high overhead, and they provided enough light for him to see Char grinning.

"I could still tell."

Jonah scowled. "Yeah, well, it's not like that. She's just a friend."

"Uh huh." Char's grin widened. Jonah glared at her, which only made Char grin more. Jonah felt his face heat even further, and he looked away to hide his embarrassment. Then he glanced at Char again as he realized she was relaxing against a headstone, completely at ease.

"Aren't you scared to be in a cemetery at night? Most people would be scared."

Char's forehead wrinkled in confusion. "No. Why... should I be?"

"Most people think hanging out in cemeteries is weird." Even Irene, who had been dead, had been afraid to go to the cemetery alone, insisting he accompany her while she looked for the tunnel to the other side.

Char shrugged. "In Victorian times, hanging out in cemeteries was considered normal. People used to have picnics in them."

Jonah stared at her, surprised for the second time by her knowledge of obscure facts, and then smiled despite himself. "Exactly."

Char smiled back.

For some reason, he suddenly felt self-conscious, so he twisted around to check on the progress of the coffin-reclamation work. Still working.

It was a warm, July night, and the little frogs known as Spring Peepers were peeping their hearts out. Though it was late, traffic noises still sounded, though in the distance, muffled here by the trees surrounding the cemetery. A hot wind stirred, rustling the leaves and drowning out the cars. It lifted a dark strand of Char's hair, blowing it across her face, and she brushed it back behind her ear.

"So," Char said, "you're in college?"

Jonah looked at her in surprise. Char shrugged. "Auntie told me... at dinner."

The burgeoning goodwill he had started to feel toward her evaporated, replaced by guardedness. "Yeah," he said curtly, hoping Char would be discouraged from probing further, though, given her track record to date, that seemed highly unlikely. While it was true he'd enrolled—at his parents' insistence—in the local community college six months ago, neither his parents nor Madame Majicka knew he'd dropped out shortly thereafter—at about the same time he'd moved into the magic shop.

"So you're eighteen?" She gave him an assessing look. "You don't look eighteen."

Jonah shook his head. "I'm not. I'll be seventeen in October."

"Wow, you graduated young."

"I skipped a couple of grades."

"What's college like? Do you like it?"

Jonah shrugged. "No, not really." He racked his brain for a way to turn the conversation from himself. He had no doubt that simply saying he didn't like to talk about himself would make Char even more determined to talk about him.

"Really? Why not?"

Jonah shrugged again. "I don't really have anything in common with anyone there. It's like high school, only with more partying and hooking up. Everyone is so juvenile, you know?"

"I wish I could tell you that I do know," Char said, "but I've never been to any kind of school."

Now it was Jonah's turn to be confused. "What do you mean you've never been to school?"

Char lifted a shoulder in a gesture of resignation. "I have purple hair, and I see dead people. Do you really think anyone in their right mind would let me anywhere near normal kids? I'm homeschooled."

That didn't sound bad to him, but clearly Char was expecting sympathy for this revelation. "Sorry." That hardly seemed an adequate response, though, so he added, "You haven't really missed much. School is boring. It took them a year to teach me stuff I could have learned in a week if they'd just given me a textbook and let me read it myself."

"Yeah. I suppose that's the advantage of home-schooling — I get to learn as fast as I can. I don't have to wait for the slow people to catch up. But there's other stuff you get at school that you don't get at home — like friends and dances and boyfriends and things like that."

"Only if you're popular," Jonah said, unable to keep a note of bitterness out of his voice. Embarrassed, he checked the workers' progress again, wishing desperately that they'd hurry up and finish.

Thankfully, Char fell silent — for a moment.

"So, you're doing the out-of-body thing again," she said. It wasn't a question. Jonah warily glanced at her, not sure where the conversation was going next.

Char chewed her lip, eyeing him speculatively. "Can I ask you a question? Earlier, when we met, you said that you had forgotten you were out of your body. What did you mean? I mean, how can you possibly forget that?"

Jonah shrugged and adjusted his position, trying to find a comfortable spot against the stone. "I spend so much time out of my body it just feels natural to be like this, you know? In my body is when it's weird, because I have to eat and go to the bathroom and sneeze and stuff. Without a body, I don't have to do any of those things."

"So... you do this kind of stuff a lot, then?"

He listened to the Peepers, enjoying the feel of the cool stone against his back, a relief from the muggy night air. For a moment, the world was comfortingly peaceful, even the traffic sounds dying away. He was silent, letting the stillness wash over him. He wished Irene was here to enjoy it.

Of course, Irene would probably think hanging out in a cemetery was weird.

Char looked at him expectantly. He sighed. "It's not really all that different, being out of my body. I can do pretty much all the same stuff. The food tastes different, but you get used to that after a while."

"Okay, but don't you think that's a bit dangerous to go days without eating or... peeing? Your spirit form may not need sustenance, but your body still does."

Jonah sighed again, louder and more theatrically. "Thanks, *mom*, but I'm fine. Look, why don't you go back to the shop? Madame Majicka will be mad if she finds you snuck out."

Char opened her mouth to argue, but a sudden movement of the group of ghosts breaking down the coffins drew Jonah's attention. He grabbed Char's arm, cutting her off. "Shhh! Look—they're getting ready to go."

Jonah waited until the group of coffin-reclamation workers had moved a ways off before he rose to follow. Char also got to her feet.

"What are you doing?" he asked.

"Coming with you."

"Oh, no you don't. You—"

The group of ghosts paused at the cemetery gate and watched Jonah and Char warily.

"Shit!" Jonah grabbed Char's arm and pushed her toward a headstone. "Get down. They'll see you."

Char raised an eyebrow. "They don't know me—they won't think I'm following them."

"Get down!"

"Okay! Okay!" Char raised her hands in submission and sank into a crouch behind the stone.

The group of ghosts hesitated for a moment longer and then passed out of the cemetery, pushing carts laden with the materials scavenged from the ghost coffins. Jonah waited a few seconds and then started after the group. Char followed as well. He glared at her, but there was no time to argue. The group wasn't going to wait for him—they'd said he could tag along when they crossed through the doorway to the afterlife, but only if he didn't interrupt their work or hold them up in any way.

Thankfully, Char behaved herself, keeping quiet as they followed the ghosts at a safe distance. Several blocks later, the group paused in front of a large stone church and then proceeded to pass, in twos and threes, straight through the church's closed front door—a beautiful, double entry painted a vivid red. As the last group, pushing a heavily laden wheelbarrow, paused before the door, they cast a look over their shoulders, signaling that it was time. Jonah darted forward to catch up to them.

"Jonah!" Char cried, but he didn't stop. He grabbed hold of one side of the wheelbarrow and held fast as the group moved forward and passed through the door.

There was a feeling of dissolution, as if he was melting, a moment of suspension, as if he was caught between two states, and then a flowing back together, and he found himself in a gray void, surrounded by mist. The mist pressed in on him, and there was no sense of up or down, just a vast, empty nothing. Behind him stood the door he had passed through, floating disconnectedly in the mist. The ghosts had disappeared.

Jonah silently swore. This wasn't where he wanted to be.

Every time he had passed through a doorway to the afterlife the same thing happened – he found himself stuck between the realms. Moving through the different planes of existence wasn't exactly magic – there was actual science behind it. In the same way you couldn't just take a fish out of water and expect it to live, you couldn't just take energy accustomed to existing in a physical state and suddenly thrust it into a non-physical state. There had to be a transformation of some kind. Which is where the various mechanisms for transferring a spirit from one plane to the next – tunnels of light, red doorways, river-crossing ferries – came in. Like giving a fish lungs, these doorways acted upon the spirit's energy, transforming it so it could exist in the next environment. Only, something seemed to prevent it from working on him. When Irene had crossed over, she'd gone through the tunnel of light – a tunnel he couldn't see, and when he passed through a red door, he just ended up in a formless void. Someone or something was blocking him from crossing over.

He had hoped that hanging onto a ghost when they passed through would give him a boost and help him reach the other side, but clearly not. Instead, this entire evening – and the huge bribe he'd given the ghosts – had been a complete waste. With a growl of frustration, he turned around and passed back through the floating red door.

Back on the sidewalk in the land of the living, four of the ghosts he had been following were collecting a bundle of materials that had been left behind. They must have passed through to the other side and then returned again while he was stuck in the void between worlds.

"Nice try, kid," one of the ghosts said with a malicious chuckle as he swept past Jonah and back through the door.

Char was standing off to one side, out in the open and not even trying to hide, watching the ghosts. Jonah shot her an annoyed look – she was supposed to be hiding. She shrugged, her expression clearly saying there wasn't anything she could have done to avoid detection.

Jonah grabbed the arm of the next ghost, a tall, wiry, twenty-something guy with slicked back hair and a toothpick dangling from his mouth. "I want to try again," he said.

"Look, you paid, we tried, it's over."

"It's not over, Hector; it didn't work."

The ghost shook his arm loose from Jonah's grip. "Well, you deliver me another thousand converted ketchup packets and a case of Scotch, and then you can try again."

"Oh come on, do you know how hard it is for me to get liquor? I'm not old enough to buy it! Ask for something else." Five cases of ketchup packets weren't all that easy to obtain, convert, and carry either, but at least he could legally get those.

"Those are my terms, take 'em or leave 'em."

"Jonah—" Char broke in, her voice worried, but he held up a hand to silence her.

"Give us a break, kid," cried a weaselly-looking ghost as she brushed past Jonah.

Jonah crossed his arms over his chest and glared at Hector. "You know, you can only pay for so much with coffin parts. Eventually, you're going to need something else, and you're going to have to come to me to get it. You might want to keep that in mind."

"Oh, well, I'll be waiting for that day to come."

His friend chortled. "With bells on!"

"With bells on!" Hector brayed as he passed through the doorway. "Good one! With bells on!"

Bells were used to drive away evil spirits. It was a joke, a double entendre. Cute. Apparently this passed for high humor in the ghost world.

Jonah bit back a retort, his lips compressed to a thin line as all of the ghosts burst into laughter, the sound hanging in the air as, one by one, they passed through the doorway and faded from sight.

After the last one had disappeared, Jonah turned away, sighing heavily. He hadn't really expected this to work, but it would have been nice if he'd at least learned something from it. Instead, the entire evening had been wasted. Another dead end. Another day lost.

As he turned, he saw Char, shifting anxiously from foot to foot. Annoyance at her following him and barging into his business returned.

"Come on," he said, "Let's go."

"What just happened?" she asked, not moving from the spot. "I've never seen a spirit actually pass through a solid object before!"

"It doesn't matter — it didn't work."

Char darted in front of him and planted herself in his path. "Oh no!" she said, hands on her hips. "You owe me some answers! What the hell is going on?"

"Owe you? I don't even know you!"

Jonah tried to brush past her, but Char blocked him. "You're working in my aunt's shop, living in her house, so you owe me an explanation — I need to know you're not a crazy person."

"Or what?"

Char narrowed her eyes. "Or I'll tell her that you're sneaking around cemeteries at night, trying to find a doorway to the other side, that's what. Believe me, Auntie has definite *views* on that sort of thing."

Jonah stopped dead in his tracks and stared at Char, assessing whether or not she'd really rat him out to Madame Majicka. Ironclad determination glared back at him from her eyes. He exhaled sharply. "Look, it's simple. The door on the church is red, right? Red doors are 'doors of the dead.' When a ghost passes through one, they cross into the spirit realm. It's been that way since the Ancient Egyptians who put red granite doors in the tombs of their dead. And that's why you see so many churches with red doors."

Char's expression was a mixture of disbelief and confusion. Jonah sighed. "Look, I'll show you." He grabbed Char's hand and pulled her toward the door.

She dug in her feet. "What? No way!"

"It's perfectly safe."

"I'm not dead! And technically, neither are you."

"I'm telling you, it's safe. Don't be such a baby."

Char succeeded in wrenching her hand free, and she stopped short. She reached out and slapped the church's door with her hand, the smack of flesh on wood resoundingly solid. "Uh, not entirely, Chief. I can't pass through doors."

Jonah frowned. "Oh. Right." He looked at the door again and then at Char. "Sorry, I forgot—I don't hang out with the living much."

"See, that right there is kind of weird."

Jonah sighed wearily and turned away. "It's not that weird. Look, I'm trying to help someone, okay? And to do that I need to find a way into the spirit realm. See? Perfectly reasonable explanation."

"Who are you trying to help? And how is finding a way into the spirit realm going to help?"

Jonah hesitated, trying to think of a plausible lie.

"This is about a girl, isn't it?" Char said with a knowing look.

His face must have given him away because Char laughed. Jonah scowled. "She's not a girl—she's in her thirties."

Char raised an eyebrow. "So, we're talking MILF territory here."

His face went hot. "It's not like that! She's just a friend."

"Wait... is this about... what's her name? Irene?"

Jonah's scowl deepened, and he turned away, shoving his hands into his pockets. "It doesn't matter anyway—it never works. When I go through a red door, I just end up stuck between the two worlds." He started walking, heading back to the shop, leaving Char to follow—or not.

It couldn't be much past one a.m. Here, on the street by the church, the peacefulness of the cemetery's blowing wind and peeping frogs had faded away, leaving only city stillness—the drone of air conditioners, the electric buzz of the streetlights, and the absence of people. The moon was still overhead, but here the city lights outshone it, making it just another dull glow in the sky line.

For a second, Jonah heard nothing from Char, and then there was the scamper of feet running to catch up.

"Well, maybe that's the wrong door," she said as she drew even with him.

"You know you look like you're talking to yourself, right?"

Char shrugged. "I'm wandering the streets in the middle of the night with purple hair. No one is going to bat an eye at me talking to myself. Besides, there's no one around."

Jonah rolled his eyes but had to admit she was right — the street was deserted.

Without missing a beat, Char returned to her original point. "So, what about trying another door?"

"I've tried many." He never passed a red door without stepping through it, just to be sure.

She glanced at him out of the corner of her eye, and he could see her mentally calculating just how many doors that might be.

"Well, maybe it's the wrong time of day. Have you tried going through at midnight?"

"Yes."

"At noon?"

"Yes."

"At three a.m.?"

"Yup."

"The Hour of the Wolf?"

"I've tried every time of day and night."

"Well, maybe at the full moon —"

"I've tried every phase of the moon, every day of the year, and every hour of both equinoxes. I've tried all the days traditionally associated with the dead being able to leave the underworld, and even once during an eclipse. Nothing. It's always the same." That, however, didn't stop him from continuing to try. Last week, he'd spent an entire day passing back and forth through the red door at the Athenaeum Library just as quickly as he could, in an attempt to test the doorway at every minute of the day. It had been a grueling twenty-four hours and had revealed no new information. He'd been stuck between realms every single time.

Char grew quiet. Jonah glanced at her; she was looking at the ground, chewing her lip. He tensed, waiting for her to blurt out whatever annoying or discomfiting thing she was thinking. Instead, she peeked up at him and said quietly, "I'm sorry."

She seemed genuinely sympathetic. Guilt for snapping at her washed over him. "Look, I'm sorry—I didn't mean to bite your head off. It's just... I've been at this a while. And I'm pretty much an expert on this stuff, so I've tried all the obvious solutions."

Char gave him a tentative half-smile, but there was still a worried look behind her eyes that he didn't like. She might be sympathetic to his concern for Irene, but she clearly still disapproved of how much time he was spending in the ghost realm—concern she'd threatened to share with her aunt.

He lapsed into a moody silence, contemplating just how he was going to keep Char from following him again. Char, for her part, seemed to have been cowed into silence, or, at least, didn't feel compelled to offer any more "helpful" suggestions regarding red doors. They turned onto a main street and despite Char's blithe retort that she didn't care if people thought she was crazy, there was just enough foot traffic to keep her from starting a new conversation. They ended up walking in silence for the rest of the return trip— which was perfectly fine with Jonah.

Five

Irene, falling through the water, sank beneath ocean waves and plummeted towards the bottom like an anchor. She thrashed wildly, trying to right herself and rise to the surface before her air ran out. Her heart jack-hammered in her chest, slamming into her breastbone so hard she thought it would shatter.

She clawed desperately at the water, but her legs and arms didn't seem to be working properly. It took a moment for understanding to filter up to her brain: she hung in the water, upright, but simply floating, suspended between the surface and the bottom. No amount of effort propelled her up or down. Gravity had disappeared.

Surprise deadened her terror, making way for rational thought. She pushed hard with her arms and managed to twirl in place. Sensory input began to filter through the haze of panic, and she took in the eerily beautiful world around her. The water was a clear and brilliant blue-green and seemed to stretch on endlessly in all directions.

Schools of brightly colored fish in rainbow colors of all shapes and sizes swam placidly by.

She was breathing normally.

Andras was nowhere in sight.

She experienced a moment of transcendent calm, feeling both in the world and out of it, as if seeing it from within and from above. She just had time to think, "This is really weird," and then the world changed again. The water shimmered and rippled, and she was once more back in the field of wheat, standing on solid ground and perfectly dry.

Andras was on his hands and knees, gasping for breath. Instantly, she dropped to his side, steadying him as his body tried to vomit up the water he imagined he had swallowed.

"Easy, easy," she said, her hand hovering over his back for a second and then settling to gently rub it. She expected him to bark at her or pull away, but he did neither. She wasn't sure if he even noticed her ministrations. He remained doubled over, and he gasped for air, close to hyperventilating. "We don't breathe, so we can't actually drown," she said softly. "It's all in your head." She repeated this over and over, supporting him all the while, as his breathing gradually slowed.

The irony of the role reversal—her reminding him the dead didn't have physical bodies—wasn't lost on her. She chuckled. "Shake it off, big fella, just like you always tell me to."

Andras, still on his hands and knees, glared at her, coughing hard as he brought up the last of the imagined water. He managed to gasp out, "What in the name of all that is holy happened?"

The full impact of everything they had just experienced finally hit her, and she sat back on her heels, limp and loose-limbed as the adrenaline left her. The butterflies and then the fish and then drowning—a shudder ran through her as she contemplated their situation. The plane they were on was completely unstable. At any moment they might be dumped off it for good.

"I'm no expert, but I think it's like when we found that short-cut to that place that looked like an Indian village. I think we probably accidentally fell down a rabbit hole and crossed onto a different plane for a moment."

"And the snow and the butterflies?"

"I think... look, it's just a guess, alright? But I'd say it's like when we were walking and our feet were sinking through the ground. We've gone so far from the physical realm that our brains can't even compensate any more. Our brains are just kind of making it up as we go along, doing their best to approximate what they think is happening."

"Then what is really happening?"

"Again, I'm not really the expert..." She shrugged helplessly, wishing Jonah was here. He was the one who got this stuff, not her. Even as she had that thought, she realized it wasn't entirely true. She did have a theory on what the butterflies and fish had been — together, Jonah and The Guide had given her enough knowledge to be reasonably certain she understood how things worked around here. The problem was she didn't want to share her theory with Andras because he wasn't going to like it. However, she knew Andras wasn't going to move from the spot until he had some sort of explanation.

She plucked a stalk of wheat, fiddling with it to avoid making eye contact. She wished she could just make something up. Unfortunately, she wasn't any good at lying, and even if she was, Andras could read her like a book — he'd know she was bending the truth. She heaved a sigh and took the plunge.

"Well, The Guide said... The Guide said that everything is layered together, in the same place. We're technically still in the land of the living; we're just in a different plane or a facet or something so we can't see the living. Or maybe it's that we can't see them in the same way as before because we experience the world differently now that we don't have bodies — you know, the no-eyes-and-ears thing.

"I think... well, I think maybe the snow and the butterflies and the fish are other people on other planes — maybe even living people. We can't see them properly because we're not on the same plane, so our brains make up a shape for them because it doesn't quite know what they are." She risked peeking up at him to see his reaction. He knitted his brows in confusion and doubt, so she added, "It's like the sleepers in the tents in the Indian Village — they looked like they were asleep to us because they were on a different plane than us, so we couldn't see them properly."

She felt a pang of longing deep in her gut. The land of the living was so close and yet still so out of reach, just beyond her ability to get to it, separated from her by the thinnest layer of reality, and yet it might as well have been a million light years away. One of those fish — or even one of the snowflakes — might have been Jonah or her mother or her friend Alexis, all going about their lives back in the land of the living. Of course, there was an equal possibility one of them had been her grandmother, her father, or even Andras's brother going about their business on a higher plane of the afterlife. There was no way for her to know — or, at least, no way yet. With a little more time to study them, she might be able to figure it out.

Andras had shifted to a sitting position, but his expression still showed that he didn't understand. "Are we at the mercy of these 'rabbit holes', then, or is there a way we can navigate around them?"

While she was relieved, in a way, that he hadn't understood what she was saying — that they were, in some way, still in the land of the living and one rabbit hole away from returning to it — a part of her was disappointed as well. She was just kicking the can down the road, delaying the inevitable parting of the ways.

"The Guide said that in order to navigate the afterlife, we have to learn to see without eyes, to hear without ears." She had no idea what that meant, exactly, though she'd been trying to figure it out since he'd first said it to her. The closest she'd ever come was tapping into the "internal compass" — which was highly unpredictable and mostly uncontrollable.

"Then you must learn to do this — and quickly."

"I'm doing the best I can!" she shot back, stung by the criticism. "Maybe you should give it a whirl if you don't like the rate I'm going." Lips clamped together hard, she climbed to her feet and turned her back on him as she roughly dusted herself off. Furious tears scalded her eyes, and she made a show of surveying the landscape while she tried to pull herself together. Couldn't he see she was doing the best she could? She'd been dead all of five minutes. It wasn't like she'd had eight hundred years — unlike him — to learn this stuff.

She tried to work up a full boil of righteous anger and found that she couldn't because as much as she wanted to deny it, Andras was right — she was the one who had been given the knowledge of how to navigate the afterlife, so it was her responsibility to get them out of here.

Taking a deep, steadying breath, she looked around. The butterflies were gone. The fish were gone. The sand was gone. Everything looked as it had before: wheat and burning, brittle light — and the beckoning castle in the distance. For the moment, it appeared to be safe to proceed on their way. She grabbed her bag from where it lay at her feet and then set off, trying to call up the internal compass. She had never used it to navigate *around* things before; usually, once she found one of the wormholes, she either got sucked down it involuntarily or purposely slid down it. She wasn't sure if, once she located one of the tunnels, she could avoid it.

She focused on slowing down her breathing and emptied her mind of all thoughts but the castle. The rhythmic swish of the wheat seeped through her, filling her with a bone-deep feeling of peace and calm. She inhaled deeply, closed her eyes, and reached for the warm, flame-like glow of the internal compass nestled behind her breast-bone as she slowly exhaled.

"What are you doing?"

Andras had drawn abreast of her.

She cracked one eye and glared at him. "I'm doing what you told me to — I'm trying to learn how to use my ghost senses."

She closed her eyes again and immediately tripped, staggered drunkenly, and bumped into him. He let out a hastily smothered guffaw even as he caught hold of her and helped to right her.

Her eyes flew open, and she gave him a furious look. "Shut up! At least I'm trying!" She defiantly closed her eyes again, but now the moment was ruined. She could feel Andras watching her — and laughing — and it made her too self-conscious to focus.

Just as she gave up and opened her eyes, Andras pointed. "There is something, just there," he said.

Irene looked where he pointed and could see something brown in the wheat. She veered off course to take a closer look. It was a tiny rowboat of varnished wood, barely large enough for two people, just sitting there in the wheat. It was in impeccable condition, the sides gleaming brightly in the bronze light; it looked like it had never been used. Irene raised an eyebrow.

"What's a boat doing here? There's no water."

Andras's lip curled in suspicion. "Nothing here is as it seems."

"Yeah, so you keep pointing out."

Irene circled the boat, studying it from all sides. The wheat it sat on wasn't even flattened; it just bent around the boat.

"We should continue on our way," Andras said. "This is of no use to us."

"I'm not so sure," Irene said, her brow puckered in concentration. Andras was right that nothing here was as it seemed; things were also rarely present without a reason. This boat had a purpose — the trick was figuring out what it was. "You know what, get in."

"What? Why?"

"Just trust me. I think this might be a doorway to another plane."

"I thought we were going to avoid those."

"Not if it's a shortcut out of here."

"Are we to row through the wheat?"

"Will you just get in?"

Andras quirked an eyebrow suspiciously.

"Oh for God's sake — if it turns out to be nothing, the worst that happens is we get to sit down for a few minutes."

"That is not the worst that can happen."

Irene shook her head at him and then climbed into the boat, dropping into the seat in the bow. Reluctantly, Andras climbed in and gingerly sat himself mid-ship.

Nothing happened.

"See?" Irene said. "Nothing bad happened."

The boat began to rock gently.

"Are you doing that?" she asked, grabbing onto the sides of the boat. Beneath them, the wheat had turned to water. In fact, all the wheat had turned to water. They were on the edge of a large lake of glass-smooth water, black as night. On the shore, bordering the lake in all directions, stood twisted, bare-branched trees, not unlike apple trees, of stark, gleaming, solid white. They shone almost as if they were made of plastic. The sky overhead was a delicate, rosy pink, as if it were sunrise.

"Holy crap," Irene said, craning her neck as she looked around. They had to be really far from the physical plane now—the scenery here was straight out of a Tim Burton movie.

The boat glided gently forward, away from the shore.

Andras's face turned ashen, and he gripped the sides of the boat until his knuckled turned white. "What is happening?"

"Uh, well, I was right," Irene said. "It's a tunnel to another plane." She shot him an apologetic look. She tried to exude an air of confidence, but her hands clutched her bag tightly as her heart pounded in her chest. She hoped this hadn't been a mistake.

They skimmed along gently but at significant speed, and the breeze was cool and refreshing on Irene's face. She tilted her head up, letting the wind blow through her hair as she studied the strange landscape around them. They appeared to be heading for a large, dark island, thickly covered with the strange, white trees, rising gently and standing only a few feet above the water's surface in the center of the lake. As they drew closer, Irene could see that the island was edged in a vast expanse of black sand, increasing the starkness of the bone-white trees that covered it.

In another moment, they had beached, the boat bumping gently against the shore, and came to rest with a crunching sound against the sand. Irene and Andras kept their seats, waiting apprehensively for whatever was about to happen next.

Nothing happened.

"Uh, I guess we're here," Irene said.

Shakily, Andras rose to his feet and awkwardly stumbled out of the boat. Then he held out a hand to help her out. She wobbled unsteadily on her feet, the rocking of the boat throwing her off balance, and impatiently, Andras reached in, wrapped his hands around her waist, and lifted her out. She squawked in surprise as, just as quickly, he set her down, practically dropping her as he snatched back his hands like they'd been burned.

"Watch the manhandling!" Irene said, straightening her dress.

Andras just frowned at her.

Irene could hear voices. She shushed Andras and cocked her head. "I think there are people up ahead," she said. The land, transitioning from black sand to short black grass, sloped upwards as it moved away from the shore, the white trees growing more plentiful until they turned into densely-packed forest.

Irene started forward with Andras behind her and followed the sound. The black grass crunched softly under foot as they mounted the gentle slope and approached the edge of the wood. Irene stopped to touch a tree – though it was knobby and gnarled, the surface was smooth as silk, without texture. Irene wasn't sure what that meant, except she was pretty sure it wasn't actually a tree.

At the top of the rise they stopped short in surprise as they came upon a scene straight out of a medieval tapestry. In a clearing amongst the gleaming white trees – these with dense clusters of bright pink leaves – stood a massive oaken dining table, large enough to seat thirty or more. Around this table, seated upon massive, hand-carved chairs like mini-thrones, were richly dressed men and women, resplendent in long and lavish flowing robes and gowns of velvet and damask in shades of vermilion, plum, garnet, hunter, and the like, all edged with embroidery, lace, and fur. The women wore Renaissance style hats of one or two peaks from which trailed gauzy veils, and the men wore large, floppy, velvet and ermine hats.

The table was heaped with luscious fruits and roasted meats and goblets of jewel-colored liquids, possibly wine, though the platters were covered over by a layer of fallen pink leaves, which fell lazily from the trees like tinkling musical notes, giving the impression that the platters hadn't been touched for years. Bird-song permeated the grove, sweet and gentle, filling Irene with a sense of peace and tranquility.

Irene had a strange yearning to join the party at the table — to sit down with them, to drink from one of the cups, and to sample the food on the table. Her stomach rumbled — not with hunger so much as longing — and Irene put a hand to it, as if she could quiet it with the gesture.

The men and women around the table had been talking languorously, though Irene couldn't make out their words — she thought they might have been speaking a foreign language — but as they became aware of Irene's and Andras's presence, the conversation slowly trailed off and then died.

"Uh, hello?" Irene said, cautiously, stepping forward. There was no trace of friendliness from the people. In fact, the atmosphere of the entire area seemed to be growing less friendly by the second. Even the bird-song had stopped.

Thirty pairs of eyes slowly swiveled to face Irene and Andras.

Irene gasped and stepped back. Now that they diners faced her, she could see what she hadn't been able to see before: each person had the head of an animal — a goat, an ox, a horse, a fox, a cat, a crocodile...

A horse-headed woman in an apricot-colored robe rose to her feet. "You don't belong here," she said harshly, her frigid tone turning Irene's blood to ice.

"I'm sorry… we got lost…" Irene said, clutching her bag tighter as alarm snaked through her.

"This place is not for you," said a jaguar-headed man in carnelian robes, also rising to his feet.

Irene took a step back. The naked hostility was apparent now.

"I think we should go—" she said in an undertone to Andras.

"Agreed."

There was a movement at the table, and then something whistled through the air, striking Irene on the shoulder hard.

"Ow!" she cried, as the projectile dropped to the ground—a rock. "Hey!" she cried angrily, rubbing the bruise, but then another rock hit her, this time thudding dully against the side of her head. Andras grunted and flinched as he, too, was hit.

"You don't belong here," the men and women at the table said, each rising one by one. More rocks followed. Irene backed away hastily.

"Alright! Alright! We're going!"

The diners were all standing now, intoning "you don't belong here" in unison as rocks rained down on Irene and Andras.

"Come on!" Andras shouted.

Following his lead, Irene turned and ran, rocks pelting her head, her shoulders, her back, her legs as she fled.

They reached the beach and then the boat. Irene hopped in as Andras shoved off and then jumped in after her.

"Go! Go! Go!" Irene shouted, thumping the sides with her hands. Andras grabbed the oars and pulled hard, heading for the far shore. Irene had no idea if the boat would take them back to the plane with the wheat field or not. For all she knew, it was a one-way trip and they were stuck on this plane.

Irene was facing the beach they had just evacuated, and she watched breathlessly to see if the diners from the grove had given chase.

Long moments ticked by in which the only sounds were her harsh breathing and the splash of the oars in the water.

The beach remained empty.

Irene slumped down in her seat with relief.

"What's the worst that can happen?" Andras mimicked angrily, still pulling hard on the oars.

"Oh, shut up!" Irene said.

One they were mid-way back to shore, Andras pulled in the oars, letting the current pull them forward.

To Irene's relief, the water slowly turned back into wheat. In another moment, they were sitting in a stationary rowboat in a field of wheat, back in the land of the golden light. Andras jumped out of the boat so fast he tripped and nearly sprawled on his face. Irene climbed out more slowly — and gracefully. She was shaking all over, though.

Irene would have liked to sit down, at least until her legs stopped trembling like Jell-O, but Andras was glaring at the boat like he thought it would attack at any second and muttering in Spanish. She wanted to laugh, but it really wasn't funny. Everywhere they went in the afterlife, there were things attacking them — usually for no discernable reason. She was really starting to get sick of it.

Andras turned to her. "We should not linger," he said.

"Well, hang on," she said thoughtfully studying the boat. "It might be possible that shortcuts work in more than one direction. We just went higher up, but maybe we can go backwards, too — to a lower plane." *Possibly, even to the land of the living.* "The Guide did say that everything is layered together. So maybe it's not just an escalator, but an elevator, too."

"To what end?"

Irene's heart sank. Right — Andras would not go backwards, only forward.

"Look, it's either this or wandering through the endless hay field some more. This is the first concrete thing we've come to."

Andras shook his head. "What if you cannot control it? Or we drift even further from our goal? What if we get stuck and cannot return? The ferry of the dead brought us to this place for a reason."

"And what if that reason was so we could find this tunnel? Maybe this place is just a big inter-dimensional transit hub, like Grand Central Station or something. Maybe it brought us here just so we can connect to other ferries to other places."

Andras stubbornly shook his head again. "If that were the case, would not these 'ferries' be more obvious? Instead, this 'portal' as you call it is half-hidden here, obscure and forgotten."

Irene wanted desperately to argue, but she did have to admit he had a point. The rowboat wasn't as readily apparent as, say, the castle, which appeared to be the real goal of this plane. Like the tunnel to the Indian village on the last plane, this short-cut did seem to be incidental, or, perhaps, more accurately, meant for someone with better afterlife navigation skills than she possessed. She had no doubt that if she knew how to use it, it would prove invaluable. The problem was she didn't know how to use it.

She ground her teeth in frustration. She felt stupid and inept—why didn't she know how to use it? When, exactly, was she supposed to have learned how to use it—before she left the land of the living? On the last plane? The Guide had helped her immensely, teaching her much more than most dead people learned about the skills she'd need to navigate the afterlife, and yet, it was still only half as much as she needed. Jonah had said that the living used to prepare the dead—burying them with the tools and knowledge they needed to navigate the afterlife. When she got back to the land of the living, this was definitely one of the practices she'd make sure to reinstate. No more dead people sent off unprepared. Instead, they'd get buried with money and food and clothes and incidentals and companion animals and an instruction manual, damn it.

Irene glanced longingly at the boat. Given enough time, she could probably conquer the navigation problem. The Guide had seemed to think so. And here was the perfect opportunity to try. All the other short-cuts she'd found by chance – and they seemed to move around. This was the one stationary one she'd found.

She could elect to stay here, tell Andras to go on without her. Then, with unlimited time and no interruptions, she could focus all of her attention on trying to master navigating the planes of the afterlife – and returning home.

But what about Andras?

Guilt rolled through her belly; she couldn't just abandon him.

She sighed heavily and turned away from the boat. Andras stepped back and gestured for her to precede him – away from the boat and onward to the castle. She scanned the horizon for the castle – no closer for the distance they had already traveled – and then set off toward it once more. Irene saw Andras glance at the rowboat and cross himself as they left.

"It wasn't that bad," she said, shifting the beach bag into place on her shoulder. "At least there were people on that plane – here's there's just nothing."

"I think I prefer nothing," Andras said.

"Well," she conceded, "they were kind of snooty. I think we weren't evolved enough for them."

"Perhaps we should avoid any more short-cuts," Andras said dryly.

"We have to get off this plane somehow. Unless you propose that we build ourselves a little house and just live here forever?"

"Wherefore would we need a house?" Andras said. "We have no need of shelter – there is no rain, no cold, no insects."

"No, just storms of fish and snow," Irene said, just as dryly. "Aren't you cute today, making jokes and everything!"

Andras grunted, but one side of his mouth curled up slightly.

Irene laughed despite herself.

Any relief they felt, however, at returning to the placid wheat fields was soon replaced by unease at the increasing number of shadow workers. Soon the landscape was full of them, working in row upon row upon row. Their blank, shadowy faces gave Irene the heebie-jeebies, and she found herself holding her breath as she and Andras passed them.

"Do not look," Andras said in an undertone as he dipped his head close to her ear, "but we are being followed."

Irene glanced over her shoulder. They were, indeed, being followed — by a lone shadow.

Andras hissed in aggravation. "Why can you never do as you are told?"

"I'm sorry!" Irene whispered furiously. "I couldn't help it. It was just instinct."

Andras made a raspy, disgruntled noise.

"Instead of growling at me, why don't you think of a plan?"

"We could ask it what it wants."

"It's a shadow. I don't think it has a mouth."

"Technically, neither do we," Andras replied.

"This is no time to be cute."

They were beginning to attract attention. The shadows threshing the wheat were stopping their work, one by one, slowly straightening up to turn their blank, featureless faces to Irene and Andras.

The shadows began to move. Slowly, sweeping through the wheat as if it were mist, the shadow workers headed toward them. Irene turned, and there were shadows coming from behind them as well. They were coming from all directions now, encircling and closing in on them.

"Uh, Andras…"

"I see them," Andras said grimly. He stopped walking and held up a hand in a placating gesture. "Pax Verbotum. Peace be with you," he said in the incantation that had always soothed the Hungry Ghosts on the last plane.

The shadows slowed but didn't stop.

"What do you want?" Irene asked, surreptitiously sliding the bag from her shoulder and then plunging a hand into it to plumb its depths for a weapon of some kind. Her hand closed around the tire iron.

There was no answer, not even the whisper of wheat as the shadows moved through it. All was silence. Irene's heart thundered in her ears.

"What do you want?" she cried again, whipping around to confront the lone shadow that had been following them. It, however, was gone, melted into the solid wall of shadows surrounding them. Irene whirled back around to face the shadows jostling to draw closer to them. She yanked the tire iron out of her bag, holding it in front of her with one hand like a sword.

Andras moved sideways, positioning himself back-to-back with her, and raised his fists defensively.

As one, the shadows stepped closer, tightening the circle, and Irene jabbed warningly at them with the tire iron. The shadows didn't stop. Irene jabbed again, connecting with the closest shadow. The tire iron passed through it as if it were air. The shadow didn't even flinch.

Irene stabbed at the shadow again and, again, the tire iron passed right through it.

It's not real, she thought. *They're just shadows.*

She turned her head toward Andras, still back-to-back with her, to tell him that the shadows weren't real, when the closest one reached out and touched her. She felt an odd tug, as if someone had yanked on the back of her jacket. She whirled around, but there was only Andras behind her. She felt the tug again and once more, turned around, but still nothing. She turned back to Andras, who was looking over his shoulder as if he, too, had felt a tug on the back of his clothes.

"Let's get out of here," Irene said, unease spreading through her.

"Agreed," Andras said.

They pushed through the ring of shadows, passing right through them with only a bit of resistance, as if the shadows were somehow sticky.

Irene glanced over her shoulder as they race-walked away. The shadows stood where they were, unmoving, as if intently watching them depart. Irene shivered and put on a burst of speed.

Six

"What are you doing?"

Jonah cringed as Char's voice cut into his concentration. He was on the dead side of the store, which was mercifully devoid of customers. He hunched over a notebook set on a wooden display table, where he'd managed to clear some workspace amidst the clutter of the shop.

He glanced up just long enough to take in her outfit — today she was wearing a black, short-sleeved t-shirt with some kind of cartoon zombie doll over a long-sleeved purple t-shirt, black shorts over black and white leggings, and the combat boots — and then he put his head back down, trying to concentrate harder on the ledger he was working on in the hope she might take the hint and go away. "Inventory," he said curtly.

"Oh. Do you need any help?"

Jonah put his head down even farther, letting the curtain of his hair hide him from view, until his nose almost touched the book. "No."

He heard her come closer, and he gritted his teeth. The girl just didn't give up. Suddenly, she was beside him and had stuck her head under his arm, so that it was practically under his nose. She was so close that Jonah could pick out the individual strands of purple in her black hair. He dropped his pencil and pulled back, alarmed to find her so close. Hadn't she ever heard of personal space?

Char straightened up and tossed back her hair. "Let's go out and do something."

"I'm working!" He enunciated each word hard.

"Let's go to a movie," she said, clearly not taking no for an answer.

"There's nothing playing." Jonah gently, but firmly, pushed her out of the way and then resumed his spot in front of the book.

"Well, we could go to Faneuil Hall or take a Duck Boat tour. Something. Anything."

Jonah made a face and kept working.

"Okay, fine, if that's not your speed, then show me some ghost stuff."

Jonah didn't even look up as he answered. "You're alive; you can't get into ghost places."

"Well, show me how to do that meditation thing and then I can!"

Jonah sighed deeply. "Your aunt wants this done by this afternoon."

"Oh, Auntie doesn't care."

"Where is your aunt, by the way?"

"She had to go to a coven meeting."

Jonah's head snapped up. "Coven? She's into witchcraft?"

Char doubled over with laughter. "No! That's just what I call it. She's at a Chamber of Commerce meeting."

Jonah gave her a disapproving frown and returned his attention to the inventory.

"Oh, all alright," Char said with the theatrical tone of one being made to suffer some kind of unbearable burden. "Fine. I'll help you finish the inventory."

"Swell."

"Tell me what you need done," Char said blithely, ignoring his sarcasm.

Jonah sighed and handed her a box of polished stones. "Here, put that back."

Char took the box from him and crossed the room. She put it down and then snatched two items off the counter and held them up. "Don't you know anything? You never put these two next to each other!" She was holding two different crystal pyramids that were indistinguishable except for the color.

"Why? What happens when they're next to each other?"

Char set one of the pyramids on the counter very carefully. "They open a portal to a hell dimension."

Jonah perked up. "Really?"

Char laughed. "You should see your face right now."

Jonah glared at her. "Very funny."

Char, still chuckling, crossed the room and deposited the other pyramid on a shelf containing various dried herbs. "You don't put them together because they cancel each other out, and then there's no point to having them."

Jonah made a non-committal noise.

"You're the one that's so into metaphysics and ghosts. How come you don't know that?" She plopped onto a stool across from him.

Jonah shrugged. "I don't know; the only part that interests me is ghosts and the afterlife."

Char cocked her head and raised an eyebrow. "So the living can just go suck it?"

"Yeah, I guess."

Char made a "tsking" noise that reminded him of Madame Majicka. Then she jumped to her feet. "Here—I'll tell your fortune." She crossed the room, grabbed something off the counter, and returned a second later. As she sat down, Jonah could see that she had a deck of Tarot cards. She grinned at him as she pulled out the cards and shuffled them. She paused to tuck her long hair back behind her ear and then laid out the cards.

"Let's see... oh dear, this doesn't look good." She made a face.

Curious despite himself, he craned his neck, trying to see the cards. "What?"

"It says here you're going to end up a crazy old hermit, living with your seven cats in a one-room apartment over a bakery."

Jonah screwed up his face in annoyance, and Char burst into laughter. "Wait, no, sorry, I had that wrong. It's twelve cats."

"Shut up!"

Char laughed even harder. "Actually, it says you're going to settle down and become... an accountant."

Jonah grabbed the nearest thing at hand—a packet of incense—and threw it at her.

"A rock star?" Char amended as she ducked the projectile.

"Oh yeah? Well, what do the cards say about you?" he asked as he put down his pencil and came around the table to stand beside her.

Char scooped up the cards, shuffled them, and relaid them out. "They say I'm going to marry a rich, Italian super model and spend my days lounging by the pool."

"Yeah, right!"

Jonah looked at the cards, studying the various brightly colored designs but couldn't make heads or tails of them.

"No, wait, sorry, looks like I'm actually going to be a famous race car driver, but unfortunately, a freak shopping cart accident will result in an injury to my pedal foot that will bring my career to an abrupt and untimely end."

Jonah, caught in a cross between a scoff and a laugh, choked. Char grinned at him.

"Okay, be serious," he said. "Do it right."

Char's grin widened. "For real?" He nodded, and she shifted in her seat, getting more comfortable, as she scooped up the cards. "Okay." She shuffled and then laid out seven cards in a row. She studied them for a moment, her brow creased in concentration. "Man!" she muttered.

Jonah leaned forward eagerly. "What? What do you see?"

Char's lips pursed, and she cast Jonah a dark look. "Death. Judgment. The Tower. The Hanged Man. The Wheel. I've never seen such single-minded cards in all my life."

"What do they mean?"

"Change. Change. Change. Transformation. Journeys…"

Jonah's heart thumped unsteadily, and a prickle of excitement surged through him. That sounded like he was going to find a way to cross over. What other kind of journey involved change and transformation—and she'd mentioned death.

His excitement, however, was dampened by Char abruptly scooping up the cards with a sour expression. "This stuff is all bullshit anyway. They're cards. What do they know?"

Her abrupt change in mood caught him off guard, and he frowned in confusion. "I thought you said this stuff wasn't bullshit?"

"The crystals and stuff aren't. Tarot cards are," she said as she stuffed the cards into the box and then crossed the room to return them to the shelf. "You know, I'm still kind of confused about why you're trying to find a doorway to the other side anyway."

So… apparently he wasn't the only one who thought the cards were talking about his search for Irene.

His excitement increased, but remembering that he had to be careful what he said around Char, he kept his voice calm and neutral when he spoke. "I told you… I'm trying to help my friend."

"Yeah, Ms. what's-her-name. But I thought she had crossed over?"

"Yeah, she did, but now she's in trouble."

Char paced around the room now, restlessly poking at various items. She picked up a book and then set it down without looking at it as she scoffed. "How much trouble could she be in? She's dead."

"What do you mean? There are all kinds of danger in the afterlife."

At this, Char paused. "Like what?"

"What do you mean, 'like what'? Haven't you read any of the stories?"

"Oh… yeah, I guess. I just never really thought about it."

"Never thought about it? What do you mean you never thought about it? You're psychic! You deal with the dead every day."

Char shrugged. "My concern is for the living, not for the dead."

Jonah scowled. "You sound like your aunt."

Char grinned in response. "Why thank you."

Jonah's scowl deepened. "It wasn't a compliment."

Char stuck out her tongue. Then her expression turned thoughtful again. "Okay, but still... if she's on the other side, then how do you know she's in trouble?"

"Trust me," he said. "She's always in trouble." His mind flashed through the litany of scrapes he'd had to save Irene from — getting in a fight with a couple of homeless guys, being thrown out of the library for being too loud, being attacked by Samyel in an alley, being attacked by Samyel in the middle of the shopping district, getting caught breaking into Madame Majicka's shop, getting stuck at the River Acheron because she didn't have any coins for the ferryman... really, the list was nearly endless.

"Oh God, she's one of those helpless, damsel-in-distress types?"

"Uh, no. Nothing like that. She... I don't know.... It's hard to explain. Just... trust me. She's in trouble." Irene's propensity — a word he'd learned from her — for getting into trouble stemmed from her temper, not from helplessness. Without a cooler head around to moderate her impetuosity, Irene had a tendency to run smack into problems.

Char flashed him a doubtful look. Jonah sighed heavily. "She sent me a letter."

"What did it say?"

"Stuff."

"If I'm going to help you, I'm going to need specifics."

"I don't want any help. In fact, I specifically said I don't want your help."

"Yes, but you clearly *need* help since you can't find a way across by yourself."

Jonah opened his mouth to argue, but Char crossed her arms over her chest, her eyes flashing with that, "I'm-going-to-tell-my-aunt-if-you-don't-cooperate" look.

With a growl of frustration, he reached into the back pocket of his khaki pants, pulled out his wallet, and produced the carefully folded sheet of paper that had ripped his heart in two. He hesitated for a second and then held it out to Char. She crossed the room in two strides and took it from him with a questioning look. He waited while she read through the words burned into his memory:

Dear Jonah,

This will be my last letter. I'm leaving the rocks by the river so that future arrivals will always have a way to get a coin so they can cross. Someday, very far in the future, when you finally make it here, I hope you'll see the altar and think of the woman you once helped.

We both know I couldn't have gotten this far without you, but now it's time for us to go our separate ways. Don't send me any more letters – I won't read them. Stop visiting my grave. I need to move on, and you need to forget about ghosts and the afterlife. It's not good for you to spend so much time with the dead. You need to live your life – your real life. Go out and see and do and experience everything the world has to offer before it's too late. Life is short, Jonah; the afterlife is forever.

Jonah's fists clenched at the cold, remorseless words, written without so much as a sign of a tear to show that it had been as painful for Irene to write them as it had been for him to read them.

Char looked up from the page. "Uh, seems pretty clear to me that she *doesn't* need your help."

"Of course she does!"

"Last I checked, Chief, 'stop writing to me,' isn't code for 'please come and save me from mortal peril.' When a woman says to leave her alone, she means leave her alone. Even I know that."

Jonah snatched the letter from Char. "Irene would never have written that letter unless she was forced to."

"Wow, way to be persistent." Char's voice dripped with sarcasm.

"Look, I know her, okay?" He carefully refolded the brittle, worn paper as he spoke and replaced it in his wallet next to Irene's other letters. "And I'm telling you, she would never have cut off contact like that unless something was really wrong or someone forced her to."

"And what... then she just sat down to wait for you to come rescue her? She sounds like a real princess."

Jonah tensed, a flash of anger searing through him. "Don't talk about her like that. You don't even know her!"

Char put up her hands in surrender and took a step back. "Okay, okay. Chill!"

Jonah turned away, shoving the wallet into his pocket, and returned to the inventory ledger, his temper starting to boil over at Char's invasive questions and mocking.

Abruptly, Char stood up. "I'm hungry. Let's go get something to eat."

"What? No." Even if he'd been starving, he wouldn't have gone with her. Besides the fact that she was annoying, every time he spent five minutes with her, she blackmailed him into spilling his guts. He was painfully aware of the fact that until he turned eighteen, he had limited freedom to do as he pleased; if his parents found out he wasn't in school, if he lost his job and apartment at Madame Majicka's, if people found out about his unusual hobby, if, if, if... There were more ways than he could count that he could get in trouble and even more ways his ghost-hunting activities could be curtailed — he could be forced to return home to his parents, sent to prison, or even confined to a mental hospital.

Impatiently, he shoved back the cuffs of his long-sleeved t-shirt and picked up his pencil. "I'm busy," he said.

"Oh, come on," Char said, "you need to eat a sandwich or something. You're rail thin. You'd be cute if you weren't so bony."

Despite his resolution to ignore her, Jonah found himself staring at her, his mouth hanging open in surprise. "Do you ever filter any of the stuff that comes out of your mouth?"

Char shrugged, completely unabashed. "I told you — I'm homeschooled; I haven't been socialized. Now are we gonna go get something to eat or what?"

The bell over the door jangled. Startled, Jonah and Char both looked to see who it was at the same moment. Jonah thought he had locked the shop, but realized he'd only locked the side for the living. He recognized the ghost coming through the door, too. It was hard not to — powdered wig of cascading curls, black silk cut-away coat and matching knee breeches over a vest of gold silk, frothy white neck scarf folded in a waterfall of ruffles, white silk stockings, and black, heeled shoes with gold buckles. He was one of Jonah's customers — the ones that Madame Majicka didn't know about. Damn it, he didn't need this with Char here.

"Hi, can I help you?" Char said brightly, moving to intercept the man, but the ghost ignored her. He stepped up to the table beside Jonah and plopped a plastic grocery bag down on the counter.

"Two coats and a lamp," the man said with a grand flourish.

Jonah bit his lip to keep from groaning out loud. He glanced at Char, trying to find a way to keep her from finding out what was happening. "Look, William —"

"*Sir* William," the ghost corrected, holding up an imperious finger.

"Sir William," Jonah amended. "Now isn't a good time —"

"What's going on?" Char asked, coming closer and peering at the bundle on the counter.

"Nothing," Jonah said quickly. He picked up the bag and thrust it at the ghost. "We don't take lamps." He pushed Sir William toward the door.

"It's a perfectly good lamp," Sir William said, digging in his heels. "It was working just the other day."

"Yeah? And will it still be working after I cross it over and you take the ghost version away?" Jonah asked, trying to move the resisting man toward the exit. "No lamps."

Jonah managed to get Sir William to take two steps towards the exit, his gold-buckled shoes clicking loudly against the floor tiles. Char was still hovering beside him, looking back and forth between the two men, a worried and confused frown puckering her brow.

"And the coats?" Sir William said, still stubbornly refusing to move fast enough.

"And where'd you get them?" Jonah asked, knowing perfectly well what the answer would be. Sir William was a kleptomaniac and a cheat. He'd pull every trick he could to get a bargain or something for nothing.

"Why, the poor box, of course," Sir William replied, mercifully taking three more steps toward the door.

"You can't steal donations left at the church!" Jonah cried in exasperation. He counted the steps remaining. Just four more and Sir William would be out the door. Jonah shoved harder.

"It wasn't at the church," the ghost retorted with asperity. "What do you take me for?" Jonah took him for someone who had been caught stealing from the donation boxes at all the local churches too many times to count. "It was outside the Goodwill."

Jonah yanked opened the door. "No," he said firmly and with one final shove, pushed Sir William outside. He slammed the door closed so hard the bottles on the nearby counter jumped and rattled. He turned the lock for good measure; the bolts slid closed with a satisfying thunk.

Jonah slumped against the door. His relief, however, was short lived. Char crossed her arms over her chest and cocked one hip. "What was that all about?"

"Nothing."

Char pursed her lips and her eyes glinted dangerously. She tossed her head, sending a ripple through her long, black hair. "Oh really? Maybe I should tell my aunt about your 'nothing'?"

Jonah straightened up, grinding his teeth in frustration. "You know, that's growing old real fast. You can't just blackmail people into doing what you want. Maybe I don't want to tell you. Maybe it's none of your business."

Char grinned, totally unabashed. "Oh, boo hoo. Don't be a sore loser. Just tell me."

"Irene never resorted to blackmail," Jonah muttered, brushing past her. He moved to the other side of the room, putting the long, low counter where he'd been working on inventory between them.

"Oh, that's right, Saint Irene," Char said, the corners of her mouth turning down in disapproval. Then she perked up. "Does this have to do with her?"

He slumped against the counter. "Oh, my God, you are so annoying! Do you know that?"

The steely glint in Char's eyes returned, and Jonah had no doubt she'd make good on her threat to tell her aunt about his visitor. Frustrated, he straightened and began scooping the inventory materials into a pile as he talked. "I need money. So I trade with ghosts. They bring me living stuff, I cross it over for them; they get the dead item back, I keep the living shell, which I pawn or sell on eBay or whatever. Then I use the money to buy the stuff I need." It was mostly true. Char didn't need to know that the "stuff" he needed was travel expenses for a trip around the world to visit the various possible portals to the land of the dead.

Char frowned. "Isn't that illegal?"

"How's it illegal?"

Char's frown deepened. "I don't know—where do the ghosts get the stuff they bring to you? They must steal it."

"I don't take stuff that's clearly outright stolen from donation boxes and stuff."

"And the stuff that's only sort of stolen?"

Jonah shrugged. "How am I supposed to know if it's stolen or not?"

Now Char looked outraged. "Jonah! That's terrible! You can't just—"

"Look, if people don't want ghosts to steal their stuff, then they should put charms on their house so ghosts can't get in. I'm not responsible for what the ghosts do."

"Yeah, but if they couldn't trade the stuff, then they wouldn't take it."

He finished collecting the inventory-related items and dumped them in a pile in a cubby under the counter. Then he moved around the store, straightening items so he could avoid looking at Char as he spoke. "Not true. Ghosts have been stealing from the living for forever. They aren't dumb. A lot of them manage to figure out how to convert it to dead stuff on their own—they leave it on their own grave or at a general shrine. Where there's a will, there's a way. Besides, a lot of the time, the stuff is scavenged from the trash or whatever. It's not stolen."

Char frowned doubtfully at him. "Yeah, well, I don't think Auntie would approve of you using her store for your side business—"

Jonah spun around, leaned forward, and pointed a finger at Char to punctuate his words. "Yeah, and you're not going to tell her, either."

"Oh yeah? Says who?"

"Because if you do, I'll get fired, and then you won't have anyone to hang out with." Jonah watched in satisfaction as Char's eyes widened in surprise and then narrowed in annoyance. His little threat had hit home. *Ha*, he thought smugly, *two can play the blackmail game*.

It would hurt him more than her to leave the magic shop—he'd have to find another place to operate his trading business and a new place to live—but Char seemed so desperate for a friend she apparently hadn't noticed that little flaw in his argument.

Char leaned back on her heels, studied him for a moment, and then crossed her arms over her chest. "Fine," she said tightly, "I won't tell. But if I think for one second you're doing anything illegal or that might put my aunt or the shop in jeopardy, the deal's off!"

"Fine," Jonah said, trying, and failing, to hide his smile of triumph.

Char matched his smug look with one of her own. "Can we go get something to eat now?"

Seven

There were shadows everywhere now, and Irene and Andras walked past rows and rows of them, all of which stopped to stare as they passed.

"Andras…" Irene said urgently, not really sure what she wanted Andras to do about the shadows.

The shadows were more plentiful here, and a few hundred feet ahead, Irene could see a thick cluster of them. In the middle of the cluster was a man, solid like her and Andras. The man shouted as the shadows encircled him. Before Irene or Andras could react, the man flailed wildly, as if struggling to break free from someone holding him though no one seemed to be touching him. The shadows surged forward, and then the man disappeared. One moment he was there, the next he was gone, leaving only empty space where he'd been a moment ago.

Irene gasped, her hand flying to her mouth. At the noise, the shadows turned as one to stare at her and Andras, as if they had heard. The menace they exuded was palpable. Irene took an involuntary step backwards.

Andras grabbed her wrist, his fingers biting into her flesh as, in one motion, he yanked her sideways, away from the shadows, and turned to run. She stumbled and tripped. Dimly, she heard him shout, "RUN!"

And then she ran.

They zigzagged through the wheat, running from the shadows. Everything passed by in a blur — wheat, clusters of shadows, more wheat. Irene ran without seeing, propelled on fear and instinct, her bag slamming into her hip with each step. There was no plan, no thought, no goal, beyond survival and escape. The only thing Irene knew for sure was that every way they turned led to more shadows.

They ran and ran, past endurance, past ability, past everything but the burning pain of exhaustion. The haze of the passing scenery became monochromatic — gold, gold, gold.

Irene finally stopped, doubling over to gasp for breath, sure she would die from the screaming, wrenching pain in her lungs as she gulped in giant lungfuls of air.

Andras drew to a halt beside her, calm and collected. "You are not out of breath; you have no need for air." He said it firmly, but gently, and he placed a comforting hand on the small of her back, warm and reassuring.

Irene tried to laugh but choked as she struggled to breathe, hands on knees. She opened her mouth to retort when a movement behind Andras caught her eye.

It was a shadow.

With a startled cry, she straightened up and jumped back. Andras immediately spun around to see what was behind him. The shadow was faster, though, and it skirted around behind him.

"Behind you!" Irene cried.

Andras spun the other way, but once more, the shadow eluded him. He spun again, this time continuing in a circle. The shadow continued to move as well, circling him.

Irene began to laugh. "Stop, stop," she called breathlessly. She pointed behind him. "It's *your* shadow."

Andras tried to look, but, of course, couldn't twist far enough to see completely behind himself. He looked like a dog chasing his tail. Irene laughed even harder. Andras stopped trying to see his own shadow and, instead, glared at her. Then he pointed behind her. "You have one as well." Startled, Irene copied Andras's movements, trying to see behind herself. She realized a second after she turned what she had done and stopped. She thought she detected a smirk on Andras's face, and she narrowed her eyes. Andras's face remained carefully neutral, but there was definitely a twinkle in his eyes now.

She shifted her attention back to the shadow lurking behind Andras. "Do something," she said. "Raise your hand or something so I can see if that really is your shadow."

He cast her a dubious look but complied. The shadow mimicked the movement. Irene gestured with her hand, indicating Andras should continue moving. He raised his other arm and then flapped both like a bird. The shadow moved in time with him. Irene narrowed her eyes as she studied the shadow hard, not entirely convinced it belonged to Andras. Andras sighed and lifted one leg and then began to dance a jig.

Irene laughed. "Okay, okay, I guess it is your shadow. Though," she said the laughter changing to a thoughtful frown, "that doesn't look like a normal shadow. It's standing behind you. I mean... standing, like... standing."

Andras, studying her shadow with the same intensity, slowly nodded. "A shadow is cast against something – the ground, a wall. It does not follow behind like..."

"Like a body double or a stalker," Irene finished. "I know." She shifted from foot to foot uneasily. "Well, I guess shadows in the afterlife behave differently?" She tried to look at the sky and assess the angle of the sun, but that made her eyes water. "Why wouldn't they? I mean, there's no sun, so I'm not even sure why there are shadows." *Or how a ghost could have a shadow.*

She thought of the shadows that had attacked the man.

Or why there are shadows without people.

She shivered. Something definitely wasn't right. What had happened to the man when he'd disappeared? It had looked like he was being attacked, but the shadows never seemed to touch him.

Irene sidled closer to Andras's shadow, but Andras turned to see what she was doing. The shadow moved with him. "Hold still!" she said.

Andras complied, and Irene cautiously approached the shadow again. Slowly, she put out her hand, reaching for the shadow. She hesitated for a moment, and then in a rush of fatalistic determination, she plunged her hand into it. As with their attackers, her hand passed right through as if the shadow wasn't even there.

"Hang on!" Irene said. She plunged a hand into her bag and dug frantically, finally coming up with a sheaf of papers — letters from Jonah. She riffled through them. "Ah ha! I thought so!" she said triumphantly. "In his last letter to me, Jonah mentioned that the Egyptians thought that people were made up of five parts — including the shadow!"

"What does that mean?"

Instantly, she deflated. "Uh, I don't know exactly." When Andras gave her an exasperated look, Irene put her hands on her hips. "I don't see you bringing any knowledge to the table."

"All things in time."

"Ha. Ha. Seriously, remind me what it is you bring to this expedition?"

Andras's mouth turned down, and Irene feared she'd hurt his feelings. "I was just joking," she said in exasperation.

Andras's eyes locked on hers and, suddenly serious, he took a step toward her, closing the distance between them. "I know. I have learned that it is not the things you say but the things you do not that matter."

Irene swallowed hard, unsettled by his sudden closeness and took a step back. "What is this — when did you become Sigmund Freud?"

"You use words like a shield; you hide behind them."

"Why does everyone I meet feel the need to psychoanalyze me?"

One side of Andras's mouth tilted up, and his eyes softened. "Because you are such an interesting specimen."

"Specimen?" she sputtered in surprise. "Where the hell did you pull that word out of? No, seriously," she said, trailing after him as he turned away and set off once more, "since when do you use words like 'specimen'?"

"We should not linger," Andras said over his shoulder. "Those shadow creatures may find us."

Reluctantly admitting he was right, Irene gathered her stuff, and they set off once more. However, the idyllic peace of the endless wheat fields was broken. It no longer felt like they were alone; instead, it felt like they were being followed by a couple of Mafia hit men. Irene cast furtive glances over her shoulder at the two shadows following them as they walked.

She and Andras had wandered off course when they'd run, and now they angled back toward the castle, which stubbornly remained in the far distance. No matter how far they travelled, it never seemed to get any closer. Irene narrowed her eyes as she studied it in the far distance, but close scrutiny didn't reveal any clues as to the castle's purpose or how to reach it.

She turned her attention back to the letter clutched in her hand and read as they walked, combing it for any clues as to what the shadows might be or how to defend against them. "Jonah says here that the Egyptians believed people were made up of five parts—including the shadow. The shadow served as a kind of replacement body for the spirit after the person died. Do you think that's what these things are?" Irene gestured to the shadows walking behind them.

Andras shrugged.

"But if that's our ghost body, then why aren't we in it? Why is it over there when I'm over here?"

Andras shrugged again.

"And why would they attack us? It doesn't make any sense." She frowned. "Maybe it's like the Uglies or the Hungry Ghosts? Maybe they're ghosts who have forgotten who they are—they're all body, no spirit? Or maybe—"

Andras nudged her and pointed. "There is a village."

At first, Irene thought it was another throng of shadows, but she soon realized these were not shadows but people, like her and Andras — and lots of them. She thought Andras had been exaggerating when he'd called it a village, but as they drew closer, Irene realized he was right. Not only were there people, there were shaggy goats, sturdy draft horses, plump sheep — most roaming free, but some contained in wood-slatted corrals — cooking fires with spits and kettles, smiling women grinding grain on large, flat stones, and even what appeared to be a stone well, complete with wooden bucket.

The village, spread out over a sizeable area, was situated on a kind of reverse oasis — the ground had been cleared of all wheat and was now nothing but an island of dry and dusty dirt amidst the endless golden fields. Scattered throughout this clearing were ten or so large, Bedouin-like tents — large, untanned animal hide canopies stretched over tall poles that were more like small houses than the tiny, nylon, weekend camping shelters Irene was familiar with — not that she'd ever been camping in her life, but she had flipped through an L. L. Bean catalog once or twice.

These tents had their flaps flipped open, revealing their contents, and as Irene passed, she saw tapestries, rugs, and blankets, mountains of cushions, braziers of incense, small, ornately carved wooden tables, stools, earthenware ewers and cups, and more. The furnishings were, for the most part, plain and serviceable, but more than enough to create a very snug and comfortable home in the afterlife. Irene's mind boggled as she considered the fact that everything here had been carried through from the land of the living, most likely by being buried with their owners — these people had all really planned ahead for the afterlife.

As for the people themselves — they all seemed friendly, though not particularly inviting. They smiled and raised their hands or nodded in greeting as Irene and Andras passed, but none stopped what they were doing to speak to or approach them.

Irene took in their clothes, their physical features, their hair styles — primitive sandals, robes of rough, faded, hand-woven fabric closed with a bit of rope or a plain sash, scarves over the women's heads, thick beards and shaggy heads of hair on the men — and tried to figure out where in time these people were from. In truth, they reminded her of extras from the movie "The Ten Commandments," and she half expected Charlton Heston to appear at any moment.

Irene stopped to watch several women clustered around a large, flat rock, grinding something between it and a stone rolling pin. Irene guessed they were probably grinding wheat into flour. Good God, that wasn't their job in the afterlife, was it? They'd never be done — the wheat fields were endless.

One of the women, in her twenties, with soft, brown curls and laughing eyes, looked up and smiled.

"Uh, hi," said Irene, not really sure how to open a conversation. "How's it going?"

Irene hadn't quite figured out how communication worked in the afterlife — though she had a lot of theories. Andras had lived in twelfth-century Spain. There was no way he had ever learned English, and even if he had, it wouldn't have been any form she would understand. She hardly understood Shakespeare, and that stuff had been written only four hundred years ago. And yet, she and Andras were perfectly able to communicate. Even stranger, she'd had no problem holding a conversation with a Chinese philosopher who'd lived over two thousand years ago or with Ancient Greeks.

This had all seemed weird to her until she'd realized none of them had bodies — which meant they didn't have mouths or vocal cords. They shouldn't have been able to communicate at all. But the fact that they could meant they were communicating in some way other than spoken language. What that way was, however, she had no idea. Since they were pure energy now, maybe it was through vibrations that mimicked sound waves. Or maybe it was mental telepathy. Or, quite possibly, everything here was simply a figment of her imagination and she was imagining all of it—including the conversations.

"Aw ibetj," the woman said, inclining her head.

Okay, well, at least these people talked, unlike the ones at the Indian Village she'd stumbled into on the last plane. It was a start.

"I'm sorry, we're a little lost—can you tell me where we are?" Irene asked.

The woman smiled wider. "These are the things of Masudmensah."

"Masudmensah?" Irene looked at Andras for help, but he had wandered off to talk to a group of men tending a flock of speckled sheep with long, pointed horns. She hissed in frustration and then racked her brain—she didn't know any afterlife deity named Masudmensah. She tried another tack. "What are you all doing?"

"Making bread."

"I meant what are you all doing here—in this land? Are you waiting for something?" Unlike the people at the river on the last plane, these people didn't really seem to be waiting for anything—or lost. They seemed to have set up household and were living here permanently—quite happily it seemed.

The woman didn't seem to understand the question. She looked at her two companions for help. One of the women smiled and moved over, making room for Irene. She patted the ground. Andras was still talking, so Irene plopped down, covering as much of her lower half with her short skirt as she could.

The women were looking at her expectantly. Irene wasn't sure what they wanted her to say. "Soooo... heard any good jokes lately?"

The smiling woman to her left smiled wider and passed Irene the shallow stone bowl of grain that she was working. "Uh, thanks?" Irene said. She had no idea what they expected her to do with this. She set it down and dug in her bag for a second. The goats and sheep had reminded her of the cow she'd seen when she'd arrived in this land—maybe it belonged to these women and had wandered off.

At the very bottom of the bag, she found what she was looking for—a tiny, origami cow that she'd picked up during Ghost Festival while she was still in the land of the living. She pulled it and a cheap Bic lighter out of her bag.

"Here," she said to the women. She turned around, lit the lighter, held the flame to the cow until the paper caught, and then set the burning effigy down on the ground behind her. The paper went up in flames instantly, emitting a small puff of smoke. Instead of dissipating, however, the smoke continued to grow, expanding upwards and outwards, elongating until a head, torso, four legs, and a tail were discernable in the swirling vortex. In a moment, the smoke solidified and a full-sized cow—light brown in color with wide, liquid brown eyes—stood there, placidly chewing its cud.

The women gasped and laughed, as if Irene had just performed an entertaining magic trick. And then, as if the sudden appearance of a cow out of nowhere was nothing special, then went back to working their grain mills. The woman to her left reached into a nearby basket and pulled out a small, cracker-like round, which she handed to Irene. Irene took it to be food, maybe what passed for bread. Not wanting to offend, she took a bite—the texture was rough, like stone-ground wheat, which was the only pleasant part of it. The item was like cardboard—dry and tasteless. Irene managed to swallow the bite without choking and pasted a smile on her face. "Mmmm… thank you," she said thickly, the cracker having turned to paste in her mouth, gluing her tongue to the roof of her mouth.

She remembered she'd seen a well nearby. She excused herself and then race-walked over to it, relieved to find the bucket, sitting on the ring of stones surrounding the well, full of water. Irene grabbed the ladle sitting beside the bucket, filled it with water, and drank greedily.

Andras materialized at her shoulder. Irene coughed as she cleared the last of the cracker from her throat. "Don't try the crackers," Irene said thickly.

"They water the livestock from that bucket," Andras said. Irene sputtered and nearly dropped the ladle. Then she realized he was trying to get a rise out of her. She lifted her chin and met Andras's look with a steely one of her own. "I can't get germs from sheep—I don't have a body," she said, and then purposely lifted the ladle and took another long, slow drink.

Andras laughed.

"Did you find out anything?" Irene asked.

"We are in Yaaru, awaiting Anpu, who will lead us to Ma'at."

Irene stared at him, impressed despite herself. "How'd you get all that?"

Andras shrugged. "Men like to talk about sheep."

Irene stared at him. "I don't even know what that means."

Andras's lips twitched, but he didn't elaborate. Irene grimaced and turned over the information he'd provided. The only word she'd recognized in there was Ma'at—the Egyptian goddess in charge of weighing the hearts of the dead. "Does Ma'at live in the castle?" she asked with a quiver of unease.

"No. Asir lives in the castle."

"Who the hell is Asir?"

Andras shrugged. "Heathen beliefs."

Irene rolled her eyes. "Okay, well, what do you want to do? Do we keep poking around here and see if these people know anything else, or do we keep going?"

"They seem a simple people. I do not think they know anything that will be of help to us. Their beliefs are their own."

"You know, we might all be heathens and unbelievers to you, but you'll notice we're all sharing the same afterlife. You might want to think about that."

Andras's mouth turned down in displeasure, but he regarded her steadily for a moment. "Why did you give the women that cow?"

Irene shrugged, not sure how to explain the impulse to give the women a gift. "I don't know. I just felt like it. It seemed appropriate. There's a lot of things people can call me, and I'd cop to most of them, but stingy isn't one of them. I have all this stuff with me and thought I'd share it. Besides, seriously, what am I going to do with a cow?"

Before Andras could respond, there was a commotion nearby — shouts, rushing people, and the tramp of marching feet.

Irene turned just in time to see the villagers moving aside for four burly men in the short, white skirts of Ancient Egypt who had the unmistakable appearance of soldiers — copper bandolier-like breast plates, shiny silver-colored helmets, and short swords. And they were heading straight for Andras and Irene.

"Uh, time to go," Irene said to Andras, taking several steps back.

It was too late, however. The soldiers surrounded them. They saluted smartly, but their eyes were unyielding. The tallest one took Irene by the arm right above the elbow. "The lord Masudmensah requests an audience," he said. Refusing didn't seem to be an option.

Eight

Char stood in the doorway, watching him with worried eyes as Jonah stuffed items into his backpack. "You're going to try to cross over to the other side again, aren't you?"

Jonah glanced up and then quickly looked away without pausing, hoping she'd get the hint and leave. He'd hoped to get out the door before she finished breakfast; unfortunately, no such luck.

"Let me go with you," Char burst out abruptly.

It was just as he feared: she was going to insist on following him, and if he refused, she'd just try to blackmail him into letting her go. Only, he had no intention of taking her with him today. He was going to visit Irene's grave and Irene's mother—two things he absolutely intended to do alone.

He tried to keep his tone calm and nonchalant. If Char suspected he was keeping something from her, she'd press all the harder to find out what it was. "You can't. You're alive, remember? You can't cross into the land of the dead." Jonah moved to the desk, grabbed a handful of books, and then returned to cram them into the backpack as well. He planned on staying in Salem all day so he could get some work done—without interruption.

"So teach me the meditation thing so I can go with you."

Jonah paused, startled by her request. "Why would you do that?"

"Because someone has to keep you out of trouble."

He stared at her, trying to judge the real motivation behind her request. Char dropped her eyes, avoiding his gaze by focusing on a loose thread on her sleeve. She took hold of the thread, worrying it between her fingers. "Is she worth it?" she asked abruptly, still not looking at him.

A prickle of discomfort went through him, and he quickly resumed packing, rearranging items in his backpack with more force than necessary. "It's not like that."

"No, of course not. You're just willing to go to the ends of the earth for this woman for no reason." Char's voice dripped with bitterness, and the set of her jaw became mulish.

Jonah's scowl deepened, and he shoved another t-shirt in the bag. "Because she's my *friend*. And she needs me. She needs help."

Char quietly watched him. He did his best to ignore her, but he could feel her eyes on his back as he moved about the room, contemplating, assessing, *judging*.

After a while, she said, "So, are you going to let me help or not?"

"Not," he said automatically.

"Why?"

Jonah glanced at her over his shoulder. "Because it's too dangerous."

"Well, if it's dangerous, maybe you shouldn't be doing it either!"

"I am perfectly capable of taking care of myself." He yanked a sweater out of a dresser drawer and slammed the drawer shut. "And I'm more than capable of deciding how I spend my time and who I spend it with."

Loosened by the slamming of the drawers, a picture stuck under the frame of the bureau's mirror fluttered to the ground at Char's feet. She stooped and picked it up before Jonah could react. He hesitated, torn between protectively snatching the picture back and accidentally piquing Char's interest even further by trying to hide it from her. He waited tensely as she studied the picture intently, scrutinizing every detail. Jonah knew the picture by heart: a girl — maybe sixteen — with dark, free-flowing mahogany-colored hair and long, slim legs. She wore a short field hockey uniform and was striking a pose somehow both cocky and sultry, as if she couldn't quite decide between the two. Jonah felt a tug at his heart as he remembered that smile — she'd never outgrown that expression, and he'd seen it on Irene's face many, many times.

"Is this her — the woman you're so crazy about?"

Annoyance and, oddly, disappointment at Char's reaction flooded through him. He sighed and grabbed the picture, sliding it carefully into the front pocket of the backpack. "How many times do I have to tell you? It's not like that."

"I thought you said she was old, like in her thirties?"

"It's an old picture."

"Ah. I assume Ms. Hot Stuff aged well?"

Unbidden, his face heated, and he turned away to hide the blush. "She didn't look... people look different when they're dead."

"Oh? And how did Ms. Hot Stuff look?"

"She looked..." Jonah, turning back towards the bed, paused and let the flood of memories wash over him: soft, brown eyes and the steely glint that came into them whenever someone told her she couldn't do something; a thick mane of hair and the way she impatiently ran a hand through it when she was frustrated; a clear, smooth voice and the little hitch that came into it when she was moved by an unexpected kindness but didn't want to show it. He became conscious of Char watching him, seeing way more than he cared to share, and he scowled. "Anyway, age is irrelevant when you're dead. You're just a blob of energy —"

"They don't look like blobs to me; they look like people."

"That's because you want them to look like people. Because it's less scary. It's familiar. And because they want to look like people, because they don't want to be dead." The backpack was full, and he still had a stack of books he needed to add. He violently dumped the bag's contents in a pile and then restarted packing from scratch, talking as he angrily shoved items in the bag. He wanted out of this conversation, and if he could have just left without taking anything with him, then he would have. Unfortunately, he needed supplies in case his attempts to cross through the red door of the First Church in Salem worked and something to occupy him if it didn't.

Talking about afterlife mythology seemed safe enough – Char couldn't read anything into that – and maybe it would distract her long enough for him to get out of here without any more uncomfortable questions, so he kept talking as he repacked the bag. "The ancient Romans thought that we look the way we think we look, that we project the image we want others to perceive. And it's true. Think about how someone looks when they're confident versus when they're shy. Big difference. And it's all because of what they project.

"But that's only half the story. The truth is that what we see is a combination of what others want us to see and what we want to see. The dead stuck here, on Earth, are still clinging to life. They pretend they're still alive, that they still have bodies. So that's what they project, and the living want to see the familiar shape of a human body, so that's what they see." He paused in his packing, his goal of leaving as quickly as possible forgotten as he delved further into one of his favorite topics. "However, when you're dead, you're really just a blob of energy – you don't actually look like anything."

"Well, okay, but I don't see how that makes age irrelevant –"

"Age has to do with the physical, with the body. When you're dead, you leave your body behind. All that's left is the energy that was inside you. How old is that energy?"

Char shrugged. "As old as the person?"

"Wrong. We originally get our energy from our mother – when we're developing in the womb. And where did she get it? From her mother. And her grandmother got it from her mother, and so on. If you go back far enough, that energy came from the creation of the universe — so how old is that? The energy inside us is as old as time itself. So technically, we're all the same age."

"I can see you've given this a lot of thought," Char said dryly.

"Exactly. So if I could just find her —"

"Ah, see, now you took it to a creepy place again."

Jonah threw up his hands and spun away from her, silently cursing himself for letting her draw him back into a conversation. "It's not creepy! Christ!" He glared at her for a moment. "You know, if it was your mother or your aunt trapped in some Hell place, I doubt you'd be so cavalier about just leaving them — or about people questioning why you want to help them."

Char had the decency to at least blush at that. He grabbed the backpack off the bed and pushed past her. "And for your information, I'm not even going to try to get through the doorway today, okay? I have some personal things to take care of — if that's alright with you."

Jonah expected Char to try to stop him or, at least, to follow him as he descended the stairs and exited the shop as quickly as he could, but to his surprise, she didn't.

He scowled ferociously as he stalked down the street toward the commuter rail station, fuming. He was still fuming when he bought his ticket and boarded the train bound for Salem. Once slumped in a seat, his knees up, his backpack hugged to his chest, a vague feeling of unease and guilt — though he couldn't identify why he felt the latter — settled over him. He pulled out a book, *Communicating Across the Void*, and focused intently on the words, trying, unsuccessfully, to block out everything else during the hour-long trip north.

Unfortunately, thoughts and worries about Irene's mother Deborah instantly began to crowd in, pushing out the frustration with Char. After Irene had left, Jonah had taken it upon himself to take care of her mother. The relationship was a little complicated — Deborah didn't know that Jonah had known Irene. All she knew was that Jonah's inert body had been found in Irene's house — after Irene had died. Jonah had told the police he'd seen the door open and had gone in to check on the homeowner when he'd had a seizure and slipped into a coma. Though he hadn't been charged with any crime, he'd told Deborah he'd been sentenced to community service and was required to help her out around the house. She'd accepted this story without question and he'd been visiting her two or three times per week ever since. It had been three years, but she never questioned exactly how long his sentence was supposed to last.

The visits were hard. While it helped to be in a place filled with memories of Irene, he had to be careful not to reveal that he'd known her or to show too much curiosity about her. Being so close and yet so far from her made him miss her all the more. There were so many things he wanted to know, so many gaps in his knowledge he wanted to fill.

Added to this was the pain of watching Deborah decline with each passing day. From what little Irene had said of her mother, Jonah had gathered Deborah Dunphy had never been particularly strong, but after Irene's death, she just seemed to give up. Outwardly, she hid it well, but every visit, Jonah noticed Deborah seemed to have slipped a little further away. He didn't know how much longer she'd be able to continue living alone. She had a sister-in-law, Betty, but since his link to Deborah was tenuous at best, he was loath to interact with Betty more than necessary. He'd talked to her a few times and dropped as many hints about his concerns as he could, but there wasn't much more he could do — after all, he was supposedly a stranger, just there to do community service.

As he approached Deborah's house, he fished the key out of a pocket of the backpack and let himself in the front door. Deborah came into the living room as he entered and stopped short, a combination of surprise and confusion on her face, as if she'd been trying to remember something. Jonah had the impression she'd been wandering from room to room, something she was prone to do more and more lately.

"Hello, Mrs. Dunphy," he said, slipping off his backpack. Surreptitiously, he looked Deborah over, but she was neat and well-dressed as always—soft, graying curls neatly framing her aged yet still beautiful face, lemon yellow cardigan and matching blouse, navy slacks, and the ever-present string of pearls around her throat. She might forget to eat, pay the bills, lock the front door, or even who he was sometimes, but she never forgot her pearls. He suspected she'd forget everything else before she forgot those.

"School's out already?" Deborah asked vacantly, only half present in the conversation.

"Mrs. Dunphy, I graduated already. Remember? I told you."

"Oh, that's right," Deborah said vaguely, giving the impression that the information still hadn't really penetrated.

Jonah looked around at the spotless house. "Did your sister-in-law come by today?"

"Betty? Oh, yes… yes, I suppose she did."

Jonah frowned thoughtfully. "Mrs. Dunphy, are you feeling all right?" Deborah seemed more out of it than usual.

"Oh yes, yes, of course." However, a deep scowl abruptly marred her placid features. and she picked an envelope up from the coffee table and waved it in the air. "I got a letter for Irene today. Why do they keep sending stuff to her? I've called and told them she's dead! It's very upsetting. Don't they realize?" Deborah tossed the letter back onto the coffee table with a huff.

Inwardly, Jonah groaned. So that was it, then; today was a bad day. Any emotional upset tended to send Deborah into a tail spin, magnifying all the other problems—the mood swings, the forgetfulness, the confusion—that she normally managed to hide.

He picked up the letter and crossed to the trash without glancing at who it was from.

"I went by her house today," Deborah said absently.

Jonah looked at her quickly. "Awww, Mrs. Dunphy... you shouldn't—"

"I don't like what those new people have done with the yard," Deborah burst out angrily, her mouth twisting almost into a snarl.

Jonah thought quickly, trying to find a topic of conversation he could use to head off a full-blown meltdown.

"Your mother called," Deborah added, on a roll now. "She says you haven't been home to see them in weeks. Why don't you visit your mother?"

Jonah cast around desperately, trying to find a way to derail Deborah. "Are you hungry? I could make us something."

"No, I don't want anything to eat!" Deborah snapped. "I just had lunch."

Jonah assumed that was a slip of the tongue; it was only a quarter to noon, much too early for Deborah to have eaten. "Look, why don't I go out and see if I can fix the shed door, and then we'll play some cards or something, okay?"

Deborah sat down heavily on the couch, as if the strength had vanished from her legs. She clasped her hands in front of her and then after a moment, surreptitiously wiped away a tear, reclasping her hands when she was done.

Jonah stood there, feeling helpless. It had been almost four years since Irene's death, but the cut of it was still fresh for Deborah. She didn't have the benefit of knowing that Irene lived on or that Irene had visited her several times after she'd died. For Deborah, the death had been sudden and shocking and final.

Even four years on, any little thing could set Deborah off—the arrival of a random piece of junk mail addressed to Irene, the discovery of an old picture or memento in the back of a drawer, or the sight of someone who looked like Irene on the street or on the television. One never knew when the moments would strike—Deborah had once gone to pieces over a box of cookies; they had been Irene's favorite when she was a child.

Seeing her like this killed him. He wanted desperately to tell her that Irene was alive, that he had been helping Irene, that he was watching out for her and trying to make sure she was safe and okay. But he couldn't. He knew he couldn't — and holding that secret was like a knife in his heart as he watched Deborah twist the pearls in her hands, her lower lip trembling.

"You know, the holidays are coming soon," Deborah said suddenly. "We should go up to the attic and bring the decorations down."

Jonah wasn't sure which holidays she meant — it was late July — but at least it was a distraction. "Uh, sure, just show me where they are, and I'll carry them down."

That seemed to do the trick. Deborah was instantly on her feet, all thoughts of Irene seemingly having disappeared. She led him up the stairs to the second floor and then up a second flight to the attic. It was stifling up there. After twenty minutes of hot, sweaty searching, they finally located a box of fall decorations. Jonah was relieved. Deborah wasn't too far off; it was a little early to break out the fall stuff, but at least she was in the general ballpark as to the time of year.

Jonah picked up the box and headed for the stairs, but Deborah wasn't quite ready to go yet. "Where's that pillow Irene made?" she said, pushing against a large box, trying to move it aside.

"Here, let me." Jonah set down the box of decorations, crossed to Deborah, and lifted the box out of the way. He scanned the labels of the boxes that had been behind it and then popped opened the one labeled "Misc."

"Here, is this it?" He pulled out an old, frayed pillow — a basic square made of a cheerful red fabric, to which white cotton balls — to simulate a beard and hair — and a pair of "googly" eyes had been affixed.

Deborah, who had sat down to rest on an old trunk, took it gingerly from his hands, as if it was as fragile as a Fabergé egg. She chuckled. "Oh, this thing is hideous," she said, though fondly. "I don't know why I kept it. Irene always wanted me to throw it out."

"She wasn't much into crafts, huh?" It wasn't really a question. There wasn't anyone he could envision as less likely to engage in crafts than Irene.

Deborah chuckled. "No. Not at all."

Jonah sat down on a box. "Tell me something about her."

"Well, she was stubborn as an old goat."

Jonah choked back a laugh, coughing into his hand to hide the sound. It was true, but he couldn't say that since Deborah didn't know that he'd known Irene.

"Are you alright?"

"Uh, yeah. Just some dust," Jonah said, waving a hand in front of his face and faking a cough.

"Oh." Deborah eyed him suspiciously for a moment.

"Tell me something *good* about her," Jonah said quickly.

"Good? Hmm, well, let's see…" Deborah seemed to be racking her brain.

"Oh, come on," Jonah said. "You're her mother! There must be something you liked about her!"

"Well, you have to understand—Irene could be… difficult…"

"Yeah, true, but that's one of the best things…" The words just slipped out before he could catch them, and Jonah silently castigated himself.

However, Deborah didn't seem to notice the slip-up. Her mouth twisted into a grimace. "Well, I don't know about that. Irene was very… independent. My God, I never saw such a stubborn, independent child. Always wanted to do things herself. Couldn't accept anybody's word for anything—had to find out on her own. If you told her it was raining, she'd have to look out the window to see. If you told her the stove was hot, she couldn't just take your word for it, oh no. She'd have to put her hand on it to be sure."

Jonah ducked his head to hide a smile. That was Irene to a "T." Oddly, the things Deborah was finding fault with were the things he liked best about Irene. She didn't take "no" for an answer, and she made sure to find out the truth for herself, rather than just take other people's word for it. As for being stubborn — well, at least Irene didn't give up. She didn't let anything stand in her way; she fought for what she wanted and for what she believed in.

Deborah was quiet for a moment. "She wasn't a cuddly child. Never wanted to be held. A normal child, when she falls and skins her knee, cries for her mother. Not Irene. Oh no! If you so much as offered her a Band-Aid, she'd get huffy, like you'd insulted her in some way." Deborah's frown deepened, and she shook her head.

Jonah's amusement faded, replaced by a slinking feeling of unease. Deborah's anger and disapproval were making him both uncomfortable and angry. Her assessment of Irene's character was pretty dead on, and yet, completely wrong. Instead of seeing strength of mind and self-reliance, Deborah saw only stubbornness and distantness. Instead of tenacity and loyalty, she saw only a tendency to be argumentative and willful.

"Mothers and sons are different," Irene had said once, a bitterness in her voice he hadn't been able to explain. "But mothers and daughters — then there's no pleasing the woman."

A fierce protectiveness washed over him, and he felt his face heat. The need to defend Irene became almost overwhelming. He wanted to tell Deborah off and point out all the ways she was wrong about Irene. Fine, so Irene was independent and also didn't handle frustration well — her first response both to being mothered and to being frustrated was generally an impulsive flare of anger, which quickly burned itself out. All anyone had to do was wait a few minutes, and then she was fine, ready to channel that impressive stubbornness into more productive uses.

Jonah sprang to his feet, feeling stifled, and paced, his back to Deborah. Irene really wasn't all that difficult to deal with once you got to know her. In fact, fighting with her had been one of his favorite parts of their time together; trying to out-argue and outsmart her had been become a kind of game since Irene refused to ever give up or give in, resorting to cheating — bullying, diversions, and change of subject — when she couldn't outwit him, and he'd loved seeing what crazy thing she'd say just to win an argument. Often she'd resorted to the absurd just to win, and the funny part is that, by that point, they both knew she was being absurd, and it stopped being an argument and became a joke instead.

Deborah, not appearing to notice his sudden agitation, sighed. "Well, these boxes aren't going to move themselves, I guess." She stood up. Jonah took several deep breaths, forcing himself to calm down. Revealing that he'd known Irene would not do anyone any good, and yelling at Deborah would hardly change the past. Plus, he'd promised to take care of Deborah; yelling at her could hardly be considered caring for her. He swallowed his anger, picked up the box of fall decorations, and followed her back downstairs, where the two of them hung the decorations, mostly in silence.

To Jonah's relief, Deborah was tired when they were done and decided to take a nap. Jonah said his goodbyes and waited until he was outside to call Deborah's sister-in-law.

"Mrs. Long? It's Jonah... Jonah Johnson. Yeah, I'm fine. Yeah, she had a bad day today; some mail came, and she went by Irene's house — maybe you should stop by later, make sure she's okay." He listened as Betty raged against the stupidity of the postal service, the callousness of junk-mail senders, and the wishy-washiness of her sister-in-law. He finally managed to get off the phone after extracting a promise from Betty to send one of her sons or daughters over to check on Deborah later.

He hefted his backpack higher on his shoulder and set off, heading for the cemetery, his stomach tied in knots. Deborah's revelations had been ugly, and he couldn't get the taste of them out of his mouth. Head down, he walked hard all the way to the cemetery.

As the familiar rolling green hills came into view, the tension eased though it didn't disappear. As always, he felt a flash of something. Irony? Grief? He was never sure — as he dwelled on the fact that his first outing with Irene had been to this very cemetery. They'd gone to look for the tunnel to the other side. He'd shown up at her house out of a strange sense of guilt and empathy—she was a ghost but didn't want to admit it—and some curiosity, too. After all, he'd never met a ghost before. She had been his first. At that point, she'd been just an abstract concept, simply "that ghost woman"—until the cemetery. There had been a moment there when she'd talked about the moral dilemma of digging up and displaying mummies, and she had suddenly become something else—she'd become a person, with thoughts and feelings. There had been something shy and a little vulnerable in her admission that she thought it wrong, and he'd liked that. It was that moment when he'd first noticed her chin would tilt up challengingly if she said something she thought someone might laugh at. Later that evening, when she'd asked—no, goaded—him to walk her home when he would have otherwise just left her alone, she'd thought him rude. He hadn't been a "sweet boy" or a "nerd" or any one of a hundred single-item labels he'd been called all his life. She'd treated him like an adult, like someone of value—she'd wanted his help, his company, and his protection—and he'd liked that, too. That's when he'd noticed her eyes were a soft, golden brown.

He crossed the expansive, green sward, heading for Irene's grave, passing her parents' plot—where her father was buried—on the way.

Irene's grave stood alone, an unremarkable and modest headstone of granite engraved with her name and birth and death dates. In front of the headstone, however, had been erected—by him—a statue of an angel, delicately holding a bowl in supplicating hands. To it he had affixed a plaque in bronze, which he'd had to save up for a year to buy, with a simple inscription: *Leave a penny and a prayer for the dead.* The bowl was always overflowing with coins.

Most people left the coins in memory of a loved one who had passed. What none of them realized was that the statue was actually connected to the land of the dead, and the coins — well the spirit or essence of the coins — were sent to the other side to be used by the dead to pay a ferryman for passage to the afterlife.

The coins were rarely disturbed. At first, Jonah had thought it was sentiment — the same reason people didn't take the money from a fountain — but then he realized it had to do with the coins themselves. Once the spirit or essence of the coins crossed over to the land of the dead, the physical shell left behind was just as lifeless as a dead body. That seemed a strange thing to say, that an inanimate object like a coin could be "dead," but there was a definite feeling that surrounded the coins of the vitality having left them. They were dull, faded, old and worn, and some part of the brain registered this and caused an instinctive avoidance of them. Eventually, the coins would pass from the world. They would fall to the ground and, unnoticed, would sink into the earth. Some might perhaps be picked up by scavengers and sold for scrap. Either way, the departing of their essence had marked the end of their useful life.

Deborah didn't know about the statue — she'd never been to Irene's grave after the funeral. Deborah's sister, Betty, had stopped coming to maintain the grave after the first year; all the work of maintaining it now fell on Jonah, which was fine by him — he could arrange it to his satisfaction, the way Irene would have liked it.

He knelt by the grave, opened up his bag, and fished inside until his hands found the package of black licorice — Irene's favorite candy. He pulled out the candy and set it on her grave. She'd told him to stop writing, but she hadn't said he couldn't still send her things. Without knowing where she was or what she was facing, though, he was shooting in the dark as to what she might need. He'd sent her a nail file and some paper clips a while ago, thinking she could use those to pick the lock if she was locked up somewhere. Irene struck him as the kind of person who probably knew how to pick a lock — she had a lot of strange, unaccountable skills like that. Knowing her, she'd learned how to do it in order to sneak out of the house when her parents grounded her or something. He'd also sent her a large letter opener — it was as close to a dagger as he could find. Now, he mostly just sent comforting items — like her favorite candy. Just little things to let her know she wasn't alone, that help was coming.

He sat back on his heels and brushed his hands across the stone's face to remove non-existent dirt, his fingers lingering over the lines of her name. His breath caught in his throat, and an ache started deep and low in his chest, as it did every time he came here. He had once promised her he wouldn't let any monsters get her. It had been a half-joking promise, meant to relieve the tension of the moment; however, there was a part of him that had meant it, that would always mean it. And now she was God-only-knew-where, facing God-only-knew-what kind of monsters and torments. His mind flashed through all the stories of the underworld — Sisyphus and the stone, Prometheus and the vultures, unworthy souls torn to pieces by hippopotamuses, harpies, furies, and Cerebus, the three-headed dog that guarded the afterworld gates. The horrors of the afterlife were almost too numerous to count. Why had he let her go? He should have tried harder to stop her. He should have begged her not to go. He should have promised to take care of her and stay with her so she'd never be alone. He should have told her about all the terrible things that awaited on the other side so she would have been too scared to leave. He should have stood in front of the tunnel, blocking the entrance with his body and preventing her from going. He should have grabbed hold of her as she entered the tunnel so he would be pulled through, too. He should have…

There were a million things he could have done, and he hadn't done a single one. He'd stood there, pitiful and silent, sad and powerless, like a child, and she'd left. She was out there now, because of him. And she was out there without him, cut off from even sending him letters because of… something. Something bad. And she was all alone.

He shuddered and closed his eyes, leaning his forehead against the cool, smooth stone. "I'm trying," he whispered, clutching tightly at the pain in his heart to keep it from breaking free. "I'm trying everything I can to find you." His voice broke, and he trembled with the effort to keep from breaking down. "Just hang on a little longer, okay?" The rough stone cut into his hands, but he didn't let go, as if holding onto the stone would allow him to hold onto her; once he found her, he would never let go again. "Wherever you are, whatever's happening, just hang on a little longer. I'm coming. I promise."

Nine

The four Egyptian soldiers surrounded them, implacable, one holding tight to Irene's upper arm. Andras tensed, giving off an air of coiled readiness. Irene expected him to launch himself at the men, but, instead, he glanced at her, as if checking that she was okay, and then he gestured for the soldiers to lead the way.

The hand on her arm was firm but not hurtful, so Irene matched her pace to the soldier's and let him lead her. The guards retraced their steps, returning the way they had come from farther in the village. As they walked, the number of tents and people — and horses and sheep — grew, multiplying exponentially. This really was a village — or quite possibly a town.

Soon, it became apparent that everything they'd seen so far was arranged around a central structure — a pavilion similar to the villagers' homes except this one was as large as a circus tent and open on three sides. The soldiers seemed to be taking her and Andras to it.

The soldiers slowed as they approached the periphery of the pavilion. Inside the pavilion, Irene could see, above the heads of the bustling crowd between her and it, a square dais — large enough for a man to lie down on — covered in animal hides and plush red pillows richly embroidered in gold thread. Seated stiffly upon these cushions, cross-legged, his hands resting on his thighs, was a man in his early thirties—the very embodiment of Egyptian hieroglyphs. His smooth, hairless chest was bare except for the thick collar of heavy gold and turquoise links that lay across his collarbone. Matching cuffs of hammered gold adorned each bicep and each ankle, and around his waist he had a knee-length skirt of yellow cloth held in place by a belt of golden discs. His dark hair was closely cropped, as was the thin goatee-like beard covering his chin, and his eyes were darkly rimmed with kohl. He would have been good-looking except for the indolent, bored expression upon his face. Behind him a row of five servants—each clad in a short skirt or dress depending on their gender—pulled on ropes operating giant overhead paddles, creating a gentle breeze within the pavilion.

The area outside the pavilion was a hive of activity with people bustling back and forth; Irene wasn't sure if these people were servants or villagers—maybe they were both. As they approached the crowd, the soldiers stopped. The one holding Irene's arm released her. Then the soldiers snapped to attention and waited. Irene wasn't sure if she and Andras were supposed to stay there or continue on. Two women hurried forward and strewed flower petals at their feet, backing away toward the pavilion, laying down a path of petals as they went. Irene glanced at Andras for guidance. Andras shrugged, offering no assistance. She responded with a look of entreaty; this was more his arena than hers. He'd been a knight and lived during a time when there had been nobles and royalty and stuff like that. He knew more about the etiquette of such situations than she. The owner of the pavilion appeared to be a person of some importance, possibly even royalty, and she wasn't sure what to do.

Andras scowled and stepped forward, following the two women through the crowd. As Irene and Andras reached the edge of the pavilion, two burly male servants, both with shaved heads and dark, lowering brows, stepped in front of them, blocking their path. Behind the two men, servants filed into the pavilion, filling the space between them and the dais and all around the dais as well. The amount of people filing into the pavilion seemed impossibly large, and yet they still kept coming.

Irene hesitated, not sure if the two burly men were threatening or not, and waited, hoping for instructions. The man on the dais clapped his hands, twice, and the two servants blocking the way forward dropped to their knees and bowed, heads to the ground three times.

"The noble lord Masudmensah welcomes, you travelers. He offers you his hospitality though meager may it be. May it find favor with you."

The servants scooted backwards, still on their knees, each pivoting ninety degrees — one to the left and one to the right — as if they were a pair of doors swinging wide. Irene swallowed hard as she looked over the crowd of unblinking stares directed at her and Andras. The man on the dais — the one Irene assumed was Masudmensah — clapped his hands again. Instantly, the servants in front of the dais parted like the Red Sea and dropped to their knees, leaving a pathway open for Irene and Andras to approach.

The nobleman waved them forward. This close, Irene could see that he had rings on almost all of his fingers and his skirt was lavishly embroidered with gold thread around the hem. His eyes were like Andras's — so dark they were almost black — and his face, while not scowling, was not welcoming either.

Irene and Andras came forward and then stopped when they reached the edge of the dais. "Uh... hi?" Irene said. "You wanted to see us?"

Masudmensah clapped his hands together again, once, twice, and then the servants on either side of the stairs leading up to the dais held out their hands. It took a moment for Irene to understand this was an invitation to take their hands and climb the steps. She did so and then assumed she was meant to sit on the pillows as their host was doing, so she dropped to her knees as gracefully as she could in her short dress. A second later, Andras dropped to his knees beside her, his hands resting comfortably on his thighs. He inclined his head. "We thank you for your hospitality. May God bestow blessings upon you."

Irene looked askance at him, surprised he seemed to know what to say and do, and that he seemed completely at ease.

Their host made a complicated pattern of gestures, touching his fingertips to his forehead, his lips, and then the sky, as well as tracing figures in the air, and instantly, two women servants from outside the tent came forward with large platters heaped with food—figs, dates, fruit, and cheese—which they held out above the heads so they were reachable by the people on the dais.

Their host motioned to the platters of food, encouraging her and Andras to eat something. Irene's stomach was flip-flopping with nerves, but she didn't want to be rude—in movies, they always said the locals would take offense if offerings of food were refused—so she helped herself to the most innocuous-looking piece of fruit she could find. Andras took something that was small and brown—possibly a fig.

Their host watched them intently, if not a little indulgently, and Irene felt a bit like a specimen under a microscope. She wasn't sure if she was supposed to talk or not.

As soon as Irene had finished eating her piece of fruit—some kind of melon—a servant sprang forward with a small bowl of copper and held it out to Irene with her fingertips. Irene glanced at it with confusion. Andras raised an eyebrow and proceeded to demonstrate, dipping his fingers into the bowl to wet them and then wiping them on a proffered cloth.

Ah, okay, finger bowls. She'd seen this in a movie once. No big deal. Irene copied him, wiping the fruit's sticky juice from her fingers.

As soon as Irene took her fingers from the drying towel, their host clapped his hands several times, and more servants sprang into action, bringing forth a ewer of water, another of wine, and three goblets, as well as a small wooden chest. The servant placed the chest in front of

Masudmensah and backed away. Another servant, a young woman, knelt down beside a large zither-like stringed instrument and began to stroke the strings, filling the pavilion with slow, lilting music.

Their host undid the clasp on the chest the servant had placed before him and opened the lid, revealing a sparkling assortment of jewelry—rings, bracelets, necklaces, ankle cuffs, and more, all made of gold and some set with colored stones. He tipped the chest, spilling the contents onto the pillows in front of them and then gestured to the items.

"Uh, very nice?" Irene said, again glancing at Andras for guidance. So far, she wasn't really sure why the man had sent for them with armed guards when everything seemed so amicable. Her nerves twanged, waiting for the other shoe to drop.

Andras shot her an exasperated look and then took a bracelet from the pile, grabbed Irene's arm, pushed up her jacket sleeve, and slipped the bracelet on her wrist. Then he gave her a meaningful look, followed by a look at her bag.

She was floundering here, but she was guessing this was some kind of ceremonial exchanging of gifts, so she dug in her bag, not sure what an ancient Egyptian prince might like. He had plenty of jewelry, so her earrings, watch, and cheap bangle bracelets hardly seemed worthy. He might like the ornate room divider—a decorative touch for his pavilion—but it was currently in origami form. Lighting it on fire and turning it into the real item would probably freak him out—and get her condemned as a witch. He seemed to have enough food, so she ruled out her red bean paste buns and licorice. Make-up—no. Ballpoint pens—no. Perfume—maybe.

Finally, she settled on a neon orange disposable cigarette lighter. She pulled it out and flicked it on to demonstrate how it worked and then passed it to their host. He took the lighter carefully, studied it with suspicion for a second, and then fumbled with the mechanism until it caught. He held it lit for a second and then ran his hand over the flame, verifying it was hot. He burst into laughter. He passed the lighter to a servant and then spread his arms wide.

"Greetings, friends!"

He gestured animatedly for a woman hidden amongst the cluster of servants to the side of the dais to come forward, and she did so, bowing her head slightly.

"My lady wife," he said. The woman, as ornately dressed as Masudmensah and decked with as much jewelry, was slim, though rather plain, with heavy, thick eyebrows and a nose too large for her face. The woman bowed and then backed away, disappearing back into the cluster of servants who closed ranks around her, hiding her from view.

Their host gestured broadly, sweeping his arm expansively. Instantly, all of his servants dropped to their knees and sat watching Irene and Andras with intent, expectant faces. "Tell me news, travelers, of the marvels you have seen.

"Uh..." said Irene. "I'm not sure we've seen any marvels..."

Andras elbowed her in the side.

"I mean... well, there's not much out there... mostly just wheat and shadows."

"Have you seen nothing of what lies beyond the fields of Osiris?"

Irene assumed that he meant the wheat fields. "Uh, no, not really. We just got here, in fact."

Their host's face drooped with disappointment, and he stroked his beard thoughtfully.

"Uh, what about you?" Irene said hurriedly, feeling that this was probably not a guy you wanted to disappoint. She had the uneasy feeling that a man used to having a small army of people obey his every whim was not a man who bore disappointment well. "Have you seen anything interesting... like maybe a way out of here?"

He laughed hard, like she had just told a very funny joke. "This is yaaru – paradise. Why would I leave?"

"Aren't you worried about the shadows? Don't they attack you?"

Masudmensah laughed again and waved a dismissive hand. "Bah! When the sheut come to demand tribute for Osiris, I send one of my servants."

Irene's jaw dropped. "You sacrifice them to the shadows?"

"Of course." He said this as if it was the most ordinary thing in the world.

Irene's hackles rose; Andras was shooting her warning looks with his eyes, but she didn't care. "And what will you do when you run out of servants?"

Masudmensah gave them an indulgent smile and spread his hands wide, gesturing to the hundreds of servants surrounding him. "Better to ask what I will do when the stars no longer shine in the night sky or when the sun no longer rises and sets — praise to Ra, may he reign forever and ever." Their host sobered. "Though, truth be told, I begin to wish I had not brought so many. It is taking a very long time to work my way through them all."

"You could try not feeding them to the shadows," Irene muttered.

Their host's expression turned shocked. "But it is my duty to care for them. How else shall they reach paradise? Ones as lowly as these would never be called to serve the great lord Osiris. It is only through my intervention and my sacrifice that they are able to gain immortality."

Irene felt like she was missing half the story; Masudmensah seemed genuinely confused by her affront at him feeding his servants to the shadows. However, before she could try and work her way through the tangle of information, their host brightened and snapped his fingers. "Heru!" he exclaimed and then snapped again. There was a bustle of activity in the back of the tent and then a short, slight woman, about Irene's age or a little younger, came forward and passed something to Masudmensah. The servant then dropped to her knees and put her forehead to the floor.

Masudmensah held the object out to Irene reverently, laid across both hands; it was a short stick, about an inch thick and a foot long, worn smooth on all sides and painted white. Irene raised an eyebrow. Their host thrust the stick at her again. Tentatively, Irene took it, holding it gingerly between two fingers and her thumb. "Uh, thanks?" she said, wrinkling her nose.

"I give you our most loyal Heru," Masudmensah said with a bow. His tone was regretful, almost sad, as if it hurt him to give her the stick.

"Uh, thanks... Heru," she said addressing the stick. What the hell did Heru mean?

Andras nudged her and then nodded at the servant kneeling at the foot of the dais.

"Heru?" Irene asked.

The servant cringed even lower, if that was possible. "Nemet-i!" she said.

"Oh... oh!" Irene said as she realized what Masudmensah was offering her. "Uh, thanks, that's really generous, but I don't need a slave, thanks..." She tried handing the stick back to Masudmensah, but he looked horrified. "No, seriously, I don't want—"

"You refuse our gift?" he said, a note of outrage creeping into his voice.

Andras nudged her, hard, in the ribs and bowed, grabbing her arm, and pulled her into one as well. "Pax verbotem. Peace be with you. We accept your gift with gratitude."

"And peace be with you, my friends." Their host spread his arms wide. "I offer you shelter, should you desire it. I would be pleased to have you join my retinue."

Andras bowed again. "Regretfully, we must decline your generous offer and continue on our travels."

Masudmensah seemed to accept this as expected. He nodded and clapped his hands, clearing the servants from the dais and opening a path out of the pavilion. "I shall detain you no longer then."

Andras stood, tugging Irene to her feet as well, and then backed toward the steps and down them, tugging Irene along with him. Hurriedly, as if he expected Masudmensah to change his mind, Andras headed for the exit, dragging Irene. She stumbled over her feet, protesting the whole way. "Hey, wait... hang on... what am I supposed to do with Heru? Will you let go of my arm?"

They were out from under the canopy now, and Andras turned and walked through the servants, heading out of Masudmensah's camp and continuing on their original trajectory toward the castle.

"And what about all these people?" Irene asked, sweeping an arm to encompass the village. "Aren't we going to help them? You do know what he did to get all these people here, right? He had them buried with him! That's what they did, you know. Kings and nobles — they'd have all their servants killed when they died and embalmed in their tombs so they'd have servants in the afterlife. How sick is that?"

"Just keep walking until we are safely away," Andras said in a low voice.

Irene glanced over her shoulder, a prickle of fear running down her spine. Masudmensah wouldn't actually attack them for refusing to stay with him — would he? As angry as she was, Andras had a point — they couldn't really fight an entire village by themselves.

Irene glanced behind her again, looking for Heru. The woman trailed them, following a short distance behind. Irene clutched the stick tighter and sped up.

Once well clear of Masudmensah's camp — and sure they were well clear of any shadows — they stopped to catch their breath. Irene was still seething about the visit with Masudmensah.

"Why'd he drag us to see him — by force — if he was just going to turn around and send us on our way?"

"A show of force," Andras said. "A warning in case we were there to challenge him."

"And showing off his treasure chest and his wife and then giving me this?" she asked, indicating the white stick.

"He was boasting—showing off his wealth."

"So that's it? He was basically just peeing on a tree?" When Andras's brow knit in confusion, she added, "Showing off. Marking his territory."

Andras nodded. "In my time, this was quite common. It is a way of knowing who you are dealing with and determining relative rank and power."

"Yeah, I suppose…" Irene wasn't so sure. She and Andras had been traveling alone, clearly without a retinue or army. Masudmensah had to have known they weren't a threat. She might mark up the entire incident to vanity—Masudmensah might have been showing off just for the sake of showing off—except for his question of whether or not they had seen anything beyond the wheat fields. She suspected he'd been curious to know what awaited in the "Great Beyond."

Heru stood a little way off, looking uncertain. Irene's heart pinched with a mixture of pity and bewilderment. Now that she could study Heru properly, she could see that the woman's robe was clean and neat and of good quality. A thick, silken cord of blue was fastened around her waist like a belt, the long ends dangling free and ending in large tassels. Her thick, curly hair, plaited in a complex braid, shone as if it had been rubbed with oil, and a blue ribbon was wrapped around her head like a headband. There was a thin bracelet of silver around her ankle.

Well, at least the woman didn't look like she'd been mistreated. Irene sighed and beckoned Heru forward.

"What is your will, mistress?"

"What are you doing?" Andras asked.

"You can't honestly think I'm going to keep a slave, do you? That's another thing that's illegal in my time."

"Your time sounds very dull," Andras muttered.

"Oh, let's see—equal rights, no slavery, no cholera, no small pox, no bowing and scraping to noblemen, no risk of getting your head chopped off by random people with swords. Gee, I don't know, I think my time sounds pretty fabulous compared to yours."

Andras opened his mouth to argue, but Irene held up a hand to silence him. Heru shifted uneasily from foot to foot, her eyes lowered to the ground.

"Your wish, my lady?"

Irene held the stick out to her. "I don't want this. You take it."

Heru's eyes widened in fear, and she shook her head.

"Take it," Irene said. "Go on. I'm setting you free. You aren't a slave anymore."

"Your pardon, my lady, but I am not a slave; I am a free woman."

"You were a servant in that man's household?" Andras asked.

Heru nodded. "Yes, my lord."

"What's the difference?" Irene asked. "It seems like Masudmensah thought he owned you since he thinks he can just give you away."

"He was showing me great honor, my lady."

"Honor? How do you reckon that?"

"You have no other servants; therefore, I have now been elevated to the position of chief of your servants. Moreover, as your only servant, I will be sent to the fields of Osiris much sooner than if I had stayed with my lord. This is, indeed, a great honor."

Irene shook her head. "I can't even..." She threw up her hands and looked at Andras for help. The whole conversation was making her skin crawl.

Andras's expression remained unchanged—placid and inscrutable.

Irene shook her head again with a growl of frustration. She held out the stick to Heru again. "Okay, well, you're not a slave... servant, anymore. You're free to do whatever you want."

Heru's look of fear turned to one of scorn, and her lip curled up in a sneer. Irene turned to Andras, holding the stick out to him. "Fine, you take it."

Andras simply raised an eyebrow and crossed his arms over his chest. With an exasperated sigh, Irene threw the stick down on the ground. Heru let out a long, piercing howl of anguish and threw herself down, head to the ground, wailing loudly. "No, my lady, no! I beg pardon if my words have displeased you."

Alarmed at Heru's piercing cries, Irene bent down, urging Heru to stop, to stand, to calm down, but Heru resolutely refused. Irene looked at Andras for help, but Andras simply shrugged. "She is your servant."

"I don't want a servant—that's the point!" Irene retorted.

Finally in desperation, she snatched up the stick again. Heru immediately fell silent, watching Irene intently.

"Look," Irene said, thinking maybe she hadn't been clear. "Look," she said again, shaking the stick at Heru until Heru had transferred her gaze from Irene to the stick. Irene grasped an end of the stick with each hand and, bringing it down across her knee, broke it in two. The crack of it breaking was startlingly loud in the silence that fell at the same moment.

Irene showed the broken stick to Heru and then threw the pieces on the ground. "Now do you understand?" she asked. "You're free."

Heru stared at her for a moment as if she couldn't quite believe it. Irene smiled encouragingly as understanding bloomed across Heru's face. In the next instant, Irene's smile vanished as Heru sprang to her feet and began cursing at her.

"You daughter of a hyena! You unemptied chamber pot! You whore! You filth!"

Irene backed away hurriedly as Heru advanced on her. Heru stooped to snatch up the broken stick and then threw each half at Irene in quick succession. Irene ducked away as Andras stepped in front of her, knocking the sticks aside.

Heru tore at her robe as she continued to shout insults. "May you be raped by jackals! May your heart be eaten by wild dogs! May your name be blotted from every scroll, from every record, from every temple, from every plaque! May none speak your name from this day forward! May you dwell in Duat for ten thousand years and then ten thousand more!"

"Enough!" growled Andras, grabbing Heru by the arm and shaking her. Heru wrenched free and bent down, her hands searching among the stalks of wheat. She straightened and with a quick motion threw something at Irene.

A rock.

It hit Irene squarely on the forehead, the dull thud of it striking her skull echoing inside her head. She narrowly ducked the second rock that came barreling toward her.

"Stop it!" she cried, raising her arms to shield her head as Heru quickly followed with another set of rocks.

Irene dodged away, zig-zagging back and forth and trying to stay out of Heru's range, nearly blinded by the throbbing in her head from the rock that had hit her. Andras bent over and then straightened, holding the tire iron. He advanced on Heru and extended the tire iron, like a sword, to Heru's throat.

"Go, before you are no longer able."

Heru's eyes blazed with anger, and her lip curled in a snarl. She hesitated a moment, as if she was going to refuse, and Andras pressed the point of the tire iron harder against Heru's throat. Irene could see the indentation it was making in Heru's skin. Andras's eyes blazed, and there was no hesitation in them. Irene stopped breathing.

Heru's sneer deepened, but she backed away a couple of steps, then a couple more, and, finally, she turned and fled, shouting curses over her shoulder.

"May you never know a day's joy from this day forward!" was her final insult.

Irene found she was shaking as she watched Heru disappear into the distance. "What the hell was that about?" she asked wrapping her arms around herself. "I was just trying to help."

"Your way is not the only way," Andras said, impatiently, but gently, too.

"What's that supposed to mean?"

He tossed the tire iron to the ground and then stepped close, gently taking her face in his hands and tilting her head slightly so he could look at the lump on her forehead. One hand left the side of her head to gently sweep the hair away from the bruise, his touch feather light as his fingers trailed through her hair and down the side of her face. Irene shivered again.

His dark eyes were unreadable as he contemplated her for a moment. He seemed to be searching for the right words. Then, almost abruptly, he released her and stepped back, re-opening the gulf that normally separated them. "In many cultures, it is an honor to serve. Service provides purpose and place. To take that from someone is to deny them worth and recognition. It is the greatest insult that can be leveled."

Irene felt her face heat, angry and embarrassed that Andras was once again rebuking her like a child. "Masudmensah feeds his servants to the shadows! He treats them like cannon fodder — I'd think Heru would be glad to be spared."

"They do not see it as mistreatment. Their sacrifice ensures their place in Heaven."

"That's bullshit! That's Stockholm Syndrome, that's what that is!"

"Does it matter? The end result is the same — Heru believes you have denied her entry to paradise, regardless of whether or not it is true. Now she believes you have condemned her to an eternity in Hell. Worse, you have made her feel as if she has no value."

Irene tried to blink back scalding hot tears of humiliation. She had screwed up — again. "I was just trying to help."

Andras's expression softened, which, in a way, was worse that the scolding because now he was pitying her — poor, adorable Irene, always so clueless, always so stupid. She waved him off and went to retrieve her bag. "You know," she said angrily, "morality is a lot more black and white in my time—it's another thing we have over you."

"Is it really?" Sarcasm dripped from his tone.

Her statement was ridiculous, and she knew it. Things were rarely simple, and trying to treat them like they were had been part of how she'd ended up with very little to show for her life. Her shoulders slumped. "Well," she said, "we like to think it is." She sighed and combed her hair back from her face again. "Should we go after her?"

Andras's voice was gentle when he replied. "To what end? She will not listen now. Her fate, for good or for ill, is her own."

Ten

Jonah paused at the intersection to get his bearings. He had slipped out of the magic shop early this morning — he seemed to be living his life in mornings now, spending the afternoons as far from the shop as he could and hiding in his room in the evenings — before anyone else was awake, with a long list of errands — *personal* errands that he needed to do without Char.

It was the prime of Boston morning rush hour, and commuters crammed both the streets and the sidewalks. Jonah, in his ghost body, did his best to not get trampled. The good thing about the crowd was that no one noticed when an unseen person bumped into them; the bad thing was that it made it hard to stay out of people's way.

He turned down a side street, cut through an alley, and turned onto Arlington. At the next corner, a tall, slim, handsome late-twenty-something man in a Ramones t-shirt and dark shades sat on a folding chair behind a card table with a sign advertising Tarot Card and Palm readings for five dollars. He slouched in the chair, reading a tattered paperback romance novel. He looked up as Jonah approached but didn't close his book.

"Hey, Lucien," Jonah said.

Lucien muttered a greeting in return, barely moving his lips as he spoke.

Lucien was psychic but tended to avoid the dead, if he could. The dead were bad for his fortune-telling business since potential clients tended to steer clear of a guy who appeared to be talking to himself.

"You got my stuff?" Jonah asked.

Lucien inclined his head slightly, nodding at a duffel bag under the table. Jonah knelt down and opened the bag, revealing two bottles of Scotch and a box of cigars.

"A little early in the day to be tying one on," Lucien remarked in his lilting Cajun accent, holding his paperback up to block his face so passersby couldn't see his lips moving.

"It's not for me," Jonah replied. "They're for the Baron."

"Why you want to go and get mixed up with that hoodoo stuff?" Lucien shook his head.

Jonah ignored this comment. He pulled a stack of cash — living, not dead — out of his pocket, fanned it so Lucien could see it was all there, and then placed it in Lucien's hand when he reached for it. In his ghost form, no one could see Jonah. His ghost aura distorted the light around him, obscuring anything he held — the most the living would see was an occasional glint, like light bouncing off a mirror — but the aura only extended so far. If he held anything "living" too far from his body, it would look like it was floating in the air.

He slipped the money into Lucien's hand, and Lucien curled his fist around it and then shoved it into his pocket. Jonah made sure no one was walking by and then leaned over the bag, enveloping it in his ghost aura, and picked it up. He straightened up, the bag clutched tightly to his body. "Thanks!"

Lucien grunted.

Jonah turned and headed down the street, continuing on to the storage locker that he rented several blocks away. It was tricky trying to juggle his keys and the bag without anything "showing," but he managed to get the storage unit's door open without mishap. Once inside, he set down the duffel bag and removed the contents, setting them on a shelf alongside a plastic container of special dust guaranteed to summon Baron Samedi, the voodoo guardian of the underworld, and the instructions for drawing the veve or symbol for summoning him.

Jonah looked over his growing stash of supplies: food, candles, matches, two winter coats, some gloves, two umbrellas, a couple of sleeping bags, and a tent—all of it dead. He'd rented the storage locker to hide his supplies from Madame Majicka, but now with Char sniffing around, it had turned out to be a smart precaution. All of the items here were dead—except for the recently added scotch and cigars—and, therefore, invisible to the living. To anyone not psychic, the locker would look empty.

He was mostly going by instinct, collecting whatever he thought might be useful based on the descriptions of the various planes of the afterlife. Technically, the dead didn't need any of this stuff, but Irene had insisted on continuing to think of herself as a physical being, one that required food and clothing and shelter, so he wanted to be sure to bring whatever she might need.

The absolute essentials were on the shelf where he'd placed the Baron's items: ancient texts, traditional items of offering to the various underworld deities, dozens of various types of proven effective ghost and demon repellents, and a sword. These were going to save Irene.

He took one last look around and then exited the storage unit, making sure the door was securely locked behind him. Then he left, heading back out to the main street, heading toward the library.

"Boo!"

Startled, Jonah turned to see who had spoken and then stopped short. His jaw dropped open. Standing behind him was Char. She beamed at him. "What are you doing here?" he asked, amazed and a little confounded as to how she could have possibly found him.

Char's expression turned guilty.

"Did you follow me?" Jonah asked in growing outrage. What had she done—wait by the shop's exit all night just so she could catch him if he slipped out? Had she been following him when he'd stopped to see Lucien? When he'd gone to the storage locker? "I told you—"

"I just thought you might need some help."

Jonah ground his teeth. "I told you I don't need any help. Besides, you can't get into ghost places—" He did a double take, staring hard. "Oh no! You didn't! How on earth did you—"

Char shrugged. "The page was bookmarked, Jonah. It wasn't hard to figure out that was the meditation you'd talked about."

Jonah was at her side in three strides, anger at the invasion of his privacy coupled with genuine anxiety about her safety making him furious. He grabbed her by the arms and shook her. "Damn it, Char, I'm not kidding. This isn't a joke! There's stuff here you know nothing about!"

She jerked away from him, glaring at him. "I was just trying to help!" She jammed a hand into the front pocket of her black jeans—today topped by a t-shirt with a white skull and crossbones and the ever-present combat boots—yanked something out of it, and thrust it at him. "I just came to bring you this. Here."

Jonah hesitated, looking at the fist-sized, translucent white crystal that she held out to him. It was threaded on a leather cord like a necklace. "What's that?" he asked suspiciously.

Char glared at him, her mouth set with a combination of sulkiness and belligerence. "It's a focusing crystal. It'll help concentrate your psychic energy."

Jonah stared at the crystal in disbelief. "You went through all that just to give me a stupid—"

Char's glare turned dangerous, and she angrily thrust the crystal at him again.

She stood there, holding her chin high, but her lower lip trembled and she refused to meet his eyes. It struck him that she genuinely wanted to help and that he'd hurt her feelings. She looked small and fragile, and his anger instantly dissipated, replaced by guilty regret. He sighed in resignation and gingerly took the crystal from her, holding it as if it might explode. "Uh, thanks." He tried to smile gratefully, but apparently he wasn't quite able to manage it because Char rolled her eyes.

"I think that will help," she said earnestly. "You know, with your getting stuck between worlds."

This was obviously going to need a longer conversation. Jonah looked around for somewhere out of the way of the crowd where they could talk. He gestured to a side alley with his head and tugged on her sleeve to indicate she should follow him. They wove their way through the steady stream of hurrying people and then stepped into the cool hush of the alley.

Jonah held up the crystal. "So how is this supposed to help me?"

"It's like you were talking about—the dead are pure energy, right? That's why they can cross to the other side. You, on the other hand, aren't. Even in your ghost form, part of your energy gets left behind—in your body, I mean—to keep it alive, right? That means that small amount of missing energy is the problem. So I think the crystal will help by concentrating the energy that does leave your body and making it stronger—hopefully, strong enough to get through to the other side."

"Huh." Jonah hefted the crystal in his hand, considering. Surprisingly, her explanation made sense—a lot of sense. Energy—the answer had been there right in front of him the entire time.

He tried not to get his hopes up—he'd been disappointed more times than he could count by things that had seemed like sure-fire answers. However, even if the crystal didn't work, Char's theory gave him new avenues to explore.

He smiled, feeling the grin spread slowly across his face. "Cool! Thanks! How does it work?"

Char visibly relaxed and grinned back at him. "You don't have to do anything special. Just wear it close to your body."

Jonah considered the crystal for another moment and then looked at Char. "Why are you doing this? Why would you help me? Weren't you warning me just the other day that you thought I shouldn't do this, that it's too dangerous?"

"Yeah, well, you're not the only one willing to stick their neck out for a friend, you know."

"You don't even know Irene."

Char flashed him an impatient look and rolled her eyes again. "I'm not talking about her."

The earnestness of Char's admission — and the unbridled intensity with which she was now regarding him — took him by surprise, and he wasn't sure how to react. He flushed, growing uncomfortably warm, and took a step back. "Oh." To cover his confusion, he bent his head and busied himself with tying the crystal's leather cord around his neck.

"Come on," Char said quickly, as if equally uncomfortable, "let's go try it out. Look, I brought one for me, too." She reached under the collar of her t-shirt and held up a similar crystal.

He was just about to agree when a flash of silver across the street from the alley caught his attention. The throng of hurrying commuters had thinned, and at just the instant he happened to glance toward the street, a gap in the crowd had revealed an object he'd seen a million times in his dreams. His heart stopped.

The blood thrummed in his ears as he stared past Char, not believing his eyes. Like a sleepwalker, he began to walk as if drawn to the object against his will. Char, the crystal, and everything else faded away until the entire world had focused to a solitary point: the silver BMW parked across the street. "It can't be..." he said in a half-whisper, his heart jolting awake to thunder in his ears.

"What are you —" he heard Char say, but he pushed past her on shaky legs, lurching like the undead, still not able to believe his eyes. He expected the car to vanish at any moment like a mirage. He paused at the alley's mouth, afraid to draw closer, afraid for that moment of crashing

hope when he discovered it wasn't actually her car. Only...
it was her car. He was sure of it. It was Irene's.

The realization hit him like a blow to the stomach, and
he stumbled forward, breaking into a jog. Had she made it
back by herself?

"Hey, I may be a ghost, but I'm not invisible!" Char
shouted, the words sounding tinny and far away.

He slowed as he approached the car, first looking at the
license plate and then stooping to peer in the window. "Oh
my God..." He heard footsteps behind him, and he spun
around. Char stood there with a "What the hell?" kind of
look on her face. She shrugged and shook her head,
gesturing for him to explain himself. "I can't believe it," he
exclaimed, barely able to speak coherently. It was Irene's car.
It was definitely her car—which meant she was here. She
had come back.

He scanned the area eagerly, looking for her in the
undulating crowd of commuters heading to work. Instead,
his eyes landed on the unwelcome sight of a vaguely-
rumpled man in his early twenties, his dark hair slightly
tousled as if he had just gotten out of bed, quickly
approaching them from down the street. A cigarette dangled
from the corner of the man's mouth, and he was surrounded
by the ghostly aura of the dead.

Ernest.

Jonah's hands reflexively curled into fists as anger
threaded through him. He may have only been a kid at the
time and might not have fully understood all the nuances of
why it was happening, but he'd been all too aware of where
Irene was going every time she'd snuck out of the hotel
room they shared: she'd been going to Ernest's room. And
every time she came back from visiting him, she'd been
worse than before she went—restless, anxious, itching for a
fight, and drinking more. All the ways she showed she
didn't give a crap—that she wasn't sad, that she didn't feel
guilty or ashamed, that she wasn't scared—only she did, and
she was. Being with Ernest had just made her feel worse
about herself—and both he and Irene had known it, which

just made her do it all the more so she could prove that it didn't. Watching her downward spiral into utter self-loathing had just about killed him. He'd tried everything he could think of to pull her out of it, to put a stop to her visits with Ernest—threats, pleading, diversions—but nothing he'd done had helped. It was just one more thing he hadn't been able to stop from happening, just one more way he had failed. And then, finally, she had left.

"What are you doing with my car?" Ernest glared at Jonah for a second, and then recognition dawned across his face. His manner instantly changed from annoyance to one of bored insolence. He reached up, removed the cigarette with a careless movement of his hand, and nonchalantly blew a cloud of smoke. "Junior," he drawled, his voice dripping with disdain. "Long time, no see."

So he remembered. Good. "Where's Irene?" Was this why Irene had cut off contact, because she had returned—and was with Ernest? Jonah's fists clenched tighter, itching to wipe the smirk from the other man's face.

"Jonah?" Char tugged on his sleeve, but he shrugged her off, barely registering her presence, never breaking eye contact with Ernest.

Ernest took a drag on his cigarette, regarding Jonah carefully, searching his face for something. "I wouldn't know. I haven't seen her for years, not since she said she was leaving, going to the other side."

Ernest's words were like a dash of cold water, drowning both his anger and his burgeoning hope that Irene had returned. His shoulders slumped, though relief that she wasn't with Ernest tempered the blow. He relaxed slightly, his fists unclenching. He took a deep breath and forced himself to speak in a calm, or, at least, non-belligerent, tone. "Then why do you have her car?"

"Jonah?" Another, more insistent, tug on his sleeve. Again, he shrugged her off.

"She gave it to me," Ernest said.

"Oh." Jonah scanned the car, remembering his and Irene's many white-knuckle-inducing drives together. What he wouldn't give for even just one more. "I wondered what happened to it," he said lamely as an awkward silence descended between them.

Ernest smirked and took another drag on his cigarette. "Well, it's not like you were old enough to drive it."

Ernest was baiting him, mocking, as he had four years ago, his youth and inexperience. The image seared indelibly in his brain of Irene in the bar with Ernest—leaning forward, her eyes dark and intent, her long, bare legs crossed, one over the other, exposing an expanse of thigh, her hand straying to her hair, to her throat, to the dip in the neckline of her dress—played over and over in his mind.

"What do you want me to say," she'd asked. "That I was with Ernest and we were humping like rabbits?"

No, she hadn't needed to say; he'd known.

Jonah struggled to control the frustration rising up from somewhere deep inside of him. "Have you heard from her?" he asked evenly, his hands reflexively balling into fists once more.

Ernest hesitated for a minute, looking Jonah up and down as if he was debating whether or not to answer. He took a long, slow drag on his cigarette, as if purposely stalling just to aggravate Jonah even more—which Jonah had to admit was working. Finally, Ernest released a long stream of smoke out of the side of his mouth and shook his head. "Not since the night she gave me the car. She said she was leaving. I haven't heard from her since."

Grim self-satisfaction rolled through him, and some inner devil gave birth to an unstoppable need to gloat, to wipe the arrogance from Ernest's face. "Really? That's funny, because she sent me a bunch of letters."

Jonah could tell he'd hit a nerve: the other man's face twisted into an ugly scowl, and he tossed his cigarette with an explosive movement. Jonah smirked, his smugness growing.

Ernest took a step toward him.

"Jonah!" Char's voice was growing more insistent as she tugged, for the third time, on his sleeve.

Ernest's eyes slid to Char and then back to Jonah, and he sneered, his eyes flashing with menace. "It's good to see you're sniffing after girls your own age for a change."

"Oh, funny, you're one to talk! What are you, a hundred and ten now?"

"You have some nerve, you know that? If it weren't for you, she'd still be here, and her and I would —"

"Her and you? Ha, that's a laugh. I bet she doesn't even remember your name."

Ernest's face twisted into an ugly snarl. "You know what? You have this comin'." He hauled back and nailed Jonah in the jaw. Pain exploded in Jonah's head, and the crack of his teeth slamming together was audible. He stumbled back but managed to stay on his feet. His head rang, and the world swam before his eyes for a moment. He straightened up and touched his lip, sneering at Ernest as he did so. He was a ghost; ghosts couldn't bruise, couldn't bleed.

He dropped his hand and stiffened, the ever-present anger and frustration bubbling just below the surface that he'd kept bottled for three long years flash-freezing into a cold fury. Ernest's upper lip lifted in derision, and that was the last straw. He launched himself at Ernest with a growl of rage, and the two men slammed together, fists flying.

Far away, barely penetrating the pounding of the blood in his ears, Jonah heard someone cry, "Jonah! No!" Dimly, he felt someone grab him by the back of the shirt, hauling at him with all their might. "He's not worth it!"

Jonah managed to land a few solid blows, his knuckles burning from the impact, before Char was able to pull him away just enough for Ernest to jump back, out of arm's reach. "That's right," Ernest said scornfully, directing his words at Char. "Why don't you get him out of here before I knock his teeth in?"

"You bastard!" Jonah yelled, thrashing wildly to break out of Char's grip. "You just had to touch her, didn't you? You couldn't leave her alone. There's a million other women out there —"

"Oh, well I was hardly her first, was I? Believe me —"

"You son of a bitch! When I'm through with you —"

"Jonah!" Char cried, refusing to let go of his shirt. Ernest stood his ground and smirked.

Jonah fought against Char's hold. "Let me go!" he snarled, twisting and flailing so he could pull free of her grip.

"Not until you calm down!"

They struggled together for a few minutes. Finally, Jonah jerked free, the fabric of his shirt sliding out of Char's fingers. He yanked his shirt back into place, breathing hard. He opened his mouth to ask Char just what the hell she thought she was doing when he heard a car door slam and the sound of an engine starting. They both whirled around to see Ernest behind the wheel of the silver BMW. He gave Jonah a syrupy sweet smile accompanied by a wave of his fingers and then roared off.

"Bastard," Jonah muttered, noting with satisfaction that Ernest was now completely rumpled and looking the worse for wear. Figures — the smarmy weasel had slunk off rather than fight.

Char stared at the retreating taillights for a moment before turning to glare at Jonah. "Let me guess... Ms. Hot Stuff's boyfriend?"

A new wave of roiling hot fury flowed over him, and he practically snarled his response. "Hardly. He's just some skeevy guy she hooked up with in a bar." Still breathing hard, his need to pummel Ernest not nearly abated, he stalked away from Char, pacing until he could get his heart rate under control. Faintly, in a far distant part of his mind, the idea that he'd just made an idiot of himself glimmered, and he shoved the thought away, even as the acrid tang of self-anger burned in the pit of his stomach. He yanked down his shirt and rammed his fingers through his hair, trying to smooth it down.

"Wow. Just... wow," Char said. "The more I hear about this woman, the more I want to punch her. She's got you dangling on a string, and then she's got that guy lined up —"

Jonah rounded on her. "Shut up! Just shut up! You don't even know her!"

Char glared at him, arms folded over her chest. "Or what—you gonna hit me, too?"

The words were like cold water tossed in his face, and he stopped dead in his tracks. He stared at Char for a moment as the anger ebbed away. "No, I'm not going to hit you." He stuffed his hands in his pockets to keep them from curling into fists and turned away. "Jesus, you're such a drama queen."

"Me? Hey, it takes one to know one, Chief. I'm not the one having fistfights in the street—over a woman who's not even here anymore!"

"Just shut up. You weren't there, Char. You don't know."

Char held up her hands in mock surrender. "Oh, that's right, we can't say anything bad about Saint Irene."

Jonah rounded on her. "Why do you do that? Why do you make fun of her and try to tear her down? And why do you ridicule me for being worried about her? Huh? You said you wanted to be my friend and to help me. So help already."

Char had the grace to look repentant, her expression taking on a guilty tinge.

"Come on, let's go," he said, impatiently, sick of the conversation, sick of wasting time, sick of the day. "The faster we get back to the shop, the faster I can get back to what I was doing." He jerked his head in the direction of the magic shop, indicating she should start walking.

However, Char didn't move. Instead, she cocked her head and asked, "Jonah, how long ago did Irene cross over?"

Jonah, already turning away to start walking, hesitated and then turned back, suddenly wary of Char's abrupt change in manner. "What? Why?"

"Well, it's just that that guy said that you weren't old enough to drive then. So it must have been a while ago."

Jonah pursed his lips, knowing what was coming next. "Look, I don't need any more snarky—"

Char crossed her arms over her chest and narrowed her eyes. "Jonah?"

He gritted his teeth. "Almost three years ago."

"Wait, so you met this woman when you were... fourteen?" Char's voice dripped with incredulity.

Jonah drew himself up, and his voice turned dangerous. "Whatever you're about to say... don't."

Char didn't need to—her face said it all. She held up her hands, though, as if in submission. "Okay, so she's been gone almost three years. And how long ago did she send you that note?"

Jonah's lips compressed into a thin line.

"Jonah?"

"Eight months ago," he said tightly. "Can you just drop—"

Char stared at him. "Eight months? Uh, Jonah—"

"Look," he said, cutting her off, knowing she wasn't going to let this go without an explanation. "I think time passes differently on the other side. She crossed over, and I didn't hear from her for almost two years. Then I started getting notes, and she acted like no time had passed at all, like she had just arrived on the other side. So it might have been eight months since that last note for me, but it might have been only a day for her."

Char gaped at him. "But you don't *know* that, not for sure. She could be dead—I mean actually dead—by now."

Jonah's lips compressed even further. "Hence my annoyance at having to waste time dealing with you every day."

Char flushed and dropped her eyes. "You don't have to be mean about it. I was trying to help."

"I don't need any help."

Char, still looking down, pursed her lips. "So you've said. Repeatedly."

"And yet, we keep having this conversation."

Char's scowl deepened. He cut her off, hoping to put an end to the discussion. "Look..." he paused as a cloud of vapor rose from his mouth as he spoke, as if it were winter and he could see his breath, "... can we... just..." He trailed off, completely distracted by the stream of vapor. It was July. Why could he see his breath?

The answer became apparent a second later. The temperature was dropping precipitously. He could see Char's breath, too, curling from her mouth and nostrils as she breathed hard in anger, strung by his tone and words. There was only one thing he knew of that could account for that kind of sudden drop. He lifted his eyes to look past Char, searching for the telltale smoke-like shadows.

"Uh, Earth to Jonah," Char said snapping her fingers in front of his face. "You can't doze off in the middle of a conversation just because you don't like what I'm saying —"

"Shut up for a second," he said, though kinder than he'd said it before. He spun around, scanning the area frantically. Across the street a dark mist roiled and flowed along the sides of buildings and out onto the sidewalk, over and around the living who took no head of it, heading for them. An Ugly. Terror rolled over him. "Oh, shit. Char..."

Char followed his gaze to the oozing shadow as it flowed toward them. "What the hell is that?" she cried.

Jonah backed away, preparing to run; Char, however, remained rooted to the spot, gaping at the cloud in confusion. Jonah grabbed her hand, yanking her backwards.

"Run!" he shouted at her.

Eleven

Irene shuffled the collection of papers in her hand — letters, scribbled notes, and a hand-drawn map, which were fast becoming her handbook to the afterlife — looking again for a particular paragraph she knew she had seen.

They had been trudging toward the castle forever. Okay, maybe it only felt like forever, but the castle didn't seem to be getting any closer. After the incident with Heru, Irene hadn't really felt like trying to make conversation — though Andras wasn't scowling, she still felt like she was in the dog house.

So instead, she'd pulled out all the various tidbits she had written down about the afterlife and, keeping one eye alert for shadows, was combing through them, looking for clues as to where they might be and what might await them at the castle.

Irene glanced at the building uneasily. It had changed again; instead of silver and white, it was now cream colored, made of precisely cut blocks of stone, austere and unornamented but stately and refined. "I think the castle might be the Hall of Judgment Jonah kept warning me about," she said, "where they weigh your heart on a scale."

Andras didn't seem to be listening. He was gazing at the castle with a strange, thoughtful look on his face.

"I said, that castle might be —"

"It is Ucles."

"Ucles? What's that?" She flipped through her papers, looking for a reference to the unfamiliar word.

"The seat of my order. Home, if you will. One of the fairest holdings in all of Christendom." Andras was silent for a moment. Though he didn't stop walking, his pace slowed and the military stiffness of his carriage relaxed. "I saw it only a few times, but its beauty stayed with me. The castle was made of white stone, without ornamentation. The stones needed none. Their beauty was in their starkness, in their natural perfection. Inside the keep, everything echoed—the tramp of our boots on the stairs, the ring of spurs on the cobbles, the rattle of swords in their scabbards.

"Outside, the hills—grass-covered save for the occasional jutting boulder—were gentle and rolling for as far as the eye could see. There are few trees in Ucles, and those that do grow there are low, thick, shrub-like things with dark green needles. From the parapets, everywhere is unrelenting green, except the sky, which is always blue.

"Everywhere, from the blades of grass outside to the pristine cloth on the altar, there is a sense of orderliness and authority and a feeling of peace and sanctity. Princes, kings—they all came to kneel in supplication in our hall, humbled before God."

Irene was quiet, afraid the slightest sound would shatter the moment. Andras had never before spoke of his life; in fact, he'd never spoken like this at all. His voice had taken on the cadence of a storyteller, deep and low, and the richness of it drew her in and held her breathless with anticipation for whatever he'd say next. His words rolled over her like molten honey, warm and almost sensual, and she lost herself in them, wanting him to go on talking forever and ever.

She could see everything he described. Around them, the world shimmered and faded, replaced with the images Andras painted of rolling green hills and in the distance, a shining white castle. She could hear and see and smell it all—the pine-like scent of the green-needled trees and the clean, fresh smell of grass contrasting sharply with the dusky smell of horses and leather and the damp, musty smell of stone-cooled interiors; the snapping of the pennants in the breeze, the snorts and stamps of the sweaty-flanked horses in the courtyard, the ring of steel on steel as the men practiced their swordsmanship, their hauberks flashing in the sun.

"Despite the reverence, Ucles was a hive of activity, messengers coming and going all hours of day and night. The pages often would forget themselves and run through the halls in their haste, and sharp-tongued though indulgent admonishments from their elders followed on their heels."

"You miss it," Irene said softly.

"No," Andras said shortly, his eyes, hard and unyielding, meeting hers. "It was just stones."

Andras looked away and lapsed into a moody silence. Irene glanced at the castle, seeing it in a new light. To Andras, the castle was Ucles, and Ucles meant duty. In fact, even Heaven meant duty to him—for Andras, Heaven was joining the Saboath.

When she'd first met Andras, he'd rescued her from a pack of Hungry Ghosts and then offered to guide her to the river where she could catch the ferry to the next world. It had never occurred to her until now that Andras had found the river and then voluntarily returned to the woods—over and over again. She'd accused him—on several occasions—of simply sitting down by the river and waiting for God to rescue him, but that wasn't true. Instead, he'd made a conscious decision to help others—to continue his duty as a knight. One might say he'd continued with the burden of duty, except, to him, it wasn't a burden—it was a way of life and a part of him, so deeply ingrained it was like breathing.

"You are making a face," Andras said.

Irene shrugged and dropped her gaze, letting her hair sweep forward to hide her face. "I was just thinking... about the people I left behind." Alexia and LaRayne, her two closest friends, had been with her the night she had died—they had let her drive drunk, and then they both had been left to live with that fact. Irene had never even bothered to see how they were doing, how they were coping and getting on with their lives. And then there was her mother—Irene had at least gone to say goodbye, but in the end, she'd still left. Her mother was getting older, not able to fully care for herself, and Irene had still left. And Jonah... Christ, Jonah. She should never have left him alone. If anything happened to him, it would be entirely her fault.

At the time, Irene had left the land of the living because it seemed the right thing—the grown up thing—to do. Instead of futilely holding onto her old life, she'd made a conscious decision to let it go, to accept that she was dead and move on. Now, however, she could see that it had been the selfish choice. There had been other options—she could have acknowledged she was dead and let her old life go and still upheld her responsibilities to those she loved, to those who had loved her. In fact, hadn't she been hurt when she realized her father, who had died ten years earlier, hadn't stuck around to watch over her and her mother? And then she'd up and done the same thing.

She glanced again at the castle. The Guide had said she could return to Earth, but not as she was now, not as Irene Dunphy—and she'd accepted that, too... sort of. She didn't want her old life back, not now; anything seemed better than living the sad, pitiful life of a ghost in the land of the living. However, the Guide had said she'd retain some element of her old self, some "Irene Dunphy-ness," which she thought meant she would at least remember her old life even if she couldn't return to it. Now, however, she wondered if she would remember. What if she forgot it all—the good, the bad, the lessons learned? What if she forgot the people she was returning for?

"You are thinking of home,"Andras said with a trace of disapproval.

"No... well, not in the way you mean. I was just wondering how one gets into the guardian angel business."

"One has to be very angelic," Andras said, completely deadpan.

Irene was going to rebut that premise with a list of all the movies and books featuring people sent back to Earth to help the living in order to redeem themselves but forgot what she was going to say when the waist-high wheat abruptly gave way to a yawning chasm, the ground dropping off into oblivion. The wheat hid the drop off until they were on top of it, and Irene's momentum carried her a couple of steps past Andras to the very edge of the precipice. Andras grabbed the back of her coat to keep her from falling and gently drew her back three steps to safety.

In the far distance, across a canyon at least a mile wide, Irene could make out the castle, situated on solid ground.

The canyon was a great, vast, emptiness, so deep and so wide it was more like an empty ocean than a canyon. The sides dropped so steeply that those closest to her couldn't be seen, and those on the other side were so far away Irene couldn't have described them — were they colored, were there striations, were they rough or smooth? For as far as she could see, there was just a big empty nothing.

Cautiously, she crept forward to balance on the cliff's edge, anchored firmly by Andras's hold on the hem of her jacket, and peered over. Her eyes widened, and she gasped as she beheld a burning river of fire fifty feet below. Not a molten flow of lava and not flames burning on the surface of water, but a burning, searing aurora borealis of yellows and reds filling the canyon as far as the eye could see.

Andras crept closer, coming to stand beside her so he could see what had made her gasp, though he kept a grip on her coat. Silently, they regarded the fire-filled canyon together. This high above the flames, they remained quite cool, unable to feel the heat of the inferno below.

"Well, crap," Irene said when she was finally able to articulate words. "I'm out of ideas."

"We must find another way," Andras said, but his tone was less assured than usual.

Irene worried her bottom lip with her teeth and shook her head. "There's only one place in the stories with a river of fire that I know of: Tartarus. And if I remember correctly,

Tartarus was an island." Irene pointed to the river of fire below and then followed it with her finger as it flowed past them to the right and continued around in an arc, as if the canyon indeed circled an island.

Andras went very still. "Then our first instinct was correct. We are in Hell."

Irene had been thinking the exact same thing, but she gave him a disapproving scowl. "Don't be so negative. Remember, everything here is a metaphor. That's probably not even actual fire. It's probably symbolic of regret or puppies or a summer breeze or some crap like that."

Andras swept an arm toward the fire in invitation. "Do you wish to test that theory?"

Irene grimaced. "Not especially." She surveyed first the flames and then the castle once more. How on earth were they going to get across? Her heart sank. It seemed impossible.

She racked her brain, trying and dismissing various ideas. Finally, only one remained: "You know... I do know a guy who could fly us over this canyon," she said slowly, knowing Andras wouldn't like it any more than she did. In fact, the very idea made her skin crawl. But what choice did they have? They needed to call on Samyel.

Samyel, the strange "man" she'd met in the land of the living and who had offered to be her guide in the afterlife in exchange for her bringing him through the tunnel with her, had turned out, to her horror and surprise, to be a Nephilim. Immediately upon arriving in the land of the dead, he'd revealed his wings—as he flew off and left her behind.

Andras's response was just as emphatic as it was fast. "No."

She had no idea if his promise—to come if she called him—was actually worth anything. For all she knew, it had been an easy lie to trick her into helping him. Or it might be a convenient way to invite him to show up and kill her. However, at the moment, there didn't seem to be too many other options. "Look, he owes me a favor. I mean, he promised to show up if I called him, at least—maybe. Sorta.

That's got to be worth something. We could at least give it a try—"

"No."

"There's two of us and one of him. We could take him if he—"

"NO."

"Well, what do you suggest since we aren't going to last long with those shadows out there? There's no place to hide and no place to go."

"Perhaps we should pray," Andras said.

"Are you kidding me?"

Andras's expression said that he was not. He turned away from the chasm, went down on one knee, and bowed his head. Irene rolled her eyes and turned away, throwing up her hands in frustration.

"This is hardly the—" She interrupted herself as an idea came to her. "Oh shit—pray!" She looked up at the sky and shouted, "Hey, how about a little help here?"

Andras's eyes popped open. "That is not how it is done—"

"I'm not talking to God," she said. "I'm talking to the Guide." She turned her face back up to the sky. "Hey! I know you can hear me!"

Something small and hard dropped out of the sky and hit her on the head. "Ow!" she cried, her hand flying up to rub the sore spot. "Why do people keep throwing things at me?" Her eyes followed the object as it landed on the ground, bounced once, and then rolled to a stop. She snatched it up.

It was an acorn.

"Very funny!" she shouted, shaking the acorn at the air. In the next instant, a deluge of acorns rained down on her, as if someone had upended a bucket of them over her head. She covered her head with her arms as the hard little projectiles sleeted down, bouncing and rolling every which way. She remained hunched over, arms over her head, for a few moments after the downpour ended, just to be certain. Cautiously, she straightened up, shaking acorns from her hair, the neckline of her dress, and the folds of her coat. She pressed her lips together in a flat, humorless grimace. Apparently, the Guide thought he was being cute.

"Okay, fine, I get the message," she said loudly. No help was forthcoming. She was going to have to figure this one out on her own.

Andras was staring at her with horror, his eyes wide. The rain of acorns hadn't touched him, only her, and she realized that from Andras's point of view, it probably was pretty strange to see a localized storm of acorns. "He thinks he's being funny," she said, by way of an explanation. "The Guide," she added when Andras didn't seem to understand. When he continued to look confused, she added, "You know, the Guide."

Andras, still kneeling, mutely shook his head.

"Big, round, bald guy in a toga?"

Another shake of the head.

"Didn't you see him? At the altar, before we left the last plane?"

Andras's expression remained blank and uncomprehending.

"If you never saw him, then why did you act like you knew what I was talking about this whole time? I've mentioned him like a dozen times since we arrived here!"

"I thought you were referring to the boy."

"HE HAS A NAME!"

"You seem to be upset. Perhaps we should take a rest break."

"I'm not up —" Catching on to what he had just done — turning her earlier words back around on her — she raised her hands and pantomimed choking him. "Oh, you! This is no time for jokes!" She flailed her fists in the air, venting her frustration with the Guide's lack of help and Andras's inappropriate joking.

Andras rose, poorly hiding a grin.

Irene flipped her hair back over her shoulder and straightened, assuming an air of command. "Never mind. We're just going to have to find a way across by ourselves."

She picked the bag up off the ground, shook off the acorns that had pooled on the top of it, settled the straps on her shoulder, and prepared to set off.

Andras began to lower himself back into a one-legged kneel. "I am not yet done praying."

Irene was about to make a sarcastic retort when a movement in the distance caught her eye. "Oh yes, you are!" she cried, pointing. "Shadows!"

Twelve

Jonah took off at a run, dragging Char behind him, racing down the street, searching frantically for a safe place to hide. The throng of morning commuters had long since thinned, though the sidewalk was by no means empty. He dodged around people, not caring if he bumped into them. Speed, not stealth, was the object now. Outrunning the Ugly was their only chance.

Char's hand gripped his painfully, but he didn't let go. Adrenaline pulsed through him, lending speed to his legs. They rounded a corner and then another and then another. Char tripped and then stumbled, nearly knocking him down.

"Come on!" he shouted, tugging frantically on her hand, feeling the freezing cold of the approaching Ugly deepen.

Char tried to right herself, to get her legs back under her, but she couldn't. She stumbled again and gasped, struggling to catch her breath. "Jonah... stop..."

"No!" he shouted, yanking her forward. "We have to run!" Char didn't seem to understand the danger, and he had no time, no breath, to explain.

The crowd was too thick here, impeding their progress. Dark swirls of shadow curled up the building on one side of them and the cars on the other, working to encircle them and cut them off. The air he pulled into his lungs burned; it would only be mere moments until the Ugly was on them, searing them with cold as it sucked the life from them.

He spied a small hole-in-the-wall shop, a hair salon, easily overlooked, across the street. He dragged Char forward and headed for the store. He didn't pause as he slammed into the door. It gave way, thank God, and they tumbled inside. He leaned his weight against the door, urging the spring-loaded closing mechanism to go faster. The door clicked shut, and he collapsed against it, panting.

Inside, the receptionist and a customer — her hair in pink rollers — stared at the door, which had appeared to open and close of its own accord, in confusion and surprise, and then they looked at each other. The receptionist shrugged. "It does that sometimes. We think it's vibrations from the subway."

Char doubled over, trying to catch her breath. "What is going on?" she managed to gasp out.

"Uglies," Jonah said shortly, peering through the door to check the street outside. He peered around the neon-pink lettering, squinting at the dark, gray, fog-like mist roiling past the shop.

Char looked, too. "What is that?" she asked.

"Bad news," Jonah replied.

"Can you be more specific?"

Jonah stepped away from the door and motioned for Char to follow. She frowned but complied. They moved further into shop as Jonah took in their surroundings. It was all very… pink. Pink salon chairs, pink and white tile floor, pink plastic capes, and pink covers on the dryers. Two stylists, both in their twenties, worked on a couple of middle-aged women while a third swept the floor. Jonah waved at the various women. "Hello?" he said. No one reacted. Good, no psychics present.

He threaded his way through the store and looked for a couple of empty seats out of the way. He suddenly froze, however, as a thought occurred. "Shit! Where's my backpack?"

They both cast around the salon, but it was nowhere to be seen. Jonah groaned and collapsed into an empty chair. "Crap. It's still back where we ran into Ernest."

"Jonah, can you focus for a second?" Char said. "Who cares about your backpack? What is out there?"

Jonah sighed. "That is known as an Ugly; it's a really unhappy dead person—a Chindi, Suanggi, or You Hun Ye Gui. And I am focusing—I care about my backpack because the only defense against an Ugly is *in* my backpack."

"Defense? What do you mean?" Char's eyes were wide. "Why are you so scared of it? What will happen if it catches us?"

Jonah gave her a meaningful look and lifted up his t-shirt. An angry, red pucker of scarred flesh crossed from his right shoulder to his left hip, obliterating most of the skin on his chest. Char gasped, tears springing to her eyes. "Oh my God," she whispered, one hand to her mouth. "You said the spirit realm was dangerous, but I had no idea…"

Jonah dropped his shirt with a frown. "Yeah, well imagine what they're doing to Irene."

Char shook her head. "Jonah, you have to stop doing this. You can't put yourself in danger like this—"

"Look, that thing could be out there for hours. You're going to need to say your wake-up word. You'll go right back into your body, which is safe and sound at the shop."

"And what about you?"

"I need to go get my backpack."

"Jonah, no! You can't go out there."

He shrugged off her hand on his arm. "I'll be fine. Could you maybe give me a little credit? I've been doing this for four years. I know what I'm doing."

Char, her eyes wide, shook her head, and he was surprised to see tears swimming there.

"Hey," he said, putting a reassuring hand on her arm, "it's okay. I know how to deal with them. Look, you go back to the shop; I'll get my bag and meet you back there, okay?"

Char frantically shook her head. "You can't send me out there alone—"

"I'm not sending you 'out there.' I'm sending you back to the shop —"

"Well, then, you can't expect me to leave you here alone!"

"Will you just do what I say?" he said, raising his voice to talk over her.

Char crossed her arms over her chest and glared.

"You're about as scary as a Chihuahua," he said.

"I'm not going to let you go out there alone, Jonah."

"Oh yeah? How are you going to stop me?"

"I'll tell my aunt."

"You know what? Go ahead. It'll be annoying to have to find another job, but it won't be the end of the world."

"Oh yeah? Well, when Auntie finds out what you've been up to, she'll bind your spirit to the land of the living — then you won't be able to go and find Irene. She can do it, you know."

Jonah's jaw dropped open. That was the last thing he had ever expected Char to say. "That's not possible," he said, a stutter of uncertainty creeping into his voice.

Char cocked an eyebrow. "You want to find out?"

"You wouldn't dare," he said, half incredulous, half fearful. The threat was so huge, so ludicrous, so terrible, he could hardly believe it.

"You want to bet?" Char asked, puffing up with anger. "You were right when you said that if I really cared about someone, I'd do anything to protect them. Even something as rotten as that."

Jonah tried to temper his tone so he didn't antagonize her. "Look, that's sweet, but you don't even know me, so to say that you care about me..."

Char's expression didn't change.

He tried another tack. "Look, I'm not about to leave my backpack out there for some ghost to scavenge — there's stuff in there I need. So I have to go out there, but I don't expect you —"

"We go back to the shop together, or we go after your bag — *together*."

There was no hesitancy in Char's eyes. Fear, yes, but hesitancy, no. He sighed and ran a hand through his hair before getting up and crossing to the front door again to see if the Ugly was still there. It was. He watched the gray, formless mass swirling past, one might say pacing, gauging the Ugly's size and strength.

He returned to Char, who'd had to vacate her seat due to a customer nearly sitting on her. The two of them moved farther back into the shop, hovering near the sinks to stay out of the way.

"Is it still there?" Char asked.

Jonah nodded. "Yeah. They're pretty tenacious. Once one sees you, they're pretty hard to shake."

"Can we wait it out? It'll have to give up and go away eventually, right?"

"Ha," said Jonah. "How do you think I got the scar? It was lurking outside a red door I had gone through. It must have seen me go through and decided to lurk around until I returned. I came through the door, back into the land of the living, and it grabbed me. I didn't even have a chance to react."

Char's eyes were as big as saucers. "Holy crap. How did you escape?"

The corner of his mouth lifted in a half-grin. "Bike messenger."

"Huh?"

"A guy went by on his bike and happened to ring the bell, which distracted the Ugly long enough for me to escape."

Char was looking at him with a mixture of admiration and astonishment, as if she thought he was both bad-ass and out of his mind. A little thrill of pride tingled through him. He supposed a harrowing escape from an afterlife monster was kind of bad-ass. He grinned, and she grinned back.

He nodded to the far end of the shop. "Let's see if there's a back door or another way out." They made their way through the shop and down a narrow hallway, picking their way through a clutter of boxes, broken equipment, and a pile of dirty laundry, to the back, where they found a heavy metal door with a pad lock on it.

"That's a fire code violation," Char said, as Jonah tugged on the padlock to no avail. It was solid.

"Well, we'll be sure to report them when we get back to the magic shop," Jonah said dryly.

Char stuck out her tongue and then asked, "So now what?"

Jonah thought hard for a moment. "Are you sure you won't just go back to the shop?"

Char shook her head firmly "no."

"Okay, well, let's see if we can find some bells."

"Huh?"

"You know, something that jingles."

"I know what a bell is. Why do we need one?"

"It's the only defense against an Ugly. Bells drive away evil spirits. Look around and see if you can find one we can use." They started to move in separate directions, and he gave her an additional piece of advice. "Be careful not to make too much of a commotion. You don't want to scare everyone."

A mischievous look crossed Char's face. Jonah shook his head. "I know what you're thinking, and yeah, it sounds fun, but it loses its appeal when they start throwing things at you, trust me."

They spread out and searched the shop, high to low, doing their best to surreptitiously open the various cupboards and cabinets in the small salon, which all ended up just holding hair styling products—hair dye, shampoo, conditioner, gel, mousse, and the like. The search was slow due to the need to keep the customers and staff from seeing cabinets opening and closing on their own, as well as the need to keep out from under foot. It seemed to Jonah that every time he went to open a cupboard door, one of the staff decided they needed something out of that exact same spot, and he'd have to dodge out of the way to keep from being bumped into. Finally, after forty-five minutes of excruciatingly slow and tedious searching, the only thing they had come up with was the old-fashioned front desk bell which sat on the counter by the cash register. Jonah waited until the receptionist wasn't looking and then swiped it. He gave it a few test dings, startling the receptionist, who looked around for the source of the sound. Luckily, his ghost aura covered it, hiding it from view.

"I don't think this is going to cut it," Jonah said, his frustration mounting at the puny tone the bell gave out.

"Then what are we going to do?"

"I think you should go back to the shop —"

Char folded her arms over her chest. "We already talked about this. If I do, then you come, too. Forget about the backpack, Jonah."

"I can't," he said. "That stuff is irreplaceable." When Char looked doubtful, he added, "No, really. The afterlife book is in my bag, and without it, I'm not going to be able to rescue Irene."

Char sighed. "Okay, fine, then tell me what to do."

"Are you sure?"

She nodded. There was fear in her eyes, but resolution, too, and he couldn't help but admire her determination to stick with him no matter what.

"Okay, then follow me," he said, in deadly earnestness now. "I mean, right behind me. And if I say run, you run — back to the magic shop, as fast as you can, okay? You don't stop, you don't look back, not for anything. You say your wake-up word, and that's it, okay?"

Char paled, though she was trying to look stoic, and it suddenly occurred to Jonah that despite the fact she was psychic, this was all completely foreign to her. Running from Uglies, camping out with homeless squatters, and dealing with angry ghosts were all weekly occurrences for him, and, in the grand scheme of things, not that big a deal. He was used to it, and most of the time, hardly considered any of it dangerous.

He took one last look out the door, assessing the situation. The Ugly still flowed past, but at least it wasn't pressed right up against the building — there was enough room to open the door and take one, maybe two, steps, before they'd run smack into it, which was more than enough time and space to make a dash for it with the help of the bell.

"Ready?" he asked Char. He nodded to the door. She turned and faced it, standing side by side with him. "On the count of three, yank it open." Char nodded, and softly, he counted aloud. "One... Two... THREE!"

The minute Char's hand touched the door handle, Jonah began beating on the bell with one hand while holding it in the other. The gray mist, hovering on the other side of the door, seemed to pale, almost fading to nothing, and Jonah pushed Char forward with his shoulder. "Run," he shouted. "Straight through it. RUN!"

He saw her close her eyes, and then they were pressing forward, passing through the Ugly, at a flat-out run. In the split second it took to move through the Ugly, a lifetime passed — a lifetime of agony. The searing pain of burning cold sizzled through him, slicing through his skin and blistering his organs and bones. There was a rushing, roaring sound in his ears, blocking out all other sounds, as if he stood in the middle of a raging hurricane.

Char stopped short, and Jonah plowed into her, pushing her forward. There was only one thought now: forward, forward, forward. They needed to get clear. The bell wouldn't weaken it for long and if it reformed while they were still in the midst of it, they would be dead. His hand ached, but he didn't stop hitting the bell as he ran, head down, sneakers pounding against the pavement. He didn't know where they were going — just forward, through the creature and out the other side to safety, as fast as they could.

It was like running through taffy — thick and sludgy, pulling at his legs, slowing him down. The Ugly was strengthening, growing darker and more solid by the second as it became inured to the bell. The Ugly was too strong. Jonah tried to shout at Char to hurry, but now his head and arms felt like they were pushing through taffy as well, and he couldn't get his tongue to form words.

In an instant, one realization became blindingly clear: they weren't going to make it.

He heard a shriek of pain from Char at the same moment a searing, red-hot agony sliced through him. Distantly, he registered a flash of color to their right. Summoning the last of his strength, he slammed his hand on the bell over and over, trying to hold off the Ugly for a few seconds longer. "Char! Red!" he managed to gasp, forcing the last of the air from his lungs. He wasn't sure she'd heard him, but then she changed course, angling to the right. He heard her cry out in pain once more as they hit the red door, one right after the other, and passed through it.

There was the sensation of falling through water, then flying apart, his molecules separating into a billion pieces, and then a sudden reversal, the billion pieces flying back together.

Then there was only darkness.

Thirteen

The shadows in the distance were getting closer.

Andras grabbed her arm and pulled her down into a crouch, using the wheat to hide them. Irene had no time to point out that the waist-high stalks weren't going to afford them much of a hiding place; Andras set off, moving at a cross between a crouch and a crawl, away from the shadows. They were trapped between the fire-filled canyon on one side and the approaching shadows on the other, leaving them no choice but to follow the curve of the yawning chasm. Irene knew she didn't have to point out that if they were on an island, with no place to hide and no place to run, then they weren't going to last very long against the shadows—she could tell that Andras, by the grim set of his jaw and the way he kept following the curve of the canyon with his eyes, was well aware of the problem.

There had to be a way across the gorge—Irene was sure of it, just as she'd been sure on the previous plane that there was a way across the river. The afterlife wasn't meant to trap the dead—the dead did that on their own through their fear, short-sightedness, and inability to let go of the past. No, the afterlife was meant to be traversed—it was, in a way, a giant grist mill, sorting and transforming the souls of the dead into new, more suitable forms. Therefore, there had to be a way across the canyon—she just had to find it.

She tried to blot out the urge to continually check to see where the shadows were—were they getting closer, had they seen her and Andras, were they giving chase—and, instead, focus all of her attention inward, to her internal compass. She couldn't keep moving while she closed her eyes, so she left her eyes open but tried to lose focus, gazing through her surroundings instead of at them. She breathed in slowly and deeply, focusing on the sound of her breath and the rising of her chest as it filled with air. She released the breath just as slowly, focusing on the feel of her chest deflating. Slow breath in. Slow breath out. In. Out. She sank down through layers of consciousness and reached for the place deep within herself that connected her to what lay far beyond her. She touched it, feeling its banked fire, so cold and distant.

She calmed her mind, letting it fill with nothing but an image of a bridge across the fire-filled canyon, as she poured into the compass all of her longing for reaching. Within her, the flame flickered and then began to glow. The concentrated warmth of it moved through her, spreading out through her arms and her legs to the very tips of her fingers and toes. Her pulse quickened with excitement.

It began to snow.

She tried to ignore the snowflakes swirling through the air, to not lose hold of her concentration. However, Andras—and his visible agitation at the snow squall— was harder to ignore. She tried to block him out, to stay focused on the flame.

Too late; the damage to her concentration was done. The flame wavered and then died back down as quickly as it had arisen. Irene sighed, defeated. So close—she'd been so close that time.

She could try again, but only if Andras stopped scowling at the sky and stomping around in the wheat. She put a restraining hand on his arm, signaling he should stop walking for a moment.

"Look," she said as they halted, "things aren't that bad, okay? The snow isn't going to hurt us. The butterflies aren't going to hurt us. Even the flying fish aren't going to hurt us.

So, let the world spazz out; it's fine. It's not doing any harm; it's just weird. So ignore it. Just stay focused on avoiding the shadows and looking for a way across the river, okay?"

Andras's scowl deepened, directed at her now. "And you, who must always arrange the world to her satisfaction, you are not upset by these strange and unnatural things?"

"I'm from New England. We don't consider weather weird until it's hailing, snowing, and lightning all at the same time."

Andras's eyes narrowed into a laser-hot glare; apparently, this was no time for jokes. Irene sighed. "Look, it's all strange and unnatural, okay? It's been strange and unnatural from the beginning, before I even left the land of the living. I'm talking to a guy from eleven-ninety-five, for cryin' out loud. Today, alone, I've been chased by ghost-easting shadows, found myself in the mythical land of Tartarus, and a disgruntled ex-slave attempted to put a curse on me. I'm sorry, where exactly in the grand scheme of things does a freak snowstorm fit on the weird-shit-o-meter?" She patted his arm, half comforting, half dismissive. "Come on, buck up, will you? You've faced Hungry Ghosts and invading armies without so much as batting an eye. This is a million times easier."

The furrow between Andras's eyebrows deepened, but at the same time, one corner of his mouth lifted slightly. "Perhaps," he said softly, "we should visit my time. I would dearly love to see you face down an army of Moors. In all honesty, I am not sure which side I should pity."

Irene flashed him a mirthless grin, though she was glad he was in a joking mood again. "There ya go, that's my big, strong crusader. Insult me all you want if it makes you feel better." Her teasing was short-lived, however. As soon as the words were out of her mouth, Andras raised an arm and pointed to something behind her in the distance, pulling her around behind him as if to shield her with his body as he did so. Irene spun around to see what he was pointing at.

Shadows.

She and Andras turned as one, intending to run in the opposite direction. Irene hit a tree face-first, hard, and bounced off. She fell backward and landed on her butt. Dazed, she looked up, trying to understand where the tree had come from. Her eyes traveled to the top; it wasn't a tree — it was a stalk of wheat as big as a redwood. On the heels of that thought was the realization that the ground was shaking.

Andras loomed over her. He grabbed her by an arm and hauled her to her feet. "Run!" he shouted over the rumbling of the earth. Around her, the wheat was shooting skyward, dwarfing her and Andras as the stalks became as big as trees.

She was on her feet in a second, stumbling drunkenly as the ground heaved beneath her. She clung to Andras, trying to keep her balance. Together, they staggered forward, only to jump back as a wheat-stalk tree erupted in front of them. They dodged around it and ran, stumbling, through what was now a towering, golden forest.

"What is happening?" Andras shouted, head down, shielding himself with an arm as he ran.

The world shifted, the air rippling with the oil-on-water sheen, and they were falling into absolute darkness, down, down, down, and then, just as suddenly, they were suspended against a field of stars in the vacuum of space. They hadn't stopped running, their adrenaline fueled legs pumping on auto-pilot as they blindly ran from the shadows, and now, without gravity, each stride was weightless and bounding. They leapt like gazelles and floated like feathers in the fathomless, silent dark.

Irene's head spun, disoriented by the sudden transitions, bewildered to find herself hurtling through the cosmos. It was all too fast, too much. She wanted to run through the stars to safety, to the familiar, and at the same time she wanted to stop, to assess, to study, to analyze, to grow familiar with these strange new sensations. But there was no time. She took another step forward and fell, falling, falling through space. She landed hard, once again face-first, on the ground. She lay there, stunned, the wind knocked out of her.

Beside her, she heard Andras groan, and with effort, she rolled over. Every muscle in her body trembled from the combined effects of adrenaline and fear, and she wobbled like a newborn filly standing for the first time as she sat up.

Andras climbed to his feet, his face ashen. He stood for a moment, and Irene had the impression he was testing to see if his legs would hold. He looked around and then down at her, his face grim. Tight-lipped, he held out a hand. Apparently, they were no longer in any danger from shadows.

She let him pull her to her feet, and she was relieved to see that the world had stopped shifting. They were once more amidst the placid field of wheat. Andras glared at her.

"Why are you giving me that look," Irene demanded. "You act like what just happened is my fault."

"Can you not make it stop?"

"I'm sorry! I'm not doing it on purpose. It seems like it happens every time I try to navigate us to a shortcut off this plane."

"Then perhaps we should avoid shortcuts."

"I don't know how else we're going to get out of here. If we can't find a tunnel to another plane, we're toast. We can't cross the bridge to the castle, and sooner or later, the shadows are going to get us."

Andras didn't look convinced.

Irene wanted to shake him. "You're the one that supposedly has an in with God," she said, infuriated by his pig-headed insistence on doing things the long, hard way. "Why don't *you* make it stop?"

Andras drew back as if she had slapped him, and instantly she regretted the words. She took a deep breath and smoothed down her dress, trying to get a handle on her emotions. "Okay, look, why don't we just sit here and rest for a minute, okay?"

She expected Andras to say they should keep moving, but for once, he didn't argue. They plopped on the ground, and Irene dug through her bag, not looking for anything in particular, just for something that would soothe or comfort her and help her get her focus back. The only way they were going to get out of here was if she could find a bridge over the river — and soon. She had thought the shadows were the most dangerous thing here, but now she wasn't so sure. It seemed just as likely that Andras, who had always been so steady and unflappable, would crack under the pressure of dealing with the unstable world as it was that they'd be caught by the shadows.

Her hand touched the magic mug that would fill with whatever she wanted, and she realized she hadn't yet had a drink since stepping foot on this plane. She also realized she didn't want one, either. Not even now, after they'd been chased by shadows and the world was falling apart around them. She thought maybe she should feel some sort of satisfaction in that, but instead, she just felt ambivalent. Maybe because giving up drinking was such a small part of what she still needed to do. There was still so far to travel, so much redemption to be earned.

She pulled the mug out and turned it over and over in her hands, not really seeing it as she thought back over everything that had happened to her so far. She thought of the various times she'd drank from this mug and then back before that, so the last drinks she'd had on Earth. She remembered the fight with Jonah, when he'd smashed the bottle of vodka at her feet, and before that, in the bar, when she'd gone home with Ernest, and back before that to the night she'd died.

Andras dropped from his usual position of looming over her during rest breaks into a crouch beside her, his face creased in concern. "What is wrong?"

Irene shook her head. "Nothing..." Even if she'd been able to articulate exactly what she was thinking, she wouldn't have, not to him.

Andras remained crouching, his eyes boring into her with worry.

With a sigh, she threw the cup into her bag and began digging through it, blindly searching for something, anything, that would remind her of home, of comfort, of the soothing feeling of calm that would help her call up the compass so she could guide them out of here.

"Go away," she muttered, not looking at him. "I'm practicing my ghost senses so we can get out of here."

She felt, more than saw, him move away, breathing easier the instant he was no longer scrutinizing her. Her hand, plundering the depths of her bag, touched the blanket and then, beneath that, cellophane. She moved aside the blanket and saw the package of bite-sized black licorice pieces that Jonah had sent her. She smiled. That would do the trick.

She pulled out a piece and popped it in her mouth, closed her eyes, and chewed slowly, savoring the chewy texture and deep sweet, biting flavor. She took a deep, calming breath, letting the tension flow out of her, and she relaxed, sinking into the silence that descended over the usual inner din as she focused on the feel of the licorice in her mouth, the taste of it on her tongue. She ate another piece and then another, letting the taste draw her deeper into herself, following the physical sensations to the emotions they evoked — pleasure, satisfaction, happiness — and then deeper still, until she had turned completely inward.

A sense of deep-seated calm took hold, and the world around her faded away. Though her eyes were shut, she had the feeling she was no longer in the field of wheat. Instead, she was floating in a vast emptiness, enveloped in a darkness that was absolute. She was all that existed. There was nothing else here — no stars, no planets, no cosmic dust, not even atoms; just her. She was a single point of being, and yet, she was everything, the alpha and the omega, the all and the nothing. She was everywhere, and she was nowhere — she inhabited a place out of time and out of space, neither existing nor non-existent. She was... and that was all.

I am everything that ever was and ever will be.

The Guide's words flowed over and through her, melting and melding to her, solidifying her, strengthening her, as pure and absolute as she was at this moment. There was no other thought than that; it was a simple and profound truth, the secret of creation, the secret of life, distilled into one absolute certainty. She existed. She was the sum total of creation.

And in that moment she understood.

Her eyes flew open. For a moment, there was only blackness, and then ever so slowly, the world drifted back. She could see the world rebuilding around her, layer by layer, flying together like an explosion in reverse, until at last, she sat once more in the field of wheat beside Andras.

Andras was staring at her, studying her face with a strange intensity. Irene wasn't exactly sure what had just happened. She felt disoriented and light-headed.

"Did I just go somewhere?" she asked.

Andras shook his head. The "fangs and tentacles" look was back again, so she turned away and shut her eyes, as much to blot out his expression as to stop the world from bobbing before her.

Instantly, she felt an inexorable pull back toward the expanse of nothingness. She resisted, staying rooted in the here and now of the wheat field. She wasn't sure, but the pull felt a bit like one of the "wormholes" that let her move between planes of the afterlife, and she didn't want to get separated from Andras by accidentally sliding down one without him. Slowly, she opened her eyes and looked around. Everything looked the same—and completely different.

Now the wheat was both wheat and not-wheat. It was an illusion of wheat, and she could see that it was an illusion, a wheat-esque glow super-imposed over something else. She had the distinct feeling that if she concentrated hard enough, she'd be able to see it for what it really was—trees or rocks or planets or oxygen molecules or people or Duende or Pooka-esque cats or Hungry Ghosts or Nephilim or some yet undiscovered thing existing on another plane.

She tried to focus harder, to see past the long stalks to what was below, but the harder she looked, the less she saw, the underlying images fading, leaving nothing but solid wheat in their wake.

Irene frowned and stared harder, trying to recapture the images that had floated just below the surface only a moment ago, but Andras broke her concentration by touching her on the arm.

"Are you well?" he asked.

"Peachy," she said, still frowning. "I can almost see..." She trailed off as the banked, half-hidden flame of her internal compass gave an odd kick—not exactly a flicker, but not a burst of warmth either. More of a "ping," like the returning bounce back of sonar waves. She touched her chest and then looked up quickly, her eyes straining to the distance. "There's something up ahead," she said, climbing to her feet. Another burst fluttered in her chest, and she was sure now, even though she couldn't see anything, that she was sensing something up ahead—something on this plane. She shouldered her bag and started forward, her pulse quickening.

Andras didn't move. "How do you know?"

She paused, impatient to follow what the compass was telling her before she lost the rare moment of clarity it was providing. "I don't know—I just do. I think I'm finally getting the hang of this ghost senses thing." She couldn't explain it, but it was as if she were "hearing" something with her nerve endings, rather than her ears. There was no other way to explain it other than the fact that she was "feeling" a sound. Her breath caught, and she tried not to focus too intently on the sensation, lest she lose her hold on it, and instead, focused on relaxing her mind and keeping the feeling floating somewhere between subconscious and conscious notice.

Without a word, Andras climbed to his feet. Irene gave him a grateful smile, relieved that he was trusting her for once rather than arguing. Just as quickly, the smile was wiped from her face when Andras immediately crouched down in the wheat, dragging her down with him.

Her calm and concentration shattered. The pinging sensation in her chest disappeared, all of her physical senses resolutely snapping back into place. "What the — what the hell are you doing?" she hissed, instinctively lowering her voice as Andras furtively glanced over the top of the wheat stalks.

"There is something moving... over there." He indicated the direction she'd been indicating to go with a curt nod of his head.

Irene instantly stiffened. "Shadows?"

That was not what she had been sensing; of that she was sure. Whatever she had been sensing was something she was supposed to find, something that would lead her home. It had had that familiar, warm feeling of comfort and goodness, of being right and fitting and meant to be. However, the path to what she'd been sensing was now blocked by whatever Andras was seeing.

Andras's eyes narrowed as he studied whatever he saw. "No..." He squinted hard. "It is not dark. In fact, it is..." He abruptly stood and took off, striding through the wheat.

"What the... where are you going?" she hissed frantically, but he was already out of range. "Damn it," she muttered, rising to a half-crouch and following after him as quietly as she could.

Irene could see now what Andras had been looking at. It was a person. Two people actually — real people, like her and Andras, rather than shadows. Irene straightened and darted forward, waving frantically to them. "Hello!" she called. "Hey, wait!" The ghosts paid her no mind and continued on toward the edge of the canyon. In the next instant, Irene gasped as the pair walked right off the edge of the cliff.

She darted forward, but Andras grabbed her arm and held her back. Rather than plummeting into the inferno below, as Irene expected, the two strangers hovered in the air for an instant. Then they began to float across the chasm and were soon lost to sight.

Irene's jaw dropped open. "What the..." She darted forward, and Andras grabbed her arm again, as if afraid she was going to throw herself over the edge. Exasperated, she shook him off. More slowly, she approached the spot where the ghosts had leapt off. When she was a few feet from the edge, she understood how the ghosts had crossed the canyon: there was a whisper thin wire stretched across it, a kind of suspension bridge about a hair's breadth thick. Irene stared at the bridge in disbelief. "Are you shitting me?"

Jonah had told her a story, an afterlife myth, about a bridge the width of a hair that the dead were required to cross. She hadn't actually thought it was true — which was stupid of her. All the stories were true — literally true. She'd learned this lesson already — several times, in fact. How many more times did she have to be told?

She rolled her eyes skyward. "Oh come on! You have got to be kidding!" She stared at the razor-thin bridge, and her heart sank. There was no way to cross that.

Irene turned to Andras to make a snarky comment when she was arrested by the sight of a line of ghosts flowing toward the bridge. Up close, she could see that these ghosts were translucent and half-formed, merely the suggestion of people with heads and torsos fading away below the shoulders into shapelessness and then disappearing altogether. The ghosts paid her and Andras no mind, and Irene realized they probably couldn't even see her — these ghosts were on another plane of existence.

Keeping a wary eye on the crowd, in case she was wrong about them being on another plane, Irene crept to the edge of the bridge, trying not to look down into the river of fire. She wasn't sure which would be worse: plummeting to the ground or plummeting into the fire.

She surveyed the bridge carefully, even getting on her hands and knees to peer under it.

"What are you doing?" Andras asked, a note of exasperation in his voice.

Irene circled around to look at the bridge from the other side, "I'm thoroughly assessing this bridge from every angle *before* I throw a nutty. It's a new thing I'm trying."

Andras raised an eyebrow, but the corner of his mouth quirked up the teensiest bit as well. Irene grinned and then resumed her examination. Finally, she straightened up and dusted off her hands.

"And?" Andras prompted.

"Yeah, it's really just a wire stretched over a canyon filled with fire."

"Did you really believe it would turn out to be anything else?"

"Not really, but I was hoping."

The corner of Andras's mouth turned up again. "Can we continue our journey? This is clearly not the way, and we should not linger."

Irene crossed her arms and surveyed the bridge with dissatisfaction. "I'm not so sure about that... I think this *is* the way. Jonah told me about this — a bridge the width of a hair. There was something about your heart needing to be as light as a feather and you'd float across, but if you'd been bad, your heart would be heavy and you'd fall to your death or get ripped apart by demons." Irene frowned, not entirely sure she had the story straight. "Or something like that."

She reached for Andras, putting a hand on his back and pushing him toward the bridge. "Here, why don't you test the bridge, see if it will hold you."

Andra sidestepped her hand and shot her an incredulous look. "Why me? I am near eight stone heavier than you."

"Because you're the saintly one — if anyone's heart is lighter than a feather here, it's yours."

Andras growled, but he stepped to the edge of the bridge. Tentatively, he put one foot on the wire, which immediately began to bounce unsteadily. Andras hastily withdrew. "I do not believe this bridge would hold our weight even if we could balance on it. This is impossible. It is not the way."

Now it was Irene's turn to growl with exasperation. "Okay, fine. Then I guess we—"

There was a shout in the distance. Instinctively, she and Andras both turned toward the sound.

"What now?" she asked.

Andras immediately broke into a run. Irene didn't even bother to try and stop him—she knew it was futile. Once a knight, always a knight. She raced after him, the bag bumping awkwardly against her hip with every step.

The source of the shouting was soon apparent. Shadows had surrounded a group of ghosts, solid like her and Andras. The attackers had hold of one woman's shadow, and Irene could see the inky shape flailing to free itself as the attackers pulled it free. The woman screamed and then winked out of sight.

Irene wanted to hang back, but Andras plunged into the melee, leaving her no choice but to follow. She threw herself into the fray, punching and kicking at the attacking shadows in an attempt to drive them back or, at least, hold them off long enough for the ghosts to escape, but her hands simply passed through the dark shapes.

A man to Irene's right cried out, and Irene turned just in time to see a group of attacking shadows latch onto the man's shadow and pull it away. As soon as his shadow was separated from his body, the man disappeared. The man's shadow, which still remained, stopped struggling against the attackers, and they let it go. Irene's eyes widened in horror as the man's shadow instantly turned to the nearest ghost and attacked, grabbing hold of the woman's inky black ghost body.

Irene felt a pull behind her, dragging her backwards. She tried to whirl around, but was prevented by something holding onto her. She twisted and looked behind her; the attackers had hold of her shadow. She flailed, trying to knock them away, but, as before, her fists passed right through them like they were fog. She was jerked back violently with a ripping, tearing pain that seared along her back from head to foot as if someone had reached in and attempted to yank her spine from her body. She screamed.

She tried to fight her way free, flopping and flailing like a beached fish, her fists and feet as useless as sacks of air against the shadows. She managed to pull free long enough to spin around and away from her attackers, and as she did so, she felt something heavy move with her, a counterweight throwing her off balance. She moved again, side-stepping an onrushing attack, and realized the weight was from her own shadow. She could feel it. It moved as she moved, but with mass and weight, and it was like she was wearing a backpack full of water, the shadow's weight overbalancing her.

Two attackers latched onto her shadow, and she could feel that, too, the pressure and pull of them like someone catching hold of her sleeve.

She flailed at the shadows, trying to punch them, push them, shove them away, anything to make the increasing pressure and pain stop. As she twisted and fought, she caught sight of her shadow; it was diagonally behind her now instead of directly behind her, and as she raised a leg and kicked at an attacker, so did her shadow. Her leg passed through her intended target; her shadow's leg, however, connected. The attacking shadow fell back, momentarily stunned.

Irene lashed out again, punching hard with a fist, and her shadow's fist connected with an attacker's jaw. Elation sizzled through her, bringing with it a second wind. With a triumphant cry, she summoned her flagging strength and pulled free of her attackers. She pivoted, lining her shadow up with one of the attacking shadows, and air-boxed, aiming her shadow's fists at the attacker. Her shadow's right hook connected, knocking the attacking shadow back.

She whirled around, looking for Andras, giddy with excitement, ready to shout this new information to him. She spied him through the confusion and air-boxed her way through the shadows. She was almost there, just a couple of arm length's away. She opened her mouth to call to him, to show him how to fight his way free, when a pair of shadows grabbed hold of Andras's shadow. Andras's shadow flailed, as if alive and independent of Andras. Andras gave a strangled cry of pain and then, with a ripping sound, the attacker pulled Andras's shadow away. The attackers swarmed it, and it disappeared from view.

Time seemed to stop.

For a moment, it seemed as if nothing had happened, as if Andras had suffered no ill effect from the loss of his shadow. Then Irene watched in horror as Andras winked out of sight.

Fourteen

It was dark.

Jonah realized it was because his eyes were closed. He had squeezed them shut when they'd run through the red door. There had been that moment, as always happened when he went through a red door, of suspension, of feeling, just for a fraction of a second, as if he ceased to exist and then, just as quickly, popped back into existence. Only, this time, it had been more pronounced – not a tiny, infinitesimal blip but an actual countable quantity of time in which he had been suspended between life and death.

Cautiously, he opened his eyes.

Then he gasped.

Every time he'd passed through a red door, he'd ended up in the same place – the endless void of swirling gray mist. He'd spent hours in that nowhere place, walking in various directions, without any results. There was never any variance in the void, and he'd come to suspect that, even though he thought he was walking, he wasn't actually moving at all. Instead, it was entirely possible that each time, he was simply suspended between realms, his molecules exploded without the power to re-coalesce, leaving him as nothing more than a free-floating consciousness trying to make sense of its surroundings.

This time, however, was different. He found himself standing at the far end of a sweeping, gravel driveway, wide, smooth, and bordered on both sides by a perfectly manicured lawn of seemingly infinite size and a long row of symmetrical hemlock trees. It was night and wrought-iron lamps lit the way. The drive ended in a flourish of stone steps leading to what could only be described as a palace. Warm, inviting light blazed from the windows and the open doors.

Something gripped his hand painfully. He looked down and saw that his fingers were interlaced with Char's. He looked up into a wide-eyed gaze of astonishment.

"Where are we?" Char asked, goggling at their surroundings. He tried to disengage his hand from hers, but she had him in a death grip.

"I think we crossed over when we went through the door," he said. He finally managed to shake her loose. He rubbed his hand to soothe away the numbness as he slowly turned in a circle, taking in everything. The terror of a moment ago gave way to a rising wave of elation. He tried to hold down the excitement building inside of him; he'd been trying to cross over to the land of the dead for almost a year, only to meet with disappointment every time. Best not to get excited until he was sure.

"So this is the afterlife?" Char asked, her eyes wide, mimicking him and turning in a circle. "Wow! Pretty swanky! No wonder you like spending so much time here!"

Jonah shook his head. "I've never been here."

Char looked incredulous. "What? Never?"

Jonah shook his head harder. "I told you—every time I ever went through a red door, I just ended up in a gray void."

"So what changed?"

Jonah was at as much of a loss as she was. He had no idea why this time was different. He ran through all the variables. It couldn't have been the Ugly; they had chased him into the void before. He hadn't done anything differently before going through the door—hadn't used any charms or ghost wards, hadn't said any incantations or prayers. The only thing different was Char. He frowned at her thoughtfully, eyes narrowed. Was just the presence of another person enough, or was it that she was psychic? Maybe that was it.

"What?" Char said, her expression becoming wary. She took a half step back. "Why are you looking at me like that?"

Then it dawned on him. Being psychic wasn't the only unique thing about Char. She had also given him something, something he'd never had with him before in any of his attempts. "Holy crap!" he cried. He reached under his collar and pulled out the crystal she had given him. He let it rest on his open palm as he stared at Char, his eyes wide. "Char, your crystal—it worked!"

Char looked from him to the crystal and back again. A grin slowly bloomed across her face. "I told you I could help!"

Jonah returned the grin, feeling it spread from ear to ear. He grabbed Char's hand, unrestrained excitement washing over him. "Come on! Let's go!"

He set off at a fast walk, which soon turned into a jog, the gravel crunching loudly underfoot. With each step, his heart beat faster, and his jubilation grew. His feet hardly touched the ground. He was really here. He was really going to see Irene again. Would she look the same? Would she recognize him? Would she be glad to see him?

The faint strains of an orchestra playing a waltz floated out of the open doors, growing louder as they approached. Jonah, still holding Char's hand, mounted the wide, sweeping stairs, and then paused in front of the pair of liveried footmen flanking the top, the dusky red of their jackets gleaming brightly under the lamps encircling the perimeter of the flagstone patio that extended from the stairs to the French doors of the palace.

"Whoa," Char said, giving him a wide-eyed look.

Jonah had to admit, the pomp was impressive.

The double set of glass doors before them was standing open, and invitingly, beyond the threshold, there was music and laughter. The two footmen stared past Jonah and Char as if they couldn't see them. Jonah took this to mean it was okay for them to enter. He stepped forward, and Char's hand tightened on his. Jonah glanced down at her. There was a hint of uncertainty in her eyes, but she didn't show any signs of wanting to back out. Jonah flashed her a reassuring smile and gave her hand a squeeze. Then they stepped inside.

It was as if they had entered one of the fabulous palaces from history—Versailles or Topkapi. Everything was silk and crystal and gilt. A short, opulent hallway, papered in palest blue silk and adorned with ornate mouldings and woodwork, led to a large ballroom that was like something from a movie. The walls of the ballroom were sumptuously papered in wine-red damask and the ceiling was painted in gold gilt that followed the swirls and flourishes of lavish mouldings. Gilded chandeliers, glinting like diamonds, dripped from the ceiling. In a far corner, a string quartet played. Before them, a throng of men and women dressed in velvet and lace danced a dizzying Viennese waltz, moving so fast they were little more than a blur.

Char and Jonah just stood in the doorway and gaped until polite coughs from a pair of waiters in white wigs forced them to move inside. They scampered in and moved to the side, squeezing up against the wall as they tried to get their bearings, their eyes taking it all in.

"Whoa!" Jonah said, the words escaping in a long, slow exhale.

"Double whoa," said Char.

Cautiously, still not quite certain where they were or whether they were welcome, Jonah edged to the right and Char followed, never letting go of his hand. They crept around the periphery of the room, trying not to attract notice.

Elegantly dressed ladies and gentlemen holding flutes of champagne gave them courtly nods as they passed, as if the appearance of two teenagers—one in the decidedly modern fashion of Dockers and a long-sleeved t-shirt and the other in a black t-shirt with a skull and crossbones on it and knee-high, platform combat boots with purple laces—wasn't in the least bit strange.

Jonah relaxed as he slowly became acclimated to their surroundings and realized that they were neither going to be attacked nor thrown out. A pair of dancers whirled past so close the woman's swirling dress brushed against Char's legs. Mesmerized, Char and Jonah paused to watch the couple, their eyes following the dancers around the room.

"Do you see Ms. Hot Stuff anywhere?" Char asked, craning her neck.

Jonah shook his head. "I don't think this is her kind of dancing." He still wasn't sure this was the afterlife. He wasn't sure where else they could be, but he didn't want to jump to any conclusions just yet.

He pointed to the far end of the room. "There's a doorway down there. Let's see what's through there."

The next room, wallpapered in white silk and hung with white flowing, gauzy drapes, was empty, save for a dais upon which rested a trio of harps, from which emitted a gentle, soothing melody played by unseen hands. Scattered upon the floor around the room were plush, white pillows, mounded like clouds. "Wow," said Char. "It's so... white!" Her voice echoed in the empty space.

There was something unnerving about the vast, empty white-on-white room, especially since the previous one had been so crowded.

"Why's it empty?" Jonah asked.

Char shrugged. "Probably because it's kind of boring." She pointed across the room to the wide, open doorway that led to yet another room, and they hurriedly crossed to it.

This new room was as large as the red ballroom they had first crossed through, and like the ballroom, filled with people, though the atmosphere here was very different than the previous two rooms.

This room resembled a rustic, though endlessly huge, hunting lodge, complete with exposed wooden beams and stag and boar heads on the walls. The room was filled with thick-necked men and women, dressed in animal pelts and rough leather breaches. The middle of the room was taken up by an enormous table made of rough-hewn wood planks. Jolly, carousing men and women guzzling from tankards squeezed together on the wooden benches that ran the length of the table on both sides. Everyone sang merrily — shouting the words at the top of their voices — clanging silverware and cups on the tables, stopping only to take sloppy drinks. The singing, laughter, and raucous jeering were deafening; Jonah had an urge to clap his hands over his ears just so he could hear himself think. People danced here, too, though in more of a wild, raucous country dance, than the smooth, gliding waltz of the previous room.

"Holy crap!" Jonah said in a breathless whisper. "It's Valhalla!"

They had barely stepped into the room when they were accosted by a man, large, red-faced, and laughing, who thrust an enormous, carved horn set around the rim and tip with silver and red jewels and full of strong smelling ale at Char. "Skaal!" he cried.

Char shot Jonah a quizzical look, but before Jonah could say anything, the man thrust the horn at Char again, sloshing half the contents down her front. "Drink up, little woman!"

Char shot Jonah a grin brimming with mischief and reached for the horn. "Well, if you insist!"

Jonah grabbed the horn from her hand and thrust it back at the man. Then he grabbed Char's hand, dragging her away before the Norseman could say another word.

"What is wrong with you?" Char cried, trying to pull her hand free of Jonah. "You might have offended him. When in Rome..."

"Don't you know anything? You never eat or drink anything in the underworld. You get stuck there if you do."

"Ew!" Char cried, managing to pull free. "Great." Theatrically, she wiped both of her hands on her shirt, as if trying to rid herself of cooties. Jonah rolled his eyes and started forward again, jostling and shoving his way through the unruly crowd, toward a doorway at the far end of the hall.

They tumbled through this new doorway into what turned out to be a walled garden — shockingly silent after the previous room.

"Whoa," Jonah said in a hushed tone, turning in a circle to take in the idyllic scene. Neatly trimmed hedges and clusters of colorful flowers were carefully arranged around paths lined with mosaic stepping-stones, statuary carved with leering faces, and stone fountains. Heaping mounds of luscious, ripe fruits, haphazardly piled, dotted the landscape, perfuming the air with a delicious aroma. People in loin clothes lounged here, lolling on the ground and feeding each other from the piles of fruit.

Beside them was a mud-colored lump of stone carved with a crude and grotesque dragon or serpent surrounded by a highly-stylized depiction of the sun, and Jonah ran a reverent hand over it. "Tlalocan," he whispered to Char.

"Huh?"

"Mayan afterlife."

He had no doubt now; they were definitely in the afterlife. Or, more correctly, they were in all the afterlifes at once. Mayan, Christian, Norse, Dao... they were all here. Which meant this place was vast — and somewhere in all this vastness, was Irene.

There was a doorway at the far end of the garden, and he gestured to it. "Come on," he said, striding resolutely forward.

"Can't we slow down a bit, take a look around?" Char asked, breathlessly trying to keep up with him.

"Let's find Irene first." Char's expression drooped with disappointment, as if he'd just told her she wasn't getting any presents for her birthday. "Believe me, I want to look around, too. And we will — but after we find Irene."

They crossed through the arch and found themselves in another crowded ballroom, this one wallpapered in pale-yellow silk. The dancers here were not dancing in pairs as those in the red room had; here they were involved in some kind of group dance, weaving in and out in a complicated pattern, occasionally pairing off to turn in a circle, clap, or make some other movement, and then returning to the intricate steps of the dance.

Char giggled and turned to Jonah. Sketching him an awkward bow, she said, "May I have this dance?"

Jonah scoffed. "You're a girl—you're supposed to curtsy."

"Oh, come on," Char said. "I've never been to a dance before. Please?"

Suddenly realizing she was seriously asking him to dance, Jonah gave her a dubious look. "First of all, this isn't really that kind of—"

"Just one dance! Please?"

Jonah gestured wildly at the dancers. "I don't even know how to dance like this!"

"Who cares? That's not the point."

Jonah groaned in exasperation. Char, taking this as acquiescence, squealed with delight and grabbed his hands, twirling the pair of them in a wide circle. Jonah stumbled, managed to catch himself, and then grinned despite himself as Char laughed.

They didn't bother attempting to copy the dancers in the center of the room; neither of them had any idea where to begin. Instead, they simply twirled back and forth at arm's length in their corner of the room, first one way and then the other, like children.

Char's hair flew about her in a dusky halo, and her face was aglow with delight. Jonah could feel his grin spreading, not just across his face, but down through his chest to his insides. Char gazed up at him with a look of such pure happiness that the feeling seemed to jump from her to him, and for a moment, Jonah felt almost weightless, the crushing ever-present lump in his chest lifting.

The room, the chandeliers, the dancers grew blurry and then faded to the background, and for a moment, they were the only two people in the world. Nothing existed but them. Jonah's insides gave a strange kind of lurch, and his stomach flip-flopped, like the ground had suddenly given way beneath his feet. Before he could fully register the feeling, Char wobbled and then collapsed against him, laughing.

"Oh my God, I can't breathe," she said, between gasps of laughter. "I'm so dizzy." She hung onto Jonah's neck for support, leaning her head against his shoulder as she tried to catch her breath. Reflexively, Jonah's arms tightened around her. An odd feeling came over him, and he wasn't sure if he wanted to hold her tighter or push her away.

A touch on his arm made him start, and he sprang away from Char, feeling guilty. A woman of indeterminate age — not old but not a girl, either — and elegant bearing stood beside them. She was dressed in a flowing gown of emerald green trimmed in silver, shirred and ruffled in an elaborate, graceful display, and her dark, tightly curled hair was ornately coiffed, braided throughout with various gems. She was flanked by two attendants, women in fluttering, jewel-toned gowns, one of pink and one of blue. Then Jonah noticed the golden circlet resting on the woman's head.

Disconcerted, he stepped back. "Your... your... highness," he said, flailing for an appropriate title.

"Highness?" the woman crowed in delight with a tinkling laugh. She beamed at him, her eyes sparkling like jewels. Then she held out a hand. "May I have this dance?" The woman glanced at Char. "That is, if you don't mind."

Char darted a confused glance at Jonah and then back at the woman and shrugged.

Jonah's eyes widened, and he took another step back. The woman laughed again. "I don't bite."

"I'm sorry, it's just... I don't know how to dance."

The woman's smile gentled. "Then we can look foolish together."

The two attendants glared at him, silently telegraphing a threat should he refuse. Not sure he really had a choice, Jonah helplessly took the woman's hand. She gave him another smile, this one reassuring, stepped closer, and put a hand on his shoulder, leaving him no choice but to put his free hand on her waist. He'd never held a woman around the waist before, let alone danced with one like this, and his hand fluttered indecisively over her hip before coming to rest.

The woman took the lead, moving them slowly into the throng of dancers in the middle of the room in a series of leisurely, waltz-like steps. Jonah tensed, sure he was about to trod all over her dress or her feet. However, to his surprise, he was able to follow the woman's lead, moving his feet in the small steps without too much trouble. The woman's expression turned serious, the gentleness of a moment ago fading away, leaving only a brusque, business-like demeanor in its wake. "To what do we owe the pleasure of a visit from a spirit walker?" she asked. "We haven't seen one of your kind in a long time."

"Spirit walker?" he asked. He stumbled slightly as his concentration on moving his feet slipped. He grimaced and looked down, trying to get his feet back in order. The other dancers were still engaged in a group dance, but none seemed to notice the lone pair of dancers waltzing in and out of the crowd.

"You are not the first member of the land of the living to peek into the world beyond. In my time, they were quite common."

Jonah's eyes jerked back to the woman's face. "In your time?"

The woman laughed, the notes rippling up and down the scale. "Very subtly done, to be sure, but I'm not going to tell you my age."

"I wasn't… I didn't mean… I mean—"

The woman smiled at his confusion. "So, what brings you here?"

He didn't see any need to lie—not that he was sure he could anyway. Something about her demeanor and the way she seemed to gaze right through him to his innermost thoughts made him suspect she already knew the answer to her question. "I'm looking for someone… a friend."

"Oh? And how fares your search?"

Jonah frowned. "Not great so far. But I'm just getting started."

There was a sliver of steel in the woman's voice now when she spoke though her tone was still gentle and friendly. "You may seek your friend, spirit walker; attempt to discover the mysteries of the dead, if you will, though I fear it will do you no good. We have passed beyond you; you are but a ghost to us. You move like a shadow in the night, your cares and concerns of no import to us. We have no desire to return to the land of the living. Do not seek to disturb the revels of those who rest here most willingly."

Jonah swallowed hard, aware that he was being threatened. However, he met the woman's eyes with a steely look of his own as he said, firmly, "I'm not trying to disturb anyone... I just want to find my friend and make sure she's okay."

The woman's look softened minutely. "All here are well. None abide unhappily." The woman stopped dancing and released him, just as the music ended. As if by magic, her two attendants reappeared at her sides, while at the same time, Char materialized — somewhat possessively — at his.

The woman curtseyed gracefully. "I shall keep you from your search no longer." Jonah attempted to execute a stately bow, but by the time he had straightened up, the woman was gone, having melted back into the crowd.

"Who was that?" Char asked.

Jonah, stared thoughtfully into space, running through all the various sovereigns of the afterlife. He gave a slow, half-hearted shrug. "I think she might have been Persephone."

Char raised an eyebrow.

"Queen of the underworld," he added.

"Ah. What did she want?"

Jonah shrugged again, but underneath the nonchalant veneer was a thread of worry. The woman had been warning him — about what wasn't entirely clear, though he had a suspicion. In the stories, the dead were never allowed to leave the underworld. Often, the living came to reclaim a soul from the afterlife, and the cost to do so was quite high if the ruler of the underworld let them go at all. The fact that the woman had found him so soon after they had arrived suggested the entrance to the afterlife was watched—and guarded. She'd been warning him not to try and take Irene back to the land of the living with him. Well, she could threaten him all she liked; he'd get Irene out of here one way or another.

"Come on," he said, jerking a hand for Char to follow him across the room to the next doorway. "We need to keep going."

They crossed through the doorway and found themselves outside, standing in a vast, rolling field that disappeared into the distance. They blinked rapidly, blinded by the sudden sunshine and crisp, fall-like air.

"Whoa!" said Char, quickly checking that a doorway back inside the palace remained behind them. Reassuringly, there were two doorways in the brick wall behind them, set a few feet apart.

"Double whoa!" said Jonah.

They strained their eyes looking into the distance, but there was nothing to see—just an endless, rolling field of close-cropped grass.

In the next instant, though, the ground shook beneath their feet, and a noise like thunder sounded in the distance. They tottered and flailed to keep their balance.

"What is that?" Char asked, clutching Jonah's arm and pressing close to him.

Jonah scanned the area and noticed a cloud of dust approaching from their right. In another moment a herd of horses and riders galloped past, dirt flying from the horses' hooves. Jonah and Char cringed and turned away, trying too late to shield their faces from the muck.

"Ewww!" Char cried, wiping a lump of dirt from her nose. She looked at Jonah and laughed as he pulled a clump of grass from his hair.

"Welsh or Native American afterlife," he said dryly, turning to the doorway behind them.

This entryway led to a multi-floored library, innumerable shelves lining the vast walls stretching higher than the eye could follow. There were people here, sunk deep into over-stuffed, leather-lined armchairs and immersed in reading. The only sound here was the hushed and reverent whisper of pages turning. They tiptoed through this room, looking for a doorway, which they found in a corner opposite where they had entered.

"Shouldn't we check the entire room?" Char asked in a hushed undertone as they approached the door. "For Irene, I mean."

Jonah scoffed. "Irene hates libraries."

Char rolled her eyes. "Why am I not surprised?"

The next room took them outside again to another walled garden, this one more wild and free than the Mayan one, with fruit trees twined with vining plants. The people here, naked, strolled leisurely through the garden, arms locked about each other.

Char and Jonah, unable to stop themselves from staring in a combination of fascination and embarrassment, exchanged wide-eyed glances.

"Eden?" Jonah said.

Unable to hold it in any longer, Char burst into laughter. Jonah grinned and, heads down, eyes averted, they hurried toward the next doorway. Char continued to laugh, unable to get her giggles under control. "You don't want to look for Irene in here?"

"No," Jonah said emphatically.

They tumbled through the doorway and found themselves in another ballroom, only this one was wallpapered in navy blue and ornamented with silver leaf on the walls and ceiling.

Jonah gazed around the room, taking in the whirl of dancers, the elaborate gowns, the wigged footmen passing amongst the guests with trays of champagne.

"Are you starting to get a 'Masque of the Red Death' vibe?" Char asked.

"Huh?"

"It's a story—"

"By Edgar Allan Poe, yeah, I know."

"Yeah, well this place is starting to remind me of that story—the way there's all these people in these differently themed rooms, and they're all partying like there's no tomorrow."

Jonah turned this over for a moment, comparing where they were with what little he knew of the story, trying to understand Char's comparison. "You think Edgar Allan Poe was here?"

Char's eyebrows shot up in disbelief. "What? No, I wasn't suggesting—"

Jonah nodded, the idea growing on him. "It makes sense. He wrote about death a lot—must be because he could visit the land of the dead, like me. Heck, maybe he even had the book that I have!"

Char shook her head and rolled her eyes. "I was going more for a sense of forced gaiety in the face of impending doom, but, sure, your rather strange and far-fetched idea works, too."

"Doom?" Jonah scoffed. "There's nothing creepy here. In fact..." He scanned the room, his lips pursed as the subtle thought that had been nagging at him since they'd arrived finally crystalized. Setting aside the fact that Irene wouldn't be caught dead waltzing or in a library or wandering naked in a garden, and that her letters had indicated she was outside, at a river, there was another glaring indication that they weren't in the right place: Valhalla, Heaven, Eden, Tlalocan... they all had one thing in common. They were where the happy dead went.

Disappointment sizzled through him, instantly souring the happiness of a few moments ago. "You know what—let's go." He turned back toward the doorway through which they had just come.

"Go? Wait... you mean we're leaving?"

"Irene's not here." Frustration burned like acid in his gut. He pushed blindly through the throng, numbness and anger warring within him. All that time, all that effort... for nothing. He was back to square one.

"What do you mean? This place is huge; we haven't even searched half of it yet."

"I can tell she's not here. This isn't where she went." Bitterness bubbled over, and he desperately wanted to punch something. He tried to tamp the feeling down; he'd give vent to his feelings in private, away from Char's prying, mocking eyes.

"How do you know she isn't here?" Char said, a note of insistence creeping into her voice. "We've hardly even looked."

Jonah stopped dead in his tracks and gestured wildly to the rooms around them. "Look around. These people are all happy. This is Valhalla and Elysium and Eden—the places people go to carouse and rejoice and celebrate a life well lived. These people don't mind that they're dead. In fact, they're thrilled. It's one endless party."

"And let me guess—Irene was not happy to be dead?"

Jonah turned away from her with a scowl and resumed heading for the doorway back the way they had come. "No. She was pissed. This is the last place she'd be. No, she's somewhere else." Waiting at a river to pay a coin to a ferryman—that sounded like the Greek or Egyptian afterlife to him. And if she hadn't then crossed into Elysium, that left Tartarus or Hades—basically Hell. He'd been right to worry. She *was* in trouble.

They crossed into the previous room, navigating carefully between the jostling throng. Jonah barely paid attention as his mind worked furiously.

"What do you mean, someplace else? Where else do the dead go when they cross over if not here?"

Jonah's scowl deepened. As usual, Char wasn't getting the hint that he didn't really want to talk anymore. "Lots of places."

"Like where?"

A pang went through him as the ever-present image of a burning lake of fire burned in the forefront of his mind. "In one of her letters, Irene said she was in a city and then in a forest—a dark, creepy forest. Based on the description, I think she was in the place where the Restless Dead go."

"Sounds charming."

Grimly, he said, "Exactly."

And then she took a boat to Hell.

"Look, I'm sure she's fine," Char said hurriedly, in an obvious, though fruitless, attempt to reassure him.

He stared straight ahead as they wove through the crowd, trying to block out the nagging worry growing inside of him.

They crossed back into the Norse room and then into one of the gardens and then into an unfamiliar room. Jonah paused for a second, trying to get his bearings. "Did we come through here before?" he asked.

Char shook her head. "I think you took a wrong turn out of the garden."

There had been only one way out of the garden—Jonah was sure of it. A feeling of unease started to take hold of him as he turned around and headed back through the doorway they had just come through. He stopped short the second they stepped across the threshold. Instead of passing back into the garden where they had just been, they now stood in the white room with the harps.

"What the..." Jonah looked around, his unease growing. "Wasn't this just Tlalocan?"

Char stared at him, her eyes wide, and nodded.

"Come on," Jonah grabbed her hand, a sinking feeling spreading upwards from the pit of his stomach, and headed for the far end of the hall. In all the stories, getting into the Underworld was easy; it was getting out that was hard. He recalled Persephone's warning, and his stomach lurched. He sped up and they passed through the doorway into another unfamiliar room.

"Wasn't this where Valhalla was?" Char asked, but Jonah didn't pause—he just strode resolutely forward, his jaw set, dragging Char with him. They passed straight through the room and in the next instant found themselves back in the blue ballroom.

"I don't understand," Char said. "How could we possibly be here again?"

The sinking feeling was getting worse, giving way to an uneasy sense of inevitability. However, he refused to admit defeat just yet.

"Maybe it's a different room that just looks like the room we were in before?" Char said, clearly grasping at straws.

They turned around and headed back through the doorway they had just come through. It should have led to the room they were just in—the white room—but instead, they found themselves back in the blue ballroom.

"But... but... this is impossible!" Char cried, stopping dead in her tracks. Jonah tried to tug her forward, but she yanked her hand from his grasp. "What the hell is going on?"

Jonah tried to keep his face and voice perfectly neutral as he spoke—to keep both Char and himself from panicking. Panic wouldn't do either of them any good. "The rooms move. Nothing's fixed."

Char stared at him, the color draining from her face. "You say that like it's no big deal."

Jonah bit his lip and didn't meet her eyes, hoping that she couldn't hear the hammering of his heart. "It's a big deal," he said, his voice tight.

"How are we going to get out of here if we can't find our way back to the entrance?"

He didn't answer—couldn't answer; he didn't know.

More forcefully, Char said, "Jonah?"

But he didn't have to say anything—he knew she could see it in his face.

They were stuck.

Fifteen

"Andras!" Irene screamed, lunging for him, only to be dragged back as if by an anchor. Her shadow was under attack. Blind fury quicksilvered through her veins, and she struck out, directing her shadow's arms and legs with frenzied movements. Right. Left. Right. Left. Round-house kick. She'd lost track of the other ghosts. She'd lost track of Andras's shadow. The only thought thrumming through her head was getting free.

Two of the attackers fell back, and Irene dove through the opening and then, head down, she took off, running as fast as she could. In a moment, she had outpaced the attacking shadows, leaving them far in the distance.

Exhausted and out of breath, she stumbled once, twice, and then fell to the ground, landing on her hands and knees. She panted, trying to catch her breath, sobs intermingling with her ragged breathing. Her brain refused to work. She could form no coherent thoughts under the onslaught of panic, grief, and disbelief. Her mind churned, replaying her last image of Andras — his look of surprise, his sudden stillness, his blinking out of existence.

"Stop it," she cried out loud, cradling her head as if she could somehow stop the thoughts with her hands. "Just stop it!" Impatiently, she wiped at her eyes. This was no time to cry — Andras might still be alive. Just because he'd disappeared didn't mean he was dead.

Slowly, painfully, she regained control of her body, forcing herself to sit up, forcing herself to breath normally, forcing her brain to think. She climbed to her feet, where she swayed unsteadily as she surveyed the vast, empty fields stretching in all directions. The ever-present light breeze ruffled her hair, and impatiently, she brushed the hair from her face.

"Andras!" she shouted and then again, louder, "ANDRAS!" She bellowed his name for a third time, but the sound just died, unanswered, in the air.

She turned in a circle, straining her eyes in all directions in the searing golden light.

See without seeing.

If her regular eyes couldn't see him, maybe her ghost eyes could. She took a deep breath, held it for a second to steady her racing heart, and then released it. She breathed in again, slowly, and then exhaled, clearing her mind with each breath. Inhale. Exhale. In. Out. She closed her eyes and reached for the guiding fire, filling her mind with the solid, immovable wall that was Andras.

The flame flickered, tiny but sure. She latched onto the feeling, focusing her entire being on it. She took a deep, centering breath, pulling air down deep into her lungs and holding it there for half a heartbeat before releasing it just as slowly. She quieted her mind and thought of Andras, picturing his face in her mind's eye. She concentrated on every aspect of him that she could—his fathomless black eyes, his broad shoulders, his ridiculous clothes. His solidness, his dependability, his stoicism, the rare flashes of wit and humor. The way it felt when he was with her—aggravating, argumentative, condescending. Calm, assured, safe.

The flame within her sparked for a moment, making her heart jump with hope, but then just as quickly it turned to a warm, soothing glow that spread throughout her body, gentle and comforting but with no intensity, no clear indicators, no direction. It was if her internal compass thought she had already found Andras.

Did that mean it didn't know where he was?

Did that mean he was dead?

No!

Irene tried again and then a third time, with the same results: Andras was nowhere, or maybe he was everywhere. Either way, the compass was no help.

She closed her eyes and held herself still, trying to fall back through the layers of senses to the still place beneath sight and sound and taste, to the vast nothing underneath it all where she could sense everything on this plane, focusing on everything — or anything — rather than just on Andras. But she felt nothing — no indication of any living presence. A crushing certainty descended on her as she gave up trying to use her ghost senses. Andras was gone. Dead. Killed by the shadows.

NO!

She refused to believe that. She couldn't — she wouldn't — believe it. He was out there somewhere. He had to be. Stupid, arrogant, tight-lipped bastard that he was, he was out there.

She clenched her fists as, once more, panic welled up within her, and she wildly grabbed at memories of every time Andras had pissed her off — calling her 'woman,' glaring at her whenever she'd stopped to rest, sermonizing about her need to find God — to fight off the fear. Anger was good. Anger she could deal with.

Other memories intruded — Andras cradling her in his arms and carrying her to safety after a fight with a Nephilim; Andras tenderly kissing her forehead after Ian had left; Andras taking her hand and vowing to stay with her until she had reached the end of her journey.

With effort, she wrestled her emotions under control. There was no evidence that the shadows had killed Andras. Perhaps, instead, he had fallen or been pushed through one of the cracks between afterlife realms. Or maybe he had been made invisible by the shadows — after all, she'd seen that other ghost's shadow remain and join the fight after it had been separated from its owner. If the shadow remained, and was still alive, then why shouldn't the corresponding ghost be, as well? In fact, hadn't Jonah's scribbled letter about the Egyptian beliefs said as much?

But if so, how was she supposed to find Andras? She didn't even know where to start.

She could feel her heart rate climbing as panic returned, and she took several deep breaths, forcing herself to stay calm. There were options. Lots of options, lots of places to start. She just had to think of them. Think, damn it!

Okay, well, what would Jonah do?

Jonah would know what the shadows were and how to deal with them.

She ground her teeth. Okay, fine, what would Andras do?

Andras would pray.

She turned her eyes skyward. "If you're going to help me," she whispered to the air, knowing the Guide could hear her wherever she was, "now would be the time to do it."

Silence.

Thick, loud, silence.

"Oh, come on," she said. "No more games. No more jokes. No more riddles. I need your help. *Andras* needs your help."

She expanded her prayer outward, reaching out to the Guide, God, or any deity that might hear her.

Pleasepleasepleasepleaseplease, she silently prayed, pouring her entire soul into that single word. *If you really are God, you have to help me.*

The silence was absolute, and time ticked by slowly. Even her heart seemed to stop.

And there was no answer.

Disbelief washed over her, followed by blind, unreasoning fury. Andras had devoted his life to God, and now, when he needed God most, He was nowhere to be found... which meant either there wasn't a God—and Andras's life and his afterlife and all his piety and selflessness had been for nothing — or God was a bastard who didn't deserve Andras's sacrifices.

"Fuck you," she shouted to the air. "Fuck you!"

She lashed out at the only thing at hand — the wheat. She grabbed handfuls of it and ripped it free and then threw it with all her might. It impotently fluttered to the ground, which only enraged her more.

She spied her bag and snatched it up, upending the contents on the ground in a frenzy and then threw the bag down beside the scattered items. She dropped to her knees and clawed at the pile, scattering items right and left, wildly sifting through them, looking for something, anything that might help her. Tire iron? Pepper spray? Matches? Paper? Perfume? Blanket? Red bean paste buns? Another horse? Some birds? Junk, junk, junk.

She spied Jonah's last letter to her, and she snatched it up with a cry. Hastily, nearly tearing it, she opened it and scanned the words, sure there was something there that would help her find Andras.

Her elation was short-lived. *A person was made up of five parts* — yes, she knew that. *The heart, the spirit, the shadow, the body, and the breath* — got it. *After death the spirit joined with the shadow to become the Ankh* — check. None of this explained how a shadow could exist without a person or why shadows would attack a ghost or what happened if a ghost lost their shadow. She crumpled up the letter and threw it on the ground. It hit the ground, bounced, and then disappeared into the wheat. The moment it disappeared from view was too like the sight of Andras vanishing, and she turned away, squeezing her eyes shut to try and blot out the memory and the tears it raised.

Something about the act of turning was reminiscent of her and Andras trying to see their own shadows, and she wondered if her shadow was still behind her. She had assumed it was because she hadn't disappeared, but she realized now that didn't necessarily follow. She turned to look over her shoulder, twisting first one way and then the other, but the shadow, if it was still there, evaded her sight.

She glanced again at the pile of scattered items and spied her compact. She grabbed it, flicking it open in one practiced motion. She angled the mirror this way and that until she could see the shadow behind her.

She studied the reflection, but it revealed no answers to her. It was just a shadow.

"How do I find Andras?" she asked the reflection in the glass. The shadow didn't respond. "Can you hear me?" she asked, directing the question over her shoulder while still keeping the image in the compact's mirror in sight. "Tell me how to find him."

The shadow remained impassive. Irene wasn't even sure it could hear her.

She was wasting time. Andras was out there, of that she was sure, and he needed her – of that she was even surer. And she wasn't going to find him by praying, by reading letters, or screwing around with her shadow; she was going to find him by getting off her ass and going after him.

Her lips compressed into a thin line. Fine. She'd get Andras back, and she'd do it herself. No God. No Guide. No Jonah.

She assessed her options. There weren't many. There was Masudmensah – he'd said something about the shadows serving Osiris and that somehow losing one's shadow led to entering paradise. He must know something about what happened to a spirit after it lost its shadow. Only… Irene had lost Heru, and Masudmensah probably wouldn't be too happy about that. He wasn't likely to help her after she'd basically thrown his "gift" away – but maybe Heru would, if Irene could find her.

And she could always return to where she'd last seen Andras. If she couldn't fight the shadows, then the only other choice was to let her shadow be taken so she could end up wherever Andras had gone.

And, of course, as a last resort, she could try calling on Samyel for help.

Irene sifted through the items she'd scattered over the ground and picked up two origami birds. She grabbed a cigarette lighter, lit it, and held it to one of the paper birds. As it caught fire and began to burn, she held her breath. She wasn't sure this was going to work.

As the paper burned down to her fingertips, she let it go, tossing it into the air. A breeze caught it and swept it upward as it turned to ash. The ashes broke apart with a puff of smoke, but instead of a rain of sparks and dust, a pair of wings unfolded and a small, brown sparrow emerged, beating its wings to keep aloft.

It circled overhead while Irene quickly lit the second origami bird on fire; from its smoke, a tall, graceful, pure-white crane emerged. The crane stood still, regarded her solemnly.

"I need you to find a woman named Heru," Irene said to it, feeling a little stupid. She had no idea if this would even work—could the bird even understand her, and, if it did, would it do as she asked?

The crane continued to regard her for a moment, and then it turned, spread its wings, and with a mighty heave, launched itself into the air.

Irene held out her hand to the sparrow, which immediately began to spiral down to her, chirping the entire time. It landed on her outstretched hand and turned its head to regard her with one beady eye.

"I need you to lead me to where I last saw Andras," Irene said.

The bird chirped, but didn't move.

"Andras," Irene said, enunciating carefully. "Where he disappeared."

The bird still didn't move.

"Okay, fine, find me a big group of shadows, then," Irene said.

The bird chirped but still didn't take off. Impatiently, Irene shook her hand, tossing the bird into the air. With a disgruntled chirp, the sparrow took flight. It circled overhead for a moment and then spiraled higher until it disappeared from sight.

Irene stooped down and stuffed everything back into her bag. She hunted among the wheat for Jonah's letter, reluctant to leave anything he'd given her behind, but she couldn't find it. She didn't want to delay any longer as every second could mean Andras was getting farther and farther away from her.

She wasn't sure if either of the birds were going to come back — and come back having accomplished their mission — and she didn't want to waste time standing around waiting. At least she could try returning to the bridge and start her search from there. She surveyed the horizon, trying to orient herself, and realized everything looked the same. She had no idea which direction she had come from. She took a deep breath, closed her eyes, and reached for the internal compass, filling her mind with thoughts of the razor-wire bridge and the stream of ghosts flowing over it. The flame burst to life, pointing the way. She took one step, then another, and then broke into a run, covering ground as quickly as she could.

The butterflies reappeared. Then the snow. She ran through both without stopping. The fish replaced the butterflies, iridescently sparkling in the bright sunlight. Irene focused harder on the bridge and the blinding light and the light breeze caressing her face and the stalks of wheat scratching and tickling her thighs as she ran, trying to anchor herself in this plane so she didn't slide off. The fish faded away, replaced by a single solitary butterfly. It flitted ahead, and Irene almost thought it was trying to lead her, but she didn't dare focus on it, afraid it would pull her down a wormhole, away from Andras.

Soon, the crowd of faded, half-formed ghosts flowing over the wire bridge was in sight, and Irene slowed to a walk. In the distance was a black dot, growing larger by the second — shadows.

Overhead, she heard a sparrow's chirping cry. She looked up, and her sparrow was circling above her. When it saw that she had seen it, it swooped low, dipped a wing, and then rose again, lazily circling toward the shadows in the distance. Irene's heart sped up—those must be the shadows that had attacked her and Andras!

She had no plan other than to confront the shadows and get Andras back. She had no idea exactly how she was going to do that, but then again, seat-of-the-pants, making it up as she went was pretty much her modus operandi. She'd figure something out.

Irene straightened her back, seated the bag more firmly on her shoulder, and then, head down, marched resolutely forward. To reach the shadows, she had to pass through the throng of translucent specters in line to cross the bridge. Irene started through them and then stopped.

The ghosts were crossing the bridge.

She had thought the reason these ghosts were see-through and only half-formed was because they were on another plane. But the bridge was clearly on this plane—and the ghosts were crossing it. That had to mean that the ghosts were on this plane then.

After death, the spirit and the shadow combine to form the Ankh, Jonah's letter had said.

To cross the bridge made of wire, the spirit's heart must be lighter than a feather, he'd told her back on Earth.

The *spirit's* heart—not the ghost's heart, the spirit's.

If a spirit plus a shadow equaled a ghost, then a ghost minus a shadow had to equal a spirit. It was basic math—two minus one left one.

And the spirit had to weigh less than a feather.

She had told Andras that they were pure energy now, without bodies, but that wasn't entirely true. She had weight and mass—while still in the land of the living, she could pick things up and open and close doors and bump into people and generally carry on like she still had a body and took up space.

Or, perhaps, more accurately, her shadow had weight and mass and took up space. After all, it was her shadow that could punch and kick and hold onto the other shadows. Her spirit passed right through them.

Which meant one thing: to cross the bridge, a ghost had to lose its shadow.

And the bridge was the only way off this plane as far as she could tell.

In the time it took to think these thoughts, the throng of shadows and the stampede of ghosts—solid like her—fleeing in terror before the pursuing shadows had grown closer, and now there was no time to formulate any kind of plan of action beyond "run like hell" because they were heading straight for her.

It was like being in the middle of a cattle stampede. She had only a moment to register the massive crowd before they were upon her, coming at her from all angles. In an instant, she was in the thick of the chaos of fleeing ghosts and attacking shadows, deafened by the shouts of terror and screams of pain. She struggled vainly against the crowd as she tried to get clear but was buffeted from all sides. It was all she could do to keep to her feet as people came at her from every direction, ghosts, spirits, and shadows all mingled together in a blur of fast-moving bodies. The tangible and intangible intermingled, and she could no longer tell who had a shadow and who didn't, what was an attached shadow and what wasn't. It was chaos, the air so thick with the faded essence of phantasms she couldn't see more than a few feet in front of her. She stumbled and nearly fell, kept upright only by the tight press of bodies around her, and was carried along by the fast-moving flow.

They were being herded, the multi-directional streams of running ghosts converging into a single flow. A second later, Irene realized they were being herded toward the cliff. She dug in her heels and skidded to a stop, a hair's breadth from toppling over the edge of the cliff. Irene teetered there, windmilling her arms to keep from falling over. A woman, solid like Irene, ran right off the edge of the cliff beside her, the woman's flailing shadow the last thing Irene saw before the woman disappeared from view. A man to Irene's right teetered on the chasm's brink, then seemed to regain his balance. He looked over his shoulder at the approaching shadows and then, without hesitating, turned back to the canyon and jumped.

"No!" Irene screamed, trying to catch him. Her fingers brushed his arm, and then he was gone, falling away from her into the inferno below. Around her, others followed suit, running or jumping over the cliff's side and disappearing into the flames. Their anguished screams, like the howling of a storm-lashed wind, drowned out all other sounds. Irene turned and attempted to battle her way through the crowd and away from the canyon's mouth before she was knocked over the edge.

She was jerked backwards, as if she'd reached the end of a tether, and knife-like pain shot down her spine. Icy terror sizzled through her as she struggled to break free of the shadows holding her. She air boxed viciously, trying to blindly direct her shadow's blows at the attackers holding it. The pressure on her lessened, and she sprang forward. She kicked out indiscriminately, and the shadows fell back, creating an opening. Irene dashed through it. She ran as hard as she could at a stumbling, drunken gait on legs no longer able to hold her, the shadows right behind her. Her own shadow dragged behind, slowing her down as it strained toward the attackers.

She was racing back toward the canyon again and she swerved away, trying to change directions and head for safety. The air in front of her shimmered, and then Andras was there, blocking her way. He pointed to the gaping chasm of the canyon. In her head, his voice sounded: *Jump!*

There was no time for thought, no time for argument. The shadows were on her once more, ripping and tearing at her, peeling her ghost body away from her layer by layer. Blindly, her legs obeying before her brain could make up its mind, she turned to the cliff and jumped.

Sixteen

"Oh my God," Char said.

"Don't panic," Jonah replied, though it came out more like a command than a reassurance. "Look, we can just say our wake-up words and we'll go straight back to our bodies."

Char stared blankly at him. "Wake-up word? What do you mean?"

Jonah tensed, sure she had misunderstood him. "Tell me you set a wake-up word when you said the incantation?"

Char weakly shook her head. "I must have missed that part."

The words were so awful, so gut-grabbingly terrifying that his brain couldn't process them at first. She had to be joking. Only... she wasn't. He could tell by the look on her face. He grabbed her by the arms and shook her hard. "Damn it, Char! That's the only way to get back into your body! You're such an idiot! I told you not to mess around with this stuff!"

Char angrily wrenched herself from his grip. "Stop it!" she cried, shoving him away with both hands.

He stared at her, seething with anger and frustration and fear. It wasn't supposed to be like this. Irene was supposed to be here. And she'd be happy to see him. She'd need him to fix whatever problem she'd run into, and he'd do it, and then it would be like old times. They'd laugh and make fun of each other, she'd say something snarky, and he'd shut her down with a dead-panned retort. They'd argue, he'd outwit her like he usually did, and they'd explore the afterlife together, but properly this time—exploring for the sake of exploring, just for fun and just because, rather than on a schedule with time tables and restrictions and the constant underlying knowledge that they'd soon be saying goodbye.

Instead, he was back to square one. No, worse than square one because now they were stuck here, and even if he found a way to get them back home, he'd still have to find a way to get Char back into her body. For all he knew, there wasn't a way, and she was stuck as a ghost forever.

His gut clenched at the thought.

That sobering realization was enough to dispel his anger and disappointment. He breathed hard through his nose and ran a hand through his hair. He surveyed the room they were in, assessing options.

There weren't any that he could think of, other than to keep walking through the rooms until they randomly hit one with an exit. Without a word, his face stony with determination, he turned and set off once more, weaving around people as he headed for the far end of the room and the direction that Eden was supposed to be. Behind him, Char followed, muttering, "Oh my God" under her breath over and over, ruining his concentration.

Jonah gritted his teeth. "Will you stop that?" he said.

They marched in a straight line, going from room to room. Valhalla, the red ballroom, Tlalocan, the blue ballroom, and the library all flashed by as they passed through.

"Jonah…"

Jonah marched grimly on.

"Jonah…"

They passed into yet another room.

"JONAH!" Char grabbed his arm, forcing him to stop. "What are we doing?"

"If we just keep going in a straight line, then eventually we have to pass through all the rooms and end up at the beginning again, right?"

Char shook her head. "We've passed through Valhalla three times already!"

"Okay, fine." Jonah spun around and re-crossed into the room they had just left—the blue ballroom—and this time they found themselves in the library.

"What are we going to do?" Char asked, her voice rising in pitch.

"I don't know yet."

"Oh my God! Are we stuck here?"

"I don't know yet," Jonah said, hoping she'd get the hint to shut up. Her panic was grating, and there was a small—and growing—part of him that couldn't forget that it was entirely her fault they were stuck here. If she hadn't followed him, if she hadn't screwed up the incantation, if she hadn't blackmailed him into bringing her along, he'd just be able to say his wake-up word and end up back in the land of the living, no harm, no foul.

"We're stuck, aren't we?"

"Look, just give me a minute—"

"Oh my God, we are stuck!"

Jonah rounded her. "Shut up for a second, will you, and give me a minute to think!"

Char opened her mouth to respond, but Jonah cut her off. "Look," he said, struggling not to shout at her, "let's find some place quiet so I can sit and think."

Char glared at him, a mixture of accusation and fear in her eyes, her lips clamped tightly shut. He didn't give her a chance to say whatever angry thing she was thinking. Instead, he turned and led the way through the nearest doorway.

They crossed several rooms before they reached a garden—Tlalocan. They found a secluded corner amidst the lush, green vegetation and fragrant mounds of ripe fruit and sank down on a pair of small boulders, each carved with a variety of Mayan symbols—stylized suns, leering faces, and geometric patterns that repeated over and over. Jonah slumped on his rock, chin resting on one fist as he stared into space, his mind working furiously to recall everything he knew about the afterlife — and more importantly, how one left the afterlife.

"Are we dead?" Char asked bleakly.

"No."

"Are you sure?"

"Pretty sure." He was only half paying attention to her hysterics, hoping that if he ignored her, she'd calm down on her own, like Irene would have.

He thought about his bag, annoyed at himself for having dropped it. Surely there was something in there that would help them. "If only I had my bag right now," he muttered.

Char didn't reply. Then, after a long pause, and in a thoughtful voice, she said, "You packed a lot of stuff in that bag."

It didn't seem to be a question, so Jonah made a non-committal noise of assent.

"Because you knew this might happen," Char said, her voice oddly flat and unemotional. "That's why you packed so much stuff. You knew you might get stuck here."

Something in her tone warned him that she wasn't calming down at all; in fact, just the opposite. Jonah tensed, and his eyes warily slid to Char. She sat rigidly on her rock. Her face was white, two red spots standing out on her cheeks, and her hands were clenched in her lap.

"You knew," she said as soon as he looked at her, her voice rising sharply. "You knew, and you let me come with you anyway!"

Astonished, Jonah's jaw dropped open. "Let you come? You forced me to bring you. *I* told you not to come. *I* told you it was dangerous, and *I* told you not to come."

There was a sudden, chilling silence. Char began to tremble with anger from head to foot.

"You're seriously willing to die for this woman? Seriously? All this, just for her?"

"I'm not the one—"

"Liar!" Char shouted, jumping to her feet. "You're such a coward. Just admit it already!" Char trembled like a leaf, her hands clenched at her sides. She was breathing hard, and her nostrils flared.

"Knock it off," he said. He glared at her, and Char glared back. The only sound was Char's harsh breathing as they each attempted to stare the other down.

"Say it," Char rasped. "I want to hear you say it."

"I told you to—"

"SAY IT!"

Jonah went rigid, every muscle in his body tense. Slowly, he lifted his eyes, meeting Char's blazing anger with a steely look of his own. Coldly, deliberately, so there could be no mistaking his meaning or his resolution, he said, "Yes. I would do anything for her—*anything*."

Char's eyes narrowed, and her voice grew as cold and hard as his. "Even die?"

Something inside of him snapped. He had gone somewhere beyond anger, beyond rage. He'd gone so far into it he had come out the other side to a place where there weren't any emotions, just cold, hard, barren facts. He stood up, his limbs stiff and mechanical—every part of him was empty, as if it this body was no longer his, as if it belonged to someone else—and woodenly closed the distance between him and Char.

Char's eyes widened as he approached, and she looked like she wanted to take a step back, but she held her ground. He moved in close so they were standing toe-to-toe. He looked down at her, letting the conviction in his words show in his eyes.

"Even die," he said, enunciating each word carefully.

Char exploded, her words nearly incoherent as they burst forth in a torrent. "You are the most selfish person I have ever met—"

"Selfish! How do you figure that?"

"—you haven't just risked your own life, you've risked mine! And for what? Some stupid woman who doesn't even want to talk to you anymore! And what about your family and your friends—if anything happens to you, don't you think they'd be devastated? How could you do this to them? How could you—"

"Oh, you know what, don't stand there with your purple hair and your crazy clothes and tell me you don't know what it's like to feel invisible—"

"So, what? One day Auntie—or even me—was going to find you dead in our spare room—"

"—and to wish desperately that there was someone, *anyone*, in the world who got you, who understood you, and if you did find such a person, that you wouldn't do anything—*anything*—for them. Even die!"

"—and then what? We'd have to call your parents and tell them... what? That you'd rather be dead than—"

His voice rose above hers to a full-throated bellow. "No one was ever supposed to know—it would just look like a heart attack!"

The truth was finally out, and it hit them both simultaneously. He wasn't just willing to die—he'd been planning on it. Shock seared them both into silence. Jonah panted hard like he'd just run a marathon. For a second, he wasn't even sure what he'd said. Then he felt a jolt of horror as he realized how much he'd revealed—to both Char and himself. Char looked just as horrified.

He stumbled backwards and slumped back down on the rock, cradling his head in his hands. Emptiness washed over him, leaving him numb. For a moment, he was silent as he contemplated the hollowness he felt. For three long years, he'd held those words inside, desperately wanting to tell them to someone—*anyone*—and yet terrified to speak them aloud—even to himself.

He looked up. Char was watching him, still with the same look of horror on her face.

The way she was looking at him—he couldn't stand it. Words bubbled up, wrenched deep from inside. He wanted to explain, wanted her to understand—so she'd stop looking at him like that. "My whole life, I've been invisible—like I'm a ghost. It's like I'm not even there, you know? At school, I was ignored—I didn't even get beaten up for lunch money or bullied into doing people's homework. Half the time, my teachers couldn't even remember my name—they called me John or Jimmy or Joe. One called me J.J.—not like a nickname, but because all he could remember were my initials." Resentment sizzled through him, and his fists clenched at the memory.

"At home it was the same. My parents hardly paid attention to anything I did. My dad signed me up for a summer football camp one year. I told him I didn't like football. You know what he said? 'Course you do!' Like I don't know what I like. Like he knows better than me what I like."

Char's look of horror had turned into a kind of creeping dismay, as if he'd sprouted fangs or tentacles, and his insides twisted at the look in her eyes.

"And Irene?" she said quietly.

He swallowed the sudden lump in his throat. "Irene was different. She's the only person who ever treated me like a real person. She asked my opinion, she listened to my advice, even argued with me. She noticed when I wasn't around. That's certainly a lot more than my parents. I mean, Christ! I disappeared for days, even weeks, at a time, and they didn't even notice. I made up a story about going on a field trip to France so I could skip school to help Irene, and they were like 'Okay! Have a good time!' What are they, idiots? Of course I wasn't going to France!" He gave the ground a vicious kick, the festering, long-held resentment sparking once more within him.

Char dropped bonelessly to her own boulder and stared at him, her face full of sympathy. "Oh, Jonah…"

Jonah looked away again, unable to stand the look of pity, which was somehow worse than the look of horror she'd had only a moment ago. "I know what you're thinking. But it wasn't just me. It was the same for her, too. I know it was." Char had never seen the way Irene kept everyone at arm's length—everyone but him. With him, she'd let her guard down and had shown flashes—brief, to be sure, but increasing in frequency and duration—of her true self: warm, funny, and vulnerable.

Jonah could feel Char's look of doubt, and a quick glance at her out of the corner of his eye confirmed his suspicion. "You weren't there!" he burst out angrily. "You never saw—" He bit off his words and glared at her furiously, indignation temporarily overriding everything else. When she didn't challenge his statement, his anger subsided, leaving him hollow once more. He deflated. Softly, he said, "I felt like a real person when I was with her. I wasn't invisible, and I wasn't ignored, and I was allowed to have thoughts and feelings of my own. And now she's gone." His insides ached as if he'd been punched, and his arms curled reflexively around his abdomen, cradling it as if he could somehow hold the pain in.

"Oh, Jonah…" Char's voice cracked. He looked up. She bit her lip, and there were tears swimming in her eyes. "I'm sorry. I'm so sorry." She didn't seem to know what else to say—and really, there was nothing else that could be said. It was pathetic and depressing and horrifying all rolled together.

Jonah shrugged and, avoiding looking at her, tried to surreptitiously wipe a sleeve across his eyes.

"I get it," Char said softly. "I really do. And I get why you want to find her so badly and even risk your life to do it. In your place, I guess I'd do the same."

"But?"

Char shook her head. "No but… well, not exactly. I get why you want to find her. I get why you miss her. But Jonah, if your places were reversed, would you want her to risk her life to come after you? If I cared about someone that much, I wouldn't want them to risk their life for me. I'd feel like crap if anything happened to them."

Jonah started to shake his head, to protest, but Char cut him off.

"Maybe she meant what she said in that letter—that she doesn't want you to come after her. If she really is your friend, then she wouldn't want you to risk your life like this.

She'd want you to live your life and do all the things she never had a chance to do. You said she was pissed at being dead. The last thing she'd want is for you to be dead, too."

Jonah shook his head harder. "Irene wouldn't do that. She would never say that kind of cheesy, clichéd crap, and she *never* tried to tell me what to do or acted like she knew what was best for me, like I was just a stupid kid."

"You were fourteen! You *were* just a stupid kid!"

He started to protest and then stopped. The last thing Irene had said to him was, "Maybe wait until you're older to look me up." He'd thought it an invitation. It had never occurred to him that maybe she'd meant just the opposite — that she didn't want him to come after her at all. Jonah clenched his jaw so tight it ached. "Maybe. But she never treated me like one. And she never said stupid shit like, 'Oh, hang in there; it gets better' or 'You're still so young; you have your whole life ahead of you.' "

"I know you miss her, but people die, Jonah. All the time. The reason we're not supposed to know what's on the other side is so we let them go. That's how it works."

He jumped to his feet and gestured to the garden around them — to the relaxing people, the restful breeze, and the luscious fruits. "But that's the thing — it's not how it works. The dead are all around us; we've just shut our eyes to them. But we don't have to let them go — "

"Yes we do! The dead aren't alive, Jonah, not really. They don't make or create or invent — they just scavenge from the living. And they don't grow or change — how many dead do you see still wearing what they were buried in for cryin' out loud. I mean, look around you! Look at this place; there's a reason all the stories describe the afterlife as eternal and unchanging. The dead are the past, Jonah. They're what's come and gone. And that's why we have to let them go. Otherwise, they'll pull us down with them. We'd be so focused on the past we'd never look at the future."

Irene's words echoed in his head: *Life is short. The afterlife is forever.*

He stubbornly shook his head. "I just want to know that she's okay. What if she is in trouble? What if she's in Hell or being tortured or attacked by demons? How am I supposed to just go about my life knowing that there's a chance that the one friend I've ever had, the one person who ever gave a crap about me, is being tortured or worse? If there's even the tiniest possibility she needs help and I ignore that, how could I ever live with myself?" *Especially since it's my fault she left in the first place.*

Now Char looked exasperated. "And what if she is? Do you know how to fight demons or release someone from purgatory?"

Annoyance flashed through him. "Not yet. But I'll figure it out."

"Or die trying?"

Jonah didn't bother responding. They both knew the answer to that.

Char sighed. "And then what? You two will live happily ever after? Because I don't really see —"

"I know."

"I mean, she'll still be dead —"

"I *know.*"

"Even if you do overcome the age thing, which I really don't —"

"I KNOW!" Jonah jumped to his feet and began pacing, his hands jammed in his pockets. "You think I don't know? You think I chose to feel this way or that I like feeling this way? Trust me — I don't."

Char was silent and she appeared to be contemplating his words, her eyes growing sadder and sadder. Several long minutes passed in which there was only silence. When she finally spoke, her voice was soft. "Jonah, the thing is, I'm not like you. I don't want to die. I'm not ready — not by a long shot. I mean, jeez, I haven't even been kissed yet. I don't want to die before that happens."

Guilt washed over him. In the past, his experiments and plans had only ever involved himself. He'd never wanted, never expected, anyone to get hurt. "Look, if it makes you feel any better, I'm not particularly keen on dying just yet either. That's a last resort. So don't worry. We're not done just yet. I'm going to get you out of here. I promise."

He had no idea how he was going to make good on his promise, but now that he'd given his word, he'd have to find a way. He looked around, racking his brain for ideas on how to get them home.

"Okay, look, I can just say my wake-up word and get back to my body. So why don't I do that and then see if I can wake you up?"

"But what if you can't?"

"Then I'll come back."

Char shook her head vehemently. "No! Don't leave me here alone!"

"Char, I promise I'll come back—"

"Even if you do, how will you find me? Everything keeps moving around. You could spend a lifetime going from room to room and never find the one I'm in!"

Jonah frowned thoughtfully. "Well, I have a spell that lets me find things—I should be able to locate you."

"Yeah, you can locate me, but what if you can't get to me?"

"Well, we can test it out…"

Char sprang forward and clutched his arm. "No! Please, don't leave me here alone, Jonah. I mean it!"

He was surprised by the terror in Char's eyes and struck by the realization that she was depending entirely on him to fix this. Irene had never needed him in quite the same way— Irene was more stoic, more self-reliant. Even when she had needed his help, she would rather have died than admit it. Irene responded better to antagonism than sympathy; it got her fight response up, made her strong and resolute. The few times he'd offered to comfort Irene with a hug or reassuring word, she'd refused. Well, refused wasn't quite the right word. More like bit his head off.

He didn't think antagonism would work on Char, though; in fact, it would probably have the opposite effect. He tentatively put a hand on Char's shoulder, searching for something reassuring to say. "Don't worry, Char. I won't leave you. I promise."

To his relief, that seemed to work. Though the look of fear in her eyes remained, Char let go of his arm and rocked back onto her heels. "What are we going to do?"

Jonah thought hard for a moment, surveying the landscape around them for any obvious answers, and then an idea came to him. If they couldn't go *through* the mansion to find the exit...

He grinned. "If I learned one thing from Irene, it was to never take no for an answer — even if it means making up your own rules and doing things your own way. So... what would Irene do?" He held out a hand to Char.

Char shot him a questioning look as she gingerly put a hand in his. "What?"

Jonah pointed at the wall surrounding the garden. "We go over."

Seventeen

She expected annihilation — flesh-melting flames or bone-crunching impact. Instead, there was falling. Endless falling, first through heat and then through cold, through a blinding flash of light and then, finally, through a long stretch of darkness. There was no sensation of either falling quickly or slowly, of plummeting or floating, only of falling.

Finally, she landed — on her back — hitting the ground hard. The impact knocked the wind from her lungs, and there was an audible crack as her head slammed into the solid surface beneath her. Stars danced before her eyes as pain ricocheted through every inch of her.

She lay there, stunned, as, slowly, the world came back into focus. The first thing she realized was the stars weren't before her eyes. They were far away pinpricks of light, far overhead. She blinked, trying to orient herself. She was on her back, and it was dark. Tentatively she tried moving her right arm. She braced, expecting pain, but there was none.

You're dead, she reminded herself. *You can't feel pain.*

Telling herself that had never worked in the past, but this time she felt oddly numb, as if she was detached from her body. She wiggled her fingers and then moved her arm more fully. Then she repeated the movements with the other arm. Then she tried her legs. Everything seemed in working order. Relieved, she sat up.

She took a fortifying breath and then looked down at herself, expecting to find something wrong. However, everything was intact—no broken bones, no torn dress, not even a missing shoe.

The memory of Andras appearing before her, exhorting her to jump, flashed across her mind, and she twisted around, searching for him.

"Andras?"

Her voice echoed with a dark, hollow quality, as if she was in a cavernous space.

There was no reply.

"Andras?" she repeated louder and then shrank from the cacophonous sound of her voice echoing as it bounced from surface to surface.

Her heart sank. Had she hallucinated Andras?

There was a strange sensation of comforting familiarity, almost as if the air vibrated, and Irene felt a hand brush across her shoulder. The hairs on the back of her neck stood up, and she whipped around, looking for who or what had touched her. Though the light filtering down from above was faint, Irene could see that there was no one there. The air vibrated again, a feeling reminiscent of the charge before a lightning storm, and she definitely felt as if someone was near. She jumped to her feet.

"Andras?" She craned her neck in all directions, searching for him in the darkness, certain he was nearby. The air twanged harder, as if in response to her calling his name, but there was still no one there.

Irene's eyes had adjusted to the darkness now, and she could make out details of where she was. A feeble shaft of light made its way down to her, just bright enough to illuminate the space around her. Here, at the bottom, the grand chasm that had been so insurmountable above had narrowed to fifteen feet across and surrounded her on all sides. The walls, made of what appeared to be obsidian, were as smooth as glass and dark as night. Irene slowly turned in a circle, examining the walls for openings—there were none. She looked up, her eyes following the walls up and up and up...

She froze.

A very long way up, the river of fire flowed above her, blotting out the rim of the canyon. The pinpricks of light she had seen were the reflection of the underside of the river, sparkling and shimmering as it undulated overhead.

Irene's heart stuttered and then stopped – the way out lay thousands of feet straight up.

She stumbled forward to the closest wall, patting wildly at the surface, testing the solidity and searching for an opening as she made her way around the space. Her fingers met nothing but unyielding rock.

"Oh shit," she muttered over and over, her breathing coming in short, sharp gasps. She was at the bottom of a well, miles underground. No one knew where she was – no one cared. There was no one looking for her, and even if there was, how would they ever reach her? She would die down here – no, not die. She didn't need food or water or even oxygen. She would live down here... forever.

"Andras!" she shouted as panic overwhelmed her. "ANDRAS!" Her words reverberated throughout her prison and then died away, smothered by the cavernous heights of the slick, unclimbable walls.

She was completely and absolutely alone.

Her legs wobbled, and she leaned her forehead against the wall for support, counting heartbeats in the stillness to keep from clawing at the rock. Was it finally time to call Samyel? Would he be able to find her, let alone reach her, if she did? Would he even help her?

I am here.

Andras's voice sounded in the air all around her or perhaps in her head. It seemed to come from both everywhere and nowhere simultaneously. Irene whirled around. "Andras?" No answer. "Andras? Where are you?"

The air quivered like a plucked bow string with what felt like uncertainty.

Here.

Relief washed over her. "Oh my God, oh my God, you're alive. You bastard! Do you know how much you scared me? I could strangle you, you know that..." Irene's brow furrowed as she realized she was talking to herself. Andras was nowhere to be seen. She moved around the small space cautiously, hunting for unseen corners or crevices where he might be concealed. "Andras?"

I am here.

"You're going to have to be more specific. Here where?"

Can you not see me?

"No, I can't see you. Where are you?"

The air vibrated again, this time with the heavy, slow oscillation of confusion.

I see you.

Okay, that was a little creepy. Irene eyed her surroundings again. The space was only fifteen feet wide and about the same length. There was nowhere for him to hide. She looked up, just in case he was floating above her or standing on a ledge somewhere higher up. Nothing – the walls were smooth all the way up until they were swallowed by the river of fire high overhead. "Well, that's great, but I can't see you."

I am here.

He sounded frustrated, so Irene decided to let it go for the moment. She didn't need to see him. The important part was that he was alive and that they were both in the same place. That fact finally struck home, and she went limp with relief as gratitude washed over her: Andras was alive. She sagged against the wall.

Are you alright?

"What? Oh, yeah..." She combed the hair back from her face and exhaled, feeling the tension flow out of her. She smiled, hoping he could see her relief. She was having a hard time reconciling the fact that she heard Andras without being able to see him and that his voice was inside her head, rather than coming from a particular spot. It made him seem strange and omnipresent, which was a little thrilling and a little intimidating. She didn't know where to point her face when she talked. Could he see her expression from anywhere? Or maybe he couldn't see her expression at all. If so, was he reading her emotions the way she was reading his? She shifted from foot to foot uneasily, discomfited by the idea that Andras might be able to read her thoughts.

"In case it's not obvious, can I just say I'm really glad you're not dead?"

Now there was the airy quivering of amusement.

I am *dead*.

"You know what I mean! This is no time for jokes. You've turned invisible—"

I am not *invisible*.

"Well, I can't see you, so I don't know what you'd call it then."

I am *here*.

"Yeah, so you've said."

There was a twang of confusion.

I *am* here.

Unease stirred in the pit of Irene's stomach. Something was wrong. Andras was repeating himself.

"Where is here, exactly?" She turned in a circle as she spoke. "Can you describe what it looks like?"

I am...

"Yes?"

I am...

As she turned, the air shimmered and rippled, and two lines of wood and canvas market stalls dominoed into view down the length of a fathomless corridor as the canyon walls faded from sight. Strings of multi-colored lights stretching from the top of one stall to the next followed suit, twinkling into existence and then snaking their way down the line of stalls. A thronging crowd of ghosts shimmered into place and then, finally, vast, dark shapes cloaked in shadow materialized inside the stalls — merchants selling their wares.

Irene whirled back around, but now the stalls, lights, vendors, and crowd extended in both directions, the canyon having disappeared completely. Irene looked up; the river of fire had also disappeared. Overhead, beyond the feeble glow of the strings of lights, there was only inky blackness.

The crowd pushed past Irene, knocking her from side to side. She stumbled out of the way, pressing her back against the nearest stall as she tried to make sense of what she was seeing. Panic started to set in, and she gripped the hard, wooden edge of the stall behind her for support, the rough surface biting into her hands.

"Andras?" she whispered urgently, but the warm, comforting feeling of his presence—the feeling that there was someone else with her, even if she couldn't see him, and the thick, quivering potentiality of the air—had dissipated, leaving nothing but emptiness behind. Andras was gone.

What was happening? Where was she? Had she slipped through another wormhole? And more importantly, where was Andras?

Irene whirled around, craning her neck to see over her shoulder. If she'd lost her shadow, then that might explain what had happened: instead of falling when she'd leapt off the cliff, as she had thought, she'd floated across to the next plane like the other ghosts. However, try as she might, she couldn't see behind herself. She looked around, searching for her bag, and then realized it was nowhere to be seen. She darted back into the crowd, ducking under and around shoppers, as she hunted for it. Had she had it with her when she'd landed on the canyon floor? With a sinking heart, she realized she didn't remember seeing it. She had dropped it sometime before she'd jumped.

She sagged against the nearest stall and groaned as her legs threatened to give out. That bag was everything—her only weapons, her only valuables, her only tangible reminders of home. She looked around, searching for a way out. She needed to get back to Andras, back to Tartarus.

Nothing apparent jumped out at her—there was only inky darkness, the bustling crowd, and the market stalls. She scanned the area for solo shadows or other signs of danger, but found none. Here, the ghosts were like her—solid and real, unlike the half-formed ghosts that she'd seen floating across the chasm on the wire bridge. Their shadows were present, but fainter, harder to see against the inky black night, the darkness of which was barely penetrated by the strings of lights hanging between the stalls. Strangely, halos of brightly colored balls of light floated over each ghost's head. Irene looked up and saw a dozen such balls of electric blue circling her like a small solar system. She tried to wave them away, as if they were flies, but the lights simply scattered and then reformed.

Everyone seemed to be in a hurry—those not pushing their way through the crowd were engaged in rapid-fire patter with the shadowy figures inside the stalls. The balls of light overhead zoomed back and forth between the people in the stalls and the people in the crowd—as if they were being traded or exchanged.

However, the longer Irene watched, the less sure she was that the people in the stalls were merchants; none of them displayed any wares, and the words they shouted, what Irene had first thought were come-ons and sales enticements, were confusing and nonsensical.

"Hunger? Hunger? You have Hunger?"

"Colors. Buying colors. Bring colors!"

"Smells. All smells here."

The voices coming from the shadowy "merchants" were high-pitched and screechy, like a flock of angry crows, with a grating, wheedling quality. Irene cringed at the sound. She had the urge to clap her hands over her ears though she suspected that wouldn't blot out the voices. They seemed to be in her head, much like Andras's had been

A voice sounded in her ear, low and private, meant just for her. "You have fear. I will take."

Irene let out an involuntary cry of alarm and whirled around. One of the vendors stood at her shoulder. It had stepped out from the shadows and was fully illuminated in the dim light, and for the first time, Irene could clearly see what was manning the stalls. It looked like a giant vulture— black, hulking, and massive. It loomed over her, hunched and grotesque, with a disturbingly human face, pinched and shrewish, with a hooked, beak-like nose and cruel, razor-sharp talons for hands.

Oh my God, it's a harpy, Irene thought wildly. She gasped again and backed away. She bumped against something solid and couldn't move any farther; she was trapped between the creature and a stall.

"Give. Give fear. I will take," the harpy wheedled, motioning with its claws in a give-me motion.

Irene shook her head, not sure what it was asking her for, and pressed herself as hard as she could against the wall, trying to sink into it or through it or somehow disappear. The creature loomed up, its suddenly outstretched wings flapping angrily, and it bellowed at her, "GIVE!" The foul bellows of its breath assailed Irene, choking and suffocating her, and she turned her head, shielding her face with her arm. The harpy towered over her, screeching and rending the air with its wings, and Irene's heart jack-hammered in her chest. The creature stretched out one clawed hand to her, and without thinking, Irene ducked under its outstretched wing, diving into the crowd. The harpy turned with a screech of rage, but a passing wave of shoppers swept Irene away. Distantly, she heard one last ear-splitting screech before the harpy disappeared from view.

Irene moved with the crowd, race-walking as far from the harpy as she could. Finally, she risked a glance over her shoulder. The harpy had not followed. Her heart slowed, and she took several deep, calming breaths.

She kept moving, but at a walk now, her eyes and ears peeled for a way out of the strange market, but the likelihood of finding such a thing lessened by the moment. The line of stalls stretched on endlessly, hardly more than barely discernable dark shapes against the general darkness. The bare-bulb lights strung overhead and their sickly yellow glow from stall to stall only managed to illuminate the area to about the level of dusk. The stalls butted up against each other, leaving no openings to get around behind them and see what might be back there in the impenetrable dark—

perhaps more stalls, roads, endless fields, canyon walls, or possibly nothing at all.

Perhaps she had chosen the wrong direction. She backtracked, returning to her original starting point — ducking past the stall of the harpy that had accosted her — and then continuing on to see what lay in the other direction. The same thing: an endless double row of stalls and a thronging crowd.

She kept walking, on and on.

"Fear! Fear! I take fear!"

Irene couldn't be sure, everything looked the same in the dim light, but it seemed to be the same harpy as before. She had walked in a circle. That meant there was no beginning and no end to the stalls, just an endless loop. There was no way out.

She moved out of the crowd to press back up against a stall. Numbly, she closed her eyes, trying to ignore the crowd and the screeching and the whizzing balls of light as she reached for the compass, trying to sense Andras or a way off this plane or anything of note at all.

Nothing.

The flame resolutely stayed banked, and even without it, she could feel a lack of "tingle" in the air, which meant the compass wasn't going to work.

She was stuck.

She scanned the market stalls again, watching the interactions between harpies and the individuals who approached them. She thought maybe there were some kind of transactions going on — the two parties would talk for a moment, and then balls of light would exchange places, whizzing from one person to the other. She suspected that if she wanted to get out of here, she was going to have to find out what, exactly, was being exchanged.

A movement beside her caught her eye. Irene squeaked with surprise and jumped sideways.

Her shadow.

It was beside her, dark against dark, barely discernable in the dusky gloom where the light didn't penetrate, standing against the wall in the same pose as she. Pressed up against the wall as she was, the shadow had no room to stand behind her; it had no choice but to stand beside her. She stared at it a moment, a small measure of relief easing the tightness in her chest. At least she still had her shadow.

Irene knew it was stupid, but she couldn't help herself. She raised a hand and watched in fascination as the shadow mirrored the movement. Irene tilted her head, waved her arm in circles, and stood on one leg; the shadow mimicked each movement. Finally she laughed; she had to. This was the dorkiest thing she'd ever done in her life. She raised a hand, and when her shadow copied the movement, she moved her hand in for a high-five. "Good job," she said to it as their hands met—and then passed right through each other. Jonah would laugh his ass off if he could see this; it was just the kind of thing that he'd find hysterically amusing.

Jonah.

Home.

Andras.

She sighed and pushed away from the wall, heading back into the fray once more. She turned to the nearest passing ghost, a woman, and tried to get her attention. "Excuse me, can you tell me..." But the woman didn't even pause and continued on by. Irene tried several more times to flag someone down, but each time, she was either ignored or brushed off. The ghosts all seemed to know exactly where they were going and were in a great hurry to get there.

With no other choice, Irene reluctantly drew closer to the nearest stall, hoping to eavesdrop on an exchange. A youngish-looking ghost woman was haggling with the harpy there.

"You give taste?" the harpy said.

"What is it you have?" the woman asked.

"Salt," the harpy replied, leaning in towards the woman, staring at her greedily.

The woman nodded. "Fine."

A ball of light from each party flew out and was exchanged, zipping from one solar system of circling orbs to the other. The woman went still for a moment, staring vacantly into space. Then she turned away and continued down the row of stalls.

That had been as illuminating as... nothing. Another ghost was approaching the harpy, who stretched out its wings and cried enticements to the passing crowd. Irene waited, wanting to see another exchange.

The harpy at the adjacent stand noticed Irene's interest and immediately tried to entice her over. "Your memories good! I take! Come, you give!"

Irene's heart fluttered with fear, and she backed away, shaking her head. "Uh, I'm just looking—"

The harpy suddenly straightened up, adding another three feet to its already impressive height, and spread its wings, screeching in excitement. "Drowning! You have drowning!"

The merchants at the stall on either side perked up at this, turning their attention to Irene.

"I buy!" all three shouted simultaneously. "Give me! Give me!"

Her heart in her throat, Irene shook her head more insistently and backed away faster, blindly bumping into passing ghosts as she did so. "No, I—"

"No go!" the three shrieked. "No go! We buy! Good price!"

Irene bumped into something and came to an abrupt stop. She was against a stall, and its owner joined in the chorus as well.

"Give! Give!" the harpies all squawked.

"Look, I don't know—"

"We give! Give good! Give good!" the harpies cried in a deafening chorus.

"Give? Give what?" Irene cried desperately, hoping she could convince them she didn't have whatever they wanted or vice versa.

"Ice! I give you ice!"

"I have tides! I have tides!"

"Vapor! Good Vapor! You like!"

Irene had no idea what they meant. Tides? Like the ocean? How could they possible give those to her? And in exchange for what? They'd said something about memories and about drowning—that they'd wanted her to give them drowning. How did she give someone drowning? It made no sense.

She kept shaking her head, scrabbling backwards against the stall that blocked her escape.

"Give us drowning!" the harpies cried more stridently.

"I don't know what you want!" she cried. "I don't have any drowning." Only... she did. Drowning was how she had died. Irene paused... were they asking for her to share the memory of drowning with them?

The harpies hadn't pounced on her like she expected, and though they kept screeching at her, they didn't seem to be attacking either. Just wheedling and cajoling. Warily, Irene decided to test out her theory. "You want to buy one of my memories?" she asked cautiously. "A memory of drowning?"

"Yes! Yes!" the harpies screeched in chorus, shaking their wings in agitation.

So she was right!

Something clicked in her brain; she had stumbled into an Indian village on the last plane; there had been people sleeping in tents, images, possibly memories, flashing in the air over their heads, while another person sat nearby, watching the images. Irene hadn't understood what was happening, but had thought maybe it had to do with final judgment—maybe each watcher was reviewing the person's life. Something about that explanation hadn't satisfied, though. The images flashing in the air had been disjointed and intangible—a jumble of emotions and ideas, rather than the memories of people and places.

Perhaps, instead, what she'd actually been seeing was a marketplace—perhaps even this marketplace. Maybe what she'd been seeing was people selling and buying experiences. She'd stumbled into that village by accident — she'd fallen down a wormhole and temporarily found herself on a different plane of the afterlife, one she wasn't equipped to navigate or understand because it had been too advanced for her. Perhaps now she was seeing the same thing, only she was seeing it from different angle or with a better understanding.

She edged away from the harpies, putting some breathing room between her and them. She was on more solid footing now that she knew what they wanted, and she suspected she knew how to get back to Tartarus now, too. One of them had to have the memory of how to get out of here.

Unfortunately, the only memory of drowning she had was of her death, and she wasn't about to share that. It was too personal, too shameful. She shook her head. "No, I don't want to sell that one." There had to be something else they wanted.

The first merchant who had spoken ruffled its feathers. "You sell others? Sell sunlight? One memory — just one! You have others. Many others. Sell? Yes?"

Irene hesitated; she wasn't entirely sure what she was agreeing to, but no matter how you sliced it, selling her memories seemed like a rather big deal. "Am I just letting you see the memory or am I giving it to you?" she asked warily.

"You give!" the first harpy shouted, and then the others picked up the cry, alternating their voices in a continuous din.

Irene clapped her hands over her ears. "Okay, okay! I get it."

"You have others!" one of the harpies said. "So many others. So give one. Just one!"

So she'd lose whatever memory she traded. That put a slightly different spin on things. Cautiously, she asked, "Okay, fine, I give up a memory of sunlight in exchange for... what? What do you have?"

"Grass!" shouted the harpy whose stall she had backed into.

"What, like marijuana? You're selling drugs?" The memory of drug use? That seemed like a bit of a letdown — though she supposed for a ghost it might be a good deal. With no body, ghosts couldn't experience physical sensations — they could only remember. If a ghost had no memory of a particular sensation, then the only way to experience it would be to buy a memory of it.

Hmmm…. a risk free way of experiencing all the things you never got to try in life. Now this might actually be interesting… She thought of Amy, the ghost woman who spent all her time trying to experience things vicariously through the living. Irene made a mental note of another person she would now be able to help when she returned to the land of the living.

The harpy screeched in outrage. "Not drug! Grass! Grass! Plant!"

The memory of… grass? Irene raised an eyebrow. "I think I have all the memories of grass that I need, thanks." She'd seen plenty of lawns in her life, and she'd just spend untold hours traversing an endless plain of wheat — which was basically just really tall grass. She was all full up on grass at the moment.

She inched sideways, trying to surreptitiously move around the harpies so she could melt back into the crowd. The grass-seller put out a claw to stop her.

"You like! Trust! Trust! Try! Try!" it cajoled in a low, deep-throated wheedle.

Irene hesitated. She supposed trading one memory of sunlight for one memory of grass was a simple enough way to figure out first-hand what was actually going on in the market. A memory of grass seemed harmless enough.

Yeah, right. Since when did anything in the afterlife ever turn out to be as simple and straightforward as it sounded?

She took a deep breath. "Okay," she said, having the distinct feeling this was actually going to turn out to be a bad idea.

Eighteen

Since Char was so short, Jonah cradled his hands to give her a leg up. She gave him a doubtful look. "How are you going to get over?"

"Just look over the wall and tell me what you see."

Grimacing, Char allowed Jonah to boost her up. She balanced on her tiptoes and peered over the edge. "I can't see anything. It's dark."

"What do you mean it's dark?"

"I mean it's night or something. It's pitch black."

"Okay—climb up on top of the wall."

Char shot him another doubtful look but pulled herself up. Jonah went a few feet down the wall and, using a rock as a stool, managed to climb up as well, and then he inched his way back over to Char. Seated side by side, their legs dangling into the void, they stared into the inky darkness spreading before them. There was literally nothing out there—no stars, no trees, no ground. It was almost like looking into the gray mist between realms, except this was an impenetrable black.

Jonah took hold of Char's hand. "Hang on, okay?"

Char looked at him as if he'd lost his mind. "Are you suggesting we jump?"

Jonah grinned.

"Oh no—" Char started to say, but he didn't give her the opportunity to protest. He pulled them both forward as he pitched himself off the edge of the wall.

To his surprise, it was an extremely short drop—only about a foot. They hit the ground—grass to be specific—landing heavily on their feet. Jonah blinked in the sudden sunshine and realized they were back in the endless field where they had seen the horses and riders.

"Crap."

"Are you out of your mind?" Char said, stepping away from him as if he was contaminated in some way. "You don't just jump off a wall without knowing how far—"

That was just the sort of thing he would have said to Irene. The irony of the situation struck him, and he began to laugh.

"What's so funny?" Char wrinkled her nose in suspicion.

"Nothing," Jonah said. "It's just weird to be the crazy, impulsive one for once."

Char raised an eyebrow. "It's not saying a lot for our prospects if I'm the sane and normal one." She took hold of a strand of her hair and waved it at him. "Purple hair, remember?"

Jonah shrugged. "The purple isn't that weird. I kind of like it."

Char's eyes widened, and her hand stilled. "You do?"

Jonah snorted. "Don't get crazy, okay? We need to focus on getting out of here."

Char hesitated, eyeing him for a second as if she didn't want to drop the subject, and then relented, releasing her hair with a sigh. "Yeah, well here's a crazy idea." She pointed to the brick wall running around the outside of the palace—the only feature of the landscape other than grass. "If we follow this all the way around, then we should find the entrance—and the way home—again, right?"

Jonah surveyed the landscape, taking in the uninterrupted plain spreading before them. If there was a way out of the afterlife that way, then it wasn't visible from here. He wasn't so sure he agreed with Char's logic that following the wall would take them around to the front again since everything here moved around, but it was easier to start there than to blindly wander off onto the plain.

"Okay, yeah, sure," he said, and they set off, keeping the building on their right. They walked in silence, passing several doorways, which they ignored.

"So," Char said, suddenly serious and gazing everywhere but at him, "tell me about Irene—the real Irene, the one no one but you knows."

"Why?" he asked, immediately suspicious.

Char shrugged and still didn't look at him. "Well, since I'm risking my life for this woman, I guess I should know something about her."

"Oh." Jonah turned this over for a moment. He doubted Char's out-of-nowhere desire to talk about Irene, but it seemed rude to say so. He desperately searched for a way to change the conversation.

"Come on," Char said when he hesitated. "Tell me something about her—something good."

Her words so closely echoed the ones he'd spoken to Deborah just a day ago that he experienced a moment of déjà vu. The same feeling of protectiveness toward Irene that he'd experienced then welled up inside of him.

"Well... she likes to argue. She has a pathological need to be right." He snorted. "She says the craziest stuff just to win an argument. It's fun to provoke her—just to see what insane thing she'll say next. The stuff that comes out of her mouth sometimes..." He shook his head and gave a dry chuckle that mixed equal parts amusement and exasperation. He'd always been both horrified and impressed with how inappropriate she'd been at times, never censoring herself due to his age. Certainly, he'd never met anyone before or since who had treated him like an equal to the same extent. "She makes this kind of frownie face whenever she's presented with something she can't argue with. You can see the wheels turning and turning and turning as she tries to find a flaw, to find a way to argue herself out of the corner. And when she can't... well, she never admits that she's wrong. She'll just revise her opinion and keep going like that was her opinion the whole time."

Char cast him an incredulous look. "This is what you look for in a girl?"

Clearly, he wasn't explaining it right—the goofy humor, the battles of wits that were a strange mix of fight to the death and exercise in the absurd, the comradery, the freedom to just be themselves—without worrying about what the other person would think. He frowned, trying to find the words to convey what he meant. "It's not just that. It's a million things. Like how she hates for anyone to think she's weak or afraid. She'll do stupid stuff—like picking a fight or throwing a tantrum—to hide when she's scared. She never asks for help, not even when she really needs it."

This will be my last letter...

Pain sliced through him as if someone had punched him in the gut, and he swallowed hard again, trying to quell the growing thickness in his voice. He kept talking because it was easier than stopping and hoped Char didn't notice. "She's funny—she's got this really dry sense of humor, and she's good with the clever come-backs. She's smart, and she sticks to her guns, and when she makes up her mind to do something, she does it—no matter what. Irene can do anything she sets her mind to. If she wanted, she could kick down the whole world. But she's not tough, you know? She's kind of vulnerable and sweet..."

He had to stop; it was getting too hard to keep going. He lapsed into silence and waited for Char to say something. The wall stretched out endlessly before them, the bricks unrelentingly even and well-cemented, showing no signs of coming to an end. Soon the silence stretched out, too.

He cast Char a sidelong glance, wondering what she was thinking. Her brow was furrowed, her eyes fixed on the wall. Finally, she said softly, not looking at him, "If you two were so perfect for each other, then how come she left?" There was a catch in her voice.

He didn't know how to answer that. Irene had left.... because. Because she was afraid of staying — afraid of letting him down, afraid he'd let her down, afraid of things getting hard. "It's complicated."

Char turned to look at him, and there was a fierceness in her eyes he hadn't expected. "If I had someone like you in my corner, I would have never left. I would never give that up." Startled by the sudden ferocity in her tone, Jonah stumbled over his feet and then stopped walking. Char instantly dropped her eyes as a blush suffused her face and ears.

Jonah watched the blush spread down her neck, not sure what to say. He didn't have a chance to unpack her words or her sudden embarrassment, however, because her expression quickly changed to one of mischievousness as she raised her eyes, now sparkling with merriment. "Did you ever... you know..." A sly grin spread across her face. "Kiss?"

Now he knew she was purposely trying to be provoking.

"Let's stop for a second," he said. "I want to see what's over the wall here."

"You're changing the subject."

"Yup." He made a cradle with his hands and held it out for her to step into.

"So did you?" Char said, not moving from the spot.

He shook the cradle at her, urging her to give him her foot.

She rolled her eyes and complied, putting her foot in his hands and letting him boost her up.

"What do you see?"

"Nothing, it's dark, like before."

He lowered her back down to the ground.

"I don't get it," she said, as she landed. "Why is it dark when I look over the wall? Shouldn't I see a garden or whatever? It was dark when I looked over the wall from the other side, too, like it was night, but it's mid-day here."

"It's not actually a wall. All these places we're seeing, they're all separate from each other."

"What do you mean?"

"This isn't one big, linear place. You're thinking of it like the physical plane, and it's not. It's a lot of different places, and we're traveling between them every time we step through a doorway. There's a sensation, really subtle but there, when we go through a door. Did you feel it? Like you're toothpaste being squeezed out of the tube."

Char nodded. "I just thought it was motion sickness."

"No, it's because we're actually traveling between realms of the afterlife. That's why you can't see over the wall."

"Then why did you make me climb up there and look?" she asked, exasperated.

"Well, it was just a theory. I wanted to confirm it." He tried to hold back a grin but couldn't. "And I wanted to see if I could make you climb up there."

She narrowed her eyes and pursed her lips in mock outrage and swatted at his shoulder. He dodged out of the way with a laugh. She narrowed her eyes even more and pantomimed putting her arms around someone while making theatrical fake kissing noises. "Oh, Irene, I love you, mwah, mwah."

"Okay, that's just... disturbing. Look, this wall doesn't seem to be leading us anywhere. It just stretches on and on. Maybe we should try checking in the field."

Char stuck out her tongue but followed him away from the wall and into the open field without comment.

He scanned the horizon, looking for any features that might help them escape or at least identify which version of paradise they were in. However, the grassy plain was featureless—there was an endless blue sky with a smattering of clouds, and the endless sea of ankle deep grass, yellowed and thin as if at the end of summer or parched by lack of rain. A light breeze ruffled their hair, but that was the only interruption in the otherwise uniform landscape. For a hunting ground, it seemed terribly devoid of game — there weren't even any birds in the sky.

The landscape wasn't getting any more populated as they continued farther away from the wall either. Jonah suspected that without some idea of what they were looking for or in what direction it might lay, they could wander out here forever without finding anything but grass and the occasional stampeding horde of huntsmen. If the way out was this way, they had little hope of finding it unaided.

He pointed to the ground. "Look, why don't we rest for a minute." He needed to stop and think.

Without waiting for an answer, he plopped down. Char joined him a second later, leaning her back against his. He glanced at her, disconcerted by her closeness. After a moment, he relaxed and leaned into her, grateful for the support.

"Auntie is going to flip when I don't show up for dinner," Char said absently as if she was thinking out loud.

Jonah didn't say anything. There really wasn't anything to say. Madame Majicka was going to flip out about a lot of things if they didn't get back soon — or find a way to get Char back into her body.

Several long minutes passed.

"How long do you think we've been here?"

Jonah shrugged.

Another long silence.

"Jonah… you said you thought time passes differently on this side — that a day here could be like three years in the land of the living."

"Yeah."

Another silence.

"Does that mean we've already been missing for years back home?"

Jonah's brow furrowed. "Oh. Uh…" He searched for some kind of plausible lie.

Char groaned and slumped back against him. "Great."

"Probably not," Jonah said quickly. "I'm sure it will be okay."

"You're a terrible liar."

"It doesn't feel like it's been that long. Just a few hours."

Another silence.

"Isn't that the point—that it only feels like a day here when it's been a year back home?"

"Well..."

Char groaned and let her head fall back, cracking her skull against his in the process.

"Ow!" Jonah cried, turning around to give her an exasperated look.

Char grinned. "Sorry!"

Jonah felt the corners of his mouth turn up in an answering smile despite himself. A question that had been bothering him for some time bubbled up. "How did you know how to pronounce the words of the spell?"

"What spell?"

"The meditation thing for separating your spirit and your body? It took me months to figure that out, and it was mostly trial and error."

Char's expression turned incredulous. "It's a meditation, Jonah. You don't have to speak it, you just have to feel it."

"Huh?"

"Boy, you don't know anything, do you? A meditation is just a way to channel energy, to focus it into a particular shape or direction. The words are just a guide, a kind of framework, for shaping the energy, so you don't need to actually speak them."

"Oh." He turned this over for a moment.

"Why do you sound disappointed?"

Jonah shrugged. "I don't know... that just makes it seem sort of common, like anyone could do it."

"Anyone who knows what they're doing could."

Jonah wrinkled his nose.

"What?"

"I don't know. It's just... I like that this stuff is special, that it's secret, and I'm the only one who knows about it."

"That sounds pretty lonely to me."

Jonah shrugged again.

Char's expression changed, growing serious. She studied him for a moment, her eyes flitting over his face.

Jonah shifted under the uncomfortable scrutiny, not sure what she was looking for.

"The thing is, have you ever even given anyone else a chance?" she asked abruptly. Her face flooded with red as soon as the words were out, but she didn't drop her eyes.

"What do you mean?"

"I mean have you tried actually, you know, getting to know someone else—another girl, I mean. You might actually find someone who's, you know, obtainable."

Now Jonah felt his own face heat. "What, you mean like dating? I've been a little busy—trying to save my friend and all."

Char turned to fully face him, her expression serious. "I mean an actual chance. 'Cause, you know, you haven't really given me a fair shake."

Jonah shrugged yet again, this time just lifting one shoulder in a half-hearted response. He wasn't really sure what Char wanted him to say.

"Gee, thanks."

It dawned on him that Char was trying to say that she liked him—in a romantic sense. Jonah's face heated even more, and he felt like both a jerk and an idiot for not understanding sooner. "Sorry, I didn't mean it like... I just meant... I don't... I've never..."

Char heaved a theatrical sigh of exasperation. "Why, yes, Jonah, I'd love to go on a date with you after we get back to the land of the living and reintegrate my spirit into my body. Thank you for asking."

Jonah wasn't sure if she was serious about going on a date or was just trying to get a rise out of him—it was hard to tell if she was actually as forward and "unsocialized" as she claimed or if she just came out with half the things she said just to have a laugh at his ensuing discomfort. He also wasn't sure how he felt about a date with Char—or about Char in general. In the short time that he'd known her, every thought of her had pretty much focused on how to avoid her.

Since it wasn't a topic he could really think about at the moment, given that there were a lot more important things they needed to be thinking about, he decided to change the subject. He stood up and dusted himself off. "Speaking of which, it's time we got back to work. Clearly, wandering out here isn't getting us anywhere. I think we need to go back to the palace."

Char rolled her eyes. "Nice change of subject. Again."

Jonah ignored the comment, refusing to be side-tracked. "There was a library in the palace. There might be something in there to help us. And, if that doesn't work, then worst case, we can ask Persephone for help. So we're not out of options yet."

"So you'll get back to me on the date thing?" she said as she climbed to her feet.

Before he could respond, however, the ground began to shake. The rumbling grew louder, as if of an approaching thunderstorm, and Char took one faltering, off-balance step towards him. "What is that?"

Jonah pointed to the rising cloud of dust in the distance. "I think the hunt is returning!"

"Should we maybe head back inside, then?"

Jonah hesitated. "I don't think they're dangerous. This is the happy afterlife, remember?"

"But still…"

Jonah vacillated. The hunt members might be able to tell them if there was a way out. On the other hand, those horses were big and growing bigger by the second, and the warriors' faces didn't seem to be all that friendly. "Yeah… maybe you're right."

Too late. The hunt was now between them and the palace and closing fast. "Uukhai!" shouted a fierce Mongol warrior in heavy furs as his horse skidded to a halt beside Jonah. He shook his spear in the air, and the others, representing a dozen different cultures and periods in history, took up the cry as they drew closer.

Char cringed and clutched at Jonah's shirt as she half hid behind him. "I don't think they're friendly."

Too quickly to stop, the Mongol warrior leaned down, grabbed Char by the back of her shirt, and hauled her up and across the saddle in front of him like a sack of potatoes.

"Hey!" Jonah cried as Char flailed and shouted, "Help!"

The warrior shook his spear again, and with a triumphant note in his voice, he let out a piercing cry. Jonah jumped forward to grab Char but was knocked back as the horseman twitched his reins, causing his horse to wheel away and break into a gallop. The other warriors followed suit, all shaking their spears in the air and yelling exaltations. Jonah managed to grab hold of a warrior's leg, a Celt if Jonah had to guess, as his horse took off, Jonah's fingers desperately digging into the man's stiff animal-hide leggings. Jonah gritted his teeth as he held on with all his might and tried to keep up with the horse. He stumbled, found his feet, stumbled again, and then he was being dragged by the horse and rider. The horseman grinned down at him, and for a moment, Jonah thought he was going to help. Then the warrior swung the butt end of his spear, knocking Jonah free. Jonah hit the ground, the impact reverberating in every bone, and tumbled over and over endlessly before finally coming to rest.

There might have been pain, but he didn't stop to think about it. He bounded to his feet, and was off, chasing after the riders. His legs pumped as he hurtled across the plain like an Olympic sprinter, chasing the cloud of dust retreating into the distance.

It didn't matter. They were too fast and soon had outpaced him. Reluctantly, he slowed to a halt. Desperately, he scanned the never-ending horizon, his heart hammering in his chest. It wasn't supposed to be like this. This wasn't how the afterlife was supposed to be. People weren't supposed to die.

He tried to clamp down the rising fear. This was the happy afterlife. The huntsmen wouldn't—they *couldn't*—

hurt Char, right? Maybe it was just a game, like capture the flag.

Yeah, right. If that were the case, then why hadn't they taken him, too?

He stared at the horizon, trying to gauge how far the Hunt might have traveled by now. Every second of delay seemed interminable, and yet, he wasn't sure that his continuing to chase after them on foot was going to accomplish anything. By the time he caught up, they could have already done any number of horrible things to Char.

He frantically looked around, hoping for something, anything, that might help him catch up to the huntsmen. There wasn't even a dry stick that he might use as a weapon. The only thing in sight was the palace. Though he felt like he'd been running for miles, the brick wall surrounding it was still in sight. Hope glimmered through him. Maybe someone inside could help — direct him to the camp, show him a shortcut, help him overpower the men and get Char back.

He was in motion again, racing for the wall and then running along it, looking for an opening, any opening, back into the palace.

He ducked through an opening, into a garden. "Help!" he cried to the first person he saw, a woman, lounging under a tree. "The Hunt has my friend!" The woman's brow furrowed, signaling she had heard him, but she didn't seem at all alarmed — or even interested — in his statement. "Did you hear me?" he said. "I need help. The men on horseback, outside, have grabbed her!"

The woman stared blankly at him, unperturbed. Jonah spun away from her and approached a nearby couple. "Hey! Hey you!" he cried. "Help!" The couple gave him the same blank look as the woman. Exasperated, he raced for the nearest doorway, skidding through it into Valhalla. Thank God! The dead here were warriors — surely they'd help.

"Help!" he cried, trying to be heard over the din. He grabbed the arm of the nearest man, sloshing the man's drink on the way to his mouth. "The Hunt has my friend. Please help! We have to get her back!"

"Skaal!" cried the warrior, raising his drinking horn and guzzling down its contents.

Jonah's fear and anger bubbled over, and he knocked the cup from the man's hands. "Didn't you hear me?" he said.

The man laughed and clapped Jonah on the back. "Skaal!" he cried, grabbing a cup out of another man's hand and passing it to Jonah, who slapped it aside and pushed free of the man's hold, shoving his way through the crowd to the door. What was wrong with these people? Didn't anyone understand what he was saying? Or did they just not care?

You are but a shadow to us.

Persephone's words echoed in his head, and understanding dawned. He was a ghost to these people, barely registering in their perception. Nothing he said or did here would make any difference — he couldn't get through to them.

The panic returned; he wasn't sure where to turn next when a second realization hit, stunning in its obviousness.

Persephone.

Of course.

If anyone could help, it would be the ruler of the underworld.

He'd last seen Persephone in the blue room, but she could be anywhere. How long would it take him to find her in the ever-changing maze of rooms? Every second felt like an eternity. What would the warriors do to Char in the time it took him to find the queen? And would Persephone even help him? In the stories, the ruler of the underworld always demanded a price for his or her assistance — a labor to perform some kind of impossible task, a quest to retrieve some kind of unobtainable object, a sacrifice like the hero's heart or most treasured possession or first-born child, servitude or even enslavement for a hundred or even a thousand years. Whatever it was, it was always steep. What would Persephone's price be, and would he be able to pay it?

He ducked through an opening, into another garden, dashed through it, and continued on through a doorway, shouting Persephone's name. He skidded to a stop in the library, scanning for Persephone, then continued on, calling her name in every room. Valhalla, the red room, the white room, the blue room... Where was she?

He was well aware of the passing of every second as he raced from room to room, searching wildly for the queen or one of her attendants. Every minute he wasted increased the likelihood he'd never see Char again.

He crossed through the white room, and then just as he stepped through the doorway into the next room, he was struck by a thought—what was the point of the white room? It was as empty as ever, with nothing but the mounds of white pillows and the dais with the self-playing harps. For the first time, however, he noticed the two chairs on the dais—chairs or possibly thrones.

It was too late, however; he was already through the doorway to the next room when the realization that the white room might possibly be a throne room struck. He dashed through a doorway and blindly raced on crossing doorway after doorway until he had circled back to the white room. He skidded to a halt and looked around wildly for Persephone, but the room was as devoid of people as it had ever been.

He honed in on the dais, approaching it cautiously as he looked around for a trap of some kind. He half expected someone to appear out of nowhere to stop him from getting too close, but nothing happened. Everything remained unchanged, the room quiet and empty save for the softly lilting music of the harps.

Now that he was closer, he would see that one of the harps, the largest one, sitting squarely in the center, was not playing. Slowly, Jonah reached out and touched the strings.

Instantly, the other harps fell silent as a sound like a trumpet blast rang out. Jonah stumbled backwards, doubting the wisdom of his action as the room began to shake. Pillows began to shimmy across the room, and the silk drapes swayed wildly as the rumbling increased. He thought about running, but it was too late to change his mind now. The woman in green, Persephone, queen of the underworld, was rising, impossibly, up through the floor of the dais. Not from an opening in the floor, but through the floor itself, as if it was no more than water or mist.

She looked stern and impossible and grew taller by the second. No longer was she the kindly woman who had asked him for a dance or even the stern woman warning him not to disturb the dead. Now there was a fierceness about her, her face devoid of any warmth or kindness. Jonah took another step back and then another, not believing his eyes. The dais and even the room around him seemed to dim and become less solid while Persephone herself became more solid and real than anything surrounding her. She seemed incredibly tall, too, certainly taller than when they had danced, and there was something alien and terrifying about her now, her face all sharp angles and planes. She stood before him, towering and proud, regarding him with a cold, hard gaze that seemed to look right through him. He stepped back another two steps, his breath catching in his throat. The room continued to shake.

"Speak," she said coldly, and her voice was honed steel, hollow and commanding, echoing dully in the empty room.

Jonah's mind stumbled through its trove of afterlife knowledge, desperately trying to recall the words to invoke a boon from the ruler of the underworld. Was there a traditional greeting or gift that was supposed to be offered to soften the ruler's wrath at being disturbed? He couldn't remember.

The room continued to rumble and shake, and one of the harps fell over with a discordant clang, barely discernable above the sound of the earth trembling. Persephone, too, still seemed to be growing, and now she towered over him by a foot.

"I'm sorry to bother you," he managed to stutter out. He wasn't sure if he should bow, but it didn't matter anyway; his whole body had gone stiff with fear. Was it his imagination, or was she still growing taller, rising higher by the second? Now she seemed to loom over him, impossibly tall.

He tried to hold his voice steady and failed. "The members of the Wild Hunt have taken my friend, the other spirit walker, who was with me. Please, I need your help to save her."

"And what will you give me in return?" Persephone's eyes were like bottomless pools of darkness, drawing him in to drown in their depths. He tried to break eye contact and found he couldn't. He was rooted to the spot.

"Whatever you want," he said desperately. "I don't care. Please, just hurry, before they hurt her."

Persephone's mouth curved into a cruel smile. "Beg," she said, hard and flat.

"What?" he said, taken aback by both the demand and the merciless way it was delivered.

"I said, 'beg'." She took a step toward him, and instinctively, he backed away. Her eyes glittered and all the angles of her face seemed sharper now, as if all the softness had been stripped away. "Offer me riches," she said, with another step toward him. "Offer me power." Step. "Offer to be my slave." Step. "Offer your life."

It was as if all the air had been sucked from the room. He couldn't breathe. He was growing dizzy, and the room around him seemed to shift and blur. She stepped again, this time through the edge of the dais, and she was on the floor now, advancing on him, and he held up a hand to ward her off. "Stop," he managed to gasp out. She just smiled, and now her teeth were sharp as knives. She reminded him of someone from long ago, and at first he couldn't remember who, and then it came to him: Samyel, the man he'd suspected of being a demon. The man who had gone with Irene to the land of the dead.

The color was leaching from Persephone's dress, the vibrant green now the barest whisper of celadon and even that was fading fast, while Persephone herself seemed to glow. The intersection of her gleaming, pale flesh and the blinding white of her gown became indiscernible and then seemed to burn, like the incandescent flame of a filament. He raised a hand to block the searing, burning light. The world around him shuddered and changed. They were no longer in the white room; they were in the library, and the ground still shook.

"Wha... what's happening?" he managed to gasp out, still backing away on unsteady legs as she approached.

"You're falling," she said, and she was taller now than she had been moments ago, so tall her head pressed against the vaulted ceiling. The world shifted and blurred once more. Now they were in the blue ballroom.

"Wha... what?" He bumped against a chair, and he tripped, stumbled once, twice, and then righted himself. When he straightened, they were in the Aztec Garden. She was so tall now he had to crane his neck to see her face. And now she was spreading, growing wider as well as taller, blinding white but with a darkness above and behind now, as if she was crowned with a halo or perhaps a pair of wings.

"You tried to cross into my realm and failed, and now you're falling, falling between worlds."

"No," Jonah said, even though he didn't really understand. He hadn't tried to go anywhere—just the opposite. He'd tried to call her to him.

He fought to stay upright on stumbling, unsteady feet and to stay conscious as the world shuddered and changed around them.

Persephone stretched out a long, gleaming white hand. She was close enough to touch, but somehow the stretching of her arm went on for a long time, as if it was reaching out to him from a great distance. Distantly, through the dizziness and confusion, he felt her talon-like fingers graze his chest as they closed around the crystal at his neck. Her touch burned like red-hot pokers, and he cried out, twisting away from her and the searing pain. There was an audible "snap!" as the cord broke. The world shuddered once more.

Then everything went dark.

Nineteen

As soon as Irene agreed to the exchange — the memory of grass for the memory of sunlight — the other harpies growled in frustration and turned away. A red ball of light circling the harpy's head zoomed toward Irene and was exchanged for a blue ball of light from her. "Uh, wait," Irene said, reflexively reaching up to snatch her blue ball back as she was assailed by a sudden onslaught of buyer's remorse. Too late. Memories slammed into her, flooding her mind, over-riding and replacing her own thoughts.

Minute vibrations — layers upon layers: subtle, overt, erratic, steady... so many sensations.

Sensed not heard.

Sensed not felt.

No light. No dark. No sound. No warmth. No cold.

No understanding of these things.

No skin. No fingers. No toes. No eyes. No mouth.

No me. No I. No self. No boundary between "me" and "not me."

Unheard of concepts. Unknown and undreamed.

Instead, only the constant vibration of sensing, akin to a dowsing rod seeking water. Not from her, though. From outside. From around. From above and under and beside. From near. From far.

The world was layer upon layer of vibrations, each with a distinct "taste." Everything was vibrating — her roots in the soil sensed the vibration of molecules of water, separate and distinct from the vibration of dirt. And in between, the vibration of movement, of things categorized as not dirt, not rock, not water. Ants? Grubs? Earthquake? Irrelevant. Not dirt. Not rock. Not water.

Above, the vibration of water molecules in the air, the vibration of particles of light. And in between – the vibration of movement, of things categorized as not water, not light. Human footsteps? Grazing animals? Lawnmower? Car? Irrelevant. Not water. Not light.

Every tremor, every throb, pulsed through her, conveying a hundred different pieces of information. But not on her skin. Not in her fingers and toes. In her. Part of her. From root to tip, the sensations flowed, as deep a part of her as the knowledge of not dirt, not rock, not light, not water.

As quickly as it had come, the sensations faded, leaving her once more in the center of the market, once more human, once more Irene Dunphy. Irene stared at the vendor in confusion and wonder.

"Grass," she said slowly, wonder and awe washing over her. "I was a blade of grass." Grass hardly seemed like the kind of thing to inspire wonder and awe, and yet, that was the only way to describe what she was feeling. Grass has always seemed so… flat and uninteresting – it was just *there*, static and inanimate. But what she had just experienced showed otherwise – grass had… feelings, for lack of a better word. Not emotions, exactly, but senses. It was aware of its world and it had… wants and, to an extent, made value judgments about things in its surroundings. Grass, for lack of more precise word, was sentient and alive – but sentient and alive in a completely foreign and amazing way.

Irene turned to the harpy, her mind reeling with questions – not the least of which was how what had just happened was possible, but the harpy was no longer paying attention to her. Another customer had stepped forward, and the harpy was haggling.

Irene could still feel the grass memory under her own, flashing in and out of consciousness as sight was replaced momentarily with vibrations, as her feet standing firmly upon the ground were replaced with roots burrowing deep, as her head was replaced with photo receptors seeking the set of vibrations that indicated sunlight. Her brain was having trouble reconciling the memory, attempting to translate the experience into human terms and understanding and finding the task impossible.

Irene had never really given much thought to what it might like to be something other than human. She'd always thought people who went gaa-gaa over how smart their dogs were because the thing had figured out how to open the fridge and steal food or escape from the backyard or who talked about their cat's feelings and desires were sad — and a bit delusional. Honestly, how smart could a dog or cat — or snake or rabbit or goldfish — really be? But now, she had to wonder. Grass — *grass*, for God's sake — knew when it was being walked on and it could identify what was doing the walking. It didn't have language, like humans, to label the various things it came into contact with, but it knew the difference between a harmless bug and grazing cow, for instance.

Irene realized she was shaking, and she wrapped her arms around herself, trying to push the grass memory out of her conscious mind, to focus on being human so she could quell the sensory overload. She slowly turned in a half circle, surveying the endless line of stalls. A different experience at every stall? How could there be so many? Were they all this intense?

Now that the initial shock was wearing off, she found her curiosity piqued. Eyes narrowed in thought, she stepped away from the grass-seller and wandered down the line of merchants, listening to their patter with a new understanding.

"Tides! I have tides!"

"I have yellow! Yellow here!"

"Have wind! Good price! Good wind!"

"Ice! Yes, yes! Ice! You want?"

"I give dirt! You like!"

Irene couldn't imagine that the sensation of being dirt was terribly exciting, but a bunch of customers clustered around the stall seemed to indicate otherwise. Sales seemed to be brisk if the dizzying whirl of colored balls of light whizzing back and forth was any indication.

Irene was curious, but, at the same time, she held back, afraid of diving in. Under normal circumstances, she'd be all for this — hell, the things she'd tried when she was alive just because it was new and different and people were doing it at a party or at the club or at the bar or at the resort — but if she'd learned one thing so far, it was that the afterlife was designed to strip away one's humanity. The entire point of all of these afterlife planes was to break people down into their component parts, leaving only that which was essential — the individual's unique element or trait — so it could be recycled and passed on. It was hard enough to hold onto her memories of life on earth — the things driving her to return — hard enough to remember what rain or cashmere or the sun felt like. To frivolously sell off those memories in exchange for strange, alien thoughts that had no relation to her own would be crazy.

And yet... so many people were doing it.

And it was tempting... very, very tempting. Everything being sold here was so strange, so alien. And, in a way, it was an avenue to experience life in the land of the living from a different angle. Might make her appreciate the things she missed even more, really...

A harpy reached out and snagged Irene's arm. "You will like blue," it hissed at her.

Being a color? What would that be like?

Besides... she was supposed to be finding a memory that would help her get back to Tartarus and Andras. She couldn't do that if she didn't actually buy anything.

"Okay, sure, I'll take some blue," she said.

"You give? Give blue?"

"Oh, sorry, I thought you were selling."

"Yes, yes, Give blue."

"You or me?"

"You. Me. Yes. Give. Blue. Yes."

Irene frowned in confusion, stymied by how to get the conversation out of the endless loop it seemed to be stuck in. The harpy seemed to realize she was confused because it squawked loudly and shook its wings impatiently. "You give. I give. Yes. Blue. Light for same. Water for same. Color for same."

"Oh. You want one of my memories of blue — what it looks like — and you'll give me... the memory of what it feels like to be blue?"

The harpy screeched in what Irene took to be assent.

"Uh, okay. That seems weird, but fine, let's give it a whirl." Irene was pretty sure it didn't feel like anything in particular to be a color, and even if it did, colors weren't sentient in any shape or form, so how would they even know what it felt like? It didn't seem likely these were actually memories, then, but more like a simulation of an experience.

She felt let down by that thought.

As soon as she assented to the trade, two balls overhead zipped between her and the harpy, exchanging places. In the next instant, memories slammed into Irene.

She hummed. With every fiber of her being, she vibrated, her atoms oscillating in perfect synchronization, creating an internal music only she could hear, though it wasn't a sound as her human mind had thought of it. This was music felt rather than heard, like breathing or a heartbeat, something integral and primal to her being.

There was nothing else.

There was no width, no depth, no height.

No movement, no stillness, no forward, no back.

There was only the hum.

Perfect. All encompassing. Eternal.

As the memory faded, Irene felt a moment of disorientation as width, height, depth, time, sound, taste, and smell rushed back in. There was a transformation — a turning inside out and upside down and expanding outward and inward simultaneously — that her human brain couldn't quite process, an impossibility for a three-dimensional creature of the physical plane to understand existing in one-dimension and vice versa. Even if she were blind or deaf, she would know, in every fiber of her being, that she took up space, that she had weight and mass, that she acted upon objects and they acted upon her. As a ray of light, however, these concepts had no meaning. The two states — human and light — were mutually exclusive and mutually incomprehensible. Her brain wrestled with the paradox, trying to reconcile the new memory with the old, trying to integrate it into the rest of her experience. There was pain and a moment of panic as she phased in and out of the two states, unable to settle on either. Her mind finally decided on human, and stuffed the light memory to one side, a strange and isolated bubble awkwardly left to fend for itself like an unsettling dream.

Irene glanced up at the halo of lights circling overhead and saw there were now two red ones amongst the numerous blue ones. In theory, she had now sold two memories. She hadn't counted the number of blue balls she'd had when she started, so she had no way to know if she had lost any. She tried to rummage around in her memories, to figure out what the harpy had taken, but she knew that would be impossible. Had the harpy taken a second, a minute, a day of memory? In the thousands upon thousands of hours of memories containing sunlight or the color blue, how would she recognize which second or minute or hour was missing, if any? What if it had taken more — a month, a year, several years? Would she be able to tell? And what kind of blue had it taken from her — the memory of a crayon, a memory of the sky, the ocean, an important piece of clothing, a loved one's eyes?

Irene turned away from the stall and scanned the market once more, this time taking note of the percentage of red and blue balls above the buyers' heads. It was a mixed bag, but Irene noted with alarm there were some ghosts who had far more red than blue. Irene also noted that humans didn't seem to be trading with other humans — only with the harpies.

Irene shivered — these people were selling their humanity, their memory of what it meant to be human and to experience the world through the lens of human perception — and for what? To experience the world as dirt or grass or light beams? Her initial enthusiasm for the idea of selling memories to gain new experiences faded. It was all well and good if the buyers were gaining memories of human experience, but trading away humanity for memories of things they'd never be? What kind of person would do that?

The thought flickered across her brain that Andras might. He counted his time on Earth very cheaply, only too happy to forget about it and move on. She wasn't so sure, however, that he would trade those memories for such a trivial and useless thing as what it felt like to be dirt. In fact, he'd probably consider it a sacrilege to imagine yourself, even for a second, as anything other than human because that would somehow be insulting to God.

Andras.

Irene glanced over her shoulder, checking that she still had her shadow. She did. Whatever the memory trades were about, at least it didn't seem to affect that.

She continued down the row of stalls, listening to the sales patter, trying to figure out who might have a memory that would help her get out of here.

"Star! I have star! You want? I give! Good price! Good! Good!"

The wheedling cry caught Irene's attention. *Star? Like... a star?* Now that might actually be interesting.

She approached the vendor. "How much?"

"Anger. Give anger!"

Anger she could do. She had plenty of that; she'd spent most of her life angry.

She was a little surprised by the harpy's request because she had thought the trades involved different facets of the same thing, and she wasn't sure how anger related to stars, but she supposed it didn't really matter. Being angry for being a star seemed like a good trade. "Okay, fine."

She watched as a red ball zipped from over the harpy's head to hers, and then the memory flooded through her.

Light and heat exploded inside of her, overloading her senses. Everything went black except for the fiery inferno that she had become. The entirety of her world was light, glorious light – raging and fierce, devouring… devouring… devouring. She was a star, and she burned with exquisite fire. There was no body, no thoughts, no sounds, no sights – just white-hot burning. It seared through every atom of her being, and she throbbed with it, ached with it, exploded with it. It was pleasure so intense it was pain, pulsing through every atom of her being, pushing her higher and higher, past the point of endurance, and still it came, and she never wanted it to end. She was glorious and infinite, devourer of cosmos, magnificence incarnate.

The fire winked out as quickly as it had come, and she cried out as her body spasmed, wracked by the aftermath of the pleasure-pain. She collapsed, landing onto her hands and knees, trembling and shaking, unable to get control of her body, as the market swirled back into view.

She gasped as another spasm of pleasure rocked her body, and she had to bite her lip, hard, to keep from crying out. Embarrassment heated her face even as a completely different type of warmth suffused the rest of her. She tried to push the sensations to the back of her mind, to get control of her thoughts and her body, but each successive wave rocking her made that impossible. She groaned and bit down harder on her lip as another flare pulsed through her.

Slowly, the sensations faded, leaving her depleted and exhausted. She balanced on her hands and knees, the crowd eddying around her, unable to summon the strength to move from the position. The hard ground cut into her palms, and her arms trembled from the effort to remain as she was, but she was afraid that if she unlocked her arms, she'd fall flat on her face.

Taking a deep breath, she rocked back, pushing up with her hands, and managed to get herself into a kneeling position. She sat back on her heels, breathing slowly in and out as she tried to calm the twanging of her nerves endings.

"Holy fuck," she said, still dazed and reeling from the sensory overload.

Slowly, she climbed to her feet, groaning at the pain of cramped limbs. The harpy was watching her with what Irene thought might be a smug expression. She felt her face heat again.

"What the hell was that?" she asked, but she already knew. The memory was seared in her mind — the vast nothingness in which there was only the magnificent fire that was the entirety of her being. There had been no thoughts, no consciousness, no conscious self, just the all-consuming inferno creating and destroying her over and over and over.

She had been a star.

She exhaled hard, forcing herself to breath in slow and deep so that she stayed rooted here rather than slipping back into the orgasmic pleasure of the star memory.

She had been a star.

The harpy squawked with pride. "You like? Yes? My memories good, yes?"

"*Your* memories?"

Not a simulation.

Actual memories.

Like her own.

Experience.

Sentience.

A conscious understanding of and interacting with the environment.

Life.

Not as humans knew it, not as humans even imagined it possible, but life and, more importantly, sentience, on a thousand different planes of existence that humans didn't yet dream of or understand.

Until they died.

Irene stared at the harpy, trying to wrap her mind around the truth. "That's impossible," she said. How could this thing in front of her have been a star?

And what was it doing here if it had been?

It wasn't the creature's physical appearance that was confusing her — she understood that everything she saw was a precept, a construct of a mind trying to make sense of the non-physical realm of the afterlife. The wheat in Tartarus hadn't been wheat; she had seen through it with her "ghost eyes" to its true form: energy and heat and light. The part of her that had been human had wanted it to be wheat because that was how it was used to contextualizing the world — in terms of physical constructs. And she understood on some level that she no longer had a body, no longer had lungs and legs and hair and eyes — she was nothing more than a ball of energy now, too — but she still thought of herself in terms of lungs and legs and hair and eyes because that was how her human mind needed to frame things. It had no other way of understanding the world.

That part she got.

The part she didn't get was how the creature before her could have once been a star. How could a star have memories, and more importantly, how could a star — or a blade of grass or a ray of light — be standing here, before her, as a sentient being? Stars and grass and light weren't *alive* —

Another memory surfaced and slotted into place like a puzzle piece: on the last plane, she and Andras had been attacked by an angel, a Nephilim, and when Irene had asked why one of its kind, Samyel, had been on Earth among the living, the angel had corrected her, saying, "your living."

Your living — meaning humans.

The angel had been telling her that there were other kinds of life, other planes of existence, other things besides humans that lived sentient lives.

Irene shuddered and took a step back as the truth hit her. *Jesus.* This wasn't the afterlife — not as humans thought of it. The afterlife was a human-centric concept — a world for and about humans after they had left their physical shell. This, however, was so much more. The world as humans experienced it was so small, such a tiny part of existence, such a tiny part of what lived and died and transformed. Death had granted her access to the actual world — the entirety of creation that existed beyond the narrow precepts of human experience and understanding.

"The Romans thought we are all gods, and that time spent on Earth is a prison. When our time is over, we return to being gods."

She remembered the words, spoken to her so long ago, and her heart lurched.

The stories were all true.

The Chinese were right. The Egyptians were right. The Buddhists were right. The Aztecs were right.

The Romans were right.

Irene turned in a half-circle again, surveying the market for the third time, and she finally understood what the humans were doing – they were learning.

Learning how to exist as beings of energy and light.

Learning how to exist in one or two or ten dimensions.

Learning how to traverse the planes of the universe.

Learning how to take their place among the pantheon of creation.

What type of person traded their memories of being human for memories of other types of existence? One that was ready to move on, to move forward, to be reborn.

Irene turned back to the harpy, her eyes wide, reassessing the creature's outward appearance, trying to see past the physical form to the true form, the star, beneath. The harpy ruffled its feathers and blinked at her. "More? You want more? I have more."

Irene shook her head, not sure she could survive more of the same. She backed away from the stall, not sure what to do now.

You have to go forward to go back and back to go forward.

She wasn't really sure which way was up now. Which way – forward or back – was the way she needed to go? Learning how to be less human might help her get out of this market, might help her learn how to travel across the planes of the afterlife faster and more efficiently. At the same time, it might also make her forget why she wanted to go back to Tartarus and back to Earth. It might also make it impossible for her to do so – once she learned how to exist as a non-physical being, would she ever be able to return to the narrow confines of the physical? Once she had been a star, the wind, an ocean, could she ever be satisfied just being human?

She understood now what the guide had meant when he'd said she could return to Earth, but not as herself and that she had to go forward to go back. She could shine down, as a star, on her mother and LaRayne and Alexia and her old boss and all the other people living their lives on Earth or touch their faces as a breeze or tickle their feet as a blade of grass. And due to the unique, defining thing that made her Irene, she'd be a stubbornly glinting star, or a particularly stubborn and forceful wind, or a tenacious blade of grass growing where others had been unable to take root.

Or, she could hang onto her humanity and the reasons she wanted to return and be forced to take the long, slow way back. The people she loved might be dead by the time she figured out how to navigate the planes of the afterlife or found the right combination of rabbit holes and short cuts to take her back. And once back, she'd still only be a ghost; she might be able to give her ghostly existence the purpose and meaning it had lacked when she'd last been on Earth by watching over her family and friends and helping out other ghosts in trouble like Amy and Ernest, but, in the end, her existence would still just be a pale shadow of what it was when she was alive and what it could be if she embraced everything offered here.

A ghost watching over her family unseen or experience the blazing glory of a star?

To feel the breeze on her face or to be the breeze?

To touch her family without them knowing she did so or to touch her family without her knowing who they were?

It was an impossible choice.

Her eyes raked across the market, not really taking anything in, not really seeing the landscape before her. They darted from stall to stall, grasping for anything to hold onto, anything that would help her make sense of what to do next, of which path to choose.

The hum and burble of the market seemed to fade away, leaving only the sound of her heart in her ears. Across the market, an opening appeared in the crowd — a spontaneous parting as if the people all moved aside in the same moment; in the middle of the opening stood the Guide.

"You!" Irene cried, darting toward him, relief and anger swirling together at the sight of him.

The Guide motioned to the stall beside him, pointing at it purposefully. Then he began to fade from view.

"What? Wait a minute..." She put out a hand, trying to grab hold of him, to stop him from disappearing, but in the next moment, the crowd closed up around him, and he was gone.

"Damn it!" Irene cried, scanning the area, but the Guide was truly gone. She wasn't even sure he'd really been there. Maybe she had imagined the whole thing. She turned to the vendor that the Guide had pointed at. "Okay, fine, I'll take one. How much?"

"Cheap! Cheap! Only costs spring rain."

"Okay, fine, whatever. Do it."

There was the swish of memory balls exchanging and then darkness. For several long moments there was nothing but dark, pure and absolute.

No sensations.

No thoughts.

No feelings.

Just... darkness and a sense of gathered potential, almost a sense of waiting and anticipation — if she'd had any understanding of such a thing.

And then...

And then...

And then...

There was yearning. For something she couldn't name but absolutely knew. A yearning towards that vast, nameless something that was both her and necessary for her to become her.

There was separation now, an unfurling. Tip up, roots down. Stretching, reaching, striving.

Up.

Up.

Up.

There was resistance, a hard, unmovable wall blocking her path, blocking her way towards the vastness calling her, and she pushed against it with the frail, trembling stem that was her being.

The pushing went on for a long time with no discernable change. Then all at once, the resistance gave way. A crack, that was all she needed. She pushed through, one infinitesimal step at a time.

The yearning increased, driving her now, and she reached out with every atom of her being, letting the yearning pull her towards her destination. Below, she sprouted roots, which sank, thin and shallow at first and then deeper and thicker, hardening and lengthening to immoveable anchors, holding her burgeoning height and weight firmly.

She was dividing now, tendrils branching out in multiple directions, harvesting life with her wide green leaves. And still she yearned, reaching, stretching, striving.

Up.

Up.

Up.

Become. Become. Become.

The memory of being an acorn faded, the market filtering back into view. The yearning, however, remained.

Because it was hers.

Because it had always been hers, always been a part of her.

Even when she hadn't recognized it, even when she hadn't consciously been aware of it, it had been there.

Always and forever.

Inside her. Inside everyone.

Her stomach ached, as if the wind had been knocked out of her. She doubled over, curling her arms protectively around herself, trying to hold in the pain, the sense of loss. If it escaped, she would crack open like a walnut, spilling her insides everywhere. Tears ran down her face.

She'd asked a question — *should I go forward or backward* — and the universe, in the form of the Guide, had answered: there really was only way she could go.

With effort, she climbed unsteadily to her feet. Around her, the market—stalls, vendors, shoppers, and all—was fading away, disintegrating into darkness. She spun around as she tried to hold onto the plane before it disappeared completely, but now she was in a narrow hole, fifteen feet across. She looked up—she could see the underside of the river of fire a long way up. When she looked down again, she was surrounded by obsidian walls. She was back in Tartarus, once more stuck in the bottom of the canyon.

Shakily, she crossed to the nearest wall, running her hands over the smooth surface to verify its validity. "This isn't better than the market!" she muttered, silently cursing the Guide for not at least dumping her back at the top of the canyon.

She swiped at her tears and took a deep breath, wrestling her emotions back under control. She still had to rescue Andras. In his present state, he very likely couldn't exist outside of this plane. Before she did anything else, she had to get his shadow back.

She stepped back from the wall and surveyed the small space, looking for any signs of Andras.

"Andras? Are you still here? Andras?" She prayed he hadn't also slid off this plane—she'd never find him if he had—or worse, dissipated into the ether. She wasn't sure how long he could stay together without his shadow.

I am here.

"Oh thank God," she said, putting a hand on the wall to steady herself as her knees went weak with relief. "I thought I'd lost you!"

I did not leave.

"No, I know; I did—but not on purpose. I fell through one of those cracks between planes again." Irene slowly pivoted in place, scanning with her ghost senses for any other tunnels or openings that she might use to climb out of the canyon and back up to Tartarus. "While I was gone, I don't suppose you figured out a way for me to get out of here?"

You are not trapped. There was a note of question in Andras's voice, as if he didn't quite understand her dilemma. She could feel the change in his emotions as if it there was a sudden change in the weather. The slow, sonorous oscillations of Andras's default state of collected and tightly checked emotions gave way to a short, sharp humming that she took for perplexity.

Technically, he was right. She wasn't trapped; the market was the main way out of here. However, she didn't want to go out that way. She needed to get to Tartarus, to get Andras's shadow back, and then get Andras to the castle. The castle was Ucles, and Ucles was duty. For Andras, that was Heaven.

Irene surveyed the smooth walls once more and then closed her eyes, relaxing her mind so she could look past the walls to see their true underlying nature.

Did the boy mention this place?

"Hmmm?" Irene asked absently, only half listening. Her mind skimmed over the shapes and textures that made up the walls, and she probed deeper, focusing on the taste and feel of Tartarus and trying to find anything that matched, any tunnel or bridge that would lead back there.

The boy, Andras repeated impatiently.

"Boy? What boy?" Irene retorted just as impatiently, trying, and failing, to hold onto her concentration.

The air vibrated hard with irritation. *I apologize,* Andras said, sounding more annoyed than contrite. *Jonah. Did Jonah mention this place?*

The strange note of insistence in Andras's voice gave her pause. Confused, and a little worried, she opened her eyes as she shook her head, turning away from the wall to where she supposed Andras stood. She frowned. "Andras, I don't know what you're talking about. I don't know anyone by that name."

Twenty

Jonah opened his eyes. Everything was fuzzy and indistinct. His head throbbed and his body felt like it had been through a meat grinder. He lifted a hand to his head with a groan, forcing his eyes to open all the way.

He was standing in the middle of a formless gray mist, in what appeared to be the void between the land of the living and the land of the dead, the one on the other side of every red door he'd ever stepped through. He took two steps forward and instantly a familiar door loomed before him, confirming his suspicion. He put a hand to his neck and then groaned. The crystal Char had given him was gone, stolen by Persephone.

Char.

He had to get back to the land of the dead. His stomach dropped at the thought that it might already be too late. He yanked open the door dashed through it, tumbling out onto a familiar Boston street, back in the same location where he and Char had been chased through the door by the Ugly a lifetime ago.

He took off at a run, heading for the magic shop, his mind clear of all thoughts but one: get another crystal and return to the land of the dead. No matter where Char was, he would find her, and he would find a way to save her.

His feet pounded against the pavement as he ran blindly through the streets, bee-lining for the magic shop. He was gasping for air by the time he skidded to a halt at the back door. Just as he reached for the knob, the door was thrown open from the inside.

He blinked in surprise as Char stood framed in the doorway by the fading afternoon sunlight. His stupor was broken by a squeal of delight from Char as she threw her arms around his neck and squeezed tight.

"Oh my God, I'm so glad to see you! I was just going back—"

"How did you get here?" he asked, stunned to find her in the last place he expected to see her. "Are you okay?" He stepped back so he could look her over for injuries. "How did you get here?" He realized he was repeating himself, his words tumbling out in confusion.

She laughed, though it was thin and watery like she might burst into tears at any second. She was a ghastly shade of white, and she was shaking. "Yeah, actually, it was kind of funny," she said with no trace of humor in her voice. "We hadn't gone very far when I suddenly felt like I was falling. Then everything kind of faded away and became all gray and misty. I thought I had fallen off the horse and gotten a concussion or something. Then I saw a door floating in the mist and realized I was in the void between worlds. Though I didn't know how it happened or why, I was glad to get away from those guys. I wanted to go back and find you, but that's when I noticed my focusing crystal was gone. It either fell off from all the bumping around on horseback or maybe got knocked off when they grabbed me, I don't know. What must have happened is that as soon as I lost the crystal, I lost my hold on the land of the dead and got sucked back to the in-between place. I knew I couldn't get back to you without first getting another crystal, but I was afraid to leave in case you showed up. I hung around for a while, waiting for you, then I went through the door, back into Boston, and finally I ran back here to get another crystal."

Jonah sagged against the side of the building. His legs gave out as relief flooded through him and he sank to the ground.

"Jesus, Char... I can't even tell you how scared I was..."

Char laughed, and this time she sounded more like her usual self. "Awww, were you worried about little ole me," she said. When he shot her a rueful look, she playfully batted her eyes and struck a cutesy, fawning expression like a 1950's movie heroine.

He just shook his head, still not quite able to process that they were safely back in the land of the living. The full brunt of what had happened hit him, and he laughed mirthlessly as he cradled his head in hands. Defeat washed over him.

"What's so funny?" Char asked.

Jonah couldn't look at her. "You were right," he said grimly. "I'm a total failure. How am I going to save Irene when I'm totally useless?"

Char sank into a crouch beside him and put a hand on his arm. "Jonah—"

"No, seriously, this was a disaster," he said, still cradling his head. "I couldn't even find a way over to the other side— I needed your help with that. Then we got stuck over there, and I couldn't find a way back—it was pure luck, you losing your crystal and mine getting stolen, that we both managed to get back here in one piece. To top it off, I was attacked by an actual demon and didn't do so well." He glanced down at his chest and saw that the neck of his t-shirt was in tatters. He peered through the holes in the fabric and saw several deep slashes in his skin.

Char noticed, too. Her eyes widened. "Oh my God, what happened?"

Jonah shook his head as he adjusted his shirt collar, covering up the wound. "Persephone. Or, at least, that's who I thought she was. Now I don't know."

Beg. Offer me riches. Offer to be my slave. Offer me your life.

Her face, cruel and mocking, loomed up in his mind's eye, sending a shiver through him. Why had she taken his crystal? It had sent him back to the land of the living—had she meant to do that? Had she known Char was already back here and was actually trying to help him, or had she really attacked him, stealing the crystal for her own ends?

His mind flashed to Samyel, the strange "man" he and Irene had met. Samyel had agreed to help Irene if she took him with her through the tunnel to the other side. Jonah had wondered about that—was Samyel somehow stuck here?

Now Jonah thought maybe he'd traveled here from another afterlife plane and couldn't get back. Alternatively, maybe he'd had a crystal and lost it, or maybe it didn't work on him. Perhaps that was why Persephone needed a crystal—to escape from where she was or to cross into somewhere else... perhaps even to the land of the living.

Dread slithered through him, and he shivered again.

"So what are you going to do?" she asked.

He shook his head again—he didn't know what he could do—as he slowly got to his feet. He shoved the thoughts of Persephone and Samyel from his mind. There were other problems to solve first. "It doesn't matter. At the moment, there's something way more pressing than Irene."

Char's eyebrows rose in surprise as she straightened up. "Oh?"

"Uh, did you forget that we still have to figure out how to get you back into your body? Escaping from the land of the dead was the easy part, remember?"

"Oh. Yeah." Apparently, in her relief at making it back safely from the land of the dead, Char *had* forgotten about her predicament. She looked down at herself in confusion.

Jonah grunted. "See? I told you it's easy to forget when you're out of your body. Not so weird now, is it?"

Char stuck her tongue out at him in response.

He grunted again, even as a slow grin spread across his face. His joking mood was short-lived though, as reality crashed back in on him—they needed to go in and face Madame Majikca.

Jonah sighed, the grin fading as quickly as it had surfaced. The blood-thundering fear of Char's kidnapping and his run-in with Persephone were replaced with a dull, hollow, dread as he imagined Madame Majicka's anger at what had happened. He glanced toward the shop's interior. "Have you seen your Aunt? Is she pissed?"

Char shook her head. "Auntie's not here."

Jonah lifted an eyebrow. "Really?" It wasn't unusual for Madame Majicka to not be around, but he and Char had been gone for a while—at least for the better part of a day; it had been morning when they left, and now it was late afternoon. Was it really possible that Madame Majicka hadn't noticed? Maybe he'd have a chance to fix this before she returned.

He jerked his head toward the door, indicating they should go in, and winced as the movement caused the slash marks around his collar bone to burn. He was exhausted, he ached all over, and he wanted nothing more than lie down and take a nap, but there wasn't time. They needed to figure out how to fix Char as soon as possible. He entered the shop with Char on his heels and headed upstairs. In his room, Char's body was on the bed, curled up against his on top of the white coverlet, as if the two of them had fallen asleep together. Jonah groaned.

"Really? What would your aunt have thought if she'd found us like this?"

Char grinned. "She'd think we'd been fooling around."

"Yeah, and she'd murder me!"

Char raised an eyebrow. "Are you kidding? She'd be thrilled. Why do you think she told me she suddenly and urgently needed my help at the shop? She was trying to fix us up."

Discomfort at the thought of Madame Majicka playing matchmaker for him heated Jonah's face. "Ugh... really?"

Char glared at him. "Gee, thanks."

"Sorry. I didn't mean—"

"Yeah, yeah," Char said with a wave of her hand. "I know."

Jonah went to the bed and looked down at Char's body. Then he looked at his own. For the first time, he noticed how gaunt he looked, the bones of his wrists sticking out in sharp relief against the thinness of his arms, visible where his long-sleeved t-shirt had ridden up. Char was right that the body had needs—food, exercise, sunlight. Char's inability to return to her body wasn't just an inconvenience; there might be very real health consequences if she stayed out of it for too long.

Char followed him to the bed, creeping closer until she stood staring down at her own body. "It's kind of weird to look at myself from this angle," she said absently. "Is that really what my chin looks like?"

Jonah cast her a worried glance. She seemed strangely disinterested. Maybe she was going into shock, the reality of the situation finally hitting her. "Maybe we should go to your room," he said.

Char shook her head, though she crossed to the desk and sat down, back to the bed. "No, it's okay. The bodies are here."

"Okay, well, let's see if we can fix this. We should try the obvious, first."

He grabbed Char's body by the shoulders and shook her. Then he looked at her. "Feel anything?" he asked.

Char, having twisted around to see what he was doing, shook her head.

He tried shaking her again. "Do you mind if I get a little rough?" he asked.

Char smirked.

Exasperated, he said, "Be serious."

She grinned and gestured for him to proceed.

He hesitated, then gave her hair a tentative tug.

"Oh for cryin' out loud," Char said, getting up and crossing to the bed. She grabbed a handful of hair and gave it a vicious yank.

"Maybe pinch or slap yourself?" Jonah suggested.

Char proceed to try both, first pinching her arms until she almost drew blood and then slapping herself hard in the face.

Jonah shifted uncomfortably. "This is…" He trailed off.

Char nodded. "Weird. And disturbing."

"And, also, not working."

Jonah pulled the black afterlife book from the arms of Char's body. He perched on the edge of the bed, the springs creaking in protest, and flipped pages. He paused to recite a spell for reviving the dead. Nothing happened.

"I'm not sure I pronounced half these words right," he said. Char had said pronunciation didn't matter, but he didn't really understand how the spells, er, mediations, worked without pronunciation—just one more thing he apparently needed to learn. He tried again, altering his pronunciation, and then a third time. Still no effect.

Reluctantly, he moved on, turning more pages in the book. He tried a spell to reconstitute broken items and one to reanimate the dead.

"That's not going to make me into a zombie is it?" Char asked nervously.

"Would that be worse than being a ghost?" Jonah asked.

Char shot him a warning look. "This is hardly the time for jokes."

Grimly, Jonah replied, "Who's joking?"

It didn't matter—the spell didn't work anyway. Jonah turned to the last page in the book and then returned to the beginning to flip through a second time. He reviewed every page slowly and carefully, but nothing jumped out at him. In fact, he was finding it hard to focus on anything in the book, the pages swimming before his eyes as his concentration wandered. Finally, he slammed the book closed. "Let's go downstairs. Maybe there's something in the shop we can use."

"Like what?"

"I don't know. Like the crystals, maybe."

They trooped downstairs and, starting with the ghost side of the shop, began searching for something that might help. Jonah racked his brain for any bit of ghost lore that might help them as they looked. He wandered about the shop, picking up items at random and then putting them back down again. "We should check the other side. This stuff is all for ghosts—there's nothing to help a ghost get back into their body once they're really and truly dead."

They crossed through the bead curtain to the living side of the store. Jonah looked at the array of crystals on a nearby table. "Do these all do the same thing, or do the different colors mean different things?"

"They're pretty much all the same—for concentrating energy and such."

Jonah picked one up and held it in his hand. It didn't feel like anything in particular—not warm or cold, just heavy. "We probably don't want one of these then—we want to weaken your ghost form, not strengthen it." He set the crystal back down. "Can you think of anything that might help?"

"Like what?"

"I don't know, like the crystal helped to get us to the other side. You know more about this psychic stuff than I do."

Char gave him a hopeless look. She picked up a pack of incense and then slapped it back down in frustration. "This stuff is all about awakening your third eye and harmonizing your energy and such. It's about getting out of your body, not into it."

"Well, crap." Defeated, he looked at Char, hoping she had a suggestion. "I don't know what to do."

With obvious reluctance, she replied, "As much as I hate to say it, I think we're going to need Auntie's help."

Jonah groaned and slumped against the counter. "Your aunt is going to kill me."

Of course, they were both assuming Madame Majicka could fix this. What if she couldn't? Jonah grimaced, dreading the thought of how Madame Majicka was going to react. He'd taken the job at the shop because it had ideally positioned him to continue his search for Irene, but it hadn't been all cold calculation. He liked Madame Majicka, and she was going to be disappointed in him. He'd learned quite a bit about dealing with the dead from her, and apparently, she'd cared enough about him to try fixing him up with her niece. She'd given him a job and a place to live, and she'd trusted him to run the shop when she wasn't around. He'd even come to enjoy receiving advice over a cup of tea. He hated the thought of losing her respect and even more, of losing her friendship.

He sighed. "Well, what do you want to do while we wait for her to come back?"

Char gave a one-shouldered shrug.

Jonah mimicked the movement, feeling the same way. "Honestly," he said, "I'd love to just to go to bed. I feel like I could sleep for a hundred years."

"Sounds good to me," Char said. "I feel like I've run a hundred miles."

They silently made their way back up the rough, wooden stairs and down the narrow hall. Jonah headed for his room, but then paused at the door when Char made to follow him. He shot her a quizzical look.

She gave him a look of indignation mingled with pleading. "Oh, come on, I don't want to be alone! I'm already freaked out enough as it is—I'm a ghost! What if I start to fade away or get sucked over to the other side?"

"That won't happen."

"How do you know?"

"It's never happened to me, and you used the same spell!"

"That doesn't mean anything! I'm a girl, and I'm psychic—so things might work differently on me."

Exasperated, Jonah pushed open his bedroom door and then gestured for Char to enter. He followed her in and then headed for the desk. "Look, I'm going to check the book again, one last time, okay?" He didn't wait for a response as he settled himself at the desk. Behind him, he heard the bed creak as Char sat down.

He flipped the book open to a bookmarked passage in the middle. The page contained the meditation that allowed him to separate his spirit from his body. It also held additional text that he had never been able to translate, illustrated by three drawings: the first was the outline of a stick-figure person, the second was the same stick figure with blue lines radiating from it, and the third was the same figure as the first, only colored in with heavy, black ink. He had long thought that the three illustrations on this page referred to the three states of being: fully alive, the in-between state of someone in the meditative trance, and fully dead. As the middle passage contained the meditative trance that allowed the living to separate their spirit from their body, he suspected that the remaining two, untranslated passages, contained information or incantations related to the other two states. In fact, one of the passages could be instructions for how to return the spirit to the body. Unfortunately, in the five years that he'd had the book, he'd never been able to translate the passages. They were written in some obscure, dead language.

He attempted to study the passage, but try as he might, his eyes just couldn't seem to stay on the page. He'd start to read and would suddenly find himself skimming the words, not really seeing or understanding them. He'd refocus, and a moment later, the same thing would happen. After several tries, he realized why — the book was dead. The essence or spirit of the book had been in his backpack — the backpack that he'd lost after the fight with Ernest. Without its essence, the physical shell of the book — like the coins left on the shrine at Irene's grave — was empty and lifeless, mere junk and of no further use. He groaned and threw the book down on the desk. He'd lost the most valuable thing he'd ever owned. That book held all of the knowledge ever collected about the afterlife. With it, his search for Irene had been hard enough; without it, there was no way he could succeed.

"What's the matter?" Char asked from the bed.

Jonah shook his head, unable to speak. Misery washed over him.

"Jonah?"

He heard the bed springs creak, and he forced himself to push the thoughts aside. He didn't want to talk about it — it hurt too much. Besides, Char wasn't going to want to hear about this; she had her own problems—and he should be focusing on those right now.

He stood up and crossed to the bed. "Nothing," he said, forcing a reassuring smile to his face. "I just remembered I lost my backpack is all."

Char was sitting to one side of their bodies, so he climbed onto the other side of the bed and settled himself against the headboard in the narrow strip of unoccupied mattress. Char stared at him, her knees drawn up to her chest, with a look of wide-eyed misery. The fact that she might be stuck permanently had clearly set in, and he could tell she was terrified. He sighed and opened one arm in silent invitation

Instantly, Char sprang up and moved closer, climbing awkwardly over their bodies in the middle of the bed so she could curl against him like a kitten. He stared down at the top of her head, picking out the individual strands of mingled black and purple. She shivered, her face buried against his shoulder. He put his arm around her and gave her a reassuring squeeze. "Don't worry, Char—we'll figure something out."

She made a guttural noise, almost like a hiccup, and he thought maybe she was crying. Guilt washed over him anew. He searched for something to say, something that would reassure her, but he couldn't imagine what would make this better.

He rested his head against the headboard and began slowly and methodically going through his inventory of afterlife knowledge. Somewhere in his brain had to be the answer—in something he'd read or seen or heard.

However, his brain refused to cooperate. Instead, now that it was quiet and he had time to think, the memory of his encounter with Persephone kept cropping up. No matter how he tried to stop thinking about it, the image of her growing and spreading and rising over him with the unfurling darkness behind her crept to the forefront of his mind, making his heart hammer and his back prickle with cold sweat. His new wounds burned as he recalled her slashing him.

You're falling... falling between worlds.

For some reason, Persephone's words terrified him — even more than the woman herself. He recalled the terror of Char's kidnapping and of the encounter with Persephone, and a shiver of fear snaked through him. That had been the happy afterlife. Imagine what the unhappy one looked like.

He tried to shove that thought away as, for the first time, he realized there really and truly might not be anything he could do to help Irene. In all his imaginings of where she might be or what might be happening to her or what it would be like when they were reunited, he had never imagined failing — he never didn't find her, never didn't save her.

Eventually, despite the fact he was in his ghost body and technically didn't need sleep, his eyes grew heavy, and he fell asleep. He slept like the dead. When he woke, the sun was full overhead, light streaming through the gauzy lace curtains over the window. Char was still curled up against him, and by all appearances, she, too, had slept soundly through the night. As soon as he moved, she awoke with a start, looking around in confusion, until her memory caught up to her. Her shoulders slumped. She didn't say anything, just cast him a worried look, and then they both got up and made their way downstairs to face Madame Majicka.

The walk down the hall and then the stairs was the longest of his life. His stomach roiled with a slurry of anxiety and regret. When Madame Majicka found out just how much he'd betrayed her trust, she would throw him out — if he was lucky, that's all she'd do. His shoulders sagged as he imagined the look of disappointment on her face.

They reached the bottom of the stairs, and Jonah hesitated, delaying the moment of reckoning for as long as he could. Finally, he took a deep breath and forced himself forward. He scanned the living half of the shop, but there was no sign of Madame Majicka. Exchanging a glance with Char, they headed for the ghost half of the store. They pushed aside the bead curtain and stepped through. However, to his surprise, Madame Majicka wasn't there either. In fact, the shop was closed, locked up tight. They returned through the bead curtain and double-checked the living side, only to find that it, too, was closed. Jonah and Char exchanged confused glances and then headed towards the stairs to look for Madame Majicka there. They didn't have to talk to know where they were headed—Madame Majicka hadn't been in his bedroom and wasn't likely to be in Char's. There was only one other place she could be: her bedroom. They both hesitated outside the door to her room, and then, screwing up his courage, Jonah rapped on the door.

Silence.

Jonah rapped again.

Still no answer. Hesitantly, he cracked open her door and peered in. "Hello?"

Empty.

Jonah and Char exchanged another silent look of confusion and growing alarm.

"This isn't like Auntie. She would have told us if she was going somewhere."

Jonah wasn't so sure—he wouldn't put it past Madame Majicka to swan off without telling them—but he didn't tell Char that. Instead, he just shrugged.

"Maybe..." Char hesitated and then visibly swallowed hard.

"What?"

"Maybe we were gone a really long time."

Jonah frowned. "If we were gone a long time, wouldn't they have moved us to the hospital or something? That's what happened to me last time someone found me like this."

Char didn't seem convinced, so they hunted around for something that would tell them the date. They found Char's cell phone in her room, but the battery was dead.

"Where's the charger?" Jonah asked, trying to remain calm.

Char was tossing things about, clearly growing more and more agitated by the second. Her room was a mirror of his — plain wooden desk, chair, three-drawer wooden bureau with a mirror, and a wrought-iron bed. Char kept her room a lot neater than his, though — the desk was clear, and the bed was made.

"Why would it be in your sock drawer?" he asked as socks flew past his head.

"I don't know!" Char snapped, yanking t-shirts from another drawer.

"Will you just stop for a second and think. It's not going to be in your dresser. How about a suitcase or backpack or..."

"Ah ha!" Char cried, pulling a tangled cord from amidst a jumble of shirts. She shot Jonah a triumphant look and then crossed the room to a free outlet.

The phone was completely dead, so it didn't come on right away. Char impatiently tapped her foot. "Come on... Come on..."

"Will you chill? I'm telling you it hasn't been that long."

There was a "Ding!" as the battery received enough juice to power up the phone. Char jabbed frantically at the buttons and then froze, staring at the screen with wide-eyes.

"How long?" Jonah asked, a knot in his stomach.

"Three days," Char whispered.

Jonah exhaled in relief. Three days. Not terrible. Long enough for Madame Majicka to have noticed they were gone but not long enough to have completely upended their lives.

"Three days," Char repeated.

"It's not that bad."

Char shot him a look that said she disagreed.

Jonah held up his hands in surrender. "Okay, fine, but this doesn't answer the question of where your aunt is. By this time, she'd have to know something's wrong. I can't believe she'd leave us alone." Jonah looked at the phone. "Can you text her, tell her we're back?"

Char shook her head. "Auntie doesn't have a cell phone."

"Doesn't have a cell phone?" Jonah echoed.

Char shrugged. "She's not good with technology. You might have noticed she still has one of those old-fashioned cash registers with the push buttons and the bell."

"I thought that was just for ambiance."

Char shook her head. "No, that's for Auntie."

They stared at each other, neither sure what to do next. Finally, Char said, "Well... this is anticlimactic." She gave Jonah a helpless look. "What do we do now?"

Jonah shrugged again. He really and truly was out of ideas.

They stood there for a moment and then by mutual, unspoken agreement, wandered back down to the shop. They each plopped down in a chair and sat there, limp and unfocused.

The minutes ticked by slowly.

Char began to drum her fingers on the table. "Being a ghost is kind of boring."

"Ayup."

He cast about the shop for something to relieve the tension.

A bell tingled. Jonah glanced at the front door, but it was closed. No one had entered there. It must have come from the other side of the shop. Jonah looked at Char, tensing slightly. "We locked the door yesterday!"

"Maybe Auntie came home last night after we went to sleep and then left again this morning?"

That made no sense to him. They'd been gone for three days. If Madame Majicka had seen that they had returned, she wouldn't have just left them alone again. And if she hadn't realized they'd returned, then that meant she hadn't been checking on them. Didn't she even care that they had been gone?

In a moment, he had his answer as Madame Majicka, followed by a bevy of women dressed in stylish, smart clothes in somber, serious tones, swept into the room.

"Oh, really, you two!" she said, as soon as she saw Jonah and Char.

They both jumped to their feet.

"Auntie!" Char cried. She dashed to her aunt and threw her arms around her.

"Oh, hush," Madame Majicka said, wrapping her arms around Char. "There, there, my dear, don't worry."

"I'm stuck!" Char said in a small voice, her face buried against her aunt's shoulder. "I can't get back into my body!"

Madame Majicka was looking at Jonah over Char's head, and Jonah could barely meet her eyes as he tried to explain. "I—" he said, but Madame Majicka cut him off with a sharp, slashing gesture. He cringed, guilt and shame coursing through him, and all the fight went out of him. He hung his head. "Can you fix it?" he asked, hoping against hope that the answer was yes. He lifted his eyes just high enough to see her toss her head.

"Of course I can fix it."

Jonah's head jerked up. "But how? I tried everything!"

"Well, you might know a great deal about the dead, my dear, but, lucky for you, I happen to know quite a lot about the living." She set Char away from her, and Jonah cringed again as he saw Char surreptitiously wipe away tears.

The women accompanying Madame Majicka were filling the shop. There seemed to be no end to them as they crowded into the small space, talking in hushed tones as if they were at a funeral. One of the women touched Madame Majicka's shoulder. The psychic turned to the woman, who whispered something in her ear. "Oh, yes," Madame Majicka replied. She raised her hands, clapping them together twice, to get everyone' attention. "Ladies, if you please, up the stairs, first door on the left. You, too, Char."

Jonah watched them file out, his heart shuddering in his chest with both hope and dread. Madame Majicka seemed very certain she could fix this, but what if she was wrong?

The psychic gestured impatiently for him to proceed up the stairs as well. Swallowing his fear, he crossed the room and slowly headed for his bedroom, step by ponderous step, Madame Majicka on his heels.

The women all moved quietly and solemnly, filling the narrow hallway with an air of reverence. The noiselessness of the procession was broken only by the sound of his shoes scuffing on the carpeting. He felt awkward and ungainly, too big for his shoes and too small for his clothes. The women seemed to move as a unit, following a pattern or unspoken command, in a graceful and well-rehearsed dance, making him feel even more clumsy and wooden with every step he took.

The feeling that he was somehow intruding and unwelcome only doubled when he entered his bedroom. The women knelt in a circle around the bed where Char's body lay. Char, herself, stood at the foot of the bed, near to the circle but outside of it. Jonah squeezed inside the doorway, unsure how to proceed, but Madame Majicka put a hand on his back and pushed him forward into the room. "It wasn't a push you needed," she said as she stepped past him to approach the bed. "It was a pull."

Jonah's face creased with confusion. He wasn't sure he was allowed to ask questions, but was saved from having to by Char.

"What's going to happen?" she asked.

"You two were pushing on the door the wrong way; you were trying to shove your spirit back into your body from the outside when what you really needed was to pull it back in from the inside. Lucky for you, I was already planning to pull you both back." She gestured to the women assembled around the room.

Char's forehead creased in confusion. She looked around the circle of women and then at her aunt. "I don't understand."

Madame Majicka pulled a crystal — not unlike the one he and Char had used to travel to the other side — from her pocket and set it on Char's body — the one on the bed — in the center of her chest. She gestured for Char to come and stand beside her.

"Think of it like fishing," Madame Majicka said. "We're going to pass a psychic rope through your body for you to grab onto and then pull you into your body by it."

The women joined hands, starting with a woman on the far side of the bed who took hold of one of the hands of Char's body and ending with the woman to the right of Madame Majicka putting a free hand on the psychic's shoulder. The women on either side of Jonah each took one of his hands as well, pulling him down to kneel beside them and incorporating him into the circle.

Madame Majicka reached a hand out and took one of Char's ghost hands in her own. "Char, my dear, concentrate. Feel the thread of energy connecting you to your body, and feel us pulling on that thread, guiding you back. Understand?"

Char gave a short, sharp nod, as if afraid to move at all.

Madame Majicka bowed her head, and the women followed suit, as if they were all praying. The psychic reached out her free hand and put it over the crystal resting on Char's body. Everything went still.

Jonah held his breath, waiting, his eyes fixed on the bed, and found himself unconsciously trying to will Char back into her body.

For a long moment, nothing happened. The hands holding his gripped tighter, and yet, nothing seemed to change. A surge of panic shot through him. Whatever they were doing, it wasn't working.

Then he felt it—a tingling warmth, faint but discernable, running through him like a current. He focused on it, trying to amplify the feeling, trying to dump some part of himself into it to make it stronger. He had no idea if anything he did made any difference, but still, he concentrated as hard as he could, pulling the current into himself from the right and willing it to flow from him to the person on his left.

Char's body twitched, and as it did so, Char's ghost form blinked out of existence. Jonah sucked in his breath, but a moment later released it in a relieved woosh as Char, once more in her body, sat up on the bed. She blinked and looked around, seeming disoriented. Then she looked down at herself, an expression of incredulity spreading across her face. She patted herself. "I'm back? Oh my God, I'm back!" She turned to Madame Majicka and threw her arms around her neck. "Oh, Auntie!"

"Oh, my dear," her aunt murmured, holding Char. "Hush now. You're fine."

Jonah caught Char's eye, and he smiled. "Hey."

Char pulled out of Madame Majicka's arms and scrambled off the bed. She bounded across the room and threw her arms around him. "I'm back! Look, it's me!"

Jonah wrapped his arms around her, returning the hug. Char was trembling from relief and another surge of guilt washed over him.

Life is short. The afterlife is forever.

The enormity of what had almost happened engulfed him, and he buried his face in Char's hair, squeezing her tight. For several long minutes, they clung to each other, unable to let go.

Around them, the women rose to their feet and filtered out of the room. Madame Majicka murmured a word of thanks to each of them.

"Char, my dear," Madame Majicka said, "run down and put the kettle on, will you? I think this calls for tea."

Reluctantly, Char stepped out of Jonah's arms with an anguished look. They both knew what was coming next.

"It's not his fault—" Char said in a rush, but Madame Majicka cut her off. Gently, but firmly, the psychic said, "The tea, Char."

"But Auntie—"

"It's okay," Jonah said to Char. "You should go."

Char's shoulders slumped. With one last rueful look, she turned and left the room.

Jonah's heart sped up, dread making it thump unevenly. He knew what was coming, but that didn't make it any easier. He was about to lose everything—his home, his job, his friends—and suddenly he realized how much he didn't want to lose those things—and not because of how it would hinder his search for Irene but because of how much it meant to him. Somehow, in the midst of everything—abandoning his "real world" life, searching for Irene, and the "adventures" with Char—he'd built a life, an actual life, that he enjoyed. Maybe it wasn't traditional—it didn't include college or many living people—but it held important work and hobbies and friends. A pang of regret went through him, and he desperately wondered if there was anything he could say to make Madame Majicka forgive him.

The psychic regarded him for a long moment, her thoughts unfathomable behind the inky black of her eyes. Finally, she said, "The dead are a tricky business."

"What do you mean?" he asked cautiously.

She gave him a soft, sad smile. "Well, you see, they're dead and yet they're alive, they're corporeal and ethereal, ephemeral and eternal, existing everywhere and nowhere at once. They remain here with us, and yet they're gone, beside us and yet always out of reach. It's a terrible paradox and a fabulous duality that, alas, the living can never hope to aspire to. We, you see, have to be one or the other, I'm afraid."

He scuffed a toe against the floor, avoiding her eyes. "I know," he said quietly.

Madame Majicka regarded him for a moment, her eyes dark and unreadable. "Do you? Then, I suppose we'll see, won't we?" She paused, seeming on the verge of saying something else, and then she appeared to think better of it. "Well," she said, instead, "I'm sure the tea is ready." With that, she swept out of the room.

Jonah stood there, hands in his pockets, not sure where this left him. He'd expected Madame Majicka to yell—to tell him that he was reckless, that he had disappointed her, that he'd needlessly endangered Char—and she hadn't. Maybe she'd be back, after she drank some tea and said goodbye to her guests. Maybe she was just waiting until the other women were gone to shout at him and throw him out.

He looked at his body, lying prone on the bed, unsure what to do next. He spoke his wake up word and sat up. He was stiff from lying prone for several days, and he twisted and stretched, trying to work the kinks out. He climbed off the bed and then looked around the room, taking in how numerous the books and papers were compared with the clothes and personal items.

A bone-deep fatigue washed over him, and he felt for the first time how thin and frail his body was. Weak and tired, he returned to the bed, curling up on his side and pulling a blanket over him for a long overdue nap. Within seconds, he was fast asleep.

Twenty-One

Andras's emotions buzzed like a hive of angry bees, alarm bordering on panic, rolling off of him. *What do you mean you know no one of that name?*

Andras's panic was beginning to scare her. Irene's heart rate ticked up a notch, and a cold prickle raised the hair on her arms. "What do you mean, 'what do I mean'?"

The silence went on a little too long.

"Andras?"

Perhaps it is for the best.

"Perhaps what is for the best? Will you stop talking in riddles?"

It does not matter. I was mistaken.

Irene's hands flew to her hips. "What do you mean you were mistaken? You seemed pretty certain a second ago. Who are you talking about?" She looked around the cavern wildly, trying to glare everywhere at once.

You need to focus. You must get out of here.

"You're changing the subject!"

That does not make me incorrect.

Irene inhaled and then exhaled slowly and theatrically. "Sometimes, you are the most aggravating person on the face of the Earth, do you know that?"

Now there was amusement, warm and teasing like a summer breeze. Irene pursed her lips. "That's fine, go ahead and laugh at me. But the longer I'm stuck down here, the longer it will take to get your shadow back, bucko."

There was hesitation now, the questioning deepening. *I do not understand. What do you mean 'get my shadow back'?"*

Irene huffed and put her hands on her hips again. "Well obviously we need to get it back."

To what end?

"What do you mean 'to what end'? To put you back together so you're not invisible anymore!"

And how do you propose to do that?

She was on less firm ground here, and her voice faltered a bit. "Well, I've been thinking about that. There's a… story. A fairytale, I guess. There's this girl named Wendy, and one night she wakes up to find a boy in her bedroom, crying. She asks him what's wrong, and he tells her that he's lost his shadow. It's become separated from him somehow. They catch the shadow, and the girl sews it back onto the boy —"

Waves of skepticism, deep and rolling, emanated from Andras. *How does one sew a shadow?*

"Apparently with needle and thread. Anyway —"

The skepticism deepened.

Irene gritted her teeth. "Yes, I know it sounds ridiculous, but I didn't make up the story. The point is there might be a way to get your shadow back."

Andras didn't seem convinced. The skepticism lingered, layered on top of the slow oscillations of Andras's default emotional state. However, there was something else — a quavery quality she couldn't quite place. Uneasiness? Something withheld? A guilty conscience?

She was getting used to the feeling of Andras's emotions as a physical sensation. Now that the novelty was wearing off, she could pick up nuances, a type of flavor and texture to the strange extra-sensory perception that seemed to simultaneously be both external and internal to her. She concentrated, trying to hone in on the feeling, trying to bring it into sharper focus so she could identify the worrying tinge to Andras's silence.

How are you going to get out of here?

Andras's words cut into her concentration. If she didn't know any better, she'd think he was deliberately trying to distract her, to keep her from probing too closely. She pursed her lips, torn between her desire to find out what Andras was dodging and acknowledging that Andras was right — getting out of here was her most immediate concern.

Irene?

"What? Yes, I'm thinking. Okay, fine, yes, getting out of here." She turned and studied the unending walls surrounding her. "I'm going to need your help. I need you to look for an opening."

If you cannot see it…

"I'll be able to see it — if you point it out to me. If I know where to look, then I think I'll be able to get my ghost eyes to work. I think."

I do not —

"Have faith."

Andras heaved a theatrical sigh.

"Just look for something that doesn't belong, like the music in the dead forest or the butterflies and the fish in the fields. All those things were cracks between planes. They're doorways. I can't sense anything here because I'm not on a high enough plane. But you, now that you've lost your shadow, I think you're higher up than me. So you should be able to see something. Once I know where to look, I'll be able to focus on it."

You seem quite confident suddenly in your ability to navigate between planes.

"I understand the mechanics of it all perfectly well, thank you very much. It's the practical application that I've been having trouble with. I can't always see the doors, but once I stumble across one, I have no trouble going through it."

There was a thick, contemplative silence. Something in her gut told her Andras wasn't looking for an opening; she would bet her bottom dollar that he could already see a way out. He'd already said as much, in fact. Instead, he was contemplating her — assessing, thinking, picking and choosing what to do next

Her skin prickled with unease—why was he keeping something from her? And why was he hesitating to help her get out of this canyon? He wasn't thinking of leaving her here, was he? She bit her bottom lip; she couldn't imagine that Andras would ever just up and abandon her like that. He'd vowed to stay by her side until she reached her destination, and he was nothing if not a man of honor. He would fulfill that vow or die trying—of that she was certain. So what was giving him so much trouble?

"Andras?"

He seemed to reach a decision because the worrying hesitation in the air vanished, and his voice was decisive when he answered. *Turn around. Walk straight at the wall. A little to your left. Yes. There.*

She moved to where he indicated and stared at the wall, preparing herself to concentrate. "Okay, here goes."

She took a few deep, controlled breaths and then sucked in one long, slow breath and closed her eyes. She emptied her mind, listening for the far away silence that existed beyond her, beyond her breathing, beyond her thoughts, beyond the confines of her conscious self, beyond the confines of her unconscious self to the world of the blade of grass, of the color blue, of the burning star. She searched for the hum, the pull of those dimensions, and then she refocused her concentration, directing that energy into imagining herself at the top of the chasm, back in the land of the shadows.

What are you doing?

"Shhhhh.... You're ruining my concentration."

Yes, but—

"Have faith," she said, allowing herself a small smile. Then she blocked him out, closing her mind to his presence. She re-centered, letting stillness settle over her once more as she reached through the layers of existence, focusing all her energy on tying together the disparate threads of learning that had brought her to this moment:

Everything is connected. Everything exists together. Layered together, existing in one space.

Including the exit from this cavern.

Walk with purpose. Decide where you want to go, and then let the destination pull you to it.

I need to return to the bridge to the castle.

Nothing here is real.

There are no walls. There is no cavern. There are only ladders and tunnels — ladders and tunnels back to the land of shadows.

The yearning of the acorn and of the human soul are the same.

Follow the yearning.

Eyes squeezed shut, she dug deep, until she felt the yearning pulling her forward.

Slowly, still holding onto the silence and the pull, she opened her ghost eyes. The darkness and the walls and the far away river of fire overhead faded away, simple and irrelevant constructs. She looked through them to the space beyond, the layers upon layers of atoms — the same atoms in each layer, just arranged differently each time.

She stretched out her hands, which were no longer physical hands limited by skin and nerve endings, and touched the smooth, slick obsidian walls, which were no longer physical walls, and then beyond, probing beneath the surface with her senses, searching for any give that indicated a doorway between planes.

Her fingers sank into the obsidian, passing through it like mist. Her fingers stroked over the threads of creation, teasing apart the different textures, until at last she touched one that kicked up the flame in her chest.

Bingo!

Slowly, she opened her physical eyes, allowing a small smile to play about her lips as she reached out and grabbed a handful of hard-packed dirt and let it crumble between her fingers.

"Told you I could find it."

It wasn't much of an opening — just a crack really — but it was enough that she could change the construct in her mind, transforming the insurmountable obsidian into moveable dirt.

Long, slow notes of admiration rolled over her, and she smiled at Andras's approbation. She was going to make a smart-ass comment but then decided to let the moment stand.

She contemplated her next move, looking up and letting her eyes travel all the way up the very long ascent to the river above. "This is going to suck." She was going to have to use her bare hands to dig handholds and footholds in the dirt and climb out, the long, slow, hard way. It was all metaphorical, really, her brain's representation of her efforts to squeeze herself through this thin crack between planes, but that made little difference. The real journey was going to be as arduous as the metaphorical one.

If she'd been pure energy, like Andras was now, she'd easily be able to slip through this narrow crack. However, because she still had her shadow — and its associated weight and mass — she was going to have to squeeze through here, and it was going to be slow and painful going. In a way, it pretty much mirrored the sprouting of an acorn, pushing itself through the soil to reach the surface. Irene frowned, wondering if the parallels were coincidence or not. Maybe the Guide had used that metaphor with her so long ago because he'd foreseen the day when she'd make this climb. Maybe her brain had chosen these constructs to represent the journey because of the prominence of the acorn metaphor in her thoughts. Maybe it was all gibberish and didn't matter anyway.

She looked up, measuring the distance she needed to climb. Then she took a deep breath, stepped up to the wall, and began to dig. The dirt was rock-free but hard-packed, and it didn't come loose easily. She dug her fingertips in and scratched away at the dirt. Andras was hovering — that was the only way she could explain it. He was agitated, worried, the emotions emanating from him a confused jumble. The vibrations got stronger and then weaker and then stronger again, like the ebb and flow of a tide going out.

"Just say whatever you have to say," Irene said irritably, her fingers already tiring.

There was a deep, thick, ponderous silence. *It is nothing,* he said at last.

She ground her teeth in frustration at his sudden secretiveness. She would have probed further, demanded a proper answer, except it was taking all her concentration to force herself to keep digging. Her fingers already ached from scratching at the hard dirt, her skin rubbed raw and her joints protesting the treatment. She tried to ignore the pain, emptying her mind of everything but the need to keep going, and focused on breathing deeply and evenly.

Silently, she chanted over and over, "You don't have skin. You don't have joints. There is no pain. There is no fatigue."

After about what she guessed was ten minutes, she had dug four shallow holes—hand and toe holds. Andras had remained quiet the entire time, retreating into a kind of watchful silence.

Irene stretched up on tiptoe, wedged her hands in the hand holds, put one foot in a toehold and then boosted herself up until she could put the other toe in its corresponding spot. She balanced there, precariously pressed against the wall for a moment, assessing whether or not the dirt would hold her weight and whether or not she had enough strength to sustain the position while she dug the next set of handholds.

After a moment, feeling it was safe to proceed, slowly and deliberately, she freed a hand, stretched up, and began to scrape at the dirt above her. Within moments her arm was trembling from the effort, her legs were shaking, and her back was screaming in pain. Defeat washed over her; there was no way she was going to be able to make this climb.

"I can't do it," she said. "This isn't going to work."

Immediately she felt a presence behind her, as if Andras stood directly behind her.

Yes, you can.

"No, I really can't." She looked down, trying to find her way back down. Something brushed against her backside, and she froze.

"What are you doing?" she asked suspiciously.

Supporting you.

"With your hand on my ass?"

Andras's voice was matter-of-fact, but the air was fuzzy with amusement. *I am beyond such things now.*

She felt the brush against her backside again. Andras's amusement increased.

I am merely boosting you up.

"I suppose you think you're being cute," Irene said, not sure whether to laugh or be exasperated.

The air turned heavy with smugness. *I was quite adorable as a child. My aunts frequently remarked upon my exceptionalness in this area.*

Irene glared into the dark. "I'm going to kill you when I get out of here, you know that, right?"

She felt pressure along her back, as if Andras had leaned forward and now pressed against her. His voice, low and throaty, sounded right in her ear, sending a shiver down her spine.

When you get out of here, you may do as you please.

"Is that a dare?"

Andras laughed.

"Don't think that I don't know what you're doing," she said, both grateful and annoyed at him trying to goad her into continuing on.

Is it working?

"Yes. I'm going to get out of here just *so* I can kill you." She attacked the dirt with renewed vigor.

Andras's amusement increased. *Beware letting the iron of anger enter into your heart, for it will cloud your judgment.*

Irene grunted as she stabbed the dirt with her fingers. "Is that some kind of proverb or something?"

When I was a boy —

"Wait, what's this?" Irene stopped, turned toward where she thought Andras was, and nearly lost her balance. She immediately felt a steadying hand on her back as she grabbed for the dirt.

Attend to your work!

"Are you actually going to tell me something about your life? Voluntarily? Without me begging or fishing or pulling teeth or—"

As long as you keep working, I will speak of my life. When you stop, I stop.

She felt the gentle pressure of Andras's presence behind her again—and then expectant waiting.

Irene sighed, theatrically, for show, so he didn't think she was so easily led, but reached for the dirt above her again as relief and gratitude for his assistance washed over her. It struck her then that, for the first time, he was helping her, as a partner and an equal, instead of ordering her around or stepping back and expecting her to lead. She smiled as she scraped at the dirt, a happy flutter in her stomach.

Andras began to speak.

When I was a boy, my brother beat me in a foot race. I was angry at having lost, so I picked up a rock and threw it at him. However, my aim was poor and the rock missed my brother — by a good distance. Instead, it struck a maid carrying a pail of milk to the kitchens. The maid dropped the bucket, and the milk was lost. When later I made confession to the priest, he spoke those words to me, and I have remembered them ever since.

Irene tested to see if the next set of "rungs" in her ladder would hold. Then she hefted herself up and began digging the next set of holes. "That was a rather anticlimactic story."

Oh, I was also punished—first by my nurse, then by my father, and finally by the priest.

Irene grunted in response as she attacked the dirt. "Is this the same brother you spoke of before—the one with the child bride?"

Yes, the same brother.

"Any other siblings?"

There was my brother and me and two sisters.

"What were your sisters like?"

As gay and lively as song birds and just about as much use. They were as serious and steadfast as butterflies and, verily, as great a pair of straw-brained ninny hammers as might be found, as cosseted and spoiled as any dowager's lap dog, and surely the most unrepentant coquettes in all of Christendom, flirting with every man through their lashes.

"They hardly sound like 'demure ladies of the court,'" Irene said.

Andras laughed, the sonorous, deep sound rumbling through Irene's insides like warm honey.

That they were not. They were whirlwinds of tumult and catastrophe and most likely gave their husbands no end of grief and misery.

There was no censure in Andras's tone, only fondness. Irene smirked as she hefted herself up to the next set of handholds.

"No doubt made that way by their overly indulgent older brothers."

No doubt, Andras agreed amicably.

"It's funny; I doubt you'd be so fond of any other woman who acted that way. I always thought you'd expect your wife to be the demure, subservient type."

Andras laughed again. *Yes, many a man turns a blind eye to behavior in his relatives he would not stand in other men.*

"Or women."

Or women, he agreed good-naturedly.

Irene shook her head but couldn't help laughing. "Wow, this is a whole 'nother side of you. Sense of humor. Laughter. Playfulness. A weakness for batted eyelashes. Who knew?"

Death has sobered me.

The words were dead-panned, but the air vibrated with humor still. Her lips twitched as she focused on testing her next set of handholds.

"So you were a smart-ass back then, too?"

I was a hot head.

"You weren't somber and religious like you are now?"

Oh, I was that — but I was also a hot head, overly confident in the righteousness of my convictions and easily offended, itching for a fight at every turn.

Irene grinned. "And that's different from now... how?"

She felt the pressure against her backside again. *You have much faith that I will not drop you.*

Irene chuckled. "At this point, I'm not sure that wouldn't be better. At least I'd get to sit down and rest."

Andras's tone changed, suddenly deeply earnest and serious. *You need not fear; I will not let you fall.*

A strange tenderness washed her at his concern, bringing a catch to her throat. "I know," she whispered, all teasing fleeing. "I know."

They both fell silent. Long minutes ticked by, the quiet thick and suffocating. Irene kept her eyes focused on the dirt in front of her as she mechanically scratched at the earth above, a strange dual lightness and heaviness from Andras's words and presence settling over her. With her face so close to the dirt, she could no longer see anything but blackness. Her fingers were coated and grimy, and they were lost in the darkness as well. The night pressed in on all sides, like a coffin.

The effort to continue digging was becoming too much. Her arm shook uncontrollably, and her fingers hurt to the point of raising tears to her eyes every time she curled them into the dirt. "You promised me stories," she said, to distract herself from the pain.

Andras didn't hesitate. *My name, de Cordoba, refers to the land of my ancestors. However, it was conquered by the Moors in the eighth century, and my forefathers left to settle in Castile. We had a great holding there, and my father was a member of Alphonso's court. As the younger son, I did my duty by joining the Order.*

Irene's heart pinched. "They made you become a knight?" She'd asked Andras once about becoming a knight, whether it was by choice or not, but he'd only said that it was an honor to join. She'd assumed he'd voluntarily become one.

It is the duty of the younger son.

"Oh." There was a lot he wasn't saying—perhaps expecting her to simply understand. Only, she didn't, but she didn't want to interrupt his story to ask questions for fear he'd clam up.

My order had holdings all over the kingdoms of Castile and Leon, but I spent little time at any of them. In my early years with the Order, before the war, I was on the road, accompanying pilgrims on their way to the cathedral of Sant Iago – Saint James.

On the northern route, there is a stop – the Cruz de Hierro. The Iron Cross. Pilgrims who carried nothing but the clothes on their backs would yet carry a stone with them from their home to leave at the cross. The stone was said to represent the pilgrim's sins, and leaving it at the cross was an act of absolution though some said the stone was one's burden – the thing one could not let go of – and to lay down the stone was to lay down the burden and let go at last. Though either version is a heresy – only through confession and penance may one be absolved of one's sins – I secretly preferred the latter explanation.

His words surrounded her, buoying and holding her up as she inched her way up the wall, one painful fingerful of dirt at a time. Stab, scrape, dump. Stab, scrape, dump. Over and over and over again.

Imagine the tired pilgrim, footsore and heavy-hearted, having traveled untold miles on such a long, hot, dusty road, toiling under the burning sun for weeks. His feet most likely have blistered and bled, and his clothes are travel-stained and worn. He is hungry and thirsty and tired in his bones. His limbs threaten to give out, and he thinks he can walk no farther. He will fail. He will not reach Santiago and the great cathedral. His despair grows, and he does not know how he can go on. And lo! He espies something rising in the distance – a great cross of iron atop a rough, wooden pole, thirty-feet high. To see such a sign from God in that moment, affirmation that he is still on the path, that God is with him always, and that his goal is closer than he thinks! His flagging strength is renewed, and he forces his legs forward as he climbs the hill to the cross.

His honey-rich voice flowed through her, filling her with a comforting warmth. The scraped-raw pain of her knuckles, the ache in her fingers and toes as she clung to the dirt, and the trembling of her arms and legs all drained away. The dirt, the dark, the canyon, and even the fear faded, leaving nothing but his voice, filling and sustaining her.

He climbs the tower of pebbles surrounding the cross's base, as thousands have done before him. He kneels in gratitude to God, and there, beneath the azure sky with the magnificent countryside laid out below him, he pulls out the rock he has carried and lays it down, and in laying it down, he feels his burden – this thing he has not been able to let go of – fade away, taken from his shoulders by God, who hears his prayer. His fatigue leaves him, and he realizes he could walk a hundred, a thousand, a million miles more because God is with him always, and suddenly, feeling light as a feather, he descends the pile of rocks and continues on his way, his heart lightened and once more full of hope.

Irene became so focused on what he was saying that she forgot to turn her head as she dug. Dirt rained down on her, and she turned her head quickly, to avoid being blinded. She coughed hard as she sucked up a lungful of the fine dust, nearly losing her balance in the process. The pressure from Andras's presence instantly increased.

Careful.

Irene clung to the wall, bolstered by Andras, until the coughing fit passed. Awkwardly, she wiped her eyes against the shoulder of her jacket, trying to clear the tears surfaced by the choking coughs. Once she could see again, she shifted her weight, trying to find a more secure stance.

Are you ready?

"Yeah, I'm good." She resisted the urge to look up or down to measure the distance accomplished, the distance left. She was already spent – any distance would look insurmountable. There was no option but to continue on, head down, blindly digging until she was done.

She pictured Andras's iron cross and the scene he had described – then she imagined herself as the pilgrim, climbing the slippery, shifting pile of rocks to lay her pebble at the top. She imagined the relief at letting go and finding peace at last.

You are not digging. Are you already weary of my tales?

Irene smiled weakly. "No," she said softly. "These stories are good – much better than your usual ones." Using every ounce of will power she possessed, she raised her arm and once more stabbed her aching fingers into the dirt.

Twenty-Two

He exited the train in Salem with a heavy heart. He'd waited the rest of the day and all night for the other shoe to drop. He'd expected Madame Majicka to return to finish reaming him out, but she hadn't. Nor had he seen Char. He wasn't sure if they were waiting for him to seek them out or if they were giving him the cold shoulder.

Either way, he couldn't take it anymore and had slipped out of the magic shop early that morning. He'd briefly checked the area where he'd lost his backpack but unsurprisingly, there was no sign of it. Ghosts were scavengers — the backpack would have been scooped up almost as soon as it hit the ground.

It took only a few minutes to walk to Irene's mother's house. In the past, he'd never questioned whether or not he should cross over to find Irene — it went without question. But now, for the first time, he was forced to ask himself: what would happen to Deborah if he wasn't around? Her sister-in-law Betty did as much as she could, but she was busy with her own family, and she lived an hour away. Betty had already raised the possibility of Deborah coming to live with her, which Deborah had emphatically refused to consider.

He let himself in and found Deborah in the kitchen, sitting at the kitchen table with a mug of coffee warming her hands. She had all the appearance of a woman who had simply been sitting there, staring into space. She looked up as Jonah entered.

"Oh, hello, Jonah," she said. Then her brow creased. "Is it Wednesday already?"

"Hey, Mrs. Dunphy. No, it's Sunday. I had some free time, so I thought I'd stop in and say hello."

Deborah made a non-committal noise and took a sip from her mug. Jonah watched her for a moment, suddenly feeling reluctant to speak. Gingerly, he slid into the seat opposite Deborah.

"Mrs. Dunphy... I... I might not be able to visit you for a few weeks—" His life was in tatters. At the very least, he needed time to find a new place to live and a new job, and until then, it was going to be hard to find the time to visit Deborah. Or maybe, just maybe, he'd pack up everything in his storage locker, go through the nearest red door, find Persephone, and force her to tell him how to reach Hell.

Deborah sharpened up at this and looked at him in horror. "Are you in trouble again?"

Jonah shook his head. "No, I'm not going to jail or anything like that. I just have some stuff to take care of." He paused and then added, in a rush, "I might not be back for a while."

"Oh?"

She didn't seem particularly interested in this piece of news. Jonah wasn't sure she'd understood, so he tried again. "I won't be able to come by and check on you for a while. Maybe months." He tested out the feel of the words and the idea of never seeing Deborah again—as would happen if he crossed over. His stomach hitched with guilt.

Deborah made another non-committal noise and took a sip of her coffee. When she was done, her eyes drifted to the window, and she stared out. "Just like Irene," she murmured. "Always tearing off somewhere." Then her voice grew firmer and became laced with bitterness. "She was always too busy to visit. Then she went away for good."

Jonah grabbed Deborah's bony hand, squeezing it tight in his own—it was an impulse, so fast, it surprised him, as well — and words — deliberate and fierce — rushed out. "Irene didn't mean to go away. She didn't want to; it just happened. If it was up to her, she never would have left."

Deborah, startled, looked down at Jonah's hand on her own for a moment and then turned her face away, looking stubbornly out the window. Her chin trembled.

Jonah tightened his grip. "She was a better person than you give her credit for. Irene has — had — a lot of good qualities. She's fierce — she doesn't put up with crap from anybody; she's a fighter — she doesn't give up, no matter what; and she's loyal — she looks out for people even when they don't look out for her."

Deborah's chin went up half a notch, and there was a thread of anger in her voice. "She was like her father."

"She was like herself. Maybe she wasn't what you expected or even what you wanted, but that doesn't make her a bad person."

Deborah spun to face him, her eyes wide — with shock or anger, he couldn't be sure. She stared at him, emotions rolling across her lined face: pain, confusion, defiance. Jonah braced, expecting anger, but instead, Deborah abruptly began to cry, fat, swollen tears rolling down her face. She pulled her hand from Jonah's and used it to grasp the string of pearls at her throat.

"She was always so angry. I don't know why. Why she was so damn angry all the time?"

Jonah didn't know how to explain to Deborah about loneliness, about the bitterness of not being accepted for who you were, about the soul-crushing despair of expectations you could never meet. However, as he stared at Deborah's face, the pain etched deep in the lines there beneath her paper-thin skin, he realized he didn't have to. Mother and daughter were more alike than they knew.

"She wasn't angry at you," he said softly. "She was angry at herself." The words seemed to come from somewhere outside himself, as if sheeting down to him from the universe, and as he said the words, a sudden and vast understanding overcame him. Immediately, his own anger, the tightly wound bud of desolation and despair that he'd clung to for as long as he could remember, dissolved, replaced at last by a feeling of calm.

Deborah lifted eyes, full of questions, to his and searched his face. "You knew her." It wasn't a question.

Jonah clasped his hands and squeezed them between his knees to stop their trembling. "Yeah, I knew her."

Deborah dropped her eyes, her hand still on her pearls. Vaguely, as if the information wasn't really all that important, she said, "You never said." Deborah's brow was furrowed, and as she absently stared at the table, she seemed to be trying to make this information fit with what she thought she'd known of her daughter's life.

They sat there in silence for several minutes, their heads bowed in an impromptu memorial service. Memories of Irene flitted through his mind, and Jonah had no doubt that Deborah was also thinking of Irene. However, for the first time since she'd left, he felt calm, rather than angry, accepting, rather than despondent. He glanced at Deborah and suspected she felt the same. She seemed calmer now than she ever had, the tight lines of tension that defined her body seeming to have disappeared. Irene was never coming back—and they both knew that now.

They sat like this for some time. Finally, Jonah stood up. "I have to go," he said.

Deborah gave him a faint smile. "I know." She stood, too, and stepped closer, taking his face in her hands. With a sudden, sad urgency, she said, "Be good, Jonah."

With a heavy heart, he turned for the door, and then, without looking back, he left.

He wasn't sure what he felt by the time he reached Irene's grave—mostly numb, but there was a strange calm, too, that he couldn't quite identify. Maybe it was resignation, maybe it was acceptance. He only knew that it didn't hurt, and it didn't feel hollow—the two feelings that had been his constant companions for as long as he could remember.

He brushed at Irene's headstone, wiping away any traces of dirt and noted with satisfaction that the bowl remained overflowing with coins.

"That's beautiful."

Startled, Jonah looked up. It was a woman, in her mid- to late-twenties and with a cardigan sweater wrapped around her, as if she was cold, despite the warm July sun. She pointed at the statue. "It's beautiful," she repeated. "Is that your mom?"

"Friend," Jonah said hurriedly. "Just a friend."

The woman nodded though she didn't really seem to have heard him. "My dad... he..." She glanced down at her hands, which were busy twisting a tissue in circles. It was then that Jonah realized her face was tear-stained.

"I never got a chance to tell him I loved him," the woman said, her voice cracking. She didn't really seem to be talking to Jonah so much as simply talking aloud. "I wish... just once, you know? Just one more chance to talk to him." She stopped and made a wet, hiccupy noise. She swiped the back of her hand against her nose.

Jonah's heart pinched in sympathy. "You should write him a letter."

"I do... I mean, I did — once." The woman gave a half-hearted shrug. "I know it doesn't mean anything; it's not like he can read it, but I just thought... I mean, it's nice to think..."

"He — your dad — he got it. The letter," Jonah said. In the past, he would have shied away from this conversation, his reluctance stemming from a complicated mixture of wanting to keep ghost stuff for himself and fear of ridicule or censure. But now, somehow, he didn't care. He didn't want to keep it private, and he wasn't afraid of people finding out. He climbed to his feet, his confidence in his decision to speak growing.

The woman stared at him, her mouth slowly opening and then staying that way.

He nodded and gave her an encouraging smile. "Anything left on a grave gets sent to the person buried there. So, if you left it on his grave, then he got it."

The woman was quiet for a moment. She dropped her eyes, and her shoulders shook. She was openly crying now. "It's nice to think so," she said in a low voice.

"No, really," Jonah said earnestly.

"The letter never went anywhere. It wasn't even carted away by the wind."

Impulsively, Jonah reached out and took one of her hands in his. "The physical letter stays there, so you don't know that it's gone, but trust me, the spirit of the letter — it gets to the other side. You should keep writing to him. Let him know how you're doing."

The woman had raised her eyes again. Tears were still rolling down her cheeks, but she was no longer sobbing. She stared at him hard, her eyes searching his face, as if she thought he was pulling her leg. Jonah let her look.

Unexpectedly, the woman stepped close and put her arms around him, hugging him tightly, and then just as quickly released him. She flushed, as if embarrassed. "Thank you," she said, sniffing hard. She pulled the cardigan tighter and then turned around and walked away.

He watched her leave, and then he, too, headed for the exit. It was time to start moving forward again.

He returned to the magic shop, slipping back to his room unnoticed. He stood there for a moment, torn about what to do next. The empty physical shells of the items from his lost backpack were laid out on the desk. They were all junk now, but he was loath to part with them, in case there was any way they could be saved. He crossed to the desk and picked up the black book of afterlife knowledge. He ran a hand over the bark-like cover, so familiar to him after five years of constant study. He wondered if it was possible to restore the lost "spirit" of the book to the physical shell, the way Madame Majicka had returned Char's spirit to her body.

The picture of Irene as a teenager was on the desk as well, staring up at him. He picked it up, studying the delicate lines of her face, the cocky smile, the something a little sad despite the smile lurking in her eyes.

He sank into the chair, the picture unbearably heavy in his hand.

He understood now why Irene had left. There had been nothing here for her anymore. She'd told him that, but he hadn't understood. Not until now, when he stood to lose everything that connected him to the land of the living.

The truth of the matter was that he could travel to the afterlife and find Irene, slay whatever demon was holding her captive, and offer to bring her back to the land of the living, and she wouldn't come. His idea that she'd be satisfied just to have a place to live had been incredibly naïve—and just plain dumb. Of course she'd need more than that. Living was more than just getting up, getting dressed, and existing. She'd tried to tell him that, too—in that stupid, awful letter.

"You thinking about Irene?"

Jonah's head snapped up. Char stood in the hallway, peering around the doorway into the room with a shy, uncertain air about her. Jonah jumped to his feet, suddenly feeling self-conscious, as if he'd been caught doing something wrong.

He lowered the hand still clutching the picture, half hiding it behind him. "Yeah." He hesitated, reluctant to voice his thoughts.

"You're not giving up looking for her are you?"

"No." He glanced at the picture once more. The desperation and guilt were gone; only resolve and determination remained. "I'll never give up looking for her. I still need to know she's okay. But I think I need to go about it a little differently." If this little adventure had taught him anything it was that Char had been right that he was woefully unprepared to rescue anybody—himself included—from the other side. He needed a lot more preparation and training—particularly in areas that he'd previously thought irrelevant and useless like crystals and meditation. Up until now, he'd been going about his search for Irene as if he were dead—spending his time as a ghost, cutting himself off from the living, planning to sacrifice his life if necessary. Maybe it was time to see what the living had to offer.

Char's eyes narrowed with alarm and suspicion, and she came fully into the room, all of her shyness erased. "What do you mean?"

Jonah gave her a reassuring smile. "I think maybe I shouldn't keep trying to do it alone. I need help, and I have a lot to learn. I've been thinking—Persephone called me a 'Spirit Walker.' She said there have been others like me, the living who could cross into the afterlife. I want to try to find some of them. Maybe they can teach me—"

Char crossed the room in two strides, putting an eager hand on his arm. "And I'll help! My cousin is like a super psychic and knows a lot of occulty, weird stuff. I'll talk to him and see what he knows."

Jonah's brow knit, not sure Char understood what he was saying. "You'd do that? Even after everything that happened?"

"Of course. That's what friends are for, right?"

Relief bubbled up inside him at Char's words—she wasn't mad at him—and he couldn't stop the grin that spread across his face. "You know, you're pretty cool for a chick with purple hair."

Char's expression changed to one he couldn't quite read—it seemed to be a mixture of surprise and pleasure—and then she grabbed his shirt front with both hands and pulled him close. She pressed her lips to his—hard.

She'd taken him by surprise, and he wasn't sure what he was supposed to feel or do. Char's lips were warm and soft, but the feeling of them on his was foreign and strange. He thought maybe he wanted to kiss her back but also that he didn't, and he thought maybe he was kissing her but maybe he wasn't. Mostly, he wanted more time to think about it, but then her lips left his, and she was standing before him, beaming. "I've wanted to do that since we met."

"Really?"

Char's grin broadened. "Yeah." Then she gave him a playful shove. "Hey, you hungry? Want to go get some Chinese?"

"Aren't you grounded or something?"

"What? Why?"

"Your aunt—she isn't furious? I kind of assumed I need to pack and leave…"

Char waved a dismissive hand. "Auntie? Nah, she isn't mad. Apparently, getting stranded is a classic rookie Astral Projection mistake. She just wishes we'd asked for her help before trying it ourselves. That was the only part she was upset about."

"Oh."

Char peered at him. "You're not really going to leave, are you? I'm still here for two more weeks, and you owe me a date."

"A what?"

"You promised to take me out on a date when we got back."

"I don't think I did, actually…" he said, but this time he was only teasing. His smile widened.

Char poked him in the ribs. Then her grin turned devious. "Come on. I'll race ya!" She didn't wait for a response—she simply took off, trailing laughter behind her.

"Hey, no fair!" Jonah started to follow when he suddenly remembered the photo in his hand. He glanced down at it for a moment, studying the familiar lines of Irene's face. Then he tossed the photo on the desk and raced after Char, their laughter ringing throughout the shop.

Twenty-Three

She'd been climbing for forever. Thought and feeling and memory drifted away, leaving nothing but the certainty that this is what she had always done, that there was no other existence but this. Hazy, distant recollections of a life lived without climbing, a life away from the cold, hard press of the dirt against her chest and face teased at her like a half-remembered dream, but she knew that wasn't real. This, the climbing and the endless night, this was real.

She could no longer tell where she ended and the cavern began. Maybe she was the cavern. Maybe she was nothing at all. In the still dark, nothing else existed — there was only her and the disembodied voice of a figment of her imagination she called Andras. She half-listened while it spoke of strange, alien things like trees and sunlight and mountain peaks, all the while understanding less and less of what it said. Her mind began to wander; slipped loose from the confines of her physical self, it meandered in the drifting byways of space. She floated on a river of dreams, wandering the imaginings of stars and light beams and water molecules, half dreaming, half waking. She was everywhere and nowhere at once. Time and dimensions — up, down, thick, thin, tall, short — lost all meaning.

Not much farther now, the figment said.

To what, she wondered muzzily.

To the way out.

The figment spoke gibberish. Way out of what? There was no out. There was no in. There was just existence.

Irene... Irene, you must return to your body now. You are almost there.

She shuttered her mind, trying to block out the words. They made no sense—return to what? To where?—and besides, she didn't want to. She was happier here—drifting and timeless, beyond limitation, beyond pain, beyond sorrow. Here, there was only being—perfect and absolute.

I know... but this is not what you truly want. The figment's voice was heavy with sorrow. *Return now, so that you can exit the canyon to safety and resume your journey home.*

She ignored the figment's cajoling. It was a trick—a lie, a deception, a return to pain and sorrow and loss. Here, she was warm and safe and comfortable.

I... There was a pause, a reluctance to speak, and then at last, guilt, as if making a confession. *There are a great many things I would have shown you—happy things—had we visited my time. I would have liked to share them with you. I am sorry now that we will not have that opportunity.*

The figment's words were growing more confusing by the moment. Now they sounded like a goodbye. She tried to ignore them, to shut out the sound of the voice, but the sorrow in its tone drew her back to herself, despite her intentions. There was the faintest tingling in her limbs, like pins and needles—wait, what were arms and legs? Why did she have them?

I wish... I wish I was to be the one with you until the end.

The taste and texture of the murky depths began to change. The dark undulated and pulsed and then began to swirl and eddy. There were variations to the darkness now—a lightening and then the faintest tinges of colors—red and orange.

The pins and needles feeling grew stronger and the memory of legs and arms, fingers and toes, returned. She resisted, trying to push the memory from her, to cling to the warm, safe, comfort of floating in the vastness of space.

It was too late, however. Pain was flooding through her, and now she could once more tell the distinction between herself and the canyon wall, could feel the rough dirt pressed against the bare skin of her chest and throat, feel it pressing the thin fabric of her dress against her breasts and belly.

The world swayed and turned beneath her, and she was dizzy, as if she could feel the Earth hurtling through space. She clung to the wall as memories flooded through her, a hundred competing voices and a hundred different lives — a human woman, a burning star, a striving acorn, a twanging color.

The competing lives grew louder and louder until they were a painful din, drowning out everything else. Outside of herself, there was a rushing, roaring sound, as of a waterfall. The combination of sounds pummeled her, growing into a maelstrom that buffeted her from all sides. She squeezed her eyes closed, trying to curl in on herself in order to shut out the noise.

No, do not retreat.

Through the din and confusion came a sensation of familiarity, of comfort. She lurched toward it, latching onto it. A sensation rose over the noise — a touch on her arm and back, as if someone cradled her in their arms — and she focused on it, letting it lift her over the cacophony.

Andras? she whimpered, the thought no more than a whisper.

I am here.

I can't... there's too much... She tried to curl inward again, to shut out the noise. She felt him grab her arms and pull them away from her head, keeping her from curling in a ball. She whimpered in protest, turning away from the noise and into the darkness.

There is no pain, Andras said as both reassurance and command.

The red and orange light was growing steadily, seeping under her eyelids to burn her eyes. She whimpered fretfully, twisting to pull her arms free, twisting away from the light and noise and pain, yes, definitely pain.

Rough vibrations, as if Andras shook her, pinning her to the wall so she didn't fall, rocketed through her, sending searing pain through her head, as if her teeth had slammed together. Teeth? What were teeth?

She pulled harder against the force holding her from retreat, holding her from pulling further away. If she just let go, if she fell back, through the darkness, to the calm quiet of the canyon floor she could rest, she could sleep, she could leave this noise and pain and harsh light behind. She could curl into a ball and stay safe and warm and free forever. She struggled, to open her hands, to release her hold on the wall.

It is not pain; it is simply a return to the physical. You must not retreat from it. It is your only salvation — you must turn into it, rather than away — or you will never be able to return home.

Home? What did he mean? This was her home — the vast cosmic nothingness was her and she was it, and that was where she lived.

Andras shook her again, sending another cascade of teeth-rattling vibrations through her. This time, anger sparked at the rough treatment, at the battering, and she struck out, twisting and attempting to kick as she was held, pinned, against the wall.

Yes. Good. Now open your eyes.

She squeezed her eyes even more tightly and thrashed her head from side to side, trying to break free, to retreat from the torture. The one thing she was sure of was that opening her eyes would destroy her. Already, she could see fire seeping under the seams of her eyelids — a burning brightness so intense it would incinerate her if she looked upon it.

You must open your eyes. Now!

"No!" she said, and though the words came out wispy and faint, her voice dusty from disuse, it was her voice and her words, and the sound of them, pulled her the rest of the way into her body. Her conscious mind flooded into the woman-shaped space bounded by skin and bone and shoes and coat.

Her eyes flew open, and she gasped as the world came into focus. Pain flooded through her as light assailed her eyes. She had reached the river of fire, or more accurate to say, she was in the river of fire. The opalescent glow of the fiery undulations dazzled as the river flowed over and around her. In the heart of the flames were diamond glints that might have been stars or galaxies or memories or actual diamonds—they were tiny, or maybe they were far away, and flashed so briefly it was hard to tell. The fire didn't burn; it wasn't even hot, and she reached out a hand and ran it through the flames, cupping them and then dribbling them out again, and the sensation was impossible to describe—neither hot nor cold, neither wet nor sticky. If she had to use a word, it might be soft or plush, but those were completely the wrong words anyway.

You are getting distracted, Andras said. *Focus on the doorway. Continue to the surface.*

Irene grunted and reached up, not sure why, and her body, on autopilot, followed the motions to dig, and then she remembered digging and handholds and the long climb. She climbed up one more set of rungs and then reached up to dig again. Instead of solid, hard-packed earth, however, her hand touched nothing but air. She strained, reaching as far as she could to feel around, but there was nothing there—no dirt, no rock, no resistance. Nothing.

It took her a moment to understand. Then her brain adjusted, remembered why she was climbing, and came to a realization: she had reached the top of the canyon wall. She looked up, clinging tight to the handholds with her fingers and toes so she didn't lose her balance and peered into the darkness, wondering why she couldn't see anything. Why wasn't there any light if she had reached Tartarus? Where was the searing, golden glow?

She reached up, felt around, and traced the edge of the hole that was the exit from the canyon. She felt around for something to hold onto as she pulled herself up and over the edge. There was nothing concrete—just grass. She did the best she could, digging in her fingers and pulling herself to freedom. She scrabbled the last little bit, caught between momentum and gravity, and for a second, she feared gravity would win. She kicked at the wall, scrabbling to find a purchase with her feet, and she pushed hard with her arms, pulling herself up until she was over the tipping point, until she flopped forward, three quarters of her out of the hole, and then finally, the last little bit, her feet knocking dirt back over the edge as she scrambled forward on all fours to free-fall down out of the sky as the world suddenly shifted dimensions and planes, and she landed on the ground, face-down and panting.

She groaned as she lay there. Sensory input filtered through, slowly at first, in disconnected bits and pieces. The press of the hard ground against her face and legs. The pins and needles of restricted circulation in her hand trapped under her stomach. The tomb-like stillness of the air.

"Andras?" she said, and the movement of physical speech felt alien and strange.

I am here. There was relief in his voice.

With difficulty, she rolled over, and stared up at the sky. Tiny, far away pin-pricks of light. For a moment, she thought it was the river of fire, which she had just crawled out of, and then she realized it wasn't the far away glint of the river or Tartarus at all but stars.

Grass. She'd felt grass as she'd simultaneously climbed up out of the hole and fallen down out of the sky onto the ground. She moved her hands beside her, and yes, that was definitely grass under her.

There was no grass in Tartarus.

Irene bolted into a sitting position and looked around.

She lay on a flat, grassy plain on a finger of rock thrusting up from the deep canyon surrounding it on all sides. Overhead, the night sky was filled with the cold, thin light of distant stars while colorful ribbons of light danced in the air around her—the fire-filled river she had seen from above when she stood on the edge of the canyon in Tarturus and looked down, was now an Aurora Borealis of red, yellow, and orange dancing just above the horizon all around her. The way the plateau thrust up into the sky, she felt as if she was surrounded on all sides by nothing but stars and firelight, as if she floated in the void of space. Unlike when she ran through the cosmos in Tartarus or floated in the void as a star, she was decidedly human now, rooted in her body, in her physical self, and she felt very small and very alone against the backdrop of space.

"Andras?"

I am here.

She didn't really have anything to say; she'd just wanted reassurance she wasn't alone. She climbed to her feet and turned in place. Behind her, a wooden suspension bridge, the kind movie villains were always cutting the ropes of as the good guys raced across, stretched across the gaping canyon to the solid land on the other side; on that far end of the bridge stood the magnificent castle she and Andras had been trying to get to from Tarturus. The bridge connected to a sweeping, gravel driveway, wide, smooth, and bordered on both sides by a perfectly manicured lawn of seemingly infinite size and a long row of symmetrical hemlock trees. Wrought-iron lamps lit the way from the bridge to the castle's entrance. The gravel path ended in a flourish of stone steps leading up to a flagstone patio, upon which liveried footmen waited to greet visitors. Warm, inviting light blazed from the windows and the open doors.

Irene's heart fluttered in excitement at the grandeur and beauty of the castle, at the welcoming ambience, of the feelings of safety and comfort it stirred. Just as quickly, her elation evaporated. "Wait, Andras, this isn't right... we're not in Tartarus." They had bypassed the land of the shadows — and the opportunity to put Andras back together.

No, we are not.

His tone was flat; there was no surprise in it. Fear slithered through her. "What did you do?" she cried. "You showed me the wrong tunnel!"

It was a 'shortcut.'

"The wrong shortcut! How am I supposed to get your shadow back if we bypass Tartarus altogether?"

The thick, heavy feeling of guilt and furtiveness was back in the air.

Understanding washed over her. Her shoulders slumped. "You did it on purpose."

The oppressiveness increased.

"Why? Why would you do this? Why would you lead me here? You know we have to go back to Tartarus to get your shadow."

Irene, you know as well as I that you cannot return to the land of shadows. It is too dangerous. You risk losing your own shadow — without which you cannot return to the land of the living.

"I don't want to return to the land of the living. I want to go on with you!" The memory of being a star, a blade of grass, an acorn — the glorious, magnificent, life-altering sensations — bubbled to the surface along with her desire to experience them again. She had known, as soon as she'd experienced the acorn memory and recognized the yearning inside herself, that after she'd helped Andras get back on his own path, she would be returning to the marketplace.

No, you do not.

"Don't tell me what I want!" she snapped, wiping furiously at the scalding tears of anger and frustration that had sprung up.

You have forgotten. You sold more than you meant to — and have lost something dear to you. You wish to return home — to someone who needs you.

"My mother and Alexia don't need me, not really —"

Not them. There is another. At first I thought it was for the best. It was a selfish thought, though. I see that now. I wanted you to stay with me, but I understand now that cannot be.

Irene shook her head vehemently, as if she could shake away the truth. She was angry — he was talking in riddles, and he'd tricked her and taken away her ability to make her own decision — but, at the same time, there was a tangle of relief mixed in, too. Leaving him, whether to return to the physical plane or to the market, had been eating her up inside. She'd wanted there to be another option, one where they could stay together. She'd wanted to find a way for them both to have the same goal and want the same things. The only way for that to happen, though, would be for one of them to give up what they wanted — or for one of them to become someone they were not.

Andras, however, had taken the guilt and pain of that decision upon himself. Instead of forcing her to choose, he'd made the decision for her, for both of them. This way, they both got what they wanted — without guilt or regret. Now, there was no choice but to separate and go their own ways. She couldn't follow him, and he couldn't follow her.

"I could fight you on this," she said, not ready to just give in. "I could refuse to cross that bridge. I could just sit down here and refuse to leave. Or I can try to find another way back — climb back down the hole or find another crack between planes."

You could, he said placidly, as if her threats were worthless — which they were. She couldn't find the cracks between planes without him.

She turned away from the castle and the bridge, the pangs of loss almost too great to bear. She turned her eyes to the sky and watched the ribbon of fire in silence, giving her brain some time to sort out her thoughts and feelings. She and Andras lapsed into a companionable silence, and Irene sensed that Andras watched the sky, too. She wondered what it looked like to him, now completely unfettered by human eyes. As a being of pure energy, he was able to see so much beyond her now. Everything hidden to her, everything she'd been able to sense but not see, now lay open to him. She felt a twinge of jealousy.

They remained that way for some time; Irene was reluctant to leave, delaying the inevitable parting of the ways. She'd known it was coming; she just hadn't known it would be this hard.

"So," she said, finally, turning away from the night sky, "what happens now? I can't just walk away and leave you like this."

You will not have to. I will be with you – always.

Irene shook her head again. "Andras, as soon as we cross that bridge, you're going to disappear the moment we reach the other side. You'll ascend to a higher plane, and I'm going to go back down to a lower one. For all I know, without your shadow, there will be nothing to hold you together at all. You may lose all cohesion and just become part of some great big, collective consciousness."

And yet, I will still be with you.

"That's not how this works. Even if that were true, I won't be able to hear you – "

Have faith.

She felt a feather-light brush against her face, as if Andras had cupped her cheek.

We will see each other again. Of that I have no doubt.

The warm comfort of his laughter brought doubts crashing down on her, driving home the reality that they were really about to go their separate ways, that she was about to lose the best man she'd ever known. She choked back the tears that had risen to obscure her vision. She wasn't ready to say goodbye to him, to lose the strong, steady presence that had become the rock on which she leaned. She bit her lip as her courage faltered. She knew it was selfish and unfair of her, but she had to ask anyway. "Are you sure I can't change your mind?"

There was a gentle touch on her shoulder. Certainty radiated from him. *You will not be alone. I promise you this. I will always be with you.*

Yes, he would. He might be the wind that touched her face or the sunlight that caressed her skin or the certain something in the air that felt comforting when she was alone, but no matter the form, it would be, in some undefinable way, him.

She took a deep breath and managed to get her tears under control. She dried her eyes on her sleeve and stared out at the vast starry sky, searching for the words to express what she wanted to say. "Thank you – for everything."

Hold out your hand.

Brow furrowed in confusion—and a bit of skepticism—Irene complied with the strange request. Her hand grew warm and then a small, beach-stone-sized rock appeared in her palm.

"What this?" she asked, looking at the rock but seeing nothing of note.

It is the thing I was not able to let go of.

His story of the pilgrims walking the path to Saint James—and placing down their burdens.

She was too overwhelmed by the gesture to say anything. Her fingers closed protectively around the small, smooth stone.

Do not be thankful. It is a burden, and I pass it on to you.

She gave a watery laugh. "Gee, you couldn't have given me something cheerful, like a happy memory or something?"

All my happiest memories are of you. I will not trade them for anything.

A blush spread through her from head to toe, and the tears welled up again, but she laughed, too. "Christ, where were you when I was alive?" she muttered. "I bet you were a good kisser, too."

Andras laughed.

Irene squeezed the rock again and then tucked it into one of the jacket's pockets for safe keeping. She took a deep breath. It was time to go.

"Okay, then," she said, steeling herself.

Are you ready?

She nodded. "As ready as I'll ever be, I guess."

She moved to the edge of the bridge and stared out across the gaping chasm to the castle in the distance, watching the fire dance in the sky. She relaxed her mind, allowing the various eddies of sensation to flow past her, reaching for the ever-present pull of the internal compass that guided her. She found it and latched on, trusting it to pull her across the canyon to the castle. She looked down at the rickety bridge, and her heart leapt to her throat. Was she really going to attempt this?

"Don't let me fall," she whispered.

Never.

She raised one foot and held it over the bridge, hesitating to take that first, terrifying step.

Do not think. Do not walk. Just float.

Sucking in a deep breath, she closed her eyes and stepped off the cliff.

She squeezed all her senses shut, blocking out all sensory input, refusing to ask her senses if she was falling or not, and instead, focused on the castle, picturing herself standing before the gates and willing it to be so. She felt the tug within her chest as when she slid down one of the wormholes between planes, and she let go, turning herself over to the pull of the next plane. There was the sensation of the world flying past and then of falling and then of nothing at all.

She waited, but nothing happened. She kept her eyes squeezed shut, afraid of what she'd see when she opened them, wanting to hold onto the illusion, the hope, that she'd made it.

"Andras?"

No response.

She didn't have to ask for him again. She could feel it — he was gone. The warm, comforting presence that had filled the air around her and the space inside her was gone, leaving only emptiness behind. She was alone.

Slowly, she opened her eyes. She stood before the long gravel path before the large, wrought-iron gates, beyond which stood the gleaming castle-mansion.

The gates were open, and before them stood the Guide in his usual garish multi-colored toga, the warm light spilling from the castle's windows reflecting off his bald head, his hands clasped in front of him and a smile on his lips.

"Well, Acorn, glad to see you made it."

She smiled, relief flooding through her. "Were there any doubts?"

His grin broadened. "No, not really."

315

Irene drew closer, hesitating before the gates, intimidated by the imposing size of the edifice behind him.

"Don't worry, there's a room at the inn for you." He nodded toward the open windows, through which could be heard the sounds of raucous laughter and song above the strains of lilting waltz-like music. "It's a hell of a party — or, more accurately, dozens of parties. You sure you don't want to join them? There's bound to be one you like, and it's not too late to change your mind."

There was a time when that would have been welcome news. In fact, wasn't that what she had originally set out to find a thousand lifetimes ago when she'd left her home in Salem — a place where the party never ended, a place filled with the happy, carousing dead, drinking away the afterlife without a care in the world?

Now, though, the scene held no interest for her. Instead, she felt a longing for home and for… someone or something she couldn't name. A person, maybe; someone who needed her. Well, truthfully, there were lots of someones — and she was going to help them all. The resolve that had faded during her long climb through the dark flooded through her, returning full force.

"Actually," she said, turning away from the warm, inviting sounds, "I was more wondering if you had any openings in the guardian angel department."

The Guide smiled. "Good choice." He stepped closer and put a companionable arm around her shoulders, ushering her forward through the gates. "You know, I think we might have a halo in just your size."

EXTRAS

WHEREAFTER Discussion Guide

1. How does *Whereafter* compare to the previous two books in the series? Were there any surprises? Any disappointments?

2. In *Whereafter*, we finally get to see Jonah's point of view/the story is no longer solely Irene's. How did you feel about this change? Did your perceptions about the relationship between Irene and Jonah change now that you've seen Jonah's side of the story?

3. How did the Jonah of *Whereafter* compare to the Jonah of *Hereafter*? Did you feel like he was the same person? Other than being three years older, did anything else seem different or changed about him?

4. For the first time, Jonah's depression (and suicidal tendencies) is dealt with head-on, and he is forced to acknowledge it. Was the fact that he was suffering from depression a surprise to you or did you already know? Did you know he was suicidal? Do you think being forced to acknowledge his depression and talk about it helped him? Do you think Char did enough to help him address his depression and suicidal thoughts? What more could she have done?

5. *Whereafter* introduces new character Char — how did you feel about Char? Did you like her or find her annoying? What did you think about the relationship between Char and Jonah? Do you think they will end up as a couple?

6. How is Jonah at the end of the story compared to how he was at the beginning? Do you feel that he grew or changed or did he remain static? What about his desire to continue visiting the afterlife? His feelings for Irene?

7. How does Irene in *Whereafter* compare with Irene in *Hereafter* — is she more or less sympathetic than in *Hereafter*? In *Thereafter*? Has she grown/evolved since the first book, and if so, how?

8. For the first time in the series, at the end of *Whereafter*, Irene finally has a concrete goal — to return to the land of the living to help the people she's left behind. How did you feel about this goal? Was it worthy or "too little too late"? Do you believe she'll follow through on this goal? What will it change about her or for her if she does? If she doesn't?

9. How would you describe Irene and Jonah's relationship in this book compared to in *Hereafter*? As compared to *Thereafter*? In what ways has the relationship changed? In what ways has it remained the same? Do you think this relationship, as presented in *Whereafter*, is good for each of them or bad? Why? What do you hope happens to this relationship over the rest of the series?

10. In *Whereafter*, Andras reveals a great deal about his history as well as his philosophy and principles. Did any of what he revealed change your opinion of him? Does it change your reading of any of his actions or statements in *Thereafter*?

11. By leading Irene away from Tartarus, Andras ensures Irene won't be able to restore his shadow. Do you think his action was self-sacrificing (protecting Irene from losing her own shadow so she could return to the land of the living) or self-serving (ensuring he won't be forced to follow Irene to the land of the living, which he doesn't want to go to)?

12. How would you describe Andras's and Irene's relationship in this book? Would you describe it as a romantic relationship or as something else? How does it compare to their relationship in *Thereafter*? If you see the relationship as romantic, do you like them as a couple? Do you think they are good for each other?

13. In many ways, *Whereafter* is more philosophical than the previous two books. Do you agree with this statement? Why or why not? If you agree, how do you feel about this change? Do you wish the book had been more action-oriented, or did you like the more philosophical bent?

14. In *Whereafter*, Irene believes that she and Andras are in Tartarus. Do you agree that is where they were? How does the Tartarus of Whereafter compare to the "real" Tartarus/other descriptions of Tartarus? How does it differ? How is it the same?

15. Andras criticizes Irene for setting Heru free. Heru herself is distraught by this action as well. Did you agree with Irene's decision? How else might she have handled this situation?

16. Which afterlife myths did you recognize in *Whereafter*? How were the myths similar or different from the way you knew the story(ies)? Which myths

were new or unexpected? What was your favorite part of the afterlife, as depicted in *Whereafter*?

17. Some readers felt that the version of the afterlife presented in *Hereafter* and *Thereafter* was depressing or bleak. How did you feel about the version presented in *Whereafter*—was it hopeful or bleak? Was it more or less hopeful than the afterlife of *Hereafter*? Of *Thereafter*?

18. What are some of themes in *Whereafter*, and how did these compare to the themes of *Hereafter* and *Thereafter*? Did any of these themes resonate more strongly with you than the others? Why or why not?

19. Overall, did you feel that *Whereafter* was a hopeful or a bleak story? Did it have a "happy" ending? Why or why not?

20. Did you have any favorite quotes or scenes from the story? What made that quote or passage stand out to you?

21. What events in the story stand out for you as memorable? Was there any foreshadowing and suspense or did the author give things away at the beginning of the book? Was this effective? How did it affect your enjoyment of the book? Has the author foreshadowed things to come in the remaining books of the series?

22. The *Afterlife Series* is planned to be six books total. What do you think will happen to the characters next? What do you wish would happen to the characters? How would you like to see the series progress? What, for you, would be a "happy" ending, given that Irene is dead?

About the Author

Terri Bruce has been making up adventure stories for as long as she can remember. Like Anne Shirley, she prefers to make people cry rather than laugh, but is happy if she can do either. She produces fantasy and adventure stories from a haunted house in New England where she lives with her husband and three cats. Visit her on the web at www.terribruce.net.

Keep up to date with all the latest news and sign up to be notified of new releases in the Afterlife Series at:

Website/Blog:
http://www.terribruce.net

Connect with Terri on social media:

Facebook:
http://www.facebook.com/pages/Terri-Bruce-Fan-Page/325830544139030

Twitter:
http://www.twitter.com/@_TerriBruce

WHENAFTER (Afterlife #4)

In The Afterlife, Nothing Is As It Seems...

Just as she's found the doorway from the Great Beyond back to the land of the living, Irene Dunphy's plan to return home as a guardian angel is derailed by a surprise attack from an old enemy.

Swept into the afterlife plane inhabited by the Nephilim, Irene is forced to call in a favor from the mysterious Samyel — the Nephilim who used her to bring him to the afterlife and then promptly abandoned her. He's her only hope of survival and escape — if he can be trusted to deliver on past promises. But will Samyel help her — or betray her?

Coming Soon!

Pride Publishing books by L.M. Somerton

Mountain Rescue
Black Dog
The Portrait
Stroke Rate
Chemical Bonds
Owned by the Sea
Testing Lysander

Tales from The Edge
Reaching the Edge
Living on the Edge
Dancing on the Edge
A Double-Edged Sword
Rough Around the Edges
Scorched Edges
Driven to the Edge
Binding the Edges

Investigating Love
Rasputin's Kiss
Evil's Embrace
Tarot's Love

Warlocks
Elemental Love
Elemental Hope

The Wyverns
Mantrap
Deathtrap
Rattrap
Sand Trap
Steel Trap

Anthologies
Racing Hearts: Keeping the Luck
His Rules: Tagging Mackenzie

TESTING LYSANDER

L.M. SOMERTON

Testing Lysander
ISBN # 978-1-78686-361-4
©Copyright L.M. Somerton 2018
Cover Art by Cora Graphics ©Copyright June 2018
Interior text design by Claire Siemaszkiewicz
Pride Publishing

Published in 2018 by Pride Publishing, United Kingdom.

Pride Publishing is an imprint of Totally Entwined Group Limited.

TESTING LYSANDER

Dedication

To finding *your* passion

Chapter One

"You need your head read, young man. You treat photography like an extreme sport."

"And your bedside manner needs some work, Doc." Brock winced and gritted his teeth as another needle punctured his flesh.

"Would you rather I patted your head and gave you a sugar lump?"

"Is that what you did in the army?" Brock often thought that his doctor forgot he was now dealing with delicate civilians.

"Most squaddies would run away screaming at the sight of a needle if it didn't mean disciplinary action. I often wish the same principles could be applied to my patients here."

Brock squirmed. "I don't remember vaccinations ever being this painful and I've had enough of them over the years"

The doctor grinned. "Baby. Okay, that was the last one. You can pull your trousers up."

He peeled off his gloves and threw the used syringe into a special bin that his nurse held out for him.

"You may experience some flu-like symptoms over the next twenty-four hours, and you'll probably get some localized bruising, but if you feel any worse than that, give me a call. When are you traveling?"

"Ten days' time." Brock smiled and got to his feet. "Then I'll be out there for four weeks. I know I should have come in sooner."

"Yes, you should. Still, better now than not at all. Well, good luck. Stay safe. Bring me back another picture for the wall in reception."

Brock pulled the consulting room door closed behind him but still overheard the doctor as he said, "Colombia! I don't know whether he's brave, stupid or just too young to know any better!"

Brock waited for the nurse to respond, but nothing happened.

"Linda! Quit mooning over him and get the room ready for the next patient."

"But he's so gorgeous, Doc. I could definitely be tempted to get unprofessional with him!"

Brock winced. *Not in this lifetime.*

The doctor chuckled. "Forget it! He's more likely to go for me than you."

There was a groan. "Oh, for goodness sake, I know it's a cliché, but I'm going to say it anyway. Why are all the pretty ones either married or gay? That is a serious loss to womankind."

Brock shook his head, stepped away from the door then headed for the exit. He didn't mind the comments. Linda said the same thing every time she saw him, and, as he used his brother's house a lot when he was traveling, that was frequently. Outside the surgery, the weather was doing its best impression of a tropical

monsoon, though without the heat. The rain beat down onto pavements already awash after days of continuous downpours. In the distance, thunder rumbled ominously and the sky had a threatening purple hue that spoke of more rain to come.

Brock looked up just as lightning split the sky. The rain got even harder. He turned up the collar of his waterproof coat and grimaced at the trickle of cold water that immediately slid down his neck. In seconds, his hair was soaked and plastered to his head. He hunched his shoulders and lengthened his stride toward home — though it wasn't strictly *his* home. He was just house-sitting while his brother, sister-in-law and two young nephews spent their annual fortnight's holiday on one of the Balearic Islands — he couldn't remember which one.

Brock spent such a lot of time traveling on photographic assignments that he'd never bothered to get his own place. When he was in England, he spent the time with his brother's family or returned to his mum and dad's rambling old place in Northumberland. Their house was so big, and they were both so busy with various pet projects and charities, that he could probably have lived there full-time without them even noticing his presence. Brock smiled to himself at the thought — he was very fond of his eccentric parents.

He soon arrived at the edge of the new estate where his brother's house sat on a decent-sized plot, halfway down a tree-lined avenue. Despite the miserable weather, he felt uncomfortably warm and was glad to make it to the sanctuary of the front hall, where a small puddle gathered around his feet as he stripped off dripping outdoor clothes and boots. Feeling progressively worse, he caught his reflection in the hall

mirror and grimaced. His skin appeared clammy and his hands shook a little.

"Bloody vaccinations," he muttered. He climbed the stairs slowly, passing a number of his own framed photographs, and headed for the guest room bed. "Better just sleep it off." He grabbed a towel from the en suite, gave his hair a rub then stripped to his underwear. Drawing the curtains, he frowned at the sheets of driving rain. He could just make out the shape of a man sheltering under a tree opposite the house. "Blimey, he must be soaked." Despite his desire to get into his comfy bed to sleep away the after-effects of his inoculations as quickly as possible, Brock shrugged into his dressing gown then went back downstairs to the hallway to grab an umbrella. If the guy had to be outside, at least he could stay a little drier. By the time he went to the front door, the man was gone. Had he even been there, or was it a side-effect of the injections the doctor hadn't warned him about? He trudged back to the bedroom, finished pulling the curtains closed then took off his robe. He slid gratefully between cool sheets as his body reacted to the cocktail of drugs swimming through his system. Sleep came quickly and he drifted into dreams of distant jungles and the amazing pictures he would take.

* * * *

Outside, under the dripping tree, Kyle Dawson shifted uncomfortably. He had just been treated to a glimpse of the most tempting body he'd seen in some time and his cock had started dancing to its own tune despite the cold, damp conditions. He shook water droplets from the caped shoulders of his long, waxed coat and tilted the brim of his hat forward a bit further.

Kyle knew exactly where the subject of his observation had been that day, indeed for the last two weeks, though today was the first time he had gotten close to Brock's home.

He closed his eyes and recalled the details of the file he had been given. *Lysander Brock, known as Brock to his friends* – parents clearly had a thing for Shakespeare because his brother's name was Ferdinand. *Six feet tall, blond hair, blue eyes* – stunning blue eyes in Kyle's opinion – *one-hundred-eighty pounds* – all completely edible – *aged twenty-five. Permanent address listed at his parents' home in Northumberland. Professional photographer with work published in every travel and wildlife publication worth reading. Very well-traveled, with skills that included caving, climbing and hiking. Currently unattached. Two previous boyfriends known, neither particularly serious.*

Or deserving, Kyle thought grumpily.

He pictured the photo hidden in his inside pocket and licked his lips. He knew he should be maintaining a cold, clinical approach to the task ahead but, for Christ's sake, this guy was stunning and there was no harm in dreaming. After all, he'd been chosen for the job specifically because he was also gay. His bosses had thought he would blend in better if he needed to follow his quarry to gay pubs and clubs, though, in the end, that had not been necessary. Lysander Brock led a very quiet life when he wasn't working.

"You'd have no chance, you idiot," Kyle muttered under his breath, "even if you weren't about to ruin his day."

He looked around to make sure he was unobserved then crossed the road. The appalling weather worked in his favor, as very few people were out and about. Confident that there was no one around to witness his

swift journey across the garden and, through the unlocked gate, he slipped down the path at the side of the house and into the back garden of the property. Tall hedges and mature trees shielded it from the neighboring houses, giving him all the time in the world to pick the lock on the door and slip into the kitchen.

Kyle found the back door key on a wall hook. He relocked the door, slid the additional bolt shut and tucked the key into his pocket. Taking his time, he removed his wet coat and hat and hung them over a chair. The layout of the house was stored in his head so he moved confidently to the front door to set the deadbolts. Secure in the knowledge that Brock would not be able to run, he crept up the stairs and peered around the door of the guest bedroom. Kyle had to bite down on his lip as he saw the young man in the bed, sound asleep. Brock had pushed the covers down to his hips, one arm was flung out to the side and his smooth, hairless chest rose and fell gently as he breathed. His face was a little flushed but, other than that, he seemed at peace. Kyle resisted the temptation to pull the covers down a little farther, backed away then crept downstairs to the kitchen. He took one of the chairs set around the kitchen table and turned it so that he could face the door to the hall then he settled down to wait.

* * * *

When Brock awoke, it was already very dark. For a moment he couldn't remember where he was then it all came back, along with awareness of a pounding headache hammering at his temples. He climbed carefully out of bed, trying not to jog his head too much, and stretched.

"I need aspirin. Lots of aspirin," he whispered, and felt his way along the bed to the door. He didn't bother to dress—he was wearing a pair of dark gray trunks and had no intention of doing anything other than taking painkillers, swallowing a glass of water and returning to his cozy bed.

After a quick visit to the bathroom, he fought momentary giddiness and descended the stairs, gripping the banister. The darkness was soothing and he didn't need lights to find his way around, so he made it to the kitchen where he grabbed tablets from a drawer without too much fumbling. He took a tumbler from the draining board then pulled open the door of the fridge to get a bottle of water. The bright light from the fridge's interior lit the room with a blue-white glow, giving shape to the dark figure seated in a chair across the kitchen units from him.

Glass shattered across the tiled floor as Brock dropped the tumbler.

"Who the fuck are you?"

He groped for the knife block but soon realized that it was gone and there was nothing else to hand that he could use as a weapon.

"Please calm down, Lysander. I don't intend to hurt you unless I have to."

The voice was deep, sonorous and scarily calm.

"How do you know my name? Who are you?" Brock felt extremely vulnerable, semi-naked in the company of an intruder who had a clear advantage over him.

"Come over here and sit down. Then I'll tell you."

Brock shook his head and edged away then he turned and ran for the hall. He yanked at the front door but it was locked and there was no sign of the key to release the deadbolts. The stranger followed him into the hall and now stood blocking any other escape route. Brock

turned and pressed himself back against unyielding wood.

"There's nowhere to run. The back door is locked too. Now, come and sit down."

His voice betrayed no sign of impatience, but there was an edge to his tone that suggested the man was used to being obeyed. Brock tried to calm his pounding heart and played for time. "Can I at least put some clothes on?"

"No. I like you just the way you are." The intruder examined him from head to toe, pausing a little too long in the middle. "Nowhere to hide any sharp implements." He gestured at the kitchen door and waited for Brock to move.

The gap was narrow and Brock was forced to brush against him, the skin-tight fabric of his trunks rucked up to expose the curve of his ass and he thought he heard a hiss of frustration behind him.

Brock sat at the kitchen table and tried to ignore the sensation of cold wood against his thighs. He winced as the light went on, remembering the reason he had come downstairs in the first place.

"Would you like those painkillers now?" the intruder asked, placing a fresh glass of water and the tablets on the table.

Brock nodded. There was no need to refuse them just for the sake of being awkward. He swallowed the pills and kept his hand wrapped around the heavy glass, thinking it might provide a useful weapon.

"I'm not going to be able to trust you, am I?"

Before Brock could react to the words, the stranger produced a pair of rigid handcuffs, pulled Brock's arms roughly behind the chair and locked his wrists into unyielding metal bracelets.

"Better. Now we can talk without me wondering what you'll try to brain me with."

Brock tested the security of the cuffs but they were bruisingly tight and he soon realized that struggling was futile. His captor sat and smirked at him, though his eyes seemed to drift hungrily downward at regular intervals.

Brock took the opportunity to take a good look at the man opposite him. He was tall, maybe a couple of inches taller than his own six feet, and more heavily built—very muscular. He had short, dark hair and smoky gray eyes. No beard, but enough stubble to suggest that shaving once a day would not be enough. Brock had to admit that he was very good looking, even with the scar that ran from the corner of one eye, down his cheekbone. Dressed all in black, it was clear that he was in good shape. Arms jutting from rolled-up sleeves were firm and tanned, dusted with dark hair. Against his will, Brock's dick gave a little jerk. It obviously didn't care about the circumstances and knew what it liked. He peeked up into amused eyes.

"So, now you've had a good look, do you think we can be friends?"

"Fuck off." Brock was defiant but he shivered a little, though whether from fear, cold or arousal he wasn't too sure.

"Are you cold?"

"Do you care?" Brock snapped back a little quicker than sense would have dictated considering he was handcuffed to a chair in his underwear. However, he was feeling angry, humiliated and vaguely feverish, so to hell with the consequences.

"Feisty, aren't you?" The stranger threw a sheaf of photographs onto the table then walked around it to

stand behind Brock. "Perhaps these will make you a little more compliant."

Brock's stomach knotted as he took in pictures of his nephews on the beach and in their school uniforms, his brother at the gym and his parents in their garden. They had all been taken in recent weeks.

"My organization wishes to engage your services. Agree to help us and your family will never know that they are being watched. There will be no need for things to become...unpleasant."

Brock knew when he was beaten. There was no way he would put himself before the safety of his family. Two large hands curled over his shoulders and squeezed, warm breath caressed his neck and a deep voice sounded in his ear.

"Do we understand each other?"

He didn't respond. The man grabbed his hair and yanked his head back.

"All right! I understand."

His head snapped forward as he was released. Brock trembled as his tormentor stroked his arms and chest before pinching his nipples hard.

"Good. I'm glad we're going to be friends."

Brock squirmed in his chair, willing his cock not to react to the sensation of strong hands on his body, but it was no good. Fear did not stop it visibly hardening beneath his trunks, pushing against the thin material until it created a lewd bulge.

There was a deep chuckle from behind him. "Mmm. Very nice."

Ashamed of his involuntary reaction, Brock dipped his head, his face heating.

"Look at me." The voice was sharp enough to make Brock obey. The stranger had moved around him and taken the seat opposite.

"We are going to be spending some time together. You need to know why."

"Is there any point in asking you to free my hands?" Brock really wanted to cover his bulging crotch.

"Absolutely none. I'm enjoying the view far too much, so shut up and listen."

Brock's groin fired up again at his tone and he groaned and whispered to himself, "For fuck's sake, find some self-respect."

Kyle stared at him with knowing amusement.

"You can call me Kyle. *You* are my new best friend because my organization needs some pictures taken and you are the chosen photographer. It's as simple as that."

"Pictures of what, you son of a bitch?"

"That information will be given to you when you need to know. In the meantime, you will pack a few things. In the morning, we will be going somewhere where it's easier for me to keep an eye on you. "

"Oh good, that sounds like fun." Frustration at his helplessness gnawed at Brock's mind.

"There's no need for sarcasm. Now I expect you'd like to go back to bed?"

Kyle walked over and released him from the handcuffs. Brock massaged his sore wrists and tried to ignore the cool grip on his upper arm as he was led toward the stairs. His captor was so close behind him that he could feel Kyle's thighs brushing his ass as they climbed upward.

"Do you need to use the bathroom?" Kyle asked.

Brock shook his head. Kyle pulled him into the small en suite regardless.

"Well I do, so come in here where I can watch you."

The cuffs came out and Kyle attached one bracelet to the towel rail and the other to Brock's wrist. Facing him,

Kyle unzipped his fly and released a large cock unencumbered by underwear. He turned away with a sly smile and relieved himself before zipping up and turning back. He washed his hands thoroughly before releasing Brock's wrist and pushing him into the bedroom.

Kyle wrapped an arm around Brock's chest while the other hand dipped to massage Brock's arse through the fabric of his trunks. Brock shuddered and fought Kyle's hold, but he was too strong.

"Get your hands off of me!"

"Keep still. I'm thinking." Kyle obviously didn't need his hands to think. "I need to sleep, and I know I can't trust you to behave, so this is what we'll do." He pulled the covers back and shoved Brock down onto one side of the bed.

Once Brock was flat on his back, Kyle yanked his arms above his head, cuffing them to the wooden headboard. Brock glared up at him and got a look of barely restrained lust in return. Then Kyle turned away and undressed, stripping to bare skin. His body was hard all over, muscles defined, his thick cock erect. Brock turned his head away, refusing to display any interest in the view.

Kyle gave a low chuckle as he slid into bed next to Brock and pulled the covers up. He turned on his side and pushed a few stray tendrils of hair away from Brock's face then slid one hand beneath the sheets and began to explore Brock's body, touching and stroking his way across his chest and stomach. He dipped lower, tracing the pelvic bone to the waistband of Brock's trunks.

Brock bucked his hand off and snarled, "Very fucking brave, aren't you, when I can't fight back."

Kyle smiled patiently. "I'd like you to fight me, Lysander. I'd like to feel you struggling beneath me as I fill that perfect ass and fuck you senseless. I think you'd enjoy it too, though our situation means you must take the moral high ground and pretend otherwise."

Kyle turned away and began jerking his cock with smooth, rapid motions until he came with a grunt of satisfaction. When he returned from cleaning himself up, he took a peek beneath the covers, much to Brock's embarrassment.

"It's a shame you can give yourself no relief from the rather sizeable problem you have there, Lysander. I'd be very happy to oblige, but, as you've already pointed out, that wouldn't be fair. I have no intention of forcing myself on you. I think in a few days you'll be begging me to fuck you." He turned over and closed his eyes. "Sleep well."

Within minutes, Kyle was asleep, leaving Brock to suffer the discomfort of his own unrelieved need. He tugged on the unyielding metal cuffs and swore under his breath but it was no use. He stared daggers into the back of a dark head until he finally drifted into an uneasy doze.

* * * *

Wet heat, steamy humidity that soaked through clothing and sapped his strength surrounded him. The jungle was full of movement, unexplained noises and dripping, vibrant vegetation. A canopy stretched beneath the trees formed a shelter of sorts and slung underneath it was a large hammock made from netting. The edges of the scene were ragged and Brock knew he was dreaming, but he didn't fight it. In the way of dreams, he was suddenly naked, his body slick and

shiny with moisture, damp, blond locks clinging to his face. His muscles seemed more defined, his raging erection painfully hard as he watched Kyle stroll out of the trees. Kyle didn't pause but grasped Brock's neck and kissed him roughly, his breath as hot and sweet as the jungle air. He pressed Brock back to the hammock and waited while he climbed in. The fine net dug patterns into his skin as Kyle forced Brock's hands through holes that then held him in place. Kyle pushed the edge of the net back until Brock's backside was at the very edge and threw his legs over the suspending ropes. On his knees, Kyle leaned in to Brock's exposed ass and stabbed with his tongue, probing and testing the resistance of his small, dark entrance. The hammock swayed as Brock jerked and twitched, thrusting his ass wantonly toward the pleasure of that tormenting tongue. Kyle stood and stripped, positioned his huge cock then thrust forward. Heat upon heat enveloped Brock's body as his tight passage gave way to the massive intruder. Entangled in the netting, he screamed with pleasure and pain as Kyle used the swing of the hammock to add to the force of his penetration. Eyes bright with lust and concentration, Kyle leaned forward to wrap one hand tightly around Brock's slick shaft. He shouted his triumph and thrust again and again until…

* * * *

Brock awoke to a cool flannel being pressed against his forehead. He was soaked with sweat but shivering with cold at the same time and fought the clinging embrace of tangled sheets.

Kyle's deep voice penetrated his confusion. "Calm down. The fever's broken. You reacted badly to the vaccinations."

A fresh cloth replaced the first. Kyle used it to wipe down Brock's glistening chest and stomach.

"Try to sleep now. Everything will be fine."

The words were reassuring but, somewhere in his subconscious, Brock knew that things were far from fine. He was vaguely aware as Kyle tidied the covers and pulled them up over him. The last thing Brock heard was Kyle apologizing.

"I'm sorry, Lysander, but there is no other way."

Chapter Two

Brock woke to the sound of rain pattering against the windowpanes. He turned to look at the clock on the bedside table and winced as rigid metal dug into his wrists.

"Shit."

The events of the previous night came flooding back and he was filled with a combination of despair and resignation. Next to him, the bed was empty and he heaved a sigh of relief. He'd been thrown off balance every time Kyle touched him, wanting more while at the same time resenting every uninvited contact. He had vague memories of waking in the night and fever dreams that had soaked him in sweat and left him feeling weak and drained.

"I need a shower." He felt sticky and stale.

Kyle chose that moment to appear around the en suite door, a towel wrapped around his hips, broad chest glistening with water droplets. He gave himself a quick rub-down and bent to retrieve his clothes. Brock

couldn't restrain his whimper as he was presented with a perfect view of a tight backside and muscular thighs.

Kyle turned and smiled at him. "Good morning. Are you feeling better?"

Brock had to hook his tongue back into his mouth and stop himself from drooling. Kyle was completely unselfconscious, standing there in all his glory. Even soft, Kyle's dick looked huge to Brock, but in perfect proportion for the man's height. Kyle pulled on his trousers then came to stand by the bed, looking down on Brock with laughing eyes.

"I'll let you use the bathroom if you give me your word not to do anything silly. No trying to run and no attempts to fight me."

Brock nodded and groaned with relief as his wrists were released. He rolled out of bed, grabbed clean underwear from a drawer and stalked across to the bathroom without a backward glance.

The shower was a joyful experience. Soap and shampoo had never felt so good, but Brock couldn't get the image of Kyle's stunning, naked body out of his mind. He braced himself against the wall with one hand and wrapped the other around his painfully stiff cock. He jerked harder than normal, punishing himself for his lack of control, until he came with a gasp against the tiles. He rested his forehead against the cool ceramic and groaned. *Why does this man make me feel this way?* He should be angry, scared of what was happening to him, but all he felt was a guilty desire to get up close and personal with that hard body. He was also really curious about the mysterious job Kyle needed him to do. It involved photography, it had to be risky and that pushed his professional buttons in the same way that Kyle pushed his personal ones.

"If you're finished…you need to get ready. There will be a car here to pick us up in less than an hour."

Brock jumped at the sound of Kyle's low tones coming from the doorway. How long had he been standing there? From the self-satisfied expression on his face, long enough.

Brock stepped from the cubicle, grabbed a towel and rubbed vigorously, trying to ignore Kyle, who stood and watched, his eyes never leaving Brock's body. Brock pulled on black shorts and wished that he'd chosen less clingy underwear. He gave his hair a final rub then combed it with his fingers. He shaved quickly, cleaned his teeth then turned to the door.

"Can I dress?"

His face heated as Kyle examined him.

"I'm tempted to say no — but you are very distracting in that state, so please do." Kyle leered.

Brock dressed in jeans, a black T-shirt and a soft black pullover that he loved. He pulled on socks and boots, watched constantly by Kyle.

"Pack a small bag for the next few days then come downstairs. I'll make you some breakfast. Oh, and pack as many pairs of those shorts you're wearing as you like. They look good on you."

"Screw you," Brock muttered under his breath as he carelessly threw clothes and toiletries into a leather holdall. He found his least attractive pajamas and shoved them in the bag too. Tartan brushed cotton, a present from his mother, should conceal everything of interest to Kyle. Brock glanced in the mirror. Tousled blond hair shaded his eyes and deepened the shadows under them. His skin was paler than usual and he appeared tired and stressed. Sighing, he turned toward the door and headed downstairs, where the smell of

frying bacon assaulted his nostrils and elicited loud grumbles from his stomach.

Kyle had clearly been exploring the fridge because he served up a remarkably good plate of bacon and scrambled eggs with warm toast on the side. Coffee bubbled away in the percolator and delicious aromas filled the room.

"I'll let you have a cup if you promise not to throw it at me."

His smirk made Brock want to do exactly that, but the allure of his addiction meant Brock would have promised anything in exchange for a mug of his favorite blend. He hoped that his curt nod didn't betray him—Kyle would no doubt take full advantage of his weakness and bend him over the nearest table. Brock's arse clenched at the thought and he tried to switch his concentration back to the coffee.

Hot, bitter silk slid over his tongue and he sighed his appreciation. "Oh God, that's good!"

His obvious pleasure brought a grin to Kyle's face. "Just the kind of comment I'll be expecting in bed."

Refusing to rise to the bait, Brock sat at the table and ate in stony silence. He kept his gaze directed at his food and attempted to focus on the fact that Kyle was his enemy and not a deliciously dominant potential boyfriend. It just wasn't working. He pushed his plate away and made eye contact.

"Why don't you just tell me what this is all about, Kyle? Has it not occurred to you that I might help you without the threats?"

To his surprise, Kyle didn't deny him straight away. He looked thoughtful, as if he were weighing some options, then he disappeared into the kitchen and Brock

heard him muttering on the phone. When he came back, he gave Brock a stern look.

"Fine. I can see you're going to be nothing but trouble if I don't tell you. I had reservations from the start about taking this approach."

Brock didn't push. He let Kyle take his time.

"For some time, the British and American intelligence services have been attempting to locate the base of a subversive terrorist group funded by the Colombian drug trade. A high-tech spy drone has taken aerial pictures of what we believe is their headquarters but it's in a remote, inaccessible area. The only way of getting anywhere close undetected is via a virtually unexplored cave system. Access to the caves can only be reached by crossing terrain that would be challenging to the average mountain goat."

Brock felt strangely excited. "I'm guessing that you need photographs of this base and you want to use my officially sanctioned expedition as cover."

Kyle took a sip of his coffee. "What we are asking you to do is dangerous. If you are caught, you could be taken hostage and your actions would then come to the attention of various government interests. We have to make sure there is a plausible reason to justify your presence in the country and a trail that could prove you have been coerced."

"Who is 'we' exactly?"

"That's the one thing I can't tell you. My organization handles certain…difficult tasks…for the British government and its allies — things that can't be done above the political radar."

Brock frowned. "So you're telling me that your strong-arm tactics are all a ploy? For my own protection?"

Kyle nodded. "That's right."

"You should have told me the truth from the start, Kyle, but, I have to admit, I'm intrigued."

Brock was silent for a while as he reflected on what he had learned. Kyle was one of the good guys. That meant that lust at first sight was not such a bad thing. This could turn into an amazing adventure in more ways than one.

"I should be furious at how you've deceived me," Brock said quietly.

"Should?" Kyle sounded hopeful.

"I don't even have any way of knowing that you're telling me the truth."

"No, you don't."

"But I believe you. Whatever shadowy organization you work for seriously needs to work on its contractor engagement policies, though." Brock's lips quirked into half a smile.

"I'll pass that back to management," Kyle said with a straight face. He gazed intently at Brock. "So you'll do it?"

Brock grinned. "Yes, I'll do it. I'll take your pictures because they will do some good and because there are only two other photographers in the world with the skills needed to do this."

"There's a major adrenaline junkie hidden inside that beautiful body, isn't there?"

Brock ducked his head. "Nobody else will ever get the chance to take pictures like these."

"There'll be no recognition. You understand that, don't you?"

"That's not why I take pictures, Kyle. Sure, I make a good living, but the satisfaction comes from capturing the perfect shot—freezing a moment in time that will

never be repeated." Brock looked up from beneath his lashes.

"I'm glad you know the truth, but we still have to maintain the illusion that you are an unwilling participant in all this. Until we are tucked away in a safe house, I'll have to treat you like a hostage," Kyle said blandly.

Brock's face heated. "That doesn't sound so bad," he mumbled.

"I think there are some very interesting fantasies dancing around inside that pretty head of yours, Lysander. You and I are going to get along just fine."

I really hope so. Brock kept that thought to himself.

While Brock fetched his bag from the bedroom, Kyle cleaned up the kitchen. When Brock returned, Kyle looked at his watch. "Okay, time to go. It's best you don't know where we're going, so you'll be blindfolded once we're in the car."

Brock waited in the hall while Kyle took their coats and Brock's bag to a waiting car. Kyle returned and escorted him down the drive and into a low, black saloon with deeply tinted windows. There was a driver in the front and a blackened screen between them. Kyle clicked the locks shut and turned to Brock. "This compartment is soundproof. The driver can't hear us, so it's okay to ask me questions, though I'd rather you wait until we get to the safe house. I'm going to blindfold you now." He produced a length of dark cloth and made to tie it around Brock's eyes but Brock flinched away.

"Hey, it's okay to be nervous. I'm not going to hurt you, but this is non-negotiable," Kyle said, his voice soothing.

Brock held still as the cloth went around his eyes and was knotted tightly behind his head.

Resigned, Brock leaned back against the seat and breathed in the scent of polished leather, only to jump out of his skin as Kyle rested his hand on Brock's thigh and began to stroke.

Brock tried to push Kyle away, but his hand was immovable.

"Consider this a training exercise in self-control, Lysander. You're going to have to follow my orders on this mission, so let's see how you manage with a simple one." Kyle brushed against the hardening bulge in Brock's trousers. "Keep nice and quiet."

* * * *

A long car journey in total darkness was not the best experience Brock had ever had. As soon as his mind wandered into thoughts of whether or not he could trust Kyle, he would be jerked back to reality by a new assault as Kyle traced the ridge of his cock or rubbed his thigh. Every time Brock moved his hands protectively into his lap, they were shoved aside. He sat in silence, bearing the delicious torment as best he could, muscles rigid with tension. His every involuntary reaction got a low chuckle or satisfied murmur from Kyle. Brock bit down hard on his lip and fought back the urge to curse.

When the car finally rolled to a halt, Kyle got out. Brock heaved a sigh of relief as the locks clicked down, leaving him alone. He hadn't been able to relax for a minute of the journey and now he had to deal with his achingly hard dick and a desperate need to come. Lack of sight magnified his other senses and, though he

hated to admit it, he loved the feeling of being powerless.

Brock guessed that ten minutes passed before the door opened and cool air washed into the interior of the car. It was awkward to climb out with his eyes covered and he struggled until a firm grip clasped his biceps and pulled him forward. The grip did not release, but guided him along a path of some kind. He could hear the rustle of leaves in the breeze and Brock sensed that mature trees surrounded him. There was no traffic noise or any identifiable sounds, other than those of birds and the distant bleating of sheep, all of which were cut off as they entered a building and the door shut behind him. He flinched at the sound of locks clicking and heavy bolts sliding into place.

"You look very pretty in a blindfold, I'm loath to remove it, but I suppose I must."

Kyle unknotted the strip of cloth and pulled it away from Brock's face. Brock blinked a few times while his eyes adjusted to the light. He took in his surroundings. They stood in a narrow corridor and a set of stairs rose in front of them. To the side was a single door, suggesting that they were in a small cottage of some kind. Kyle opened it and beckoned Brock into a cozy lounge-diner with a wood burner well alight in the fireplace. The soft lighting came from small lamps as heavy external shutters covered the window. There was a decent TV, a DVD player and a bookshelf carrying a selection of recent thrillers and fantasy novels.

"As you can see, there are films and books to keep us amused—I hope your taste is similar to mine," Kyle said. "A few days here won't kill us. I just need you off the radar for a while. In a moment, you can ring your

mother and let her know that you are taking a short trip with friends. Don't tell her anything that may give away what we're doing, Brock—that's in all our interests."

Kyle handed him a cheap mobile phone and watched while he dialed the number.

Brock imagined his mother cleaning flour from her hands before picking up the phone at the other end. She was often up to her ears in baking.

"Hi, Mum."

"Lysander, sweetie, how lovely to hear from you. Is everything okay?"

As he heard her voice, Brock's hands began to shake and he couldn't prevent the slight tremble in his voice as he answered.

"I'm fine, getting ready for the trip, you know. I had a bad reaction to the jabs, but a day in bed seems to have sorted it. I'm just ringing to let you know that I'll be out of contact for a while. I'm going climbing with a few friends, as I won't see them for a while after I go to Colombia."

"Sounds lovely, dear. You be careful. No taking silly risks."

"Of course not, Mum. I may not be able to get in touch from Colombia, so it could be a while before we speak again. Give my love to Dad." After a few more exchanges, he said goodbye and handed the phone back to Kyle, whose expression was carefully neutral.

"That was harder than I thought it would be."

Kyle smiled at him sympathetically. "Unfortunately, in my world, lies are a necessity. My parents think I'm a security consultant. Now, do you need to text your brother?"

"No, he's used to me disappearing."

Brock sat on the edge of the sofa and put his head in his hands.

"This is starting to feel unreal. Perhaps I'm still reacting to those jabs. I'll wake up soon and you'll be gone."

"And there was I thinking that I was the man of your dreams."

Brock felt a spike of desire and took a deep, ragged breath. He didn't want Kyle to see him as weak and emotional. He steeled himself to look up and met a gaze that spoke of understanding and sympathy.

"I'm not an unfeeling monster. I do understand what you're going through." Kyle's words were barely audible and he turned away quickly.

"Come on, I'll show you upstairs then we'll have some lunch."

Two bedrooms and a bathroom made up the first floor. One bedroom was a small single. It contained the kind of bed that Brock decided would have fitted well in a very dated hospital—one with a green metal frame and a thin mattress covered by a frayed sheet. In addition to the external shutters, the window was barred. There was no bulb in the light socket and no door.

"Mine, I presume?" Brock stared into the unfriendly space and grimaced.

"Well. It would have been." Kyle grinned.

The other bedroom was much larger, dominated by a double bed with a metal scrollwork headboard and luxurious covers. There was a wardrobe and a small linen press along one wall, and Brock's bag sat in a corner.

"The choice is yours—you can either sleep in here with me or in the other room. I won't force you to share

a bed with me, though I won't pretend that I don't want you to."

Brock's face heated.

"You could order me to sleep in here, couldn't you?"

"I could, but I won't. It's your decision. Of course, once you're in here with me, there will definitely be orders to follow."

Brock swallowed and changed the subject. "I'm hungry."

"Mmm. Me too."

The diversionary tactic hadn't worked, as Kyle was clearly not thinking about food. His eyes were fixed on Brock's as he moved closer. He placed his hands around Brock's body and pressed his thumbs into the groove at the top of his hipbones. A butterfly pinned to a display board couldn't have felt more trapped than Brock did at that moment. He tried to pull away, but Kyle was very strong and held him in place with ease, grinding his thumbs in harder. Brock could feel his cock swelling and his temperature rising. He wanted to resist, but Kyle had pressed the switch in his brain that responded to control. It felt so good to be held by strong hands, to know that Kyle could take him by force if he wanted to.

Kyle patted Brock's perfect arse and let him go. He'd made his point. Brock fled down the stairs and Kyle watched him go with a smile. Brock's responses turned him on in a way that he hadn't experienced in a long time. Brock was so pretty — part of Kyle wanted to bury his head in that soft blond hair and whisper words of comfort. The other part wanted to tie Brock down, tear his clothes off and hammer his arse until he screamed.

Intuition told Kyle that Brock would enjoy the second option more.

Kyle waited a few moments for his iron erection to subside a little then followed Brock downstairs. His quarry was curled into the corner of the sofa with his head buried in a book, blond waves falling forward to conceal his face. Kyle didn't bait him any further but went into the kitchen to prepare some lunch. He returned about fifteen minutes later with bowls of steaming soup, warm crusty bread and mugs of tea.

"I hope this is okay."

He put the tray down on the coffee table and picked up one of the bowls. Brock put his book on the floor and took the soup from him. "Thank you. It smells delicious. Is it homemade?"

"Yes. I find cooking therapeutic. There's a freezer full of soups. Feel free to help yourself."

"This is amazing." Brock dipped a chunk of bread into his bowl and ate it with relish.

"I did lunch—you can cook dinner."

"You might regret that decision."

Kyle gave a short laugh. "As long as you manage not to burn anything, I'm sure it will be fine. It's difficult to go wrong with pasta and there are homemade sauces in the freezer you can choose from."

"Okay, it's a deal."

Brock ate the rest of his lunch in contented silence then glanced over at Kyle.

"I've been patient and you have my word that I will get you the best pictures I can. But I want to know more."

Kyle looked at him thoughtfully. He cleared the dishes away then returned from the kitchen and sat next to him on the sofa.

"I'll tell you more soon, I promise. I have orders to follow too. My bosses know that you are now a willing participant, but they still have to be cautious."

Kyle slipped off his boots and socks and swung his legs up so that he was leaning against the opposite arm of the sofa, knees bent so that black denim hugged the curve of his arse. He pushed his toes underneath Brock's thigh and wiggled them into a comfortable position.

"You look tired. Are you still feeling the effects of the jabs?"

"I feel weak and I have a headache, nothing serious. I'm tired because I didn't sleep well for some reason." The sarcasm was evident in his voice.

"Then you need to rest. Come here."

Kyle parted his legs and patted the space between them. Brock froze and shook his head slowly. Kyle decided to see if his intuition was accurate, that Brock just needed a reason to submit to him.

"Remember I said there'd be orders to follow if we shared a bed. The same applies to sofas. Now come here."

Silently Brock turned and shuffled backward into the space waiting for him. Kyle pulled him back so that he was lying against his chest then pinned him into place with his thighs. He leaned forward and breathed in the scent from Brock's hair.

"Relax. Close your eyes and pretend that I'm your dream man."

He could feel Brock trembling, muscles tensed as he ran a finger along his defined cheekbone.

"So beautiful..." Kyle resisted the urge to stroke and touch every inch of Brock's body. He was already hard enough that Brock must be able to feel Kyle's erection

pressing into his lower back. He wondered what Brock was thinking, hoped that he was secretly enjoying their closeness.

Brock could hardly breathe. Kyle's ample cock was digging into his spine and all he wanted was for it to move lower. Kyle touched his face and he had to fight not to turn into his warm palm and nuzzle there. He felt lightheaded and dizzy, but he didn't think the inoculations were to blame. Blood left his head and descended to his groin as if gravity had increased its pull. He swallowed and tilted his head back, exposing his slender neck in an act of trust. He trembled, but not from fear, and gasped as soft lips sucked the sensitive skin above his collarbone then moved to his neck. Kyle encircled his chest with a strong arm and held him in place as he bit down gently at first, then harder, into the juncture between neck and shoulder until Brock cried out. Kyle's grip on him softened and he pulled back, rubbing a thumb over the sore place on Brock's neck. Brock knew he'd been marked and, God help him, he liked it.

Some of the tension left Brock's body and he relaxed against Kyle's firm chest. His lashes fluttered and he slipped toward sleep, his exhaustion compounded by the emotional exertion he had been through. He turned his head and snuggled against Kyle's body, enjoying the spicy scent that permeated Kyle's pullover, and drifted into his dreams.

Kyle knew that Brock must have been utterly spent, both emotionally and physically, and that he shouldn't read anything deeper into the position he now found himself in. However, in the weeks he had spent

learning about Brock's life, following him and observing everything he did, he'd come to realize he was deeply attracted to the younger man. It wasn't just physical lust either, though he couldn't deny that it was part of the equation. He had fallen for the whole package — Brock's sense of adventure, his passion for his work, his sensitivity. Blond hair and those beautiful eyes were the icing on the cake. Kyle ran his fingers down the scar on his own face. He felt rough and ugly in comparison. If they'd met through normal means, he was sure Brock wouldn't have spared him a second glance, yet here he was with this gorgeous creature asleep on his chest, rising and falling as Kyle breathed gently so as not to disturb him. It felt wonderful, yet at the same time was the worst possible torture because he knew it couldn't last. He was fooling himself if he thought Brock would ever want him. He sighed and closed his own eyes, one arm still protectively wrapped around Brock's chest.

* * * *

When Brock stirred a couple of hours later, he was still curled against Kyle's body. For a few delicious moments, he allowed himself to believe that it was his boyfriend who held him so securely. Just the thought of all that toned muscle making contact with his naked flesh was enough to make Brock painfully hard. He wanted to feel the rake of stubble across his skin. He wanted to be thrown down and taken hard. Counter to all logic, he hoped that Kyle would lose patience and do what his eyes continually threatened. The way in which their lives had collided was shocking, but,

despite everything, Brock liked this man who had gatecrashed his world.

Carefully, Brock lifted Kyle's arm away from his body and slid forward. With a sigh of relief, he stood and crept toward the stairs. He needed to splash cold water on his face and another part of his anatomy would benefit from a dousing as well.

* * * *

The rest of the day passed without drama. Brock cooked dinner. They watched a movie from separate chairs. Neither man mentioned what had happened that afternoon, but the livid bruise on Brock's neck bore testament to that brief escape into sensation. Kyle felt ridiculously protective. "You look exhausted."

"I'm shattered. Is it all right if I go to bed?"

Kyle nodded. "Of course. I need you fit and well. Get ready and I'll be up soon."

Kyle gave him fifteen minutes to use the bathroom then followed him upstairs. Brock sat on the edge of the single bed in the small, cell-like second bedroom. He wore dark pajamas in some kind of tartan pattern and his pale bare feet rested on the floorboards. Frustrated, Kyle sighed. "You don't have to do this, you know."

"Yes, I do." Brock gazed directly at him, blue eyes glittering. "Much as I'd love to jump into bed with you, Kyle, I have to know you want me for the right reasons. It's not like we've just come back from a dinner date, is it?"

Kyle scowled. "Fine. It's your choice. Lie down."

Kyle went to the other bedroom and came back with a heavy blanket that he placed over Brock.

"Those pajamas are your way of torturing me, aren't they? Tell me you don't normally wear them."

Brock smiled sweetly. "I usually sleep naked."

Kyle turned and stalked from the room, muttering expletives under his breath. He went through his pre-bed routine with a raging hard-on and a head full of Brock. He got into bed and spent an hour tossing and turning and beating the hell out of his pillow. All he could think about was Brock, cold and alone, in the other room.

"Bugger this."

He threw back the duvet and sat on the edge of the bed. He was wearing black shorts that did little to disguise the prominent bulge testing the elasticity of the fabric and he debated covering up a bit more. "Fuck it." What he had in mind did not require more clothing. He crossed to the dresser and hesitated before picking up his handcuffs and the flick knife that sat between his comb and coin tray.

"This is a really bad idea."

He prowled across the landing to Brock's room, where he wasn't surprised to find him awake.

Kyle didn't say a word, just yanked the covers off the bed and loomed over Brock's helpless form. He tugged Brock's arms up and cuffed him to the bed frame. In his hand, the knife glinted in the dim light. As he climbed onto the bed and knelt across Brock's thighs, Brock yanked on the cuffs, rattling the chain. He looked wide-eyed and expectant rather than scared. Kyle rested the tip of the knife in the hollow at the base of Brock's throat and glared.

"Pick a safe word. I assume you know what that is."

"I've never needed one before."

"Well, you do now."

Brock gulped. "Aconcagua. Not a word I'm likely to scream in the throes of passion."

"It'll do. Now…I really hate these fucking pajamas."

Kyle slid the knife down until it met the resistance of a button. The blade slipped through the threads and descended to the next. In seconds, all five buttons had been sliced free, allowing him to push the gaudy cloth back and expose golden skin and small dark nipples.

"A little better."

Kyle trailed the knife down twitching stomach muscles until it reached a tartan waistband then followed it round to a slim hip. Slowly, he drew the blade down the entire length of the leg seam, slitting the fabric with ease. Then he did the same the other side. He started on the arm seams and, when he was done, pulled the ruined garments from Brock's body.

"Improving all the time."

Brock's sweet whimper was all the encouragement Kyle needed. He licked his lips at the sight of tight trunks hugging a barely restrained erection and he ran the tip of the knife across the bulge. He pushed one finger beneath the waistband and stroked Brock's abdomen. Brock's muscles tensed beneath his touch and small moans escaped his compressed lips. Kyle slit the elastic at each side and tore the fabric so that only tattered rags covered Brock's cock and balls. He stroked his thumb down the exposed flesh between hip and thigh and Brock bucked, losing the remnants of material covering him.

"Perfect."

Using just one finger, Kyle stroked lightly. He circled the gleaming tip of Brock's dick and spread the liquid down his shaft. He fondled his swollen sac then paused. "One word and I stop."

The silence was telling. The only sound was the rapid breathing coming from Brock's parted lips.

Kyle wasn't as gentle with his mouth as with his fingers. He plunged his head down and pulled back with fierce suction. Brock tasted bittersweet, his flavor spreading across Kyle's tongue as he licked. Kyle nuzzled Brock's inner thighs as he transferred his attention to smooth, firm balls then returning to swallow him with confident skill. He pushed Brock's thighs even farther apart, taking him deep. Brock's back arched as Kyle used his teeth to make an impression in delicate flesh.

Brock's needy moans grew more urgent, telling Kyle that he was close. Kyle renewed his efforts. He rode the movement as Brock bucked. He pushed Brock down and mouthed him harder. As warm fluid coated his tongue, Kyle swallowed greedily. Finally he pulled away and sat back. Brock's pretty eyes were squeezed shut. The muscles in his arms were hard and defined as he pulled on his bonds. He looked stunning.

Kyle wriggled out of his underwear. "Look at me, Lysander." He kept his tone gentle but firm and Brock responded. He opened his eyes wide as Kyle moved until his cock touched Brock's lips.

"One word and I stop." Kyle held his breath then let it out with a hiss as Brock parted kiss-bruised lips. Kyle didn't hesitate. He fucked Brock's mouth with controlled aggression. He wanted to own the beautiful man beneath him—possess him, mark him. To Kyle's surprise, Brock responded as best he could, using his tongue as much as Kyle allowed. Kyle intended to pull away before he came, but the moment arrived with such force that he flooded Brock's mouth with his cum.

Brock didn't struggle or fight it. He swallowed again and again, taking every drop.

After a few recuperative seconds, Kyle clambered off the bed.

"Don't go away." He grinned at Brock's irritated expression and headed for the bathroom to clean up. He took his time, enjoying the thought of Brock lying there, restrained, the taste of Kyle's cum lingering on his tongue.

When Kyle returned to the bedroom and released Brock's wrists, Brock sat up and ran a hand through his tousled hair.

"I…we…shouldn't have…"

"Stop thinking. Use the bathroom then get to bed — the other bed." Kyle issued the order in a tone that brooked no argument and Brock meekly did as he was told. When he was done cleaning up, he joined Kyle in the main bedroom and slipped beneath the covers, lying as far away from Kyle as possible. Kyle grunted and dragged Brock closer. He spooned against Brock's back, making sure that his semi-soft cock rested in the channel between Brock's arse cheeks. He flung his arm over Brock's warm body, held him in place then dropped into sleep.

Chapter Three

It was raining again in the morning—relentless, heavy rain from a low, oppressive sky. It was dark enough that when Brock woke, he thought for a while that it was still the middle of the night. He listened to the drumming beat against the window and glanced at the clock—six-thirty—not early for him. He turned onto his back and froze as warm fingers brushed his thigh. "Oh shit."

In a rush, the previous night came back to him. Strong hands on his body, a demanding mouth doing things to his cock that he had never experienced before.

"My willpower is about as strong as melting jelly," he muttered under his breath. Kyle had given him the chance to stop it and he had stayed silent. Now here he was, millimeters from the man that had driven him to an incredible orgasm, a man he should not desire. Instead he craved his touch almost as much as he wanted to run and hide from his feelings.

"Good morning. You think too much." Kyle's voice broke into his thoughts, deep and amused.

Brock didn't look at him. "What do you mean?"

"I can hear the cogs whirring—you're trying to understand why you like me. I'll give you a way out—you were chained to the bed and couldn't stop me."

He raised one knee and put his hands behind his head.

"You would have stopped if I'd asked you." Brock's voice was quiet but sure.

"Of course."

"I didn't ask you to stop—because I didn't want you to."

"Is it so hard to accept that you're attracted to me? Or do I repulse you? Was it just a physical reaction last night? I know I'm not the prettiest man in the world…maybe I'm just not your type?" Kyle sounded hurt, but resigned.

Brock turned onto his side and gazed at Kyle. It was time to face up to the truth of how he felt.

"You're gorgeous, Kyle. How could you not know that?"

Kyle swallowed. "Not like you—you're beautiful."

Brock flushed. He'd been complimented on his appearance by plenty of men, but none of them had ever made him feel the way Kyle did. He turned onto his back again and closed his eyes. "I've never felt this way about anyone before. I can't look at you without wanting you to touch me. Just the sound of your voice makes me nervous. Last night, when you took control, it felt amazing. You could have done anything and I would have let you."

"Now you tell me!"

"It can't happen again, Kyle. It can't."

"Are you finding it hard to ignore the fact that so far I've stalked you, invaded your privacy, broken into your home, threatened your family...?"

Brock snickered. "You're not doing a great job of promoting yourself. But no, that's not it. I don't know you. Such sudden, intense feelings scare me. I can't ignore that."

Brock flinched as Kyle snaked a hand across his bare stomach and stroked his skin persistently.

"I think I could make you ignore it."

Brock groaned. "I know you could. That's the problem."

He clambered out of bed, avoiding Kyle's steely gaze, and pulled on underwear and jeans before turning to face him.

"I'll do what you ask because you are in charge of this mission. I'll even sleep in this bed if you insist on it. But please don't touch me again. I need time to understand why I feel the way I do." He turned away and left the room.

Kyle clenched his fists in frustration. He loved his job, but sometimes it seemed to get in the way of any chance he had for finding real happiness. He sighed. It had been a nice dream while it lasted. He wouldn't give up—that wasn't in him—but for now the mission had to come first. He got up, showered and dressed quickly. Downstairs, he found Brock sitting at the small dining table eating a bowl of cereal. He didn't make eye contact but Kyle detected a slight blush highlighting pretty cheekbones. Kyle grinned, pleased that Brock wasn't going to find it easy to resist his feelings.

In the kitchen, there was a pot of coffee brewing. Kyle poured himself a mug and slammed a couple of pieces

of bread in the toaster. When it was done and slathered in butter, he carried his breakfast through to the dining room and joined Brock at the table.

"So, today you get to show me why you have the reputation of being the best in your field."

Brock glanced up curiously. "Today? What's happening today?"

Kyle chewed on his toast. In between bites he said, "Have you ever heard of Imber?"

Brock frowned. "Yes, of course. I did a series of location shots a couple of years ago on lost villages. The magazine I worked for wanted to feature Imber but couldn't get permission from the military."

Kyle sipped his coffee. "The village was evacuated in November 1943 to facilitate training of American troops for the D-Day landings. The village has remained in military occupation ever since. It's only accessible to the public on a few days per year."

"I remember now. Weren't the villagers told they would be able to return to their homes after the war but then never were?"

"That's right. If you looked on a map now, you wouldn't even know the village was there at all. There's just a big blank space."

"So, what does this have to do with me?"

Kyle stared at Brock. "Do you ever regret your career choice?"

Brock rubbed a hand through his hair. "No. Never. The fact that I can make a good living doing what I love never ceases to amaze me."

"How did you know that you wanted to be a photographer?" Kyle pushed a little, trying to get Brock to reveal some personal details.

Brock chewed his lip. "I wanted to be a wildlife photographer from the moment my father gave me a disposable camera and pointed out the squirrels romping around our local park. From that moment, I was hooked. School and university provided opportunities to develop the skills that give me an edge. It's a competitive field."

Kyle drummed his fingers on the table. "Your reputation has been built on your willingness to shoot in the most inhospitable, inaccessible places on the planet. In the last two years, you've taken assignments in Alaska, Irian Jaya, Vietnam and Botswana."

"Yes, and in a few weeks I'm supposed to be heading to the cloud forests of the eastern Andes to photograph a range of local wildlife and explore some of the deep cave systems in the area. I have a commission from *National Geographic*."

"Yes, I know, which is the perfect cover for our mission. However, my employers are keen to test your abilities first."

"In what way, exactly?"

"There is a church in Imber, kept in reasonable repair because it's Grade One listed. It's called St. Giles. The tower was built around 1400 and there are even some ancient wall paintings that have survived." He paused. "The church tower provides the perfect vantage point to observe military activities going on in the area. Tomorrow night, a small anti-terrorist unit will be engaged in training exercises in and around Imber. You are going to take pictures of them."

Brock looked incredulous. "Without them knowing?"

Kyle nodded. "I want you to trespass on military property—at night—climb a crumbling church tower without ropes and yes, take pictures of a bunch of elite

troops who will be mightily pissed off if they catch you."

"Oh."

"Yes, oh."

"What happens if they do catch me?"

"I'll disappear from your life and you'll be able to take your trip as planned. We will seek alternative help for the mission in Colombia. Oh — and someone will get you out of military custody, of course."

"Charming. So it's succeed or get dumped? I'm not sure I like the options."

Kyle shoved his chair back and was behind Brock in an instant, yanking his head back by the hair. "You don't have a choice. I don't question my orders and you will not question mine. Understand?" Kyle resisted the urge to bend down and give Brock a punishing kiss as he fought Kyle's hold.

"Let me go!"

"Show some respect or I'll put you over my knee."

Brock ripped himself from Kyle's grip, sacrificing a few golden strands of hair. He sat, trembling, his face flushed.

Kyle grinned. "Or maybe that's what you want?"

"Fuck off, Kyle. Show me what camera equipment I'll be using so I can start to prepare. The sooner this is done, the better."

* * * *

Brock jerked awake, heart pounding, and for a moment couldn't remember where he was. Lights streaked toward him, blue-white out of the darkness, then flashed by. A car...he was in a car...and the hood Kyle had put over his head when they'd left the cottage

was gone. He groaned and rubbed at his eyes. "How long have I been asleep?"

"An hour or so. We're nearly at the drop-off point." Kyle looked utterly relaxed, one hand on the wheel, the other resting on the gear stick. "There are glucose tablets in the glove compartment. I suggest you take a couple now."

Brock found the packet and chewed a couple of the chalky tablets. "You want any?"

Kyle shook his head. "I'll be dozing in the car while you're romping around Salisbury Plain."

"Good to know. I wouldn't want you to be biting your nails worrying about me," Brock said, with more than a hint of sarcasm.

"We're here." Kyle pulled in to a deserted garage, switched off the headlights and drove to the rear of the building. "This place was abandoned years ago. It'll be easy enough for you to get back to and it's highly unlikely that any patrols will pass — military or local plod." He turned off the ignition. "Let's get you ready."

Both men got out of the car and circled around to the boot. Brock wore matte black climbing gear with a hooded fleece over the top. He had on light hiking boots and thin gloves. Every inch of his pale skin was covered, apart from his face. Kyle opened the boot and rummaged in a bag. He pulled out a stick of camouflage paint. He smeared the black goo over Brock's cheeks and rubbed it in.

"Better. Make sure you keep the hood up, your hair is like a fucking Belisha beacon." He handed Brock a small rucksack. "Right, in here you have climbing shoes, camera and a bottle of water. Here's your map — " He handed over a small square of laminated paper. "Keep exactly to the marked route. You'll be crossing a

live firing area and there may be undetonated shells. Do you understand me, Brock? Do not stray from the path."

Brock shouldered the pack. "You *do* care." He pulled on a pair of night vision goggles and let his eyes adjust to the eerie landscape.

"You have five hours. You may not need it all, but that's the safe limit for darkness. It's a cloudy night and there's no moon, so conditions couldn't be better. Forecast said there was a chance of rain. Remember, some of the ground is boggy. Take your time—you don't want to pick up an injury."

Brock shrugged the pack into a more comfortable position. "We've been over this a hundred times. I'll do what I have to do. I'm good at this, remember? That's why you want me to help you."

He moved to the edge of the building and checked for traffic. There was no sign of life or light for as far as the eye could see. He sucked in his breath as Kyle gently squeezed his shoulder.

"Be careful."

Brock shrugged off Kyle's touch and sprinted across the road, into the darkness.

Finally alone, Brock found running through the night therapeutic. Being close to Kyle had made him jittery and tense. He longed for the man's touch. Running gave him time to think, to analyze the way he felt. From time to time he glanced at his little route map, but he had memorized every feature and so far it proved to be accurate. The path hugged crumbling walls and fence lines, skirting open spaces as much as possible. Brock kept low and tried to move at a steady pace, grateful for the night vision goggles that allowed him to negotiate the rough terrain safely.

At one point he saw a line of figures moving in the distance and ducked into a ditch, holding his breath. He crouched in the damp, muddy channel for what he thought was a safe time then poked his head out cautiously. It was all clear, so he carried on, heart pounding. He couldn't get caught. Someone was watching over him because he had just crossed a narrow rutted track when a tank rumbled over a nearby ridge and sped down the hill toward him. Brock threw himself down and froze — careless of the boggy ground. Scant feet away from his prone form, the hunk of metal trundled past without stopping. *Too close.* Brock pushed down a sob of relief and carried on.

When the church finally came into view, Brock found a relatively dry spot and changed into his climbing shoes. He took the small camera Kyle had supplied from his pack, hung it around his neck, then stashed the pack — and his boots — under a bush. The biggest obstacles between him and his goal were the rolls of razor wire that blocked the lanes around the tiny hamlet of Imber. Abandoned buildings loomed from the darkness like a scene from the apocalypse. Brock shivered and focused on his goal, moving carefully toward the church. This was where things got unpredictable. Though Kyle had shown him pictures of the tower he had to climb, he hadn't been able to tell him about the condition of the stone. Brock had to climb freestyle, without ropes, and he didn't like the uncertainty. It was dangerous.

He paused at the base of the squat tower and looked up. Black forms flitted in and out of the uppermost window like shadowy confetti. His destination was apparently home to a colony of bats. He took a moment to double-check the settings on his unfamiliar camera,

an expensive model designed to cope with the lack of light without a flash, and took a couple of test shots, which seemed fine.

Adjusting the camera strap around his neck, Brock then felt for his first hand and toe holds and started upward. The ancient stone held firm and there were plenty of niches to dig his fingers into. As climbs went, it was one of the easiest he'd tackled from a technical perspective, but his heart still raced with the fear of being seen. Just below the opening that the bats were using, there was a narrow projection in the stonework. Brock used the extra stability to hold on with one hand and pull himself over the ledge. The rickety floor of the tower room was thick with bat guano and Brock cringed as his thin climbing shoes sank deep into the muck. He hunkered down and rested his camera on the ledge. He found himself assessing the angle and proportions of the scene below and shook his head. *Just take the pictures, you idiot! Aesthetics are not important right at this moment.*

He had to stay frozen in position for what seemed to be an endless time before anything happened but, after a while, an armored vehicle trundled into the road alongside the church. A few minutes later, heavily camouflaged men came into view. The group gathered briefly, then fanned out and began searching the area. Brock snapped away, mindful of his precarious position but still determined to get good shots. He had no idea what the soldiers below him were doing and he didn't care. A couple of them were using equipment that resembled sophisticated metal detectors, so he made sure to get close-ups of the kit. He also zoomed in on faces where he could. When he was satisfied that

he had enough shots, he ducked inside the tower room and waited for the noises below to cease.

Every few minutes, Brock took a peek out of the window. His muscles were beginning to ache in his crouched position, but he didn't want to sit in three inches of bat shit. When the soldiers finally moved away, he climbed down the tower in slow, steady increments, breathing a sigh of relief as he hit solid ground. He stretched out his cramped muscles then ran back to the place he'd left his pack. As he changed his footwear again and stowed the camera, he heard the distant sound of men's voices. Frantically, he looked around. There wasn't much cover, just a drainage channel lined with barbed wire. There was no choice. He flung himself down into the narrow depression, clamping his mouth shut as razor-sharp barbs pierced his clothes and the tender flesh beneath.

"Who was it said they saw something?" A gruff voice sounded far too close.

"Private Jacobs, sir. Said he thought there was movement at the church tower window. He was too far away to say for sure, though."

"Fine. Let's take a gander. He does realize that there are about ten thousand fucking bats living in there?"

Heavy footsteps moved away. Brock risked rolling backward a fraction. Barbed wire had wrapped itself around his forearm and another section pierced his hip. He didn't dare pull it free. He hardly dared breathe and it seemed like an age before the soldiers returned.

"I have bat shit on my boots, Private. Tell your colleague he'll be cleaning them off when we get back to barracks. There's no sign of anything happening here…"

Brock didn't catch the tail end of the conversation as the soldiers moved away. He lay in his uncomfortable hiding place for twenty minutes until he was certain that they were gone. He extricated himself from the wire, wincing as the metal thorns ripped his skin. There was no time to check the damage. He had to move. The delay had cost him valuable time—he'd be lucky to get back to Kyle on schedule.

Brock's muscles ached and he could feel the seep of blood down his arm as he ran. He prayed that the pictures he had taken were good enough. Thoughts of Kyle filled his mind. Brock could fight his attraction but he couldn't deny it. He'd like to photograph Kyle's handsome, scarred face. Take pictures of his hard, muscled body. He could imagine the subtle lighting and the angles. Black and white would work well. His cock jerked happily and Brock moaned. Now was absolutely *not* the time. To compound his misery, it started to rain, lightly at first but then more steadily, giving him a thorough soaking. He was muddy and exhausted by the time he reached the road opposite the abandoned service station. He crouched low before crossing and circling behind the dilapidated building.

The car was still there, dark and silent in the shadows. He edged toward the vehicle, hugging the wall, then pulled open the door and slid into the passenger seat. The instant the door clunked shut, the locks engaged. Brock slumped back in his seat, utterly drained.

"You got the pictures." Kyle's comment was a statement, not a question, and Brock didn't answer.

"Turn toward me."

Brock didn't have the energy to resist as Kyle slipped a hood over his head.

"You have to be fucking kidding me? I got your pictures. I came back. I did everything you asked."

"You did, and I'm impressed. However, you still can't know where the safe house is and it will be light soon."

"You're paranoid," Brock muttered stubbornly.

Kyle started the car. "I suggest you stop bitching and rest." He reached into the back seat and grabbed a thick, fleecy travel blanket. "You're wet and cold. You need to warm up." He tucked the blanket around Brock's body and turned the heater up to full.

* * * *

Despite his discomfort, Brock had slipped instantly into sleep, lulled by the heat and thrum of the car's engine. When he awoke, dawn had arrived and, with it, a few shreds of light that seeped beneath the edge of the hood. He shifted and moaned as clammy clothing chafed his skin. He ached everywhere.

"Couple of minutes and we'll be back," Kyle stated. "You can take off the hood, there's nothing around here to identify where we are." He turned the car through a gate and onto a well-maintained track. Brock guessed they were heading for a farmhouse and he was proved right when they crested the brow of a hill and some buildings came into view. They looked old—the main house more a cottage than anything. There was a scattering of outbuildings as well and Kyle pulled the car up in front of what appeared to be a stable block.

Brock grabbed his pack, wriggled free of the blanket and levered himself out of the car. Kyle took his arm gently and pushed him toward the house, letting go only to use his keys and open the door. He immediately locked it behind them.

Brock dumped the pack and sagged against the door. "I'm too tired and sore to think, let alone climb those stairs."

Kyle helped him off with his fleece, his fingers lingering on Brock's skin a little too long.

"Fuck, you're bleeding. Why didn't you say anything?" Kyle pulled at Brock's top until he lifted his arms and allowed Kyle to remove it, revealing the angry tears in his skin that ran from elbow to wrist.

"I wasn't in the mood for conversation."

"Do you have these anywhere else?" Kyle probed at the wounds delicately.

"Right leg. Had to lie on razor wire."

"Jesus. Go and take a shower. I'll be up in a minute with the first-aid kit." Kyle stomped toward the kitchen, muttering under his breath.

Brock couldn't be bothered to think anymore, it was too much effort. He dragged himself up the stairs and stripped the moment he entered the bathroom, dropping his clothing carelessly in a pile. He clambered into the shower and let the hot water wash away mud and blood in a gory stream. He summoned the energy to shampoo his hair and lather some gel over his tired limbs. When he was done, he wrapped a towel around his hips and sat on the edge of the bath, head in his hands. Kyle came in, carrying first-aid supplies. He put antiseptic, cotton wool pads and gauze next to the sink as Brock watched him nervously.

"Stand up."

Brock stepped away from the bath. Kyle grabbed the towel and yanked it free, leaving Brock naked and exposed.

"What the hell!" Brock turned, frantically looking for a way out.

"Keep still." Kyle snapped the order and something in Brock's mind responded. He stilled, his face heating, and placed his hands protectively over his crotch.

"Hands at your sides. You don't hide yourself from me."

"I… No, I'm not doing this," Brock stammered even as his hands seemed to move of their own accord.

"You'll do as I say. That's what you want, isn't it? Deep down, you want me to tell you what to do. Being obedient makes you feel good."

"No…" Brock tried to deny it but his hardening cock betrayed him. Kyle's touch was torment as he treated the dozens of small cuts on Brock's arm and leg.

With the first aid complete, Kyle took a step back. "You're exhausted and injured. You need to rest."

Kyle didn't make eye contact and when Brock retrieved the discarded towel and wrapped it around his hips, Kyle made no move to stop him.

Brock pushed past Kyle and headed for the bedroom. He yanked the curtains closed to shut out the early morning light, dropped the towel and slipped into bed.

Kyle paused inside the bedroom door then stripped off his own clothes. Brock watched him with tired exasperation. He couldn't stop himself admiring Kyle's body and that made him feel even more frustrated. When Kyle joined him in bed, Brock edged over as far as he could, leaving a gap between them, and turned away.

"I had to test you," Kyle murmured. "What I need you to do, the real mission, is too important to leave to chance. I had to know that you could handle pressure and difficult conditions. I'm sorry you got hurt."

Brock's head was swimming. Everything seemed fuzzy and indistinct. He longed to be comforted and

held tight. Kyle must have sensed his need because he pressed hard against Brock's back and pulled him in to an inescapable embrace.

Brock shivered as Kyle stroked his hair away from his face.

"I could hold you like this forever, Lysander. I don't think I'll ever be able to let you go," Kyle whispered.

As Brock drifted into sleep, he wondered if Kyle was talking about when the mission ended — or something else. Something he no longer wanted to resist.

Chapter Four

For Brock, the following day passed in a daze. His injuries were sore, but superficial. He napped, ate, read and took another long bath, which gave him a lot of time to think. Kyle checked on him every now and again but spent his time poring over maps and documents. More and more, Brock found himself watching Kyle's every move, wondering what it would be like to be with him unrestrained by his fears. As darkness fell, he made a decision.

"Kyle?"

"Yes, Lysander."

"I think I might go and lie down."

"Are you still tired?" Kyle sounded concerned.

Brock nibbled on his lower lip. He gave Kyle a coy glance from beneath his lashes. "No. Not tired at all."

Kyle stared at him, eyes sparking with desire. He stood, his lips curving into a predatory smile. Brock took a step backward.

"I should escort you upstairs."

"You should?"

"I don't think you should get over-excited without me there to keep an eye on you."

"You just want to watch?" Brock chuckled.

"You little…"

Brock ran for the stairs, Kyle on his heels. Kyle tackled him to the bed then wasted no time in stripping him bare. Brock sprawled on the bed, panting. He was hard, his cock clearly signaling his willingness to play. Kyle stripped, taking a lot more time over it than he had with Brock. Brock eyed his impressive erection. He licked his lips.

"Don't make the mistake of thinking you're in control, Lysander." Kyle grabbed two spare pillows. "Lift your ass." He shoved them beneath Brock's hips, lifting his backside off the mattress. "Now, spread your legs."

Brock's breath hitched. He bent his knees then spread his thighs, exposing himself to Kyle's scrutiny. He watched as Kyle slicked two fingers with a coating of lube. His ass clenched in anticipation. Kyle climbed onto the bed next to him.

"You have no idea what you've started, do you, Lysander?" Kyle rubbed a slick fingertip over Brock's exposed hole. Without warning, he plunged two fingers into Brock's channel, then stilled. Brock took a few frantic breaths, relishing the burn. He bucked his hips, trying to achieve deeper penetration, but Kyle gave his aching dick a smack.

"Be still, or I'll find a nice, heavy cock ring and you won't get to come for hours."

Brock whimpered, but Kyle's words just made him harder.

Kyle's sense of satisfaction deepened when Brock stopped trying to take charge. "That's it, beautiful. Behave yourself."

Brock scowled. "You have two fingers in my ass. Are you going to do something with them or do you have a sudden case of digit paralysis? And call me Brock, for fuck's sake!"

Kyle gave an exaggerated sigh. "Still so rebellious. Do you have somewhere else to be?" Kyle pressed the bundle of nerves inside his lover's body that let him exert control with just a touch.

"I... Oh!" Brock made a sweet little squeaking sound.

"You have a lot to learn," he said. "This seems to be an opportune moment for your first lesson." Kyle stroked the silky inner walls of Brock's channel, stretching him fractionally.

"You have got to be kidding me!" Brock squirmed. "Are you trying to make me hate you?"

"Stop trying to take more than I'm prepared to give you. Be still." Kyle put just enough force into his voice to alter his words from suggestion to command. Brock stopped moving instantly.

So beautifully receptive. Ripe to be taught and molded. He has the potential to be the perfect submissive. Kyle continued to move his fingers, enjoying Brock's inner heat and his quiet, needy whimpers. "That's much better. It's good to see that you're not untrainable."

Kyle ignored Brock's snort of indignation and took the opportunity to give him a thorough examination. Brock's slender form was stretched down the center of the bed while Kyle lay, propped on one elbow, next to him. The pillows beneath Brock's hips tilted his pelvis, allowing Kyle easy access to his ass. Brock's dick pointed toward the ceiling, lewdly displayed by his

position. His legs, dusted with a fine covering of golden hair, were spread wide, his knees slightly bent.

He has the legs of a climber. Kyle admired the lean muscle that plumped Brock's calves and thighs. Strength was apparent in every gentle swell and curve. His feet and ankles were slender, almost delicate, and a virtually imperceptible twitch pulsed in the smooth arch of his instep, betraying his arousal. Kyle grinned and scissored his fingers. Brock's toes curled and his hips lifted a fraction.

"Please…"

"All in good time. Begging won't do you any good. You need to learn patience." Kyle shifted his gaze to Brock's rigid shaft. The head gleamed with pre-cum, the tiny slit glinting with promise. Kyle dipped his head and took a taste. Just one flick of his tongue and Brock's salt-sweet flavor exploded across his taste buds. He hummed his pleasure. "You taste delicious."

Brock's eyes were squeezed shut, his teeth digging into his swollen lower lip.

"Open your eyes. Look at me," Kyle ordered. "Now tell me why you've changed your mind about me."

Glints of blue appeared beneath a shield of golden lashes.

"Now? You want to talk now?"

Content that Brock was paying appropriate attention, Kyle went back to admiring his prize. A pair of smooth, plump balls tempted Kyle to squeeze them but he resisted. There was plenty of time to play. The hairless sac looked flushed with heat, the skin stretched taut. He liked the bare skin. The hair at Brock's groin was cropped short but eventually it would have to go. Kyle's fingers twitched as he imagined taking a razor to the golden strands. He'd slipped into a daydream

and forgotten momentarily where his fingers were. Brock moaned and bucked. Kyle shook himself out of his mental meandering and chuckled.

"I'm curious. You've been fighting your attraction since we met, you said you'd share a bed if you had to but that was it. Now here we are and you were the one that instigated naked playtime, not me."

"Oh God! Fine. I decided that life's too short. If you dump me when this is all over, then so be it, but in the meantime I don't want to spend every moment frustrated and wondering how things could be between us."

"Well, I for one am glad you've seen the light. Finally. Time for three, I think." He withdrew his fingers and applied a fresh coating of lube. Brock's body sucked him in greedily as he pressed three fingers forward. "So needy. So hot and tight." Brock's abs rippled as he drew in a deep breath. Kyle leaned down and licked a damp trail from Brock's belly button all the way to one peaked nipple. He bit down firmly.

"Fuck! Kyle... You can't... I'm going to come!"

Kyle bathed the imprints left by his teeth with his tongue, soothing the redness. "Not until I say you can." He withdrew his fingers from Brock's grasping channel and gloved his cock, adding more slick. He knelt between the V of Brock's legs and hoisted one of them onto his shoulder, twisting Brock's body slightly to the side. His penetration was swift and assured. He thrust deep, then paused. Brock looked almost feverish. His eyes were bright, his cheeks flushed pink. His tousled blond hair spread across the sheet in a wild tangle of strands. The tip of his tongue peeked from between parted lips.

"Hard! Want it rough..." Brock cried out.

Kyle didn't have a problem with that request. He put all his focus into the snap of his hips. Brock's position allowed Kyle to drive deep, pegging his lover's gland with every thrust. Brock gasped and clawed at the sheets. Calling on every ounce of willpower he possessed, Kyle held back his own release as long as he could but the pressure as Brock's inner muscles squeezed his cock soon became too much to bear. The fiery burn of orgasm flooded his body and he came with a triumphant yell.

"Please, please, please..."

Brock's desperate begging brought Kyle back to reality. He grasped Brock's slender dick and gave it a couple of rough, clumsy jerks. The lack of finesse didn't matter. Brock shot into his hand with an anguished moan.

Kyle's arms shook as he held his weight away from Brock and took a few panting deep breaths. Carefully he withdrew from Brock's body and lowered his lover's leg to the bed. He rolled to one side and collapsed.

"We need to pack plenty of lube for the trip," he mused.

"Don't you think we're going to have other things on our minds than sex? You know...ruthless terrorists, risk of death..." Brock's laugh sounded a little hysterical.

"Plenty of sex is essential. It'll ease the stress. It's a requirement of the mission. Did I not mention that?"

"No you didn't." Brock yanked the crushed pillows from beneath his hips and tossed them onto the floor.

"It's in the small print, alongside the line that says you have to do as you're told." Kyle stretched, enjoying the burn of well-worked muscles. "Now, much as I'd like to keep you tied to my bed for the rest of the day,

we need to get up. There's a lot of planning to get done."

Brock shrugged. "Well, you keep telling me that you're in charge… I think you should take the lead and warm up the shower." He rolled onto his stomach and rested his head on his folded arms.

Kyle couldn't resist. Brock's smooth ass practically yelled 'Spank me!' He planted a couple of smacks across the curve of rounded cheeks and laughed at Brock's offended yelp.

"There's room in the shower for both of us. I'll even let you scrub my back if you're good."

"If *I'm* good?" Brock protested. "You're the one leading me astray."

Kyle grabbed an ankle and yanked Brock to the edge of the bed. "Get up, or I may be tempted to tow you to the bathroom by your dick."

"All right, all right! I'm coming."

"Well, you will be soon enough. Get that pretty pink behind into the bathroom. I'm feeling the urge to taste you again."

That got Brock moving. He scrambled off the bed and ran the few paces across the landing to the bathroom. By the time Kyle caught up to him, the water was running and Brock's gorgeous body was beneath the spray. For a moment Kyle just stood and watched as Brock ran his hands through his wet hair. A little pang of self-doubt squeezed Kyle's heart. Brock was gorgeous. He could have any man he wanted. *Why the hell would he fall for a scarred, possessive bastard like me?* Maybe his responses, which seemed so unstudied and natural, were just a reaction to an extreme situation. It wasn't as if they'd just met in a bar or at a dinner party. Kyle had invaded Brock's home, cuffed him to a chair

and threatened his family. He'd forced him to go through a risky test of his abilities and he'd gotten hurt as a result. Kyle could clearly see the tracks of scabbed cuts that marred the pristine skin of Brock's arm and thigh, left there by the British Army's brutal barbed wire.

"Aren't you coming in?" Brock asked.

Kyle looked into Brock's clear blue eyes and saw no doubt. He allowed himself a little hope. Happy ever after wasn't on the cards for him but maybe happy for now was good enough for a while and if, when this whole affair was over, Brock ran for the hills... Well, Kyle wouldn't blame him. He stepped into the shower and gripped Brock's hips, pulling him close to his body. Brock came willingly, pressing against him. Kyle couldn't remember the last time he'd been so close to another human being, let alone a man as desirable as Brock. He dropped to his knees and caught the shiny droplet of water hanging from the end of Brock's dick with his tongue. Without hesitation, carefully covering his teeth with his lips, he took Brock's length into his mouth.

"Oh God!" Brock staggered a little and balanced himself by leaning back against the tiles.

Kyle kept a firm hold of Brock's hips, holding him in place. Kyle might've been the one on his knees but he still controlled the situation. He sucked long and hard, relishing the clean, salty taste of Brock's skin. Determined not to gag, he paced himself, taking Brock a little deeper, sucking and swirling his tongue in lazy circles. Under Kyle's ministrations, Brock's half-hard dick gradually stiffened once more. Through the pounding water, Kyle could hear Brock's sweet moans. Beneath his fingertips, Brock's muscles quivered. Kyle

would have stayed there, quite happily, for some time but Brock tugged on his hair.

"Have to come… Please…"

Kyle grinned around his mouth full of cock. He dipped his head and the blunt crown of Brock's dick hit the back of his throat. He swallowed. Brock gasped and came with a hot gush into Kyle's mouth. Kyle swallowed again and again, milking Brock dry, catching every drop of his lover's warm seed. Only when Kyle was certain that Brock was utterly sated did he let Brock's now-drooping penis slip from between his lips. He gave the tip one last kiss then got to his feet. Brock immediately fell into his arms.

"Legs don't work… You've turned me to jelly."

"Good. That was the general idea so I must have done something right." Kyle chuckled. He held Brock up with an arm around his waist and used his free hand to squeeze some gel from the bottle hanging from the shower rail. The scent of lemons replaced the aroma of fresh cum. Kyle soaped Brock down, paying careful attention to his pretty cock and balls. Brock groaned pitifully.

"Stop! It's so sensitive down there. You'll get me hard again…"

"Why would that be a problem? Anyway, it's my go. Getting you off has made my dick jealous."

"I'm impressed by your recovery time," Brock said. "For an old guy, you have considerable stamina."

"I'm not that much older than you, cheeky brat." Kyle moaned as Brock gave his burgeoning erection a few lazy strokes before palming his balls and giving them a gentle squeeze.

"Let me help you along a bit." Brock rubbed the sensitive skin behind Kyle's sac.

Kyle groped for the waterproof lube and a foil-wrapped condom. "Can you open this?" He pushed the little square package into Brock's hand. There was some cursing as Brock fought the slippery foil, but then the rubber was free and Brock managed to roll it onto Kyle's erection on only the third attempt.

"We need to get tested. Want you in me without the barrier," Brock muttered. "It'll feel amazing. I know it will, and it'll be a damn sight less frustrating than grappling with condoms."

For a few seconds, Kyle couldn't move. He'd never barebacked with anyone. That Brock wanted to take that step with him meant everything. All the connotations of trust, monogamy and commitment flashed through his mind. His need to fill his lover became desperate. Clumsily he got the cap off the lube and managed to squeeze a dollop into his hand before dropping the tube into the shower tray.

"That's going to go everywhere…" Brock commented.

"So long as it gets to the important places," Kyle said roughly. He slicked his cock and swiveled Brock in his arms. "Not too sore for this, are you?" The need to take care of Brock overrode even Kyle's desperate urge to claim him again. Brock's garbled response was unintelligible but he shook his head, sending droplets of warm water flying everywhere. Kyle got the message loud and clear.

Penetration was smooth and easy as Brock's body welcomed him.

"Still tight. You fit me like a glove."

Brock bent forward limply, letting Kyle control the pace.

"Feels so good…"

"Feels fantastic. Love that you're all stretched for me... I'm not hurting you, am I?" Kyle kept up a steady thrusting rhythm.

"No. Need more. Harder."

"You really like it rough, don't you?" Kyle pistoned his hips in and out—piercing Brock to the core. He imagined what it would feel like without the rubber. There was no question that it would be even better. Fueled by the thought of taking Brock with nothing to separate them, Kyle was overwhelmed with the sudden ferocity of his orgasm. His hold on Brock's hips tightened. In a day or so, Brock would have ten small bruises marking his flesh and Kyle liked the idea of that. Brock needed his marks. He thrust a couple more times, muscles corded, spine bowed, wringing the last tremors of orgasm from his body. He brushed his hand up Brock's slippery skin and tweaked a nipple, hard. Brock grabbed his dick with a moan.

"Can't come again... Can't." But he did.

Kyle's cock softened and he slipped from Brock's grasping channel. The water raining down on them had grown tepid and Brock shivered in his arms. Kyle helped him from the shower and wrapped him in a warm towel before disposing of the condom. Brock rubbed at himself half-heartedly. Kyle chuckled. "You're almost asleep." He slung a smaller towel around his hips and helped Brock get dry. "Can you manage to get yourself dressed?"

Brock scowled. "Funny. This is all your fault. You've worn me out."

Kyle crooked an eyebrow. "My pleasure."

Brock's lips twitched and he smiled. He ducked his head and looked at Kyle from under his lashes, his creamy cheeks flushed with pink. He exited the room,

leaving Kyle with the urge to laugh out loud from sheer delight.

* * * *

Brock stood in the kitchen waiting for the kettle to boil. He leaned against the cabinets and hoped that the trembling in his thigh muscles receded soon. He didn't need any reason for Kyle to keep teasing him.

"Blushing like a fucking lovesick teenager. What the hell is wrong with me? The man's a pain in the ass." He shifted a little, enjoying the ache. "Literally." He sighed. "You're falling for him, Brock. Falling hard. Dangerous territory."

"Talking to yourself? Should I be worried?"

Brock jumped as Kyle's voice sounded from the door. He chuckled nervously. "Maybe. You have to admit that I must be a little mad... Agreeing to photograph South American terrorists."

"Certifiable." Kyle reached into a cupboard and brought out a couple of plates. His tight T-shirt rose a little. Even that tiny glimpse of bare skin was enough to distract Brock from his task.

"If you hadn't... I mean if... Oh hell, never mind," Brock stumbled over the words.

"Talk to me, Brock. It's okay. You can ask me anything."

Kyle's gaze was so steady and unblinking, his voice so calm. It gave Brock confidence to put voice to his thoughts.

"If you didn't...*like* me, would you have gone through with the whole charade of forcing me to do the job in Colombia? Would you have left me thinking that my family was under threat if I didn't comply?"

"I have a job to do, Brock, and it's an important one," Kyle replied. "You and I are only a small part of this operation. It's taken a very long time to set this up, a great deal of time and money. My employers are demanding people and they don't like excuses so yes… I would have gone through with it."

Brock leaned on the counter, needing the support.

"I'm sorry if that upsets you, but I won't lie." Kyle took a couple of steps back. "Not anymore. I needed you to agree to the mission and I took a chance that you would do it willingly if you knew a bit more about it. I shouldn't have done that. It went against protocol and all my training — but I had a strong feeling about you. If that feeling hadn't been there, I would have let you think that you had no choice."

"I don't know how that makes me feel. I suppose deep down I knew that would be your answer and I don't want you to pretend otherwise. I think I just want to be more important to you than the job." Brock spooned fresh ground beans into a cafetière and poured boiling water onto them. He set out a couple of mugs. "It doesn't matter."

"Of course it matters."

Brock flinched as Kyle pressed against his back and massaged his shoulders.

"You are *very* important to me and not just because I need you. When this is all over, perhaps you'll let me show you?"

"When this is all over, we could both be dead," Brock commented.

Kyle worked Brock's muscles harder. "Either one of us could walk under a bus tomorrow. Nobody can predict the future — I wish I could — but believe me

when I say I will do *everything* in my power to keep you safe."

"I want to get to know you better, Kyle. This has all happened so fast. If we do make it back, I want to start again. Take it slow."

"Sounds good. I'll look forward to our first date." Kyle stopped his massage and pulled Brock into his arms. "You do put out on a first date, don't you?"

"Are you suggesting I'm a slut?"

"Only for me and only when I tell you to be."

Brock squirmed, trying to escape Kyle's grip.

"Hold still."

Brock responded to the order instinctively. He relaxed and rested his head on Kyle's shoulder. *Fuck it. I finally found the perfect man for me, but in a couple of weeks he could be gone. This could end thousands of miles from home, with a bullet or a knife.* "I shouldn't give in to this."

"To what?" Kyle asked.

"To you. I'm not stupid, Kyle. You're not just dominant in the bedroom. You want a submissive."

"That shouldn't scare you... You're a natural sub."

"Maybe..."

"Maybe nothing. You are a responsive, stunning submissive. You just haven't found the right man to bring it out of you — until now."

Brock tilted his head back and looked into Kyle's dark eyes. There wasn't that much of a height difference between them, but in Kyle's arms Brock always felt more delicate. Kyle was much more muscular than Brock and Brock always felt that Kyle was holding himself back, aware of his strength and that he could hurt Brock by accident.

"It's true my previous relationships haven't been particularly satisfying, but that doesn't mean I think of myself as a submissive."

"It's not something you have to think about, sweetheart. Just accept it. It's who you are, not a decision you have to make. Your previous boyfriends" — Kyle sounded as if he had a nasty taste in his mouth when he said the word 'boyfriends' — "were undeserving of your grace. Power exchange is not something to be played at or taken lightly. It's the ultimate act of trust and it honors me that you place your body into my hands."

Brock had to admit that his world had never felt more right than when he allowed Kyle to control him. "Wait a minute... How the hell do you know about my previous relationships?" He pushed Kyle away.

Kyle scrubbed a hand through his hair. "Choosing you for this job wasn't a decision taken overnight. I followed you for months and researched every aspect of your life. How do you think I knew where to find you at your brother's house? I know all about you — the awards, the front cover stories, the respect that other professional photographers have for you. I even know all about the crazy risks you take to get the perfect shot. The test I put you through on Salisbury Plain was a walk in the park compared to your day job."

Brock frowned. "Every time I put it out of my head that this is just a job to you, something reminds me. That's not going to change. It's probably best that I accept things for the way they are. I'm not going to build my hopes up about a future beyond Colombia. I'm just going to take each day as it comes."

"If that's the way you want it..."

"It's the way it has to be." Heart heavy, Brock went back to making coffee and breakfast.

Chapter Five

With breakfast done and the dishes tidied away, Brock followed Kyle through to the lounge-diner. He pushed down his sadness about Kyle's job being such a wall between them and focused on the mission.

"We have a lot of work to do today," Kyle said. "To begin with, I want you to take me through all the stages of expedition preparation." He settled into an armchair and sipped from a second mug of coffee. "Oh God, that's good!"

Brock shook his head. "You and coffee... Anyone would think you were sipping on ambrosia."

"But I am. Didn't you know that? Dear me, Lysander Brock, your education has been sorely lacking in so many important areas. All that honey stuff is nonsense. The Greek gods drank coffee. Did you know that ambrosia was supposed to confer longevity?" Kyle leered.

"I think that referred to long life, not... Oh my God! Why am I even engaging in this conversation? Can we please get back to reality and talk about Colombia?"

"It wasn't me who changed the subject." Kyle had another sip of his drink. "I need to know all the details about how you plan an expedition, however boring or insignificant they might seem to you. I'll be traveling with you as your assistant and, if I'm to make a credible attempt at passing as that, I have to sound like I know what I'm talking about."

"Fine. Get comfortable then because this may take a while." Brock took the seat opposite Kyle. He didn't want to get too close because he would end up mesmerized by Kyle's eyes, or his denim-hugged thighs, or... *Fuck. Concentrate, you idiot. Try to keep the life-threatening situation in your head.* Brock caught Kyle smirking at him, looking as if he knew *exactly* what Brock was thinking about. Brock sighed.

"I'll try to go through this in roughly chronological order." He paused and sorted through the stages of preparation in his head. "As the photographer on any expedition—whether mine or someone else's—I have three main responsibilities. The first is to make a comprehensive visual record of the entire expedition from preparation through to the time we return home." He counted off on his fingers. "Second is to produce visually stunning images that satisfy my sponsors and that suit their publications. Have you ever even read *National Geographic*?"

"Of course," Kyle replied. "My dentist's waiting room has a whole stack of them."

"You might want to buy a couple of recent editions to read on the plane." Brock let sarcasm flood his voice.

"Sweetheart, I've read almost every magazine you've ever had anything published in. Research, remember? What's the third thing?"

"Sorry?"

"You said the photographer — that is you — has three responsibilities. You've only given me two."

Brock rolled his eyes. "Oh. The third is to work in a manner that respects the peoples, cultures and environments the expedition encounters — to ensure that other photographers coming after me don't have a hard time because of something I've done."

"Hmm. Not sure you're going to be able to fulfill that last one," Kyle muttered.

Brock chose to ignore him. He didn't want to think about what he was getting into until he had to, and he still had a few days to pretend that this was just another expedition.

"Do you consider yourself a wildlife photographer or landscape?" Kyle asked.

"Neither. Wildlife was my first love, but I've switched more and more to landscape. I've done a bit of portraiture and other odd projects for friends as well. I'm just a photographer."

"Okay, I was just interested," Kyle said. "What comes next?"

"So, equipment. I normally travel with both weather-sealed digital and conventional film cameras."

"Really? I'd have thought digital is the only way to go these days." Kyle seemed genuinely curious.

"It is, really, but I love my old manual camera. It feels like a betrayal to leave it behind. I enjoy the anticipation of developing the film to see what I've managed to capture. I admit that digital is cheaper and the images are easy to transmit via satellite phone, but they are

reliant on battery power. I imagine you'll be happier if I have a back-up, even if film is easily damaged in transit."

"We'll need to transmit the images as quickly as possible, so it has to be digital," Kyle said. "When you go through that cave system, you'll want to be carrying as little as possible, but I can see the value of a back-up under more usual circumstances. You'll need to take everything you normally would, regardless."

Brock leaned back in his seat. "I'm assuming that I need to keep up the pretense of a genuine expedition?"

"It won't be a pretense. You can still take all the pictures you need for your commission. In fact, it's essential that you do everything you would do if that was your only reason for traveling."

Brock realized that he was tapping his fingers on his knee and slammed his hand down. He hit himself a bit too hard and the sharp pain made him draw a quick breath. Kyle came and stood behind him and began to massage his shoulders.

"Try to relax. This is what you do. It's your profession and you are very good at it. You don't need to worry about anything else…yet. Keep going… Tell me what you need to consider next."

Brock sighed. Kyle's hands on his tense muscles felt fantastic, but inevitably his cock responded, making him feel anything but relaxed.

"Okay, first I need to plan my photographic needs. I make a comprehensive shot list with notes and priority gradings for all the pictures that will be needed. This requires discussion with the publication editors, which I'm sure you'll be glad to hear I've already done. The list helps to fix in my head what I need to be looking for. Sometimes that's a specific animal, which makes it

a very short list. Other times it can be a bit wider. It depends on whether the shots are to support someone else's article or whether the entire piece is built around the photography. I sometimes supply stock shots for background images because original stuff is always in demand. Then I also have to think about post-expedition needs, publication timings, promotion—that kind of thing."

"You'll need to keep a low profile for a while when we get back. I hope that won't be a problem?" Kyle asked.

Brock caught a hint of the ruthless professional Kyle was. Kyle would probably lock him up if he had to and not think twice about it rather than let him do anything to jeopardize the outcome of the mission.

"It takes months for the articles to be prepared. The shots from this commission aren't scheduled for six months. I prefer to stay behind the scenes anyway. I rarely make public appearances."

"Good."

Kyle attacked a particularly tough knot and Brock winced. "I'm so glad my fame and fortune are top of your agenda."

"It's a cunning plan to keep you all to myself."

That didn't sound so bad. Brock attempted to re-focus on expedition preparation.

"Once I know what my picture list looks like, I need to select and prepare the right equipment. Then it's my least favorite task—packing."

"I've never met a man yet that gets pleasure out of ramming assorted crap into luggage," Kyle said. "And I include myself in that generalization."

"Then it's a good job you don't have to help because all this stuff has been done already," Brock said a little impatiently.

"I know." Kyle stroked the back of his neck, making him shiver. "But I need to understand. Every detail. So carry on and there may be a reward waiting for you when you're done."

Brock tipped his head back in an attempt to see Kyle's expression and found himself firmly kissed. Kyle gave his hair a tug, sending an erotic shiver through Brock's body.

"Focus, love." Kyle resumed his seat across the room and, though Brock would have preferred to be in his arms, he remained a safe distance away.

"You can't kiss me and then tell me to focus. It's not fair."

Kyle put his elbows on his knees and steepled his fingers. He came up with his best innocent-puppy look.

"Oh good grief! Fine. I have to trust the equipment I take on any expedition. I have to be so familiar with each camera that I am able to use them blindfolded, so I know which way to turn the dial for a shorter shutter-time, where the button for holding auto-exposure is which way to adjust for longer focal lengths and so on. Are you listening?" Kyle's eyes seemed a little glazed.

"Sorry, I got distracted when you used the word blindfolded. Please carry on."

Brock grabbed at the fabric of his jeans. He needed to do something to occupy his hands. "I test all the equipment using the different combinations, with various lenses, with and without flash, using different exposure modes and settings to ensure that it is all working fine. I don't want to be discovering problems in the field."

"You got me at flash that time." Kyle's grin was wicked.

Brock plowed on with determination. "I take a whole load of stuff, as well as my cameras. Everything goes into hard cases so that none of it gets damaged in transit. I usually carry the cameras as hand luggage, just to be safe, and then I have a special padded backpack for trekking with lots of separate compartments. I take extra batteries for everything and chargers for when power is available—a lightweight tripod for static shots, cleaning kit, jeweler's screwdrivers to fasten loose screws, spare lens caps… Is this too much detail? It's not exactly exciting stuff."

"The more detail the better. Carry on. I'll stop you if I don't need to know." Kyle crossed his legs at the ankles and relaxed into his chair.

"I take spare cables, memory cards and a portable hard drive but other than that, I try to travel light. The more I take, the more there is to get lost or stolen."

Kyle nodded. "As I said, when we get to the less public part of the expedition, you're going to have to travel as light as possible. It will just be the two of us, on foot. I calculate that it will take us two—possibly three—days to get from the area of your official shoot to where we need to be to get shots of the terrorists. Will it be a problem to replace one of your support team with one of mine?"

Brock frowned. "It could be. I have a contract with a couple of guys I've worked with in South America before. I trust them. They're really good at smoothing the path locally and they are already on the ground out there setting everything up. It would look very odd if I dumped either one of them at such a late stage."

Kyle frowned. "How about if you *added* someone to the crew, rather than take someone away? A specialist, for example."

"What kind of specialist?"

"How about a naturalist or—even better—a herpetologist? You could say that you picked up an additional commission to photograph some of the local wildlife."

"That would work. My guys are exhibition leaders. They're great if you need to survive in the jungle with a couple of matches and a Mars Bar, not so good if you need to identify a plant species or some kind of creepy-crawly."

"They sound like my kind of people." Kyle grinned. "Creepy-crawly? Is that some scientific term I haven't come across yet?"

"Would you me prefer to use creepius-crawlius? I hate insects, okay?"

Kyle fell about laughing. Brock put his head in his hands. "You're never going to let me hear the last of this, are you?"

"It's just so…" Kyle dissolved all over again.

"Laugh it up, tough guy."

"World-famous adventuring photographer is afraid of bugs. Priceless." Kyle wiped away a tear.

"Have you seen the size of the nasties that live in the jungle? Huge, massive, hairy… Ugh."

"Until you got to the last part of that sentence, you could have been talking about me."

"I swear your ego is as big as your… Nope, not going there. I need some more coffee." Brock got up and headed for the kitchen, Kyle's laughter trailing after him.

* * * *

Brock scooped more ground coffee into the cafetière, then filled the kettle and put it on to boil. At the rate he and Kyle were absorbing caffeine, the two of them would be awake half the night. He grinned. That wasn't a bad idea at all. He may have resigned himself to this being a short-term thing, but he was sure as hell going to enjoy it. It wasn't every day a man like Kyle walked into his life.

He took two mugs from the draining board where they'd been left to dry from breakfast and put them on the counter top, fiddling with their position until the handles were aligned and perfectly parallel. The mugs were a sunny yellow color with a daisy pattern around the rim. Ceramic cheerfulness wasn't enough, however, to dislodge Brock's thoughts from the dark track they were heading along.

Talking about the trip and all the planning that went into each and every expedition made the danger a bit more real. Brock had spent many months refining every detail of his expedition. The Colombian cloud forests were not a destination to be taken lightly and he was well aware of the risks of traveling in such an inhospitable area. As a legitimate trip, it was still a dangerous undertaking. Add into that the secret mission Kyle had enlisted him for and Brock thought he might need to up the cover on his travel insurance.

"Not that any insurer in the world is going to give me a policy that covers this trip," he muttered.

"Stop worrying," Kyle said from the doorway.

"Stop following me," Brock snapped back. "I need a moment of panic, if it's all right with you?"

Kyle chuckled. "You thrive on adventure and danger. Don't try to tell me that this trip doesn't excite you, because I know it does. Forget about the terrorists and concentrate on the territory you'll be accessing. You'll get pictures no other photographer is ever likely to see through a lens."

"There are good reasons why people don't venture into certain parts of the world," Brock said dryly.

"And better reasons for taking that extra step, as you well know. This isn't the first time you'll take risks for pictures. I've seen your work, Brock, remember? You're even crazier than I am. The shots you took in Irian Jaya—in the Jayawijaya mountains. You had to have been dangling off the rock face by your fingernails to get those pictures."

"Not the same thing, and you know it." Brock poured boiling water into the cafetière, then gave the coffee a stir before depressing the plunger. "Let's get back to the expedition ahead of us rather than reliving the past. What else do you want to know about my preparations?" He poured two fresh mugs and handed one to Kyle.

"Let's go and get comfortable and we'll go through all the travel arrangements. I've made a few changes that I need to tell you about." Kyle about-faced and went back to the lounge. Brock took a few deep breaths and followed to find Kyle settled at one end of the couch.

"Come and sit with me."

It was an order, not a request. Brock looked longingly at the chair on the other side of the room.

"Now, Brock," Kyle said. His tone remained mild but Brock was under no illusions that if he didn't do as he

was told, there would be repercussions. Kyle's mug sat on the low coffee table, untouched.

"Put your coffee down, Brock. You don't need it. Making it was just a way to distract yourself."

Fuck, he knows me too well. Brock's hand trembled a little as he placed his mug on the table. Tiny ripples disturbed the surface of the liquid but soon settled into stillness. He sat next to Kyle, back stiff, keeping clear space between them, but Kyle pulled him firmly down so that Brock leaned against him. Brock shuddered and sighed. The rhythm of Kyle's breathing calmed him and he relaxed into his hold.

"There. I've got you. Stop over-thinking everything and let me do the worrying for you."

With Kyle's strong arms around him, Brock's dick inevitably hardened. It was so fucking difficult to think straight with Kyle's hands on him.

"I have a colleague who'll be perfect to join the expedition. He's an American and he looks like a stereotypical mad professor. He has a photographic memory that I'm very jealous of, so if I get in touch today he can mug up on the area we're going to and meet us there."

"Sounds good. Now why do you need me to go through my travel plans if you've already meddled with them?" Even to his own ears, Brock sounded petulant. Kyle didn't miss the tone either. He unfastened Brock's jeans and lowered his zipper, then took a firm, almost painful hold of his cock. Brock drew a quick breath. The hold just made him harder.

"This would look pretty in a cage, don't you think?" Kyle said conversationally.

"You wouldn't." Even as he said it, Brock knew that Kyle almost certainly would.

"I fucking would—in an instant. So stop acting like a brat… Or perhaps you want me to punish you? Is that it, Brock? Another distraction?"

"I don't want—aagh!" Brock yelped as Kyle got a hand around his balls and squeezed. "Don't…"

"For however long this lasts between us, Brock, these are mine, to do with as I wish."

Brock squirmed in Kyle's hold. *I should fight this. Arrogant bastard. I should refuse to submit to him.* But he couldn't. Rough handling was exactly what he needed.

"Yes, Sir."

The pressure on his balls eased a fraction.

"You can call me that as often as you like. Travel plans. Talk me through them." All trace of Kyle's softer side was gone. Brock shivered with need. He fought to ignore Kyle's touch and focused instead on the details of his expedition plan.

"I'm booked on a scheduled flight from Heathrow to Miami in three days' time. Business class. I have a hotel booked in Miami for one night before catching a flight from there to Bogotá. I have another night booked there before my internal flight to Cartagena. From there it's a helicopter ride into the interior. There's an airfield that can take helicopters and small planes. That's the closest I can get by air to where I need to be and that's where my expedition team will meet me. We carry on from there overland by Jeep to an area called Antioquia and Las Orquídeas National Park, where the camp is. After that, I travel on foot. Most of the equipment is being sorted locally. My cameras are coming with me as hand baggage." Brock's breath hissed between his teeth. "Fuck, Kyle! I can't think while you're doing that."

"You don't need to think. Recall should be automatic and you need to learn the new plans as if they were your own."

Brock couldn't help himself. He pushed into the warmth of Kyle's grip, silently begging for more. Kyle's grip slackened.

"Nope. Work first. Play later."

"What you're doing isn't playing?" Brock's voice rose to a squeak as Kyle scraped a nail across the sensitive skin of his sac.

"No, it's a demonstration of man's ability to multi-task. It's a myth that only women can manage more than one thing at a time."

"I'd prefer to perpetuate the myth," Brock replied. The heat and tightness in his balls had his full attention. He moaned when Kyle released him and tried to grab Kyle's hand so that he could put it back where it belonged. Instead, Kyle grasped Brock's wrist and twisted his arm behind his back, trapping it between their bodies. Desperately, Brock tried to get hold of his aching dick with his free hand. It got the same treatment as the other one and he was left with his rigid dick exposed to the air and no way of finding relief. Kyle wrapped an arm around him, pinning him in place. Instead of making him want to escape, the restraint turned Brock to a pile of submissive goo.

"Not fair!" Brock whined.

"No complaining now. Accept my control. If you're good, I may let you come...eventually," Kyle responded.

Kyle's words had completely the wrong effect. Brock gasped as an orgasm snuck up and took him by surprise. Untouched, his cock pulsed and spurted streams of cum in an arc onto his lap.

"Fuck, fuck, fuck... I didn't do anything, Sir, I promise!"

Kyle chuckled and the deep rumble vibrated through Brock's body.

"Note to self... Keep disobedient sub in a nice, tight cock ring...or permanent chastity—either works for me." He lifted Brock to his feet. "Go and get cleaned up, then perhaps we can get back to business?"

"Yes, Sir." Brock smiled. He didn't look back at Kyle and took a couple of steps forward.

"You might think you're safe, knowing that I can't see the smug expression on your pretty face, Brock, but I won't underestimate your capacity for rebellion again. Believe me."

Brock shivered at the unspoken promise in Kyle's words. "No, Sir." He made sure there was an appropriate amount of deference in his tone. "I'm sure you won't."

Chapter Six

"Explain to me why you've bumped us up to First Class, Kyle. Not that I'm complaining." Brock sank back into his plush leather chair, stretched out his legs and looked around the hallowed sanctum of Virgin Atlantic's First Class lounge. "But we're traveling on the same flight that I booked. Aren't we supposed to be inconspicuous?"

Kyle conjured up an expression that was meant to communicate patience and tolerance with Brock's naivety. It involved raising an eyebrow.

"There's significantly more gossip and idle speculation in Business Class than there is in First. The stewards in First Class are hand-picked and trained to be discreet. It's a legitimate business expense and one my organization is more than happy to pay. We will arrive rested and more alert. It will also get us out of the airport at the other end a hell of a lot quicker and with a lot fewer questions, because we'll get priority

disembarkation and our bags will be offloaded before anyone else's."

Brock grinned. "There endeth the lesson?"

"Cheeky brat. If need be, I can find us a private bathroom, spank your behind and let you sit through a ten-hour flight shifting from one cheek to the other." It was Kyle's turn to grin as Brock winced and shifted in his chair as if imagining an aching ass. Kyle took the opportunity to give Brock an appraising examination. To a casual observer, Brock appeared relaxed. He wore comfortable beige cargoes and a pale blue open-necked shirt that highlighted the color of his eyes. His blond hair was a little tousled and very sexy. It hadn't escaped Kyle's notice that Brock drew a lot of admiring glances from both women and a few men. The lounge attendant in particular had far too much time on his hands and was using it to cast lascivious glances Brock's way. Kyle allowed himself to imagine putting the guy in an arm lock and squeezing him into unconsciousness. His thoughts must have been reflected in his expression because the young man flushed to the roots of his ginger hair and found something else to gawk at. Kyle switched his attention back to Brock. He knew his traveling companion wasn't nearly as comfortable as he appeared. Brock was a bundle of nerves. A certain cure would be to tie him to the nearest flat surface and fuck the anxiety out of him, but that wasn't really an option. Kyle chuckled. Knowing his countrymen, he could probably do whatever the hell he wanted and no one would bat an eyelid.

"Care to share the joke?" Brock asked.

"Just pondering the eccentricities of the English."

"Really?" Brock sounded dubious. "Then why does that guy over there look like he's expecting an

assassination attempt?" Brock nodded toward the attendant, who was polishing a table to within an inch of its life.

"He was ogling you." Kyle decided that should be enough explanation.

Brock shook his head. "And I suppose you gave him the patented Kyle death glare?"

"Death glare?"

"Uh-huh. Brings new meaning to the phrase 'if looks could kill'."

"He shouldn't have been watching you." Kyle had an unexplainable urge to pout. "At least not like he was undressing you with his beady little eyes."

"He doesn't have beady eyes."

"You shouldn't be taking any notice of him either," Kyle growled.

"You take possessive to whole new levels, don't you?" Brock stood and gave him a challenging stare. "I'm going to get a drink. Would you like anything?"

Kyle wanted to throw Brock back into his chair but he knew damn well Brock was baiting him. Well, he could act like a grown-up. Revenge could come later—in a Miami hotel room.

"An orange juice would be nice, thank you. Freshly squeezed, with ice."

"That smile is scarier than the whole growly thing." Brock appeared a little pale.

"Payback's a bitch, sunshine. See if your new friend can rustle up some snacks while you're over there. I'm feeling peckish." He watched as Brock strolled across to the attendant and had a brief conversation. They both cast nervous glances in his direction and a warm sense of satisfaction spread through his bones.

"Just as it should be," he muttered happily. "That boy needs to learn his place."

Brock returned with tall glasses of juice for both of them. He sat down and threw across a bag of macadamias.

"Thanks, I love these." Kyle ripped open the packet. "Have you ever had them fresh from the shell? Delicious."

Brock sipped his drink, then ran his tongue across his lower lip.

"I'm not keen on nuts."

"Really? These are great, but half the fun is cracking the shell and freeing the tender center from its protective case." Kyle chomped on a nut and kept his unblinking gaze fixed on Brock. His lover's cheeks were pinking nicely.

"You're not talking about nuts anymore, are you?" Brock whispered.

"Very perceptive... Well, not the kind that grow on trees anyway."

"You are *not* putting me in chastity," Brock hissed.

"The idea's making you hard, isn't it? We'll see... If you can avoid ogling any more men during this trip, I might let you off." Kyle shrugged. "Then again...maybe not."

Brock frowned. "This is going to be the longest flight in history."

Kyle chuckled. "I'm sure there will be some good films playing to keep you entertained. They have great privacy screens in first class. It's almost as good as having your own room. You could take in *Deep Impact... Max Payne* is quite good, or you can't go wrong with *Die Hard*." Kyle kept a straight face as Brock coughed and spluttered into his juice. Kyle was

looking forward to the flight. Having a few hours to contemplate all the things he would do to Brock on their return home was a rare pleasure and his imagination needed a workout.

* * * *

The flight was comfortable and the time passed quickly. Once Kyle had scanned the faces of the other First Class passengers and decided that none of them constituted a threat, he felt able to sit back and enjoy a few hours of relaxation. In his head, he ran over the meticulous plans he had put in place for the next two weeks, plans that had been many months in the making. There was a great deal riding on this mission and a huge weight sitting on Kyle's shoulders. He was used to the pressure. Brock, however, was not. Kyle had no doubt that the young photographer was brave, resourceful and tenacious. He'd been tested mentally and physically during previous expeditions to hostile parts of the world, but this trip was different. Risking his life for his country was part of Kyle's job. Brock didn't normally operate with the threat of an unpleasant death hanging over his head.

Kyle glanced across to his companion. Brock had his head buried in a back issue of *National Geographic* that he'd brought with him. As if sensing Kyle's gaze, Brock lifted his head and smiled.

"This is a really interesting article... Listen." He began to read. "'Observed in the wild, tucked away in museum collections and even exhibited in zoos around the world, there is one mysterious creature that has been a victim of mistaken identity for more than one hundred years. A team of Smithsonian scientists,

however, uncovered overlooked museum specimens of this remarkable animal, which took them on a journey from museum cabinets in Chicago to cloud forests in South America to genetics labs in Washington, DC. The result—the olinguito (*Bassaricyon neblina*)—the first carnivore species to be discovered in the American continents in thirty-five years.'" His eyes sparkled. "Can you imagine what it must be like to discover a new species?"

Kyle shook his head. "I spend my time discovering secrets, sweetheart, and, though those secrets often involve sub-species of human, they aren't exactly rare. More's the pity."

Brock rolled his eyes and continued to read out loud. "'A team, led by Smithsonian scientist Kristofer Helgen, spent ten years examining hundreds of museum specimens and tracking animals in the wild in the cloud forests.' They discovered this…" He reversed the magazine and displayed a photograph of an animal that seemed to be a cross between a house cat and a teddy bear.

"Cute," Kyle muttered.

"Cute? That's all you can say? Do you have any idea how rare it is to discover a new mammal? This one comes from the same family as raccoons, coatis and kinkajous. It weighs about two pounds and is native to the cloud forests of Colombia. If we're really lucky, we might get to see one."

Kyle gave Brock what he hoped was an encouraging smile. It was good for Brock to have something else to think about other than their mission.

"It's amazing, isn't it? The discovery of the olinguito shows us that the world is not yet completely explored, its most basic secrets not yet revealed. There must be

more species out there to be discovered. Of course, most of those will be in the deep ocean, but who knows what's lurking in the remote forests of the world. These Andean forests are so amazing. There must be loads of cool species to discover yet."

"Maybe you should get back to more wildlife photography, give landscape a rest for a while?" Kyle knew that Brock loved both. He'd seen every shot Brock had ever had published — spectacular vistas from all around the world, often taken from incredibly dangerous positions.

"I don't think so," Brock mused, clearly having given it some thought. "I don't have the patience to specialize in wildlife photography, but I've had some luck on my trips. I think the animals I've taken pictures of are so surprised to meet a human that they just pose for me because they don't know that they need to run away."

Kyle imagined Brock, halfway up a rock face, coming nose-to-nose with some startled creature, and laughed. "I prefer to rely on planning rather than luck."

"You're no fun." Brock pouted and Kyle wanted nothing more than to take that plump lower lip between his teeth and bite down.

"You'll find out just how much fun I can be when we get to Miami. You, me, a luxury hotel room and plenty of time before our next flight. I have interesting plans for that tender little behind of yours."

Kyle looked up as a very red-faced steward cleared his throat. He stood in the aisle with a silver tray in his hands, two glasses of iced water on it.

"Drinks before your meal, Sir. Just water, as requested."

Kyle winked at him. The steward chewed on his lip and gave him a shy smile in exchange.

"Let me know if you gentlemen would like some company in Miami." The drinks were delivered and Kyle watched as the steward's neat little butt, encased in uniform trousers, swayed back down the aisle.

"Stop staring at his ass," Brock grumbled.

"Why? He's cute in a sweet, twinky kind of way. Not really my type but nice enough to watch."

"You're incorrigible. So what is your type then?"

"Oh, I don't know… Tall, blond, likes to call me Sir."

Brock blushed almost as brightly as the steward.

"Who said I like it?"

"You like it." Kyle sipped his drink and studied the menu.

For the remainder of the flight, Kyle kept the conversation to safe, innocuous subjects. Brock was a voracious reader and provided a running commentary on any interesting articles he came across. He also showed Kyle the photographs he liked and pointed out the compositional flaws in most of them. It was an interesting insight into Brock's personality that Kyle valued. It was something that months of observation hadn't told him. His sub—for that was how Kyle couldn't help but think of Brock—was a stubborn perfectionist, passionate about every detail of his craft. That passion would stand him in good stead in the days ahead.

* * * *

The descent into Miami was smooth, as was passage through immigration and passport control. As they walked out through the automatic door into the Arrivals hall, a crowd of people holding up signs on assorted cards waited behind a rope barrier. At the

back of the group, a nondescript man in a Miami Dolphins cap held up a small card with 'A. Smith' written on it. Kyle nodded in his direction and the man moved toward the doors.

"That's our ride," Kyle said, and followed.

"You had this arranged? Why Smith?" Lysander asked quietly.

"Just follow me. The fewer questions you ask, the better." Kyle scanned his surroundings as they made their way toward short-term parking. He had no reason to believe that anyone would be watching them, but it was in his blood to be suspicious. He had no intention of risking Brock's life if there was even a hint that the mission had been compromised.

The car the driver took them to was a sleek BMW with tinted windows. Once their luggage had been stowed in the trunk, Kyle and Brock settled into the back seat. The car smelled of leather and polish, a scent that Kyle felt very at home with. He contemplated fucking Brock there and then but decided that he didn't need to provide their chauffeur with in-car entertainment. Kyle leaned forward. "You know what to do?" he asked.

"Yes, sir." The driver nodded and started the ignition. He slipped the car into gear and pulled smoothly away. "The office made everything clear."

"Good. Nice ride… You prefer the stick shift?"

"Doesn't everyone?" The driver grinned, directing his gaze at the rear-view mirror so that Kyle could see his expression without him having to take his eyes off the road by twisting around. "Much more responsive, should the situation require it."

"Let's hope it doesn't." Kyle settled back and rested a hand on Brock's thigh.

"Are you expecting trouble?" Brock asked, sounding a little nervous.

"No, not at all. Car chases in downtown Miami are really not my favorite form of entertainment. Don't worry."

Brock closed his eyes. "Okay. I can't wait to get to the hotel."

"Feeling tired?" Kyle checked his watch. "Eight o'clock—that makes it one in the morning back in England."

Brock yawned. "I could nap."

Kyle smiled as Brock leaned against him. He pulled him closer and Brock didn't resist, just snuggled in with a contented sigh.

My God, he's converting me into a cuddler. I do not *cuddle.* Still, it felt good in the cool air-conditioned interior of the car to have Brock's warm body so close.

The car wound its way through the evening traffic and pulled up in front of the Palace Hotel. Kyle gave Brock a gentle shake.

"We're here, Brock. Let's go."

Brock grumbled but followed him out of the car onto the pavement.

"The driver will bring in our bags. Let's go and check in. The sooner we're in the room, the sooner I can stuff my dick up your ass." That woke Brock up.

"Fuck, Kyle! Tell the whole street, why don't you?" Brock scanned the area with a scowl but his cheeks were flushed and his trousers were tented.

"It's too warm to be standing around out here." The Florida humidity was enough to sap anyone's strength. Kyle pushed his way through the revolving doors into the hotel lobby and strolled over to the reception desk.

He tipped the driver when he placed a couple of bags next to Kyle's feet. The man briefly raised his cap.

"Have a good stay, sir." He headed back out to the car and Kyle completed check-in. He declined a porter and handed one of the bags to Brock. "Here you go."

"But this isn't—"

"The lifts are over there," Kyle interrupted and led Brock across the lobby. Once in the lift, which was free of other passengers, he pressed a finger to his lips and gave Brock a warning glower. The bell rang and the doors opened out onto the ninth floor.

"We're in nine three seven—this way." Kyle strolled down the carpeted corridor with Brock trailing behind him. Kyle slipped the electronic key card into the door lock and pushed it open. He ignored the beautiful view and the plush appointments and instead switched the TV onto high volume and began unpacking the bags.

"Are you going to tell me what's going on, Kyle?" Brock sat down on the end of one of the two beds. "These aren't our bags."

"To all intents and purposes, this is our hotel and we need to make it appear as if we are staying here. We won't be, though. Keats, that's our driver, will be waiting in the underground parking garage with a different vehicle and he'll be taking us on to another place where we *will* spend the night. Our bags are still in the trunk. It's all precautionary, but normal practice in my line of work." He glanced at Brock, who looked a bit stunned. "Here, put these wash bags in the bathroom. Wet the sink and spray a bit of deodorant around. Make it look used."

Brock did as he was asked and disappeared into the small en suite. A few minutes later, the toilet flushed and Brock heard the taps running. Brock reappeared,

drying his hands on a towel, which he flung onto the end of the bed. Kyle pulled back the covers on both beds and rumpled the sheets.

"That will do. We just need to leave the 'Do Not Disturb' sign on the door and we're done. It won't stand up under expert scrutiny, but to a casual observer, it looks like there are people staying in the room. Let's go."

They took the stairs and didn't come across a single soul as they descended nine floors to ground level, then two more to the basement garage. A quick flash of headlights told Kyle which car to head toward and a few minutes later they were back on the road, this time in a nondescript Ford. Kyle put his arm around Brock's tense shoulders and pulled him close.

"Not long now, love."

Brock sighed. "Really? This is just the beginning. I feel a bit sick."

"Jet lag. Don't worry, a few hours' sleep and you'll feel better." Kyle tried to sound confident but he knew that Brock's nausea was more to do with stress than lack of sleep. The cloak and dagger antics were a necessary precaution and there was little Kyle could do to protect Brock from the pressures of his world. Even if he had the power to call off the mission, he wouldn't do it. He was convinced that Brock had the inner strength to cope with the challenges ahead and, for the next few hours at least, he would make sure that his mind was occupied with much more entertaining thoughts.

Chapter Seven

Brock awoke in gradual increments, pulling himself from vague dreams of heat and mist and hundreds of shades of green. For a moment he couldn't work out where he was. He lay on sheets of the highest quality cotton and cool air brushed his bare skin. He didn't recall undressing and a momentary stab of anxiety twisted his gut into a tight coil.

"Relax. You're in Miami, safe and sound."

Kyle's deep tones sent a little shiver of desire down Brock's spine. He rolled onto his side and drank in the sight of the man sharing his bed. The sheet reached only to Kyle's waist. Bare-chested, he lay propped on his pillows, with one arm behind his head. The other stretched across Brock's pillow. Kyle played with Brock's hair, pulling it gently.

"Have you been awake long? What time is it?" Brock glanced around the room. He could hear a clock ticking but couldn't see it anywhere.

"It's just after eleven in the morning, local time, and I woke up about half an hour ago. I got to the shower and back without you even noticing, sleepyhead."

"It's the bed's fault… It's too comfortable."

Kyle chuckled. "I'll bring you back here one day for a proper holiday. I've always wanted to explore the Art Deco District."

"Sounds lovely." Brock's stomach rumbled. "Something tells me I need to eat."

"Why don't you go and freshen up and I'll order some room service."

"Okay." Brock's disappointment at not sharing a shower with Kyle was offset by the thought of an imminent food delivery.

By the time he'd showered, shaved and brushed his teeth, Brock felt one hundred percent better and a hell of a lot more alert. He remembered little of arriving at the hotel the previous night and now he got the chance to see just how luxurious the place was. The bathroom was all marble and polished chrome, the towels thick and fluffy. He ignored the robe hanging on a hook and settled for one of the towels slung around his hips. He was just about to go back to the bedroom when there was a light tap at the door. He stayed in the bathroom while Kyle dealt with the room service delivery but ventured out as soon as the snick of a latch signaled that the waiter had departed.

"Oh that smells good. What did you order?"

"Pancakes with strawberries and syrup, hash browns, scrambled eggs and bacon. There's freshly squeezed orange juice and an industrial-sized vat of coffee."

"I've died and gone to heaven. The only thing that could make it better would be if you took off that robe." Brock fluttered his eyelashes at Kyle.

"Lose the towel and I might oblige." Kyle didn't wait for Brock to obey. He pulled the towel away himself, leaving Brock bare.

"Hey! What about you?" Brock protested.

Kyle raised an eyebrow and dropped the robe. Underneath he had on a pair of clingy black shorts.

"Not fair," Brock sulked.

"Seems perfectly reasonable to me," Kyle replied. "Now eat, because my cock has a pressing appointment with your ass and it doesn't like to be kept waiting."

Brock enjoyed every mouthful of his breakfast, though he ate it quickly. He sat on the bed with his knees drawn up in an attempt to hide his burgeoning erection. Every now and again he cast a shy glance at Kyle, whose predatory expression sent tremors of desire through Brock's entire frame. He nibbled on a strawberry and fought back the urge to smile. Kyle was getting impatient. His fingers tapped on one muscled thigh and his underwear was straining to contain his cock.

"Enough." Kyle piled all the crockery in a heap on the discarded tray and dumped it onto the stool in front of the dressing table. "You're a tease, Lysander Brock, and for that you need to be punished."

"What did I do?" Brock protested.

"You converted the simple task of eating a piece of fruit into a pornographic act — a serious offense." Kyle removed the belt from his discarded robe. "On your knees."

Brock debated whether or not to obey for all of ten seconds. Kyle was unbelievably sexy when his inner Dominant came to the surface. All Brock wanted to do was submit, to hand over all responsibility and allow Kyle to use him as he wished. His cock ached as he

shifted to a kneeling position in the center of the bed and held out his hands for Kyle to bind.

"Behind your back, I think. I don't want you to have any opportunity to touch yourself," Kyle said gruffly.

Brock crossed his wrists in the appropriate position and kept still as Kyle tied his hands.

"Good. Now keep your knees together and bend forward." Kyle positioned a couple of pillows beneath Brock's chest so that he was supported and his face wasn't pressed into the mattress. Brock sensed the displacement of air too late to prepare for the sharp blow to his ass. He yelped as a narrow line of heat seared his skin.

"What the fuck? Did you pack a cane, Kyle?" *How the hell did he get that through customs without comment? And if he packed a cane, what else has he got hidden in his bag?*

"Address me correctly."

"Ow!" A second strike had Brock wriggling down the bed in an attempt to escape, but the pillows hampered his movement.

"Keep still." Two more blows punctuated Kyle's words.

"Fuck, that stings… Sir."

"I don't hear your safe word." The next two hits were harder. "I want your ass nice and warm before I fuck you. No bruises, though—not with the journey we have ahead."

Brock detected regret in Kyle's voice and his buttocks clenched at the thought of a more aggressive spanking.

"In fact…" Kyle stroked Brock's abused flesh. "I think I'd better stop now. You have an attractive rosy glow back here."

"I'm so glad you're enjoying yourself, Sir." *Oh, and so am I!* There was no way Brock would admit to Kyle that

he was so turned on his dick could hammer nails. The restraint, the pain—even Kyle's tone of voice—combined to put Brock into a state of submissive bliss. The only thing that could possibly make it better would be a damn good fucking.

A couple of well-lubed fingers penetrated Brock's ass with little finesse.

"Oh! Yes... More, Sir." Brock pushed back as best he could but Kyle was never going to let him take control. Kyle withdrew completely.

"No! Sir... I'm sorry. I'll be good."

"Well that'll be a first."

The crinkle of foil told Brock that he was going to get what he wanted—and soon. He wondered again what it would be like to take Kyle bare. *Good. Really good. Do I trust him that much?* The sudden realization that he did trust Kyle enough crashed over Brock in an overwhelming wave. He already trusted Kyle to keep him safe in bondage, to respect his safe word. Going bare was just another step along the path.

"If we make it out of this, we could get tested," he said quietly.

Kyle stilled and Brock worried that he'd gone too far with his suggestion.

"No one else will ever get to touch you, so yes, we will. I decided that when you mentioned it in England."

Brock sucked in his breath as Kyle pushed the blunt head of his gloved cock against Brock's hole. Such a controlling statement should have made his erection wilt. Instead, it made him even harder.

"Fuck me, damn it."

"For a man with his hands tied and his ass in the air, you are awfully demanding."

Brock wiggled his butt, trying to encourage Kyle to press home his claim. His balls ached. His need to come was all-consuming, beating down any sense of self-preservation he'd ever had.

"Fuck. Me."

Brock smacked him hard and thrust forward at the same time.

"I need to get you a gag." Kyle grabbed Brock's hips and proceeded to pound his ass until Brock saw stars, planets and whole fucking galaxies. Bent over and bound, all he could do was take what Kyle delivered. His shoulders ached and his muscles flexed as he attempted to break free of the ties around his wrists. They were soft but immoveable, adding to his delicious frustration. Kyle's grunts mixed with his own whimpers and cries as the unstoppable surge of orgasm shot through his body. He came hard and Kyle helped him along by grabbing Brock's dick and tugging roughly.

Brock panted through his release, hardly able to suck in enough air. Kyle's punishing rhythm didn't let up. Brock pressed his forehead into a pillow and bit back a scream. His eyes watered. He clenched his ass, bringing a yell from Kyle, who went rigid and grunted, filling the condom. For a few seconds the only sounds were of gasping moans and a ticking clock. Brock breathed to the clock's beat and gradually settled. A gentle tug on his wrists told him that Kyle was untying him. His hands came free as Kyle slipped from his body. Brock slumped forward onto his face with a happy, sated sigh.

"Just going to deal with the condom and fetch a washcloth." Kyle stroked the back of Brock's calf before moving away. Brock hummed. The best part of a scene,

however tame and obviously excluding orgasm, was the aftercare that Kyle provided. For a rough, physical man, he could be surprisingly tender. Brock dozed until the heat of a wet cloth pressed against his skin.

"The heat and pressure will make sure you don't bruise. Are you sore?"

Kyle's caring concern sent a pleasant shiver over Brock's sensitive skin.

"I'll be feeling you for a while." He grinned and rolled over.

"You like that, don't you?" Kyle smirked.

"Ask me again when we're trekking through the cloud forests." Brock studied Kyle and admired his hard, muscled body. There were several small scars and he wanted to learn the story behind each and every one, preferably while licking and kissing them. He longed to be held and, as if Kyle had read his mind, he climbed into bed and pulled Brock against him.

"We have a few hours still before we have to leave for the airport. We should take advantage while we can and get some more rest."

"Sounds good to me." Brock snuggled against his lover and tried to forget that it might be the last chance they got to hold each other in comfort for quite some time.

* * * *

Flying time from Miami to Bogotá took just three hours and forty-five minutes. Everything ran to schedule and, other than a short delay waiting for their baggage to arrive on the somewhat creaky carousel, arrival at El Dorado International was painless. Brock followed Kyle toward the taxi rank, taking in the sights

and sounds of a country he had read about extensively but never visited before.

"I love that they call the airport after a mystical city of gold," he said, as the two of them joined the short queue for a cab.

"You're a romantic at heart, aren't you? Do you fancy life as an explorer searching for lost treasures?"

Brock laughed. "I think you're more suited to being the next Indiana Jones than I am. I'll just take the pictures of you in action."

The next cab was theirs. Kyle heaved their bags into the trunk and gave directions in rapid Spanish to the waiting driver, then they both got comfortable in the back of the car.

"We're about ten miles northwest of the city center. The drive to the hotel shouldn't be too bad at this time in the evening, although traffic here is never good."

"You've been here before?" Brock asked.

"Several times."

Kyle didn't expand and Brock thought it best not to question him further. He could only imagine the kind of reasons Kyle might have for his frequent visits to South America. Best not to know.

"Are we staying at the hotel I booked or have you changed the arrangements again?"

"No major changes from now on. The arrangements — on the whole — remain as you planned. The precautions in Miami were just that — precautions. There are a lot of curious eyes on the ground there that I wanted to avoid. Here we'll be watched regardless of where we stay, so we must be what we purport to be — a photographer and his assistant in transit."

"Well, my local team recommended The Orchids. It's not the cheapest place but it's smaller with a good

reputation for service. It's in the Candelaria district, which I really wanted to see."

"It's an interesting part of the city, and there are plenty of good restaurants if you know where to go. We should be able to get some great tapas tonight." Kyle licked his lips, making Brock laugh.

"Hungry?"

"Absolutely. But I won't keep you out too late. We can't lie in quite as long tomorrow morning as we did in Miami. The flight to Cartagena leaves at midday. This will have to be another place added to our list of return visits."

The taxi dropped them off in an unassuming street outside an arched wooden entrance. When Kyle rang the bell pull, a small window set into the planks opened and an elderly man examined them. Kyle gave their names and the doorman's suspicious expression broke into a wide smile.

"Welcome, welcome, *bienvenidos*, gentlemen. We have been expecting you."

The large wooden door swung open on silent, well-oiled hinges.

"Good evening. My name is Santiago and it will be my great pleasure to see to your comfort during your short stay. Welcome to The Orchids."

Santiago's English was heavily accented but impressive. Kyle replied to him in rapid Spanish and the old man grinned, exposing a gold incisor in an otherwise perfect set of teeth.

"Forgive me, *señor*, but it gives me pleasure to practice my English. I hope you do not mind?"

"Not at all," Brock answered. "You speak the language very well, Santiago."

"You are very kind. I hope that you both will point out my mistakes. Now, let me show you to your suite. You must be tired after the journey."

Brock followed Santiago through the gate into a small, enclosed courtyard strung with fairy lights and hung with lanterns. To one side, a cloistered walkway, edged with stone planters full of flowers, led to a glass door protected by intricate wrought iron.

"This is a beautiful building." Brock looked around in admiration. He pulled out his camera and took a few quick shots. "I'll have to take some more tomorrow in the daylight." He caught Kyle's knowing expression and took a picture of that, too. "What? You have to admit this place is worth a picture or two?"

"I'm just amazed that you haven't whipped that thing out sooner."

Brock's cock jerked. Kyle was staring in the direction of Brock's groin and not at his camera equipment.

Santiago gave them both a bemused shake of his head and went inside. Brock did his best not to act like a little boy on an adventure. The thrill of new sights and sounds—new images to capture—never failed to get him excited. Coupled with the hot looks that Kyle kept sending his way, his pulse raced.

They crossed a cool, marble-floored lobby to an old-fashioned cage elevator.

"We can deal with the check-in formalities when you're settled. Your suite is on the top floor," Santiago explained.

They all got into the lift and it was a bit of squeeze with the three of them and the baggage. Santiago slid the security door shut and pressed the button marked Three. The lift lurched into action and moved upward surprisingly fast. Brock was quite relieved when it

shuddered to a halt and they could all spill out onto the small landing. Only two doors opened from the area and Santiago took them across to the one on the left. He opened it with an old-fashioned, heavy key then handed the key to Kyle.

"Best rooms in the hotel, gentlemen." Santiago gestured for them to enter with a sweep of his arm.

Brock gaped. The room was stunning, decorated in pale turquoise and gold. Elaborate plasterwork edged the ceiling and an enormous, gilt-framed mirror took up a third of one wall. The furniture was mahogany, polished to a high gloss, but the star attraction was a four-poster bed swathed with deep blue velvet curtains.

"Wow." Brock hadn't expected anything close to such luxury. "Santiago, are you sure this is our room? I didn't book a suite…"

"We only have eight rooms and a wedding party booked the other seven. We put you up here because it will be a little quieter. The honeymoon suite is across the landing, but that won't be in use until tomorrow night. Your bathroom is through there." He pointed at a door in the corner. "And through the arch is a small seating area."

While Brock explored, Kyle tipped Santiago and sent him on his way. "We'll be eating out, so we'll stop at reception to register on our way. If there's somewhere close by you could recommend, that would be helpful."

Santiago nodded. "Of course. I'll give you directions when you come down." He left the room, closing the door behind him.

Kyle piled the bags on the luggage rack. "I'll think we should go straight out. If I get anywhere near that bed,

I'll only want to fuck you on it and that's not nearly so much fun with a rumbling stomach."

Brock peeked into the bathroom. "There's a tub in here that's big enough to swim in."

"I'll fuck you in that, too." Kyle pushed past him. "Unless you want to watch me pee, wait outside. I need to freshen up."

"You're such a romantic." Brock went and sat on the edge of the bed.

"Are you saying you don't want to be fucked? Scratch that… Tied down and fucked?" There was a slight echo to Kyle's words as he shouted from the bathroom.

Brock flopped back on the bed and groaned. With just a few words in that deep, growly voice, Kyle had got him hard. Again. The four-poster appeared perfect for some bondage games — nice and sturdy.

"Well?"

Brock glanced up to see Kyle, shirtless, drying his hands on a towel. He got even harder.

"I didn't say that. This bed has all kinds of possibilities."

Kyle threw the towel back into the bathroom, strolled across to his bag and rummaged around until he found a fresh T-shirt.

"It does. I can picture you, naked, stretched out for me while I fuck your mouth and leave you hard and wanting."

Brock licked his lips at the thought of tasting Kyle's thick shaft.

"Yes please."

"Well, the sooner you get ready, the sooner we can get out of here, and once my stomach is satisfied, I'll be able to focus on satisfying other things."

* * * *

The sidewalk in front of the tapas bar that Santiago recommended was peppered with welcoming, well-padded chairs arranged around cocktail tables. Most of the tables were occupied by locals drinking and enjoying the relative cool of the evening breeze. A bright, hand-painted sign declared the bar to be called Estrella's.

Inside Estrella's, noisy chatter mixed with American rock music issuing from four corner speakers. As well as more tables, there was an area of comfy sofas, a couple of rocking chairs and low tables. Brock and Kyle received a few curious glances and some smiles.

"Hey, look..." Brock pointed upward. "The roof is open."

"Must be retractable," Kyle replied. "Good idea. I've seen something similar at a place in Cartagena." He crossed to the bar. "What would you like to drink?"

"Just mineral water please. I want to be able to taste the food. It smells fantastic in here."

"Grab a table. I'll order."

There was one table open, in a back corner. Brock took a seat and surveyed the room. The chalkboard menu listed around twenty items, including flash-fried sweet peppers and a brochette of shrimp and diced tomatoes. Fried local cheese with onion marmalade sounded good to Brock, as did oxtail slider served with homemade potato chips.

The relaxed vibe was helped along by a few eclectic touches in the decor. Pop art pictures made from bottle caps lined the walls alongside etched mirrors and colorful woven hangings. A range of mismatched lamps dotted around provided light. Brock smiled as

Kyle joined him at the table. He clutched a bottle of water and another of beer labeled 3 *cordilleras mestiza*.

"Food won't be long. I ordered something of everything, so I hope you're hungry."

"I am and that sounds great," Brock said. "There are only one or two things on the menu that don't appeal to me, so you can have those. The atmosphere is good in here. Seems like Santiago was right to recommend it." He cracked open his bottle of water and took a long swallow. "Mmm. Needed that."

"It's nice to have somewhere to relax before we get to the hard stuff. There's no layover in Cartagena."

"No, we just take a helicopter into the interior and then continue overland to Antioquia. I hope I adjust okay to the altitude."

"You're fit, which will help," Kyle said. "Unfortunately we won't have time to acclimatize thoroughly. Time is not on our side once we get to the area where the terrorists are active. We need to be in and out as quickly as possible. I won't pretend otherwise… It's going to be tough. The conditions are extreme, to say the least."

Brock leaned back in his chair and directed his gaze through the open roof to the starry sky. "This expedition was always going to be a challenging one, even without the detour. I can handle it."

"I know you can." Kyle didn't say anything more as a series of small plates began to arrive at their table, delivered by an affable waiter who appeared to be at least ninety years old. Between them, they sampled everything the bar offered. The food was delicious and by the time they were done, Brock felt full and lazy. Kyle paid the bill and they sauntered the short distance back to the hotel.

When they returned to the room, the covers on the four-poster had been folded back and a single rosebud laid on one pillow. In the lounge area, a sofa bed had also been made up.

Kyle chuckled. "That explains why Santiago wasn't fazed by two men sharing one bed. Though he seemed pretty astute. I wouldn't be surprised if the second bed is just for show."

Brock sprawled on the four-poster, luxuriating in the bouncy mattress and soft sheets.

"We'd better set the alarm. This bed is so comfortable I'm not sure I'll wake in time tomorrow." *Mind you,* he thought, *Kyle probably has an internal alarm with pinpoint accuracy. Sleeps with one eye open, knowing him.*

"Stop thinking and get naked." Kyle disappeared into the bathroom and seconds later the sound of running water and the scent of oranges filled the air.

"Yes, Sir," Brock muttered with a touch of belligerence that melted away when Kyle reappeared in the doorway stark naked and gorgeous.

"Bath, bondage and a blindfold, what more could a man ask for?"

"You're very good to me, Sir." Brock couldn't take his eyes from Kyle's straining cock. "Can I add a little sucking to the list?"

"It doesn't begin with 'b' so I'm not sure." Kyle fisted his dick. "I was trying to be poetic."

"Blow job!" Brock blurted out, and started yanking off his clothes.

Chapter Eight

Brock stared out of the helicopter's windows. Even through the sound-dampening earphones he wore, the roar of the rotor blades was deafening.

Below, a vast sea of green, shrouded in mist, spread to the horizon in all directions. From the air, it was as if the entire world were forest. The only breaks in the featureless expanse of the canopy were the occasional giant trees, which stood above the rest like sentinels. *I'll bet they make great nesting sites for harpy eagles and toucans. Shots of birds in flight above the canopy would be amazing.* Brock took a few pictures, thinking that they might make good backgrounds for text boxes or the like in any future articles.

His earphone radio clicked on with a hiss of static, and the pilot's voice cut through the noise of the engine. "We're less than ten minutes out. Hold onto your lunch, landing can be a bit of a drop with the thermals around here."

Brock peered ahead, yet all he could see was the same unbroken terrain below and to the side. Surely he'd be able to see a clearing soon. The helicopter banked then swooped into a rapid descent. A cleared area of ground appeared through the mist and before Brock could even wonder which direction his stomach was traveling in, the skids settled on the ground. The pilot gave them the go-ahead to disembark. Brock tugged off his earphones and winced at the growl of the rotors. He unbuckled his shoulder harness and climbed from the helicopter, following Kyle's lead. Once clear of the whirling blades, he stretched and sized up their surroundings.

A battered jeep was parked in one corner of the clearing. A man sat in the driving seat and another leaned against the side, smoking a cigarette. Brock grinned and waved. He picked up his bags from where they'd been offloaded from the helicopter.

"My ground crew is here, Kyle. Want me to introduce you?"

Kyle nodded and picked up his own bags. "Sure. No reason to hang around here. We might as well get on."

They walked toward the waiting jeep.

"The driver is Milo. He's Venezuelan by birth but his father's American so he has dual nationality. The tall guy with the beard is Juan. He's a local but he lives in Mexico when he's not down here working. The two of them run a small outfit providing support to specialist expeditions. I've worked with both of them before. You know all this already, though, don't you?"

"You're the only one aware of that. As far as they're concerned, I'm just your assistant, along to do the grunt work."

As they approached the vehicle, the man Brock had identified as Juan walked toward them and took Brock's bag after a quick handshake.

"Good to see you again, picture boy. Glad to see all our hard work keeping you alive in Chile paid off. That was a fantastic spread in *Wanderlust*. Thanks for the plug, too. We've got work coming out of our ears."

Brock laughed. "Just so long as you keep taking my bookings. This is Kyle. He's going to be helping me out on this one."

Juan tipped his wide-brimmed hat. "Nice to meet you." He brought his attention back to Brock. "Are you sure you don't need us after we've got you to the base camp? We have all our other bookings sorted with staff for the next few weeks."

"Thanks, but we'll be fine. Kyle's an experienced climber and I want us to be as inconspicuous as possible once we get farther up into the cloud forests. I just need you there to take us out."

"We'll be there. We're just going to hang at base camp. No point wasting fuel if we don't have to."

They reached the jeep and clambered in. Kyle threw his bags in the back and sat in the rear seat next to Brock.

"You'll need to be careful. There have been some reports of bandit activity in the area you're heading for." Milo leaned back and shook both their hands.

"I'm always careful," Brock replied.

"Like fuck you are," Milo scoffed.

Kyle gave Brock a thunderous glare. "He'll be careful this time."

Milo and Juan looked at each other and broke into peals of laughter.

"Good to see you've found yourself a babysitter, picture boy. Maybe Kyle here will curb your death-wish tendencies." Juan guffawed.

"Something you want to tell me?" Kyle growled.

Brock batted his eyelashes and went for his best I'm-too-adorable-to-be-cross-with expression. "To get the best shots, I sometimes have to get into some awkward spots. You know that."

"I do. That doesn't mean we can't discuss how you should avoid taking stupid risks." Kyle placed a proprietary hand on Brock's thigh. Brock smiled. There was no way Kyle would be able to wrap him up in cotton wool for the next few days, but he was apparently going to try.

* * * *

From the landing field, it took the small team five hours to reach Antioquia. It was nearing midnight and the darkness had been virtually impenetrable since the sun went down, cut only by the jeep's headlights. The slices of light attracted every bug in a ten-mile radius, it seemed to Brock, and he was thankful for the industrial strength repellent that coated every inch of exposed skin. He and Kyle had both applied it as soon as Kyle had finished glaring at him. When they broke through into an illuminated clearing, the sudden change was startling. A rumbling generator cut through the buzz of insect life and high-powered spotlights lit a semicircle of small tents and one larger central marquee. Blue tarps covered the ground and awnings fashioned from plastic sheeting protected piles of crates.

Brock blinked, letting his eyes adjust to the light. Milo's unerring navigation had taken them straight to their final base camp. As he paused to catch his breath, Kyle and Juan walked around him. Milo rotated the jeep in a tight circle, then he and Juan began to unload. Kyle gave Brock's shoulder a quick squeeze and strolled toward the large central tent. Before he reached the structure, the flap pushed out and a figure emerged. Brock realized that this must be Kyle's colleague, though he seemed very at home in his assumed role of scientist. A shock of dark hair and a few days' growth of scruffy beard didn't hide his beaming smile as he waved at Kyle, then moved toward Brock.

"You finally made it. I was about to give up on you and hit the sack. I'm Dr. Jones. Everyone calls me Jonesy." He held out his hand and Brock took it with a smile. The man's good humor was infectious.

"Nice to meet you. I'm Lysander Brock."

"I know your work, Lysander. Very impressive." Dr. Jones pumped Brock's arm up and down. His grip was firm but he didn't squeeze Brock's hand too hard.

"Please call me Brock, Dr. Jones."

"Jonesy will do for me. Nice and easy to remember."

"Okay, Jonesy. Let me introduce my assistant, Kyle Dawson."

Dr. Jones showed no sign at all that he knew what Kyle really was.

"Welcome to camp. It's basic but functional and we have a few luxuries. I take no credit for any of it. It was already set up when I arrived two days ago. Your ground team is very thorough, Brock. Juan and Milo know what they're doing."

"This is much more than I expected. How the hell did you guys get a generator in here?" Brock asked Juan.

"We cheated. This camp was being used by a bunch of American botanists. They've had people here for over a year on some kind of cataloging project jointly funded by the US and Colombian governments. We've been helping them out with supplies and they donated their kit to your expedition. Once you guys are done, we'll just keep an eye on it. There's another scientific expedition due here in a few weeks. It'll get used by them too."

"I can understand the popularity of the location," Dr. Jones said. "Las Orquídeas National Park is one of the single most biologically diverse places on the planet. But don't get me started... You must be exhausted. I have some coffee going and I can manage fruit, cheese and crackers if you're hungry?"

Brock levered his pack from his back and put it down carefully.

"Sounds good. I need to check my cameras first. Which tent is mine?"

"I hope you don't mind, but I've put you and Kyle in together. Milo and Juan are sharing and I have the smaller single. I snore like a mountain gorilla but I'll share with Kyle if you'd prefer the single?"

"He'll be fine with me," Kyle interjected. "Check your gear, Brock, then we'll have a quick snack and turn in. It's been a fucking long day and we all need to rest."

If anyone noticed Brock's obedient response to his supposed assistant's orders, they didn't comment.

Once the gear was stowed and Brock had satisfied himself that his precious cameras were fine, the group gathered in the larger tent and settled into folding chairs with snacks and tin mugs of thick black coffee.

"So, Jonesy, do you know what the researchers were doing here? As we've taken over their camp, I'd quite like to know," Brock asked.

"Apparently their remit was to collect as many species of flowering plants as possible. They were racing an environmental clock, too. Climate change and development are unstoppable, so it's quite a scramble to understand what's here before it disappears." Jonesy sipped his drink. "It was a pretty big undertaking. What's left of the camp is just a fraction of the base that was here."

Jonesy chuckled. "I could rant on about the situation for hours, but you would all fall asleep. Northwestern Colombia is a global biodiversity hotspot because of its location at the intersection of the Chocó and the Tropical Andes, two of the richest biogeographic regions in the world. But for the better part of two decades, Las Orquídeas — like many other ecologically important areas in Colombia — has been largely off limits to scientists because portions of the park became the unofficial territory of armed groups of bandits."

"I'm aware of the problem," Brock said, deliberately avoiding eye contact with Kyle. "The British Foreign Office still doesn't advise travel to this region."

Jonesy shrugged. "Regardless, all over the mountain tropics of South America, the race is on to identify unique species. Field expeditions can be dangerous, making funding hard to come by."

"Tell me about it. I've been trying to persuade *National Geographic* to fund a trip out here for years. They only relented because the conflict has retreated from Las Orquídeas over the past several years."

"Yet the high mountain ecosystems remain besieged in a different way," Jonesy went on. "Mining, timber,

agriculture and ranching are all contributing to massive deforestation. We scientists are still at war." He raised his mug in an ironic toast. "What makes the northern Andes so special is that they have extraordinary concentrations of species within very small geographical ranges. Each one of these mountaintops has wonderfully different sets of species of plants and birds and butterflies and amphibians. Snakes, as well, of course. I'm still hoping to find a new species – or at least a variant of one."

"What kind of species might we come across?" asked Kyle.

"In Las Orquídeas, the Andean spectacled bear, which is endangered – rare jaguar, puma, monkeys, deer, amphibians, snakes and an incredible variety of birds, bats and insects," Jonesy listed species with enthusiasm.

"And that teddy bear thing you mentioned on the plane?" Kyle asked Brock.

"Oh yes, the olinguito. I'd love to get a shot of one of those. Not very likely, though." Brock said, fighting back a yawn.

"Large-scale mining and logging are the biggest dangers. Over seventy-four thousand acres of land in Antioquia get deforested every year," Jonesy said. "The bandits can make more money for less risk in these industries and bribery and corruption are rife. You'll need to take care, but who knows? Very few people venture where you're going. You might get lucky."

Brock couldn't do anything about his next yawn. "Sorry. I don't mean to be rude, but I think I need to turn in." He stood and found his legs to be a little wobbly. Kyle was instantly by his side.

"I'm pretty much fried myself. We can continue with this conversation tomorrow morning. Brock and I will be spending the day in camp getting acclimated and resting before we head off on foot.

They said their goodnights and headed across to the small tent allocated to them. Brock stripped off his boots and socks, then his clothes and lay naked on his cot. He kept half an eye open and watched Kyle making sure that the insect nets were in place before he too stripped down.

"Shows how tired I am that even seeing you naked is not increasing my energy levels." He considered his flaccid cock.

Kyle stretched out with a sigh. "I'm not offended. Don't worry. You can wake me up with a blow job."

"In your dreams," Brock muttered.

"I sincerely hope that you on your knees will feature heavily in my dreams," Kyle shot back.

* * * *

The last few days had been exhausting. Crossing time zones, sitting in airports and traveling on planes had all taken their toll. The high altitude and underlying stress further combined to make Brock feel like a wrung-out rag. Inside the tent, a blanket of heat lay over him, and, despite his exhaustion, he lay awake for a while, listening to the sounds of Kyle's deep breathing and the exotic noises of the forest. He would soon get used to it. Years spent traveling around the globe had made him adaptable and resilient and, of course, the photographic purpose of the trip gave everything an exciting undercurrent. When he let himself imagine the

pictures he might take, the other, less enjoyable aspect of the trip could almost be pushed to one side. Almost.

"Stop thinking and go to sleep," Kyle muttered.

Brock snorted. "Is that an order, Sir?"

"Does it need to be?" Quiet rustling told Brock that Kyle was moving to face him.

"Perhaps. I have a head full of…stuff."

"Stuff? Sounds uncomfortable. You're far too pretty to be deprived of your beauty sleep. Come over here."

Brock's dick perked up at the order but his brain resisted.

"No."

"Really? You choose this moment to become a disobedient brat? Don't make me come over there and get you, Lysander."

Brock knew from the use of his proper first name that Kyle was deadly serious.

"Don't call me that."

"Brock…" Kyle growled. He actually growled.

"We can't do anything here. Everyone else in camp will hear us," Brock whispered desperately.

"Jonesy won't give a shit and I'm pretty sure that Milo and Juan had us sussed from the first instant they met me. Now get your ass over here."

Brock sighed and gave in to the inevitable. He groped around at the side of his cot and found the switch on the solar lantern. Bluish light flooded the tent, making him blink.

"The nights are so black out here."

"Indeed. Now get over here and suck me. Hands behind your back."

Brock rolled his eyes but clambered from his cot and knelt next to Kyle, who was giving his thick erection some gentle attention. Brock leaned forward and

swiped the head with his tongue, gathering a few drops of pre-cum to taste. Kyle put his hands behind his head and hummed his approval.

"Do a good enough job and I might just return the favor."

"That's quite an incentive."

"I should tie your hands really but I'm too comfortable to move. Now get to work."

Brock gave Kyle's cock a flick with his tongue, making it sway before ducking forward and swallowing it down. Kyle's strangled gasp was reward enough. Brock constricted his throat, thankful that he had great control over his gag reflex.

"Fucking hell!" Kyle's hips jerked.

Brock pulled off with a long drag of his tongue then sucked hard, but just the first inch or so of Kyle's straining dick.

"You taste so good." He hummed a little, hoping that the added vibration would drive Kyle wild. He wasn't disappointed. He loved going down on Kyle, loved every expression that flitted across Kyle's face and the excitement in his eyes. Being able to touch would have made things even better. It was a special kind of torment not to be able to grip Kyle's hot shaft or feel the weight of his balls.

"Aagh!" Kyle's gasp sounded the moment Brock swirled the tip of his tongue around the smooth and rounded head of Kyle's cock. It was followed by a deep sigh as Brock slid his lips down Kyle's dick. Brock sucked and squeezed his mouth around Kyle's shaft harder and faster until Kyle's muscled body tensed.

"Close!"

Brock accepted the warning and plunged forward to deep throat Kyle again. He held still, his airway

blocked, as Kyle jerked and came in a hot stream. Brock swallowed again and again then pulled off with a satisfied smack of his lips.

"Holy fuck, you're good at that!" Kyle exclaimed.

Brock flushed with pride at having pleased Kyle. Kyle's order to keep his hands behind his back slipped from Brock's mind and he fisted his cock roughly. Two swift jerks and he shot hard, with a shuddering moan. He opened his eyes to catch Kyle's amused expression.

"What happened to 'hands behind your back'?"

Brock attempted a contrite look. "Sorry, Sir."

"Oh, you will be, the next time I have the time and opportunity to thrash your ass." Kyle stretched.

"If you were a cat, you'd be purring," Brock observed as he cleaned himself up with a tissue, then clambered back onto his cot.

"Nothing wrong with sounds of deep satisfaction. I got off in a spectacular fashion, I got to watch you on your knees and I can look forward to punishing you for disobedience in the very near future. All is good."

Brock closed his eyes, feeling much more relaxed and ready for sleep.

"*Very* good." He had to agree.

Chapter Nine

After spending a day getting used to their surroundings and exploring the periphery of the camp, both Kyle and Brock were itching to get going. For Kyle, it wasn't just the urge to get the mission over and done with but a driving need to spend time alone with Brock. He packed and re-packed his kit. He examined maps and plans until his eyes ached. He spent hours huddled in corners with Jonesy going over every detail of the mission under the pretext of a sudden fascination with the local snake population. He kept an eye on Brock as much as possible, but Brock kept wandering off to take pictures. At least he always took Milo or Juan with him. Kyle recognized men who knew what they were doing in a hostile environment. Brock was as safe as he could be with them and taking photographs kept him occupied, with less time to worry.

After a farewell dinner, they went to bed early and slept hard. Kyle suspected that there was some scientific reason as to why the brain registered a need

for rest before an extreme experience and he was grateful for it. Physically, they were ready. Mentally, he still couldn't be sure that Brock would cope with what lay ahead but there wasn't much about the trip that he *could* be sure about. All the planning in the world could be thrown into chaos by any number of unpredictable scenarios. Kyle had done his best to think of every possible event but he knew from experience that anything that could go wrong probably would.

Kyle emerged from the tent before six in the morning, just as the sun was rising. Brock followed closely behind him, quieter than usual. They sat down to breakfast with Milo, Juan and Jonesy. Everyone had risen early to see them off. The meal consisted of cornmeal *arepas* and steaming bowls of *agua de panela*, a local drink made from boiled sugar cane. Both would give them the energy they needed for the hike ahead.

With the meal finished, there was no further reason to delay.

"Ready?" Kyle asked Brock. The question was superfluous but Kyle felt the need for a little reassurance. Brock could still change his mind after all.

"Of course. I'm looking forward to it. Spectacular pictures are waiting out there and it's our job to hunt them down." He grinned. "Don't worry, Kyle, I'll take care of you."

Kyle snorted. "Of course you will."

Brock fetched his small pack. It contained only essential supplies — bed roll, mosquito netting, some dry rations, a change of clothes, machete, water bottle and filter pump. He also had his light climbing shoes, a caving helmet and head torch. He could travel for weeks in the most remote parts of the world with little else. With the wealth of the forest readily available —

from various fruits and berries to roots and edible plants to abundant game and fish—there was little need to haul additional food. All being well, they would be gone no more than four days and traveling light was essential.

Kyle's pack was somewhat bigger. He had coils of rope attached to his rucksack, along with a shiny set of D-rings and a few metal pegs. They probably wouldn't need them. He and Brock were both more than capable of free climbing the cliff face they would need to tackle. Kyle's concern was that rockfalls may have altered the landscape since the last reconnaissance photos were taken. He also had one other essential piece of equipment buried deep in his pack—a packet of coffee. There were a few other useful items in there as well. Things that he hadn't shown to Brock.

After brief goodbyes with the rest of the team, he and Brock donned their light rain gear, crossed the stream that bordered the camp on a dubious bridge made of a single log and trudged along a narrow, muddy trail into the cloud forest.

As he hiked, keeping pace with Kyle's long stride, Brock gazed around. His fingers kept contact with the camera case slung over his shoulder on a long strap, itching to take it out and frame some shots. It was as if they were hiking through a verdant cathedral. A dense canopy of woven tree branches arched overhead, absorbing most of the sunlight and casting everything in an emerald glow. Brock had read that less than ten percent of the sun's light pierced through to reach the forest floor. Because of this, the lowest level of the forest, where they walked now, was clear of vegetation. The narrow path was muddy but easy enough to see.

Here the forest was a world of shadow and decomposition — the domain of insects, fungi and roots. Brock spotted enough wriggly beasts to give him nightmares for months. He shuddered and gave silent thanks that Kyle had insisted they wear full-length trousers rather than cooler shorts.

Still, the lack of vegetation didn't necessarily make trekking through the forest an easy journey. Rotted logs and branches lay everywhere, coated with yellow mold and white mushrooms. A slick mulch of decaying black leaves threatened his footing, while protruding roots added to the risk of a twisted ankle.

The way was too narrow to walk side by side, so Brock contented himself with watching Kyle's easy lope. The man moved with enviable confidence.

"I can hear you thinking from here," Kyle called back.

"Plenty to think about. How long till we reach the cliffs?"

"If we push on, four, maybe five hours. We should be there by lunchtime if we're not delayed. Then we should be able to complete the climb in the light and camp at the top."

"Are there paths the whole way? I'm kind of surprised that we're not hacking our way through the vegetation."

"The tracks are there if you know where to look. You researched a bit about the indigenous peoples, didn't you?"

"Sure. They're called the U'wa." Brock paused and clambered over a fallen log. "They're peaceful people."

"That's right. Both the U'wa and the cloud forest are among the last of their kind in the world and that's part of the reason we're here. Industry in the U'wa territory has contributed to a climate of violence. It's an easy

situation for terrorists to take advantage of because anyone who isn't corrupt is being pulled in so many different directions that their activity goes unchallenged."

Kyle came to a dead stop and pointed up toward the canopy.

"Up there," he whispered.

Instinctively, and with slow movements, Brock pulled out his camera. On a branch just a few feet above Kyle's head sat a dark red primate.

"Wow, red howler monkey. A real beauty." Brock snapped off a couple of shots. "Not bothered by us at all." He kept his voice low but the monkey just stared at him curiously.

"They probably got used to the scientists being around. I expect there's a whole tribe of them around here somewhere. Monkeys, that is, not scientists."

He moved off quietly.

"So back to the U'wa. They consider themselves guardians of the forest and the species that live here, including our monkey friend."

"They must be in constant danger," Brock murmured.

"Yes, and from the worst kind of predators. The U'wa have stated that they are willing to die to keep oil drilling off their ancestral homelands and unfortunately that's what's happening. Terrorists need funding. Oil companies will pay indiscriminately for access to new parcels of land. The U'wa are in the way."

"So what we're doing will help them, as well as whoever it is you work for?"

"Absolutely."

They fell silent and continued to walk. Brock mulled over in his head what Kyle had said. He felt a whole lot better about their mission, knowing that it might help

the local people. Kyle had sounded very intense. He was clearly affected by the situation and that only increased Brock's affection for him. Brock was no environmental activist, but he did hope that his work helped to highlight environmental issues around the world.

Brock began to feel the burn in his calves and thighs as the route got steeper. Sweat soaked his body beneath the thin raincoat and the ever-present mist saturated his hair until it clung in tendrils about his face. He recalled the maps he'd seen back in England. This stage of the journey was particularly arduous as they had to scale the lower slopes of a heavily forested mountain before reaching the base of the cliff they needed to ascend. His boots skidded on the slippery ground and he adjusted the pack on his back to regain balance. He put his head down and trudged on, concentrating on keeping his footing. Neither of them could afford an injury so early in their journey.

From then on, the territory got more unyielding. At times, Kyle had to use his machete to cut a trail through the dense vegetation. Several times they crossed waterways clogged with debris. Brock took pictures when he could, though it was usually Kyle who spotted the wildlife first and pointed it out. Several colorful birds, a bright yellow frog and some spectacular orchids were enshrined on Brock's memory card, along with plenty of atmospheric shots of light filtering through the mist-shrouded verdure. They stopped for a break in a clearing where the land fell away to reveal a sweeping view of the endless trees. Along the side of the valley, a cliff face could be seen—a stark white streak against the green. Kyle observed cracks and

ledges running down most of the face and the silver glitter of falling water.

Kyle chewed on a cereal bar and took deep swallows from his water canteen.

"That's where we have to get to." He pointed across to the cliffs. "We need to climb up a bit farther before we head across the valley side. It will level out somewhat but the going won't get any easier until we reach the base of the rocks. Then we follow them for a quarter of a mile or so to reach the place where we can get out of the trees and start the ascent."

Brock tossed Kyle an apple. "It's going to be an interesting climb."

"It's seven hundred feet, but not technically difficult. The surface is rough. Plenty of hand and footholds. The worst part is just before the top where there's a slight overhang, but there is a route around if it's too dangerous to go over."

"I can't wait." Brock munched on his apple. "Can you imagine the shots I'll be able to get of the view? I'll bet there will be plenty of birds nesting up there, too. I love to catch them in flight. Climbing makes it feel as if I'm out in the air with them."

Kyle smiled, warming Brock's heart.

"You are amazing. You see beauty in everything, don't you?"

"There *is* beauty in everything." Brock lifted his camera and took a shot of Kyle against the dramatic backdrop.

"Even in me?"

"*Especially* in you."

"I think you should book an appointment with your optician when we get back to England. There's

definitely something wrong with your eyesight," Kyle said in a dry tone.

"I have perfect vision. Anyway, the camera doesn't lie. You'll see, when I turn that picture into a giant poster." Brock stowed his camera away. "Are you going to dawdle here all day, or are we going to get moving?" He put his hands on his hips and scowled but couldn't hold the expression, which broke down into a grin.

Kyle tossed his apple core into the undergrowth and got to his feet. "I think it might make an interesting experiment to see how far you can hike with a vibrating plug shoved up your ass. Any more cheek from you and we are going to find out."

Brock took a few rapid paces down the path.

With their goal in sight—if only in occasional glimpses through the trees—the rest of the trek seemed to go quickly. Even the plant life became less resistant to their passage and at times the path grew wide enough that they could trudge alongside each other. The effort of walking made conversation difficult but the silence between them wasn't uncomfortable. Brock enjoyed the companionship and the knowledge that every step took them closer to completing their mission. Perhaps then, they could consider a life together.

They made good time and shortly before noon, Kyle broke through the trees at the base of the cliff. Brock stepped into the open air and gasped. To one side, the sheer rock rose above them, a seemingly impenetrable wall. To the other, the world stretched out in a sea of green. Miles of forest clung to valleys and mountainsides. Nebulous clouds of mist gave everything a mysterious air but the sun, clear and

bright, lit every damp leaf with diamond sparkles. Brock couldn't resist taking a few pictures before they ate. While he framed the vistas with a practiced eye, Kyle disappeared back into the forest and came back with fruit fresh from the trees to supplement their rations.

"Tonight, we'll try to trap something so that we can have fresh meat. Rehydrated food is fine, but if we don't have to eat it, I'll be happy."

"As long as you take charge of the barbecue. I'm a hopeless outdoor cook." Brock recalled his last attempt to cook sausages on his brother's garden grill. The resultant blackened sticks of meat had been charcoal on the outside and raw on the inside. They'd all ended up in the neighbor's dog.

"Of course. But first we have to get up that." Kyle pointed up to the towering cliff.

Brock checked the ground for anything that might want to take a bite out of him, then lay back so that he could take in the climb.

"It's impressive but doable. We should be able to free climb." In his head he could picture the routes across the rock like a drawing. There were several options and a couple of good resting points. He'd tackled far more challenging ascents.

"We should, but I still want to take some basic precautions. We can't risk injury, not out here. I need to keep you in one piece."

They finished their meal and drank plenty of water.

"I'm going to feel this sloshing around inside me on the way up," Brock complained.

"Better that than dehydration," Kyle responded. "We may be soaking wet, but climbing in this heat is going to suck the moisture out of us."

"What a delightful image. Why don't we get started?"

Brock took off his boots and damp hiking socks and exchanged them for light, rubber-soled climbing shoes. He made sure his pack was secure and shifted his camera bag into a more accessible position.

Kyle made similar preparations. "You can lead."

"Really?" Brock was surprised. He'd assumed that Kyle would want to go first.

"I'm not stupid. You're a far more expert climber than I am. You can pick out the safest route and I'll follow. Just don't kick any rocks down onto my head and use the safety line where you need to." He handed over the coiled rope. Brock threw it over his shoulder and fastened the belt full of D-rings around his waist.

He grinned. "Okay, let's go."

It was glorious to be climbing rather than cutting trails and hiking. There were plenty of big moves, good holds and a few gripping run-outs on the damp rock. It was a little slicker than Brock would have liked, but the climbing got better and more solid with every pitch. Crack systems linked into horizontal breaks. The rock was generally stable with a few loose sections.

Even though Brock didn't find the climb difficult, it was still draining. In the high altitude he found it tough to get enough oxygen into his lungs. He felt the stress of sighting each new pitch and ensuring it was safe for Kyle to follow. Kyle seemed to have no difficulties at all. He followed every move effortlessly and Brock realized just how fit Kyle must be.

Brock found a number of small ledges where it was possible to stop and take a breather. Kyle insisted on some rope support while Brock twisted and contorted to get the best pictures of the spectacular view. At one

point, Brock handed the camera to Kyle and asked him to take a couple of shots.

"The magazines always like to have pictures of their photographers in action."

"Okay, but don't blame me if I get my thumb in the shot or cut half your head off."

As Brock had hoped, the bird life was spectacular. Inquisitive hummingbirds hovered around them. Swallows played and flew parallel with the walls, narrowly pulling away from impact at the very last second. Colorful parrots chattered away in annoyance at having their roosts disturbed. He took dozens of pictures and even when it began to rain in earnest, they were somewhat protected by the slight overhangs.

A storm rolled past and the skies thundered while they climbed through the clouds, making route finding a bit more difficult. It all just added to the thrill for Brock. He got some incredible shots, potential prizewinners.

Most of the climbing was free with the exception of a short traverse. After that, Brock hung from the fingertips of one hand and enjoyed the sensation of muscles stretching to their limit. He shook out the tension in his free arm before locking his other hand across a small outcrop of rock. Above him there was a short stretch of vertical cliff face before the lip of the escarpment—below him a rope showed the path that Kyle would take as he followed him up the climb. The rain made everything even more slippery and wet hands did not make for easy climbing. Handholds were still plentiful but the rock was becoming razor-sharp, insects bit at every piece of exposed flesh and the plants that grew in the crevices seemed to be uniformly covered with thorns.

Brock took a breath and began his last push toward the top. He knew that Kyle was only a few feet below him, but both men climbed in silence, making as little noise as possible. Brock winced as a sharp edge cut into his hand and gritted his teeth as his body weight opened a wound that he could do nothing to prevent. Blood slicked his fingers, loosening his grip, but he moved upward and grabbed the edge to pull himself over the top of the cliff. He rolled onto his back with relief and took a few deep breaths. As he relaxed and the adrenaline flooding his system subsided, he began to feel the throbbing ache in his hand. He closed his eyes, refusing to examine it straight away. Another body flopped down beside him and a low voice whispered in his ear.

"Climbing behind you gives me a perfect view of your ass. It's very distracting."

Brock ran his uninjured hand through sweat-soaked hair and sat up. "You shouldn't be admiring me, you should be focused on the climb. Get the first-aid kit out of that bottomless pack of yours, will you?"

Kyle instantly sat up, concern etched on his face. "What have you done? Show me."

Kyle held out his hand. Brock took it, unrolling his fingers.

"Ouch. That's nasty." He rummaged around in his pack and pulled out a first-aid kit, extracting antiseptic and bandages. "How the heck did you get that?"

"A handhold with an edge that was much sharper than it looked. I had all my weight on that hand and it was either hold on or fall."

"Well, I'm glad you chose to hold on." Kyle took charge and swabbed the cut, which ran across the meat at the base of Brock's fingers. Breath hissed from

between Brock's clenched teeth as the liquid penetrated the wound.

"Sorry, but in this climate it's important that I make sure the cut is clean. Heat, dirt… It would be easy for you to get an infection. If you start feeling ill, if your temperature goes up, you tell me immediately." Kyle placed a dressing across the cut, then wrapped a bandage around Brock's hand a few times. "I'll clean it again later. We need to get to tonight's campsite before it gets dark." He glanced at his watch. "We've made good time so far. We have about four hours of daylight left and the spot we're aiming for is about two hours away if we keep up the pace."

They both drank more water and made use of the natural facilities. They changed back into hiking boots, Brock making sure to tuck his trousers into his socks. Kyle laughed at him.

"You afraid that something's going to sneak up your trouser leg?"

Brock scowled. "Just removing the opportunity. Insects are cunning little bastards."

"That *is* true. A couple of years ago I spent some time out in Vietnam. I was having dinner in an open-air restaurant one night and felt something tickling my leg. It was a centipede. Twenty-three centimeters long."

Brock stared at him in horror. "How the hell do you know how long it was?"

"My host caught it, measured it and took a photo. I think he was hoping for the world record but he didn't get it. The biggest one on record is twenty-seven centimeters."

Brock shuddered. "And that is why I am tucking my trousers into my socks. Can we get out of here before

you start remembering other insect-related stories to scare me with?"

"Well, now you mention it, there was this one time with a bird-eating spider…"

Brock gave chase as Kyle sprinted toward the trees. Just as he caught up, Kyle turned and pulled him into a hard hug. He followed it up with a kiss that left Brock breathless.

"There will be time for more campfire stories later."

Brock pouted. "I'm hoping for more than stories."

Kyle's eyes glinted. "Well, get walking. The sooner we get there, the sooner I can check you for crawlies — all over."

Chapter Ten

After they'd walked for half an hour or so, Kyle produced a map from his pack that Brock hadn't seen him make any reference to before then.

"I thought you knew exactly which way to go? We're not lost, are we?" he asked, trying not to smile.

"No, we're not lost." Kyle raised his head from the map and narrowed his eyes. "Cheeky brat. We should come to a fork in the trail soon but it's difficult to spot. We need to take the left fork or we'll end up at a river in a gorge that's impossible to cross. I think we're pretty close... Just making sure that we haven't already walked past it."

Brock peered over Kyle's shoulder. "Well, have we? Oh, that's not a map!"

"No, there aren't any decent maps of this area. This is a satellite image taken a few weeks ago. I don't think we've missed it." Kyle traced a line on the picture with his finger. "This is the stream we crossed about a hundred meters back and this" — he followed a vague

curve that was a little darker than the surrounding trees — "is the bend we're coming up to."

"What bend?" Brock peered into the trees.

"You won't be able to see it yet — not from here — but the split in the path should be a few meters after the bend." He returned the plastic-coated sheet to his pack. "Let's get going. Keep those photographer's eyes peeled."

Sure enough, the path did begin to bend. It was very overgrown but didn't require too much hacking and chopping to get through. They moved forward slowly and it was Brock who found the junction.

"It's here, I think." He pushed aside a curtain of vines to reveal a narrow track. "Or it could just be that an animal has passed through here."

The track to the right was much clearer. Kyle explored it for a short distance before returning.

"That must be it." He double-checked their direction with a compass then stuffed it back in his pocket. "The direction is exactly right. Well done."

Brock all but glowed at the praise. It was good to feel as if he was making a positive contribution when Kyle carried much of the responsibility for getting them to their destination safely. They both shouldered their packs again and Kyle took the lead as they set off through the dense vegetation at a steady pace. Brock's natural sense of direction told him that Kyle kept them on track, moving consistently northeast. The trail they followed could hardly be credited with the name and Brock wondered whether a jaguar had made the vague separation in the plants. It would explain why it seemed to be clearer below waist level. It was tough going and even through his trousers, Brock sustained quite a few scratches from the spiky undergrowth.

After slogging along for around an hour and a half, they emerged into a small clearing.

Brock sighed with relief. He'd started feeling a bit claustrophobic and it was nice to be able to see more than a fleeting glimpse of the sky.

"This is it." Kyle dumped his pack on the ground and rolled his shoulders. "What do you think?"

Brock switched his gaze from upward to ground level and gasped.

"Wow, it's stunning." Three-quarters of the clearing was covered by water in the form of a sparkling green pool. On the far side there was a rocky outcrop, over which a waterfall cascaded into the deep basin. The water churned and boiled at its base and miniature whirlpools appeared and disappeared in the currents. Above the overhang, bare rock glistened with moisture. All around, trees crowded close.

"How the heck did anyone ever find this place?" Brock exclaimed. The scene was enchanting. "And where does the water go?"

"To answer the first question, the U'wa discovered this place and directions have been passed down through the generations. It took a combination of satellite technology and rough drawings to come up with a route. And the water goes underground from here. This whole area is riddled with cave systems and much of the water flows underground. It finally joins the Magdalena River, I believe."

"It's amazing. I wish there was more light to take some pictures."

"You'll get your chance in the morning."

The light was rapidly fading as Brock took in as much of the scene as he could. He wanted the image imprinted on his mind so he could plan some shots.

However, much as he loved the scenery, standing still rather than walking gave him time to realize how many parts of his body ached and just how tired he was.

"I think the day is starting to catch up with me." He stretched and listened to a few joints pop. "It'll be good to settle in for the night."

Kyle nodded. "Well, the entrance to the cave system that forms the next leg of the journey should be behind the falls. I'm intending that we camp back there. If we're behind the water, it should be safe for us to have a fire. We wouldn't be able to risk it out here. Though the chances of anyone being around to see the smoke are miniscule, there's still a possibility."

As he spoke, Kyle headed around the edge of the pool and disappeared behind the curtain of water. Brock followed behind. He hesitated briefly and let his ears get accustomed to the thunderous noise. The force of the falls drummed up heavy spray but he didn't get too wet as he crossed the rocky ledge behind it. It wasn't a drenching, just a cool mist that rested on his skin and clothes like liquid cobwebs.

"What's a bit more wet? I've been soaked through all day anyway," Brock muttered to himself. "I'll be glad to get out of these clammy clothes."

"And I'll be glad to help you." Kyle leered in Brock's direction. "However, there are a few things to do before we can relax."

Brock ventured a bit farther into the cave. After a few feet the floor became completely dry.

"What do we need to do?" He watched as Kyle began to empty his rucksack.

"Well, we'll need dry wood for the fire an, if you want to eat something other than field rations, I'll have to set a snare or two."

Brock frowned.

"What's wrong?" Kyle came across to him.

"It's stupid, I know, but much as I like the idea of roast meat, I don't want to kill off the local wildlife to get it."

Kyle chuckled. "Rations it is then. Reconstituted chicken supreme has always been one of my favorite meals." He squeezed Brock's shoulder. "My sweet, kind-hearted man."

Brock leaned into him instinctively and Kyle gave him a hug. Brock shivered at the contact and his cock perked into life.

"Stop! If you keep touching me, there'll be no fire, no food and a very uncomfortable night." He pressed his hardening erection against Kyle's body in explanation.

Kyle smirked. "Very nice. But you're right. That will have to wait. Are you okay to sort out the wood?"

"Sure." Brock pulled away reluctantly. As he went back to negotiate the waterfall again, he could feel Kyle's gaze following him all the way and that put an idiotic smile on his face.

Out in the clearing, the light was almost gone. Brock stared at the sky. It could have been a piece of cloth dip-dyed in midnight blue ink with the darkest color at the top and a thin edge of pale blue at the bottom. The air was warm and very still. Brock stood motionless and listened. As his ears tuned in to the cacophony of forest sounds, he realized just how much life the place teemed with. He fancied he could see glittering pairs of eyes peeking at him from behind every bush. He could visualize some great night shots but he didn't have the right kind of equipment with him.

"Some remote camera traps in a place like this would be amazing," he mused, picking out the best spots. A

twig snapped behind him and he whirled around to find a slightly damp Kyle standing there with his hands on his hips.

"I should have known you'd get distracted. I came out here to see if you'd been eaten by something."

"Sorry." Brock was glad that the dim light meant Kyle couldn't see the flush on his cheeks. "I couldn't help it. How long have I been out here?"

"At least fifteen minutes. Plenty of time for a passing jaguar to take a few chunks out of you."

"Aw, you were worried about me. That's adorable." Brock smiled.

"Don't try to beguile me with that smile. I'm out here to crack the whip, not fall for your witchery."

"Witchery? Is that even a word?" Brock fell about laughing. "All right, I'm on wood duty. I promise not to get sidetracked again."

"Good, because photographers who don't do their chores get punished. As you will be anyway if you ever call me 'adorable' again." With that, Kyle whirled on his heel and headed back to the cave. Brock swallowed and pulled at the neck of his shirt, which had grown strangely constricting.

"Bastard did that on purpose."

He soon discovered that there was plenty of dry material to gather, despite the wet conditions. Huge leaves and low branches provided plenty of sheltered spots. After a few close encounters with some scary-looking insects, he used a big stick to disturb the undergrowth before collecting his haul and he gave every piece of wood a good shake to dislodge as many crawly things as possible. He had to make several trips to ensure that they had enough fuel to last the night and he had to cover his armloads with his raincoat to keep

the wood dry—consequently, after multiple trips through the falls, he was soaked through. His last collection was done in complete darkness so when he got back inside the cave, Brock was glad to see that Kyle had already started a small blaze.

"Come and sit by the fire while I build it up a bit. You look half drowned," Kyle called.

"I am." Brock took a seat close to Kyle. "It's not cold, though, just a bit uncomfortable."

"I laid out the sleeping mats to give them a bit of an airing. They were damp, but they'll soon dry off in here. As soon as the heat builds, I'll boil some water for coffee."

As well as the glow from the flames, a solar lantern stood to one side on a low rocky shelf. A capsule of flickering light surrounded them but beyond it there was nothing but darkness and eerie shadows. Brock got up and wandered back into the cave as far as the light would allow. He could see several enticing tunnel openings and felt an almost childish excitement at the prospect of exploring them the next day.

He returned to the fireside.

"You were right about this place being riddled with caves. There are several entrances back there. I hope you know which one we need to take or we could be here for weeks."

Kyle raised an eyebrow and gave him a disdainful stare.

"Fine! You are the all-knowing guide. If I've got time, I think I'm going to freshen up a bit. I stink." Brock sniffed at himself and cringed.

"Sure. The water will take a while to boil anyway."

Brock wandered back to the falls and stripped off his clothes. The tumbling cascade was so inviting and he

couldn't wait to wash away the sweat and grime accumulated during a day's hard effort. He found a flat ledge where he could stand in safety, where the water's force was not quite so brutal, and stepped under the spray. He yelped as the chilly torrent hit his hot skin and hopped from foot to foot while his body adjusted to the temperature.

"Oh wow, this is good." He luxuriated in the sensation of cool water beating against him, running his hands through his hair and sluicing the flow across his body. Shiny droplets sprayed into the air and landed with a gentle patter on the floor behind him.

Kyle tried to stay interested in taking care of his fire but the thought of Brock standing naked under the cascade was too much to resist. Just the image in his head had him hard and aching. He gulped and drew in a deep breath, then headed toward the front of the cave. He moved quietly, sticking to the shadows, and found a spot where he could watch Brock undress. Unless Brock turned and stole a deliberate peek into his corner, Kyle could get away with indulging his voyeuristic streak.

Brock stripped off his clothes too quickly for Kyle's liking. He would have preferred more of a show but he could hardly reveal his presence and ask for it.

"Oh, that's more like it," Kyle murmured as Brock stepped beneath the spray and began to make orgasmic moaning noises. Kyle fought back a laugh. He didn't want to give himself away just yet, not when he had a perfect rear view of Brock's lithe, muscular body, all wet and glistening. Brock stretched his arms up and the muscles in his thighs and ass tightened, then he bent to rub the muddy streaks off his legs and Kyle was

presented with firm buttocks crying out for his touch. As if sensing a presence behind him, Brock swiveled around and raised an eyebrow. He was erect, despite the cold water. Kyle licked his lips and gave him a slow, lazy smile.

"How long have you been watching me?" Brock asked.

"Does it matter?"

"I suppose not. Are you just going to carry on standing there?"

Kyle interpreted that as an invitation and he had no intention of giving Brock a chance to withdraw it. He pulled off his clothes, discarding them in a messy heap, then stepped into the spray. The ledge Brock had chosen to use was not that wide, meaning that Kyle needed to stand close to him, something he was very pleased about. He took full advantage and began to slide his hands across Brock's slick golden skin, touching and kissing at will. With his chest pressed to Brock's back and his cock probing at Brock's ass, Kyle was in heaven. Brock responded by pushing back against him, inviting as much contact as Kyle could give. He sealed their bodies together, shoulder to thigh, and sucked up a mark on Brock's neck.

Brock made such delicious noises. They were almost enough to make Kyle come there and then. He wrapped his arms around Brock's slippery torso and plucked at his nipples, eliciting little groans of pleasure-pain.

"Need to kiss you." Words were hard to get out. Kyle wanted to use his mouth for kissing, not talking. Brock obliged him by rotating in the circle of his arms.

"What's stopping you?" The challenge in Brock's voice was clear. Kyle cupped the nape of Brock's neck with one hand and grabbed his ass with the other.

"Nothing at all." He pressed his lips to Brock's, demanding entry. Brock opened to him willingly and Kyle deepened the kiss. Brock's dick, only semi-erect now, pressed against Kyle's groin as they seemed to meld together and become one. Kyle dropped his hand from neck to ass and used both to massage Brock's cheeks. He separated them enough to allow cool water to trickle down the resulting valley. Using one finger, he began to torment Brock's hole, rubbing around the edge before pushing firmly inside him. Brock gasped and wriggled, trying to draw him in deeper. When Kyle pulled free, Brock's moan was one of disappointment.

"No more, not without lube."

"Want more. Like the burn," Brock complained. Tiny droplets of water balanced on his lashes. Kyle kissed them away.

"I know you do, but I'm not going to risk damaging you."

"You won't... I trust you."

Brock squirmed in his hold.

"Greedy man. I'll look after you. Don't worry. I want you, but that's not going to happen while the necessary equipment is hypothermic!"

"Then I think we're clean enough, don't you?"

"So impatient. It's not like the water's going to run out." Kyle grabbed Brock's hand and pulled him back toward the fire.

"Now who's the pushy one?" Brock protested as Kyle manhandled him across the cave.

"That's my job, remember? Please accept that I find you irresistible when you're all wet and dripping. I just need to get my cock out of cryostasis."

"The water wasn't that cold... It was refreshing." Brock shook his head like a soggy puppy and sent water flying everywhere.

Kyle glanced back at his lover's cock.

"You're only half hard. You could do with a little defrosting too." Kyle grabbed Brock's dick and used it to tow him toward the welcome warmth of the fire. Brock followed meekly, hardening with every step, much to Kyle's amusement.

"I should put your dick in a leash. It would suit you and I think you'd like it. Don't you agree, sweetheart? I could take you to The Underground, a great BDSM club I know in London, and lead you around by your cock. Naked, of course, apart from a nice collar and cuffs set."

Brock whimpered, but when Kyle contemplated him, Brock's handsome face was flushed and his eyes were bright with excitement.

"Sounds awful, Sir." Brock nibbled his lip and looked at Kyle through his lashes.

"You're a terrible liar, love."

It was fewer than thirty paces to the fireside, but, apart from his hair, Kyle was almost dry by the time they got there. Brock's longer style meant that there were still shiny rivulets of liquid on his chest as water continued to drip from his blond strands. The crackling flames cast dancing shadows across the rocks around their camping area. The dark stone was bathed in orange and red light and the air misted with tiny wisps of steam as a few stray droplets landed in the fire. Kyle reluctantly let go of Brock's now iron-hard erection and grabbed a clean T-shirt from his pack. He gave his head

a quick rub with it, then tossed the damp garment to Brock. While Brock used his makeshift towel to get a bit drier, making his dick move in a very enticing manner, Kyle searched in his pack for a condom and lube.

"Yes! Found it." His hands shook a little as he tore open a foil packet and rolled the silky sheath onto his now-straining cock. Brock grinned at him.

"You packed supplies?"

"Of course I did. They went in before anything else."

"You're far too pleased with yourself."

Kyle pushed Brock toward the wall of the cave. "This is not the time for conversation. Brace yourself, this isn't going to be gentle," he growled.

Brock giggled. "Brace yourself? Really?"

Kyle gave Brock's ass a hard slap.

"Ow!"

"Behave, brat."

Brock locked his arm muscles and braced against the stone, bending so that his butt stuck out. Uncaring of the hard surface, Kyle dropped to his knees and sank his teeth into one cheek. He didn't bite hard enough to break skin, but he dug his teeth deep enough to leave a bruise.

"Fuck!"

"Open your legs wider," Kyle snapped, getting impatient. He dragged his tongue through Brock's crack and teased his hole, pushing inside just a little way before withdrawing. "Love the way you taste." He slicked a couple of fingers and pushed them into Brock's channel. "Need to get you nice and slippery, but not too stretched." The preparation was cursory, but Kyle had no patience for lengthy foreplay. He stood, dribbled more lube onto his gloved cock and smeared it around, then lined his dick up with its

target. Brock's glossy entrance winked at him as his muscles contracted.

"Think you can keep me out, do you?" Kyle rammed into Brock. "Gonna fill you up." Intense heat surrounded his cock. Brock pushed back and Kyle drove deeper inside him.

"Hurts so good," Brock moaned.

Kyle couldn't hold back. He pounded Brock's ass with a desperation born of unstated fear for the future. Every thrust set new nerves on fire. Flesh met flesh, over and over again. Kyle grabbed Brock by the hips and used the increased leverage to good effect.

"Taking you so deep I don't want you seeing anything except a red haze in front of your eyes."

Brock cried out as Kyle forced him toward the rock, grazing his forearms as he tried to resist the pressure. Brock's internal muscles squeezed Kyle hard and Kyle fought to control his urge to come. He pulled free.

"I know what you're up to. I'm not done with you yet." The words came out in short punchy sounds, stabbing the air with a lethal edge. "Bend over and grab your ankles."

"So fucking romantic."

Kyle was banking on Brock being too dazed to do anything but obey. He shifted one arm around Brock's waist, supporting him as he bent forward. Actually, he decided, it was more of a flop than a controlled bend. He grinned. Brock was loose and pliant in his arms.

"Love you like this... Helpless and vulnerable."

"Love it when you go all Dommy on me." Brock wriggled, pushing his ass back, seeking Kyle's dick. "Empty. Need you in me."

"Your ass is begging for it."

Brock had no leverage. He couldn't fight the position. He was at Kyle's mercy and that was the ultimate turn-on. Kyle speared him deeper than before, sinking inside him then withdrawing until only the tip of his cock remained in Brock's grasping channel. Then he plunged forward again, pulling Brock back at the same time. He ground his hips against Brock's body, drilling into him, then reached for Brock's rigid dick. Instead of grasping it and giving Brock some relief, he gave it a couple of hard flicks with his fingers.

"Fucking bastard!" Brock came with a shout of indignant outrage. He struggled and fought but Kyle's superior strength made sure that he stood no chance of escape. Brock's muscles continued to spasm with the intensity of his orgasm, and he sobbed with what sounded to Kyle like a mixture of joy and frustration. The whimpers and small cries brought Kyle to the edge and tipped him over. He came with force, punishing Brock's beautiful ass with a few final jerks of his hips.

"Fuck, fuck, fuck…" Kyle gasped out the words. His arms trembled and he released his hold on Brock gradually, allowing him to sink to all fours in front of him, his breath coming in short, ragged heaves. Brock gave a short laugh and went back to sucking in air. Kyle leaned against the cave wall, needing its support.

"You okay?" he asked Brock.

"Ask me again when I remember how to breathe."

Kyle pushed away from the wall and gave Brock's ass a gentle pat as he passed.

Chapter Eleven

Kyle wrapped the condom in a plastic bag then tucked it into the side pocket of his pack before wandering back to the falls for a cursory wash. He picked up the T-shirt he'd discarded earlier and dipped a corner in the water, then wrung it out. He strolled back to where Brock was climbing shakily to his feet. Kyle pressed against him from behind and stretched his arms around Brock's waist.

"Here, let me clean you up a bit."

Brock grabbed his wrist and guided the damp cloth to the sticky bits on his skin. "Thanks. I think you broke my ass."

Kyle chuckled. "You're tough. It'll take a bit more than a firm fucking to break you."

"If that's what you call firm, I dread to think what an aggressive pounding will feel like," Brock said. He spun around in Kyle's arms and gave him a brief kiss.

"Dread or crave?" Kyle asked, then watched with interest as a pink flush spread along Brock's

cheekbones. "I think there's a pain slut hiding beneath that pretty exterior."

Brock grunted but didn't reply. He took Kyle's hand and pulled him toward the fire.

"I know it's warm, but I need to sit by the fire and let you pamper me. Well, feed me at the very least."

To Kyle's disappointment, Brock pulled a fresh pair of cargoes from his pack and slipped them on. Kyle scowled. Brock rolled his eyes.

"My tender little behind needs at least one layer between it and the rock floor, so you can stop pouting."

"I don't pout," Kyle grunted. "And I'll be seeing it again before the evening's out. I can guarantee it." He found some fresh clothes and dressed swiftly. Brock raised an eyebrow and smirked.

"If I'm cooking, it's in your interest that my best bits are protected from stray sparks, okay?" Kyle wondered why he felt the need to justify his actions. It wouldn't have occurred to him to explain to anyone else.

"I didn't say a word!" Brock held his hands up.

"Didn't need to. Now make yourself useful and build up the fire a bit. We've been away from it for too long." Kyle moved the billycan he had filled earlier closer to the flames. "Another couple of minutes and this will be hot enough for coffee."

"Excellent. I seem to have worked up quite a thirst for some reason." Brock brought an armful of wood across from where he'd stacked it against the cave wall. "This should keep it going for a while. It's good that the cave is high enough for the smoke to be distributed and there's plenty of ventilation."

"That's great. Thanks. Once we've eaten, I'll bank it up enough so that it lasts the night," Kyle said. "I think

the folding cups and ration packs are in your bag. The coffee is in mine. Can you get them?"

Within a minute they were both making pleased moaning sounds over mugs of steaming black coffee.

"Oh, that's good." Kyle breathed in the aroma. "It was definitely worth going to the effort of buying the local ground stuff. You'll never drink it any fresher than this."

"I may get withdrawal symptoms. I've never tasted anything like it. I'm so pleased you thought to pack it. Makes me wonder what other goodies are hidden in that bottomless bag of yours." Brock shifted his bare feet nearer the fire and wiggled his toes. "This feels like a boys' own adventure and I'd prefer it if reality stayed away a bit longer."

Kyle focused on heating their evening meal of reconstituted chicken supreme and rice. He didn't want to think about the real world either. Tucked behind the waterfall in the middle of nowhere, it was easy to forget. Time alone with Brock was a luxury that would be very difficult to give up. Out of the corner of his eye, he caught Brock flexing his injured hand.

"As soon as we've eaten I'll check that cut and re-dress it. Does it hurt?" Kyle said.

"Aches a bit and it's bleeding a little. Think I opened it pushing against the rock earlier." Brock grinned. "And that was definitely worth it."

"Even so, there's a significant risk of infection out here and I have no intention of carrying you out if you get sick." Kyle stirred the bubbling food a little harder than necessary. Any thought of Brock getting hurt sent sharp stabbing pains through his gut. "I think this poor imitation of food is about ready." He doled two portions into bowls and handed one to Brock. "Tuck in.

This stuff usually tastes better than it looks." He gave the contents of his own bowl a dubious glance. "Of course, this resembles regurgitated crap, so that's not much of a challenge."

Brock giggled in a way that made him sound very young. He closed his eyes, wrinkled his nose and shoved a forkful of food into his mouth. He chewed slowly. His face relaxed and his pretty blue eyes blinked open.

"It's not bad at all. I don't know how much actual chicken there is in this, but it's got me fooled."

Kyle shook his head. "Fuck, you're easily pleased." He ate his own food with a grimace.

Brock scraped out his dish and put it to one side. "I may not have very discerning taste buds, but I am fussy about other things."

"Like what?" Kyle took the bait.

"Men, of course."

"Of course." Kyle wondered where the conversation would lead. "We're not going to compare ex-boyfriend counts, are we?"

Brock laughed. He went and fetched their sleeping mats from where Kyle had rolled them out and he laid them next to each other. "No, of course not." He started to collect the dirty dishes. "You cooked, so I'll clean up. I'll go and rinse these out."

Kyle couldn't help but admire the lean lines of Brock's bare chest as he walked away. The man had a stunning body with the power to inflate Kyle's cock every time he rested his eyes on golden skin and flexing muscle.

"Get a grip, Kyle. There's a bit more at stake here than your over-excited libido." He banked the fire and used a twig to tidy up a few stray embers, then moved across to the sleeping mats. The shaped pads weighed a mere

fifteen ounces and packed down to a compact volume. Kyle knew from experience that the internal air baffles and reflective barriers kept the user nearly as warm as a propane heater.

"Technology," he muttered, stretching out on one of the pads. "Fucking amazing."

"Now you're the one talking to yourself. Is it my turn to be worried?" The amusement in Brock's voice made Kyle smile. Brock's cheek would have to be punished, of course. He couldn't allow his future submissive to get too bold. His fingers clenched into a fist of their own volition as Kyle's brain registered that he had just assumed that there would be a future for him and Brock.

"Maybe. Why don't you come here and find out?" He patted the mat next to him. "Bring the first-aid kit. I want to deal with that hand before I deal with you."

For a moment Kyle thought that Brock might tell him to fuck off. His expression implied that he wanted to. Kyle kept his gaze steady and schooled his features into a careful, emotionless blank. He wondered if he should have given Brock a little more time to assess his feelings after being taken so assertively. *He fought my hold, but I know he wanted it. He couldn't stop me and he enjoyed that feeling, I know he did.* Kyle decided to go with his gut.

"I said come here, Brock. Do as you're told or I will put you across my knee and spank what I'm sure is a very sore ass."

Brock's lips twitched as if he was fighting back a smile but Kyle's words motivated him to move.

"A spanking is one indignity I'm not prepared to tolerate just at the moment."

He walked across and knelt on the second mat, holding out his injured hand. Kyle frowned as he took

in the bloody bandage. He unwrapped it with care and examined the wound.

"Hmm. It needs to be stitched or it's going to keep pulling open. It's in such an awkward place, movement is unavoidable. It's a little red, but I don't think there's any infection."

Brock trembled. "I don't recall passing a handy casualty unit, so it's not going to get stitched any time soon, is it?"

"Yes it is. There are surgical needles and sterile thread in the first-aid kit."

Brock's face blanched to bone white. "I don't even want to know what scenarios you were imagining when you packed a surgical kit, and if you have a scalpel in there, don't tell me."

"Don't panic. I'm highly trained in embroidery. I'll do a fine job."

"Oh my God."

"If the edges were cleaner, I could use skin glue, but they're not."

Brock shunted away a few inches. "You don't sound disappointed that the less painful option is not possible. Bloody hell! You're enjoying this!"

Kyle rummaged in the first-aid kit until he found antiseptic, a curved needle and thread. "I don't get to practice very often. The last time it was on myself and that wasn't fun."

"Let me see," Brock whispered.

"What?"

"Let me see where you did the stitching. I should get to see an example before I let you stick something sharp into me."

Several witty responses to that comment came straight into Kyle's head but he resisted. Brock appeared pale and anxious, his brow furrowed.

"Fine." Kyle undid his trousers, lifted his ass so he could push them down then kicked them away. He pointed to a faint white line just above his left knee. "It's there. Got slashed with a Stanley knife."

Brock didn't say a word. He just stared. It took Kyle a few moments to realize that Brock wasn't staring at the scar at all. His gaze was several inches north of where it needed to be.

"Brock." Nothing. No response. "Lysander! Stop gawping at my fucking cock."

"Oh. Oh! Sorry," Brock muttered. "I got a little distracted."

"I'll just bet you did." Kyle yanked his trousers back up but left the fly open a little. A bit of distraction wouldn't hurt if it took Brock's mind off the needle. "Give me your hand." Kyle got onto his knees to make his position more stable. He threaded the little curved needle with a short length of thread. "I'll swab the wound first." He doused it in antiseptic. Brock yanked his hand away with a yelp.

"That stings!"

"It's supposed to. Hand."

Brock extended his arm and Kyle grabbed his wrist. "You need to keep still and not pull away. Do you think you can manage that?"

Brock nodded but he still looked pale and nervous.

"I didn't think you'd be the squeamish type. You've been injured before on your travels."

"Something else you found out during your research on me?"

Kyle gave him a sharp stare. "Yes, and I thought you'd got over the whole spying-on-you thing?"

"Sorry. I have. I understand why you did it. I'm just nervous."

"In the last ten years you've broken your collarbone, cracked an elbow, dislocated a knee and broken your left wrist—twice. You've had stitches in your scalp and both legs. Two concussions. Various strained muscles and pulled ligaments. You can't tell me you're afraid of a couple more stitches?"

"Not afraid… Just a little nervous. It's the whole lack of anesthetic and amateur stitcher scenario we have going on here."

"Trust me." Kyle rested Brock's injured hand on his thigh. "You're shaking." He shook his head. "That won't do." He lowered his zipper a bit more.

Two minutes later, the job was done. Kyle nodded, satisfied with the neat stitches. "All done."

"Oh! Really?" Brock examined his hand. "I hardly felt a thing."

Kyle rolled his eyes. "Unbelievable. I'm going to put another sterile patch over the top because these are hardly the most hygienic conditions in the world." He finished dressing Brock's hand and packed away the kit. "Now, I think we still need to have a conversation about your taste in men, don't we?"

"Do you ever forget anything?" Brock pouted.

"No." Kyle stretched out on one of the mats, putting the softer of the packs beneath his head. "Come here."

Brock lay down next to him and didn't resist as Kyle pulled him onto his chest.

"There, obedience isn't so hard, is it?"

Brock frowned. "Is that what you want then? A meek submissive who will jump at your every command?"

Kyle gave a short laugh. "Do you think that I would find you so bloody attractive if that was the case?"

"Then what *is* it you want? What do you fantasize about?"

"I thought we were going to discuss *your* taste in men, not mine."

Brock chuckled. "That won't take long. Tall, dark and Dominant. Now, back to *your* fantasies."

"Do you really need to ask?" Kyle felt strangely reticent about jumping into a response. He stroked Brock's cheek, letting the slight roughness tickle his skin. Brock colored and shivered.

"Humor me. I'm intrigued, and if you go all mysterious on me, I'll just keep plaguing you until you give in anyway."

"I'm not sure it's a good idea."

"What are you afraid of?"

Kyle shrugged and pulled Brock closer. "That you won't want to be with me anymore."

"Jesus, Kyle, how bad can it be!" Brock twisted onto his side and began to play with Kyle's chest, tracing his muscles and brushing against his rapidly hardening nipples.

"Oh, I can be very bad. For now I think I'll leave it to your imagination. You have an active one, so I'm sure you can come up with all sorts of interesting ideas." Kyle swallowed as Brock flicked a nipple. He was especially sensitive there and Brock knew it.

"You could take up being aggravating as a new profession. You know that, don't you?" Brock extracted himself from Kyle's hold and sat up, a stubborn expression pasted on his pretty face.

He might act the innocent, but Kyle suspected that Brock had a pretty good idea of what Kyle would like

to do with him. Physically Kyle was very dominant and didn't try to hide that he relished that role. From his research, Kyle knew that Brock's previous relationships had been on an equal footing.

"Tell me why you broke up with your previous boyfriends." He put his hands behind his head and crossed his ankles.

"All two of them? That won't take long. I thought we weren't comparing lists of exes?"

"We're not. I just want you to think about it."

Brock's shoulders dropped and he resumed his position curled against Kyle's chest.

"They were both nice guys. Thoughtful, considerate... Neither of them was particularly toppy. They both liked to switch. It's a perception thing, I suppose. I'm not exactly small and twinky, but topping does nothing for me. I'll oblige if it gives my partner pleasure but given the choice..."

"You prefer to be held down and fucked to within an inch of your life?" Kyle queried, already knowing the answer.

"Yes," Brock said in a dreamy tone.

"Hey! Focus." Kyle brought Brock back from whatever kinky daydream he had going on his head.

"If I must. I suppose that was the problem. I always felt that there was something lacking. Neither relationship was fulfilling for me. They were too...nice."

"Nice... A damning word if ever there was one."

"It wasn't as if I even recognized my need to be submissive in the bedroom. That didn't occur to me until I met you. I'm not naturally submissive in day-to-day life and have no intention of being that way as a general rule, but when it comes to a physical

relationship... It turns me on in a way I've never felt before." His voice had dropped to a whisper by the time he finished speaking.

"It's not something you should be ashamed of, Brock." Kyle wanted to wrap Brock up and protect him from the world.

"I'm not ashamed... A little afraid, perhaps. When you broke into my brother's house and had me tied to that chair in my underwear..."

"Mmm. That's a picture that will stick in my memory for a very long time."

"Stop it! I should have been terrified. I didn't know who you were or what you wanted. Instead, I was turned on. That *can't* be normal."

Kyle stroked Brock's back in comforting circles. "What *is* normal? We hardly met in average circumstances and things haven't been boring since, have they? This is normal for me. Most people would freak out and run for the hills. You didn't."

"I saw your reactions when you had me restrained. Your icy control, your confidence... Something in me recognized a Dominant and you made me ache in all the right places."

"Maybe my fantasies won't scare you off then," Kyle said. "I want to tempt you. See how far you're prepared to go. I want to take you to places you've only dreamed about—and I'm not talking about more forests or caves."

Brock propped his chin on Kyle's chest and gazed into his eyes.

"My limits are completely untested. I've been further with you than with any other lover... I don't have much experience, but I know that when I'm with you, I feel more alive even than when I'm dangling off a cliff with

a camera in my hand, and that's something I didn't think could be beaten. But I don't like the uncertainty of the position we're in. What future can we have together, Kyle? Once this adventure is over, I have no idea if you'll disappear from my life or if you'll find a way to stick around. I don't even know if that's possible for you in your job. I won't ask you to tell me one way or the other, because I'm afraid of what the answer might be."

Kyle wanted nothing more than to hold Brock close and give him as much comfort as possible. He couldn't give him the reassurance he needed about the future but he could try to make the present a little more bearable.

Chapter Twelve

Brock slept well — a deep, dreamless sleep prompted by fatigue and supported by the security of Kyle's arms. He woke to the eerie half-light of dawn filtering into the cave through its curtain of water. The fire had burned away to a few blackened embers and a scattering of ash. He lay quietly for a few moments, riding the rise and descent of Kyle's chest as he breathed and listened to the relentless pounding of the falls. The continuous sound of water reminded him of his bladder.

How does that work? Why does the noise of water always make me want to go? Every time. He extracted himself from Kyle's grip and got to his feet, suppressing a groan as his muscles protested the movement. He did a few quick bends and stretches, then padded outside, ducking through the spray as quickly as he could. In the early light, the glade and its emerald pool were stunning. Brock found a convenient place to relieve himself then went back into the cave to fetch his

camera. He moved quietly, but Kyle was already awake.

"Morning." He yawned. "I need coffee."

Brock grinned. "That would be your first thought—today of all days."

"And I'll bet yours was 'Where's my camera?' wasn't it?" Kyle looked at him expectantly.

"So, I'm predictable too. The light out there is just stunning. I won't be long." He grabbed his camera before Kyle's naked chest could distract him.

"Get some water while you're out there. I'll rebuild the fire and get it going. I believe we have the delights of reconstituted oatmeal to tempt our taste buds this morning."

Brock picked up the billycan and took it with him. Once he was out beyond the falls, it was hard to know where to aim his camera first. He put the can down in among some roots, then took picture after picture, delighted by the way the light reflected from so many glistening surfaces. A scurry of movement caught Brock's eye and he zoomed in to a spot at the base of a tree, rapidly adjusting his settings. To his astonishment, a small creature—no bigger than a kitten—clung to the trunk.

"Oh my God, it can't be!" Brock snapped off some shots and crept closer. The tiny creature didn't run away, just stared at him with curious eyes. Farther up the trunk, another animal scratched at the bark. Brock panned upward and realized that this must be the mother of the tiny cub on the ground. "Olinguitos. I can't believe it." The animals seemed unperturbed by his presence. The baby was so small that Brock could have fitted it onto his palm. He was so close that he

could see its tiny, curved claws and textured foot pads. It was perfectly designed for climbing trees.

Brock forced himself to move slowly backward to the cave, never taking his eyes off the olinguito baby. He desperately wanted Kyle to get the chance to see the animals too. As he reached the waterfall, he turned to find Kyle standing there, staring.

"Are those what I think they are?" he asked.

Brock nodded. "Yes! Can you believe it? A mother and baby—and they are so fearless." The two of them stood and watched the cute little creatures as they foraged for insects and chased up and down the tree. Eventually they disappeared upward and out of sight.

"That has to be a good omen for the trip," Brock said as he filled the billycan with water. "That was as good as winning the lottery." He wanted to stay and see if the animals returned, but Kyle took his hand and led him back into the cave.

"Unfortunately, we have other things to do today. Let's go and eat."

* * * *

They had a very quick breakfast of oatmeal and chopped fruit, then packed up in silence, each preoccupied with what they had to do that day. Any kit that wasn't needed was hidden behind rocks on one side of the cave. Apart from climbing equipment, head torch and camera, Brock was taking nothing else with him.

"You remember the plan?" Kyle asked.

Brock nodded. "Of course. Once we've negotiated the more dangerous parts of the route, you'll stop while I continue on alone. That's about halfway through the

route. I get to the other side of the mountain, take the pictures and retrace my steps as quickly as possible. You'll then pick up the relay and take the memory card back to base camp so that Jonesy can get it to a location for satellite transmission."

"That's right. I don't like separating and leaving you to do the worst part of the job alone, but one of us has to conserve the energy to be able to make the return trip at speed. You can then follow at a slower pace once you've recovered. You can camp at the waterfall, retrieve any remaining kit from the cave and make sure that no trace is left of our presence."

"Then I head back and meet you at base camp."

"That's right. Then if everything goes well, we can go home." Kyle re-dressed the wound on Brock's hand and stroked the sensitive skin on the underside of his wrist. Brock shivered at the contact and leaned into the searing kiss that followed.

"Be safe, Brock. I need you back in one piece."

"I'll do my best." He ran his hand round the back of Kyle's neck then reluctantly moved away.

Brock headed toward the smallest opening in the back wall of the cavern. He eyed the tiny tunnel and grinned. Kyle didn't come across as nearly so enthusiastic.

"It's called a wormhole," Brock said.

"Looks more like a fucking sewer drain to me," Kyle complained. The black entrance stood only two and a half feet high. Brock crouched and shone his head torch down the tube.

"With a backpack on, I estimate it will just be possible to crawl through these holes. It's a good job we're traveling light," Brock said. He got down on his belly and squirmed into the darkness.

Kyle stood with his hands on his hips as his last view of Brock's boots disappeared. After a couple of minutes he heard Brock shout back to him that he was good to go.

"Just wonderful." Kyle got down on his knees and gave the cave entrance another examination. It didn't get any better from his staring at it. His pack was bigger than Brock's so he pushed it into the hole, then followed Brock's example and slid forward with his arms outstretched, shoving the bag in front of him.

"Fuck, this is tight." Rock pressed down all around. He edged ahead. He cursed as he scraped his wrist on a jagged edge and twisted his upper body. His helmet ground against the rock.

"I fucking hate small holes," he muttered, clawing his way on. "I feel like a piece of that spiral pasta." He wriggled his hips, losing another shaving of skin. His bag was yanked free, then he popped out of the narrow hole into a larger cavern. He rolled onto his back and looked up into Brock's grinning face.

"Fusilli. That's the proper name for that kind of pasta. And I thought you loved fucking small holes." Brock put Kyle's pack down next to him.

"Cheeky brat. My shoulders are about a foot wider than yours. I've lost skin in there."

"Aw, poor baby. I think I may have broken a nail, so we're both equally battered."

"You realize there's nowhere to run down here, don't you?" Kyle rolled onto his knees and stood. "The locals call that passage the throat of the snake and we have to go back through there to get home. Some days, I hate my job." He stretched with a groan. "I suppose you love it, don't you?"

Brock nodded. "Don't hate me." His grin was enormous.

After the wrestling match with the narrow tunnel, they sat to rest for a few minutes. Brock leaned against the rock wall, then pressed his shoulder to Kyle's.

"Switch off your head lamp to save battery life," Kyle said. "I have spares, but the more energy we can conserve, the better." They both switched off their lamps and a palpable blackness enveloped them.

"You'd never experience this kind of blackness on the surface," Brock said softly. "Even in the dead of night, there's always some light coming from somewhere. From the stars, moonlight or firelight. Your eyes adjust and you can see after a fashion. But down here, the darkness is so thick, you can hold your hand an inch from your face for as long as you like and you won't see it."

"You're holding your hand up, aren't you?" Kyle asked.

"Of course. Have to test the theory." Brock patted Kyle's knee.

"Well, much as I'm enjoying sitting here, admiring the color black, we should get moving." Kyle snapped his torch back on and Brock blinked at him owlishly. Even with their powerful lights, Kyle could barely make out the walls around them. "This chamber is the size of a barn."

"Which way do we need to go?" Brock asked.

"Up and left," Kyle directed. He shone his lamp onto a sloping rock wall. "We go up there. There should be an opening at the top."

"Seems like an easy climb—the rock almost forms a staircase," Brock said as he moved eagerly across the chamber. He headed up first and Kyle followed close

behind. It was a bit of a scramble in places, but not difficult. At the apex of the cavern, Brock traversed a sloping ledge and disappeared into another tunnel. Kyle trailed with a little less confidence. He couldn't see the drop, but he knew it was there and that made him nervous. The passage was large enough that he could stand up and he pursued the glow of Brock's light for several hundred yards before they reached the next obstacle. The passage dropped and became a crawl space less than two feet high. Brock was already on his stomach, peering into it.

"There's some debris, but it's not completely blocked." He wriggled back out.

"I'll go first and clear it," Kyle said. "You need to conserve your energy." He took his pack off again, got onto his stomach and edged ahead. "Shit, why can't all caves be like Wookey Hole? I quite enjoyed wandering around there when I was a kid. It was pretty." He could hear Brock laughing behind him. He shimmied as far as he could. The rock ceiling seemed to press down on him, even though there was a foot of clear space above his head. Using his hands as scoops, he maneuvered loose debris around his body, pushing it out as far as he could to leave a clear way for Brock to follow. After fifteen minutes or so, he'd moved perhaps ten feet forward.

"Fuck, this is hard work." His arms ached and he was soaked in sweat but in front of him, there was no more muck to clear. Kyle pushed thoughts of the millions of tons of rock above him away and pressed on. He found time to wish that he'd had room for elbow pads, kneepads, shin pads and some kind of cock pad in the rucksack. He was getting scraped to hell. Finally he was

able to raise his head and crawl out into another bigger space.

"Come on through," he shouted through the low gap to Brock, then settled in to wait while Brock made the journey through the low space. He didn't have to wait long.

"Like a rat up a drainpipe, as my dear old dad would say," Kyle muttered as Brock cleared the passage in less than five minutes, emerging with a happy smile, shoving both packs in front of him.

"God, I've missed this. It's been an age since I've done any caving and there are so few systems left that are unexplored. You can probably count on one hand the number of people who've been down here in the last fifty years."

"I'm so glad you're having fun." Kyle moved off, relieved that the cave roof was high enough that he didn't even have to stoop, let alone crawl for a while.

After another hour of traveling through passages coated in mud the color and texture of melted chocolate, Kyle stopped on the edge of an almost vertical drop. He slid on his ass down a flowstone curtain into another, lower tunnel where the mud came up his boots and sucked at his feet as he walked. Brock followed closely, the light of their head torches mingling. After trudging through the muck for about two hundred feet, they reached a fissure splitting the floor. Kyle shone his light down through the crack.

"I can see water," Brock said. "This is where we part company, isn't it?"

"Yes," Kyle replied, trying to keep his voice steady. "I'm afraid it is."

Kyle found a dryish rock that they could both perch on while they ate some high-energy protein bars and drank sugar-laden drinks.

"The map has been right so far but there were a few more accounts to build the picture to this point. As far as we know, only a couple of people have been beyond the sinkhole and not recently. I don't have any reason to believe that it's not accurate but you'll need to be careful and be aware of crevices or other sudden drops that might not be marked once you're through the water." He regarded the luminous dial of his watch. "It's taken us four hours to get to this point—a bit longer than I'd hoped but clearing the debris in that crawl space lost us a bit of time and we won't need to do that again on the way back. Parts of the route were tighter than I would have liked. Do you have any injuries?"

Kyle had grazes on most bits of his body but he hoped that Brock's more slender frame might have allowed him to escape damage.

"Just a few minor scrapes and bruises. Nothing serious," he replied.

"How about your hand?"

"It feels okay. The stitches are holding and the gloves helped a lot. I'll be fine, Kyle, really." Brock patted Kyle's knee. "I just want to get on with this. The sooner it's done, the sooner we get to go home." He directed his head torch at the sinkhole in front of him and frowned. "I thought the map indicated a breathing space between the water and the roof of the tunnel?"

"It did, but if there ever was a gap, it's gone now. That could be because of the season and a higher rainfall level on the surface. You'll have to dive to find the

entrance to the passage." Kyle tried to keep the worry out of his voice.

"I'm sure you're right. It should still be doable. The underwater part is only fifteen meters long, isn't it?"

"As far as we know, it is. Can you do it?"

Brock nodded. "Of course I can." He handed his pack and all the bits of kit he could do without to Kyle. His camera was weather-sealed but he checked the waterproof bag around it anyway, making sure it was still secured, and tightened the strap across his chest. He couldn't risk anything happening to it.

"Right, time to leave."

Kyle leaned in and cupped his face. "Take care." He kissed him gently, then let him go.

Chimneying, his back against one wall and knees against the other, Brock slid down the crack into the frigid water. His feet didn't touch the bottom, so he was obliged to swim. The farther he swam, the more the ceiling dropped. Eventually he had to twist his head sideways in a small airway. The water — black as ink — slopped into his mouth. He took a couple of deep breaths, filling his lungs, and went under, immediately swallowed by the inky blackness. In seconds he had disappeared from view. Kyle peered down the crevice into the water for a while longer then switched off his own light and settled down to wait.

Brock pushed away the instant anxiety that came with leaving Kyle behind. The moment he ducked beneath the water, all his concentration was focused on finding the route he needed to follow. He felt the rock with his hands, inching down with his fingertips. The solid wall gave way to water. He traced the edge of the hole to the width of his arm span. It was big enough for

an easy swim. He wouldn't have to force his way through at least. He swam back to where he could take in more air then turned, dove and swam forward into the submerged tunnel with powerful strokes. He counted in his head, and when he got to fifteen began to feel the rock above him. It slowed him down but in the darkness it was the only way to know where the tunnel ended. He found the edge and pulled himself out. The surface was only a couple of feet up and he emerged into a large space that was oddly lit.

"Hmm, phosphorescence." Treading water, Brock took in the rough rocks cast in eerie green shadows. He swam to the side of the small pool and pulled himself up onto a rocky shelf. It hadn't been a difficult swim but he was now shivering from the cold.

"Got to keep moving and warm up." Brock knew that he only had a short window of opportunity to get the shots he needed. Once he reached the end of the cave, it would be late afternoon and the light would already be failing. He had no idea what he was walking into — Kyle's intelligence had been limited — but if his luck held, he would reach the outside world smack in the middle of the terrorists' base of operations. Brock sniggered at the irony of that thought. *Who in their right mind would feel lucky to be that close to a bunch of heavily armed, brutal fanatics? I must be losing it.* He wrung as much of the water out of his sodden clothes as he could and set off.

At first the route was low and narrow, dripping with moisture. Gradually it widened and he was able to stand upright. He moved quickly, heedless of unseen obstacles, taking risks he would never normally have considered. He crossed a wide cavern, hopping over a small stream that had dug a trough through the center

of the floor, and wove around the many stalagmites clustered together in various places. He kept going, his helmet light picking up all kinds of weird colors and formations. He wished he had time to take some pictures, but resisted the temptation. He climbed over a small outcropping, feeling the pull in muscles still tired from the previous day's climb. His wet, muddy clothing clung to his skin. The activity was warming him up at least, but then he had to slow down and begin searching for the exit from the cavern. In a corner, a narrow vertical crack appeared to be the only means of exit.

Brock adjusted his camera bag to a position where it was less likely to snag or catch. He needed to reduce his profile as much as possible. He shuddered. The route was daunting and it was a hell of a lot more difficult to be brave without Kyle to tease. He wondered if he could possibly wedge his body into that slit. The walls looked as if they would squeeze the breath from his chest.

He did a swift reconnaissance of the crack, edging inside and casting round with his light. He chuckled at his own nerves and pushed forward. The passage was about ten feet long, but narrowed to a tight spot near the end. Brock could see that, beyond the worst point, it widened into a decent-sized tunnel again.

"Piece of cake," he muttered, glad that there was no one to argue with his assessment. He kept his helmet light pointing to the front, leaned his back on the left wall, which was the smoothest, and maneuvered his left shoulder into the crack, one foot pointing forward, the other back. Inching into the claustrophobic space, he tried to halt the panicked flutter of his heart and just concentrate on making progress. Up ahead, more

phosphorescent light diffused around the curve of the narrow aperture. There were just a few steps to go.

The crack swallowed him up. The walls pressed, too tight even to turn his head. All he could do was slide one leg a few inches and drag his body along behind it. He counted the steps, trying to divert his mind.

"You're doing fine," he told himself. "Just a little farther."

A ghost of a smile played about his lips. Kyle would laugh like a drain if he knew Brock was talking to himself again. He moved his left foot a little, but when he tried to wiggle his body to follow, his chest jammed snug in the crack.

"Fuck." He tried to force himself ahead, only pinning himself tighter. He squirmed backward, trying to free himself, but failed.

He reached out with his hand and grasped an edge. He counted to three then blew out all the air from his lungs, shrinking his chest, then heaved himself forward. Pain shot through his shoulder but he popped free of the crack, like a cork from a celebratory bottle of Moët.

"Thank you, Lord. Fuck, that was not fun." Brock rolled his shoulder. "Just bruised." He glanced around and realized that the increased brightness was not just from glowing algae, but daylight. He turned off his head torch. Up ahead, the sun's rays filtered through the darkness from an opening to the real world. He made his way toward the golden glow and finally the passage widened into an opening. Cautiously he stuck his head out through a screen of tangled vegetation and found that the ragged hole in the rock was set into a small outcrop and there was a sheer drop of about seven feet below him. The air was still and warm, thick

with humidity but it felt good against his chilled skin. He unwrapped his camera and hid his helmet and the waterproof bag just inside the entrance. He lowered himself over the lip of the rock. His hand throbbed as it took his weight momentarily before he dropped the last foot or so to the ground, boots squelching as he landed.

Brock paused to catch his breath. He checked the wound on his hand and to his relief there was no blood seeping through the wet dressing. Kyle's stitches had held. He gave his camera a quick once-over and made sure the settings were right for the conditions.

"Okay. Now for the difficult part." Keeping low, Brock pushed forward through the undergrowth.

Chapter Thirteen

Within a few yards of the cave entrance Brock froze. He could hear men's voices somewhere close by but was disoriented and had to concentrate to work out which direction the sound came from. The last thing he wanted to do was to blunder into someone because of carelessness, so he kept still and listened. He wasn't good at being still. That was why he preferred landscape rather than wildlife photography. Mountains didn't run away in a panic if you moved an eyelash. With his life at stake, he found a new level of patience. He was grateful for the concealing vegetation as he dropped to his knees and crawled forward, inch by inch. Even the varied insect life that chose to wander across his hands didn't distract him.

As the sounds grew louder, Brock lowered himself to his stomach and slid as quietly as he could along the muddy ground. To his astonishment, when the voices became clearer, he could hear that the men were speaking English, not Spanish. Not only that, they had

American accents. Curiosity made him reckless and he edged a little farther forward. He almost gave himself away when he stuck his head between two bushes and found his nose inches from a pair of muddy combat boots. He held his breath, only letting it out when the boots moved away. *Fuck, that was close.* His view was restricted but Brock saw that he was on the edge of a deeply rutted dirt track. *This must be the road Kyle mentioned – the only one in and out of the area.* Down the track in one direction Brock observed several vehicles parked to the side. One appeared to be some kind of armored personnel carrier and there were a couple of open jeeps. In the other direction stood the two men he could hear talking. Dressed in camouflage gear, they could have passed for regular soldiers, except they wore no insignia that Brock could identify and both had baseball caps on their heads. Light machine guns were slung over their shoulders.

Hardly daring to breathe, Brock slid deeper into the undergrowth and checked his camera one more time, making sure the lens cover was open. His hands shook a little as he adjusted the settings for the shade and forced himself to calm down. He clenched and released his fingers a few times and they became steadier. He smeared mud onto his face and into his hair in an attempt to become less visible. His blond locks in particular were not an asset when it came to stealth and concealment, especially in a country where blond was not the norm. He crept back to the trackside position and for the next half an hour or so he took shots of men and guns, vehicles carrying heavy weapons and lorries loaded with equipment. The track was well used and clearly the main thoroughfare to and from the camp. There was plenty of movement for him to capture.

I need to move. These shots are all very well, but I have to get pictures of more important people, not just foot soldiers. This stuff is background, but there's nothing that interesting. Satellites have probably picked up most of this. His thoughts scattered as he weighed up all the risks and options. *In for a penny.* He'd come so far. He couldn't stop now. He couldn't let Kyle down. Much as he wanted to take his time, the fading light gave him no choice. He slipped through the trees and made his way parallel to the track in the direction the vehicles had mainly come from. The rough road widened until it opened into a clearing that housed an encampment. From his vantage point in the trees, Brock could see several tents and a couple of shacks constructed from sheet metal. Several armed men stood around the periphery of the clearing. They acted like sentries and Brock couldn't see a way to get past them without being spotted. He waited for an opportunity to get closer. A bell clanged and Brock's heart leapt. He dropped to the ground, holding back a curse as a thorny plant stabbed his knee. He watched with a grin as men came from every direction and converged on the biggest tent.

"Ha! Food time." He couldn't believe his luck. Within ten minutes, all but two of the men had disappeared inside. Brock could just hear chatter and the occasional shout of laughter. From his hiding place he managed a few distance shots, then skirted around the tents. He took as many pictures as he dared and even sprinted into a vehicle compound, to get pictures of the trucks loaded with crates and boxes. Some were marked with Russian lettering, others in English. He clambered into the back of one truck and levered a lid from a crate. He pulled off some straw packing and gasped as his digging revealed several automatic weapons.

He moved farther back into the vehicle to a bigger crate but inside that were some bags rather than weapons. Brock pulled one open and gaped at the glittering pile of gold ingots inside. He slipped a single small bar into his pocket and jumped out of the truck.

Just time to try to get into those huts, then the light will be gone. He skirted around the back of the noisy mess tent, grateful that the chatter concealed any sound he made. The voices he heard spoke Spanish with a local accent, but also English with a southern US drawl. He thought he caught some German as well. "Quite the international love-in," he muttered beneath his breath. Moving as fast as he dared, Brock crossed the compound to the biggest of the huts. Roughly constructed from sheets of corrugated iron, it had a hinged door with an enormous padlock that to Brock's delight hung open. He unhooked it and slipped inside. Once his eyes adjusted to the gloomy interior, he could make out a couple of wheeled metal cages similar to ones he'd seen in supermarkets back home. Inside them were stacked dozens of canisters, marked with strange symbols. Brock didn't have time to wonder what they contained. He took more pictures, adjusting his camera settings for the lack of light. He didn't dare use a flash but someone with a bit of computer know-how would be able to enhance the images easily enough.

He'd risked his luck by remaining so long. He edged from the hut and replaced the padlock in the door latch. Scraping and clattering from the mess tent told him that mealtime was ending. He could either hide or make a run for it.

"Shit." Running seemed like the safer option. He tore a direct line for the trees, running at full pelt, camera banging against his side. Just as he reached the tree line,

cries of alarm went up behind him and the sharp retort of weapons firing split the air. Bullets bit into the trunks around him, spitting lethal shards of wood all around. A red-hot pain shot through his shoulder and Brock staggered at the impact. He didn't pause to look back. He ran, heart pounding, for the relative security of the cave.

Brock had a rough idea of direction. The trees next to the track were thinner so he kept back in the denser vegetation. It slowed him down but meant that he was better concealed from any pursuers. The gunfire had ceased, replaced by distant shouts. He hoped that his appearance had been so unexpected that the terrorists, guerrillas — whoever the hell they were — were taking time to get organized. He tripped over a root and almost fell but righted himself in time. Creepers and brambles tore at his clothing but he ripped through them, ignoring the damage to his skin. He couldn't think of anything but getting back to the cool darkness of the cave. The entrance was well hidden and there was a chance that he wouldn't be followed. If he could get through the first narrow crevice, he doubted anyone would follow him anyway, not without collecting proper gear and finding people who knew what they were doing.

He reached the escarpment and scrambled for the lower lip of the cave entrance. It was a hell of a lot harder getting back up than it had been climbing down and every stretch sent stabbing shards of agony through his shoulder. He used the thick vegetation to pull himself up and finally, with a shuddering sigh, rolled over the edge and into the cave. He pulled the hanging plants back over the entrance and sagged against the rock wall. As he leaned back, he had to bite

back a scream. There was something sticking into his shoulder and he had just driven it deeper. Sweat rolled down his face and his breath came in short gasps. He reached back and probed with his fingers, finding a jagged shard of wood projecting from just beneath his shoulder blade. Clamping his mouth shut, he yanked the wooden dagger from his flesh.

Brock's eyes watered at the pain. He drove his teeth into his lower lip to stop himself from crying out. From outside came shouts and swearing in a range of languages. He had to move. He grabbed his helmet from where he'd left it what seemed like a lifetime earlier and rammed it onto his head. He rolled up the waterproof camera bag and stuffed it in his pocket, then turned sideways and edged his body into the narrow crevice that meant escape.

Each time his clothing caught on the rock or the squeeze became tight, Brock forced himself on, uncaring about the damage to his increasingly ragged clothes and skin. His vision blurred as sweat dripped into his eyes, stinging and making them water more. He couldn't get a hand anywhere near his face to brush the moisture away. Frantically he dragged himself forward and finally fell from the crevice.

On his hands and bruised knees, chest heaving from the exertion, and shaking with fear, Brock sobbed with relief. The warm stickiness of blood oozed down his arm but he dismissed it. He had no first-aid kit and no time to worry about a little scratch. It was hardly life threatening.

"Kyle would say to stop making such a fuss over a splinter," he muttered, his tone wry. He slowed his breathing and gathered his thoughts. The last few minutes had been spent in utter panic and it came as a

shock to him to realize just how scared he was. The possibility of being captured hadn't become real until those shouts of discovery had reached his ears.

"What the hell am I doing here? I'm a photographer, not a bloody spy." He chuckled. "Of course, that's exactly why I *am* here. Any idiot can take a few pictures — not everyone has a plausible excuse for being in this part of the world." He pulled off his helmet and scrubbed a hand through his hair. "That's why I'm the one running for my life instead of Kyle." Momentary doubt wheedled its way into Brock's head but he pushed it away. "He'd be here if he could. I know he would." The longing to get back to Kyle crashed over him and he fought back tears. "Sitting here crying like a girl is not going to get these pictures where they need to be." He patted his camera then stood up. He put his helmet back on and adjusted the beam of his head torch. "Time to get going."

Every shifting rock and drip of water had Brock listening for the sounds of pursuit, but there was no indication that anyone had followed him into the cave. He doubted that the terrorists would even be aware of its presence. If they had found the concealed entrance, it was unlikely that they would choose to venture through the crevice — not without the proper equipment and preparation, anyway. Two hours of reckless scrambling and crawling brought him back to the cave containing the pool. Brock couldn't help but grin. A short swim was all that separated him from Kyle. He allowed himself a few moments of rest. He was filthy, exhausted and battered. It felt as if every inch of his body was scratched, scraped or bruised. His shoulder throbbed horribly. He wrapped the camera in its waterproof bag and made sure it was sealed tight.

The last thing he wanted to do was ruin the memory card after all the effort it had taken to get the pictures on it. Happy that his precious cargo would be safe in the water, Brock tightened the chinstrap on his helmet and slipped into the pool. The water felt good against his dirty, heated skin. He took a couple of deep breaths and ducked beneath the surface.

* * * *

Kyle tapped his fingers on the rock and stared into the darkness. The occasional glance at his watch told him that Brock had been gone almost six hours. That had given Kyle plenty of time to sit and think. Conserving his torch battery meant that there was little else for him to do in the utter blackness. He dozed a little, but concern for Brock's safety didn't allow him to sleep. Tuned in to the silence, his ears caught the first sounds of splashing below. Kyle put on his light and got down on his belly to bend over the crack leading to the underground pool. He stared at the water, willing Brock to appear. The surface stirred, then broke. Mud-streaked, water-darkened blond hair appeared, then Kyle was gazing down at Brock's smiling, upturned face. To Kyle, his lover had never appeared more beautiful.

Brock started to heave himself out of the water but Kyle could see that he was struggling. Kyle leaned down as far as he was able, stretching out his arms. Brock grabbed hold and Kyle hauled his exhausted body upward. Brock rolled over the lip of the crevice and flopped down, breathing heavily.

"They saw me... They'll be coming," he gasped out the words. "They didn't follow me into the cave, I don't

even know if they realize the entrance is there, but they definitely spotted me."

Kyle frowned. "They'll know that the scientists' camp has been in use. There's not much that happens in the forests that their spies don't inform them of. The camp is the only other human activity for a hundred miles. They'll head there first."

Brock scrambled to his knees. "The others... They'll be in danger..."

"Not for a while." Kyle reassured him. "There's no direct route between their area of operation and our camp, remember? It'll take them a full day at least to get there because they have to drive almost to the airfield before heading back toward our base."

"Still, you shouldn't waste any time." Brock fumbled for the camera bag with trembling fingers. Kyle took it from him and removed it from the waterproof bag.

"Take the memory card and go... You'll need every second," Brock urged.

Kyle removed the card and replaced it with another one. He handed the camera back.

"Just in case. The pictures on that card will back up your story that you have a legitimate reason for being in the forest. I copied some of your stuff onto a spare card back at camp." He unloaded the contents of his pack. "Here you go—energy bars, chocolate and dried fruit. There's a bottle of water with glucose in it, too. Tastes like crap, but you'll need the energy. I want you to eat and rest before you start back. There will be more supplies for you at the cave. I won't be stopping there for long." He took Brock's hand and gave it a gentle squeeze.

"I wish we could go back together," Brock said. "I know we can't—you'll move much faster than I can at

the moment—but I don't like being apart from you."
He leaned against Kyle.

"I don't like it any more than you do, but this is the
safest option. I have to get these pictures away securely,
then we can focus on ourselves. You just need to make
sure you get out of here in one piece, or I won't be
happy."

Brock chuckled. "Still bossy. Oh, I have something
else for you." He groped in his pocket and handed over
a small object. Kyle ducked his head to focus his light
on it.

"Holy crap… This is gold! Where did you find it?"

"In the camp. There were bags and bags of these
ingots. I took pictures of them and just brought one
away. It has markings on it so I thought it might be
useful to have a sample."

"I'm sure it will be." Kyle pocketed the metal bar. He
went to his knees and took Brock's face between his
hands. "Take care, love. I have plans for you… For us."

"Thinking about that will keep me going." Brock
smiled. "Kiss me and go. I can't bear long goodbyes."

Kyle pulled him in for a long, slow kiss. Brock's soft
lips were cold, and he tasted salty. Kyle wanted to
remember that taste. He licked his lips and stood.

"I'll see you soon. When you get back to the waterfall,
it will be dark, so get some proper rest. Don't leave
there until daylight. I'll mark the trail as best I can. If
you get back to the camp and there's no one there, find
a place to hide and stay there. Don't reveal yourself
unless you're sure that it's me or one of the others,
okay?"

Brock nodded. "You be careful too, especially
abseiling down that rock face in the dark."

"I will, and the ropes will be there for you to use. I have to go." Kyle took one last look at Brock, smiling bravely in his little pool of light, then turned and jogged away.

Brock listened until all sound from Kyle's footsteps had faded into silence. Alone in the darkness, there were no distractions. His senses were heightened. Every cut and bruise made its presence felt with a vengeance. He shifted on the unyielding ground.

"I swear... Even my ass is bruised, and not in a good way." Bruises put there by Kyle would have been much more tolerable. Brock worried at his lower lip. Even deep underground, with an arduous journey ahead of him, his head was filled with thoughts of Kyle and what he would like him to be doing to him. "Must be the stress. There's no way I should be getting turned on in this situation." He shook his head. "Idiot." He picked up an energy bar, unwrapped it and tore off a bite. As soon as he started eating, he realized just how hungry he was. He worked his way through the entire stash of food that Kyle had left for him and washed it down with the glucose drink. *Kyle was right, it does taste disgusting.* He drank it anyway. He would need every ounce of energy the meal could provide for getting back to the camp.

Brock didn't rest for long. He was keen to get going. He'd had enough of being underground and craved the open air and warmth. The adrenaline that had kept him going to this point was draining away and he was starting to feel the cold. What had started out as an adventure had turned into a terrifying ordeal. His soaking wet clothes made unpleasant sucking noises as

the cloth pulled away from his skin, then immediately clung to him again.

"Uugh. When did dry clothes and a fire become the ultimate in desirable luxuries?" Brock had no illusions about how difficult his journey was going to be. Pain and cold would slow him down considerably. He made sure to pick up everything remaining from his meager meal, stuffing the wrappings and empty bottle into the small pack Kyle had left for him. He set off as quickly as he could, fixing his mind on the relative safety and comfort of the waterfall cave, tuning out the protests of his body. He prayed that Kyle would make it back safely. He wouldn't be stopping to rest and had to travel through the night to reach the main camp. Jonesy should have put things in place to make the journey easier — fixed ropes on the cliff, left supplies at strategic points so that Kyle didn't have to carry anything. Then Milo and Juan would be waiting with transport back to the airfield, which was the nearest place with the computer equipment Kyle would need to send the photos with encryption.

Scrambling and climbing through the cave system sapped Brock's strength and tested his endurance in a way he'd never experienced before. He'd been challenged physically many times in the course of his work but there had never been a threat to his life because of what he'd done. Nor had he had someone else to worry about in quite the same way. He feared for Kyle more than he feared for himself. An endless torrent of pictures streamed through his head of Kyle falling, being bitten or stung by some malevolent insect, being caught and shot by ruthless terrorists. It went on and on until tears blinded him. He stopped to rest, leaning forward with his hands on his knees. He took

some deep breaths, trying to calm his racing thoughts. *You're being ridiculous. He's trained for this. Probably does more dangerous things every week. Stop worrying about him and be concerned about yourself, or chances are you'll do something stupid and end up falling face first down a crevice.* Kyle's face appeared in his mind, dark gray eyes glinting. Cool and calm, there was no way Kyle would be panicking. He would be completely focused on his task. Brock took strength from that thought. He blanked out the pain, ignored the exhaustion and put one tired foot in front of another. Five minutes later he reached the narrow passage to the back of the waterfall cave. He dropped to the floor, wriggled through the tube and after a couple of uncomfortably tight minutes, he was through.

Straight away Brock could see that Kyle had stopped when he'd reached the waterfall. The fire was banked with plenty of wood. Next to it lay a billycan, a couple of ration packets and a plastic camera film tube containing waterproof matches. There was even a small paper packet of coffee. One sleeping mat was laid out and on it sat the first-aid kit and a large pack. On the floor next to where Brock would sleep, Kyle had arranged a group of pebbles into the shape of a heart.

Tears welled in Brock's eyes. "If I didn't love him before, it's a done deal now. No going back." Despite the urgency of his mission, Kyle had spent precious time thinking of Brock's needs. That, more than anything that Kyle had said or done since they'd left England, convinced Brock that Kyle's feelings for him were real. "God, I hope he's okay." Brock snapped a picture of the stone pattern, then walked around it. He pulled off his helmet and put it down against the cave wall, nestling his camera inside it. Then he stripped out

of his filthy, ripped clothing and walked to the falls. He stood beneath the pounding spray for an age, letting the clean, cool water wash away blood, sweat and grime.

Brock couldn't help but think back to the last time he'd showered beneath the falls. Everything seemed to remind him of Kyle. His cock made a half-hearted attempt to rise but even memories of the hard fucking Kyle had given him less than twenty-four hours earlier couldn't beat exhaustion. Brock padded back to the fire. He didn't bother to dress, just lit the wood and set the billy full of water in the flames to heat. While he waited for it to get to boiling point, he swabbed those wounds he could reach with antiseptic from the first-aid kit.

"Fuck, that stings!" There were so many minor cuts and grazes that his body was on fire by the time he'd finished. He soaked a cotton pad in the liquid, reached back and pressed it to the wound below his shoulder. For a moment his vision went white as agony burned through his body. The pain dulled to a throb and Brock remembered how to breathe. "It's probably full of dirt and bits of wood." Brock sighed. There was nothing he could do about it without help. He checked the wound on his hand and was pleased to see that the stitches had held. The edges of the cut looked a little inflamed but all he could do was change the dressing and hope for the best.

He made coffee and sipped it while his rations heated. Kyle had left him beef stew and vegetables and the food actually smelled good. "Though I could be cooking stewed snake and think it was gourmet bourguignon, the state I'm in."

By the time he'd eaten and cleared up, Brock's eyelids were drooping. He settled onto the sleeping mat, lying

on the side away from his injured shoulder, and dropped immediately into sleep.

Chapter Fourteen

Brock slept like a dead man. It was only the nagging ache in his shoulder that dragged him from unconsciousness. He moved and immediately regretted the action. Every muscle, every tendon and ligament protested. His head pounded and his skin felt hot to the touch.

"Fuck. Wound must be infected. A fever's just what I need." Brock sighed. The fire had died in the night because in his exhausted state he had neglected to bank it up. He dug around in the first-aid kit and, to his relief, found a packet of generic antibiotics. He swallowed two tablets and a couple of painkillers, then kept still for ten minutes while his various aches receded to a manageable level. Sense told him he should eat, but his stomach rebelled at the thought and he dry–heaved, sending spasms of pain through his already tender abdominal muscles. He forced himself to mix up some oatmeal, using cold water, and choked it down. He needed something to give him energy and the mixture

was going to set like cement in his stomach. It would be difficult to throw up again. He sat for a few minutes, taking deep breaths and his meager breakfast stayed put.

"Well, you can't stay here, Lysander Brock. Pull yourself together." He laughed, a little hysterically. "Now I sound like my mother." That was enough motivation to get his battered body moving. He dragged himself up and emptied the contents of his pack. Fresh clothes made a fractional improvement in the way he was feeling and it was nice to be dry, though he knew that, as soon as he ventured out into the humidity of the cloud forest, that wouldn't last. He filled a water bottle from the falls and put the minimum number of items in his pack—his camera, of course, glucose tablets, the first-aid kit and his climbing shoes. Everything else he left behind. He needed to travel fast and light.

Brock spread the fire ash until it had all but disappeared, then piled everything he was leaving behind that might betray his presence inside one of the tunnel entrances at the back of the cave. His last act was to scatter the pebble heart, though he picked up one pretty polished stone and tucked it into his pocket. After a final look around, he strode through the falls and headed into the forest.

Making the return journey alone was a hard slog and there were parts of it that Brock couldn't remember at all. The only thing that kept him going was the thought of seeing Kyle again. The climb, which had thrilled him on the inward journey, became a precarious descent where a rope was the only thing keeping him alive. Brock gave thanks over and over that Kyle had left fixed rigging in place, making the abseil a relatively

simple exercise. The muddy forest paths pulled at his boots and each step got harder and harder. By the time he staggered back into the base camp, Brock hardly knew what day it was.

The small group of tents was silent. It was obvious that no one was there. Brock made it to the tent he had shared with Kyle, shrugged off his pack, dragged off his boots and collapsed onto a cot. He managed to swallow more pills but had no energy to resist the pull of unconsciousness.

He awoke to the rumbling sound of approaching vehicles. He had no idea how long he'd been asleep, but it didn't feel like long. He guessed a couple of hours at most. Brock sat bolt upright, a sick feeling of panic churning in his guts.

"Fuck. How could I fall asleep? I was supposed to hide." He stood up and staggered as his vision went black around the edges. He felt hot and his skin was sheened with sweat. "Damn it! I cannot be ill." He crawled to the tent flap. He peered out cautiously. Several four-wheel drive vehicles and a truck were pulling into the camp and he counted at least a dozen men. "If I run now, I might just make it." He didn't have any choice. To stay where he was meant certain capture. He made a dash for the trees.

"Lupo, runner heading for the trees!"

The sharp retort of a gun sent Brock to his knees. He staggered to his feet and lurched forward again.

"Stop! Keep running and I'll blow you to pieces."

Brock considered his chances. He was too far from safety to keep going. His shoulders dropped and he swiveled around to face half a dozen heavily armed men. He raised his hands to shoulder height and waited.

"That's him, Lupo. Nobody else in the forest has hair that color." One of the group stepped forward — Brock guessed it was the one they called Lupo — and walked toward him. Brock took a couple of paces back, but his legs gave way beneath him and he fell backward into the dirt. The world spun in a dizzying psychedelic whirl of color. Brock tried his best to focus as Lupo and his men formed a loose circle around him.

Lupo gestured to two men. "Put your weapons away and pick him up," he ordered brusquely. "Be careful of him. I can't interrogate a corpse."

The two men hauled Brock up by his arms. He was barely conscious, but the movement aggravated his shoulder wound and he croaked out a scream. One of the men slapped his face hard.

"Come on. Wake up, you fucker."

"That's enough," said Lupo. "Tie his arms and put him in the jeep. Search him first."

Brock's pockets were emptied as he hung between the two men.

"Nothing but a pebble, for fuck's sake." The stone was tossed aside and Brock watched it fall to the ground. Anger sparked through him and he struggled weakly. His wrists were bound behind his back with rough cord, which bit into his flesh. His captors dragged and pushed him toward a jeep, its engine already running, and shoved him into the back seat.

There were so many men around that any attempt to escape would be futile. Not that he was physically capable of running anywhere. Brock felt nothing but despair. He had endured so much in the past twenty-four hours and now he had no idea how he would cope with whatever awaited him. *Where the hell is Kyle? If*

Lupo takes me away then no one will know where I am. There will be no chance of rescue.

He was sandwiched between two men in the back of the jeep — one was thin and wiry with a stringy mustache, the other brawny and heavily muscled. He turned to the thin man.

"You can't do this, I'm just a photographer — "

The thin man glared and caught him a hard backhanded blow across the face.

"Shut the fuck up."

Brock doubled over with the pain and to shield himself from another blow. Nobody was going to listen to a word he said, so he decided to stay silent.

Lupo climbed into the passenger seat and was soon joined by another man who took the wheel. He lobbed Brock's camera into Lupo's lap.

"This was in the tent. Nothing much else — there's some climbing gear, expedition kit and supplies for a couple of weeks."

Lupo just nodded. "Let's go."

The driver banged the jeep into gear and sped away down the track. Four bone-jarring hours later the jeep swerved to the right, ran on a hundred yards up a small sidetrack partly overgrown with bushes. It went on through a rusting gate into a concrete yard surrounded by a high wall topped with razor-wire. They drew up in front of a dilapidated building that seemed to be a small warehouse.

Brock guessed that they were somewhere close to the airfield, as it was the nearest piece of civilization. The rough road they had followed was the same one that Milo and Juan had used after collecting him and Kyle from the helicopter.

Someone urged Brock out of the jeep with a sharp elbow to the ribs. Fear crawled up his spine, making him shiver despite the heat. Lupo pushed up a roller door with a clatter and disappeared inside the building. Brock followed without resistance. He didn't want to invite any more shoves or slaps. Inside it was hot as an oven and dark.

Lupo stood in the doorway of a room on the right. He crooked a finger at Brock in summons and smiled coldly.

"Come. We are wasting time." He spoke in English with the slightest trace of an accent. He showed no emotion. Unable to do anything but obey, Brock crossed the threshold into a small room. It may once have been an office, but now it contained just a battered wooden desk and an empty metal bookcase. A bare light bulb hung from the ceiling, but it wasn't switched on. A narrow window, almost at ceiling height, provided the only illumination.

Lupo took a seat on the desk, unhooked a coiled whip from his belt and put it down next to him. He pointed at the floor in front of him. "This will do," he said to the thin man still gripping Brock's bound arms.

Lupo contemplated Brock, his face expressionless. "On your knees. Do not attempt to resist. Whether you live or die depends on the outcome of the talk we are about to have."

The thin man pushed Brock down then took out a hunting knife. He used it to cut the shirt from Brock's body, yanking the pieces roughly away.

"Leave us," Lupo snapped. The thin man pulled the door closed behind him leaving Brock alone with Lupo.

Brock knelt in the middle of the floor, cuts and bruises livid on his pale skin. Lupo circled him, then went back

to lean against the desk. He pulled a packet of cigarettes from his shirt pocket and shook one out. He stuck it between his lips and lit it with a lurid yellow plastic lighter. In the dark room, the bright color caught Brock's attention and he followed it all the way to the desk.

Lupo examined Brock like a spider might assess a fly. He picked up the whip from beside him and let the long, knotted tail trail toward the floor. Then he flicked his wrist and the whip painted a line of fire across Brock's chest. His whole body arched in an involuntary spasm and he gasped. Behind his back, his fingers clenched into fists, then his body sagged.

"You see, young man? Is your position quite clear?"

Brock dragged his gaze upward to meet Lupo's cold eyes.

"I'm just a photographer. I have a commission from *National Geographic* – "

"I don't think so," Lupo interrupted. He gave Brock a venomous glower. "Who sent you and where are the pictures you took?"

The whip snapped forward, catching the side of Brock's arm.

"Perhaps I should explain," said Lupo. "I am quite prepared to flay the skin from your body until you answer my questions, so please don't be obstinate." He paused, and his wrist lifted slightly on his knee. Brock cringed, expecting more pain, but Lupo just laughed. Brock closed his eyes, preferring not to see the whip lift again. A rhythmic tapping of wood on wood began. Brock opened his eyes a fraction and, as if he had been waiting for exactly that, Lupo struck again and again. Brock didn't even have the energy to scream. He fell sideways onto the floor and tried to make his body

smaller, less of a target. Lupo sat for a while smoking his cigarette. When he spoke again, he sounded impatient.

"You were seen taking photographs. We have your camera, but the pictures on the memory card are of nothing but trees and mountains. Who was with you? Who has the other card?" The whip lashed down again.

Through the red mist of pain, Brock thought of Kyle and it gave him strength.

"I was alone. My expedition team remained at base camp. I'm just a photographer... I didn't see anything..."

"Stupid, stubborn..."

Brock writhed as the whip struck again, catching his hip, ripping his trousers.

Brock raised his head and spoke haltingly. "I'm telling you the truth." Exhausted by the effort, he collapsed to the floor again. Tears ran from his eyes.

"Bullshit." For the first time, Lupo lost some of his calm. "Where are the fucking pictures?"

Brock managed a harsh laugh. "Go fuck yourself."

Lupo snarled and set to work again with a series of savage blows. Brock let the pain overtake him and drag him into darkness.

* * * *

Brock came around with the kind of headache that usually followed at least two bottles of wine and a damn good evening out. There wasn't an inch of his body that didn't hurt. His shoulder throbbed and the side of his face felt as if a horse had kicked him. He wondered if his cheekbone was fractured and tried to reach up to feel the wound, only to find that he couldn't

move his arms. As his mind cleared, he realized that his wrists were still bound behind his back and now his ankles were bound, too. His captors had removed his boots and left him barefoot, as well as shirtless. He lay on a rock-hard floor in an empty room with no windows. The heat in the small space was suffocating. Brock moaned softly to himself, dry lips cracking. He could taste the metallic tang of his own blood and had to fight the feeling of panic that threatened to overwhelm him. He had no recollection of being moved to this room. For all he knew, he could be in a completely different building or another town.

No. It smells the same. Feels the same. He didn't have much time to worry about it. Bolts grated and the door to his prison creaked open. He struggled against his bonds, trying to sit up. A pair of dusty boots arrived in front of his face, then his visitor nudged at his shoulder. He stilled and the man hauled him to a sitting position before cutting the ropes around his wrists. Muscles screamed as his limbs changed position for the first time in hours. Brock rubbed at his chafed skin and swore. He looked up into Lupo's grinning face.

"Eat. Drink. Then we talk some more." Lupo leaned down and locked Brock's wrists into a set of cuffs. Brock gagged as he got a whiff of fetid breath. Another man dumped a tin plate of food, a mug of water and an empty galvanized bucket next to him.

"Nobody can say that Lupo is not humane." Lupo ruffled Brock's hair in a parody of affection, then left the room, laughing as he went. Brock resisted the urge to vomit and grabbed the mug of water. The liquid was warm but to Brock tasted better than the finest champagne. He took small sips, not knowing how long it might be before he got any more. On the plate was a

heel of stale bread, a lump of cheese and an orange, sliced into quarters. Brock ate every scrap of the bread and cheese. He saved the orange until last because it smelled wonderful. It tasted amazing. The flavors burst across his tongue and the juice quenched his thirst. It felt like a wonderful treat.

Painfully, Brock shuffled upright. He managed to use the bucket, then moved it away to the farthest corner of the room. He slumped against the opposite wall and rested his bound hands on his knees. Every inch of his body protested at the abuse he had suffered. If he had the energy to spare, he would have cried. He couldn't bear to think about what Lupo might do to him next but there was no way he was going to put Kyle in danger. He had to buy him as much time as possible.

If they were going to kill me, they would have done it already. That thought gave him a measure of comfort. *I suppose I've got value as a hostage once they get sick of trying to whip the truth out of me.* He rested his aching head on his hands and closed his eyes.

Brock raised his head when the door opened once more. He was dragged back to his original interrogation room. Lupo returned to his seat on the edge of the desk and this time his friends remained with him. Brock spared a glance for the two, heavy-set, swarthy men who pulled him to his feet and stood him in front of Lupo. Lupo had a toothpick sticking from between his lips. He twirled it with his tongue as he eyed Brock curiously. Brock just wished the mad man would get on with whatever it was he had planned.

"You interest me, Mr. Photographer. What is your name?"

Brock hesitated but realized that there was no value in withholding the information — quite the opposite, in fact.

"Lysander Brock. I'm in this country with full permission from your government. I work for *National Geographic* and I'm a British citizen. You can't treat me like this."

Lupo removed the pick from beneath his teeth and spat a glob of something disgusting onto the floor.

"The Colombian government are a bunch of American sympathizers. I follow my own rules." He gestured to one of his colleagues and the man yanked Brock's cuffed hands above his head and looped the short chain over a meat hook hanging from the ceiling. Brock bit back a scream as the position pulled on his shoulder and raw back.

"Say I believe that you are what you say you are…"

"I am! I'm just a photographer. I'm not American. I'm a British citizen. You can't do this." Brock jerked desperately at the chains but couldn't flick them free, there wasn't enough play.

"Don't think to tell me what I can and can't do. Fucking arrogant Westerners. You're in *my* world now and the rules have changed. I want to know what you saw when you…accidentally came across my camp in the forest."

"I didn't see anything. I was exploring a cave system, taking pictures. I saw daylight and found an exit that I didn't know existed. I explored a little and saw some tents, then people started shooting at me and I ran."

"And disappeared. Like magic."

"I just went back the way I came."

"What's the phrase you English use…? You think I was born yesterday? You're lying. You will tell me what I want to know. Strip him."

Lupo looked on dispassionately as the ropes around Brock's ankles were cut so that his trousers could be removed. Brock swallowed bile. His stomach churned as the possibility of rape hit him hard. His head swam and only the cuffs on his wrists held him upright.

Lupo chuckled. "The pretty man thinks we want his ass, my friends." He jumped from the desk and moved so that he was face-to-face with Brock. Staring him in the eyes, Lupo reached between their bodies and took Brock's limp dick in his hand. "Lupo can get all the women he wants. This is of no interest to me." He took a step back and pulled a small glass jar from his trouser pocket. He held it up so that Brock could see the contents.

"You know what this is?"

To Brock it resembled a giant ant, dark brown with a stubby body shape.

"An ant?"

Lupo jiggled the jar, agitating the inch-long creature.

"A very special ant. This one is called the bullet ant. It is said that getting stung by one of these is like getting shot by a bullet. The pain from the sting is said to last twenty-four hours and is the most painful sting out of all the insects in the world. I have seen someone stung by one of these. He said it was like fire-walking over charcoal with a three-inch rusty nail in his heel." He gave Brock's balls a squeeze. "Tell me the truth and I might be persuaded not to stick the end of your cock in this jar."

Every muscle in Brock's body tensed as he imagined the pain to come. He clamped his mouth shut. He

would not betray Kyle. Any amount of pain was preferable to giving in.

"I'll give you some time to think about your choices, Mr. Brock." Lupo positioned the jar on the edge of the desk and he and the other two men left the room.

Brock had absolutely no doubt that Lupo was telling the truth. A single tear slipped down his face.

"I spill my guts and that psycho is going to use his little pet regardless. He'll do it for the fun of it. Punishment for not speaking sooner. Well, fuck him. What's twenty-four hours of sheer bloody agony between friends?" Talking to himself didn't help. For the first time since his capture, Brock felt truly afraid. He longed for his knight in shining armor to burst through the door, but there was no chance of that—no chance of rescue at all. He was alone and so far up shit creek that he'd need an outboard motor rather than a paddle to get down it again.

Lupo came back less than ten minutes later and he was alone.

With nothing to lose, Brock dredged some saliva from his dry mouth and spat at Lupo's feet.

"Do it, you fucker. I can't tell you anything else, so do your worst."

Lupo ran his hand across Brock's ass.

"Take your hands off me, you son of a bitch." Brock jerked his body away from Lupo's touch.

"So brave. So stupid. But my fun will have to wait a while. So many demands on my time. So many people relying on me. My pleasure must come second to more important matters." Lupo unhooked the chain and Brock dropped to his knees. "I will have more food and water delivered to you. I want you fit to feel the agony

I will inflict on you. It will be a pleasure to listen to you scream."

Brock brought his knees up to his chest, instinctively protecting his groin, expecting to be kicked or beaten. Lupo tapped his bottled torture device on the desk, pocketed it and left.

Brock lay on the hard floor, cuffed hands stretched forward, his body numb. No matter which way he turned, or how often he stretched and twisted, there was no comfortable position he'd managed to discover. He had a reprieve from more torture and that was something to be grateful for.

At least the room was cooling down a fraction. He had no idea what the time was but guessed the slightly lower temperature must have come with darkness. He sat up and shuffled across the concrete to get a little closer to the door where he could make out snatches of conversation outside.

Brock could hear Lupo talking with a couple of others whose voices Brock didn't recognize. They still didn't seem able to decide if he was more than just a photographer who happened to be in the wrong place at the wrong time. Uncertainty was good. Every hour that passed meant that Kyle had more chance to get the pictures away. Brock listened hard to the conversation, which was in a mixture of English and Spanish.

"His story about being a photographer checks out. He's done stuff all over the world."

"He's a Brit, which makes him a fucking nuisance as a hostage. They don't pay up for anyone. We could have the fucking Queen in there and their upper lips would still be starched."

"Still has possibilities. Someone else might stump up for him."

"I don't trust him." That was Lupo. "He says he was exploring an old cave system and found the exit by accident. That exit just happened to be close to our base camp? I don't fucking believe in coincidences. There's something he's not telling us."

"Well, it isn't safe to keep him here. Too much unwanted attention."

"So we take him back to the camp. I'll have another go at the bastard there. That bullet ant is pissed as hell. He should pack a mean sting and even if his story is true, it will be entertaining to watch."

Their voices faded away.

Brock lay in his prison for what seemed like hours. Strangely, the lack of action was worse. Brock was desperately thirsty. It had been a lifetime since the mug of warm water he'd had. He was hungry, too, and angry that gnawing hunger pains just added to his misery.

He started to feel sleepy and guessed it must be getting late. He thought about trying to nod off but then he heard boots approaching.

The door flew open and two men he hadn't seen before marched in. They gripped his arms—one on either side—and hauled him to his feet. One of them held a pair of filthy trousers while Brock shoved shaky legs into them. Someone tied a scratchy strip of cloth around his eyes, then his captors dragged him outside.

A gust of humid air played across his bare skin. Chips of gravel punctured the soles of his feet as he was manhandled into the back of a truck. He fell forward onto a pile of rough fabric that smelled earthy, possibly old sacks.

Brock shunted down a few feet. Two, maybe three men climbed into the back of the truck with him then a

tailgate slammed shut. An engine fired up. As the truck rumbled along, Brock tried to maintain some sense of direction. His guards chatted idly and he heard the strike of a match, followed by the scent of strong tobacco. Brock curled up and steeled himself for a long, uncomfortable journey. He didn't feel afraid — more resigned to his fate. He hoped that everything he was going through was worth it, that Kyle had gotten safely away.

Chapter Fifteen

From his hiding place in the trees, Kyle watched in cold fury as Brock was shoved into the back of a jeep and driven away from the campsite. He stayed where he was, seething with frustration, for twenty minutes to make sure that none of the armed men circled back. Sure enough, just as he was thinking it might be safe to come out, two vehicles returned and six men tore through the camp, wrecking everything they could lay their hands on. Then they mounted up and headed out again.

"Fuck." Kyle swung down from his perch, landing lightly. He pulled a radio from his utility belt and flicked it on.

"Jonesy, this is Alpha. We have a problem." There was a crackle of static, then Jonesy responded.

"The problem just passed me on the road, heading toward the airport."

"Follow them and, for fuck's sake, don't get spotted."

"Well, color me insulted. Stay put. I'll come back to you when I know where they are going."

Kyle switched off the radio and stuck it back in his belt. He wasn't good at killing time but Jonesy was in a better position to track Brock's captors than he was. Once he knew where Brock had been taken, he could make a plan to get him back. Brock's life was at stake and he had to keep his head. Much as he wanted to give chase, it was far more important that Jonesy didn't lose sight of Brock's kidnappers.

Kyle paced impatiently, his head filled with the imagined horrors that Brock might be experiencing.

"Fuck, this is getting me nowhere." He started a methodical search of the camp for any equipment that might be of use. Most things had been systematically destroyed, but he managed to salvage some energy bars, bottled water and a powerful Maglite. He ignored clothes that had been strewn everywhere, dismissing them as useless. Once he had Brock back, they would be leaving the country as quickly as possible and there would be no stopping until they were on friendly soil. In the tent he'd shared with Brock, he righted the cots. To his concern, the sleeping bag on Brock's bed was stained with blood.

Kyle's fingers curled into fists. "He's hurt. How the hell did that happen? He didn't say anything at the exchange point," he muttered, angrier at himself than at Brock. "Keeping things from me is a discussion we'll be having as soon as possible. My pretty man is in dire need of a good spanking." Kyle lay down on the bed and fancied that he could still pick up a trace of Brock's scent. *Of course he wouldn't have told me that he'd been hurt. He wouldn't do anything to risk the mission, the idiot.* Kyle sighed. He saw a lot of himself in Brock. The same

stubborn perseverance. An impressive tolerance of severe physical demands on his body. A deep-seated passion for what he believed in. Of course in Brock's case, that was all about taking the best possible photographs. For Kyle, it was a dedication to making the world a better place by taking on the dirty jobs that no one else wanted to do, but that were absolutely necessary.

"I should never have dragged him into this mess. It's too sordid for someone with such an unblemished view of the world. He's too sweet. Too innocent." He chuckled. "Well, maybe innocent isn't quite the right word. He has a kinky streak as wide as mine, even if he is only just coming to terms with it." And that was what made them so perfect together. Matching kinks. Complementary passions. His dominant, protective personality and Brock's submissive, nurturing character. Both strong in their own ways. Both in need of the balance provided by the other.

Kyle slipped into a light doze, but remained alert for any new sounds. He had to give Jonesy time to assess the situation and get back to him. He'd known Jonesy for years and trusted him completely. The man was a seasoned operative and would know to take care not to be seen. Several hours passed and the air in the tent grew stuffy. Kyle headed back outside where he found enough unbroken equipment to heat water for coffee. There were a few bananas and bags of unopened nuts strewn around the communal tent so he had a quick snack with his drink. Doing something helped pass the time and he knew full well that a watched radio never buzzed.

It was hours before Jonesy made contact. The radio crackled and Kyle grabbed it up.

"Jonesy, talk to me. I'm stewing in my own juices here."

"Charming as always. They're moving him again. I think they're preparing to head back to the forest site. Local intelligence has confirmed that the leader is a guy called Lupo. He's a vicious bastard, well known for taking Western hostages. On the positive side, he isn't interested in killing them. All he wants is money. So far, he's had quite a lucrative time of extorting money from terrified families. Two Japanese tourists, an Argentine businessman and a Dutch scientist are the victims that we know of. Undisclosed ransoms were paid for all of them. As of now, his group is not holding anyone else that we're aware of."

"So where are they now?"

"In a warehouse about an hour away from the airfield. It's well guarded and impossible to get close to without being seen. They were in there for about three hours, but they've just loaded up their vehicles and headed out. I saw Brock briefly. They put him into the back of a covered truck. He was blindfolded so they don't want him to know the route they're taking or where they're going."

Kyle paced up and down, gripping the radio.

"Was he badly hurt?" It wasn't a question of if, but the extent of any injuries Lupo might have inflicted.

"Couldn't tell. He was conscious, I can tell you that much."

It was something. "It'll be easier to get him out from the forest camp. They'll feel safer once they get back there and won't pay so much attention to him. Either they've swallowed his story about being an ordinary photographer or they've failed to get any information out of him. Brock doesn't know how we're really

getting the pictures out. I told him we needed to encrypt them with special equipment near the airport, so there's not much he *can* tell them. The pictures are gone."

"Milo and Juan will be back in Cartagena by now," Jonesy said. "They will have sent the pictures to the US and the UK. As far as they know, they're just sending Brock's commissioned work to file dump email addresses."

"Which leaves us just one job — to get Brock out. Get back here and pick me up. I'll start heading down the road toward you. Every minute we save could make a difference to Brock."

* * * *

Much later, Jonesy pulled the jeep over to the side of the track and gestured at Kyle. "This is where you get off. We're a couple of miles from their camp. I'll turn around and wait in the trees. Once you get Brock out, you're going to have to get back here as quickly as possible. Try to lead them in another direction and circle back. Then our best bet is to go hell for leather for the airport. The plane will be waiting."

Kyle nodded. Further debate was useless. He clambered from the vehicle and stood out of the way while Jonesy did a neat three point turn, then maneuvered the jeep into the trees until it was all but invisible from the road. Brock checked for a marker, something he would recognize when he got back. There was a rotten tree stump close to the edge of the track with some brightly colored fungus growing on it. He fixed the image in his head. That would do.

He hefted his small pack into a more comfortable position and grinned at Jonesy. "See you soon. Try not to fall asleep."

Jonesy gave him the finger.

Kyle set off at a steady jog, sticking to the side of the road. He didn't want to take unnecessary risks, but speed was more important than invisibility at this point. Taking a chance that no one would be leaving the camp so soon after Lupo's arrival was one he was prepared to take.

For about twenty minutes he moved through the shadows. The trees were close to the road, and so dense that it was almost like running through a tunnel. When he saw the glow of lights from the camp up ahead, he stopped. He heard only the sound of insects and the rustle of the foliage above him. He moved forward carefully, edging off the track and into the trees. Several large tents and a couple of low, corrugated shacks lay ahead, scattered throughout a clearing. The camp was lit by floodlights positioned at intervals around the perimeter, presumably run from a generator similar to the one at the scientists' base camp. There were also lights on in some of the tents, but no sign of movement.

"Where the hell is their security? Are they that arrogant about their position here?" Kyle muttered as he tried to work out which structure was likely to house a prisoner. He stilled as a couple of armed men walked past then stopped less than five meters from his hiding place. Kyle held his breath, but after lighting up cigarettes, the two men moved on. *They probably have such an evil reputation that the locals steer well clear, and let's face it, who the hell else would venture out here unless they had to? Lupo can afford to be complacent.*

Kyle dismissed the larger tents and the metal buildings. Of the smaller structures, only one stood unlit. As he watched, a single guard appeared and took up a position outside it.

"That must be it." It was just an educated guess, but that was all he had and Kyle trusted his gut. It didn't often set him wrong.

He moved off, keeping low along the edge of the trees, gradually circling the camp until he reached the point behind his target tent. He took advantage of the cover provided by the pouring rain and sprinted the fifteen meters to the canvas wall. He got down on the floor and lifted the base of the tent enough to peer beneath it. As his eyes adjusted to the dim interior, he could see a trembling figure curled up on the floor. A glimpse of blond hair told him that he had the right place and relief flooded through him. He wanted to shout and scream with joy that Brock was alive.

Kyle pulled his knife from his belt. Even under the cover of the driving rain, he was too exposed. He pushed the tip of the knife into the canvas about two feet from the ground and slid it downward. It was so sharp it slit the thick fabric as if it were silk. Once the cut was made, Kyle slid forward on his belly, wincing at every tiny sound.

He crawled across to where Brock lay, gave his shoulder a shake and immediately clamped a hand across his mouth. Blue eyes snapped open and widened. Kyle could feel Brock's hot breath on his palm. He lifted a finger to his lips, commanding Brock to silence before removing the hand gag. He pressed his lips close to Brock's ear and whispered. "Don't move."

Brock stayed completely still as Kyle leaned forward and sliced through the ropes binding his ankles. There

was little he could do about the handcuffs. Brock would have to run with them on — and with bare feet. He had trousers on but no shirt. It wasn't the ideal escape outfit, but there was nothing Kyle could do about it. If it came to it, he would carry Brock out.

"Time to go," Kyle said in an urgent whisper. "Don't move, while I check the coast is clear. Are you going to be able to run?"

Brock nodded and gave him an exhausted smile.

Kyle crawled across the tent and stuck his head out of the newly made exit. He glanced around then ducked back inside and beckoned to Brock. He waited as Brock crept across to him and squirmed through the gap then followed close behind him.

Kyle didn't look left or right. He grabbed Brock's hand and ran for the trees in an arrow-straight line. It was pointless worrying about being seen. He just ran in a stoop to make as small a target as possible, keeping Brock in front, shielding him.

Staring back through the gloom, Kyle couldn't see any sign of movement. The appalling weather was on their side. Giving Brock's arm a tug, he moved deeper into the concealing trees.

"Can you keep running?" Kyle kept his voice low.

Brock nodded. "If I have to, I'll run a fucking marathon if it means getting out of here."

"Once we get close to the road, we have to go about half a mile to the jeep. Jonesy is parked up, waiting for us. He's a much better driver than he is a runner. Couldn't risk them hearing an engine if we came any closer. There are too many of them to fight. There's not much movement at the moment, so we've got a chance at a clean getaway."

"They've been checking on me every half an hour or so, since we got here," Brock murmured. "We don't have long before they notice I'm gone. Ten minutes at most, I'd guess. Lupo has his evening's entertainment planned around me, so they're not going to conveniently forget me."

"Fuck." Kyle didn't like their odds. "We need to loop around and try to leave a false trail. They'll know you're not alone once they see the slit in the tent. I'm going to head for the river, then double back."

"Lead the way." Brock smiled.

Kyle pulled him in for a quick, urgent kiss. "You're burning hot!"

"I think my shoulder wound is infected." Brock shrugged. "I only took a couple of doses of the antibiotics in the first-aid kit you left before they found me. I'll manage. I don't feel as bad as I did a few hours ago."

"What shoulder wound? Fuck, we don't have time to discuss this but you and I are going to have a long conversation about this sometime very soon."

Brock rolled his eyes. "Best keep me alive then, or you won't get the chance."

Kyle pursed his lips but started to weave his way through the trees. Brock followed, moving stiffly. Kyle could see that he was in a bad way. He wished he had time to examine his lover more thoroughly and perform some rudimentary first aid, but it wasn't possible. Alive and hurting was better than dead.

A shout had them both dropping flat to the ground. Kyle held his breath, but it was a false alarm and after an agonizing few minutes they made it across the track and moved deeper into the forest. As soon as they were clear, Kyle started to jog and Brock followed, keeping

pace as best he could. Every now and then Kyle paused to listen for sounds of pursuit and to give Brock time to catch his breath. Running barefoot through this terrain in his condition had to be virtually impossible. Kyle was impressed at Brock's fortitude and endurance.

Every second brought some new sound, a cracking twig, a howling monkey or a screeching bird that prompted Kyle into moving faster.

The hunters raced down the track. They exchanged shouts that were mostly swearwords. Kyle kept glancing back to make sure that Brock was keeping up with him. Pale and sweating, his body covered in raw wounds and fresh insect bites, he staggered more than he ran.

"We're almost at the water," Kyle shouted. "It's our only chance. Once we're in the river, they won't come after us." He pushed hard through the thick undergrowth, trying to clear the way as much as possible for Brock. Kyle could hear rushing water. His lips stretched into a grin as he fought past some thorny undergrowth to a narrow break in the trees. Ahead, the river flowed past, swollen with recent rains. Kyle waded into the shallows near the bank and waited for Brock.

"Okay?"

Brock nodded, darting glances all around. "Time for a swim then?" he asked. "Has to be easier than running." He waded forward until the strength of the current pulled him from his feet and swept him downstream. At the last moment he grabbed Kyle's wrist and held on tight.

The noise of the hunt grew less and vanished.

For another five minutes they drifted downstream. Kyle kept as close to Brock as he was able. Brock was

pale, his forehead plastered with wet hair. A jagged branch swirled toward them. Kyle pulled Brock in front of him and lifted his left arm to protect his head. A jarring blow struck his forearm and pushed the two of them toward the shore.

Kyle let the current move them closer to the trees and as the river grew shallow, felt for the bottom. He stood and the water only reached to his thighs. He helped Brock stand, flung an arm around his shoulders and together they struggled to shore. It would be getting dark soon and they needed to reach the jeep before they lost the sun.

"How much farther?" Brock asked in a strained voice.

"Not far. Under an hour, I'd say. If my sense of direction holds true, we head inland from here and meet the airport road. Jonesy is waiting for us. He's well hidden, and it should be a while before our terrorist friends realize we've changed course. We should get well ahead of them, enough to make it to the airport."

"Let's get going. If I stand still much longer, I'm going to fall over and I don't think you want to be carrying me the rest of the way."

Kyle gazed into Brock's bloodshot eyes and cupped his cheek. "I will if I have to."

Kyle's arm ached where the branch had struck, but he dismissed the pain as irrelevant. It was nothing compared to the state Brock was in, though Brock appeared to be past the point of feeling much at all. He took as much of Brock's weight as he could and they half walked, half staggered through the dense trees.

Kyle didn't spot the jeep until they were on top of it. He almost laughed out loud with relief. Jonesy hopped from the vehicle and between them they manhandled

Brock into the back seat. Jonesy picked the lock on the handcuffs with expert ease and tossed them into the undergrowth. Kyle didn't dare to speak until Jonesy had fired up the engine and driven off at high speed.

As they bounced along at a breakneck pace, Kyle grinned at Jonesy.

"Drive like the wind, Jonesy. If they catch us, we're dead."

"Well, we wouldn't want that now, would we?" Jonesy grinned back. "I'm far too young to die just yet. There's wine, women and song waiting for me in Miami."

"You two are enjoying this far too much. You're both cracked in the head," Brock said wearily from the back seat.

Kyle turned around and mock-glared at him. "I knew I couldn't leave you alone without you getting into trouble."

"Why are you here, Kyle? What the hell are you doing? What about the pictures? I risked my fucking neck for those. You should be getting them safely home, not chasing after me."

"Don't worry! They've been transmitted by now. Milo and Juan took them as soon as I got back to camp, along with all the other memory cards you filled up."

"But that's not what you told me was going to happen... Oh, more secret spy stuff, I suppose. Better that I had the wrong information, just in case. Is that it?" Brock scowled.

Kyle nodded. "Exactly. I was concerned that our camp might be compromised, so as soon as the photos were on their way, Jonesy and I headed back from the airfield. Jonesy parked up to watch the road and I walked back to the camp, but Lupo and his men must

have passed us while we were seeing Milo and Juan off. They were already approaching the camp when I caught up with them. All I could do was hide and watch while they took you away. Not my finest moment."

"I was so tired when I got back that I forgot to hide like you told me to. I fell asleep in the tent and only woke up when Lupo and his men arrived. It's my own stupid fault they caught me."

"Don't beat yourself up," Kyle said. "Even if you had managed to hide in time, they would probably have dug you out. We need to get you to a doctor. You look like crap."

"Thanks. You're such a boost to my ego." Brock pulled the rug from the back seat around his bare shoulders. "Just get me to a plane. I won't feel safe until we're out of the country." He sagged back in the seat and closed his eyes.

Kyle took in the cuts and bruises, the blood that spattered Brock's filthy torn clothing, the rope burns and bruising around his wrists.

"Lupo really did a number on you, didn't he? I'm sorry I couldn't get to you sooner. There were too many of them at the warehouse for us to do anything." His voice tailed off.

"Did I just hear you apologize? No—they obviously rattled my brain more than I thought." Brock's eyes closed again but the corner of his lip quirked as he attempted to hide his smile.

Kyle raised one eyebrow. "I'll let that attitude pass, Brock, under the circumstances, but don't think I'll forget."

Chapter Sixteen

Brock drifted on a sea of heat and pain.

He was aware that he dreamed, but could do nothing to change the progress of the scenes in his mind. He watched the procession of distorted images and colors dispassionately. In his dream he was unable to move. Vague gray figures moved around him. He struggled to remember where he was but fighting his way back to reality was too much effort. His eyelids were heavy and deep in his mind, something told him that hiding in the darkness was safer than stepping into the light.

When dreams changed to nightmares filled with pain and captivity, he came awake, shaking, his skin damp with sweat. A weight rested on his forehead and, though it was cool on his fevered skin, he attempted to lift an arm and shove it away. Weakness overcame him, followed by a searing pain. He swore, making little sound from a throat that seemed to be lined with sandpaper. The effort sapped his remaining strength and tears rolled down his face.

A man's voice spoke but at first it was just muffled sounds rather than words that seeped into Brock's head. Gradually the sounds morphed into words that he could understand. The voice seemed familiar and he fought to remember whom it belonged to. Convinced that if he opened his eyes he would see Lupo's sneering face, Brock squeezed his eyelids shut. He couldn't take any more of the whip. He just wasn't strong enough and that made him want to cry even more at his own weakness. The weight left his forehead and coolness wiped across his cheeks. Some of his tension dissipated and he sank back into sleep.

His first impression when he awoke again was of warmth and a light breeze. He gathered his courage and opened his eyes, blinking at the brightness. Sunlight streamed through an open window and he could hear birdsong. Brock moved his head to the side and the person who'd been sitting in a chair next to his bed rose and came into his line of sight.

"Kyle." A wave of relief swept over Brock as Kyle looked down on him, gray eyes narrowed, forehead creased with concern.

"It's about time you rejoined the land of the living. Did you know you talk in your sleep? Well, not talk so much as shout and swear."

Brock smiled. He couldn't do anything else, despite the fact that Kyle was haggard with exhaustion.

"Where am I?" he asked, his voice cracking. He coughed and winced as various parts of his body protested.

"Here." Kyle lifted a plastic cup of water to Brock's lips. "Drink this."

Brock sipped the cool liquid and swished it around his dry mouth before swallowing.

"You're in a military hospital in Miami—a guest of the United States government," Kyle said. "Do you remember anything at all about the journey from Colombia?"

Brock concentrated. "I remember reaching the airfield after you rescued me from the camp. Jesus, Jonesy drives like a maniac. I'm surprised we made it there at all. After that... All I can remember are flashes and odd images."

"You were in and out of consciousness most of the way, which was to your benefit. US Air Force troop planes are fucking uncomfortable. That's how we got from Cartagena to Miami. It was a little Cessna that got us out of the forest." Kyle offered more water and Brock took a longer drink. "Those of us who were awake suffered a lot more than you did, I can tell you."

Brock chuckled. It hurt.

Kyle laid a hand on his shoulder. "Lie still and I'll go and tell the doctor you're awake. Be good... She's a bitch from hell. Keeps trying to make me leave."

As Kyle left the room, Brock closed his eyes and mentally explored his body. The worst pain was in his shoulder where the shard of wood had rammed into him. His wrists ached, as did his face. He wondered how bruised he was. Lupo had hit him pretty hard. He couldn't feel his back at all, which he tried not to worry about. The rest of his body ached, as if he had been beaten all over. He snorted. That wasn't far from the truth.

The prickle of stubble brushed his hand as he touched his face with tentative fingers. He guessed that he'd been unconscious for longer than the flight back to the States. Questions bounced around in his head but he

forgot them all when the door opened and the doctor came in, followed by a male nurse and Kyle.

The doctor, a young woman with ebony skin and a serious expression, came and stood beside the bed. She had a clipboard in her hands and lifted a couple of sheets of paper and read them before meeting Brock's worried gaze.

"I'm sure you have a lot of questions to ask, Mr. Brock," she said in a melodic, comforting tone, "but I want you to be patient and save your strength. I will give you the basics, enough to set your mind at rest so that you can concentrate on getting better. Would you prefer we talked alone?" She gestured at Kyle.

Brock reached out and Kyle came forward to take his hand. "No. I need him here."

"Very well. The man is as stubborn as a mule and refuses to leave anyway. Nothing short of a cattle prod is likely to get him out of here."

"Love you too, Doc," Kyle said with a disarming grin.

The nurse stuck a thermometer in Brock's ear and checked his watch, timing the procedure.

"You have been here two days," the doctor said, "delivered by military ambulance direct from the airport. You will remain here until you are recovered enough to travel back to England."

She paused as if deciding how much to say. "Your injuries are serious, but not life-threatening. If all goes well, you will recover completely and regain full use of your arm." The doctor smiled grimly. "We have been pumping you full of antibiotics to fight the infection in your shoulder wound. Once the infection has cleared, you will require surgery. The lacerations on your back are coated in anesthetic cream. Three were particularly deep and you may need some cosmetic surgery to

avoid scarring. I'm afraid that you will continue to be in pain for several days, though we can manage that for you." She placed a plastic device in Brock's free hand. "This controls the release of morphine in your drip. It's a controlled dosage, so you can't administer too much. You must move as little as possible but for now, rest is the most important thing. You need your strength to fight the infection. In a few days, I'll send a psychologist in to talk to you. You've suffered significant trauma and should talk it through with a professional."

The doctor contemplated Brock for a moment, then turned brusquely to Kyle. "You may stay, but you must let him rest. If you tire him out, I will call a couple of military policemen and have you thrown out."

"You are one scary woman, Doc," Kyle muttered.

She gave him a broad smile, as if he'd just paid her a great compliment, and left the room.

Kyle pulled up a chair and took a fresh hold of Brock's hand while the nurse took his blood pressure and made some notes on the chart before leaving them alone.

"The doctor seems nice," Brock said. "I think she likes you…secretly."

"Everyone likes me." Kyle grinned. "But it's you she loves. She thinks you're cute and angelic. I'm the devil incarnate."

"You're making that up!" Brock protested.

"Well you'll never know, will you, because you've been in the land of nod for two days."

"Still infuriating…" Brock smiled.

"Of course. However, I do have some sense of self-preservation so I'm not going to talk at you for long. Suffice to say that the pictures got where they were

supposed to and my employers are suitably impressed with you." His expression became serious. "As am I."

Brock's face heated. "It was all worth it then."

"Yes, it was. You'll need a thorough debriefing, but that can wait for now."

Brock snorted. "I like the sound of a 'thorough debriefing'. Though I don't think I'm wearing any briefs at the moment." He gave Kyle a coy glance.

It was Kyle's turn to blush. "Cheeky brat. You are so overdue a spanking." He shook his head. "But seriously, people back home are very excited that you've met Señor Lupo. He's been on the radar for some time, but apart from a couple of grainy images, no one even knows what he looks like."

"Well, he didn't feel the need to tell me his life story while he was torturing me, so I don't think I'll have much useful information, but I'll try. I could describe him to an artist, maybe." The words sent Brock back to the intense heat and horror of the room where he'd been whipped and worse. Sweat beaded on his forehead and a deep throb of pain crawled up his spine.

Kyle frowned. "Relax, love," he said. "I shouldn't have pushed you. It's all over now. You're safe."

Brock relaxed a little, but his eyelids fluttered with fatigue.

"The doctor's going to have my ass for tiring you out," Kyle said, peering nervously toward the door. "Now I know you're back with me, I'm going to get a shower and something to eat." He checked his watch. "Will you be okay for an hour or so?"

Brock grinned. "Of course I will. Take as long as you need. You look like crap."

"Hey! That's my line." Kyle protested. "You should reserve judgment until you've been in front of a

mirror." He stood quickly as the doctor stormed into the room. She took one look at Brock and turned on Kyle.

"Out," she ordered.

Kyle just had time to wave and blow Brock a kiss before he allowed himself to be hustled through the door. Brock listened to the doctor chewing Kyle out until their voices faded. He lay back, exhausted but happy, and drifted into sleep.

* * * *

Brock still had a huge number of questions, but Kyle insisted that they had to wait. In the meantime, Brock made good progress toward recovery. Other than a few halting trips to the bathroom, he hadn't left his bed. He was not allowed to shower or take a bath, so Kyle took charge of sponging him down. He even shaved him, balancing a bowl of warm water on Brock's lap and using a disposable razor.

"It's good practice," he said with a grin.

"For what?" Brock asked.

"For when I shave more interesting bits of you."

Brock's mouth dropped open. He had no idea what to say to that but the idea made him hard. Not that he would ever admit that to Kyle.

Three days passed and the doctor declared Brock fit for surgery. Though he wasn't looking forward to going under the knife, it was one of the steps he needed to take before he could go home and that was something he desperately wanted. He'd weaned himself off the morphine drip and now managed the twinges of pain with ordinary painkillers. His body

mended and Kyle's presence kept his mind from playing horror film repeats over and over.

Kyle, sitting in his usual spot next to the bed, glanced at his watch.

"They'll be in to give you your pre-med soon. I have a meeting in town, but I'll be back for when you wake up afterwards, so be good for the witch doctor."

"I'm always good," Brock said with a smug grin. "I won't ask who you're meeting with. Just tell me you're not doing anything dangerous."

"I'm not. I'm meeting the head honcho of the local CIA office. He has a few questions about our little 'vacation in coffee country', as he charmingly puts it."

"Your attempt at an American accent is appalling."

Kyle rose to his feet laughing. "That's exactly what he usually says." He squeezed Brock's hand. "See you later." He paused at the door. "Get that shoulder all fixed up. I won't be able to tie you up until it's healed."

Brock groaned. "Don't say things like that. Now I'll be going into surgery with a hard-on. I have to lie on my front so by the time I'm done, my dick will be broken and it'll all be your fault."

Kyle opened the door and stopped on the threshold. "You mean the dick that will be surrounded by smooth, hairless skin…? Shaved all nice and clean?" He winked and with a wave of his hand, he shut the door.

"Bastard!" Brock shouted after him.

* * * *

Kyle kept his promise. When Brock came round from his surgery and was wheeled into the recovery room, Kyle was there. It was a bittersweet moment because Kyle used it to tell Brock that he had to leave.

"I have to go back to work. I'm sorry. I tried to get a few more days' grace but I have no choice. I have to go back. There are things that need to be done and, apparently, nobody else can do them."

Brock, still feeling a little woozy, fought back his disappointment.

"It's your job. Of course you must go. I understand."

Kyle stroked his fingers, careful to avoid the cannula in the back of Kyle's hand.

"I'd rather you yelled at me than be so understanding. I don't deserve you."

"Well, that's a given," Brock replied cheekily.

Kyle smiled, but it didn't reach his eyes. He bent forward and gave Brock a tender kiss.

"Don't forget me, sweetheart."

Then he was gone.

* * * *

Brock tried to stay positive. He had a lot to be thankful for, even though Kyle's absence hurt more than any of his healing wounds. The doctor talked regularly to Brock about his progress. There would be no long-term effects from the terrible battering his body had received. She always sounded positive and encouraging but Brock wasn't reassured. All his self-confidence had disappeared with Kyle. His shoulder was still swollen and bruised and his back ached with a vengeance. His nightmares had returned and Brock had to accept that Lupo had scarred his mind as well as his body. He spent some time with a psychologist, talking through his fears, and it did help a little, but Brock knew that only time would make the horror of his experiences fade.

He was also terribly afraid that he would never see Kyle again. He was just as afraid that he would, but that his senses and his body would not respond to Kyle's dominance in the same way. His cock still stirred at the thought of being with Kyle as his submissive, but then doubts would set in. As the days passed, Brock grew resigned to never having the opportunity to test his responses again. Soon he would be able to go home. He had no way of contacting Kyle. He didn't even know if Kyle was his real name.

A consultant plastic surgeon came and talked to him about the scars on his back but Brock rejected the offer of more surgery. There were only three lash wounds that were likely to stay visible. He could live with the permanent reminder of his experiences etched on his body and he didn't want anything to cause further delay to his return home.

He made the transition out of bed and spent long hours in the hospital garden, sitting in the shade, reading or listening to music on an iPod that his nurse had lent him. As his tiredness abated, he walked more, gradually regaining his fitness until being confined at the hospital started to get on his last nerve.

When the doctor finally agreed to discharge him, it felt like Christmas. Brock couldn't wait to leave the sunshine and head back to rainy, windswept Northumberland. He'd spoken to his parents a few times and let them know that he'd been hurt, but he'd had to lie and blame a climbing accident. The lie wasn't important, as long as he could appease his mother that he hadn't lost any limbs and would be fine to travel home without an escort. The only traveling companion Brock wanted wasn't available.

Chapter Seventeen

Four weeks later

Brock walked steadily, relishing the bite of the cold air against his skin. His feet, ankles then shins sank into the moorland mud that seemed determined to hold him back. Hailstones blown by a wild, blustery wind pelted his cheeks and snuck past the shield of his coat to send icy trickles down his neck. Haworth Moor in the warmth of summer could be blissful with cheery pink foxgloves lining the bone-dry paths — the sun able to bleach all sense of brooding menace out. But today, the weather and the moor reflected Brock's dark mood and he welcomed the solitude the difficult conditions brought.

An hour earlier he'd left his car — well, his mother's borrowed Mini — in the village next to the tourist office on the deserted main street. He needed no map, having taken the same circular route many times. He followed a narrow, cobbled alley to the churchyard gate and

pushed it open. The path skirted rows of neatly kept graves to a second gate signposted *Public Footpath to Penistone Hill and Oxenhope.* He followed the signs through twists and turns until it forked. Brock chose the right-hand path, passing the sculptures of books half buried in the ground and over two dirt tracks. Just along from a couple of picnic tables, he went right by a large boulder, crossed the little stream using what was known as the Brontë Bridge and climbed a steep bank to a kissing gate.

He paused in the gap between ancient stone pillars. It was just one more thing to remind him of Kyle. Kyle's lips bruising his own, demanding his compliance. The taste of him. The graze of his stubble. Brock kicked the innocent metal and carried on. If he walked for long enough, maybe fatigue would allow him to sleep without dreaming of Kyle.

The path curved upward, leading to a ladder stile. Brock's boots slipped on the sodden, muddy wood and he banged his shin. A quick rub reduced the pain. After his experiences with Lupo and the surgery that followed, a slight bruise barely registered.

Stepping-stones, just visible above the water, took Brock across a rushing stream. The climb became more demanding as he headed toward rain-soaked ruins on the horizon.

Brock paused to catch his breath and regarded his goal.

"Top Withens. Bleak as hell." His mother had repeatedly told him that there was no evidence that the ruined farmhouse on Top Withens was the inspiration for Heathcliff's dwelling in *Wuthering Heights,* but Brock liked to think that perhaps Emily Brontë was thinking of its moorland setting when she wrote, '*One*

may guess the power of the north wind blowing over the edge, by the excessive slant of a few stunted firs at the end of the house; and by a range of gaunt thorns all stretching their limbs one way, as if craving alms of the sun.' The ruins themselves were not that interesting, but Brock loved their position. There were excellent views of the moor, looking out over a landscape where boulders faced off against each other like knuckled fists, poised to fight over the remnants of crumbled drystone walls. The vista never appeared the same from one visit to the next and it was one of his favorite views to photograph.

A group of soggy sheep huddled against one of the ruined walls. They were even more miserable than Brock. He got out his camera and settled back against the same wall. The sheep didn't seem to mind. Brock swept the sky, searching for peregrines and merlins, but even the birds were absent. He stared blindly into the distance and the rain pattered to a halt. Through a break in the cloud, shafts of sunlight lit the moors and revealed the faintest carpet of purple.

"The heather's starting to blossom." Brock captured the fleeting beauty with a few swift shots and a little of his despondency lifted.

It wasn't warm enough to tempt him to linger, so he set off back down the hill toward the Brontë Waterfalls. It wasn't a great cascade, more a series of small stepped falls over grit stone layers, but the changing light scattered rainbows through the water. Brock took a whole series of pictures, delighted that his timing had worked out so well. Framing the beautiful images made him happy, if only for a few moments. "Maybe there is life after Kyle," he whispered to himself. "In time."

* * * *

By the time Brock had trekked back to the car and driven home, his chilled skin had warmed. Inside he was still frozen. Even the car's heater going at full blast couldn't do anything about that. He pulled into the drive of his parents' rambling stone house and came to a halt in front of the triple garage. His father's Range Rover stood there too, newly washed and gleaming. The back was open, several bags piled in the space next to the dog's travel cage.

Brock climbed stiffly from the Mini to be greeted by a cacophony of excited barking. A large, woolly beast hurtled toward him, floppy ears bouncing. Brock braced himself for impact and managed not to fall over as the enormous wolfhound-cross attempted to jump into his arms.

"Grover! Get down!"

The dog settled for resting its paws on Brock's shoulders and giving his face a thorough slurping.

"Ugh. I've been gone all of a day, Grover. This greeting is somewhat excessive."

Grover cocked his shaggy head to one side and gave him a quizzical frown. Brock gave him a scratch behind the ears. "Come on, you daft walking rug. It's freezing out here and, though you might not be feeling it, I am, so get your hairy butt inside." He pushed the dog down, rescued his camera from the car and walked around the house to the back door.

Warmth and the scent of freshly baked bread enveloped him like a hug as he pushed the door open and went inside. Grover shoved past him and disappeared toward the kitchen. Brock took a left into the boot room and stripped off his waterproof jacket,

over trousers and boots. His woolly hat was almost dry, his hair beneath it damp rather than soaked. He smiled when he saw his favorite sweater lying across the radiator.

"Thank you, Mother. I can always rely on you to know what I need. Shame the same can't be said of others." He pulled on the thick jumper and gave his hair a quick rub with the old towel left in the room for just that purpose. He moved quietly in his thick socks to the welcoming glow of the kitchen. He paused in the doorway and watched as his mother pulled a tray of chocolate chip cookies from the Aga. Every available surface in the room was covered with wire trays stacked with cooling goodies.

"Mum, are you cooking for a bake sale or something that I don't know about?" Brock asked, amusement in his voice. His mother looked up, a smudge of something chocolaty across her cheek.

"Brock, honey, you're back. Did you have a good hike?"

"Cold and wet, but there weren't any others out walking in the downpour so it was peaceful."

"Get any good pictures?"

He grinned. "Of course. The cloud broke across Top Withens and the waterfalls were beautiful today. The Brontë Society have been asking me for some more shots for greetings cards and postcards, stationery — that kind of thing. I think today's shots might work for them."

"That's lovely, dear. It's good to see you a bit more cheerful. I worry about you."

"I know you do, but there's no need. It's taken longer than I thought it would for my shoulder to get better

and it's been getting me down a bit. That's all." He stole a warm cookie and juggled it in his hands.

"It must have been a bad dislocation to need surgery. It's a good job you were within range of a decent hospital."

Brock just nodded. He hated having to lie to his parents and had no intention of expanding on the fiction he'd already imparted. The less detail he gave, the less there was to trip him up later.

"So… What's with all the baking?"

"Well, your father and I are going to be away for three weeks. You'll need plenty to eat. You've lost weight, Brock, and you weren't overweight to begin with."

Brock gaped. "All this is for me?"

"Not all at once, silly boy. I'm going to freeze most of it."

A snuffling noise came from beneath the kitchen table.

"Grover! Get out from under there." An oven glove went flying in the general direction of the dog. "You are way too big and hairy to hide from me and you are not having a cookie. They have chocolate in them."

Grover gave a pitiful whine and turned his big brown eyes on Brock.

"Don't you go begging Brock that way either, you wicked dog." His mum put her hands on her hips. "Brock, honey, why don't you take Grover into the lounge and defrost yourself a bit. I'll bring you through some warm milk and cookies to keep you going until dinner."

That roughly translated into, 'Get out of my kitchen. I love you, but you're in my way.' Brock took his stolen cookie, whistled to Grover and did what his mother told him to do — always the best course of action when

she was mid-bake. When he got to the lounge, the open fire was already blazing. He threw a couple of extra logs on to keep it going and settled into the armchair closest to the flames. Grover spread himself out across the full length of the faded hearth rug, thudded his tail a couple of times then closed his eyes. Brock stretched his legs and wriggled his cold toes in his socks. They would soon be toasty warm, unlike his heart that felt like a block of ice. The fire just served to remind him of the one he and Kyle had shared in the waterfall cave and the other pleasurable activities they had enjoyed there. He sighed and wondered how long it would take for the tight pain that came with memories of Kyle to begin to fade — or at least hurt a little less.

"How are you doing, son?"

"Dad… Sorry, I didn't hear you come in." Brock smiled at his father as he took the other chair by the fire.

"Your mother's cooking," he said as if that explained every mystery in the known universe.

Grover raised his head, decided there was nothing worth getting up for and flattened his chin back on the rug. For a few moments they all sat in companionable silence, staring at the flames. Brock's mum bustled in with a tray, which she deposited on a small table between the two of them.

"Dinner's in an hour," she stated and left, closing the door firmly — a clear message to stay out of the way.

Brock picked up his glass of warm milk.

"I swear she still sees me as a five-year-old."

His dad grunted and picked up his mug of tea. "Five… Twenty-five… She just sees her baby boy. Go with the flow, son. Resistance is useless. If it makes you feel any better, I get much the same treatment. Your mother believes that the male of the species never

mentally progresses beyond adolescence and should be handled accordingly."

"Never tell her she's right, Dad." Brock lifted his glass and clinked his dad's mug in a toast. The fire crackled and spat. Brock watched the embers shift and followed a lazy curl of smoke as it drifted upward. He sipped his milk then took a bite of his second cookie.

"Mmm. Oh God… That's good!" Chewy inside, crispy outside, the cookie melted on his tongue. "With the way Mum bakes, it's a wonder you and I aren't twenty stones apiece."

Brock's dad patted his trim stomach. "Good genes."

Brock chuckled. In his dad he could see what he himself would look like in twenty-five years' time. They were uncannily alike. The only difference was their eye color. Brock had been blessed with his mother's cornflower blue, while his dad had hazel eyes. Everything else Brock had inherited was all his dad, from his blond hair to his height and build. At fifty-two, his dad's hair had lightened but not thinned. Glints of silver shone at his temples. Laughter lines crinkled at the sides of his eyes when he smiled, which he did often.

"Do you want to tell me about him?" Brock's dad kept looking at the flames as he spoke.

Brock turned toward him. "How did you know?"

"You come back from a trip you've been planning for months with an aura of sadness I've never seen around you before. I know you were hurt and the recovery must have been painful and tedious for you, but your mood has nothing to do with that. You've been hurt before, and, though I know hospital time drives you insane, you always get through it. Your melancholy is because you're missing someone—someone you got

very close to. I doubt you've switched teams in the last couple of months, so that leads me to guess that there's a special man somewhere in the world who seems to have broken your heart."

Brock put his glass back on the side table. He could still recall with absolute clarity the moment that he'd come out to his parents. Sunday lunch, a traditional roast on the table, his dad had just handed him the potatoes. He was eighteen and had blurted the words out with no warning at all.

"I'm gay."

His parents had exchanged an amused glance. His mother had pushed the gravy boat in his direction with a smile.

"Yes, dear, we know. Are you going to put those potatoes on your plate or just sit there holding the dish while everything goes cold?"

And that was why he could talk to his dad about anything.

"I did meet someone. His name was Kyle. I thought... I thought we had something special."

"He didn't feel the same?"

"I thought he did, but now I'm not so sure. Maybe it was just one of those holiday romances, not meant to last."

"Well, who knows what fate has in store for any of us? The right man for you will come along, son, and if this Kyle is in your future, who knows how things will work out? If he isn't, it's his loss."

Grover heaved himself up, came and sat next to Brock and rested his chin on Brock's knee. Brock gave him a scratch between the ears. "Thanks for your support, Grover."

"We'll be gone early in the morning, Brock. Now I know that you're going to be fine on your own for three weeks, but your mother is on the verge of canceling the cruise to stay and take care of you."

"No! You've both been getting excited about this trip for two years."

"I know that and you know that. So, make happy tonight over dinner. Convince your mother that you're not about to go into some kind of mental breakdown and we'll be off to the Med and leave you in peace."

"I don't want rid of you, Dad."

"I know. But some alone time is what you need right now, isn't it?"

Brock gave his dad a sheepish sideways glance. "A bit of solitude would be nice. I have to get my head around what I want to do next. Which commission to take."

"Well, take your time. There's no rush to go tearing off abroad again too soon."

"It's what I do." For the first time in his life, Brock wondered if that was still true. Kyle had turned his world upside down, exposed him to the possibility of using his skills to better effect. He had a lot to think about.

* * * *

Brock managed to follow his father's advice and enjoy a pleasant family dinner. His mother produced all his favorites — smoked salmon with dill cream followed by pot-roasted chicken with fluffy garlic mash and carrots. Dessert was vanilla brûlée with a cherry compote. By the time the cheese and biscuits appeared, along with a nice bottle of port, Brock could barely

move. They all relocated to the lounge and Brock's dad refilled their glasses.

"How about a toast?" Brock lifted his drink and swirled the deep red liquid around, admiring the ruby flashes in the firelight. "Bon voyage… Have an amazing time soaking up the luxury. Just please promise me that you won't come back wearing matching lilac velour leisure clothes."

His dad almost choked on his drink. "That's an easy promise to make—and keep. If your mother takes me anywhere near cruise clothes"—he made inverted comma motions with his fingers—"I'll toss her overboard."

"Seems fair." Brock and his father chinked their glasses together.

"Neither of you are too big for a clip round the ear, you know."

"Sorry, Mum," Brock attempted to sound contrite.

"Sorry, dear." His dad didn't do any better.

"You two are a bad influence on each other." Brock's mum swung her legs up onto the sofa. "Now, Brock, there are details of our landing times at all our ports of calls stuck to the fridge. We sail in two days' time…"

"And you're dropping Grover off at Ferdy's place on the way down to Southampton." There was no way his parents would leave the country without visiting their grandkids first.

"So you do listen to your old mum occasionally?"

"Every now and again." Brock smiled. "I'm going to head to bed. I'm feeling really tired and I want to be up to see you off in the morning."

"You don't have to do that, love."

Brock got up and leaned over his mum to give her a kiss on the cheek.

"I want to." He gave his dad a hug, then left his parents to their drinks. He abandoned the warmth of the lounge, pulling the door closed behind him, and crossed the house to the staircase that led to his small suite of rooms. The property had been in the family for centuries and dated back to 1595. It rambled through various extensions that clustered around the original half-timbered manor house. The house had two staircases and the one that Brock used led to what would once have been the servants' quarters. Brock had a huge bed-sitting room, a smaller room that he used as an office and a separate bathroom. It was one of the reasons he'd never bothered to move out and buy his own place. He traveled so much that it had never been worthwhile. He paid his parents a nominal rent and helped out with the never-ending cycle of maintenance that such an old property demanded. His dad still worked at the university in Newcastle and his mum had several local charitable interests that kept her just as busy. They left Brock to himself when he needed them to but were there without fail when he craved company. It was the perfect set-up. He even had his own dark room in the attic, though he didn't do that much developing himself any longer. Most of his work was done on a computer.

As he'd taken a shower before dinner, Brock just cleaned his teeth and used the toilet before stripping off his clothes and climbing into bed. He was worn out, which was just the way he wanted to be. Since getting home, his sleep had been interrupted every night by nightmares. Drifting off was never the problem. He slipped into dreams of Kyle easily enough but then they morphed into horrific, black images where Kyle's gorgeous smile became Lupo's taunting grin. Brock

dreamt of being bitten by thousands of ants, suffocating to death in darkness or drowning in a never-ending sinkhole. He awoke, soaked with sweat and trembling. Each night it seemed to get harder to disassociate the dream from reality, so much so that he was almost afraid to sleep. Physical exhaustion was an attempt to avoid the dreams.

Brock closed his eyes and let himself imagine that Kyle had tied him down and was tormenting him by flicking his cock with a soft flogger. He could almost taste the gag in his mouth, placed there to prevent him from begging for mercy. Beneath the covers he fisted his aching erection. It didn't take long for the tingle of orgasm to begin at the base of his spine. He jerked himself harder, needing the hint of pain to reach the edge. It took the thought of Kyle thrusting deep inside him to tip him over. He spilled into his hand with a despairing moan, the pleasure of the moment tainted by sadness.

* * * *

When the time came for his parents to leave the next morning, Brock had already been awake for several hours. He hid in his room, not wanting his mother to be concerned, until he heard the crunch of gravel on the drive. He dashed down the stairs, trying to make it appear that he'd just woken up. Grover was already curled into his travel cage, half asleep and snuffling grumpily as if he objected to being woken at dawn. Brock helped put the few remaining bags in the car.

"We seem to be taking enough luggage for three months rather than three weeks," his dad said with a

sigh. "Only one of these bags is mine, you know. One is full of Grover's toys and the rest are your mother's."

Brock chuckled. "Well, that's the advantage of cruising from the UK — no baggage allowance to worry about."

"And your mother has used that as an excuse to pack for every eventuality. I swear she's equipped for rain, snow, tornadoes, tidal waves and ship invasion by giant squid."

"You're going to have a fabulous time, regardless of how many sea monsters are involved," Brock said. "Take loads of pictures, won't you?"

"Trust you to think of that, son, but you don't have to worry. That digital camera you gave your mum for her birthday went down well. She'll no doubt take hundreds of snaps and then, when we get back, will bore you to tears with a detailed commentary on every single one."

"I can't wait. I'm sure Mum could give me a run for my money." He gave his father a quick hug. His mum bustled from the house, peering into her handbag.

"Passports, tickets, funny money..." She looked up and smiled as she realized Brock was watching her. "You be a good boy while we're away, Lysander. Take care of yourself properly. Three nutritious meals a day and make sure you keep that check-up appointment at the hospital." She pulled him into a tight hug.

"I'll be fine, Mum. Forget about me and concentrate on enjoying yourself. Say hi to Ferdy, Sarah and the kids for me."

"Of course, and I have your gifts from the States for them too."

"One bag we can get rid of on the way," his dad yelled from the driver's seat. "Get in the car, love, or

it'll be midnight before we get there rather than midday like we promised."

"Nag, nag, nag." After another hug, Brock's mum got into the car. Brock waved until the car disappeared from view. He went back inside to the kitchen and put the kettle on. He made a mug of tea and put a pan of milk on for porridge. His mother believed that microwaves were the spawn of Satan, so his breakfast would be made the old-fashioned way. It was comfort food, but that was what he needed and it was healthy. He didn't want to feel guilty about his diet five minutes after his parents had gone.

The emptiness of the house was a relief, the quietness soothing. Perhaps now he could get his thoughts in order and move on.

Chapter Eighteen

Brock cleared away his breakfast things, laid the fire in the lounge ready for the evening, put on a load of laundry and puttered around the house for a couple of hours. It got to mid-morning and he couldn't resist the siren call of coffee any longer. One of the results of his trip to Colombia was a craving for freshly ground coffee. He couldn't stomach the instant stuff any longer. He ground some beans and brewed a pot of Colombian roast, then sat at the kitchen table. In front of him, recently unpinned from the kitchen noticeboard, was a hospital appointment card. He sipped his coffee and made contented humming noises as the aromatic liquid slipped down his throat. He picked the card up and read it again.

"Follow-up consultation, two p.m., Churchill Ward, Bourton Military Hospital and Convalescent Facility." He tapped the card on the table. "To go or not to go?" His shoulder felt a lot better and didn't give him too much trouble apart from the occasional twinge. The

lacerations on his back from Lupo's whip had healed well and only three long, fine scars remained. "I'd just be wasting their time." It would be something to do, though, and would get him out of the house. The military hospital was near the Yorkshire coast. He could keep the appointment, then take a walk, maybe do some fossil hunting on the beach. "Mum would kill me slowly if I don't go and she'll probably call this evening to check." That was enough to make up his mind.

Brock showered, shaved and stuffed his walking boots, socks, over trousers and coat into a small pack with some chocolate and a bottle of water. He dressed in comfortable jeans and a warm, brushed-cotton shirt, then found some deck shoes to drive in. He locked up the house and threw his pack into the back of the Mini, then headed for the hospital with the postcode programmed into the satnav. He drove south, skirting the corner of County Durham, and took the scenic route across the moors rather than the main road as he was in no hurry. He lowered the car window and took deep breaths of the peat-scented air. It helped clear his head. He stopped at one of the viewpoints and took a few pictures because it was against his religion to take a trip and not capture a few images.

He got to the hospital with about twenty minutes to spare before his appointment. There were no big signs marking the entrance, just a discreet plaque on the stone pillar next to a pair of impressive wrought iron gates.

"Good job I got here early," he murmured. "The drive's so long that it's going to take me another ten minutes to get to the place. Must have been a grand stately home once upon a time." He parked the car in a

marked bay and went into a welcoming reception where he was asked to wait in a comfy seating area. To his delight, there were copies of *Outdoor Photographer* and *Shutterbug* on the low table in front of him. *This place can't be all bad. Knowing my luck they'll be ultra-efficient and running on time because I have something decent to read. Doctors and dentists are only ever late when there is only a dog-eared copy of* Needlework Monthly *available to entertain me.* Sure enough, as soon as he started reading an interesting article on a new range of lenses, the receptionist gave him a room number and directions on how to find it.

Brock followed quiet, carpeted halls and pushed through a set of double doors into a modern wing. Here everything was decorated and smelled more like the kind of hospital he was familiar with. Nurses and orderlies in pale blue and green scrubs hurried about their business, though most gave him a smile or a greeting. He found the door he needed and paused to knock before pushing it open. Inside a white-coated doctor sat at his desk. The man swiveled around with a smile.

"Come in, Mr. Brock. Don't be shy. I've been looking forward to meeting you." He held out a hand and Brock took it. The doctor's grip was firm as they shook, but not too much of a squeeze. "I'm Dr. Mick Gibson. Just call me Mick, and this is my nurse, Oliver Glenn."

Brock wondered how he had managed to miss the young man standing quietly in the corner of the room. He had tumbling blond curls, huge blue eyes and a grin that spoke of barely restrained mischief. His scrub top was lilac and covered in a pattern of tiny rainbows. Brock couldn't help but smile at him.

"Call me Olly, not that you wouldn't anyway because I'm just the nurse and not as important as Dr. Mick here, and don't worry that the doc looks a bit fierce because he's really good, honest. Take your shirt off…please."

Brock found himself undoing his buttons before his mind even worked out the jumble of words.

"Thank you, Nurse Glenn, for that glowing endorsement," the doctor said with no small amount of sarcasm. "Now, let's take a gander at that shoulder. I should say I'm a big fan of your work. That was an impressive set of pictures that you took in Madagascar. Absolutely fascinating."

"Thank you." Brock's face heated. "You're very kind."

"And you obtained this injury on another expedition, I understand. The background notes are sketchy, but that's often the case with referrals like yours."

"Like mine?" Brock asked curiously.

"You're not in the military but here you are at a military hospital. I won't ask what you were doing out in Colombia — or for whom. My interest is in making sure you are able to take beautiful pictures into the future."

"Which is why you get a full blood work-up, as well as the prodding," Nurse Glenn commented with a grin. "No saying what kind of nasties you might have picked up out there." He gave an exaggerated shudder.

For the next twenty minutes, the doctor prodded and probed at Brock's shoulder and examined his back. He manipulated his arm and asked questions about every movement, while Olly took notes. Olly then took Brock's blood pressure.

"Boringly normal," he sighed dramatically. "Blood's next." The first of several vials filled with deep red liquid. "Red." Olly huffed. "One day I just know I'm going to find green or purple! Purple would be better." He filled several more tubes, each with different colored caps.

"The results will be back in a few days," Dr. Gibson explained. "I will call you if anything shows up that needs further investigation, but if not, I'll review them with you when you come back for your next check-up. Right. I think we're done. You can get dressed."

Brock slipped off the examination bed and grabbed his shirt.

"You are recovering well but you need to take care for a while yet," the doctor cautioned. "The internal damage caused by surgery takes time to heal, and though you feel better, you could cause more damage if you over use it too soon. So absolutely no climbing or other strenuous exercise for another three weeks. Then I want you to come back and see me again. I'll give you a prescription for some mild muscle relaxants. You're tensing your muscles without even realizing it."

Brock rolled his shoulder and winced at the deep-seated ache. "It does hurt…"

"Sorry. I've given you a bit of a workout, I'm afraid. Ibuprofen should deal with the pain. Go home and take a hot bath. If you must exercise, then I'd suggest swimming and you might also like to find a qualified remedial masseur. I'm sure Nurse Glenn can give you some recommendations."

Brock did up the last couple of buttons on his shirt. "Thanks, Dr. Gibson. Mick. I'll see you again in three weeks." He took his prescription and left the room. He

was halfway down the corridor when someone called his name.

"Mr. Brock! Wait up…"

Brock glanced back to see the blond nurse dashing toward him. He brandished a copy of *National Geographic*.

"I hope you don't mind. Mick would never ask you himself because he's too professional but I'm not, and I know he'd love it if you would sign the article about your trip to Madagascar. He had this copy in his briefcase and I'm sure he wanted to show you, but honestly, people are way too shy about this kind of thing." Olly cocked his head on one side, batted his eyelashes and held out the magazine.

"I don't mind at all," Brock said with a laugh. "Do you have a pen?"

Olly produced three from his top pocket. "Purple glitter, fluorescent orange or black Sharpie?"

Brock chuckled. "I think the black will show up best, even if it is the most boring option."

Olly handed it over. "I suppose so, but in my opinion you can never have too much glitter."

Brock flicked through the magazine to the center-page spread and signed on a picture. As he handed the magazine back, an envelope fell to the ground.

"Oh… You dropped something." He bent down to pick it up and froze. "It has my name on it." He grabbed the slim envelope from the floor and looked up to see Olly skipping away down the corridor. "What the hell is going on?" Brock slipped his finger beneath the flap of the envelope and ripped it open. For a moment he thought it was empty but as he shook it, a memory card fell out into his palm. His heart pounded as he examined the tiny object. It could mean only one thing.

Or, rather, one person. "Kyle," he whispered, hating the longing in his voice.

* * * *

Brock drove home in a daze. He had no idea why the young nurse at the hospital was involved in secretly passing him information, but he was too eager to get home and examine the contents of the memory card to worry about hunting Olly down. He took the main roads home and made deep grooves in the gravel drive as he slammed the Mini to a halt in front of his parents' garage. He dashed into the house and up to his office to switch his laptop on. While it was booting up, he took a few deep breaths and attempted to calm down a bit.

"It could be nothing. Don't get your hopes up." He forced himself away from the computer. He went down to the kitchen, made himself a sandwich and cut a slice of his mum's chocolate cake, adding it to the same plate rather than having to juggle two. He made a mug of tea and carried it and his food back upstairs. The computer screen glowed brightly, taunting him. He chewed on his sandwich in defiance but the bread tasted like cardboard. He managed to choke down a few mouthfuls in the hope that eating might reduce his urge to vomit. He pushed his plate aside and picked up the memory card, turning it over and over in trembling fingers.

"This is getting you nowhere, you wuss." He shoved the rectangle of plastic into the slot in the front of his computer and waited. A box appeared inviting him to view the files. He moved the pointer over the 'Okay' box and clicked the mouse, squeezing his eyes shut at

the same time. Image after image of Kyle flashed through his head and his cock hardened. "Fuck it." Brock opened his eyes and stared at the screen without blinking, as if the action might make the images disappear. Row upon row of thumbnails covered the screen.

"My pictures..." Brock could tell without enlarging the images that they were all his shots from Colombia. Apart from the card that Lupo had taken from him, all the other cards he had filled had been taken by Milo and Juan when they left the camp. He'd lost all his camera equipment from the trip, so Brock was glad that the pictures had been saved. There were seven hundred and fifty-one of them to view—everything he had taken, apart from the ones from Lupo's base. Those were missing.

Though he was tempted to scan through all the pictures, Brock took his time. He scrolled through them slowly, sorting them into various folders. Some went together in a collection he thought would work for *National Geographic*. Quite a few went into a junk folder. Both sets would be sent to his editor because, since 2011, the magazine had insisted that all raw material be submitted, not just selected shots.

There were three pictures of Kyle that Brock had taken when Kyle wasn't paying attention, as well as a few more when he had been. Brock put them to one side for later. It was hard enough reliving every minute of the trip without having Kyle's gray eyes staring back at him. Even the pictures that Kyle had taken of Brock were there and they were remarkably good, considering his comments at the time. Brock's whole head was in the pictures and there were no thumbs straying into the corners of the shots.

Brock was pleased with how his efforts had come out. The images he'd captured during the climb he and Kyle made were particularly good and totally unique.

"My editor is going to give me a big, shiny gold star for these," he muttered. "At least something good came out of the trip. Fuck, I sound bitter." He scrubbed his hands through his hair and rocked back in his seat. "You changed me, Kyle…" With a decisive stab at the keyboard, he brought up the half-dozen images of his lover. He sighed as his heart did a few back-flips and his cock jerked to life. He slipped his fingers beneath the waistband of his jeans and flicked open the button. The zip lowered all by itself as his swelling dick fought for freedom.

"No! I don't want this." Even as he said the words, Brock pushed his hand into his underwear and encircled his heated dick with trembling fingers. "Oh fuck…" It took only a few tugs and Brock came with a hot spurt into his palm. "Damn you to hell, Kyle!" He shoved his chair back and made a quick trip to the bathroom but the lure of the pictures pulled him back. He enlarged his favorite image, which showed Kyle kneeling in the communal tent at base camp, a map spread in front of him, pointing out some feature or another. Brock couldn't remember what they'd been talking about—probably the route they needed to take. He blinked and squinted at the picture. Something didn't seem quite right. He enlarged it as far as he could before it became too pixelated and examined it again.

"What the hell…?"

The map had the British Ordnance Survey symbol in the corner. Brock practically pressed his nose to the screen in an attempt to get a better look.

"Dorset. It's a village in Dorset." Outside of the village, Kyle's blurry finger rested next to a remote property. With his photographer's eye, Brock examined the picture. An expert had altered it. The original map had been replaced seamlessly with the new one.

Brock grinned — he couldn't help himself. "Looks like I'm going on a road trip."

Chapter Nineteen

Like a child the night before Christmas, Brock could barely contain his excitement. A warm glow of anticipation enveloped him at the thought of seeing Kyle again. It was too late to set off on the long drive to Dorset that night and Brock had a few things he needed to do before he could leave his parents' house and make the trip. He spent the rest of the afternoon and evening writing notations against each of his pictures and making the final decisions about which ones to submit to his editor. The pictures of the olinguito he sent in with a separate proposal. As *National Geographic* had funded the trip, they would get first refusal on the images and Brock was sure they would want them. The baby olinguito was beyond cute and the rarity of the images made them a sure thing for an article.

Apart from one short interruption when his mum called to check that he'd been to his appointment, he just kept going. The discipline of the task kept him at least halfway calm because it demanded attention to

detail and it was past midnight by the time he finally pressed send on the email. His stomach made a loud growl of complaint and Brock realized that he had forgotten to eat. He'd had nothing since the half a sandwich at lunchtime. Even his slice of chocolate cake stood untouched on its plate. He stood and stretched, easing the kinks in his back.

"Better take some more of those pills the doctor gave me," he muttered as a twinge of pain shot through his shoulder. He jogged down to the kitchen, switching on lights as he went. "Now, what to eat..." He opened a can of chicken soup and dumped it into a pan then sawed a couple of slices from the loaf on the table. "Soup and toast will do." He made a mug of tea and ate his meal.

Too excited for sleep, he cleaned up, then went to his room to pack a weekend bag. He spent an age deciding what to pack and resorted to his usual favorites. "What the hell. Hopefully I won't be needing clothes." Eventually, he switched off the lights, stripped down and got beneath the covers. He lay there with his eyes open staring at an industrious spider spinning a web on the light fitting. He felt nervous and unsettled, excited but wary of raising his hopes too much. He was making a lot of assumptions about who or what would be waiting for him in Dorset, but he couldn't accept the possibility that Kyle would not be there. *He has to be. He will be.*

* * * *

Brock barely slept. He tossed and turned through the hours of darkness and only slipped into sleep as the gray light of dawn filtered through a crack in the

curtains. As a result he awoke feeling groggy, with a dull ache seated at his temples. He dragged himself to the bathroom, clicked the light on above the mirror and gave his reflection a critical appraisal.

"Oh God. What a state." Never one to be that bothered about his appearance, it had been a while since Brock had more than glanced in the mirror through necessity. Now he wanted to know what Kyle would see. His cheekbones seemed sharper where he'd lost a little weight during his hospital stay. His blond hair was slightly longer and more unruly, dropping in scruffy waves to his collar. His eyes were the same startling shade of blue, but ringed by dark circles.

"You could pack for a week in those bags," Brock complained, prodding at his face in irritation. He shaved, then took a long, hot shower. He tried to keep his mind blank but thoughts of Kyle kept infiltrating, sneaking round the corners of his psyche and poking his libido. "Even when I'm not with him, he's still in charge." Brock sighed heavily. He liked that idea far too much.

As he dressed, he told himself it was for comfort on the long drive but he chose a dark blue shirt that made his eyes and light hair stand out even more than usual. His jeans had a couple of strategically placed rips across the knee and thigh — less to do with design than several scrambles across rocks and through bramble-infested woods. The soft denim hugged his thighs but not quite so closely as before his journey to South America. He found a dark brown leather belt and slipped it through the loops around a waistband that sat on his hips.

Brock ate a light breakfast of fruit and cereal, drank a mug of coffee and made up a travel cup to take with

him in the car. He put his bag in the Mini and closed up the house, switching off appliances and emptying the bins. There was nothing left to do. No more reason to delay. He recognized his reticence to leave for the fear it was, accepted it and got into the car, setting the satnav by grid reference. He pulled away with a knot in his stomach and a flutter of hope in his heart.

Setting off a little later in the morning meant that Brock managed to avoid the worst of the rush-hour traffic. He made smooth progress through the motorway network toward the south and by lunchtime was already heading across Wiltshire. He stopped not far from Stonehenge for a sandwich at a roadside café, but didn't delay and within the hour, crossed the border into Dorset. Less certain about the route, he kept an eye on the satnav as it directed him down roads that soon narrowed to lanes. He was still some way from the south coast and the busy tourist spots, though the direction of travel did take him close to the Cerne Abbas Giant. The enormous chalk carving in the side of a hill tempted him to stop and take a couple of pictures, but witnessing the chalk man's huge, erect dick just made him think of Kyle, so he got straight back on the road.

He reached the edge of a small village called Crossways shortly after three-thirty in the afternoon, putting him less than a mile from his destination. On any other day, the clear sunlight and picture-postcard thatched cottages would have drawn his attention and his lens, but with his journey almost done, Brock was blind to the pretty scenery. He drove down a long lane, woods to both sides, then turned into a track that emerged from the trees into open fields. In the distance he could see an isolated cottage and some outbuildings

clustered together in a little huddle. At one time it must have been a farm but there was no signage to indicate that it still had that purpose.

On the final approach, Brock's nerves returned with a vengeance. His surroundings seemed strangely familiar and he had a nagging sense of déjà vu. As he parked in front of the honey-colored stone cottage, he realized that he had been there before, but the first time he'd been blindfolded and the second time he'd been asleep after a night scrambling around Salisbury Plain.

Brock turned off the ignition then gripped the steering wheel with both hands. He squeezed the leather-wrapped wood until his knuckles bleached white. For a split second he contemplated turning around and going home, but the thought dissipated as quickly as it arrived in his head.

"Get out of the car, you idiot. This is getting you nowhere." He pushed open the door, climbed out and shut it behind him. He wondered if Kyle had heard him arrive. Was he watching from a window? Brock decided to leave his bag in the car, not wanting to presume that he would be invited to stay. He pushed the gate open with a trembling hand and walked down the path. When he closed his eyes, the sensations that he'd felt when he made the same walk blindfolded rushed over him. The leaves of a huge copper beech standing not far from the house rustled and he remembered that sound with absolute clarity. Brock shook his head to clear it, then knocked tentatively at the front door. He moved away, not daring to look. He sensed rather than heard the door opening and gasped as a hand grasped his shoulder and spun him around.

"You came. I'm glad." The familiar deep, silky voice made Brock quiver. His mouth was too dry to attempt

a response but Kyle didn't wait for him to speak. He cupped Brock's face with both hands and pulled him forward for a kiss that left Brock gasping for air.

The moment Kyle felt Brock's smooth skin beneath his fingertips, he knew he'd done the right thing. He also knew that he'd waited far too long to bring his beautiful lover to him. Weeks of agonizing about what was right faded away as he pushed his fingers through Brock's silky, golden hair and felt the softness of his lips. Brock opened to him without hesitation, melting into Kyle's embrace, but he trembled and his stunning blue eyes were shiny with unshed tears.

"I've got you." Kyle stroked Brock's hair and held him close. "You're where you should have been all along—with me."

"I…don't understand."

Brock sounded so uncertain, so scared. All Kyle's protective instincts surged to the surface.

"There's nothing to worry about, love. Let me take care of you." Kyle pulled Brock into the hall, kicked the door shut behind them and pushed Brock against the wall, claiming his mouth again with ferocity. He wound his fingers into Brock's hair and pulled him deeper into the kiss. He wanted Brock's lips to be puffy and bruised, his cheeks pink with stubble burn. He wanted him to look owned.

"You taste amazing."

"I…"

"No. Don't speak. Just do as I say." Kyle tugged Brock toward the stairs. "Up. Now."

"You can't…" Brock's protest was half-hearted at most.

"I can. Speak again and I'll gag you." Kyle kept his voice quiet but firm. He slid his hand downward and cupped Brock's dick through his jeans, testing his response. He was rock hard and started to grind against Kyle, seeking friction. Kyle chuckled. "Still a wanton brat."

Kyle pushed Brock up the stairs to the master bedroom and paused to watch his reaction. Gentle lamplight illuminated the bed, which was clothed in deep blue silk. Kyle had deliberately created a beautiful setting but the silver chains attached to the headboard, cuffs resting on one of the plump pillows, were what gripped Brock's attention. Brock's eyes widened and he worried at his lower lip. Kyle didn't give him any time to think.

"Take your clothes off. I want to see your skin and that beautiful hair against the blue."

Brock's inner debate was clear on his face. He didn't know whether to object or run and Kyle loved watching the emotions play out as Brock's brow furrowed and his eyes narrowed.

"Your body is demanding you stay — your head is most likely fighting the urge with arguments about respect and equality." Kyle reached forward and stroked Brock's hair, which always seemed to calm him. "Stop fighting it, Brock. I know you want this. You just have to let go."

Brock's eyes glistened, but he didn't argue. He ducked his head and began to unbutton his shirt.

"You chose the perfect color. That blue suits you." Kyle let Brock struggle through the process with uncoordinated fingers and cute huffs of frustration. Brock eventually shrugged the shirt from his shoulders and dropped it to the floor. Kyle let his gaze wander

across every inch of Brock's perfect golden skin. The faint yellowing of bruises that had almost healed stood out starkly to Kyle's critical eye. Those marks were his fault. He accepted responsibility for every single one.

"You've lost a little weight." It was an observation, not a criticism. Something else that Kyle added to the list of things he needed to atone for. Brock hadn't lost any of his muscle tone, his abs were still defined, his chest firm. Kyle licked his lips. He brushed a hand across Brock's dark nipples, confirming that they had hardened into tight nubs. Brock moaned softly.

Kyle took a step back. "Now the rest of your clothes, please."

Hands a little steadier, Brock undid his belt buckle and released the studs fastening his fly. He kicked off his shoes and slid soft denim down his legs and over bare feet. As Brock's body was revealed, Kyle drew a sharp intake of breath. His iron cock pressed against his zipper, so hard it was painful. How he had denied himself Brock's body for so long he would never know. Brock's cheeks were flushed a delicate shade of pink. Kyle lowered his gaze from Brock's face to his groin. Brock had chosen to wear gauzy trunks that seemed to reveal everything and nothing at the same time. The black fabric molded to his body and his dick seemed to be doing its best to pierce the delicate weave. Kyle couldn't resist. He invaded Brock's personal space, slid his hands beneath the waistband of Brock's shorts and cupped his firm ass. He agitated smooth skin, feeling soft, downy hairs and clenching muscle. He grazed the top of Brock's crack and enjoyed the resulting whimper. Slowly he withdrew and stood back.

"I want you to take them off."

The conflict playing across Brock's beautiful features was plain to see and Kyle loved every moment of his resistance. He allowed himself a small smile of triumph as Brock slid the trunks off. He tried to cover himself with his hands but his erection denied him any modesty at all.

"It's like the first time together all over again, isn't it? You feel vulnerable… Insecure. We'll talk, I promise — but not now, not yet. Now I'm in control. No doubts, no worries… I want to show you how it can be between us. We can't talk until the barriers are broken down."

Brock's vulnerability turned Kyle on in a way he found difficult to describe. They'd made love before, but this felt so different. He stood on the edge of a precipice, peeking over, preparing to jump and wondering if the parachute would open. The thrill of it had his cock jerking with excitement.

Kyle pushed Brock's arms behind his back and circled his wrists with one hand, pinning him in place. Maintaining eye contact, he used his free hand to cradle and squeeze Brock's balls. He nudged Brock's legs a little farther apart. He ran a finger the length of Brock's rigid dick.

"So hard. So needy." Kyle caught the drop of pre-cum pooled in Brock's slit on a fingertip. Slowly. He brought the finger to his lips and sucked it clean. Brock moaned and tried to jerk against him. Kyle tightened his grip on his lover's wrists, squeezing to the point of pain. "I make the decisions, love. Behave yourself." Brock pouted and Kyle caught the word 'adorable' flitting through his mind. *I'm lost. Completely and utterly lost. This beautiful man has the rest of my life in his hands and he doesn't even know it.*

Kyle released Brock's wrists and pushed him gently back onto the bed. Brock wriggled up the mattress until his head rested on a pillow. He looked every bit as beautiful as Kyle knew he would against the midnight blue of the sheets. Bathed in the soft light of the lamps, his skin glowed. Light blond waves fanned across the pillow and his eyes glittered like sapphires.

"How did I get so lucky?" Kyle muttered to himself as he stripped his clothes off. He stood at the foot of the bed and stared down at his prize. *What if this is the last time? What if I never have this again?* He pushed the thought away and Brock's legs apart until they were spread wide, knowing that it would make Brock feel even more exposed. Brock's eyelashes fluttered gold against his cheeks. *He's nervous. Perfect.*

One of Brock's hands strayed toward his cock.

"No," Kyle snapped. "Hands by your sides." The pout returned, along with a belligerent scowl. "Is my baby about to have a tantrum?"

Brock glared at him, lips slightly parted, the tip of his tongue just visible between them. "I—"

"No! No speaking until I'm done with you. No arguing. No complaining. No begging… Though I do enjoy that. Consider it my sacrifice." For a moment, Kyle thought that Brock might protest, but his inner submissive wouldn't allow it. He relaxed back onto the pillows as if Kyle's words had released all the tension from his body.

Kyle crawled onto the bed, kneeling between the V of Brock's legs. He ducked his head and ran his tongue the full length of Brock's cock from root to tip, then reversed direction and tasted his way down until he could tongue Brock's balls. Kyle could feel the heat in the tight orbs as he savored the salty taste of smooth

skin. Brock had so little body hair that Kyle felt as if he was running his tongue across velvet. He took Brock's firm sac into his mouth and sucked, pausing to press lightly with his teeth. Brock made the most delightful little noises of pleasure and frustration. He kneaded the sheets with clenching fists and Kyle was impressed that he managed to resist the urge to thrust. Kyle pulled off and ignored the low moans of protest.

Mine. All mine. He wondered if his possessiveness reflected in his expression as he looked down on Brock. *I hope so. I want him to understand that he belongs to me.*

"Do you think you can trust me, Brock?" Without waiting for an answer, Kyle pulled Brock's arms above his head and fastened the silver cuffs around his wrists. "Christ, you look stunning." Kyle found to his astonishment that he was the one trembling now. He waited in an agony of indecision. Should he keep going? Should he wait for some kind of indication from Brock that he was okay with the way things were going?

"You remember your safe word?" Kyle asked.

As if awakening from a trance, Brock nodded. A slow, seductive smile curved his lips and he started to tug against the metal restraints. Relief flooded Kyle's system. He slipped from the bed and fetched a few things from the dresser, returning quickly to the bed.

"I've seen your blood test results from the hospital in Miami. I want you to know that I'm healthy as well." He held up a piece of paper detailing his own test results where Brock could see them. "I want to take you bare."

Brock's smile grew wider and his eyes sparkled. He nodded. Kyle almost came there and then at the thought of penetrating Brock with no barriers between

them. He gripped the base of his cock and squeezed. His strangled moan brought a knowing expression and a cheeky grin to Brock's face.

"Like that, do you? Knowing that you have me so close to the edge when we've hardly begun?"

Brock laughed, the sound joyous, and he bucked his hips. Kyle tossed his paperwork onto the floor and grabbed the lube.

"Bend your legs."

Brock obeyed, his movements eager. Kyle squeezed slippery gel onto his fingers, then spread the lubricant between Brock's ass cheeks and around his tight entrance. Brock hissed and his muscles clenched.

"Sorry. It's a bit cold," Kyle murmured. Brock rolled his eyes.

Kyle fought to keep control. Brock's spark of attitude demanded a response and Kyle wanted to drive his cock deep into Brock's body, to make him feel claimed. He needed to touch him, taste him, mark him. He wanted Brock panting, sweating and squirming beneath him, mindless with need.

"Fuck me, Kyle."

Kyle could forgive those three words, even though Brock was supposed to remain silent.

"No fucking… Making love. Nice and slow." Despite the urgent need that sent ripples of heat the length of his spine, Kyle took his time kissing and stroking every inch of Brock's body—every inch except his rigid cock. When Brock moaned and arched his back, Kyle backed off and shook his head. "Patience. All in good time. I'm not going anywhere and you"—Kyle flicked the chains holding Brock in place—"certainly aren't. Just relax and feel." Kyle stroked Brock's chest, then dragged a nail across his abs and through the groove between hip

and thigh. "Open your eyes." Kyle leaned forward and captured Brock's lips. There was nothing soft about the scorching kiss that followed. Kyle didn't ask for Brock's submission, he demanded complete surrender, and Brock gave it freely.

Kyle eased a finger into Brock's fluttering hole, slow and steady, stretching the muscles and stroking inside his channel. He withdrew, added more lube and began again. "You feel so good. Hot and tight, trying to hold onto my finger. Do you want more?" He slipped his tongue inside Brock's mouth, teasing him. He pushed a second finger into Brock's hole and began a steady sawing motion designed to torment him. Brock's shaft bounced against his belly as he rolled his hips, trying to drag Kyle in deeper. Kyle obliged with a third finger.

"Please! I can't..." Brock's plaintive cry broke through Kyle's barriers. He extracted his fingers, used the lube to slick his aching shaft, and placed Brock's ankles on his shoulders. Kyle positioned his dick at Brock's entrance. He rocked his hips, pushing just the head past Brock's guardian muscles. Inch by inch, he sheathed himself to the root, his eyes closed and his body shaking.

"I never imagined how good this would feel... So much more sensation without rubber between us. It's incredible," Kyle gasped.

"It's perfect."

Brock's passage stretched to accommodate Kyle's girth. He wrapped his legs around Kyle's waist, dragging him closer.

"Fucking move!"

With a feral grin, Kyle rocked back, withdrawing his cock from Brock's ass until only the flared head remained, then plunged forward aggressively. All-

consuming pleasure rocked him to his core. This was where he belonged and he would give up anything necessary to keep the man beneath him.

"Harder," Brock demanded.

"What happened to silence, brat?" Kyle picked up the pace, surging into Brock's body again and again. Brock's heels dug into his back. He needed to get deeper. Kyle looped his arm under Brock's knee, lifting his leg and opening him to deeper penetration.

Brock yelled his pleasure at the new angle, arching his neck and thrashing in his restraints.

"Look at me," Kyle growled, commanding Brock's attention. "I want you looking me in the eye when you come." Kyle prayed that he could outlast Brock. With every hard plunge into Brock's clenching hole, it got harder to hold off.

Kyle dipped lower over Brock's body, pressing against his chest, trapping Brock's dripping cock between their sweat-slicked bodies. He pinned him with a challenging gaze. "Let it go, baby."

Brock's mouth opened in a soundless scream, his neck corded under the strain. Wet heat hit Kyle's belly and the scent of Brock's release filled the air. Kyle let his iron control evaporate. Pleasure bordering on pain hit him like a lightning bolt straight to the groin. He screamed Brock's name as his heated release filled Brock's channel. Holding his weight away from Brock's limp body with one arm, he tangled his fingers in Brock's damp hair, holding him close, not wanting the pleasure to end.

"Perfect," Kyle whispered. He reached for the cuffs and flicked the quick release mechanism. Brock lowered his arms and wrapped them around Kyle's body, sealing them together. They stayed that way for

a long time. Kyle held Brock tightly, surrounding him with warmth and protection. It was a rare and special gift to find one person with all the qualities Kyle admired. Brock had such grace in his submission. He was strong and determined, brave and yet sensitive and responsive. He gave up control with courage that Kyle could never hope to match.

Winding his arms around Brock's neck and snuggling closer, Kyle prayed that he'd never have to let Brock go again.

* * * *

When the stickiness between them became uncomfortable, Kyle led Brock to the bathroom. They shared a shower in companionable silence and returned to the bed where Kyle lay with Brock in his arms.

"So, do I have your permission to speak now?" Brock's tone was gently sarcastic.

Kyle just raised an eyebrow and said nothing. He accepted the need to talk, but he'd rather spend more time cuddling, fixing Brock's scent and the feel of his body back into his mind.

"I missed you." Brock raised his chin and met Kyle's gaze. "I missed you so much. It hurt. I don't want to come across as needy or weak but I have to know what your intentions are, Kyle. You went to a lot of trouble to bring me here — very cloak and dagger, by the way. I need to know why."

Kyle traced the line of Brock's jaw with a finger.

"I missed you too — every minute of every day since I left you at the hospital in Miami. I haven't been able to get you out of my head."

Brock gave him a shy smile. "Why did you leave me? One minute you were there and I thought we had a future. The next you'd gone. I know you had to leave and go back to your job but I spent days wondering when you would come back, but you didn't."

"It wasn't my choice, Brock."

"You could have been dead and, for a while, so was I—dead inside. We went through so much... I know I had no right to make any claim on you, but I hoped... I thought we had something special."

Brock may as well have stabbed him through the heart. The pain of his words knifed through Kyle's chest and guilt overcame him.

"I'm so sorry—for everything. I'll understand if you just want to go."

"Of course I don't want to go! Stupid man," Brock said angrily.

Kyle winced as Brock prodded his chest.

"I want an explanation. Why am I here? I hope you haven't brought me all this way just to tell me you're leaving again or that we can't be together?"

Kyle knew full well that Brock wasn't just talking about the journey from Northumberland when he said 'brought me all this way'. Kyle had coaxed Brock along paths that he might never have otherwise explored. The trip to Colombia was the biggest, of course. Compelling Brock to use his skills for a clandestine purpose. Putting his life at risk. Brock had taken a huge leap of faith. But more important still was the journey Brock had taken into submission. Kyle had failed as a Dominant. He'd abandoned his sub at his most vulnerable—at a time when he should have been taking care of him, providing for him, making him happy.

"Fuck... I don't know how you'll ever be able to forgive me."

Brock gave an exasperated sigh. "I'm not blaming you, Kyle. You had an important job to do and I understand that, but I fell in love with you along the way and I can't let that go. Stop beating yourself up. Before you, I only dreamed about feeling metal digging into my wrists." He rubbed his reddened skin with a smile. "Being held down at someone else's whim, bondage, domination... All of that was just in a hopeful part of my imagination. I never dreamed it could be real." His voice hitched. "I can't imagine never having those experiences with you again."

Kyle gave him a serious look. "Get dressed. I'll tell you everything, but I can't do it here. With you naked in my bed I just want to tie you down and fuck you through the mattress again."

"Only if you promise to do just that later on," Brock chuckled.

"Oh, I think that can be arranged."

Kyle pulled on a pair of black jeans and a long-sleeved charcoal T-shirt. He didn't bother with underwear, much to Brock's amusement.

"Be careful with that zipper. I want those bits fully operational."

"I'll be sure to keep everything in working order." He grinned. Brock made everything better. "I'll see you downstairs. Do you want coffee or wine?"

"I'll stick with coffee, please. Something tells me I should keep a clear head."

Though he was reluctant to let Brock out of his sight—even for a few minutes—Kyle padded downstairs and brewed some coffee in the kitchen He took two steaming mugs through to the lounge, along

with a plate of chocolate Hobnobs. He sat on the sofa and hoped that Brock would join him there, rather than take one of the two armchairs. On the table in front of him sat a manila folder, stamped 'Top Secret'. Kyle eyed it like he might a rearing cobra.

Brock appeared in the doorway wearing the same clothes he'd arrived in.

"I do have a bag in the car," he said. "I'll fetch it later. Wow... Hobnobs. This must be a special occasion." He grabbed a biscuit from the plate, picked up a mug of coffee and sat on the sofa. To Kyle's joy, Brock sat so close that their thighs pressed together from hip to knee. He would have preferred to put Brock in his lap, but it wasn't practical while they had mugs of hot liquid in their hands.

"What's in the folder, Kyle?" Brock stared pointedly at the cream-colored wallet.

"Explanations." Kyle picked it up off the table and laid it on his lap. "I want you to know that if there had been any way for me to stay with you in Miami — any way at all — I would have done it. I hated leaving you there, especially as I was the reason you got hurt in the first place."

Brock patted his knee. "I was a willing part of that mission, Kyle. I knew what I was getting into."

"You did, but only after I followed you, threatened you...manipulated your natural sense of duty." He sighed. "I'm not proud of what I did to you, love."

Brock put his coffee back on the table, placed the folder on the seat next to him and scrambled onto Kyle's lap, swiveling so that his bare feet rested on the sofa. "That's better. Now, stop blaming yourself and get back to the story."

"Bossy brat." Kyle grinned. "Open the file."

Brock took it and pulled out a set of A4- sized photographs. He shuffled through them. "This is Lupo's camp, isn't it? Or what's left of it. Looks like it was bombed to hell."

"It was. Your pictures got things moving really fast. You remember the canisters you photographed?"

"Yes," Brock replied. "Were they important?"

"Very. The CIA identified them as containing a lethal, cyanide-based chemical. Released into a water supply, it could kill thousands of people. With that and the huge stash of armaments you found, an imminent attack was almost certain. An operation was put into place in days. I had to go back to Colombia and help coordinate the liaison with the Colombian government. Those photographs show the aftermath of a joint attack by US and Colombian military. Special forces raided the camp and retrieved the gas — and the gold — before the camp was wiped off the face of the planet."

"Lupo?"

"Killed in action, along with most of his men. The rest are rotting in a nice Colombian prison."

"Good. I don't remember seeing anything about this on the news, though, did I miss it?"

"No, you didn't and you never will. Our mission and everything that followed will remain secret. The repercussions will go on for some time. The gold you brought out was marked and implicates some very important people in terrorist funding activities. By the time I got back to Miami, you'd flown home. I had to spend a few days cleaning up our trail. As far as any records show, you were in Colombia on your planned expedition. You were injured in a climbing accident and given assistance by the US military as a favor to the British Ambassador."

"All very neat then. Loose ends tied off in sweet little bows." Brock sounded sad more than anything. "Why didn't you find me after that?"

Kyle sighed. "I couldn't. I was under orders from my employer and a part of me wanted to leave you to get on with your life. But I couldn't... In the end I didn't have the courage to let you go." He kissed the top of Brock's head.

"What do you mean?" Brock nuzzled against him.

"Come upstairs and I'll show you."

Brock hopped off his lap and Kyle led him upstairs to the spare bedroom. The same one that Brock had started out in on his first night at the cottage so long ago. Kyle pushed the door open and Brock gasped.

"Holy hell! This has changed..."

The room was lined with bookshelves and a large desk beneath the window held all the latest computer equipment and camera accessories.

"The organization I work for would like to offer you a job, Brock. Some very influential people were extremely impressed by your performance in Colombia and they believe you would be a valuable asset."

"I don't understand. I'm just a photographer." Brock frowned. "This is so unexpected."

"You're not *just* anything, my love." Kyle picked up a phone handset from its cradle on the desk and dialed a number. "Here. My boss wants to talk to you." He handed the phone over, gave Brock what he hoped was an encouraging smile and pulled the door shut behind him.

Kyle went downstairs and kept himself busy in the kitchen, putting together a light meal of pasta and salad. Every now and again he glanced at the ceiling, trying to picture Brock in the room above. He felt

terrible for landing such a surprise on Brock without warning, but it was the only way his employers would allow him to have any contact at all. They had arranged to get the photographs to Brock through a circuitous route involving the Secret Service. They had designed the clue to bring him to Dorset. Kyle had gone along with the plan because he wanted, more than anything, to be with Brock.

"Selfish bastard. You should have just let him go."

"And then we would both have been unhappy."

Kyle turned to find Brock walking toward him. He pulled him into a hug and for a while they clung to each other without speaking.

Kyle had to know what had happened. "Are you okay?"

Brock shook his head. "Not really. Those are scary people you work for." He rested his head on Kyle's shoulder.

"I'm a scary person, love."

"Not to me," Brock said firmly. "Your nameless boss gave me a choice. I can either accept his job offer, in which case I have to stay here so that you can induct me, as he put it. Or I can refuse, go back to my old life and you get fired."

Kyle nodded. "That just about sums it up. They don't believe I will remain effective if I'm forced away from you. They're right." He let Brock go and took their food through to the dining table. He served up bowls of pasta and sat down. "That's why I didn't give you a chance to say anything when you arrived. I wanted you to understand what staying with me will mean. I want you to know how I feel, what's going through my head when we are together. I... I like it when you submit to me. I love it when you are bound and vulnerable.

Dominating you turns me on in a way I find hard to describe." He maintained eye contact and Brock blushed as he spoke again. "I think you like it too. I know you do. But you're having a tough time accepting the way you feel. I wanted to show you how it could be between us before my boss dropped the job offer on you. I hoped it might influence your decision." He stared at his food, appetite gone. "I'll understand if you don't want to stay." He couldn't meet Brock's eyes as he waited for a response.

"If you try to push me away again, Kyle, you may be the one tied to the bed." Brock's voice was barely more than a whisper, but his smile lit up his face. "I accepted the job—and all the conditions that come with it."

"You did?" Kyle shoved his chair back and let it topple to the floor. Brock's joyful laugh warmed all the cold places inside him and the tension melted from his body.

"I did."

Kyle lifted Brock off his feet and swung him around. Then he gave him a very thorough kiss. "Then let the adventures begin."

Epilogue

Brock spread the tartan blanket out on the grass and did a quick check for invading insects before sitting down. Since his experience with Lupo, he'd developed a mild phobia about ants, even though the kind to be found on the average English hillside were a fraction of the size of the bullet ant he'd been threatened with. Needless to say, Brock had researched bullet ants and found that everything Lupo had said about them was true. Thinking about what might have happened if Lupo had carried out his threat to introduce Brock's dick to the vicious little creature was now his fail-safe method of deflating an erection in awkward situations.

"Need me to check your underwear for wrigglies?" Kyle asked, a stupid grin fixed to his handsome face. "I'm pretty sure there will be something in there to examine."

Brock huffed and lay back on the blanket. "You're supposed to be nice to me. I'm still in recovery and need delicate handling."

"Well, I can manage the handling part... Not sure it will be delicate, though." Kyle leered. He joined Brock on the blanket and began to set out their picnic. "Did you pick this spot deliberately to make me feel inadequate?"

"Size matters," Brock replied. "But no. I've always wanted to come up here and take a closer look. The Cerne Abbas Giant is intriguing. The fact that he has an enormous dick is irrelevant."

"So why are we sitting on his balls?" Kyle gestured at the chalk line curving around them.

"Are we? I didn't notice. What did you bring to drink?"

"Way to change the subject, sweetheart. We'll discuss this again later, preferably when your cock and balls are wrapped up in leather straps and you are begging me to let you come."

"Sounds like the kind of interrogation I might enjoy." Brock dug in the picnic basket and pulled out a cold beer. "Tell me you packed the bottle opener."

"Am I ever unprepared?" Kyle handed the opener over. Brock levered the bottle top off and took a long swig.

"No, I don't suppose you are. Is that one of the things you'll be teaching me? How to be ready for anything?"

"No work talk," Kyle reprimanded him. "Three weeks' holiday... Then you can worry about that kind of thing."

"Three weeks to ourselves feels decadent," Brock said. "Though I will have to drive back to Northumberland to return mum's car and collect a few things. You'll come with me?" He held his breath waiting for Kyle's response.

"You want me to meet your parents?"

"One day. Not just yet, though—they're away on a cruise so don't worry. I won't subject you to that yet."

"Then I'd love to see the place you grew up…and I'm not afraid of meeting your mum and dad…just a bit nervous."

"And there was me thinking nothing could faze you." Brock chuckled.

"Laugh it up, sunshine. You just added to your punishment quota. Now tell me about our well-endowed friend here. I need to be educated."

"I may have done a little research…" Brock admitted. "The Cerne Abbas Giant or the 'Rude Man' is one of the largest hill figures in Britain. The other one's in East Sussex, I think. He's carved from the chalk bedrock and measures in at one-hundred-and-eighty feet high."

"So who put him here?" Kyle asked.

"The first written record of the giant appears in 1751 and suggests that the figure was cut in the mid 1600s. But he's very close to an Iron Age earthwork, so a lot of experts date him much earlier."

Kyle grunted. "The most important question is why the hell does he have such a huge cock?"

Brock giggled. "That's not known, but his obvious…virility was put to use in fertility folk magic. Local women who wanted to conceive would spend a night alone on the hillside—probably right where we're sitting—and young couples would make love on the giant to ensure conception."

"I love my country. Only in England would you ever find pornography carved into an entire hill." Kyle raised his bottle in a toast. "To the giant. May his erection never flag."

"I'll drink to that." Brock tipped more cold beer down his throat. "It's a shame there are so many people

around…" He blinked at Kyle and stared pointedly at his lap. "All this talk of huge phalluses is turning me on."

Kyle's eyes narrowed. "So if I order you not to touch yourself for the next twelve hours, that's going to prove quite frustrating for you?"

"Why would you do that? That would be so cruel…" Brock's dick started to plump. "No! Now look what you've done." He flopped onto his back and groaned.

"I think we should test just how good you are at following my orders, Lysander. No touching for pleasure for the next twelve hours."

Brock pouted. "I hate you."

"Of course you do." Kyle grinned. "Just be grateful I don't have a vibrating plug to stick up your ass. Of course, when we get home I have a couple of toys that might…"

"Nooo!" Brock wailed. "Stop talking about things like that or I'm going to come regardless."

"Let's eat. That will distract you." Kyle laid out sandwiches, fruit and muffins on the rug.

Brock scowled at him, but his expression soon morphed into a smile. "I'm glad we have a chance to get to know each other a bit more." He took a careful survey of the area. There was nobody anywhere close. He walked his fingers up Kyle's thigh and slipped his hand beneath Kyle's T-shirt.

"Brock…" Kyle gave a low, warning growl.

"Mmm?" Brock began a little finger dance on his lover's abs. He gazed into Kyle's stormy eyes.

"Stop right now, or you'll be over my knee, bare-assed and begging as soon as we get home."

Brock pretended to consider that, then carried on. Kyle grabbed his wrist and held it still. He treated Brock to a punishing kiss.

"You have passion running through you like a seam of gold. For your work, for adventure... For me. I love you, Lysander Brock."

Brock all but melted into the side of the hill. "I love you too." He snuggled as close to Kyle's side as he could. "And whatever our future brings, that will never change." For a moment he wished he could capture the moment on film but then realized the memory would never fade. He didn't need a glossy picture or digital image to reinforce his love for Kyle because it was imprinted on his heart and mind.

Want to see more from this author? Here's a taster for you to enjoy!

The Retreat

Serving Him

L.M. Somerton

Excerpt

"Who'd have thought there would be so many applicants for a role where the job description includes nudity and a willingness to get your arse whipped?" Carey Hoffman leafed through the pile of paperwork in front of him. "This is a lot harder than recruiting for club servers."

"Relax, Sir. It's important we find the right people. The more applicants we get, the better chance we have of finding someone perfect." Alistair Easton, Carey's submissive, kneaded his Master's shoulders. "Our first paying client deserves the best."

"That's so good." The tension melted from Carey's shoulders as Alistair loosened knotted muscles. "Maybe we should go upstairs for an hour so that you can relieve other parts of my anatomy."

Alistair giggled. "Not a good idea if you want to invite people in for interviews this week. We have work to do."

Scowling, Carey turned to his friend and bar manager Harry Croft. "What's a Dom to do, Harry, when his sub takes charge?"

"Generally," Harry replied, "I find it's best to do what I'm told." He ruffled his sub's hair. Kai Smithson was seated on the floor between Harry's legs. "You can always spank him later, but for now, Alistair is right. We have to get through all these applications this evening. We only have one post left to fill, don't we?"

Alistair knelt at Carey's side, hands folded in his lap, his serenity in complete contrast to the noise and activity going on all around them. The Underground was always busy, but Friday nights tended to be hectic. Carey had sequestered a quiet corner for their discussion. A low table held paperwork and drinks, and cushions softened the floor for Alistair's knees and Kai's backside. Carey still found it hard to concentrate. He blamed Alistair for looking so tempting in leather trousers and a sheer silk shirt. He imagined removing the shirt, exposing Alistair's smooth skin inch by inch, then watching his lover wriggle out of the trousers…

"Carey?" Harry brought him out of his daydream.

"Sorry, I got a bit distracted. Where were we?"

"The last vacancy—if you can keep your mind on recruitment and off whatever it is you're planning to do to Alistair?" He shared a conspiratorial grin.

"Oh, yes. Right. Well, I'm thankful Mr. Wilder's requirements are not too onerous. Tor Halvorsen will act as executive chef. He cooked for Joe and Heath when they had their taster weekend with Olly and Aiden and their reviews of his cooking were first rate. Olly said, and I'm quoting here, that Tor's double

chocolate brownies were better than an orgasm after two days in chastity."

Alistair and Kai both burst out laughing.

Harry rolled his eyes. "Olly would be proud. He can create chaos even when he's hundreds of miles away. That's two extra strokes for you tonight, young man." He gave Kai's hair a gentle tug. Kai sucked on his lower lip but his eyes sparkled and he rubbed his cheek against Harry's thigh.

"Tor has recruited two kitchen assistants, both, I might add, stolen from here at The Underground," Carey said. "As Mr. Wilder is traveling alone, Tor says that will be more than adequate to cover his stay and allow for days off for each of them. Tor intends to work through and take some time off in between clients. He'll also take on training Benjy and Frank. Going forward, I think we should consider rotating the junior kitchen staff through The Retreat. Then they'll all get experience of different kinds of catering."

"That's a great idea. At least they won't be shocked by anything they see at The Retreat." Harry grinned. "Right. Goran has sorted all the drink supplies, so Mr. Wilder won't starve or go thirsty." Goran was Harry's very capable deputy bar manager. "He can always take a quick trip down there if Tor needs him for anything. It's always possible that the client will want to throw a party while he's staying. Goran's already offered to run the bar for events like that."

Carey nodded. "Excellent. Then we have Luke Redding as general manager. He's ex-forces, like Tor."

"The Retreat is going to be run like a military campaign," Harry said. "Tell me about Luke. I know he's a member here but not much else."

"He's a well-respected Dom. Kept up his membership even when he was overseas on active duty."

"Well, you do give service personnel an excellent discount."

"I do, and they deserve it. Whereas Tor was in the army, Luke is ex-Navy. Served fifteen years then took an honorable discharge to care for his father who died last year. Mother passed when he was a child so his dad brought him up. He told me at the interview that he gave himself to his career, then to his father, now it's his time. He was very open. He doesn't have to work for the money but needs a purpose. He's a very experienced manager and won't take shit from anyone. He'll be perfect for mentoring the young men that will be working at The Retreat, as well as the contractors. Management of the house and garden staff as well as all the arrangements related to housekeeping and maintenance will sit with him, and if our guests want any training in a particular technique, Luke can either handle it himself or bring someone in from the club if he doesn't feel qualified. He knows the area well too — he was based at Portsmouth for many years and the New Forest was a favorite daytrip destination."

"I hope I'll get to meet him one day," Harry said. "I'm surprised I've never come across him here."

"I'm sure you will. I intend to have post-stay debriefings with The Retreat's management team here at the club."

"Good idea. So, when you Skyped with Mr. Wilder..."

"Lorcan. He prefers to be called Lorcan."

"When you Skyped with Lorcan, did he have any special requirements for other staff?"

"I think he's going to be a low maintenance client — he was reserved, but friendly. The stay is a personal reward for selling his business. From what I could make out, he's done little else but work for many years.

He's had some training as a Dominant and has excellent references from a couple of clubs I know in the U.S. He wants to see whether immersion in the lifestyle is what he wants because, as he said, he thinks it is but he's never had time to prove it to himself."

"Sounds like he has his head in the right place."

Nodding, Carey flicked through a few applications. "I've done a full background check. There was an incident in his late teens, which I won't go into here because it shouldn't cause any issues. It marks him as a survivor. He plays hard when he has the time but that isn't often. He admits to a preference for blonds. Smaller than him and not too muscled."

"How tall is he?" Harry asked.

"Six feet one."

"That rules out three of these — all within an inch of that height. There are also several brunets and one redhead in here so I'll put them aside. That still leaves six possibles."

"Whoever we choose has to be prepared to be very flexible." At Harry's feet, Kai giggled. "Not that kind of flexible, brat," Carey chided. "Lorcan wants one man to be his personal assistant, valet and submissive. He doesn't want a lot of people around the place because his break is about getting some breathing space, so this man will be at his beck and call twenty-four seven. Experience isn't needed. I think Lorcan wants someone he can mold to his requirements, so we're looking for a relative innocent — but one who knows what he's getting into."

"And who understands the difference between furniture wax and candle wax." Harry rolled his eyes. "Talk about mission impossible."

"The housework will be light, just Lorcan's bedroom and bathroom. The contracted cleaning service will

handle the rest. We'll need someone bright enough to be an effective assistant…"

"And who doesn't mind taking notes naked, with a plug up his arse." Harry laughed. "Sorry, I'm being facetious."

"You may not be that far off the mark. Nudity and minimal dress are nonnegotiable."

"Well, that helps us narrow the field a bit more. Two of these applicants are house subs here. I know them both and I don't think either of them could be called sweet and innocent—they're a pair of brats. Of the remaining four, two have university degrees and one went to work straight from school but got very good grades at A level. The last one seems to have drifted from job to job but does have waiting experience."

"Drop him for now and ask the other three to come in. When we have time, I want to see all the applicants we've rejected for this job in case they'd like us to hold their details for future opportunities. It would be nice to be able to offer clients a portfolio of staff to choose from rather than having to go through this process all the time. That way we can also broach the subject when we recruit staff for The Underground. Whoever we choose this time will be permanently employed, but The Retreat is fully booked for months. We'll need to alternate between clients so that the houseboys can take some time off and that means we need to line up someone else for the next booking after Mr. Wilder. We can cover unexpected illness or, God forbid, walk-outs, with staff from the club in the meantime." Carey caught Alistair's eye. "What do you think, love?"

"The catalogue is a brilliant idea. I'd be happy to take pictures for it, but maybe you should ask some of the members what they think, too? You have an instant audience for research here."

"You're right, of course." Carey surveyed his club. The Underground was his pride and joy and he fully intended to make The Retreat just as perfect. "I'll leave the interview arrangements to you, Harry. Time for me to make sure my members are happy. I think the boss giving his sub a public spanking might go down well tonight, don't you?"

"You know it will."

At Carey's side, Alistair shivered. Carey stroked his hair. "Would you like that, sweetheart?"

"If it makes you happy, Sir." Alistair kept his eyes downcast but Carey could see he was smiling.

"Oh, it will, you can be sure of that and if you're very, *very* good you might even get to come. Emphasis on the *might*." Carey raised his glass. "A toast. Here's to finding someone for Lorcan Wilder who lives up to our exacting standards."

Harry pulled Kai onto his lap. He clinked his glass against Carey's. "Bottoms up!" He avoided spilling his drink by the narrowest margin as Kai shook with laughter.

"They soon will be." Carey chuckled while Alistair tried, unsuccessfully, to conceal a groan.

About the Author

Lucinda lives in a small village in the English countryside, surrounded by rolling hills, cows and sheep. She started writing to fill time between jobs and is now firmly and unashamedly addicted.

She loves the English weather, especially the rain, and adores a thunderstorm. She loves good food, warm company and a crackling fire. She's fascinated by the psychology of relationships, especially between men, and her stories contain some subtle (and some not so subtle) leanings towards BDSM.

L.M. loves to hear from readers. You can find her contact information, website details and author profile page at http://www.pride-publishing.com.

PUBLISHING